To an old HS colleague. You were my inspiration!

[signature]

My Word Is My Bonus

by

Richard Crick

Bloomington, IN Milton Keynes, UK

authorHOUSE

AuthorHouse™
1663 Liberty Drive, Suite 200
Bloomington, IN 47403
www.authorhouse.com
Phone: 1-800-839-8640

AuthorHouse™ UK Ltd.
500 Avebury Boulevard
Central Milton Keynes, MK9 2BE
www.authorhouse.co.uk
Phone: 08001974150

First published by AuthorHouse 5/2/2006

ISBN: 1-4259-2310-0 (sc)

Printed in the United States of America
Bloomington, Indiana

This book is printed on acid-free paper.

Cover designed by Sally Crick

AUTHOR'S NOTE

A number of people, some still living, some deceased, corporations, publications and other enterprises, some well-known, others less so - among them City professionals and their employers, industrialists, politicians, journalists and their works - make cameo appearances in these pages. All other characters, businesses and published materials are fictitious and any resemblance to real persons, living or dead, or real businesses, or real press comment is purely coincidental. But, as regards all persons - real, fictitious or corporate – and all references to the press, this is a work of fiction. None of the events portrayed - other than those which are a matter of public record - ever occurred.

Prologue

The British obsession with the unpredictable weather patterns which characterise their islands is best illustrated not in their interminable observation of the Atlantic fronts which successively drop their contents, summer and winter, over the already sodden landscape but in the reaction to the infrequent occasions when the weather turns 'funny'. The most spectacular example of this phenomenon in recent years was the drought of 1976. The then prime minister, James Callaghan, an unprincipled chancer, even by the heady standards set by that pair of old rogues, Harold Macmillan and Harold Wilson, before him, improbably attempted and, still more amazingly achieved, the political equivalent of a rain dance. Seeking to demonstrate his government's initiative, as the nation's gardens withered and London's double-deckers went unwashed, he plucked a nonentity by the name of Dennis Howell from his obscure sinecure as sports minister at the Department of the Environment and appointed him drought minister. During the next four days of more or less searing heat, this time-serving duffer, a man whose ineptitude was so complete that he could not have been trusted to find his own arse with both hands, organised nationwide advertisements urging the populace to limit their bathwater to no more than five inches and the City's wags coined witticisms such as "Save water, shower with a friend". On the fifth day - it was after all a bank holiday week-end - the heavens opened.

It was now 1987 and it had, for all practical purposes, been raining ever since. The blamelessness of nuclear weapons testing, to which had been popularly attributed the ghastly summers of the 1960s, was finally proven when, in October of this year, a whole generation after the signing of the Nuclear Test Ban Treaty, southern England was devastated by a stupendous and woefully unpredicted hurricane, which appeared ominously to coincide with a spectacular collapse in stock markets throughout the world. No greater proof could be required that careful observation of the British weather, and particularly its funny turns, is a valid substitute for all economic, social and political analysis.

Who's Who/What's What

(in order of appearance)

Dundas Brothers & Co Limited (Dundas Brothers), City merchant bank

Peter Davenport, corporate finance director, Dundas Brothers

Wagstaff & Co, City stockbrokers to Bottley Engineering and BMP

David Carradine, money partner, Wagstaff & Co

Max Thornhill, salaried partner, Wagstaff & Co

Bottley Engineering plc (Bottley), heavy engineering company

Timothy Phillips, corporate finance manager, Dundas Brothers

Sir Timothy Henderson-Ball Bt, chairman, Bottley

Sophie Templeton-Smythe, girl-friend of Peter Davenport

Josh & Jenny Fordyce, friends of Peter Davenport

Maureen, Peter Davenport's secretary

Tracey, Timothy Phillips' secretary

Lowe Bell Financial, financial public relations group

Stephanie Laker, Dundas Brothers internal public relations girl

Cyril Bishop, head of Dundas Brothers corporate finance division

Hank Amadeo, American director of corporate finance, Dundas Brothers

Dundas Asset Management (DAM), fund management subsidiary of Dundas Brothers

David Sellar, head of DAM

Alan Bentham, head of credit, Dundas Brothers

Alex Maguire, head of treasury, Dundas Brothers

Juan-Antonio Villareal, head of international, Dundas Brothers

Jeremy Stone, head of commercial lending, Dundas Brothers

Henry Morrissey, finance director, Dundas Brothers

Sir James Cruso, chairman, Dundas Brothers

Angus Hewat, senior partner, Allen & Overy, City law firm

Richard Cranfield, solicitor, Allen & Overy

Oliver Quentin-Archard, corporate finance executive, Dundas Brothers

Henry Pickthorne, partner, Linklaters & Paines, City law firm

Ben Silkin, deputy chairman, Bottley and director, Brocklebank Nobel, City merchant bank

Frank Griffiths, chief executive, Bottley

Stanley Holligsworth, finance director, Bottley

Rita Henderson-Ball, Sir Timothy's fourth wife

William Blackstone, corporate finance director, Dundas Brothers

Sybil Dunwoody, personnel director, Dundas Brothers

Julius Grossmann & Co Limited (Grossmanns), City merchant bank

Bill McAdam, new head of corporate finance, Dundas Brothers

Pitcairn Pharmaceuticals plc (Pitcairn), pharmaceutical company

Lord (Jock) Enderby, deputy chairman, Harcourt Properties and Pitcairn

Christopher Hennessy III, chairman, Pitcairn

Dr Robin and Julia Archer, friends of Peter Davenport

Craig and Ann Mullholland, friends of Peter Davenport

Graeme Kent, corporate finance director, Dundas Brothers

Hildegaard von Schultzendorf, secretary to Sir James Cruso

Helen Thompson, librarian, Dundas Brothers

Johnathan Tudor, chief executive, Dundas Brothers

Cindy Buckle, Graeme Kent's secretary

Festus Nyondo, corporate finance trainee, Dundas Brothers

Elspeth Watson, corporate finance executive, Dundas Brothers

Seymour Farquharson, corporate finance director, Dundas Brothers

Charlotte Mulder, corporate finance executive, Dundas Brothers

Alison Smith, secretary, corporate finance, Dundas Brothers

David Squire, founder, Squire's Homes, private housebuilder

Soo Chan, former girlfriend of Peter Davenport

Sheila, chalet girl, Couchevel 1850

The Hon. Mark Cubit, Sophie Templeton-Smythe's ex boyfriend

Stephen Harcourt, managing director, Harcourt Properties

Julian Corrigan, partner, Plummer, Goodspeed and Bleriot, City law firm

Nigel Platts, partner, KPMG, chartered accountants

*Freddie Wordsworth, co-founder, Wordsworth Wallis, financial public
relations*

David Cooper, partner, Gouldens, City law firm

Roderick King, finance director, Pitcairn

Stuart Robinson, corporate finance executive, Dundas Brothers

BMP plc (ex British Medical Products), pharmaceutical conglomerate

Lord (Arthur) Evans, chairman, BMP

Dr George Aladyce, chief executive, Pitcairn

Martin Lampard, senior partner, Ashurst, Morris, Crisp & Co, City law firm

David Stephenson, partner, trade practices, Plummers

Justin Travers-Coe, partner of Gourlay Gilfillan, stockbrokers to Pitcairn

Robert Maxwell, chairman, Maxwell Communications Corporation (MCC), publishers

Claudia Hennessy, wife of Christopher

Antony Beevor, director-general Take-Over Panel (on secondment from Hambros)

Virginia Hennessy, daughter of Christopher and Claudia

Sabine Zeitlin, mother of Claudia Hennessy

Oscar Hennessy, son of Christopher and Claudia

Gillian Wilkinson, corporate finance director, Grossmanns

Dr Lindsay Cunningham, research chemist, Pitcairn

John Addey, public relations consultant and parliamentary lobbyist

Boris, Addey's sidekick

Christopher Snaithe, case officer, Office of Fair Trading (OFT)

Dr Martin Ryan, OFT economist

Simon Masters, OFT working party secretary

Daphne Phelps, OFT healthcare industry specialist

Geoffrey Peabody, OFT consumer affairs adviser

Peter Harrington, partner, Harrington Ingram, private investigators

Peter Fraser, permanent staff, Take-Over Panel

Seamus O'Shea, Harrington's sleuth

Sally Rogers, secretary to Lord Evans

Andrea Martin, personal assistant to Robert Maxwell

Kevin Maxwell, son of Robert and director, MCC

Nicolla Duckworth, Peter Harrington's assistant, Harrington Ingram

John Soldatis, manager, Turtle Island Resort

Jacqueline Fortescue, guest, Turtle Island Resort

Jade Fortescue, her daughter

Susan Bradley, American guest, Turtle Island Resort

Milton Bradley, her husband

Igor Radziwill, guest, Turtle Island Resort

Eleanor Radziwill, his wife

Lars Stenhammar, senior forex trader, Den Copenhagen Bank

RheinHeim Bank, German commercial bank

Dantzic & Co, RheinHeim Bank's UK stockbroking subsidiary

Heinrich Röhrer, chairman, RheinHeim Bank

Stephen Gallaher, former non-executive director, Dundas Brothers and new chief executive

Tobias Hastings, private investigator, Hastings Associates

Jemima Wordsworth, wife of Freddie Wordsworth

Fay Harcourt, wife of Stephen Harcourt

Felicity Aladyce, wife of Dr George Aladyce

Carol Galley, fund manager, Mercury Asset Management

Mme Maxime Dubarry, Freddie Wordsworth's French factotum

Barclays de Zoete Wedd (BZW), merchant banking subsidiary of Barclays Bank

Wallis, Freddie Wordsworth's partner, Wordsworth Wallis

Générale des Chimiques, French pharmaceutical company

Guillaume de Fontaubert, président, Générale des Chimiques

Oberoi et Cie, Swiss private bank

Peter Lee, permanent staff, Take-Over Panel

Fidelity Trust Bank, UK bank, formerly building society

Wednesday, 16 December, 1987

Rain. Incessant rain. Not with a purpose, like it rains in Asia or Africa, so that afterwards the earth smells fertile, musty and sensual, like a lubricious mistress's bed. But like it rains in London - grey, cold, odourless, interminably miserable drizzle. It was 4.30 in the afternoon, already long dark. A foul December day.

On the fifth floor of 69 Gracechurch Street, at the intersection with Fenchurch Street, his back to an unlovely view of the grime-stained concrete tower of Barclays International, Peter Davenport was hunched over his paper-strewn desk in a glass-sided office barely larger than Davidoff's St James's Street cigar room. He was in his mid thirties, of medium height and build with thick wavy hair slightly on the fair side of brown, casually parted to the left. He wore a white shirt with bold red stripes and a red paisley tie, the jacket of a plain dark charcoal suit draped untidily over the back of his chair. The telephone at his side began to ring but he continued poring over the papers, ignoring it, until his secretary appeared in the open doorway and hustled him upstairs.

A liveried messenger in the uniform of a pre-war senior civil servant - pinstripes and black jacket - held open the door for him as he entered the sixth floor boardroom of Dundas Brothers. There were two men already there, absent-mindedly watching the rain trickling down the massive plate-glass window as they looked towards the lights of London Bridge and the scarlet on-off blinking of the brake lights of the traffic heading east and south. They turned as he entered. The taller of the two was in his early fifties, jet black hair brushed back in thick waves from a noble forehead. His features were grandly chiselled - a wide, generous mouth easily given to a broad and welcoming smile and a fine Greco-Roman nose separating blue trustworthy Celtic eyes. His dark blue double-breasted chalk-striped Saville Row suit was of impeccable cut, his Jermyn Street shirt, in a pale blue twill, the finest Egyptian cotton, his tie the broad dark red and blue stripes of the Grenadier Guards. He was relaxed, bronzed, at ease, every inch a money partner of the City stockbrokers, Wagstaff & Co.

His companion was also a partner; but that did not make the two men equal. He was much shorter, almost slight, but well proportioned, like a featherweight boxer, his features angular and hard and his eyes, though also blue, of an almost icily cruel intensity. His blond hair was cut very short at the back and the sides and, although only in his early thirties, was already forming a widow's peak on either side of a clever-looking cranium. He simply oozed intelligence; but in the *Animal Farm* that was Wagstaff & Co, it was brains good, money better.

The room in which the three men were now standing was absurdly huge, almost seventy feet in length, one whole side a sheet of glass. Opposite, where three matching doors were set flush so that they were almost concealed, the wall was panelled in a pale, warm, honey-coloured yew. Between the double doors in the middle and the two single doors on either side hung two oils in identical, heavy, dark gilt frames, late portraits by Joshua Reynolds of the bank's founders, Gordon Dundas, Lord Strathneven, and his younger brother, then Captain but subsequently Sir Alastair, both dating from 1786. They were powerful paintings, both full of the colour, fire and, it has to be said, flattery which had made Reynolds the most sought-after portrait painter of his generation. Gordon Dundas, then around fifty years old, was pictured in his ermine, bewigged and hosed, haughty and imperious. His much younger brother, not yet out of his twenties, handsome and devil-may-care, was in the brilliant blood-red, blue-lapelled and gold-braided uniform of a captain of cavalry, standing foursquare beside his charger, whose great glistening black neck swept across the lower left foreground as it pawed at the reddish earth. On the walls at each end of the room, also yew-panelled, were two more paintings, the one of a four-masted tea clipper racing across a spirited ocean, the other also of an eighteenth century sailing ship, no doubt once as gallant, foundering in mountanous seas. The artists in these cases were of no great importance but the subjects encapsulated the origins of Dundas Brothers in the tea trade. In reality, it was not until well into the nineteenth century that the financing of trade, and subsequently the financing of shipping and shipbuilding, so overtook the company's trading activities that Alastair Dundas, by then in sole charge, recognised the inevitable and Dundas Brothers assumed the nature of a merchant bank. But, in continuing deference to its origins, no coffee was ever served within the walls of No 69, only tea.

Between the two naval scenes and occupying substantially the whole room was a vast elliptically-sided table in matching yew. Thirty-five identical chairs, upholstered in dark green leather, were drawn up around it, a single chair, matching save for a higher back, positioned centrally facing the window. At each place was a green leather-bound notepad with the letters DB & Co picked out in gold at the bottom right. The table was otherwise bare save for a battalion of heavy silver ashtrays, made from the plated shell casings fired by HMS Dundas at the Battle of Jutland, laid out between each place, and a black calf-skin leather briefcase, no more than an inch and a half thick, that one of the two visitors had put there.

Though there was a mischievous dimple in his chin, Davenport's skin had the pallor of English winter. His eyes were blue and held the promise of a twinkle, but there were dark bags beneath them and, despite the automatic smile with which he had greeted his guests, his manner was brisk and business-like.

"Good afternoon, gentlemen. Thank you for braving this dreadful weather. I'm sorry we're stuck with the boardroom but every meeting room seems to be booked solid. Tell me your news." He motioned to the two naval scenes at either end of the boardroom, one with his right hand and the other with his left, and addressed the taller of his two visitors: "David, which end of this rather silly table should we be sitting? Do we have the wind in our sails or are we in peril of drowning?"

"Oh, I think somewhere in the middle would be appropriate, Peter," replied David Carradine, his large mouth breaking into a huge but mechanical smile at his riposte, as the door that led to the kitchen opened and a butler entered with tea on a silver tray.

"We have talked to a number of our friends today", Carradine began without preliminaries as his colleague opened his briefcase and handed him the single sheet of paper that was all it contained. "It would be fair to say that they were shocked by the extent of our mutual client's exposure and the gap that needs to be plugged; but, on the whole, they're being pretty grown-up about it."

Peter suppressed his natural response to this extraordinary combination of pomposity and condescension. He would have liked to know which institutions they had contacted; but knew that Wagstaff kept such intimacies to themselves. Instead he tackled his need to guage the extent of the risk he was about to run more obliquely.

"What proportion of the stock have you covered, David?"

"We restricted ourselves to around twenty per cent. We didn't want to go too wide. There's always the risk of a leak; and, with another twenty-odd per cent in the hands of the families, you can't get much further without going down to relatively small shareholdings. Whether or not we get the support of someone with only a half per cent is frankly not going to matter a tinker's cuss to the success or failure of this exercise."

"And the price?"

"We used two-for-five at 100p, as we had agreed." This was not strictly the complete truth. In their meeting the previous evening, Peter and his manager, Timothy Phillips, had tabled a schedule showing the amount of money that Bottley might raise using different combinations of price and weight. Two-for-five at 100p was the very bottom of the table. It would raise £40m, which was about right, but, compared with last night's closing price of 135p, it was a thumping discount. There could be no pretence that this was anything but a rescue. The family was not going to like it one bit. More to the point, Peter's bosses on the Risk & Exposures Committee might take some convincing that a rescue that could only be done on this basis was worth attempting at all.

"How was the market today, David?"

"Not bad overall. It was up another twenty points and Wall Street's higher too. Bottley were a penny better. All told, with the Footsie at 1690, we're almost a hundred points up on the beginning of last week; but the volumes are pitifully low and there's plenty of nervousness. And the spreads are pretty wide. In most places our client is 134 to 138 but Scrimgeours have them at 133 to nine and Laings at two to eight. The market's still torn between hoping we're over the worst and fearing we're all going to hell on a handcart."

"What about the family? I'm sure they won't be able to find £8m odd in short order. What chance the institutions coming in to pick up their rights nil paid? We really need a prior commitment if the shares aren't going to go straight down to the rights price."

"Difficult, Peter. Why should our friends pay old man Henderson-Ball 15 or 20p a share for his rights now when they might get them for a tanner three weeks down the line?"

"There's one thing that might persuade them," broke in the younger man at Carradine's side. It was the first time he had spoken. "The family at least ought to be persuaded to demonstrate their confidence in the company by undertaking a tail-swallowing."

Although the intervention had come from Max Thornhill, Peter gained the distinct impression that this was an orchestrated double act. Henderson-Ball was not going to take this price lying down. But that, Peter knew, was a pass already sold. Wagstaff would never go back to the 'friends' on whom they had tried 100p and now ask for something higher. He had given Carradine discretion the previous evening to sound out the institutions within a price range and the fact that Wagstaff had opted for the bottom end, and, Peter suspected, the bottom end alone was now a *fait accompli* . He continued to address his interrogation towards Carradine.

"Are you telling me that's what you need, David?"

"It would undoubtedly help. We'll see if we can line up some takers between now and 6.30 and let you know; but," David drew out his words slowly, sensing how Peter's brain was turning, "it won't make any difference to the price. It's 100p or nothing."

"Can you get it subbed for me, David?"

"I assume that we can rely on DAM's usual 10 per cent. It won't be easy; no guarantees; but we should get most of it away. I would have to say though, Peter, that some of our friends expressed deep misgivings about the shape of the management team. They like the new chief executive - an overdue dose of earthy common-sense - but they still think there's too much family influence. The old man ought to step down at the next Annual General Meeting and I think that must be included in tomorrow's announcement. But I'm sure that's one that we can confidently leave in your court."

*****

Peter Davenport returned to his office on the fifth floor with a claustrophobic sense of unease. The October crash had unnerved everyone and an exercise that only six months ago would have looked almost routine was now looking distinctly risky. He had never heard Carradine, or any of his partners, less certain of Wagstaff's abilities to twist arms as required. The formulae with which he was familiar included phrases such as 'reasonably confident of stitching that up', 'we would have to be very unfortunate if the funds could not absorb that' and 'subject to the market not going for a belly-flop on the day'. They never included the word 'guarantee'; but equally they never included the words 'no guarantee'. When Wagstaff said they should get it done, it was done. Only Cazenoves and Wagstaff were in this league. The sub-underwriting game was always one of a little bit of the rough mixed in with a lot of the smooth. They didn't come much rougher than Bottley Engineering in its present plight less than two months after Black Monday; but traditionally one had been able to get the institutions to step up to the plate on these occasions for fear of being dropped off the underwriting list. Wagstaff, like Cazenoves, were quick to take offence and they had memories as long and natures as blunt as computerised elephants.

Moreover, it wasn't just Peter's decision any longer. Sure, he would always have popped his head round Cyril's door, told him what was going on and got his nod. You couldn't always make out what on earth Cyril was saying; but you could normally get the drift as to whether it was a yay or a nay. Now, with all this bloody Guinness nonsense, the Bank of England had demanded that the merchant banks set up committees for this and committees for that. And what was the point of sitting on such a committee to approve your colleagues' decisions if you didn't nudge for a little variation now and again, if only to tweak their goolies. The Operations Committee of the Corporate Finance Division would probably be all right - Cyril, with his beloved garden beckoning him into retirement at the end of the year, was not going to tolerate any real change until then in the ability of one director to use his own judgement to commit his colleagues - but the Risks & Exposures Committee could be another matter. It was stuffed with the poisonous jealousies of those who saw but did not receive the corporate financiers' bonuses, the pointed steels of semi-professional back stabbers and the sharpened toe-caps of greasy pole climbers.

Peter picked up his phone and dialled an extension. "Tim, it's two-for-five at 100p.......Yes.......Yes......Yes, I know. Could you set up an Ops Com for 5.30 and a REC for 6.00. No, make the REC at 5.45. We could need a bit longer for that one. Is everyone set up for 6.30?....Fine, thanks. Oh, and let me have a copy of the latest draft of the press release"

As he put down the phone it rang immediately. It was Maureen, his secretary. "It's Sophie for you."

"Hi, Soppy, how's tricks?"

"Fine, darling. I'm just leaving the office and thought I'd pop in to Peter Jones for some pressies on the way home. It's their late night tonight. I should be back at the godown by 7.00 but we ought to be on our way out by 7.30; we're due at the Fordyces at 8.00 and, what with the weather, it could take for ever to get to Holland Park at this time of year. Any problems your end?"

"Only the usual crap. I suspect 8.00 is going to be a bit tight."

"What time's your last meeting?" she asked, a note of suspicion in her voice. "Please don't let this be one of those evenings you don't pitch at all," she pleaded.

"No danger of that, Soppy. I've just got some engineering oicks coming in who've run out of readies. I'll be shot of them by 8.30 latest. You know the Fordyces never sit down before nine. I'll be there by then. Promise. Why don't you call a cab and I'll bring the car and see you there."

"OK, but a cab would be better for you too. You know the way London is crawling with fuzz this time of year. I don't want you fastened to the end of one of their balloons on the way home. I'm intent on being knocked up in Courchevel this Christmas, not having you knocked up in Wormwood Scrubs."

"I'll do my best; but you can only get a fast black in the evening at the moment if you order it at noon. See you soon. Bye."

As he put the phone down, Maureen came in with the draft press release. "I hope you're not going to change this again," she said. "Tracey is already tearing her hair out. Lowe Bell have apparently rung through with six sets of changes in the last hour."

"Who's Tracey?'

"Tim's new secretary. She's only been here a fortnight but it's not like you not to have noticed her."

"Oh, it sounds like I must take a stroll around. Could you just get her to beam a copy of the text over to your machine, or whatever it is you girls do. I want her to keep the original but for you to produce an alternative version. Just give me a couple of minutes and I'll mark it up for you."

"OK, could I get Stephanie in to see you when it's ready? She said she only needs a couple of minutes; but it's something to do with the seating plan for tomorrow and she must see you tonight."

"Oh shit. It's the works' dance".......he pronounced it to rhyme with pants in mock working class Mancunian.

"Too right. That Sophie must be getting at you for that to have slipped your mind."

"Don't worry. There's life in the old dog yet. Wheel her in while you're typing this up."

Stephanie was Dundas Brothers' internal PR girl, which, in theory embraced everything from ensuring that the Corporate Finance Division did as good a job as any other investment bank to falsify its standing in the endless M&A league tables to organising the appearance of plentiful numbers of grouse, pheasant or other feathered offerings at a challenging height above the Chairman's invited guns during the season. It was also rumoured that she had found herself, wearing not so much as a feather boa, beneath a number of his guns from time to time in distant highland lodgings and Yorkshire moorland inns. She was slim and pert with tiny hips and an even tinier waist which she emphasised with tight wide belts and short straight skirts. Her shiny dark hair, straight and shoulder length, was either drawn back in a bobbing pony-tail or held with a bright red satin alice band. She was much taken to provocative dressing which usually took the form of thin white high-necked tee shirts stretched gloriously across her unconstrained breasts, small, round and firm. On really good days, perhaps a mite too cold for her attire, her headlights would shine out on full beam. Stocking tops and flashes of suspender-belted thigh were also occasional highpoints of an otherwise dull departmental day.

Stephanie had no sooner departed than Maureen had Max Thornhill on the line. "Peter, David asked me to give you a call about the tail-swallowing. We think we can do it like this. The family stand to be offered just over eight million shares. We think we can find buyers for 7.65 million nil-paid at 5p a share, which will give them enough to subscribe for the balance of their rights. OK?"

"Is that the best you can do, Max? Those shares have a theoretical nil-paid value of 25.7p each. The old man's not going to be overjoyed at an offer like that."

"Well, I know that the theoretical value is a bit higher; but we must expect the shares to fall quite sharply tomorrow. The extent of the problem is not in the price yet. In reality it's not negotiable."

Peter's experienced nose detected the whiff of a stitch-up - all too probably by the partners of Wagstaff itself. A quick scuttle over his calculator confirmed that, even if the share price fell 20 per cent on the news, those nil-paids were going to be worth around 9p each - a quick profit of £300,000 for the partners of Wagstaff & Co, who had no doubt already laid off the risk on their clients' discretionary funds. Still, who was he to care? His loyalty was to the awful Bottley rather than the even more awful family that controlled it.

"OK, Max. I think we'll just have to force it down their well-fed throats."

Maureen, rising from her desk just outside Peter's office, came in with with the new draft press release.

"You're due for the Ops Com in Bishop's office. They're waiting for you," she clucked. The tensions of these occasional bouts of frenetic activity when deals were in progress seemed to get to her more and more as the years progressed. She had been working for Peter for six years now, as long as he had been a director, but her hormones were conspiring against the calm assurance that ought to have come with experience.

She was blonde streaked grey, or, more likely, vice versa, and what would once have been called a handsome woman. Much given to the lifting and separation of her ample bosom, she was in her mid forties and something to do with the stress of the forthcoming menopause provoked her nipples to occasional bouts of spectacular prominence. She was inclined to blush at the obvious resulting glances; but quite enjoyed the attention notwithstanding. Whereas Stephanie in this condition set up internal calls of "come in, Rangooooooooon" as executives twiddled with the knobs of imaginary radio receivers, Maureen on such occasions induced imitations of 007 throwing an invisible trilby at a pair of all too visible hat pegs.

The Operations Committee, chaired by Cyril, passed without incident. Hank Amadeo, the only American amongst the London-based corporate finance directors, had for some reason been seconded as the independent director and was clearly baffled by the arcane mysteries of the London rights issue system. He might have hoped for some enlightenment if anyone but Cyril had been in the chair; but Cyril, reading the papers for the first time, confined his comments to: "Timothy never up to his father's mark", which Hank thought to be unnecessarily critical in front of young Timothy Phillips, who seemed to have done a competent job of preparing the papers. This was followed by "Insurers never any value when they're needed" which Hank took to be a reference to institutional investors generally; and "How much does David hold?" which passed over Amadeo's head completely and even Peter only just caught as a reference to David Sellar, head of Dundas Asset Management.

"Just over three per cent," Peter replied.

"Pity it's not in his own portfolio," Cyril threw out gruffly before concluding "that's all right then", appending the indecipherable squiggle that constitued his signature to the bottom of the minute and rising on his one good leg, an audible squeak coming from the joint of the other as he dragged it out from under the desk.

"Right, Peter, let's go and get this past those credit cretins," he said over his shoulder as he lurched out of his office leaving his stick hanging on the peg behind his door.

The Risks & Exposures Committee met on the second floor around the meeting table in the office of Alan Bentham, head of credit control, who was its chairman. The mere location offended Cyril, who felt this petty functionary had much exceeded his station in carving out a lavish corner office for himself. That he should then have been appointed chairman of a committee which dared to second-guess the princelings of corporate finance was an added insult. The other members of the committee were the heads of the bank's divisions, or their deputies if they were not available, and the finance director, Henry Morrissey. The turnout today was Bentham, Alex Maguire, the head of treasury, Juan-Antonio Villareal, the head of international, Jeremy Stone for commercial lending, Cyril for corporate finance, David Sellar of Asset Management, and Morrissey.

They were all there by the time Cyril and Peter arrived. "Nothing better to do," muttered Cyril under his breath to no one in particular.

Most of them were already sitting around the table but Villareal and Sellar were engaged in a conspiratorial discussion of their own over in the far corner by the window. Villareal, an exceptionally tall man with the confident air of a true grandee, was the heir to the Duke of Cartagena. He was swarthy and large with a mass of black curly hair, the sort of man who would look like a gorilla on the beach, if ever he ventured to leave whatever yacht he was then gracing to step amongst the masses. Apart from being blessed with dukedoms and ducats, he had also been endowed with enough brains to know how to exploit the British incompetence of anything to do with Europe. He was accordingly scandalously overpaid for an ability which in reality amounted to no more than the knowledge of five European languages and access to the boardrooms of the many continental banks and corporations which numbered amongst their directors his aristocratic cousins. When in London, he lived in some style in a grand apartment on the north side of Eaton Square; but he was more often than not jetting around the world. Somehow or another, it always appeared that he had business in Monaco when it was Grand Prix time, in Milan for La Scala's grandest opening nights and in Paris for the Prix de l'Arc de Triomphe. There was seldom significant revenue to show for any of this other than a string of unremunerative co-managements of the eurobond issues managed by Warburgs and Morgan Stanley; but, as Villareal always pointed out, this was a start-up business for Dundas Brothers and they only needed to be seen to be moving in the right circles and to maintain their investment for the breakthrough to come. Michael von Clemm and Stani Yassukovich, with whom he was working closely on the co-leads of a number of massive potential deals, had confirmed as much to him over the telephone only yesterday.

David Sellar was also tall but more slimly built. His shoulders, which were as narrow as his hips, sloped down sharply from each side of his neck; but his suits were expensively and generously cut so that the cloth appeared to swirl around him effortlessly, occasionally exposing the brightly coloured linings which were his one concession to flamboyance. His languid elegance seemed emphasised by the fact that he never appeared to be remotely hurried. Indeed the world passed him by at some level beneath what he considered worthy of his direct gaze. In this respect, as in many others, he possessed all the traditional qualities of an old Etonian - self-assurance to the point of certainty, the superiority borne of being in perpetual receipt of deference and the sort of independence of thought which can only be had from knowing that one's own personal circumstances will not in the least be affected by any decisions one takes for one's employer, right or wrong.

He came from one of those old secularised Jewish families which had infiltrated themselves thoroughly into the uppermost levels of the landed English gentry but which nevertheless never seemed to marry outside the diaspora.

Peter, whose own schooling had been at Winchester, found in him contrasts between the products of his own and the Etonian upbringing which he instinctively disliked. It was not that David was not intelligent; but he was more simply aloof than genuinely clever. It was not that he could not be an interesting companion; but he was more full of mannered wit than spontaneous bonhomie. It was not that he was not a team player; but you always knew that this was a man who was part of the team when it was winning but would be somewhere else when there were scores to be settled for losses.

As they took their places round Bentham's meeting table, Peter was maliciously delighted to see that Jeremy Stone, who he admired both for his formidable intellect and his ageing bohemian sang froid, was already well down his first Disque Bleu. Bentham was known to detest cigarette smoke and there was no ashtray to be found in his office. Stone, undeterred, had as usual taken the waste-paper basket from behind Bentham's desk and placed it beside his chair.

Peter distributed the short position paper that had been used for the earlier Ops Com and briefly summarised its contents before Bentham, who liked to conduct these meetings more formally from the chair, had a chance to say a word. At the first opportunity, he sought to bring as much order into the proceedings as his weedy Birmingham accent would permit.

"I think we need, gentlemen, to be particularly mindful on this occasion of the Chinese wall implications of this transaction. We have many relationships with Bottley across a number of divisions of the bank. This committee is, of course, entitled to straddle the Chinese walls and look down, so to speak, on everythink on either side; but we must ensure that the decision we take is in the best interests of Bottley Engineerink, as CFD's client, even where those interests might conflict with our own. For the record, could we begin by spellink out those other interests. Jeremy."

"We've organised and syndicated a number of financings for overseas projects undertaken by Bottley over the years. They have all been substantially guaranteed under ECGD arrangements and our total retained exposure on Bottley would only amount to a short million. Financially, it wouldn't matter a row of beans to us if Bottley went down the gurgler; though, as syndicate lead, it would involve us in some tiresome admin. The clearers are, of course, in over their ears with those dunderheads at Midland leading the charge as usual. Our recent syndications have been largely taken up by the Japs, who have been quoting silly margins to break into this market."

Jeremy, whose threshold of patience with Bentham had long been exhausted by the latter's role as co-ordinator of the risks run by the bank in general and his own division in particular, was already deeply bored and, following this contribution, he slouched languidly in his chair. He was around six foot but almost cadaverously thin in a way that only a man who substituted nicotine for nutrition could possibly achieve. His face was long and pointed at the nose and the chin, his hair thinning and the creases at his forehead and on either side of his mouth deeper than was appropriate to his fifty-five odd years. He and Bentham were of equal seniority in the bank but Bentham was younger. He sought to try to emphasise his hold over Stone's decisions by his insistence on holding meetings of this committee and the Credit Committee, which he also chaired, in his own office. Stone, in turn, delighted in making these meetings as noxious as possible in the certainty that Bentham's small-mindedness would not allow him to retreat to the neutral ground of an internal meeting room where Jeremy's fug could afterwards be left to fester.

Stone's little speech had given him the opportunity to ignore a growing and drooping finger of ash on the end of his cigarette, which now fell on the table and which he brushed, not entirely absent-mindedly, onto the carpet with a skeletal hand. Peter, sitting next to him, was delighted to see another little touch which conspired to keep the distinctive odour of Gallic tobacco hanging in Bentham's precious air, notwithstanding the open Air-wick on the window sill and the sickly sweet smell of cheap perfume which could only have come from some sort of regular discharge of a canister intended to tackle more lavatorial odours. With a final flourish, Stone now leaned down to ground the stub out on the leather interior of Bentham's waste-paper basket, adding another black burn mark to territory he had visited on many previous occasions and at the same time ensuring that the stale smell would linger there for the maximum possible time.

"What about you, Alex? Any treasury exposures?" Bentham asked, his nose curled up in anguished disgust at Stone's behaviour.

Alex was a shortish, round faced bachelor with small, button-like, darting, nervous eyes and gingerish hair which never appeared to be exactly the same colour two Mondays running. His skin was too smooth for his years, almost like a middle-aged baby, as if he had never had to shave. He had been with the bank from the age of sixteen, thirty-odd years ago, a barrow-boy with a brain like a calculator. He had no obvious interests beyond a two pip margin on a hundred mill of cable; but he took his summer holidays in Phuket and his winter break in Marrakesh and the former was not for the beaches and the latter was not for the casbah.

"We do most of their spot forex and a good bit of their currency and interest rate hedging. They've a good finance director and he doesn't let their exposures get out of hand - very easy with an international business operating on huge turnover and low margins. They do £700 mill annually, mostly overseas, for a profit of about £18 million. As a result we've got the thick end of £300 mill of outstanding contracts, most short-term but around fifty stretching out to three years. As it happens, though, we could close the whole lot out in the market if they went under at minimal net loss."

"Juan-Antonio?" Bentham wrestled his way nasally around the syllables.

"Nothing. They have no outstandings in the Eurobond market," he replied in tones more polished than any to which Bentham would ever aspire, in any language, and with a studied disdain for business with a company that was below the horizon as far as international financial recognition was concerned.

"And you, David?"

"We have a bit over three per cent of the shares, spread about half and half between discretionary pension funds and the high-yield unit trust. We wouldn't want any more, of course, particularly in the unit trust since I see that it's now proposed that they pass the dividend. But we haven't been approached by Wagstaff on any underwriting, so we have no commitment, what. I'll be shedding stock once the announcement gives us the all-clear to do so. We've held it for eons but its only attraction has been the dividend."

"That's not strictly speaking tr.... the case," said Peter, correcting himself in time from labelling David a liar and recalling to himself how often Sellar had been attracted to take up the invitations of Sir Timothy Henderson-Ball, Bart to lay waste the moors and rivers of the northern marches. "There is an understanding that DAM take 10 per cent of all CFD underwritings up to £15 million and this, at around a £4 millon share, falls well within that limit. Wagstaff have taken that into their calculations."

"Well they can take it right out again," Sellar snapped back. "We have a right to 10 per cent of the sub-underwriting, but no obligation to take it."

"That is not my understanding," Peter said carefully, trying to keep the temperature down. "I cannot recall an occasion when it has ever been otherwise."

"If that is the case, it is because we haven't been involved in doing rescue rights issues. I cannot be expected to put discretionary funds into an issue like this and least of all at over three times their current weighting in the stock."

Alan Bentham was torn between the gathering excitement of the occasion and a feeling that tempers were getting beyond his limited chairmanical skills. He turned to Bishop for help. "Cyril, what's your understanding of this?"

"We've done a number of these issues. I recall one for Winkley Breweries in 1968, one for Stanley Properties in 1972 and wasn't there Turner Industries around 1978 or '79," he mused, conveniently forgetting to address the question of whether or not there was an agreement between CFD and Asset Management.

"For heaven's sake," exploded Sellar, "Winkley Breweries was absorbed by Bass or some such while I was still at Oxford."

"And right piss they made too," added Stone unhelpfully, lighting one Disque Bleu from another. "That old George's Brewery in Bristol was their only serious competitor in the cats' pee stakes."

"Is there anythink we can do to resolve this one, Cyril? There's either an agreement or there isn't and we ought to know what it says." He pronounced it Midlands-style as 'sayes'.

"There is an agreement and it sayes what I say it sayes," Cyril imitated, only half intentionally. "We've had it since young David here was in shorts. James put it all together."

"Was that James I of England or James VI of Scotland?" mocked Sellar, intensely irritated by the 'young David' and for whom the history of any dynasty but his own was unimportant.

"No, our James," Cyril explained helpfully.

"Which James?" By now Sellar's exasperation was beginning to colour his cheeks.

"James upstairs." This said with a slight rolling of Cyril's watery old eyes towards the ceiling.

"What James upstairs? You sound as though you're talking about St James." A fleck of spittle showed at the corner of his mouth.

"Sir James, my boy, the Chairman, when he was head of corporate finance."

"There we are," said Jeremy Stone gleefully, "we are talking about St James. What do you say to that one, David?" he chortled, the opportunity to twist Sellar's gentrified tail being only marginally less attractive to him than a good kick at Bentham's bourgeois rump.

Sellar could see no escape. It baffled him completely that Sir James Cruso, scion of an old and distinguished Scottish family, should have taken Cyril Bishop, a barely middle class self-educated former clerk, to his heart, appointing him as his successor as head of corporate finance almost eight years ago now; but he knew that whatever Cyril could explain, and plenty that he could not, was accepted as gospel by the chairman. It was far from clear if Cyril's legendary memory was figment or reality; but he had recalled just enough obscure documents in his time that turned out to contain what he claimed, that no one would challenge him on that score between now and his garden. It was more than a suspicion in some quarters that Cyril was shrewd enough to harness this power to make every single event that he needed a precedent and every such event, once repeated, a custom.

"Well, I'm sure we can check that with the chairman in due course," said Sellar, knowing full well that he would dare do no such thing and turning immediately to a second line of attack; "but, in any event, I am far from convinced that we should be supporting this issue. It's far too soon after Black Monday to be trying to do something like this. We don't need to go pioneering with the likes of Bottley and their problems. What sort of analysis has been done to think that this issue can be got away?"

This was more the sort of question for which Peter had prepared. "There have been four significant underwritings or placements since the crash: Eurotunnel, which I would accept was a special case, BA to finance the cash alternative in the bid for British Caledonian, Mecca's 2 for 7 rights to finance the purchase of holiday camps from Ladbroke and a placing by Williams to fund the purchase of Berger Paints. There has also been a lot of bid activity generally with strong companies taking advantage of lower prices to snap up potential targets. Granada for Electronic Rentals, Honkers and Shankers for 14.9 per cent of Midland, BA for BCal, RTZ and Legrand competing for MK Electric, the KIO have been snapping up BP shares and BP itself is trying to get 30 per cent of Britoil. All this is going to feed into institutional liquidity."

"Now that's a highly selective summary, if ever I heard one, what" snapped back Sellar, who, of course, also knew his way round the markets. "The institutional take-up of failed underwritings in issues that straddled the crash took at least £500 million out of the market, the Berger Paint deal was private and will not benefit institutional liquidity one jot, the original BA offer for BCal last month was underwritten but they had to get the cash for their improved bid last week out of their own resources, twenty per cent of Eurotunnel was left with the underwriters and the Mecca rights issue, which was nothing like as heavy as this, knocked their share price to hell - and it's far from clear that they got it all sub-underwritten, what."

"We think Mecca's a helpful benchmark and we're proposing a price that draws a clear distinction between that, as an expansionist exercise, and Bottley, which is clearly a rescue. The Mecca discount was 20 per cent flat. We're proposing a discount of over 26 per cent flat, more than

20 per cent even on the theoretical ex rights price. We're allowing a lot of room for a price correction."

"What about the family?" It was Alex, looking up from his Hewlett-Packard. "I guess they won't be able to find their share and they're going to be diluted to hell. Their stake in the company is going to fall from 20.216 per cent to 14.434 per cent."

"I'm proposing to insist that they maintain their cash investment by doing a tail-swallowing. Wagstaff have assured me that they can find takers for the family's nil-paids at 5p per share."

"That's going to involve them taking a theoretical loss into the bargain of," he hesitated for just a moment as his fingers flashed over the buttons of his HP80, "£1.64 million. Strong medicine. It's certainly giving the institutions their pound of flesh. And they'll still have 21.2 million shares, plenty to lose if things go wrong. I'd go along with that if Peter can swing it."

"How about a new Chairman? Shouldn't that fat old buffer, the knight of the shires, be made to fall on his sword." This time it was Jeremy, as ever keen to kick the establishment in the cobblers whenever the opportunity presented.

"I am going to propose that he goes at the AGM next April. It's not in the draft press announcement that you have in front of you because I haven't told him yet."

"Well that should be quite fun," Jeremy smirked. "I've heard that the old sod has a temper like Vesuvius on plutonium."

"Indeed he has," Peter confirmed, his foreboding rising as the time for the completion meeting grew closer. As if to confirm its imminence, the door behind him opened and a messenger slipped a note to him from Tim informing him that everyone was now assembled upstairs in the boardroom.

"Never mind that," said Sellar, without for a moment pausing to regret the downfall of someone he would until today have labelled, if not actually a friend, at least a regular sporting companion, "I am still concerned at the shape of this issue. Even if we accept that the company needs to raise money, it would be better to do a preference issue, what. The pricing would be much more certain because of the fixed yield and the underwriting would be much less risky."

"I am afraid that the reality is that the company cannot afford to service a preference issue of this size in the short to medium term. For the next two years at least, most of the earnings are going to come from the Far East and there won't be sufficient UK tax capacity to absorb the ACT on a pref issue."

"Are you sure that you've looked at all the alternatives?" whined Bentham, desperately seeking a way out.

"We are confident that we have looked at all the *options*," Peter replied, correcting Bentham's grammar to the undisguised merriment of Jeremy Stone.

"I am still not convinced that this issue is necessary at all," came back Sellar, trying a final tack. "Are you sure you've got the sums right, Peter?"

"Unfortunately, I'm absolutely certain; and, of course, all the numbers have been gone over by Deloittes." Time was running on and he saw no point in pulling any punches. "Without this issue, David, Bottley shares could be worthless within a matter of days."

"Can Wagstaff get it sub-underwritten for us?" It was Morrissey's first intervention and typically rapier-like.

"They've sounded out the key institutions today," replied Peter, and, mentally swallowing hard, he was almost surprised to hear himself say "and they're confident of getting it away."

Even Bentham could see that this was getting nowhere and, Peter having passed him the note, he was aware that a conclusion was necessary. Lacking the skills to achieve a concensus on his own, he turned to Bishop for some help.

"Cyril, have you got anything further to add?"

"This is what we're for. No point in pretending otherwise. Nothing to do with the crash. Long-standing. Brought them to the market in the twenties. We mustn't be blown off course. Tomorrow will not wait. Not the least doubt that by the New Year, it will not all be never thought of again."

"Well that's all right then," said Morrissey, starting at first to attempt to determine whether the double negative was a triple or quadruple before eventually giving up. "This one is down to corporate finance," he added, hoping to establish where blame would lie if it all ended in tears. "Where's the minute for us to sign?"

*****

The cast in the boardroom had divided between the paper-shufflers and the decision-makers. At one end of the vast table Angus Hewat and Richard Cranfield of Allen & Overy, who were acting as legal advisers to Dundas Brothers, had pushed the chairs back against the walls and were setting out piles of documents in preparation for the signing. Max Thornhill was supplying the Stock Exchange documents and Oliver Quentin-Archard, one of Tim Phillips' executives, had a box of proof circulars from the printers together with the as yet innocent version of tomorrow's press release. Henry Pickthorne from Linklaters & Paines, who had been Bottley's solicitor for ever, was also fussing around as usual, looking ever more like a retired vicar.

Peter took in the scene as he entered and went to the other end of the boardroom where David Carradine was exchanging bonhomie with Sir Timothy. The latter was accompanied by his old mucker Ben Silkin, the non-executive deputy chairman of Bottley and, more to the point, a senior executive director of Brocklebank Nobel, which, though no longer the foremost, was still generally accepted as London's oldest-established merchant bank. His unexpected presence heightened Peter's unease. These completion meetings always involved a bit of last minute confrontation; and second-guessing from a competitor, who was under no obligation to put his own chopper on the block, was always going to be unhelpful.

"I'm sorry to be late, Chairman. Just a few formalities to process downstairs. I'll just get Tim to check that the lawyers are ready and then we'll get started."

Tim Phillips was standing a little way off with Frank Griffiths, Bottley's chief executive and Stanley Hollingsworth, the finance director. The Bottley directors, at the decision-maker's end of the boardroom, had thus divided themselves, as if by natural selection, between the patricians and the plebeians.

Peter had come across Frank Griffiths only occasionally until his appointment as chief executive earlier that year. For some years he had been running Bottley's successful Asian and Australian contracting operations out of Singapore. He was the bluffest and craggiest of Yorkshiremen and Peter could only wonder what the yellow peril must have made of him. But he had certainly got results. Nevertheless, one could not help thinking that, if there had been any male member of the

Henderson-Ball family between Sir Timothy and the twenty-six year old engineer now working on the construction of his first oil rig in the Berwick yard, known at head office simply as Mr Jocelyn, then the job would have been his. The Henderson-Balls, through a combination of commercial piracy and bucolic inter-breeding, were more wealthy than skilful and more accident-prone than prolific. The Chairman himself was now childless (or more particularly the Chairman's wives - he was currently on number four - since there were some remarkable resemblances to the squire amongst the youngsters of the parish to testify to the adequacy of Sir Timothy's own plumbing). His only acknowledged son - by wife number one - would attempt to breed no more after misjudging his approach to the private cricket ground which doubled as a landing strip on the family farm at Masham and cartwheeling his Cessna off an inauspiciously placed oak into the pavilion. He had been returning from a visit to his mistress, and the groundsman was heard unkindly to remark that it was the only occasion he could recall that Mr Bobby had returned to the pavilion having scored. The mantle had then passed to Sir Timothy's cousin, George, whose dim-wittedness was no obstacle to being chief executive of the family firm but whose twenty stone frame had proved too much for a heart that was as feeble as his mind. His death in March this year at 54 had left the board with no option but to turn to Frank , who was appointed on such grudging terms as to leave no doubt that he was only keeping the seat warm for Mr Jocelyn.

Bottley's finance function had been run for the last seven years, in an unadventurous but workmanlike manner, by Stanley Hollingsworth, who had come to the company from GEC, where he was a divisional accountant. Years of monthly submissions of capital expenditure proposals, management accounts, cash flow statements and rolling forecasts to the miserly scrutiny of Arnold Weinstock had left Stanley more or less robotic and insensible to insult. It was just as well. If the Chairman had been less well-born, he would have been the sort to refer to the finance director as 'nowt but scorer'. Within the group, most engineers had been brought up to believe that 'fucking accountant' was a single word.

Peter Davenport had done his best to get to know Frank Griffiths in the months since his return to Bottley's head office in Darlington;

but Frank was not easy with his confidences. He had expressed to Peter his general satisfaction at the state of Bottley's finances: "'Appen Stanley knows what he's about"; and his only criticism of the engineering empire that he had returned to his native Yorkshire to run was summarised in the sentence: "A few of t' lads could do wi' a course in good 'ousekeeping; but I'll knock 'em in ta shape." Peter had invited Frank and his wife to a couple of the social occasions of the English summer season; but Frank would no more be seen in tails and topper at Ascot than in a tutu on the stage of the Royal Ballet. Some said that this social reticence was on account of his wife. The formidable Mrs Griffiths, his childhood sweetheart, who would have looked even less appealing than Frank in tutu and pumps but who would have insisted on acceptance of any invitation that included the potential for social-climbing, had been dumped in Singapore in favour of a lady of Chinese extraction her husband had met in a bar in Kuala Lumpur and converted into his secretary. She was exactly half the age of the first Mrs Griffiths and more or less half her weight. With breathtaking hypocricy, given his own record, Sir Timothy Henderson-Ball had relayed the whole salacious tale to Peter as evidence of the need for Frank to be merely a caretaker chief executive - "never suitable to be chairman". Peter had been wondering what he could do next to break the ice and meet this oriental siren when, one day in mid-November, Maureen had called him out of the directors' morning meeting to tell him that Frank Griffiths wanted to talk to him urgently on the phone.

"Bit o' bother, lad, in Ras al Jamal. Whole lot went oop two nights ago. T' Arabs are trying ta finger oos."

Peter put his hand over the mouth-piece. "What the hell is he talking about?" he said to Tim Phillips, whom he had called into his office to listen in on the separate ear-piece. "It's like being addressed by a northern version of Cyril Bishop." Tim shrugged unhelpfully, muttered something about "Trouble at t' mill" and then covered his mouth with his hand to prevent any of his subsequent guffaws being detected at the other end of the line.

"'ello...'ello..can tha 'ear me?"

"Yes, sorry, Frank. I'm just getting a note-pad. Can you give it to me again?"

"Look, lad. T' refinery where we're working in t' Gulf has just blown up like t' end of a fooking James Bond fillum. There's a billion dollars worth of fooking damage and t' sheikh of Araby or whatever he bluddy calls 'isself wants some chump ta blame. T' contract engineer is flying over wi' a report. I need ye here in t' morning."

"OK, Frank. We'll be up on the early train. Could you get Stanley to run the numbers on the financial implications?"

"Too bluddy right he will, lad."

"Anything he could let us have on the fax this afternoon would be very helpful."

"Right ye are, lad. Bye."

By 11.30 next morning Peter and Tim were sitting in the boardroom of Bottley Engineering's drab offices in the centre of Darlington, with the chairman, chief executive and finance director.

The Chairman was what used to be called a man's man. Once probably athletic, he was now on the portly side of well-built and, though his ruddy cheeks were still splendidly bewhiskered, his small piggy blue eyes were the more arresting feature. For many years now, he had been a regular feature of the *News of the World*, which covered the procession of mistress to wife to new mistress to divorce court to registry office and round and round again in exquisite detail. But it had to be said that he was a genial host and Peter himself had spent some glorious sunlit afternoons under the oaks at Masham watching Sir Timothy's Invitation XI, always captained, like a faithful lap-dog, by the ubiquitous Geoffrey Boycott, taking on the various teams that were arranged for Henderson-Ball's seasonal delight. Afterwards, the gentrified guests, into which group the rhinoceros-skinned Boycott never failed to infiltrate, would repair to his grand Georgian mansion to indulge in the edible and potable elements of the old man's interests.

Peter Davenport had taken over responsibility for the Bottley account some four years previously when the latest promotion of mistress to wife was in progress. The outgoing Lady Henderson-Ball was the ex-wife of a local farmer whose mammaries had set the old boy's pulse racing as she led the champion ram past him when he was judging at the North Yorkshire Agricultural Show. It had been as much as his agitated fingers could do to pin the winner's rosette to the beast rather than to the gaping blouse of its owner; and it was not long before her husband discovered that it was not just her pedigree rams that were tupping. Unfortunately the mammaries were a snare and a delusion when it came to breeding the hoped-for replacement son and heir and, as Lady Henderson-Ball's hips widened and lips thinned, Sir Timothy turned for solace to an escort agency in Beauchamp Place, round the corner from his London flat in Cadogan Square. One evening, the proprietress of this establishment, at her wit's end when a group of visiting executives from Dai-ichi Kangyo Bank had cleared out her entire complement of girls, had presented herself, in response to his call, on the doorstep of Sir Timothy Henderson-Ball's apartment. Her looks were somewhat faded, her jet-black hair had the sort of metallic sheen that only comes out of a bottle and her breasts were no longer as firm and her belly as flat as was nature's ideal; but the tense musculature of her bra and the satin tightness of her dress still made the overall effect eye-catching. Furthermore, as Sir Timothy was soon to discover, she had a menu of tricks the like of which had never been seen in the Yorkshire dales. And that was how the fourth Lady Henderson-Ball came to be a cockney tart turned madam. Peter found her a delight, wickedly conspiratorial, shrewd and unbelievably foul-mouthed. On the occasions when he saw her, she was always taking the piss out of Boycott, forever probing his curious love-life in the smuttiest terms and leaving the super-bore floundering like a schoolboy on the end of a Wes Hall yorker. At the same time, as a lifetime of excess came to get the better of her husband's body, gout, flatulence and obesity notwithstanding, she treated him with a kindliness that was genuinely endearing and raised her in Peter's mind above the level of the bounty-hunter that everyone assumed her to be.

She would certainly not have met with the approval of the four generations of Hendersons, Balls and Henderson-Balls whose pictures now gazed down upon the group assembled in the Darlington board room; but a more dramatic picture held the attention of the six men around the table. A large aerial photograph of the site at Ras al Jamal was set out in front of them. It looked like nothing on earth; a huge expanse of tortured, charred and tangled metal splayed outwards for hundreds of metres from the clear origin of the explosion just to the north-west of the centre of the site, which had been outlined on the photograph in blue. The site engineer, his baked suntanned face etched deeply with weariness, had just finished repeating his briefing for the benefit of the bankers. Bottley Engineering were acting as sub-contractors to construct 40 oil tanks on the eastern seaboard side of the site and a dozen large pressurised propane gas tanks and associated pipework on the western side within the new refinery, natural gas liquids fractionation and storage plant which Techtel of the United States were building for the sheikh. The whole complex was due for completion early in the new year and commissioning was well advanced when suddenly, at about 2am in the morning on Tuesday, 10 November, there had been a massive explosion on the mid-western side of the site which had, over the course of a few seconds, engulfed the whole place in a stupendous fireball. The entire refinery had been destroyed with 22 workers dead or missing, a mercifully low loss of life thanks to the hour of the tragedy.

"Techtel's preliminary contention," said the Chairman, "is that the explosion originated in one of the ten pressurised tanks which we had completed and were in use, either as a result of a faulty weld or the supply of steel of inadequate quality. We have absolute proof that the welds in all the vessels which had been handed over had been x-rayed and subjected to ultrasonic checks with the latest equipment and that the results had been recorded as satisfactory. Furthermore, all materials had been certified on delivery to be fit for purpose. Techtel themselves had inspected the records and accepted the completed tanks on that basis. Whatever the cause of the explosion, it wasn't our tanks, our workmanship or our materials."

"Where on this photograph were your gas tanks?" asked Peter.

"Well, this enlargement has only just arrived and I haven't had a chance to check it yet; but I've got a perspex slide here drawn to the same scale which shows the site of the tanks," the engineer said. "I'll just position it exactly over the photograph. Right, that's just so. The tanks were built in three rows of four and this one, number eight, was the one that was commissioned last week."

Peter and Tim gazed dumbstruck at the photograph with the plan of the site superimposed on the perspex sheet above it. The eastern wall of number eight tank was the position from which all the surrounding devastation clearly emanated. It was the very epicentre of Armageddon.

"The evidence against Bottley is purely circumstantial," said Sir Timothy, breaking the silence. It was difficult to know whether he simply had such a thick hide from being caught so often with his trousers round his ankles or whether intuition had told him that this was the picture he had to expect all along. "I am absolutely confident that our site records will show our work to have been carried out according to the contract. Don't you agree, Frank?"

"I 'ope so, Chairman. It's a matter of 'ousekeeping really. Not always Bottley's best, in my opinion, as tha' knows."

"Really, Frank, this is no time for continuing that debate. The explosion must have some other cause. We cannot allow ourselves to be taken for a billion dollars on the basis of a claim which is backed by such flimsy evidence."

"'Appen, Sir Timothy, you're right; but I'd like to 'ear what our friends from t' City have to say."

No medium-sized engineering company carries the sort of insurance cover that would be necessary to provide protection from such a loss and Stanley Hollingsworth, for all his conservatism, had not made Bottley the exception. In many respects no matter. The years before final arbitration of any such claim would take Bottley into the era of Mr Jocelyn and no one would have any incentive to go beyond what the insurers would make good. Nobody was going to put Bottley under for this one. But they might just bleed it to death. The sheikh was king, parliament and judiciary in his own land; and he was also Bottley's best and biggest customer. With separate contracts for his new container terminal just down the coast at Mukaba Bay and the huge new desalination plant to feed his ambition for a desert of plenty, he was also their biggest debtor - and right now it had been made clear to Bottley by an official of his treasury that he wasn't paying. Within two months, Bottley's bank borrowings would balloon from £55 million to almost £100 million. Stanley had on his hands the one thing that his mentor, Arnie Weinstock, had not even taught him how to spell - a cash flow crisis.

"Stanley, what's the insurance position on this?" asked Peter.

"We have cover on this contract for a bit over £80 million on product liability and consequential loss. Techtel would obviously be carrying much more than that; but I doubt if it adds up to a full $1 billion. In any event, they're reserving their position and saying that they might wish to put a counter-claim on us for anything that's claimed against them. Anyway, that's not really the immediate problem, which is one of cash, as you'll have seen from the figures I faxed you down last night. We do £60 million a month in turnover and right now a third of that is in the Gulf. We do have payment insurance from the Export Credit Guarantee Department for up to 85% of the contract price; but ECGD are saying that this is not a specified event. We're the ones who are alleged to be in default on the contract, not the Petroleum Producing Authority."

"You're going to need to raise some money," said Peter.

They sat now at one end of the huge boardroom table of Dundas Brothers, the patricians on Peter's right and the horny-handed sons of toil to his left. Beyond the patricians were Carradine and Thornhill and beyond them Allen & Overy. On the other side, beyond Griffiths and Hollingsworth were Tim and Oliver and then the people from Linklaters.

"Can we just start, gentlemen," Peter began, "by looking at the schedule, with which you are all familiar, which shows the possible bases for the issue and the amounts which would be raised. Weightings along the top; prices down the side. It's been updated for today's closing mid market price, which was 136p. Wagstaff have, on our behalf, conducted discreet soundings with certain leading shareholders today and we are, as a result, proposing a rights issue of two new shares for each existing five at 100p per share."

Peter could see out of the corner of his eye that Sir Timothy's cheeks were reddening and swelling; but there was no sound and he decided to blunder on. If the old bastard was going to blow his top, he might as well get it over in one fell swoop.

"We have assumed that the families would not be able to take up the rights on the 20 million shares which they hold since it would require a little over £8 million of new money. Wagstaff are therefore proposing to buy or procure buyers for enough of these shares at 5p per share -" and now Peter was sure. He did hear the first whistle of escaping gas from the geyser bubbling on his right; but he pressed on - "to enable the families to subscribe for the balance. What we customarily call a tail-swallowing exercise."

"Young man," the Chairman began, too quietly to match the additional colour that had risen to his cheeks, "I have been in business for rather more years than you and, though I come from a line of engineers, I do have a certain amount of experience in the financial field. You haven't been associated with Bottley long enough to remember, but I was myself finance director before Stanley here, when my father was Chairman. What you are proposing, every single element of what you are proposing, is unsound, intolerable, out of the question and unacceptable."

"Chairman, it doesn't come as a great surprise to me that current market conditions have forced us to put forward a pricing level which you find disappointing; but could you be more specific about the problems you have with this structure?"

"I most certainly will. We agreed at least a fortnight ago - you were in my own office in Darlington - that £40 million would be the right amount to raise. The share price was then 134p, as I recall, and you produced a schedule very much like this one here and we talked, without demur on your part, about a one-for-three issue at 120p with the specific intention of minimising the dilutionary effect on both earnings and the family holdings. We had already put out an announcement on Ras al Jamal and the price had come back from 150p on the news. It has strengthened a little since and the whole market is up a hundred points. Oh yes, your wonderful *Financial Times* gets all the way up to Darlington, you know. We're not quite the country bumpkins you might be thinking. Now you have the gall to come to me with a price twenty per cent lower and an offer of 5p a share for the family's rights when I can see, written on your precious schedule in front of me, which I am not too much of a dim engineer to understand, that those shares are worth 25.7p each. If one of my managers put crap like that in front of me, I'd kick his arse for him. And my boys don't come in for the fancy fees you demand to feed your fucking Ferraris and your fat bonuses."

The crescendo on which this speech had ended was followed by a moment of absolute stillness, all wondering what would happen next. Ben Silkin broke it, before Peter had a chance to try to calm things down. He knew what was coming - the old soft-shoe shuffle.

"May I try to put this into perspective," Ben began, all sweet reasonableness and veteran wisdom. "I'm an old soldier and I've seen these market panics before - too many to recall over the course of fifty years in the City. This one's not as bad as even the one in 1974. The fund managers always like to claim it's the end of the earth so that they can pick up some cheap stock. Mark my words, they'll be falling over themselves to get at Bottley shares within a matter of weeks. After all, they were above 200p in July and nothing material has changed. If you chaps at Dundas don't feel confident right now, we could leave it until the New Year. January is always a good month in the markets, what with the fund managers having new money to invest, and I'm sure that I could persuade Brocklebanks to share the underwriting if you wanted to spread the load."

"Gentlemen," Peter began in response, "might I suggest that we adjourn for a few minutes for me to talk to the company separately. Tim, could you see if the Chairman's office is free?"

He got up without waiting for agreement and walked to the phone that was on a small table by the window in the corner of the room behind him. He called Maureen. Thankfully she was still there although it was well past 7.30. Sophie would be in a taxi by now. He spoke quietly, shielding the mouth-piece from the rest of the room.

"Maureen, could you please call Jenny Fordyce - you'll find the number in my book - give her my apologies and tell her that I'm running late for her dinner party. I'll try to get there later on but she mustn't hold up proceedings for me. Thanks."

As he put the receiver down, Tim emerged from the right-hand door on the far side of the room, which led straight into the Chairman's office, motioning that it was free. Peter shepherded the four Bottley men into the holy of holies, all old rosewood, discreet down-lighting, Scottish oils and sepulchrally quiet thick-pile cream carpet. Tim made as if to follow but Peter steered him back into the boardroom and shut the door. This might not be a spectacle for subordinates. The Bottley men themselves seemed undecided whether to sink into Sir James's huge settees or take up position around the small Georgian meeting table. Peter made up their minds for them, unswervingly taking the formal option. Again Ben Silkin jumped in before he could get started.

"Why don't we just agree to come back to this after Christmas? I'm sure that we can get something more sensible organised if we allow ourselves a little breathing space." The style was infinitely solicitous but it was all delivered with the unsaid condescension that this was the judgement of a man who was older, and wiser and more experienced. Ben Silkin played the part at Brocklebank Nobel that the uncles played at Warburgs; and you could see why it worked so well. Here was this man, seventy if he was a day and rich beyond imagining. If he were at your elbow in a completion meeting at eight o'clock on a shitty December evening, it could only be that he was on your side. And how could he be wrong? He was practically promising that Brocklebanks would do it if these wimps didn't have the bottle. Of course, it would take a few days to organise. That was only reasonable. But Peter knew very well that Ben Silkin didn't want this bit of business; and certainly not on better terms for the company. He just wanted to push Dundas down a hole. Peter could go through the rationale item by item; but it wouldn't make any difference. Ben would come back with his own counter arguments and, at the end of the day, it would come down to a matter of which of these two men Sir Timothy trusted. There was no way he was going to select someone who he saw as a 37 year old, slick, over-paid salary slave against crusted old money that had shot and fished and feasted (and quite possibly effed some other things besides) with him and his father and his grandfather before him for close on four decades. Furthermore, there was more than a grain of truth in what the old man had said in the boardroom. Sir Timothy had pointed out at that meeting in Darlington that one-for-three at 120p would do the trick. It was not actually at Peter's prompting; but Peter had not contradicted him, though, even then, he knew such terms to be far-fetched. He had taken the easy option of pressing on down the road and facing the crunch when it came. Even Peter had been surprised at Carradine's view of the institutions' lack of appetite for stock but he had known all along that he was allowing Sir Timothy to entertain false hopes of how smoothly Bottley could be extracted from the mire. Now there was no going back. Peter decided to tell it like it was.

"Gentlemen," he began again. "I understand all your frustration. I even understand your anger, Sir Timothy; though I would not accept that we have led you up the garden path," he dissembled with a practised absence of embarrassment. "What I think you do not appreciate is the seriousness of Bottley's position."

"For heaven's sake, young man. All we've got is a short-term cash flow problem. If we had been able to anticipate this Ras al Jamal problem, we could have stitched up oodles of bank facilities to tide us over. We only need a rights because you bankers never lend money to people when they need it, though you fall over yourselves to shove it up and down their every orifice when they don't."

"Sir Timothy, Bottley's borrowings will hit close on £95 million by the end of this month and, without the proceeds of this issue, they will go above £100 million by the end of January, and that is before the additional costs of closing down your operations in the Gulf, as now looks inevitable. You currently have net assets of around £130 million but Deloittes are going to force you to take a big write-off on the £45 million which the sheikh now owes you. Your ECGD cover doesn't insure you against a claim based on faulty workmanship. On the face of it, your year-end net assets are going to fall to less than £90 million and you're going to breach the one-to-one ratio in your bank covenants. All your bank loans have cross default clauses and the whole lot will become immediately repayable. You haven't just got a short-term cash flow problem. Deloittes are going to qualify your accounts - that's another event of default under your banking covenants. Without this rights issue, you're going to go bust."

The silence was tangible and seemed to last for ever. Ben Silkin finally broke it.

"Let's put the whole thing off for twenty-four hours and meet again in the morning. We can explore the possibilities tomorrow and, if this proposal of yours turns out to be the only solution, we can still sign it up tomorrow evening."

"No, I'm sorry, Mr Silkin. I'm not going to try to sub-underwrite an issue on the Friday before Christmas week. It gives me no leeway if I don't get it completed on the day. If we don't sign tonight, then I suggest you go round to the Midland tomorrow and ask them to put in the receivers."

Since the moment Peter had mentioned the word 'bust', Sir Timothy's cheeks, though they could not exactly pale, had at least re-assumed their normal colour. The truth, which he had tried to avoid because it all seemed so unfair, finally dawned with the word 'receivers'. He saw the last century of his family's history slipping beyond his grasp. The shame alone would be too much for him. He could not preside over such an humiliating end for Bottley. Anything which offered Bottley a chance of escape was preferable.

"All right," he said, so quietly that Peter could barely make out the words, "we'll do it."

"One more thing." Thinking of how to do this earlier in the day, Peter had not imagined feeling any sympathy for this self-important toff; but the deflated man opposite him hardly seemed worth further persecution. Nevertheless, he would have to do it.

"The major shareholders want you to step down as Chairman."

Sir Timothy no longer had the stomach to protest; but Ben Silkin was on his feet.

"No, that's outrageous!" he cried.

"It will not be necessary immediately. The AGM in April would be the appropriate time for a handover." Peter could see a spark of revival in Sir Timothy's eye. The chairmanship was actually more important to him than the millions by which his wealth was being eroded and now he could see himself slipping off the hook. Not only would Bottley rise again; but he would be there to see it through. By April the clamour would have died down, the pressure for change gone. Ben sat down again, equally devious and similarly deceived.

"But tomorrow's announcement must indicate that this is the plan," Peter said, snuffing out Sir Timothy's false hopes; but at the same time kindling the spark of another stratagem.

"You can't possibly expect Sir Timothy to step down from the chair without a nominated successor. It will look like a shambolic piece of succession planning and will damage the company."

"No, it's all right, Ben. I'm 66 now. It's not a bad age to retire from executive duties. I think that the sensible thing would be for you to step up from deputy chairman to take my position on a non-executive basis and for me to take your position as deputy."

What a cosy and tangled piece of logic, thought Peter; but, after all this grief, he was having none of that.

"With all due respect, I do not think that the succession planning message would be best presented by replacing a 66 year old chairman with one closer to 70, executive or non-executive. Would that be right, Mr Silkin?"

"You're quite right, young man," said Silkin, who had himself now seen an opening for vengeance. Dundas Brothers had stitched them up. Now he was going to ensure that they found themselves pitched into the same dark sack as their client. Bottley's survival was going to be a matter for the prestige of the bank itself.

"We must have a named replacement by tomorrow morning and one of real credibility; but we simply cannot find one from the current board; nor can we go outside at such short notice. My suggestion is that we ask Sir James Cruso to take the chair. What better decision could we take, right here in his own office?"

"Well, he's a terribly busy man, acres of commitments," stumbled Peter. "I really think it's unlikely that he could do it. In any event, I couldn't speak for him and, to be honest, I don't know where to find him right now."

"Oh, I'm sure you'll be able to track him down, Peter," said Silkin. "Why don't we just sit here while you make a few calls?"

A little after midnight, Peter Davenport and Frank Griffiths finally signed the underwriting agreement for the Bottley Engineering rights issue. Frank had uttered barely two sentences and Stanley Hollingsworth not a single word by the time they left shortly afterwards for their hotel. Sir Timothy and Ben Silkin had made a sulky departure in Sir Timothy's chauffered Rolls-Royce as soon as agreement had been secured. Sir James had been traced to the gala performance of Frederick Ashton's latest Royal Ballet production of Prokofiev's Cinderella at the Royal Opera House, where he and Lady Cruso were entertaining the recently knighted Sir Robert Scholey and his wife. The government had announced its intention to float British Steel as soon as possible only a fortnight before and Sir James was no doubt doing his bit to secure the chairman's support for Dundas Brothers to be awarded a role. Cyril Bishop had caught him in his car between Covent Garden and Le Caprice, where the party was taking a late supper. Even Cyril's tortured syntax had left Peter in no doubt of his Chairman's displeasure and the extent of personal capital that had been expended to achieve his grudging acceptance.

*****

What was apparently Tracey was still at her desk an hour later when Peter went round to the open-plan area which Tim's team occupied to check on progress. She was indeed a sight, no more than twenty-three or twenty-four but already blousey in a way which was emphasised by a mop of unruly fair waves that cascaded hither and thither to her shoulders. Her figure was not good - prematurely broad-bottomed and round-bellied - but she had that thick-lipped slightly open-mouthed pout which tends to melt a man's heart and can quickly harden other parts. Her breasts hung more pendulously than they should, enabling her to display the long deep cleavage which she knew to be the best method of broadcasting her availability. Since leaving school at the age of seventeen, she had occupied a host of secretarial jobs; and it was her proud and open boast that it had never taken her more than a fortnight to bed a boss she fancied.

She was naive enough to believe that this was still the route to an easy and well-paid secretarial future. Her first job, at BP, had failed to disillusion her. Sure, she had been caught in the beam of a security guard's torch at 10.30 one evening giving her boss a blow-job in the directors' loo; but the result of the subsequent enquiry by the personnel department had been eminently sensible. The security guard had been fired. She did not make the connection when, six weeks later, her boss was transferred with immediate effect to Cabinda; and she thought it pure misfortune that his replacement was so obviously of a different sexual orientation to herself; or perhaps just of the same orientation, depending on how you think of it.

The habitual swordsmen in corporate finance at Dundas were inclined to the maxim that such encounters were inevitable from time to time; but that it was an offence punishable by instant dismissal if the secretary were to mention it next day and particularly if she brought up the subject with the man who had skewered her. That such a rule was widespread was evidenced by the lengthy list of Tracey's former employers.

Cyril, who insisted on vetting all departmental secretaries before they were taken on, had a more old-fashioned attitude to the problem and one which he had convinced himself over the years was entirely logical.

It was inconceivable to him that his corporate financiers, almost every one bar himself Oxbridge educated, would become involved beneath their class. Address was therefore the sole criterion by which he would perform the final weeding-out of secretarial recruits. Habitation west of Trafalgar Square was basically forbidden unless it was south of the river. Essex was the territory of choice. On that basis, Tracey passed with flying colours.

Oliver and Tim sent her home to Basildon by cab around one o'clock and themselves set off for Burrups, the security printers, to check the final proofs before printing was set in motion. Peter, weary to his being, took the lift to the basement car park where his canary-yellow V8 Morgan was the last survivor, and set off for Wapping and home.

Friday, 18 December, 1987

The hole in Bottley Engineering's balance sheet which yesterday's rescue rights issue seeks to repair owes nothing to the crash but is the first such exercise of a purely defensive character since October's meltdown. The massive discount which the company has been forced to accept is a reflection of the continuing nervousness of institutional investors towards new equity investment as well as the extent of the potential damage which the aftermath of last month's Ras al Jamal explosion will do to Bottley's prospects. Whoever and whatever was to blame for that incident, there were always dangers in headlong expansion into the Gulf by a company of Bottley's limited resources. Shareholders may take comfort from the new grip which the bankers have taken over the company in the form of Sir James Cruso's appointment as chairman elect; but it is difficult to see why Dundas Brothers should think it worth laying its reputation so clearly on the line. The underwriting was, if market talk is to be believed, far from a formality and rightly so. With the share price settling yesterday a bare 8p above the rights price and plenty of selling pressure evident, shareholders could be forgiven if they decide to leave this one to the underwriters.

The Lex column piece in the *Financial Times* under a sub-heading *Blast damage* was fortunately pushed out of the lead position by Barker & Dobson's £2 billion bid for Dee Corporation, a company fifteen times larger than itself, and County Natwest's £69 million of losses in the crash. As Peter leafed through the other City columns he found them no kinder. He was just picking up the phone to Piers Pottinger at the Lowe Bell public relations outfit when William Blackstone put his dark, square-jawed face round the door.

"The gentlemen of the fourth estate appear to have bestowed on you no favours in respect of this transaction," he said in as colloquial a form of the English language as he ever mustered. "In my humble opinion, their disapprobation is a mite more surly than is warranted by the circumstances. Nevertheless, I confess to finding that Sir James has betaken himself of the chairmanship the most surprising phenomenon. You must indeed, Peter, have waxed your most persuasive to have secured for your client his not inconsiderable services."

"To be honest, William, I was simply backed into a corner by that shit Ben Silkin of Brocklebanks. It was the price for forcing that old buffer Henderson-Ball into retirement. Cyril did the biz with James. I can't say that either of them are best pleased with me."

"Mm... not necessarily the most sagacious of outcomes with the bonuses due to be resolved by the executive committee on the Winter solstice next week."

"Well, I'll just have to rely upon my shrewd suspicion that all those things are decided in November and that the last four weeks we have spent filling in staff appraisal forms for that cow, Dunwoody, is just an exercise in *ex post facto* justification." Hell's teeth, thought Peter, he's almost got me at it now before William confirmed that he was still the master of this tributary of the English language.

"I don't doubt that your incredulity is well-founded. Preterition by said lady of the sentiments we opine upon our comrades and subordinates would come as little surprise."

Poor William was a man at the mercy of his own pomposity. Few of the clients could tolerate his style or had the patience to wait for his judgement however sound. That he worked all hours of the day and night was to no avail. His existing clients spent the major part of every encounter trying to break away from the grip of his linguistic gymnastics, oblivious of the content; and his presentations to marketing targets were a torture to which no chief executive or finance director, properly forewarned, would submit. There was a distinct lack of enthusiasm amongst the executives of corporate finance to support him in these efforts. His mannered style of speech was mirrored in his physical appearance. Peter had never known a man, for example, who smoked with such precision. On his desk, his packet of Benson & Hedges was to be found in front of his telephone, perfectly aligned and squarely placed so that the flip-top end was always pointing towards the centre of the desk. His gold Dunhill was always placed on top of the packet, in the very centre of the pack, and the wheel by which it was ignited was closest to the thumb of the right hand which would operate it. Every inhalation was of exactly equal volume, the ash was flicked off after every third puff and the position in which the cigarette rested on his big brass ashtray was invariably identical. His dress was similarly impeccable but Peter had, some time ago, concluded that the whole elaborate structure of mannerism upon mannerism was essentially a reaction of nervousness and self-doubt. It was easy to label William a pompous waste of space; but it was sadder still to recognise that the City was no place for this essentially decent man.

"Anyway, what are you doing here at 7.30 on the morning after the Christmas party, William? I presume there will be no morning prayers today. In fact I don't expect many of our colleagues before mid-morning."

"I like to be in the office betimes on mornings such as this when the luxury of a little tranquility is not at a premium and some of our minions are suffering the after-effects of alcoholic dissipation. I fortunately am given neither to hangovers nor to what I believe is technically labelled self-induced reverse peristalsis."

"Well, I'll take your word for it, William. And now, if you'll excuse me, I must do what I can to mollify old Henderson-Ball. This is my last day in the office before the New Year and I have a few loose ends to tidy up before I go. By the way, you wouldn't care to look after Bottley while I'm away, would you?"

"My dear fellow, you are too kind; but I must sadly decline. I used to work on the Bottley account when I was a manager but I had something of a falling out with that unreconstructed Yorkshireman who is now chief executive."

"Yes, I can imagine that," said Peter to William's retreating back as the latter bolted for his office.

But William was right. The bonus round was looking distinctly worrying, for the bank in general, for the department, and for himself. The Brothers, having joined Schroders in defying the herd by staying out of the rush to buy stockbroking businesses, had at least saved themselves the pain of the market-making mayhem of mid October that had cost Warburgs, BZW, Grossmanns and County so dearly. BZW had already revealed results for the half year which implied £60 million of losses in the crash, Grossmans had confessed to £40 million and County, with the Blue Arrow fiasco to compound their woes, needed a fresh injection of £80 million of share capital from their parent, NatWest. But everyone had taken a bath on the BP underwriting and Dundas were looking at the thick end of £7 million, not far short of what Warburgs had revealed with their interim results a few weeks ago. Thank God the major part of the exposure had been sub-underwritten. The Americans, whose system did not permit sub-underwriting, had taken a real caning.

Peter himself had not had a bad year in terms of fees. A decent agreed offer for a highstreet retailer in the first half and the July flotation of Harcourt, the youngest and most successful of the new breed of developers. Then there was helping Cyril advise Masefield Controls when it was bought by New Jersey Signal. Peter could still not stifle a laugh when he thought of that final negotiating session in the boardroom upstairs. Cyril had been sitting in the middle on one side of the table with Peter, the lawyers and other advisers on one side of him and the directors of Masefield on the other. Opposite them, Morgan Stanley, the US investment bank advising New Jersey Signal, had turned up so mob-handed with lawyers and accountants and analysts and whatnot that they had overflowed their side of the table and were coming round each end like the horns of a charging bull. They'd been going backwards and forwards over each other's self-interested and partial valuations of the business and getting nowhere when one of Morgan Stanley's young analysts, alerted by a mention of some exceptional legal costs in the current year, had passed a note to his managing director who had then started asking some rather awkward questions about contingent liabilities. The finance director of Masefield had been forced to confess that they were on notice of a possible action by Foxboro for patent infringement. Half an hour later, the meeting was adjourned for New Jersey Signal to send for specialist reinforcements and, when they resumed, their team was so expanded with patent lawyers that some of the opposition were sitting two-deep on their side of the table. Until then Peter had felt that Chuck Arvill, New Jersey's hyperactive chief operating officer, was so pumped up with the financial equivalent of anabolic steroids that his balls would explode if he didn't get the deal done. Now Peter thought that the posse from New York lawyers, Sullivan and Cromwell, were looking sufficiently uneasy to castrate him if required.

At this juncture, Cyril suddenly shot upwards from his chair, strugglingly one-handedly at his flies, and bellowed: "Oh, fuck, my leg's fallen off!" And with this he swept around, knocking over the pile of papers in front of him, and hopped for the door, turning over his shoulder with the parting shot "Carry on, will you, Peter."

The collective jaws of the opposition dropped as one and, whether it was the shock of this event or the fact that the cascade of Cyril's papers had revealed a copy of Siebe's accounts, with a compliments slip from its chairman, Barrie Stephens, a potential rival suitor for Masefield, stapled to the cover, negotiations proceded thereafter without a hitch. By the time Cyril reappeared a half-hour later on crutches, his left trouser leg now folded up to mid thigh, the three founders of Masefield were £75 million richer and Peter was mentally banking a little less than one and a quarter million in fees.

Altogether Peter had billed his fair share; but he had to admit that he had made negligible progress on the marketing targets which Bill McAdam, shortly to take over from Cyril as head of corporate finance, had assigned to him. He felt sure that BTR were going to ditch Morgan Grenfell, tainted both by their role in the developing Guinness scandal and their failure to win the Pilkington bid; but Peter found Barry Romeril, who had taken over from Norman Ireland as finance director, an awkward man to deal with. There was no sign of him hurrying towards a decision. The reality was that Dundas Brothers had no special chance of winning a beauty parade if it came. As for Williams, Nigel

Rudd seemed disinclined to blame Schroders for failing to win Norcros although that looked like a takeover bid impossible to lose. David Challen was as firmly entrenched as ever and had just picked up another fat fee for the acquisition and financing of the Berger Paints deal.

If anything, Peter was in more danger of losing a major client than winning one. Since the poison dwarf had been installed as chairman of Pitcairn Pharmaceuticals, he had made a pretty clean sweep of directors and advisers alike. Quite apart from the summary execution of the chief executive and the finance director, Coopers had lost the audit and Wagstaff of all people had been replaced as brokers by Gourlay Gilfillan. Lord Enderby had warned Peter in an aside at Cheltenham in March that the previous chairman was on his way out, but that made it no easier for Peter to read Christopher Hennessy, the new man. He knew that John Thornton, the Goldman Sachs rotweiler, taking particular advantage of the installation of an American, had been putting up all manner of ideas because Hennessy had told him as much. Perhaps he was just trying to keep Peter on his toes, but it often felt after one of these exchanges that Dundas Brothers were hanging on by their most tender parts.

Peter's fee income was a reasonable share of the pot but the pot itself was going to be shot to hell by the BP underwriting losses. The projections for next year were not looking too clever either with no great pipeline of activity. The dozen or or so bids over the course of the last five or six weeks, worth upwards of £6 billion, had bypassed the client list of the Brothers altogether and everyone was uneasy that the great bull run of flotations and M & A, equity financings, privatisations and deals of all sorts which had led to an explosion in the number of City corporate financiers was finally coming to an end. In many ways the City deserved it. Any market that could allow Saatchi & Saatchi to propose that an advertising agency buy a clearing bank or that Peter Earl's baby Benlox should bid for Storehouse must have become so completely unhinged by its own audacity that it deserved a downfall.

Prior to the crash, Peter had every expectation of adding a bonus of around £150,000 to his salary. Now he was going to be lucky to see even £50,000. With tax on the top slice of his income at 60%, it was costing him the best part of two-thirds of his after-tax salary to service his mortgage. It was absurd that one could feel poor on a salary of £100,000; but the reality was that, by the time he had paid the service charge, rates, electricity, gas, water, telephone, not to mention insurance, petrol, the membership fees for Wentworth and the gym and Annabels, he appeared to have less left to live on than the average of the new graduate intake. The swanky chalet in Courchevel that he had agreed to take over Christmas with Robin and Craig was beginning to look like the typical folly borne of a sun-bathed, Pimms-soaked afternoon in Robin's Hampstead garden.

Peter toiled through the morning, trying to shift some of the paper that had accumulated over the last few days and assigning responsibility for his client list and anything that might happen to them over the course of Christmas week. He had a couple of terse conversations with Sir Timothy Henderson-Ball, who seemed only too delighted to be exchanging Peter's services for those of his mean-minded and humourless colleague, Graeme Kent, a man whom most in the department thought to have slightly misspelt his own surname.

Around mid-morning, the largest part of the survivors of the office party straggled in. It had, as usual, been more awful in the contemplation than in the experience. In fact, Peter had thoroughly enjoyed himself.

Stephanie had, as usual, aspired with the seating plan to give everyone a taste of the good, the bad and the ugly. In the case of Peter's table, she had put Hildegaard von Schultzendorf, secretary to the chairman, Sir James Cruso, on his right and Helen Thompson, the elegant lady who ran the bank's library, on his left. On Hildegaard's right was Tim Phillips and, between him and Oliver Quentin-Archard, Cindy Buckle, whom Maureen thought was a tart because she apparently wore no panties. Beyond Helen Thompson was Festus Nyondo, the son of the Governor of the Bank of Ghana, who had been more or less forced on the Brothers for a year's training and had no apparent attributes other than a very smart address, no doubt courtesy of some misappropriated dollop of foreign aid, and on his right Elspeth Watson. Although it was a couple of seconds before Peter recognised that the girl he had seen at the drinks before dinner, knocking down the champagne, was indeed her, she still represented, without a doubt, Peter's quotient of the ugly.

She was a nice enough girl, and had a fearsomely impressive academic record, but she had been encumbered with a barrel for a body, a mouth too full of teeth and dark fuzzy hair, parted in the centre so that it stuck out on either side like a black haystack. Her nose was more prominent than a girl would like and had one of those kinks in the middle which in men can be put down to a youthful scrummaging injury. In normal circumstances she wore no make-up to soften her unfortunate features and compounded her problems with a grotesque pair of spectacles.

For this evening she had cast aside this image altogether and was plastered with every cosmetic device known to female kind and blinking blindly behind her mascara. She had also foresworn the sort of evening sack which was the only refuge for a woman of her shape on formal occasions and instead wore what appeared to be a strapless tube of black satin, no more than two feet from top to bottom around her midriff. Below the tube every inch of her legs below the shelf of her bottom was exposed like the thighs of Ozymandias and above the tube was a cleavage of such vast proportions that at this moment it appeared that Festus would shortly follow his gaping eyes and disappear from view into the abyss.

To Peter's right and left, the women were of a very different shape, but both a little bit bad. Hildegaard, who was known throughout the office simply as the grävin, was dressed in a stunning ankle-length scarlet sheath which left little of her contours to the imagination and was topped with a single strap over her left shoulder. She was the separated wife of a landed German count from whose title she was unwilling to be divorced. She was now in perfectly preserved middle age, extremely tall, slim and elegant. An unlined aristocratic face with exceptionally high cheek bones was matched with a wide mouth filled with strong white teeth. Her blonde hair was habitually drawn tightly back and formed into a perfectly coiffed chignon. Her English was precise and grammatical but she continued to affect a German accent which she felt, no doubt, combined best a sense of teutonic efficiency with a frisson of continental mystery. She was right. There were few executives in Dundas Brothers, even amongst the senior directors, who did not approach her office with a mixture of transparent awe and often ill-concealed lust. Seymour Farquharson, one of Peter's fellow corporate finance directors known, following a chance sighting in the gents' toilets by one of the executives, as Seymour the Serpent, had the hots for her in a big way.

On Peter's other side, Helen Thompson was a lady of a very different demeanour. Tonight she was dressed in a modest, classic little black number with a small imitation emerald and diamond brooch to match her earings. She was of medium height with short expensively-styled light brown hair. Her eyes were clear and blue and her skin pure and unblemished. She was inclined to high-necked cashmere sweaters, short strings of pearls and sheath skirts, just above the knee, which showed off her slim hips and long, shapely legs. She was serious and businesslike about her job but always helpful. She was quite simply a very classy Kensington lady; which made it all the more surprising that she had asked Stephanie Laker to put her next to Festus Nyondo because her idea of a great time was to go down to Brixton, pick up the biggest black she could find and fuck him half to death.

On Peter's table good was represented by Cindy Buckle. She had been Graeme Kent's secretary for about six years which, to Peter's mind, more or less sanctified her. She was an Essex scrubber, a pretty little blonde with a bouncy bob of hair but too tarty a style with her eye make-up. She liked to wear her skirts skin-tight and it was avoidance of VPL which had driven her to the expedient of which Maureen professed, with a tinge of barely concealed jealousy, to disapprove. Her general philosophy of life was equally simple and her heart pure gold. Her sympathy went out even to Kent, whose wife she had quite rightly identified as one of the battleaxes of Britain. So much so, she had confided to colleagues over make-up reparations in the ladies' loo one morning, that the previous evening, working late, she had led him up to the top-floor flat and given him what she called a "lobster fermidor" - an oral experience of the sort a chap never gets at home. "'e was ever so grateful," was her simple conclusion to the tale.

Dinner was what it always is on these occasions - the chicken specially bred for the London hotel market with a thousand legs and a flavour indistinguishable from the accompanying bread sauce. Between courses, and at a given signal, upwards of a hundred waitresses descended on the gathering with an ear-splitting crashing of plates and cutlery. God confirmed that all was well with the world by ensuring that the obligatory spillage of sauce for the Christmas pudding went down Alan Bentham's dinner jacket, courtesy of a collision between two over-eager waitresses, and Sybil Dunwoody collected most of the contents of a bottle of red wine in her lap while stretching for the butter dish.

Peter's table, like all the others, grew steadily more raucous. He had exchanged a few risqué remarks with Hildegaard, principally on the subject of her scent - Chanel No 5, of course - and where she had applied it, at the outset but was then more or less obliged to look after an increasingly sulky Helen since Festus, to her obvious disappointment, was absolutely transfixed by what was on offer on his other side. Meanwhile Tim, notwithstanding the ten years or more that separated them, was turning the technique of a practised swordsman on Hildegaard. He was a ruggedly good-looking young man, tall and broad-shouldered with a touselled mop of curly brown hair. He had been out with a succession of stunning young women since Peter had known him and Peter had previously observed his caper of looking intently at a woman while suggestively allowing his tongue to play upon some imaginary object that he was licking. Hildegaard, the countess of cock-teasers, was loving it.

Dinner complete, the band launched into the Rolling Stones' *Jumping Jack Flash* and dancing began. Peter did a turn with Helen, then swapped her with Tim for Hildegaard and after that returned for Elspeth. She was pretty sweaty by now, Festus having jiggled her up and down in the hope that even more of her would be dislodged by the process, and had been quenching her thirst rather too deeply on the white wine. On the dance floor, she was none too steady on her pins and Peter had to do his best to keep her out of harm's way. She was not the sort of thing you would like treading on your toes. Tim, at this stage, was dancing with his secretary, Tracey, who, contrary to what one might have expected, was most soberly attired in a gentlemen's evening tail suit, stiff shirt, white tie, waistcoat and all.

Peter had returned to his table to deposit Elspeth back under Festus's wing to find Seymour the Serpent sniffing around the grävin. She had apparently excused herself from this particular dance and Seymour was trying to interest her in coming down to Hurlingham for some tennis on the indoor courts over the week-end. "Tennis!" she declared imperiously, "Seymour, I play uzzer games." Seymour's tongue looked as though it would fall into his lap.

45

Peter returned to the dance floor with Cindy to complete his duties to the ladies of his table. She barely came up to his chin but she bubbled with energy. Absent the chasm of class which separated her from Sophie Templeton-Smythe, Cindy had much in common with Peter's girlfriend, an effervescent smile, a body more curvaceous than fashion's ideal and an endless appetite for fun.

There were more and more couples on the dance floor now, Tim Phillips' team as ever to the fore. Charlotte Mulder's secretary, Alison Smith, suspiciously round-bellied for a girl not scheduled down the aisle until this week-end, was whooping it up with Tim himself. She was not yet out of her teens and fresh from secretarial college, tall, broad-shouldered and big-boned with a wide-cheeked but pretty face and long brown hair which she wore habitually in a pony tail. She came with a sad Essex accent which she shared with the young policeman, even larger than herself, who was her intended. Notwithstanding her betrothal, alcohol, even in relatively small quantities, had the effect of stimulating an insatiable desire for whichever man caught her eye. At most drinks parties after work, it would not be long before Alison, like a huge female praying mantis, had some young male, half her size, pinioned in a corner for her subsequent gratification.

Many of the men had discarded their jackets, including Oliver Quentin-Archard, who was dancing with Tracey. She had removed what had turned out to be simply a stiff shirt front with wing-collar and bow-tie attached and, as she leapt up and down to the rythm, everything was trying to get out of the top of her waistcoat. Just how much that was was then unveiled when she whipped off her tail coat and wrapped it round Oliver's shoulders, revealing that the waistcoat too was no more than a front and that she was otherwise naked from the waist up. At the moment of disclosure, Peter caught sight of Sybil Dunwoody, thumping from one foot to the other in her wine-stained sack, and he thought for a moment that there might be more appreciation on her face than censure.

An hour or so later, when the party was beginning to thin out a bit, Peter made for the bar for a night-cap. Timothy and Oliver were propped against it observing from afar the gyrations of an extraordinarily nubile young redhead who worked in asset management. Peter had seen her in Cannons from time to time and recalled that she looked even more spectacular in a thong than she did this evening in her finery. No matter, the early stages of inebriation had turned the debate which Timothy and Oliver were conducting to weightier matters as regards the subject of redheads in general. Peter, pressed for an opinion, said that he was for the moment content with his whisky, drained his glass, wished the boys good hunting, and set off to find himself a cab.

It had been close to two o'clock by the time he got home and the flat was again in darkness, as it had been the night before, save for the small spot over his desk which Sophie habitually left lit when she retired to bed without him. He hadn't been in the best of odour for failing to make the Fordyces' dinner party and thought it best to adopt a low profile. He undressed in the sitting room and used the guest bathroom before turning out the light, opening the bedroom door and groping his way through the dark to his side of the bed. He slipped beneath the body-warm duvet and snuggled up to the soft recumbent back. Sophie stirred and turned over into his arms.

"Hullo, stranger," she muttered sleepily. "Do you still live here?"

"Goodnight, Soppy," he replied and was instantly asleep.

*****

On days when Cyril's prosthesis was freshly oiled or whatever it was they did to it, it was not always apparent that the stiffness in his left leg was anything more serious; but fate had dealt him a cruel blow at the age of eighteen when he stepped on a German mine in the closing days of the war in Europe. He had used his time in hospital to read as much about banking as he could lay his hands on, and by the time he was well, was sufficiently impressive to persuade Dundas Bothers that he was going to be a clerk worth taking on. He had never looked back, riding the wave of post-war corporate reconstruction as the Brothers' back-room boy, master of the paperwork to support the deals which the well-connected young gentlemen of the firm were hatching. The sixties came along and egalitarianism was all the rage along with the white-hot heat of industrial revolution and other such Wedgwood-Bennery, and Cyril had been seamlessly metamorphosed from sergeant into the ranks of the officer class. When James Cruso took over as chairman and chief executive from the sixth Lord Strathneven in 1979, he had been the only possible choice amongst the directors to be his successor as head of corporate finance.

Peter had now been with Dundas for 12 years, all of it in corporate finance, and for eight of those years Cyril had been his boss. Sure he was ridiculously eccentric for modern tastes, caught in a time-warp that pre-dated the increasingly aggressive pursuit of fee income, the plethora of regulation and the absurd expansion of financial complexity which only a computer age could allow. But he was a canny old bird, for all his inability to express himself in plain English, and he had absorbed all these developments without turning a hair. He hated it that the young executives churned out merger schedules in minutes that would a decade ago have absorbed hours; not because he begrudged them the benefit of the technology, but because he suspected that they were making robots of themselves, blindly accepting the output as though it had papal infallibility. The argument that computers were freeing executives to spend more time thinking creatively he considered to be utter hooey.

"You're either creative or not. Don't become creative because there's nothing else to do," he barked, at this suggestion; and meanwhile he continued to extract immense satisfaction, when presented with one of these schedules, in immediately spotting without fail some figure which his logic told him could not possibly be correct. Hours later, the unfortunate would return hang-dog to Cyril's office, some elementary input error that the youngster had been staring at for an age having suddenly been revealed.

Peter was genuinely going to miss him.

Cyril had been assiduously handing over his clients and contacts for months past and today would be no different. David Squire, the founder of Squire's Homes, was coming in with his finance director and Cyril and Peter would be giving them lunch in one of the dining rooms on the seventh floor. Squire's Homes was now building upwards of 400 houses a year, principally in the south-east and was making a bucket of money on the back of the unprecedented boom. A lot of housebuilders had gone for stock exchange listings during this period and David had long been saying that 1988 was the year he expected to hit profits of around £5 million - big enough to be worth going for a flotation.

Cyril had been close to David Squire for years and the Brothers appeared to have this bit of business in the bag were it not for his impending retirement. Squire was immediately reassuring.

"We're intending that Dundas should handle the float, Cyril, and if you say that Peter Davenport is the man to do it for us, that's good enough for me."

Peter was just beginning to relax, thinking perhaps that he could afford more than the merest half glass of the excellent 1983 Fourchaume Premier Cru Chablis that was being served with their lemon sole, when Cyril upset his growing composure.

"David," he mused, "are you quite sure this is what you like?"

"Cyril, it's absolutely delicious; and this is the best Chablis I've had in years. You can taste the flint in the soil," he said, revelling in the appreciation of good things that riches had given him.

"No, the stock market," said Cyril, oblivious that his words could have been misinterpreted.

"Of course, Cyril; we've been talking about it for three or four years now, as you know. Prices may have taken a bit of a tumble; but our profits are steaming ahead. We look like making an average of close on £15,000 on each completion next year. Why delay?"

"Oh, I wasn't thinking of delay," said Cyril. "I wondered whether you should do it at all."

"Why on earth not?" said David, beginning to sound mystified to the point of mild irritation.

"You see, David, public is very different to private. Shareholders, brokers, the papers and whatnot. Can't do what you like nowadays, even when you own it. And there's getting there - reporting accountants crawling around to see who built the new tennis court and who runs the wife's car."

"What on earth do you mean, Cyril? We've got absolutely nothing to hide." By now, the tone was beginning to show that he was almost ready to take offence.

"Oh, I just wanted to warn you about the months ahead. Going public is like - what? Like examining your own arsehole really."

Bafflement was now written all over Squire's face; but Cyril was not intending to provide an explanation. Fortunately Peter had heard this one before and was able to chime in.

"You have to go through a very strange series of contortions to achieve it. And when you get there, it doesn't tend to be a pretty sight!"

"Oh, well, that's all right," said Squire with a chuckle, sounding much relieved, "I can live with that more comfortably than some pillock at Barclays breathing down my neck whenever I want to buy some more land. Frankly I've got all the money out of the company that I'll ever need; but the business simply can't generate enough to fund the land we need to buy next year."

"It's a matter," said his academic-looking finance director, who had until then barely uttered a word, "of preferring an anus horribilis to an annus horribilis."

*****

Tim was waiting by Maureen's desk when Peter came back from seeing David Squire to his big BMW. He followed him into his office.

"I've just had Thornhill on the phone. Bottley are down to 102-105. Apparently a lot of shares have been thrown at the market-makers and there are no buyers about. He's told the company."

"What's the market doing generally?"

"Not much; up a few points. BP have bid for Britoil but the Chancellor has said he will use the golden share to stop them getting control."

"That sounds just like the sort of silly advice you'd get from some arrogant Treasury apparatchik. Lawson will have to back down in due course. Meanwhile his fat buttocks stuck between the horns of a dilemma will make a very agreeable spectacle. Well, there's nothing we can do about Bottley for the next few weeks. I'm going off to the gym. You might just try to find out if it's DAM that's selling. Doesn't that little redhead you were eyeing last night work for one of the fund management teams?"

"Indeed she does."

"Aha," said Peter, "is there something you ought to be telling me about last night?"

"In my own case unfortunately not. But you might be amused to ask Festus how he's feeling today."

"I thought it was Elspeth who was drunk rather than him."

"It's not exactly his head that's bothering him. It seems that the cabbie taking them back to Festus's flat has complained that ' 'e looked over his shoulder to find this bird on 'is back seat gobbling that nigger's knob like it was a choclat lollypop.' Apparently he was so mesmerised that he drove into the back of the car in front. As you know, young Elspeth is not exactly under-supplied in the teeth department and the force of the impact caused her to give his wedding tackle a rather nasty mauling."

"How did that little bit of gossip see the light of day? It's not the sort of thing I would expect either of them to be bragging about."

"Indeed, so," said Tim, "but the car in front was full of plainclothes policemen. Two constables have been round this morning to do them for committing an act of indecency in a public place. Festus is quite relieved it's all come out because he'd decided that he ought to go and show it to the nurse and ask if he needed a tetanus jab. That, needless to say, has not gone down too well with Elspeth. She was heard shouting down the phone - 'Who do you think I am, the fucking bride of Dracula?'"

*****

For those in the City around the area of Monument and the Bank of England, Cannons, squeezed in under the arches that carry the railway lines out of Cannon Street station to the bridge over the Thames, is the gym of choice. Peter got there far less frequently than he had intended when he joined and it was a bit late now to think that an hour or two of exercise was going to prevent the first day's skiing leaving every muscle stiff and sore. Nevertheless, it seemed a good idea at the time.

The lunchtime crowd had cleared out, leaving the changing room carpet damp and the air foetid; but at least there would be no competition for the various instruments of torture. As usual, Peter chose one of a long line of treadmills and settled down to warm up. It was a strange place to spend a couple of hours. It could not really be said to be enjoyable. The bicycle and the rower, the treadmill and, above all, the step machine were boring, repetitive and sweaty. The weight machines made you feel like a wimp, surreptitiously moving the peg to halve the weight that some youth, not obviously brutish, had just been using. And surely modern science ought to be able to devise a method of exercising the stomach muscles which is not quite so deliberately painful. And yet, Peter had to admit that the combination of straining one's own body and watching one's fellows was almost therapeutic. It was like labouring in a pavement café - exertion with entertainment thrown in.

Even when the place was relatively empty, like now, there were always observations to be made. There was a lady, on the downslope towards middle age, over there on the step machine being supervised by an Aussie hunk who was for hire as a personal trainer. She couldn't be said to be doing anything to her body, on his advice, that she could not have done on her own; but perhaps the way she looked at his pecs and the occasional brush of his flesh as he showed her some new piece of equipment was enough to give an added frisson to her exertions. Strange the way the hunk was always assigned to the ladies and that willowy blonde to the men. This gymnasium lark did not look like a way to make money which required much subtelty.

Peter switched to the step machine which, in the way that it replicated the persistent bending of the knees on the piste, seemed ideal exercise for skiing. It was also said to be good for ladies' bottoms, though you never knew of course whether the girls with the shapely bums had acquired them through genetics or callisthenics. He put the one he could see in the mirror over his left shoulder, hanging by her arms from a steel bar to which she was repeatedly raising her chin, firmly in the genetics camp. She was Far Eastern, Thai or Malaysian Peter guessed, with breasts like the merest hillocks, a stomach smooth as glass and a bottom like a peach. Her light tan shoulders were beaded with a perspiration which it seemed she had no cause to expend. He thought for a moment of Soo Chan and smiled without regret.

Peter had completed three sets of weights on each of half a dozen machines, ten minutes on his abs and settled down at the back to finish off with twenty minutes on a bicycle when Hank arrived. Only an American could conceivably take himself so seriously.

Shortly after his arrival - another of Bill McAdam's recruiting aberrations - he was asked by one of the executives to provide a cv for inclusion in a presentation to Greg Hutchings, who was keen to take Tomkins into the US. In twenty years Hank had spun through the revolving doors of three major Wall Street houses and half a dozen lesser ones - all of whom had presumably found him out - two French banks, who had apparently been deceived into thinking that any American who spoke passable French must be good deep down and, to show that he could also deceive himself, had also twice run his own boutiques. The obvious failure of these enterprises was betrayed by such phrases as "merged his advisory practice into Banque Nationale de Paris" as if the latter institution was baying for his expertise rather than the reality that he had briefly crept onto that bank's payroll and as swiftly departed. But the most glorious features of his cv were saved for last in the following resounding sentence: "He is a long-standing member of the Los Angeles Rackets Club, the exclusive Brook in New York and Annabels in London and is married to a famous international beauty."

Peter had seen him a number of times at Cannons and, though the routine was always the same, watching him there was an amusement of which he could never tire. Hank would stalk into the exercise room as if he were a tiger entering a circus ring. He wore the most carefully chosen and well faded kit, preferably demonstrating, at least by implication, some former sporting glory. His favourite was the one he was wearing now, no longer truly white with a stars and stripes on the left breast, the five olympic rings across the stomach and Mexico City 1968 beneath. It was far too old for anyone to remember whether this was authentic team kit or tourist trash.

Hank would then take up position in front of one of the treadmills. It was the only machine which he ever used. An elaborate series of neck-stretching exercises were then performed in front of the mirror which had no conceivable purpose for the routine he was about to embark upon but which clearly made him feel that he looked about to release some raw animal power. Once on the machine, he began at a leisurely walking pace. During this phase a series of expressions were exchanged with the mirror - the statesman, the thinker, the athlete, the brute and the ladykiller were readily identifiable - all defined with the utmost gravitas. Finally satisfied, he would break into a slow bouncing jog, the success of which was principally measured by how perfectly his regularly coiffed grey locks, cut in something of the style of the reseeded Frank Sinatra, moved rythmically but at the same time retained their perfect order. This phase lasted no more than ten minutes and involved no perspiration. Sweating might be manly but it was not handsome. The whole thing was finished off with a further five minutes of walking during which deep breathing exercises were performed which flared his nostrils at the mirror and appeared to make him think of himself as a warhorse ready for battle.

By the time Peter reached the changing room, significantly puffed and in need of ten minutes to recover before he did anything else, Hank was emerging from the shower. They exchanged a few pleasantries and Peter stripped off, and sat on a towel. He had the impression that a glass of fine chablis and rather too much of last night's lesser quality alcohol was leeching from his pores.

He observed again the strange ritual which Americans use to get themselves dressed. You'd think it was just in the movies - or perhaps they think that's normal and have all copied it. First they put on what they call their undershorts - you can't really argue with that. But then they put on their trousers, zip up the fly and buckle the belt if they've got one. Then they put on their socks, which are usually quite long and thus require the trouser legs to be lifted almost to knee level. Then it's what an Englishman would call his vest. It's quite long and needs to be tucked inside his undershorts; so the trousers are undone, the tucking in implemented and the whole thing is done up again. After the shoes, they repeat the process with the shirt and the trousers are undone and then refastened for the third time. The shirt, by the way, is always buttoned right to the top and the reason why Americans can tolerate only those floppy shirt collars is that they fasten their tie and then fold the collar down over it. Why doesn't somebody tell them there's an easier way. And cut all their trousers an inch longer.

And then he went into the showers. There was an enormous shiny black man in there with a spectacular dong; but the curious thing about him was that he was carefully shaving his legs.

Saturday, 26 December, 1987

The weather was all to pot again. The snow had started on schedule this winter but had then just petered out so that it was only the high resorts that were skiable by Christmas. The decision to go for Courchevel 1850 was vindicated by the conditions - just about adequate snow all the way down to the village and splendid skiing at the top. But the runs down to 1300 - the lovely tree-lined Jean Blanc and Jockeys, not the most difficult but in many ways the best black runs in the Trois Vallées - were too bare and gravelly for those who valued their skis. The sunshine, which kept it warmer than it should have been so early in the season, did not augur well for those coming later unless heavy snow fell soon to restore the base. There would be enough to last them until the new year anyway. By then they would be back in London.

The chalet, a little way up the Bellecôte slope, but an easy walk from the centre once the lifts stopped for the evening, was everything that the agent had promised. From the outside it looked like a traditional structure in wood and stone; but inside it had cleverly been turned on its head so that the three comfortable bedroom suites were on the ground floor and the dining room, and the large sitting room and balcony were above with views through the pine trees onto the slopes. There was a big stone fireplace, kept, so it seemed, perpetually ablaze by Sheila, the chalet girl, who lived in half underground with the skis and boots, and large comfortable sofas on which weary bones could relax and recuperate ready for the evening's revelries. There were polished wooden stairways, solid old doors, beamed ceilings, blown-up early photographs of Victorian Alpine scenes and wonderful modern bathrooms with vast circular Jacuzzi tubs.

They had left London promptly on Saturday morning, 19 December. Peter and Sophie had been invited to leave all the arrangements to Robin, whose super-efficient wife, Julia, had, in fact, taken them upon herself. Peter had done so with some unease, knowing that Robin's practice in Hampstead provided only a minute part of the Archer family's annual income and that she had, if anything, even richer tastes than her husband. The advance payments had been pretty breathtaking; but the extent to which Julia had pushed their communal boat out was revealed as soon as they reached Geneva Airport, shunned the hordes heading for a four-hour coach journey, if they were lucky, and transferred to a twelve-seater aircraft for a thirty minute flight direct to a hair-raising landing at the Courchevel altiport. By lunch-time they were installed at the chalet, where Sheila was awaiting them with a sumptuous spread of hot fresh salmon, baked potatoes with sour cream and salads, followed by black forest gâteau. The wine was a 1984 Chassagne-Montrachet Abbaye de Morgeot, a lovely, golden, buttery burgundy, of which, amongst others, Julia had ordered a case in preference to that normally provided to guests on an all-inclusive basis.

And so it went on. Julia had organised everything but their bonking. Her bossiness seemed to grate a bit on Craig, used to running things himself and getting his own way; but Peter was perfectly content to go with the flow; and Sophie seemed so desperately keen to enjoy the first real time off that they had had together that she bounded along with every escapade as if she were a six-week old puppy.

Peter had met her in the March of that year at a dinner party held by Josh and Jenny Fordyce shortly after they had moved into their rather grand house in Norland Square. Peter had found himself sitting next to Sophie at dinner; but their liaison was not exactly planned. Peter had come with a beautiful Taiwanese girl with whom he had been exchanging bodily fluids for some months past and Sophie was accompanied by a quite well-known young upper-crust property agent, the Hon. Mark Cubit, to whom she was known to be a more or less permanent appendage. Peter had taken an almost instant aversion to the man. He was big, boastful and self confident, probably not yet out of his twenties, but going to overweight seediness in a way which only looked like getting worse. His speech already possessed the sort of gruff wheeze which implies at least sixty a day and he lit up between courses without a thought as to whether those around him were still eating. If he had been a dozen rungs lower down the social ladder, he was the sort of oaf who would have made a natural football hooligan.

It was difficult to say what made them hit it off. Peter's partner was the most attractive woman in the room by a mile and most men would have given their eye teeth to bed her; but Sophie was as effervescent as a magnum of Moët on a grand prix podium. A good bit younger than most of the party, her bright blue eyes sparkled in the candle-light and her broad and, it had to be said, tempting mouth was forever parted in spontaneous laughter to show a strong white row of even teeth. She giggled at Peter's whispered *risqué* comments on their fellow guests and she approvingly slapped her hand on his in support of his provocative contributions to a jocular debate on the future of the monarchy, notwithstanding the fact that her chain-smoking partner appeared to be the principal opponent of the republican cause which Peter had pretended to embrace with such enthusiasm.

It started over a discussion about the appropriate development of a site within striking distance of St Paul's that Cubit had acquired for a client. It was well known that plans had already been approved for a striking and original building by Richard Rogers in glass and stainless steel with its guts inside out à la Lloyds Building and Pompidou Centre; but Cubit's client had reverted to something more traditional in stone.

"The Prince of Wales," he was saying, "thinks the design much more appropriate for a building so close to the Cathedral."

Peter, who had sub-consciously been looking for an opportunity to cross swords with what he took to be an upper-class boor, could not resist chiming in. "As if his views on architecture, organic farming, Kalahari bushmen, or anything else were of the least importance alongside the opportunity to put up something that doesn't look like a scaled down version of Buck House."

"I think His Royal Highness has the right to express a view."

"Sure, but why should his profoundly inexpert opinion carry more weight than those of others. He's nothing but an overpaid supernumary without portfolio on the public purse."

"The British system may be an anachronism," Cubit had declared, "but we're bloody lucky to have it. It's cheaper than a presidency, it's popular because it's non-political and its damned good for tourism.

Moreover, now those of the princes that everyone accepts to be normal have picked themselves up attractive mates, one of whom has already confirmed her fertility and the other of whom will not be far behind," he guffawed knowingly, "its future is assured for decades to come."

"I am afraid that I beg to differ," said Peter. "As an institution it is less popular than at any time since Queen Victoria went into purdah, and declining all the time. As for the future, I don't know what's worse - the possibility that the miserable old bag who currently occupies the chair might live as long as her dipsomaniac mother, or that the next lot, who have chosen their wives with the apparent intent of genetically engineering the brain out of future generations, might get their hands on the baubles earlier than expected."

"Well, not every member of so large a family can be everyone's cup of Lapsang Souchong." And here he hesitated for a moment, thinking that he might have put his foot in it with Peter's girlfriend, sitting on his right, whose name he could not quite recall. "Indeed you may not admire any of them personally," he went on, "though I would say that you would be in a minority. But you cannot contend that your view is popular or that there is pressure for change."

"It doesn't matter. The system's doomed whether or not Big Ears and his vacant clothes-horse of a wife ever make it to the top. The question is really whether we do something about them now or wait for our children to find out that the pair of them are one banger short of a barbecue. But good riddance either way. What earthly reason is there for us to go on shovelling taxpayers' money down the throats of the Battenburgs and Saxe-Coburg-Gothas?"

"The simple reason that it's the best system there is. No country has anything better and there is no mechanism for change."

"That didn't prove much of an obstacle to Oliver Cromwell or Robespierre."

"You're not seriously suggesting...," broke in Jenny Fordyce.

"No, Jenny, not at all," Peter reassured her. "I think all their heads are so full of air that they'd bounce away down the street rather than plop sedately into the basket."

"Now, I know that you're just teasing," she said, and spotting the opportunity to bring a subject more controversial than Peter knew to a hasty close, "let's move up to the sitting room for coffee."

"I have a feeling I'm going to get into trouble for finding all that rather amusing," said the delightful young Sophie, drawing a little closer to him, as they got up from the table. For a moment, her eyes lost their sparkle and Peter thought he might have detected fear. "But, never mind," she said, squeezing his hand with an open smile, "I haven't laughed so much in an age. I wouldn't have taken you for a champion of modern architecture."

"I'm not. Actually I can't abide the jerry-built crap that arsehole Rogers designs either. I'll guarantee the Pompidou Centre will be a pile of rusting scrap and crumbling concrete before the century's out," he added with a wicked grin.

In terms of beauty, no one would have said that Sophie could hold a candle to Soo Chan. Unusually tall for a Chinese, her astonishingly shapely legs were topped by a classic hour-glass figure. A long delicate neck and perfect skin, blemished only by a small brown beauty spot on her high right cheekbone, set off wide but still oriental eyes and her sleek dark hair hung like a jet black silken curtain to the middle of her back. It was little wonder that she was now effortlessly scaling the lower rungs of the model agencies, protesting all the time that they would have to fit any photo-shoots around her studies as a violinist at the Royal College of Music.

After dinner, scattered in little groups around the Fordyces' sitting room with coffee and armagnac, Peter's eyes kept returning to the bubbly little blonde with the too curvaceous body, perched on the arm of a sofa at the far end of the room, always the centre of fun, always her eyes twinkling with delight and her vivacious buoyancy creating what seemed to be an impulsive exhilaration in those around her.

He looked from her to Soo Chan, sitting on the floor with her legs folded deliciously under her bottom in a way that only an oriental girl can manage. She was gazing up into Josh Fordyce's face, hanging upon his every word with what could only be rapt attention. Her figure-tight golden silk sheath with the intricate chinese designs in scarlet and green was slit on the right hand side to beyond a level where one ought to have seen her panties and Peter knew that the unfastened buttons at her throat were giving Josh a view of a perfect pair of small firm milk-coffee-coloured breasts the like of which he envied Peter to the depths of his scrotum.

Later that night in Soo Chan's bed he surrendered his body as usual to her extraordinary ministrations, her soft wet darting tongue, the silky smoothness of her skin on his, the body which she could manipulate and entwine around him so that it was like submitting to the touch of a masseuse with a thousand hands, legs like the tails of a hundred mermaids, tender fingers and cool, graceful hands, soft malleable breasts crowned with nipples of knotted elasticity, exploring his chest, his back, his belly and his loins, her mouth moist and luscious within her gentle lips crawling between his thighs, mouth on loin, wetness on wetness, loin on loin, sex on sex, arching up to draw him into her so deeply that she seemed almost herself to be the instrument of penetration. And all the while that she worked slowly and deliberately towards the simultaneous climax that was her goal, her ambition and her unfailing celebration of the act, Peter thought that he must be the luckiest man alive to have nothing to do but concentrate on drawing out these moments of pleasure to infinity. But afterwards, as he lay wide awake with Soo Chan's perfect face asleep on his chest, breathing lightly the sleep of the fulfilled, he could not help wondering whether all the oriental technique and the almost academic devotion to the mystique of union was actually worth more than the spontaneous coupling of a bubbly blonde; and suddenly he experienced the depressing realisation that the girl in his arms would have devoted the same degree of meticulousness to cleaning her teeth and the same lack of passion to wiping her bottom.

A fortnight later, it was the Cheltenham Festival. Peter was a guest of Stephen Harcourt of Harcourt Properties on the Tuesday, Champion Hurdle Day. Stephen had a runner in the main race in the shape of Court Dancer. The favourite had been odds on for days and, at 66-1 overnight, his horse was very much an outside bet, but it would no doubt be an occasion for a lot of fun, particularly since Mrs Harcourt was imminent with their third child and Stephen had decided to make it an all boys' box. Many of those involved in the forthcoming flotation were invited - David Carradine of Wagstaffs, who were to be the brokers, Julian Corrigan of Plummer, Goodspeed and Bleriot, Harcourt's principal lawyers, Nigel Platts from KPMG, the auditors, and the redoubtable Freddie Wordsworth of Wordsworth Wallis. Lord Enderby, who had stuck one and a half million pounds of his own money into the company on very favourable terms ahead of the flotation, was also there. He had been lined up to be non-executive chairman and looked upon this as his final chance to make himself rich beyond the dreams of avarice before he turned his toes up. The final place was occupied by a man of more professional appetite for booty - David Cooper, partner of the solicitors, Gouldens, and master of planning consents.

It was a cloudy day with a stiffish north-westerly breeze to make it feel even colder than the thermometer already claimed. Snow showers were forecast for later in the week. Peter had few qualms about attending because it was Budget Day and the prospect of Nigel Lawson doing something to reduce the level of income tax was going to keep most clients' ears firmly glued to a radio for the afternoon at least. Furthermore the coincidence of St Patrick's Day and the Champion Hurdle promised to make the whole occasion even more than usually anarchically good-humoured. As Peter approached the course, the traffic was formidable and the crowds prodigious. More or less the entire half of the Irish population that considered pleasure to be more important than politics was there and their lapels seemed to proclaim that the emerald isle had been more or less defoliated for the party.

Peter had under-estimated the time that the last few miles to the course and the process of parking would take him and, by the time he reached Stephen's box, they were all there. Indeed Freddie Wordsworth in particular seemed to have been there long enough to set some serious consumption in train. The combination of champagne with the cold northerly wind seemed to have made the limp caused by his arthritic hip - what he called his list to starboard - particularly pronounced. As Peter hung up his coat and scarf, he lurched past him.

"Ah, good to see you here at last, m'boy. I'm just off to the heads; but Stephen's keen to get lunch started before we're all three sheets to the wind."

With the drive back to London in mind, it suited Peter fine to put some food in his stomach before any further ado. Stephen took the head of the table and put Freddie, on his return, at the far end. Peter found himself between Jock Enderby on Stephen's right and David Cooper on Freddie's left, a situation which made him feel almost petite. Lord Enderby, now in his mid sixties, was a giant of a man who had cut a rumbustious swathe through the City ever since he emerged a young captain from the Army Intelligence Corps at the end of the Korean War. Since then he had graced banking parlours and government commissions, terrified financial institutions and industrial boardrooms alike and ridden markets, horses and other men's wives for four decades without ceasing. He had been brushed by rumours of involvement in the Profumo scandal back in 1963; and his avuncular friendship with Jim Slater and the collapse of his investments in Slater Walker and its satellites in the seventies had almost proved his financial undoing. Some said his survival was proof that he could emerge from a bordello smelling of incense; but the truth was more prosaic. He had lost just one less fortune than he had made - and there had been plenty of each.

David Cooper, on Peter's other side, was heading towards Freddie's girth but was even shorter. For lack of anything else to do with the money he made at the law - white-collar crime was his other speciality - he was an inveterate collector of cars and clocks, pictures and porcelain, and antiques of every description. He dealt so prodigiously that he must have had his failures; but Peter had heard only of the successes. He seemed the sort of man to whom you did not need to speak, content with an audience, not a conversation.

Stephen had organised a lunch appropriate to the weather consisting entirely (if you ignored the alcohol) of the sort of school food that you might wish that you could recollect. In reality, of course, the delicious pieces of succulent kidney and the tender steak bore no resemblance to the institutionalised muck of their collective childhoods and were accompanied by a pastry which would have seemed spun from gossamer back at Winchester.

"I see that Midland have pulled out of market-making," Jock Enderby observed, turning to Peter. "I'm told they dropped a bundle on the way. Who's next?" he asked, fishing as ever for information that he could turn to his advantage.

"Well, there are rumours that a number of people are still having major problems with their back-office admin. That sort of thing is bound to prove costly even if they're not actually making trading losses; but, since Midland were losing money, most of the rest must be in the same boat."

"Who's in the frame?'

"Kleinworts and Brocklebank Nobel are the names most often mentioned. Of course, Kleinworts got an operation that was up and running when they bought Grievsons; but Brocklebanks started from scratch and they say that it's a complete shambles."

"What can you expect of an organisation tainted by that slimy little shite, Ben Silkin. It would give me the greatest of pleasure to see him up to his ears in the brown and smelly stuff. I reckon that decision of your man Cruso to keep Dundas out of stockbroking is going to look pretty astute before 1987 is out."

"Could be; but a number of us at Dundas feel that it's going to be very difficult long-term to be a modern investment bank without a securites-trading operation. The big problem is that what we'd like is Caz and what we could afford is Panmure Gordon."

"Well, I wouldn't wish that on anyone," said Enderby, his shoulders shaking with amusement. "Except, of course, Silkin. Trust that little skinflint to try to save a nickel by setting up his own shop," he added, sublimely oblivious that his booming prejudices might carry as far as David Cooper.

"In a way you can understand it, Jock. I suspect that most people are going to find that they've bought trouble. Pardoning David Carradine over there, when you think how thick the average broker is, it's remarkable how they've taken everyone to the cleaners."

"I have to agree with you. Always thought it was the resort of the son who'd inherited neither the land nor the brain. Sickening to see the little buggers awash with dosh these days. But what's your solution for Dundas?"

"Unfortunately I suspect it will mean a loss of independence for us one of these days. We don't have the capital to compete with BZW or County if they ever get serious, still less with Wall Street. Heaven help us if the Germans and the Swiss get really interested in this market."

The steak and kidney pie was followed by a steaming jam roly-poly and custard, the latter clearly enlivened with cognac. Freddie fell upon it with gusto, claiming an urgent need to be on the quarter-deck to watch the first race but in reality bored stiff with the lecture on how to make money dealing in grandfather clocks being delivered into his left ear and keen to leave Nigel Platts, on his other side, who had unwisely

---

admitted to be more interested in cricket than the horses, as the sole recipient of this particular stream of horological wisdom.

Later on, they had all trooped down to the paddock just after three o'clock to see Court Dancer saddled up. She was a pretty young mare with a white face to offset the silky sheen of her jet black flanks. As she passed them on her first circuit of the paddock, lively and light-footed, Freddie Wordsworth observed that, had he been a stallion, she was the sort of thing he thought he might fancy. On the second, he was reassured to see her raise her long black tail and deposit a trail of steaming golden-brown turds.

"Well, I'm glad she's got that out of her sluices," he said. "It's bad enough to have to carry that little jerk over there over all those gates without having a gut full of hay slopping around in her bilges."

Finally Charlie Brooks was swung into the saddle by Fred Winter, Court Dancer deposited a final turd, and the stable girl led her away to go on down to the start. The Harcourt party turned to find their way back to the box. Peter, having noticed a loose shoelace, bent to do it up only to find himself, as he rose, face to face with Sophie. She was dressed in a dark, almost black, mink coat that fell to mid calf but was cleverly shaped to show her figure. It must have been made for her and she looked wonderful. Her long wavy blonde hair, roughly parted in the middle, cascaded to her shoulders and, as a fleeting shaft of sunlight pierced the clouds, a huge smile lit up her sunlit face.

"I thought it was you," she said, throwing her arms round his neck and hugging his face to one cheek and then the other. "What are you doing here?"

"I'm with a client who's got a runner. What about you?"

"Daddy has a leg - I think more exactly a fetlock, and the dodgy one at that - of Sergeant Pepper. We've got a big box up there for the whole syndicate. Why don't you come and join.... Oh, there you are, Mark. You remember Peter Davenport at the Fordyces the other day?"

"Of course. Good to see you," he said flatly, not even pretending to mean it and switching his cigarette to his left hand so that he could exchange a merely formal handshake. Sophie, we must rush if we're going to be back in the box for the off." And with that, he swept an arm around her furry shoulders and shepherded her away.

It was See You Then's Champion Hurdle, the 11-10 on favourite holding off a strong challenge from the US invader, Flatterer, up the famous final hill to the finish to win by a length and a half. Sergeant Pepper was pulled up out in the country and Court Dancer came a creditable last of the finishers. Out of loyalty to Stephen, everyone had backed her, except David Cooper, who said that he had put £10,000 on See You Then's nose at evens through William Hill a week before.

"I don't gamble to lose money," he said. "It's an investment with a certain likelihood of return. When I buy an Aston Martin or a Bugatti, I do so in the expectation that I'm going to get back more than I paid for it. That's why I don't buy Fords and Fiats, which simply depreciate. It's the same with horses. That nag of Stephen's will never pay her way."

"Ah, but David," said Stephen overhearing, "I don't really care. It's the pleasure of owning her, the joy of watching her run."

"I don't understand that," said David. "I don't own anything for the sake of owning it. I have the Jew's foreboding of impending calamity. I must be able to turn everything I have into cash and carry it away with me. You can't even eat that horse," he said with finality.

St Patrick's Day at Cheltenham - what a riot! The Irish, who always seemed to own this meeting, had arrived in such numbers that they overwhelmed the placid countrymen of the English shires with their whimsical eccentricity and boisterous enchantment. They sprayed the on-course bookies with wads of tenners, the stainless steel urinals with quarts of barely ingested Guinness, and the cold dank air with an exuberance which should have lifted the glowering clouds from the skies. And when Galmoy, carrying a goodly proportion of Eire's gross domestic product, won the Waterford Crystal Stayers' Hurdle at 9-2, it was several minutes before conversation was again possible, even up in Stephen's box. Peter had put a fiver on himself and was leaning over the rail to enjoy the excitement of the crowd below when Jock Enderby sidled up to him.

"As regards our earlier conversation, Peter, when the time comes I hope you'll remember," he said, lowering his voice and talking directly into Peter's ear, "to let your friends know when it would be wise to include Dundas Brothers in our portfolios."

Peter was rather taken aback by the unsubtlety of the approach and was wondering how to answer when Jock, his tongue perhaps a little loosened by indulgence, went on: "Anyway, one good turn deserves another. Don't nail your colours too closely to the current chairman of our mutually esteemed pharmaceutical friends. Short-dated stock. Mark my words. Short-dated stock."

It was getting dark when the box wound up and they went to find their cars. They had been almost on their way when it came through that Lawson had whipped two pence off the standard rate, occasioning a further round of alcoholic merriment. Peter, knowing that he really should not be driving, popped into the gents on the way to unload some champagne. As he came out, Sophie emerged from the ladies alongside.

"Well, hello again. Have you had a good day?"

"Wonderful," she beamed, " I won all of twenty pounds - and it was so good to see you again," she said, as though she really meant it. "Till next time," she smiled and, putting a gloved hand on each of his shoulders, inclined her face to him. At that moment a Catholic priest, a little the worse for wear, emerged unsteadily from the gents, a great spray of St Patrick's Day shamrock in his buttonhole, and jostled her gently as he passed. Peter was expecting a peck on the cheek but voluntarily or involuntarily, her lips brushed against his. As they parted, she smiled unperturbed.

"Ah, what a temptress you are, Sophie Templeton-Smythe. When am I going to have the chance to get you away from that boring oaf you always have in tow?"

"Mark? Oh, he's really not so bad," she said, and then added rather ominously "as long as he's sober. But I've got a pink ticket the week-end after next. He's off with his mates to Hong Kong for the Sevens. Must rush. Bye." And with that she reached up, put both her arms round his neck, and kissed him, almost lingeringly, on the mouth. No, there could be no mistake. That was deliberate.

The 1987 Hong Kong Sevens were generally reported as having belonged to New Zealand, deploying a professionalism never witnessed before in that holiday atmosphere of cobbled-together amateurs to see off the free-flowing and fun-loving Fijians; but seven thousand miles away in London, Peter Davenport thought otherwise. They had dined at Caviar Kaspia in Bruton Place, starting with the finest Scottish smoked salmon and champagne, moving on to what one might have called a comparative tasting of sevruga and beluga with blinis and Polish lemon vodka and following up with a divine brie, patisseries and coffee before walking up the road to dance at Annabel's in Berkely Square.

Sitting opposite her, it was again apparent how young she was. Her blue eyes sparkled from a face utterly devoid of the marks and shadows of either care or fatigue.

She was dressed in a pale blue trouser suit with wide lapels that plunged into her cleavage in as deep a vee as could be possible without revealing her bra. This itself was one of those wonders that lifted and shaped and generally made the best of the averagely provided young lady. In Sophie's case, blessed well beyond the norm and particularly in relation to her petite physique, the result was spectacular. Peter soon gave up trying to take his eyes off them and admitted shame-facedly that he must have a suckling complex. She giggled contentedly, acknowledging, as if it were not already obvious, that the object of a top like this was not exactly to hide one's wares. But she also confessed that she needed the long sleeves to hide the bruises.

"Peter, he's not exactly violent and he's really not as bad as you think. Oh, yes, he can be a bit pompous and self-important, particularly when he's going on about his friendship with Prince Charles."

"Oh shit, I didn't realise when I was taking the piss out of the royals the other night that I was treading on quite such tender corns. Was he very furious?"

"Not with you, particularly. Just said that the trouble with paying City slickers so much was that they got ideas above their class. But I got a bit of a going-over for finding it all so funny. I don't really know the Prince very well but I do find all that holier than thou plummy pretentiousness and tugging of his shirt cuffs a bit rich; particularly since the Army gives some ex-flame of Anne's the pay of a colonel or some such to provide his wife as mistress to the next Defender of the Faith. I think because I've said as much to Mark in the past, he thought I'd put you up to it."

"Does he hit you?" Peter asked, appalled. He knew it was commonplace but still failed to comprehend it.

"Not exactly. The norm is a tongue-lashing; but if he's drunk or very angry - and he was both after the Fordyces - he grabs me by both my arms and gives me a damned good shaking at the same time. At the moment I've got bruises where you have biceps."

"Why do you put up with it?"

"It's no big thing. He doesn't give me black eyes or slap me across the face. It's the sort of low-level violence which I imagine is pretty normal. No more than male assertiveness really. Anyway, we've been together for three years now. I suppose I've rather got into the habit. But enough of that - what of the lovely Soo Chan?"

"Finished," he exaggerated, substituting his state of mind for the physical reality. In fact he had spent the afternoon in bed with her before she raced off to catch the evening Concorde for a photo-shoot for Revlon in New York next day. They must have been keen to agree to a Sunday. From there she was flying on to Taipei to spend a week with her family.

But it was different now. For the last fortnight, he had been trying to analyse what she did to him - and what he did to her. It wasn't exactly mechanical and it was quite simply wonderful, like no woman he had ever had before. But it was almost surgical. This afternoon, she had bade him an astonishing farewell and he could still feel a tenderness induced by the repeated demands that her moist lips and darting tongue and thrusting hips had made upon his manhood. For herself there had been such wave after wave of orgasm that it was almost as if she knew that the seed she was taking from him was not for a few days but for all time. As the driver held open the door of the car that the agency had sent for her, Peter was already thinking of Sophie.

It was one of those evenings, for a man, where you knew where you were going to end up if you simply didn't make a horlicks of it. It was written all over her face that she had an inkling of it too. Not that she had decided upon it, or that she was simply there for the taking; but that she was hoping against hope that this was the very first stage of a new beginning, perhaps merely a brief experience, but something that would extract her from the tedium of being the butt of Mark's bragging, Mark's lust and Mark's temper. Peter's ambitions, if he had any, were currently no longer than his still sensitive and flaccid dick. This woman was a bundle of fun out of bed; and if she proved to be the same between the sheets, he was going to have a whale of a time.

At Annabel's they sipped champagne and giggled, increasingly absorbed with each other to the exclusion of all else. They whispered into each other's ears of nothing in particular, a gathering sexual nuance to every exchange. They danced, at first at as sedate a distance as was possible on the crowded floor but, little by little, ever closer until her arms were entwined round his neck, he could feel the softness of her breasts against his chest and, with diminishing pretence, she pressed her pelvis against the developing bulge within his trousers. It was not late when they left without discussion and, as she climbed into the taxi, she was neither surprised nor disappointed to hear his instruction to the cabbie to head for Wapping. She snuggled against his shoulder, one hand sensuously grasped around his inner thigh and almost purred with contented anticipation.

Back at his flat, Sophie explored the apartment and marvelled at the view while Peter opened more champagne. He brought their glasses over to where she stood by the window and, staring hungrily into each other's eyes, they clinked them together almost soundlessly. They had barely had two sips before they were all over each other on the sofa, their open mouths absorbing that first wonderful sensation of each other's tongues as Peter slipped his right hand within her jacket, slid it into the top of her bra and found himself effortlessly with her left breast cupped in his hand. It felt fantastic - full, soft, smooth. All thought of resistance had fled her mind as she turned her attention to the buttons of his shirt. They were scrabbling at each other now. Her jacket's two buttons were no problem and he reached behind her back to flick open the strap of her bra, her amazing breasts falling from the cups into his waiting hands. They were truly not so large though the modesty of her frame made them seem so and, after Soo Chan's perfect oriental dimensions, it was wonderful to enjoy something of a size you could truly play with. Her nipples were pink and full and boldly erect even before he took one and then the other into his mouth. She squirmed with pleasure and unashamedly reached for his zip, her tiny hand burrowing towards his underpants.

"I think we'd be more comfortable next door," he whispered, coming up for air, rising and taking her hands to pull her to her feet in front of him. Two minds with but a single thought, they reached to each other's shoulders and swept the clothes from the upper half of their bodies, his shirt falling to the floor behind him and her jacket and bra tumbling onto the sofa. They kissed but did not embrace, each using the palms of their hands to explore the other's torso; for her the firm broad shoulders and impressively flat tummy, for him the bulge of her sublime breasts, as soft as petals, as cool as glass, as malleable as ripe fruit but young and barely less firm now she was standing than when presented on the balcony of her bra.

Her hands swept once more over his stomach and came to his belt. She tore it open, released the button above his zipper and, as his trousers concertinaed to his ankles, plunged her right hand down into his underpants, grasping him there with fingers which seemed absurdly cold by contrast to the heat that was overwheming his loins. He turned his attention to her trousers in response though her bottom was sufficiently round and her trousers sufficiently tight to require him to use his hands to push them over the swelling of her buttocks. As he did so, he discovered to his delighted fascination that her panties were merely a lacy string.

No more than moments later a trail of discarded shoes and socks and trousers led the way to his bed where they lay, not yet quite naked, spinning out in time the discovery of their most sensitive parts. The glorious sensation of exploring the flesh of a new woman, enjoyed in each relationship only once, was a consuming joy that Peter rediscovered on each occasion and then apparently forgot. Maturity made for the protraction of these miraculous moments in a way that he found impossible to remember in the frantic and unrestrained couplings of his youth; and though he felt as hard as he could ever recall, unconsciously the afternoon in Soo Chan's flat had wonderfully reduced the urgency of his need and immeasurably heightened his capacity to endure the pleasure Sophie was going to give him.

It was a night to remember. They drifted in and out of sleep from time to time but, unused to sleeping with each other and lacking familiarity with each other's nocturnal movements, they tossed and turned and were repeatedly awake. On each occasion, they made love with undiminished enthusiasm.

Around ten, as she was sleeping soundly, he slipped from the bed and went to the kitchen. She was awaking drowsily when he returned still naked with a tray of freshly squeezed orange juice, soft-boiled eggs, hot toast and strong coffee.

"A girl could get used to being served like this," she purred, as he set the tray down.

"Serving is what stallions do, my darling," he said, kissing her.

"I know what I said; I come from a horsey family, remember," she answered, pulling him towards her by his cock.

"You certainly come, my darling; but it's time for breakfast."

In the shower together afterwards they were soon at it again, soaping each other's bodies and sensuously sliding slippery flesh on slippery flesh. The hero of the hour, almost bloody but still unbowed, rose to the occasion again, but the difference in their heights made penetration in a standing position apparently impossible. She was, however, not to be denied and grasping him tightly around his neck, lifted her feet off the ground and skewered herself upon him, wrapping her legs around his waist. And there, with his hands cradled beneath her bottom, they completed their first night together.

They had been together ever since. Cubit had returned from Hong Kong to find a letter, friendly but firm, sitting on the hall table of his house in Montpelier Square with his own spare keys. When he had stormed round to her flat in Chelsea, she was not at home and the locks had all been changed.

She worked for the advertising agency, Ogilvy & Mather, in the West End doing nothing in particular, so Peter could divine, other than look decorative. It was not that she was stupid - far from it - though she had no particular intellectual pretensions; but she had been brought up traditionally with prosperity and some privilege and had no particular ambition in the sense of a career. She was only twenty-four and her cravings were fortunately still for amusement and revelry rather than for marriage and children. Now her sex life was fun too, spontaneous and uncritical. Peter found in her a perfect foil, someone who could lift him instantaneously out of the pressures of his job but seemed to understood without resentment that, for him at least and for now, his work had the prior hold on his time.

Her father had returned from the Far East in his late teens to join his bachelor uncle's quite successful small clothing business, which supplied principally ties to Marks & Sparks on a more or less exclusive basis. When the old queen died in tragic and rather scandalous circumstances only seven or eight years later, her father had found himself the proprietor. The family now lived in some modest style near Sevenoaks with a few acres of land that had accommodated ponies for the children when they were young and still kept a couple of horses for her parents. The three of them, two boys and a girl, were all now adult and, as they had been separately launched into the real world, there had been enough cash on hand for each to get the benefit of a pretty soft landing. Sophie's, at the age of twenty-one, had taken the form of a long lease on a small two-bedroomed flat in Sloane Avenue Mansions, just north of the Kings Road.

They were a close family but not unfriendly to outsiders and Peter had been well received by her father as a replacement for the Hon Mark, despite his lack of a handle. As the son of an old tea-planter, he was quite tickled at the prospect of an alliance with a trusted retainer of the glorious Dundas family. The one early fly in the otherwise perfect ointment had been the family's summer holiday plans, which, immediately after Wimbledon, had swept Sophie, together with her brothers and their wives, away to a ranch in Colorado for an entire month. Sophie's mother had been keen for Peter to come too, but it coincided with the scheduled flotation of Harcourt Properties towards the end of July. He had tried at least to fit in a long week-end; but Harcourt was no sooner done and dusted than New Jersey Signal had galloped over the horizon.

The four weeks of separation had proved a turning-point for both of them. Physically, he had ached for her and she for him. On her return they fell upon each other like animals on heat, unable to get enough of each other for night after night. But something else had happened too. She had become not just a part but in reality the very centre of both the physical and intellectual sides of his existence. The totality of his life outside the office now revolved exclusively about what they did together, their mutual friends, their visits to the theatre or the cinema, the dinner parties to which they were always now invited as a pair, and the week-ends when he could snatch at least a couple of half days away from Dundas Brothers and all its works. They had even managed a full three days of shameless luxury over the end of August bank holiday, motoring up to the Lake District and staying at the Sharrow Bay Hotel overlooking Ullswater. It was still run by those two old queers who had bedecked its public rooms with antiques and *objets d'art* and its menus with the best of English cooking. And it was there one evening after dinner, replete with food and wine and still tender from the afternoon's love-making, that they decided at last to subject the London taxi trade to the crippling blow of their cohabitation.

The entire party in Courchevel consisted of experienced skiers and, in the mornings at least, they all took off together, the route (with a break for hot chocolate or whatever) invariably defined by Julia so that it culminated in a more than decent lunch around two o'clock. The first day it was all the Courchevel side, up to Saulire in the cable car, down the Combe and Verdons, up the long chair to Chenus, all over Loze and Lac Bleu on the right before descending to the Biollay chair and the Vizelle eggs to tackle the Creux and the Chanrossa on the left; and finally the Marmottes chair so that they could descend back onto the Bellecôte slope to take lunch at La Bergerie. Another day they bashed all over Méribel and Mottaret before coming back over for lunch at Cap Horn, that restaurant just above the altiport where they have every vintage of Château Petrus since the war. On still another it was the grand expedition all the way over to ski the glacier above Val Thorens and the fearsome Dame Blanche on the far side of the valley before lunch at a rather ordinary self-service above Les Menuires. On this day, of course, there was still a full afternoon of skiing to get back across the Méribel valley to Courchevel; but on most afternoons the party would divide after lunch between the doers and the doo-dooers.

Peter had no choice and wanted none. Sophie, by some way the most elegant and supple skier of the group, had no intention of giving up much before the final lift of the day and was always intent on a few black runs in the afternoon. As she skipped down the fearsome Grand Couloir from one giant mogul to the next with Peter some way in her wake, he wondered whether it was the three or four glasses of red wine that he had consumed to her two or the twelve years that separated them that gave her the advantage. No matter, he adored being with her and had decided to have her for always.

Fat chance, he thought, that for always was going to apply to the Mulhollands' marriage. Craig, recently returned to Shell's head office after a three-year stint in the Far East, was a rising management star with a thirst for experience to match his ambition. Like a hyperactive child, he was for ever at some project or other. He had got his pilot's licence whilst still at university but these days preferred the challenge of a glider to power. He had been learning to ride quite seriously and had threatened to buy himself a point-to-pointer until he discovered that, at six foot three and fourteen and a half stone, he was going to put his mount at something of a disadvantage. Now he was into painting and, on the few afternoons on which he was persuaded to return with Ann to the chalet after lunch, he was to be found on the balcony with his folding easel, brushes and tubes of paint while she was curled up in what she called infuriatingly the land of nod. To date, fortunately, they had no children; but her ridiculous baby talk betrayed that mousey motherhood was all that was on her mind.

Robin Archer was no athlete and was not a particularly serious skier. He was proficient enough but looked upon this fortnight of freedom from the grumbles of his nauseous and nauseating patients as more than just an opportunity to bash up and down the slopes. Anyone acquainted with Julia would have expected her husband's life to be organised by her from morn till night; but Robin seemed able to ignore her plans without being considered mutinous. A *modus vivendi* operated which allowed Julia to pilot the ship but Robin to come up on deck only when he felt like it. He had brought a pile of the latest crime novels out in paperback with him - 'Wolf to the Slaughter' by Ruth Rendell, 'The Choking Doberman' by Jan Harold Brunvand, 'The Old Devils' by Kingsley Amis and PD James's 'A Taste for Death' - and was happy to settle down with them for a couple of hours every afternoon. Julia was in reality far too much her own person to be offended when she was left to her own devices.

Sheila would always be ready with scones and home-made jams, delicious-looking cakes or toothsome pastries when they returned from the slopes; but in general she found that her best customers were those who had spent the afternoon doing least. Robin had a scandalously sweet tooth but quietly endured Julia's disapproving glance as he helped himself to a second slice, comfortable in the satisfaction that he had already indulged in three invisible portions before her return. Ann would emerge from her nest to climb what she called the wooden hill for something scrummy; but the rest of them merely nibbled.

The chalet girls normally had Tuesdays off; but they had all agreed that Sheila should also have the choice of Christmas Eve or Christmas Day. She was insistent on doing the works for Christmas dinner but had gratefully accepted the Thursday. That morning Robin had concocted a huge greasy fry-up of bacon and eggs, boudin noir and hash browns - an eclectic boost of saturated fat that he prescribed for the party on the grounds that your cholesterol count could not be considered high unless it exceeded that of your doctor. The morning's skiing in consequence began rather later than Julia had ordained and was conducted with a sluggishness of which she openly disapproved. They ended up on the vast terrace of the Chalet de Pierres, bathed in an unnaturally warm December sunshine, for lunch off the starchiest linen ever to grace a ski slope restaurant.

Robin, not content with the health hazard that had constituted breakfast, had decreed that the evening should also be an animal-fat fest, this time at the incomparable Bistro du Praz down in 1300 - where Charlie, the elaborately moustachioed proprietor, was on his usual exuberant form. They had begun with salads topped either with slices of warm duck breast or toasted goats cheese which they washed down with more bottles of the white Vin de Savoie than Peter cared to count. In selecting the main course, they had divided between the girls, who all wanted a fondue, and the boys, who had opted for hot fresh foie gras. The disruption that this might have caused to the seating arrangements was resolved by the simple expedient of all having both. There were three dishes of the foie gras, the first flamed in cognac, the second in armagnac and the third in calvados. Each seemed more magnificent than the one before and each swam in a *jus* of exquisite richness into which they greedily dipped their bread. The fondue that followed should have satisfied the mightiest appetite but the leisurely pace of such a dish and the continuous flow of the local red Bugey seemed designed to promote a little further indulgence. Robin's powers of persuasion were not challenged as he ordered the cheese with Grand Marnier soufflés to follow all round.

It was well gone midnight when the little minibus taxi deposited them back at the chalet. Peter was on that delightful threshold of mild inebriation that made him feel as horny as a ram and it was clear from the way that Sophie had snuggled up to him on the bench seat at the rear, burrowing into his ski jacket, that she felt much the same. Knowing nudges were exchanged all round as they, like Ann, opted out of Craig's suggested final nightcap round the fire and settled for bed. There had been something about the place - the clear almost intoxicating mountain air, the warm sunshine, the satisfied aftermath of real physical exertion, the food, the booze, the ambience and the pampering, the big soft mattress with the huge downy duvet and the grand faintly lecherous bathtub - that had got them both going from the moment they had arrived. From those early days when she had appeared a tiny bit shocked by his immediate lack of inhibition, their love-making had acquired an intimacy, an inventiveness and a spontaneity which made for fun on the grandest scale. It was not a work of art. They went at it like a pair of stoats, one on top and then the other, sideways, doggy-style, sitting in his lap, in the bath, in the shower - the cunning linguist and the man they had come to refer to as the midshipman or, to give him his full style, Mr Midshipman Fellatio Hornblower, their regular and often simultaneous companions. But here it was even more so. They were shagging before they could get their clothes off for bed, her unfastened bra flapping around her neck and her wet panties pulled to one side so that he could enter her with his trousers round his ankles; they woke in the night and their hands went immediately between each other's sleep-warmed and still sticky thighs; they woke in the morning and at once began to explore the other's state of readiness; they returned from skiing in the late afternoon and undressed each other with feverish urgency so that they finished to find the floor around the bed looking like a war-zone; and as they soaked afterwards in the bubbling Jacuzzi it was only a matter of time before the gentle soaping of each other's bodies would bring them slithering together again.

Christmas Day dawned again in perfect sunshine with Sheila back in harness, hot croissants, sensational honey that the local bees had sucked from the alpine heather, bucks fizzes, hot coffee and hugs and kisses all round. Julia had ordained only minor variations to the day's routine - a modestly later start, an imperceptibly gentler ski, and a significantly lighter lunch, albeit consisting of a sublime omelette aux fines herbes with salad and frites on the middle tier of the Bel Air's sun-basted terrace above Courchevel 1650.

That evening, back at the chalet, now infused with the aromas of Sheila's preparations, they were scheduled to assemble before dinner for champagne and to exchange presents. Julia had sensibly ordained that, in the interests of luggage space, presents were to be confined to books, CDs and inexpensive knick-knacks and that they were to give as couples; but there was still an impressive pile of gaily decorated parcels around the tree in the sitting room. As the champagne flowed and Sheila set down a huge tray of exquisite canapés, the ritual began.

The prejudices of the givers were as usual as widely represented as the tastes of the recipients. Ann, who regarded Peter as a deserving proxy for anything which she considered an excess of capitalism, had clearly been responsible for choosing his present and couldn't wait for Peter to open the package that contained his Diary of a Yuppie by Louis Auchinschloss. Robin, or more likely Julia, had chosen for him a wonderful, glossy and undoubtedly expensive book by David Stirk entitled 'Golf: The History of an Obsession'. Sophie, despite her abhorrence, had demonstrated the depths of her devotion with a grand box of Peter's favourite Montecristo Especiales. Ann's nose could already be seen wrinkling in anticipation of the assault to which it would be subjected at the end of the forthcoming feast.

Peter and Sophie had selected for Craig a wonderful book recently published by Douglas Skeggs on Monet's impressions of the Seine and, for Ann, Solti's new recording of Lohengrin with Placido Domingo, Jessye Norman and the Vienna Philharmonic. They had leavened Robin's diet of crime novels with a copy of Jeffrey Bernard's 'Low Life' and bought for his wife one of those enormously cunning new devices with a lever for extracting wine corks. They were confirmed to have been spot-on with that selection when her husband presented her with a subscription to Robert Parker's 'Wine Advocate'. Ann and Craig, knowing her passion for the opera, had bought her the new Raul Gimenez recording of the Rossini arias. Robin was also on the receiving end of lots of music though Craig and Ann's choice of the Rattle recording of Mahler's Second Symphony was not in quite the same league as his wife's impressive set of the eight discs of Django Reinhardt Django. There were CDs too for Sophie, who was considered something of an airhead by both the other girls, U2 from Craig and Ann and Stevie Wonder from Robin and Julia. Julia also managed to demonstrate her condescension towards Ann with Roy Strong's 'A Small Garden Designer's Handbook', the 'small', Peter and Sophie afterwards agreed, being applied by Julia in equal measure to the garden, the designer and the handbook.

Peter, after scouring what was left of the diminished band of London furriers, had managed to find Sophie a lovely hat in black mink to match the fabulous coat he had first seen her wear at Cheltenham. Craig's obsessive passion for military history had been rewarded with Richard Lamb's latest book on Montgomery from Robin and Julia and Michael Carver's 'Twentieth Century Warriors' from Ann. Finally, in another Julia-co-ordinated plan, Sheila was bombarded with a selection of enough perfumes to see out the remainder of the decade.

Needless to say, her dinner was a triumph; the turkey moist and succulent, the sprouts crisp, the cranberry sauce picquant and laced with eau de vie, the stuffing studded with whole jet-black morilles. Julia had selected for the occasion two magnums of 1978 Grands Echézeaux, a big, lingering, intense burgundy that they continued to drink with the creamy brie which Sheila had chosen for the cheese before switching to a luscious sweet 1976 Barsac from Château Nairac to accompany the flaming Christmas pudding. Coffee - decaf for Ann - and cognac followed with the cigars and dark chocolate truffles as they sprawled in the sitting room's deep armchairs semi-comatose with indulgence.

At some time between then and the morning, Peter removed from his mouth one or other of the parts of Sophie's anatomy with which he had regular oral contact long enough to propose marriage. Sophie, who was conversing with the midshipman at the time, conveyed a positive reply to Peter's navel representative. It was agreed that they would keep it to themselves until New Year's Eve when they would be back in London and were scheduled to be joining a party of their friends at Annabel's. There couldn't be a much more appropriate venue than where it had all more or less started; Craig and Ann, Robin and Julia would be there; also the Fordyces, who had, after all, been responsible for the introduction.

*****

"Peter, someone on the phone for you," Sheila called, knocking on the door of their bedroom, "Ronnie King, or something like that."

"OK, coming."

"What, already," giggled Sophie who was lying at the opposite end of the bath, gently massaging his balls under the water with her toes and watching expectantly as his periscope broke the surface.

Peter struggled dripping to his feet and wrapped a bath sheet around himself. It bulged guiltily below his midriff as he set off for the door and clearly caught Sheila's eye as he crossed the sitting room towards her for she handed him the phone with a conspiratorial wink.

"Peter, I'm sorry to bother you on holiday but I was catching up on some paperwork this morning and ....."

"This morning, Rod! Hasn't anybody told you it's Boxing Day?"

"Sure, Peter, but you know what it's like with young kids. Up at sparrow's yesterday morning to look at their toys and then a late night. They didn't appear much before lunch-time today and it was an ideal opportunity to wade through some of the accumulated crap. Anyway, amongst it all was the monthly return from the registrars analysing movements in the shareholders; and there's something peculiar which I don't understand. I may just be being thick; but it's been bothering me all day and I thought it was worth a call. You see the holding in Sepon Nominees is up from 6.2% last month to 14.5% now. I thought that Sepon was something to do with the Stock Exchange."

"Oh shit," said Peter, "it's the jobber's trick. Somebody's going to launch a take-over bid for you."

Sunday, 27 December, 1987

What Sophie, or more particularly her father, had disparagingly designated the godown was a former cotton warehouse in Wapping High Street which had been converted into what estate agents would title eight stunning apartments. The ground floor, apart from the entrance lobby, was given over to parking secure from the local infants who, taking advantage of the proximity of the tourist trap which constituted the Prospect of Whitby, still liked to operate a "look after your car for a fiver, mister" protection racket when given half a chance. Above, each apartment occupied half a floor of the building. Peter's was on the top left and faced slightly to the west of south before the Thames curved away north-eastwards towards Wapping Wall. It commanded a view upstream over what used to be called, in the days when this part of the river was the heart of the capital's port, the Pool of London, to Tower Bridge and Terence Conran's Butler's Wharf development on the south bank. Apart from the two bedrooms and bathrooms over on the eastern side of the apartment, it was entirely open plan, kitchen, dining area, sitting room and study all enjoying from different angles the broad sweep of the river. The original ruddy brickwork had been retained exposed where possible and the heavy beams of the warehouse roof soared like the nave of an old country church into the apex of the roof twenty feet above the polished hardwood floors. Here Peter had spread a couple of dozen or more oriental rugs in a variety of styles and colours and sizes. There were Shirvans and a Yahyali from Turkey, the former in pale blues and browns and greens, the latter in the strongest of reds and blues, its hexagonal pattern surrounding a huge central medallion in the same colours. There was a lovely Isfahan from Persia featuring the tree of life in the main sitting area, a couple of steps down from the rest of the apartment, and an all-silk Qum that hung on the wall of the study beside his pale cherry-wood partner's desk. At the entrance to the apartment was a large Sinkiang from the far north-west of China, its soft, mellow colouring picked out in a mass of geometric patterns. The dining area was given over to a large Bokhara from Jaipur in a deep, rusty pink and there were smaller rugs and runners and prayer mats scattered hither and thither, large, bold motifs from Kazak in the Caucasus, Balouchi tribal rugs in rough wool and dense Hamadans and Bijars. For furniture, he had generally stuck to the solid wooden ambience of the warehouse itself, buying tables and chairs from a gallery on the hill in Hampstead fashioned from the old Australian yarra wood sleepers used for the African railways, impermeable to termites, too heavy to float and too dense to burn. But he had also incorporated deep, comfortable sofas and chairs in a heavy coarse cream fabric from Heals and fittings in solid angular brass, black granite slabs for the kitchen work tops and lots and lots of glass. At night the huge main room, dimly lit from the big brass table lamps and concealed spots was warm and masculine and old-fashioned. At the same time, Sophie's feminine influence was evidenced by a scattering of bright cushions on the chairs and sofas and the ever-present joy of the fresh flowers which she brought home by the armful. By day, the blaze of light from the grand south facing window made it as functional and modern as a House & Garden colour spread. From each of the master bedroom, sitting room and kitchen, there was access to a solid wooden balcony, the last being of sufficient size to take enough of a table for a small dinner party under the stars.

Peter had paid a small fortune for the flat in the middle of 1986, before it was even finished so that he was able to decide its internal shape and fittings with the architect. Though the mortgage terrified him, he loved it. It was the first place he had owned in which he had been able to influence the final design and, after four years in a pokey terraced house in Islington, it was a joy. It was convenient for the office and well enough placed to avoid the miseries of any form of public transport. Above all, its view was an ever-changing panorama of the river and its traffic and of the skies above southern London.

The taxi having dropped him from Heathrow, he left his bags in the lobby while he returned his skis to the big lock-up store in the garage between his Morgan and Sophie's metallic silver mini. She had pleaded with him the possibility of returning to London, if he must, for just twenty-four hours to set in motion whatever was necessary and returning to Courchevel for the last couple of days of their holiday; but it was obvious to him that it was silly to hold out such hopes.

The day was mild but grey, the few spits and spots on the windscreen of the cab as they drove from the airport insufficient to suppress the irritating rubbery screech of the wiper blades. Up in his flat, though it was no more than mid afternoon, the dusk was already descending. He turned on all the lights and turned up the central heating control.

Peter had picked up a copy of each of the serious Sundays at the airport but had no more than flicked through them in the taxi, noting the uncomfortable prediction that the economy was now overheating too fast for Lawson to cut personal taxes very sharply in the forthcoming Budget. He quickly unpacked, made himself a pot of tea and settled in an armchair to bring himself up to date. Timothy would be here within a couple of hours. Peter smiled as he recalled their telephone conversation late last night. He had clearly caught Timothy actually on the job and, from the female moaning and sighing which filtered down the telephone, it was clear that, in her case at least, *le moment suprème* was very close indeed. There was a perfectly audible scream as Timothy, professional to the last, apparently pulled his knob out of her and announced to Peter "Okay, fire away. I was just in the middle of something; but I can finish it off later."

It couldn't be said, according to the papers, that a great deal had happened in the world. It was noted that skiing conditions were generally dismal, except at the high resorts. Someone had outraged the establishment by leaking the dreary contents of the Queen's Christmas TV message - as if it were possible to tell this year's anodyne blather from the last - and Henry Cotton, that greatest of gentleman golfers, had died on Christmas Eve. In the City, the Panel had at last done something sensible by clearing BP to bid for Britoil. The emasculated mandarins round at the Treasury had continued to intone feebly that it would use the golden share to block a transfer of control.

Around six o'clock Timothy arrived carrying two pilot's brief cases stuffed with papers.

"Is my car safe down there?" he enquired, knowing the local scene.

"Not necessarily. You'd better put it inside. You'll find plenty of room. Most people are away. Here, this is the card to operate the door."

Over the ages mankind has alighted (Peter sometimes wondered how) on any number of mechanical aids to sexual stimulation; but it was a cardinal maxim of Timothy's team that the second half of the twentieth century had hit upon the most effective stimulant yet devised. Not to be found in any of the Anne Summers sex shops which had sprung up in recent years in cosmopolitan parts of London, it took the form of a black Porsche 911 Carrera Cabriolet, though this was in reality no more than a generic. Similar hardware from Ferrari, Lamborghini, Lotus, Mercedes-Benz, BMW and even Honda, Mitsubishi and Toyota could create similar though less spectacular effects.

Naturally, not all Timothy's circle could afford the purest form of this aphrodisiac - though Timothy, still a bachelor at 31 and with several years of good bonuses under his belt, had the genuine article. Oliver Quentin-Archard had a TVR, which was perfectly adequate for the rougher end of the Sloane Ranger brigade, normally banged up in the back of mummy's Range Rover Vogue, and Stuart Robinson a Golf Cabriolet, which was effectively the bottom rung of the ladder. At the tender age of 22 and fresh out of Bristol University, there was even a young man in the department, whose father had made a lot of money out of force-feeding, murdering and eviscerating about half a million chickens every week, who had a Ferrari Testarossa. His successes among the departmental secretaries, which were many and episodic, could be put down to this monster, the general thickness of his wallet or his youthful enthusiasm; but not, by all accounts, to another item of his equipment which was generally held to be disappointingly underdeveloped.

There were about ten members of this loosely formed lads' association throughout the department. They called themselves the boys from soixante-neuf. Peter, at the age of 37 and a director to boot, was no longer looked upon as a fully paid-up member; but his continued attachment to what was now a five year old V8 Morgan was excused as a tolerable avuncular eccentricity. He was occasionally asked and less frequently accepted invitations to boys' nights out; and it was agreed that it was only a matter of time before, ensnared by the lovely Sophie, the Morgan would give way to something which could accommodate a carry-cot and a baby-buggy.

Peter fixed them drinks - a beer for Timothy and a scotch with ice and soda for himself - while Timothy parked his car. On his return, he unloaded the contents of his briefcases and sorted the papers into piles on the dining room table.

"Where do you want to start, Peter?" he asked.

"I think we should begin by looking at the current state of the defences and what we need to do to plug any gaps in our information. Then we should look at who the potential bidders might be. We can then think about how many people you're going to need to get all this done."

"And by when?"

"Well, it's a bit of a risk but I think we have to assume that a bid is unlikely until the first working day of the New Year. But that only gives us a week to get up to speed. I've arranged for us to go round to Pitcairn to see Rod King at four tomorrow afternoon."

It was three hours later by the time they had finished going through the fat grey binder which contained the master copy of Pitcairn's defence plans. It was shambolically out of date and Tim had assembled a list of missing items covering several pages of his notebook. They were hopelessly out of touch with where Pitcairn's profits were heading in the medium term and had no more idea of what was in the product pipeline than had been written up in the research of the various stockbrokers' analysts who followed the pharmaceutical sector.

"Realistically, Tim, you're hardly going to make an impression on this before tomorrow afternoon."

"Peter, it's a question of resources."

"Sure; I think you should concentrate on getting your team briefed and down to work. I think you'll need three people in addition to yourself: one to cover possible predators, one to organise the bible and fill in the gaps and one to concentrate on the pharmaceutical products, the research pipelines of Pitcairn and its competitors, where there are overlaps, where there are voids, where there are synergies."

"That should ideally be Stuart, given his background but..."

"Excellent. Good idea. Then, apart from organising everything, you can concentrate on the strengths and weaknesses analysis. That's going to have to be the foundation of the defence documents."

"But, Peter, I've got..."

"We can take this version of the bible with us to see Rod with manuscript headings for what we're going to add. I'll need to spend tomorrow morning bringing the lawyers and brokers up to speed and telling them what we need from them. I must also talk to Hennessy."

"Peter, I've been trying to tell you; I haven't got a team this week. Oliver's up in Scotland killing things, Charlotte's coming back from Barbados Tuesday morning but is taking the rest of the week off, and Elspeth is on a safari in Serengeti. I can't even reach her until she gets back to Nairobi at the end of the week. That leaves me and Stuart. I've got to organise the tail end of the Bottley rights issue and get an instruction letter out for the reporting accountants for the Squire's flotation. We've also promised Stephen Harcourt an analysis of private property companies that he might acquire. Stuart is due to start an exercise for Bill McAdam on European government stakes in industries which might be suitable for privatisation. That's a huge job that is going to take him at least the next two months."

"I'm sorry, Tim. We'll have to clear the decks. Get Charlotte and Oliver back asap. I'll talk to Bill about deferring Stuart's project or putting someone else onto it. Elspeth will have to do the work on Squire Homes and Harcourt Properties as soon as you can get her back. Apart from that we'll just have to muddle through."

"But Peter, it's simply not possible to..."

"Tim, this is going to be one of the biggest bids of 1988. Are you saying that you want me to find another manager and another team?"

"Over my dead body!"

"I thought so. Let's have another drink and then get working."

Thursday, 31 December, 1987

The New Year's Honours List had come out 24 hours early because *The Sun* had broken the embargo. The PM was said to be furious and that pompous curmudgeon that she used for a mouthpiece, Bernard Ingham, seemed to have forgotten that leaking was nine-tenths of all he did and was huffing and puffing about it being "absolutely disgraceful". More disgraceful, to Peter's mind, was that the former Cabinet secretary, Robert Armstrong, had been rewarded with a peerage for being economical with the truth during the *Spycatcher* case. What was that sixteenth century definition of a diplomat? - someone sent to lie abroad for his country. Meanwhile the bastards had the brazen effrontery to award Henry Cotton posthumously the knighthood which he had deserved for at least forty years.

A large part of the front page of *The Times* business section was as usual devoted to the gongs handed out by Mrs Thatcher to her cronies in industry and the City. Ks had gone to Ralph Robins, the MD of Rolls-Royce, Simon Hornby, the Chairman of WH Smith, Christopher Benson of MEPC and Michael Caine at Booker - not the cockney actor; he could wait for ever, thought Peter. Even that ridiculous greenie female with the unruly hair-do and the awful smelly shops had picked up a CBE. The pharmaceutical industry had, however, hit the jackpot and, under a slightly misleading sub-headline "The New Drugs Barons" were pictures of Paul Girolami of Glaxo, now Sir Paul, and Sir Arthur Evans, a new life peer. Evans, as usual gruff and unsmiling, was pictured beside the logo of his company, the three interlocking gold circles containing the letters BMP, and had immediately been popularly dubbed the Lord of the Rings.

Evans and Geronimo had not been far from Peter's thoughts all week. On the Monday afternoon he and Timothy had gone over to the West End for a meeting with Rod King at Pitcairn's head office, which occupied the elegant corner building at the north-east corner of St James's Square. The office staff had been wound down to skeletal proportions for the Christmas period and Rod came into the board room wearing a blue blazer and pink open-necked shirt. He immediately took off his jacket and hung it over the back of a chair.

"Now, explain to me. What exactly is this jobber's trick?" he began.

Rod King was a bit under six foot with an athletic build and a confident but unthreatening presence. He was in his mid forties, his short dark wavy hair now greying but his face always tanned. A strong jaw but a mischievous, almost boyish smile gave a clue both to his determination and his lively sense of fun. He had come from a senior finance function at Ford, an acknowledged breeding ground of top-class accounting men. Hennessy had put Egon Zehnder onto the job of finding him a successor to Cecil Greenacre behind the backs of his fellow directors and had dispassionately informed the unfortunate Cecil one Friday in June that he would not be needed the following week. King had started on the next Monday. The accounts for the financial year which had ended that March had already almost been finalised; but Rod set to with a will to get to grips with an industry of which he had no previous experience. What he found made him distinctly uneasy. The lacklustre results for 1985 and 1986, which had provoked the institutional shareholders to demand a change of chairman, had in reality only been achieved by writing back into profits the sort of prudent provisioning that Rod knew that every business should carry. Hennessy had already spent lavishly on firing staff and closing facilities, allowing himself the sort of clean sweep that every new broom is permitted; but Rod King had the unenviable task at the end of his first fortnight of telling his chairman that the dire set of results which they were proposing to announce were not dire enough.

"To be honest, Rod," Peter began, "I've never actually seen the jobber's trick done before; but I've discussed it with one or two people in the past as a possible tactic. As you know, holdings over 5% have to be disclosed under the Companies Act - but market makers are exempt, like jobbers used to be. So, if I say to a jobber, that is a market-maker now - 'I'm a buyer of 10% of Bloggs at 200p' - he might reply 'I can't do that size right now but could you give me until the end of the month.' He then goes off to try to build up the stake - and he registers it, as many market makers do, not in the name of the potential buyer but in the Stock Exchange's own nominee company, Sepon. The ultimate buyer, the bidder, has no declarable interest in the shares until his offer to buy is accepted and there is a contract; so, even if you put a Section 212 notice on Sepon, all you will get back is a list of market makers."

"But isn't that a sodding great risk for a broker? 15% of us is the thick end of a quarter of a billion quid. Nobody's going to take a flyer like that, are they?"

"If you think about it, Rod, it's not that much of a flyer. The bidder and the broker are in cahoots. The bidder is effectively saying 'get me as many shares as you can without moving the market too much, hide them away in Sepon, and I'll take them off your hands just before we announce the bid'.

"What about the Substantial Acquisition Rules? I thought they were intended to stop people building up stakes secretly. I suppose they don't apply to market makers either."

"Well actually they do and they are intended to stop holdings being built up so rapidly that no one discovers until too late; but they only apply to holdings of between 15 and 30%. This stake must still be below the threshold."

"It can't be that much below. There's 14.5% in Sepon in these figures I got just before Christmas."

"Sure, Rod, but they'll include holdings of other market makers. Given the SARs, you would expect the buyer, whoever he is, to restrict the size of the order to 14.9%. If it were all registered under Sepon, you would expect the total to be closer to 20%."

"Who the fuck is it?"

"Well, that's one of the things we've been doing some work on. Charlotte Mulder is co-ordinating that back in the office," he lied, anticipating her return from the Caribbean via Miami overnight, still unaware that there would be a note from Tim awaiting her arrival. "Unfortunately the list is never ending. There are four possibles amongst UK companies alone, at least half a dozen in Europe and the same again in the States. You'll find a list of our candidates in Section F of these papers. Charlotte and her team are presently preparing a profile on each one and that will be ready within a couple of days. For what it's worth at this stage and without yet being entirely *au fait* with the product fit, I would say the predator is most likely to be a UK company. You have to be a pretty sophisticated foreigner to risk a hostile take-over bid in a strange country. It might be SmithKline from the States or just conceivably Ciba Geigy or Roche from Switzerland; but I think we should concentrate on the four UK groups. Of those Wellcome is fantastically highly rated on the back of their Aids drugs but looks unlikely because a paper or part paper offer would blow a hole in the Trust's controlling shareholding; and Glaxo is an outside chance because Geronimo has always foresworn takeovers on the grounds that organic growth is superior and bids would destroy value for his own shareholders. That leaves BMP and Beecham. Beecham, over the long run, have a much more aggressive takeover record. Remember they even had a go at Glaxo in the early seventies. Their current market cap is £3.2 billion against your £1.8 and they're on a much higher PE rating. The same applies to BMP, with a market cap of £5 billion and a PE of almost 17. I'd say it's even money that the bidder is one of those two."

"Is there anything else we can do to narrow it down?"

"Perhaps. I've told the registrars to do an analysis of which brokers have been doing the recent buying. They promised to have an answer this afternoon and I've asked my secretary to call through here when they come back."

"Okay; so much for that. Now what have you got for me here?"

"Rather a lot of work, I'm afraid - a touch of the blood, sweat, toil and tears. As you know, we have had a defence bible on the stocks for the last twelve months and have been updating it as we go along," he exaggerated shamelessly. "It's now very urgent that we fill in any gaps and check it through. I feel that we should aim to have all that completed for circulation to the directors over the week-end in advance of the meeting at our offices next Monday morning. Most of it is down to us; but there are the two large areas which we need covered by you and Dr Aladyce and one each for your lawyers and your brokers."

"George will give you a presentation on the research pipeline next Monday and is having some notes prepared in layman's terms for incorporation in the bible. You'll like this one," Rod grinned at the two bankers, "he's threatening to entitle it 'Pitcairn's contribution to the problems of fer...fer...fat, fer...fer...fever, fer...fer...fucking and fer... fer...farting'," he said, imitating George's stutter. "But I hope that I've persuaded him that he doesn't need to be quite so basic."

"Yes," said Peter, chuckling back at him, "he told me over the phone this morning that the one good thing about having a bidder in the wings is that the chairman can't afford to fire any more directors. Being the irreverent sod that he is, I think that he's inclined to take advantage."

"Well, that's his problem, Peter. Mine's the numbers. The group accounts department upstairs is updating a consolidated revised budget for the year to March and our forward forecasts for the two following years. Those will be with you on Friday evening - but they will be pretty rudimentary at this stage. We won't have December's figures from the operating companies until the end of the first week in January - and then we have to consolidate them."

"Okay. Can we just flick through the bible and agree who is doing what? The defence team is all in place bar one element, which is a separate legal team for us."

"What's wrong with Plummers?"

"Nothing at all, Rod; but we have an absolute rule that Dundas takes separate legal advice when it's involved in a hostile bid. There can be conflicts of interest; and it's as well to be prepared."

"Well, that's entirely up to you. No concern of ours."

"It is in one sense. You'll be paying for them. It'll be part of our out-of-pockets; so I wanted you to know."

"Who do you want to use?"

"I think we're going to be a bit restricted for choice. Simmons & Simmons, Linklaters, Slaughter & May, Theodore Goddard and Clifford Chance are all certainly conflicted out by their relationships with potential bidders. We thought we might ask Martin Lampard, the senior partner at Ashursts. Is that okay with you?"

"I don't know the man. What's his reputation?"

"The roughest of rough diamonds. A dirty street fighter."

"Sounds just what we need. Julian Corrigan can be a bit too much of a gentleman, if you ask me; but what with the poison dwarf being a lawyer himself, I think you'd better check with him. Have you managed to get a time to see him this week?"

"Yes, I'm going down to Godalming on Wednesday."

"Good; and there's another thing here you're going to have to talk to him about. He fired Charles Barker the week before Christmas. We don't currently have a PR outfit."

"Oh shit! That's not the best of timing, is it? Had he got a replacement in mind, do you know?"

"I think, Peter, it was one of his decisive executive actions," said Rod, with a conspiratorial grin, "but it might just have been a fit of pique. To be honest, I have a theory that it's because the urinals in their visitors' loo are set a bit high up the wall and the little man can't get his little man over the top. I think he overheard someone there having a laugh at his expense because he has to wee in the crapper."

"Aren't short arses meant to have enormous dicks?" chimed in Timothy, who had until now confined his role to copious note-taking. "He should be able to hook it over the top if he's built to form."

"I am fortunately not privy to the dimensions of the chairmanical chopper, Timothy; but, be that as it may, I suggest you check out the loos of any PR outfit you recommend," Rod chuckled. "Seriously, though, do you have any ideas?"

"Well, Rod, for this situation what you need is someone who is really close to the City editors; someone who is owed a few, who can get your stories in and also keep things you don't want trumpeted out. To my mind the very best is old Freddie Wordsworth, but he's been winding down for some time and I'm not sure that he'd take on anything new. We would have to have him personally. His partner's a decent enough chap but he's an also-ran."

"Who is he?"

"Freddie? Actually, he's an extraordinary old cove, a retired submarine commander - great great grandson of the poet or some-such and rich as Croesus on the royalties from all those daffodils."

"Well that should appeal to the intellectual aspirations of our little manikin piss. What are his bogs like?"

"He tends to refer to them nautically as 'the heads', Rodney, but, in reality, the offices of Wordsworth Wallis are rather swish. They certainly contain nothing as common as a bog. Freddie is none too tall himself so we should be all right on that score."

"Sounds fine with me if he's got the organisation to do it."

"Behind a rather jolly roger sort of exterior, he's got a powerful temper. As a result he surrounds himself with a squad that hums with naval precision, and he's very good at his job. He can drink the most bibulous of journalists to death and still remember afterwards what was said.

"Okay, I'll talk to the chairman on those two. Could you get your secretary to run through the home team and check that addresses and telephone numbers are up to date?

"Section B is a draft timetable; it's really for the benefit of those not familiar with the take-over code, which I guess includes the chairman. It's all in terms of D-day plus so many days at this stage; but of course we would fill in actual dates when they became known.

"Section C contains draft press announcements in the event that a bid is made or a sharp movement in the share price forces us to make a statement. The Stock Exchange will normally insist on something if the price moves ten per cent.

"Section D is for your forecasts. At the moment, we simply have Cecil's old budgets, which date from last March. Section E is a strengths and weaknesses analysis - the sort of points to go in the defence documents and the arguments that will be used against you."

"I see that the list of weaknesses is three times as long as the strengths," observed Rod dryly.

"I think we all know what we're up against, Rod."

"Quite so, Peter; but remember Tom Thumb likes positive thinking - every problem is an opportunity and all that business school crap. I think that you'd better do some work on that before he sees this document."

"Point taken. Section F is the list of possible predators, which we've already looked at. Of course they're also the potential white knights, if it ever came to that."

"Yes, but not diplomatic to use that term with the midget at this stage."

"Sure. Section G is blank at the moment but is meant to be the same strengths and weaknesses analysis for the predators. Charlotte will have worked that up on at least the major suspects by the end of the week.

"Section H is for Dr Aladyce's work on the research pipeline and Section I is a matrix for analysing the product fit between Pitcairn and the various possible predators. Stuart Robinson, who read biology at Cambridge, is doing some work on that back at base."

"Stuart Robinson....Stuart Robinson? Do I know him? Is he that gangling giant who looks as though he's just been dragged through a hedge backwards?"

"That's the one , Rod. Not, I would have to agree, a contender for the Best Dressed Man of 1988; but, even at seven foot odd, he's more or less 95% brain."

"Okay, but keep him away from Christopher. I have enough trouble with his complexes without him thinking that one of his advisers is going to tread on him. Anything else?"

"Yes, just two things. Section J is for Plummer, Goodspeed and Bleriot. David Stephenson, their senior trade practices partner, is preparing an analysis of the OFT and MMC issues to go in here. And finally Section K is for an analysis of the shareholders' register, which Justin Travers-Coe at Gourlay Gilfillan is putting together.

"Well, that about wraps it up from our side," said Peter, scooping the papers into his briefcase. "Have you got anything else, Rod?"

"Yes, just one thing. What's all this costing me?"

"At this stage, not very much. We'd simply take account of the time involved when we come to review the year's workload in March. You'll be pleased to hear that Christmas holidays don't get charged at double time. But, if there's a bid to be defended, that's another matter. You ought to decide with Christopher and George whether you want us to be incentivised. We could charge you a flat fee win or lose or we could have it graduated depending on the outcome."

"Like how?"

"Well, say x as a flat fee plus y as a percentage of the uplift over your present market cap if you were eventually taken over at a higher price...."

".......or z if we retain our independence?"

Within Peter's briefcase, a mobile telephone began to chirrup.

"Indeed. Excuse me a moment, this could be the registrars. Hello. Yes, Maureen. Yes. Yes. Okay, thanks. I'll be back in the office in twenty minutes.

"Well, Rod, that could have been an expensive decision of Christopher to sack Wagstaffs. They've been behind almost eighty per cent of the buying in the last three stock exchange accounts."

*****

..the New Year's Eve meeting (10am, Mirror Building, 33 Holborn, London EC1) of Maxwell Communications Corporation, formerly BPCC, is likely to be extraordinary in more than name.

MCC shareholders will be asked to approve the purchase of the electronic publishing and book publishing activities of Pergamon Holdings, Mr Robert Maxwell's Liechtenstein-controlled private company which holds a majority of MCC shares.

Because of this relationship, Pergamon and directors of MCC, including Mr Maxwell, who are also directors of Pergamon will not vote at the meeting. This means that the decision will rest with independent shareholders owning a total of 48.4 per cent.

The deal involves the initial payment of $56m (£30m) to Pergamon for companies with total pre tax profits of £526,000 in the eight months to August 31, and performance-linked clauses which could raise the total to $100m.

MCC emphasised that it was negotiated at arm's length and that its independent directors took advice from

Bankers Trust, the US bank. The process was one reason, said MCC, why the negotiations took so long to complete.

So why is the meeting being held on New Year's Eve? Because Mr Maxwell had always said the deal would be completed by the end of 1987. And what the captain wants. (Clay Harris, Financial Times, 29 December, 1987).

*****

It was a brightish, mild morning that Wednesday as Peter drove down to Godalming. The A3 out of London was more or less deserted. Christopher Hennessy had suggested he arrive around eleven so that they could talk for a couple of hours before lunching *en famille*. Peter hardly thought that Hennessy would need that long. His habit was a short briefing, a shorter discussion and an instant decision which, once made, appeared to become an immutable article of faith which one subsequently questioned at one's peril.

Mrs Hennessy, an anglicised Swiss, Peter had met a couple of times before. He had persuaded Sir James that the retention of this client was worth lavishing on its new chairman a couple of precious places in the Brothers' marquee for the mens' finals day of Wimbledon. As if by osmosis, this had naturally also resulted in Pitcairn Pharmaceuticals' principal corporate finance adviser and his girlfriend occupying two more places. Wimbledon is not a form of corporate entertainment which overburdens the host with the need to make conversation with his guests. Pat Cash had predictably wiped the floor with the perennial plodder, Ivan Lendl, and it had all passed off perfectly agreeably. Claudia Hennessy, despite an accent so plummy that it could only have been inflicted on her by an English tutor, did not possess her husband's clipped self-assurance and was in every way a less competitive personality. Dark and petite, though of course at least as tall as Christopher, Peter found her decorative for her years though somewhat distant. He and Sophie had subsequently taken them to see the new Haitink production of Figaro at the Royal Opera House in early October. By that time it was clear that, after half a lifetime amongst the Boston elite, she considered herself to have settled seamlessly - or, as she put it trans-atlantically, "acclimated herself" - into the social set of upper-crust semi-rural Surrey.

Peter had not been to the house before and was following the directions that Christopher had given him over the telephone on Monday morning. Climbing the hill out of Guildford, he crossed the Hog's Back and started off down the other side before turning left onto the B3000 to follow the signs for Godalming. Soon he was winding his way through the prosperous old village of Compton. After the green, he passed the turn to the left for The Withies Inn, where he and Sophie had spent one glorious evening last summer, after the christening of a friend's baby in the chapel at nearby Charterhouse, where her husband taught modern languages. They had sat in one of the little bowers in the garden drinking Pimms and afterwards feasting shamelessly on giant pink lobsters with garlic mayonnaise. Peter could still taste them now and smiled to himself at the recollection.

A mile or so further on he passed the right turn to Farncombe and Binscombe and slowed down, looking for the turning to the left into Greatcombe Lane. There was a blue sign at the entrance - 'Single track road with passing places'. It was relatively straight and climbed a little, woodland for the most part on the left, more open country behind a rather bedraggled hedgerow on the right, which was pushed out every couple of hundred yards to provide room for two vehicles to pass. Until the previous October the road had clearly been defined by two lines of ancient trees - oaks, he thought without certainty. Behind what was left of the oaks on the left was a small plantation of younger trees, mostly saplings, which had survived more or less unscathed. On the right were open fields. But the hurricane had taken a devastating toll of the oaks themselves. About half of them were gone forever. In many cases a huge raw freshly cut stump was all that remained, together with the churned up soil and grass of the fields spattered with wood chippings. In others the earth had been ripped up as the roots tore out of the soil, the vast trees either already dismembered or lying like vast unkempt Mussulmen prostrate towards Mecca awaiting their turn with the chainsaw which was their fate. In places the road itself was buckled as it had absorbed the weight of crashing tons of vegetation. Among the survivors limbs had been torn off to reveal the pale yellow wood beneath or hung attached by ligaments which the surgeons had not yet tackled. About 800 yards down the road on the left was the south-east corner of the old boundary wall which was the next feature on Peter's directions. It was about ten feet high, composed of what looked like original sixteenth or seventeenth century bricks of the deepest russet and surmounted by something like a little thatched roof which had clearly been renewed in recent times. The walls themselves, lying on one side to the north of the sapling plantation and on the other to the west of the twin lines of oaks appeared miraculously to have taken no direct hit from the trees that had crashed hither and thither and even those of the oaks which had come down on the outer side of the wall alongside the road had failed to breach the ancient defences. Fifty yards further on a single massive survivor, badly mauled and perhaps no longer as upright as once he was, stood on the south side of the brick entrance pillars, his twin to the north no more than a scattering of wood shavings and a sad, neat stump four feet high and almost a yard across. The big black iron gates, now soldered to the twentieth century hydraulic steel tubes of an automatic opening and closing mechanism, were wide open onto a drive which swept around either side of a small plantation of rhododendrons which formed a sort of roundabout in a sea of creamy freshly-raked gravel. The walls, as far as Peter could see, enclosed the entire property. Greatcombe House itself, in brick and timber, was, as far as Peter's inexpert eye could ascertain, original Tudor, a large two-storey brick and timber mansion of not quite symmetrical construction with a slightly uneven clay-tiled roof and three distinctly Elizabethan massive square chimney-pieces in diagonally-patterned brickwork protruding to left and right and again somewhat to the left of centre. It must have been extensively renovated over the years but it looked magnificent and, thought Peter, must have cost a fortune.

To the right of the drive, still within the boundary walls, was an orchard which stretched from the front of the property and disappeared around the north wing of the house into what was presumably the back garden. To the left at first were lawns and borders but closer to the house a clutch of outbuildings backed onto the southern boundary wall. Some at least of these were garages. Two wide open doors revealed, on the left, Christopher's pale silver-blue Jaguar XJS. Peter chuckled again at the ridiculous sight, after Figaro in October, of Christopher's driver holding open the passenger door while the little man clambered onto the jump-seat in the back and swung into place the front passenger seat which was to be occupied by his wife. But perhaps such a spectacle was a thing of the past for protruding from the right of the same garage was the nose of what Peter took to be a Bentley Mulsanne Turbo in deepest burgundy, sporting the registration plate CH 111. 'I hope to God the silly bastard hasn't charged that little Christmas present up to Pitcairn just as we're about to get a bid,' thought Peter, swinging the Morgan round to a halt in front of the house but restraining himself from the temptation of a gravel-spraying handbrake turn.

It was Christopher Hennessy III himself who answered the doorbell. He was casually but almost primly attired in a pair of dark blue corduroys and a pale yellow vee-neck cashmere sweater over an open-necked blue shirt with button-down collar. The casual air was undone by the trousers which were crisply creased but, more importantly, could have done with another inch of leg. Even after several months of quite regular contact, Peter was still always initially taken aback by his dimensions. It was not just that he was short but that he was proportionately small in every way. Somehow one expected a captain of industry, even if he was under five foot three, at least to have the size of head that was normal to accommodate the human cerebrum or hands which looked as though they had spent the better part of half a century doing the sort of things that men's hands do. But in Christopher Hennessy's case, the ageing process seemed to have taken an abnormal route. It wasn't that he did not show his years, although he was the size and build of an early pubescent schoolboy. He had the crows' feet and brow furrows and shaving shadow of all middle-aged men; but he also looked intensely scrubbed, as though, even at the age of 48, nanny had just got him out of the bath, dusted him off with talcum powder and brought him down to see his parents before bed.

The generally schoolboyish air was heightened by the sort of haircut which any self-respecting public school barber could do at the rate of twenty an hour. The parting was high on the right side of the crown; but looked as though it had no particular place there. The straight light brown hair was cut too long to be neat but too short to fall in any natural style so that, at the front, it ended in a rather arbitrary line, brushed off to the left, that seemed to be designed to avoid any suggestion of a fringe. Elsewhere it was simply too long to be a 'short-back-and-sides' but too short to be anything else.

His eyes were blue, pale and almost watery but of a shape that was slightly oriental. To increase the overall air of impishness, they inclined distinctly upwards towards the outer corners. His one attempt at style lay in the spectacles, which although possessed of massive glass lenses, were invariably worn so that Christopher could look at the world over the top of them, as if they were half-moon glasses. Given the tininess of his face and the immensity of the lenses, this could only be achieved by an extraordinarily bad fit behind the ears, which enabled the bridge of the spectacles to sit on the very end of Christopher's perfectly-shaped button nose. Inevitably they regularly fell off this insecure perch but were, at such times, restrained by a string through which they were attached around his neck. They tumbled off his nose onto his chest as he opened the door.

"Hello, Peter. Come along in. We'll go through to the study to start with."

No 'compliments of the season'; no 'thankyou for coming down all this way to see me'; no 'did you have a good Christmas'. Christopher Hennessy was not into small talk.

He led the way through a hall with a grand old oak staircase climbing to a galleried floor above and into a huge beamed sitting room which occupied the whole of the front ground floor of the north side of the house. There was some serious looking art on the walls of a sort Peter thought he'd not necessarily want to live with. A fat bushy Christmas tree covered in silver balls brushed the beamed ceiling in the near corner, by the window. At the far end of the room a housekeeper of some sort was in the process of lighting a fire in the inglenook and a teenage girl with dark tousled hair was curled up on one of the window seats reading a copy of Cosmopolitan or some such. She was wired into a portable CD player which was dispensing heavy metal at a volume sufficient to be heard with little effort without the aid of the earphones attached either side of her head.

The study was at the back of the house, directly off the sitting room and connected to it by a double set of heavy wooden doors, outer and inner. Inside it was mercifully quiet. It was a large room, its ceiling striped like the sitting room with heavy oak beams. Christopher's desk, a large antique partner's table faced the leaded windows on the right hand side of the room and looked out onto the rose garden, now bare but freshly and immaculately pruned by the brothers Alfonso, the resident gardeners who apparently lived in one of the outhouses. A fax machine and a personal computer were perched, rather incongruously, on an early Victorian table to one side of the desk. The door through which they had entered was in the middle of what was otherwise a wall of bookshelves. At the farthest end of the room from the desk, under what might possibly have been an original though lesser Picasso, was a group of two settees and two armchairs covered in soft brown hide. Christopher motioned Peter to one of the sofas.

"As you know, I don't take tea or coffee myself; but would you like something in that vein, or a soft drink?"

"Coffee for me please, Christopher. I get more than enough tea at the office."

"Quite so." Hennessy walked over to his desk. He picked up the telephone and pressed one of the buttons. "Hilda, a pot of coffee and one cup in the study, and orange juice for myself."

He returned to where Peter was sitting, pulling documents from a fat briefcase, and settled himself in an armchair; or more exactly on its front edge, for to have sat within it would have left his legs sticking straight out like a teddy bear on top of a nursery toy cupboard.

"King has brought me up to date on all of your conversations over the previous few days; so we needn't go over any of that. I simply want a briefing on anything that's new, I want an explanation of how acquisition procedures work in England, I want to discuss fees and then I will take any decisions that you need from me right now."

"Rod has no doubt told you about the documents we are distributing over the course of this week-end in preparation for the meeting at our offices on Monday." Peter reached over to hand him a thick red file but Hennessy made no move to take it.

"Is this the final version or just a draft?"

"We'll be continuing to work on it over the next few days with a view to distributing it on Saturday. By then it will contain everything except George Aladyce's paper on the research pipeline, which he is going to give us with the presentation he makes on Monday morning.

This is how far we have got to date. All the gaps will be filled in by Saturday morning; but it will need constant updating over the weeks ahead if matters progress as we fear. For example, when we have the identity of the bidder."

"I'll wait for the final version. I know the product pipeline anyway. Have you made any further progress in identifying the people who have been buying our shares?"

"We put a Section 212 notice on Wagstaffs after hours on Monday evening. That's the formal request under the Companies Act to disclose..."

"Yes, yes, yes, I know what it is," Hennessy said tetchily. "Come in, come in," he continued in the same vein as he heard the outer door open.

The housekeeper put the tray down on the low table in front of Peter and handed a tall glass of freshly squeezed orange juice to Hennessy before scurrying away.

"You'll need to pour that yourself, " he said. "I don't know anything about coffee."

Christopher Hennessy was a Bostonian mormon and as such drank no tea, coffee, coca-cola, alcohol or other beverages which could be considered stimulants. He appeared to have given up proselytising on any personal level though you could even now imagine how he must have turned up on doorsteps, like a miniature version of the clean-cut boy from Utah, on his first visit to Europe in the early sixties. He had subsequently started his own law firm and had made a considerable success not only of that but also as a visiting lecturer on commercial law at the Harvard Business School. Nevertheless it had been a surprise when he had accepted an offer from Henry Kravis of KKR to become Chairman and CEO of Birkendorf Publishing after KKR had won a bitter fight for control with Robert Maxwell. The jewel in Birkendorf's crown was a mirror image of Maxwell's scientific publishing house, Pergamon Press, and Hennessy had been quick to see that the Birkendorf family had failed to follow Maxwell's lead in exploiting the opportunity to charge whatever they liked for the research publications which were a must for every serious university library in the world. Hennessy jacked up the prices to an almost scandalous degree, made Henry Kravis yet another fortune and was rumoured to have turned the modest pile of his own that he had made from the law into serious bucks. The rumour was in fact erroneous - Henry Kravis was too smart for that - and Hennessy, obsessively aware that it was his wife who controlled the family fortune, smarted from the unfulfilled ambition to make it in his own right. Nevertheless, now the rare guru who had shown that he could not only tell people how to do it, but also do it himself, he looked to the outside world like quite a catch when he was persuaded to take the chair of Pitcairn Pharmaceuticals by Lord Enderby, a non-executive director of Pitcairn, who had, with institutional support, organised a palace revolution against the previous incumbent.

Enderby's sole reward at Hennessy's hands was that he was spared the general mayhem that the new chairman had inflicted on the rest of the board. The three other non-executive directors had immediately been asked to tender their resignations and, eight months later, had still not yet been replaced. Christopher had used the lack of any restraining influence during this period to fashion the direction of the company to his will with the small-minded but enthusiastic brutality of a child pulling the limbs off a daddy-long-legs. As soon as Rod King had been brought on board in place of the previous finance director, Hennessy had quite deliberately picked a fight with the then chief executive, Charles Eve, on the subject of research expenditure. With annual costs in this area running at £90 million per annum, Hennessy had unveiled to him a plan to bolster flagging profits by the short term expedient of cutting back on the company's future life-blood. Eve, though a marketing man rather than scientist by background, had protested that research was to the pharmaceutical industry what advertising was to Procter & Gamble or Coca-Cola. He and George Aladyce, then director of research, had worked long and hard to ensure that the company got value for money out of every penny that it spent in its laboratories and Eve was determined that it should be the last item of expenditure to be subjected to any arbitrary reduction. He stuck rigidly to his budgets, as Hennessy had guessed he would, and paid the price. The terms of his severance were not ungenerous but Hennessy had insisted that the press announcement of Eve's departure refer to irreconcilable differences of approach with the new chairman over management priorities. The following day Hennessy appointed George Aladyce chief executive, asking him at the same time to launch a study into appropriate areas for an expansion in the research budget to an annual figure of £120 million by 1990.

The marketing and production directors had been the next to feel the heat. Hennessy asked them both to step down from the main board and continue with their existing jobs but as senior managers, thus cleverly disguising the attack, for the consumption of the outside world, as a move to streamline decision making and reduce central management costs. The production man, trapped by the two years he needed to round off his pension entitlement and crudely denied early retirement by his chairman, could do nothing but comply. Hennessy gambled correctly that he had no internal power base that he could use to retaliate. The younger marketing man had inevitably responded with his resignation. Now George Aladyce and Rod King were the only two executive directors apart from Hennessy himself; and both owed their appointments to him. At the next level down, the new head of marketing was in the same position, as would be the heads of production and research in due course. For the time being, Aladyce would double up as chief executive and head of research, which should keep him out of mischief.

"I haven't seen anything yet to change my initial hunch that it's Beecham or BMP," Peter continued, pouring coffee from the silver pot that had been set in front of him. "I know that Wagstaffs haven't acted for either in the past; but that in itself would be a helpful disguise for whoever it is they are backing. It also may imply that Wagstaffs took the idea to the bidder - a sort of marketing idea with the added spice of potential revenge for being replaced at Pitcairn."

"Well, if that is the case, it would confirm my view that Wagstaffs were too full of their own interests rather than their client's. Not my sort of people," he added, "to hide such behaviour behind an establishment veneer."

Exactly your sort of people, thought Peter, and I don't doubt that you loved the snobbishness of the whole set-up. But what you didn't like was that they knew the company and more particularly its shareholders better than you. And that could now be a mighty weapon in any bidder's arsenal. Not what our little friend here had in mind when he sacked them, which was probably that David Carradine and Lord Enderby were in each other's pockets - altogether too powerful a combination for a new chairman trying to consolidate his hold.

"Not very appealing behaviour, if it's true," agreed Peter, "but it wouldn't be the first time that it's happened, nor the last."

"Can't we claim that they should be barred from helping a bidder; that they've gotten too much inside information about us? What about this Take-Over Panel you have? Isn't there a rule against this? There sure oughta be."

The American linguistic quirks were so infrequently evident in Christopher's speech that they always came as a surprise to Peter. It was often as if the sort of Boston set from which Hennessy had emerged was no further distant than Chelsea. But, more worrisome than language, was the looming reality of taking a US ex-lawyer, steeped in the certainties of the SEC's enforcement of the law, into the hazily self-regulated jungle of a City bid battle.

"There's a rule regarding the need for advisers to be genuinely independent and an appendix to the Code regarding the circumstances in which financial advisers should be disbarred on grounds of possession of material confidential information. None of that, of course, would stop Wagstaffs accumulating shares unless they could be said to be acting on inside information. That seems unlikely because, as I understand it, they went even before this year's budget was prepared. I would certainly try to get Wagstaffs ruled off-side as advisers; but I would have no confidence that the argument would run with the Panel. The other side could point to plenty of precedents for former advisers being permitted to switch sides. There are likely to be bigger battles to fight in front of the Panel than that one."

"Where I come from, Peter, we fight every battle at law and we fight it all the way. This Panel must have some appeal process - doesn't it?"

"Indeed. Decisions in the first instance are made by what is called the Panel Executive, who are full-time regulators and who include a number of lawyers and accountants, who are seconded there for a period of a couple of years. The secondees always include the Director General, who comes in succession from the corporate finance department of one of the merchant banks. At the moment it's Antony Beevor from Hambros. He was appointed a couple of months ago and only took up the job just before Christmas.

"If you don't like a decision that you get from the executive, you can appeal to the Panel itself. That's chaired by a leading corporate law barrister called Robert Alexander at the moment and includes a number of worthies representing the groups who benefit from the market's processes - investing institutions, industry, etcetera. It rarely overturns an executive decision - but it does sometimes.

"Then, on top of that there's an Appeal Committee, which is chaired by a judge who sits with two other members of the Panel not involved in the original hearing; but the right to appeal is very limited - it's effectively only in cases where the Panel has found that the Code has been breached and intends to take disciplinary action or where it is alleged that the Panel has acted outside its powers. There's no appeal against a finding of fact or of interpretation of the Code itself. For all practical purposes, the Panel itself is usually the end of the line."

"But we haven't got to law yet! Where's the appeal to the Courts?" Hennessy protested in disbelief. "Didn't I read in the news the other day that Guinness are taking the Panel to court?"

"Yes, that's right. They're going for what's called a judicial review - a review by the Court of a decision by officialdom. They're not generally thought to have much chance of success. Pru-Bache appealed to the Courts over a Panel ruling at the back end of 1986 and got thrown out by the Master of the Rolls - he's the sen..."

"Yes, yes. Sir John Donaldson's an old friend of mine and I know his role."

"As far as I know, that was the first time it had ever happened to the Panel. Guinness is the second. But, in a sense, it's irrelevant to the outcome. Guinness got Distillers. They used some tactics which are outlawed by Panel rules to get there - but nobody has tried to get the outcome changed. It's just impractical to go back. Impossible to reconstruct the position before the market was deceived. What's happening now is an appeal by Guinness against a Panel ruling that it must pay compensation to those who accepted the bid, representing the difference between the winning bid and the higher figure that some of its supporters paid for Distillers shares. It's going to cost Guinness the thick end of £100 million; so you can see why it's worth one last throw of the dice."

"Okay, okay, I'd better have a look at these rules; but let me warn you, I'm going to want everything fought all the way."

"I'll send a copy of the rules down with your bible on Saturday morning. I'd leave you my copy; but it's covered in notes and jottings, and I'd be lost without it."

"Yes, do that. And could you please refer to Saturday's documents as the briefing pack. Please remember that there's only one bible as far as I'm concerned. And now, what about anti-trust legislation? I know you Brits are a bit out of step with the States on that too."

Peter kicked himself mentally for the 'bible' slip. In a world devoid of religion, it was hard to remember that something close to the edge of Christian fanaticism lurked behind this lilliputian lawyer's business-like exterior. He was further irritated by the implication that the US way of doing things was always superior and suppressed the immediate instinct to express contrition, trying hopelessly to imagine that it was too small a matter to register on Hennessy's religious radar.

"For the purposes of take-over bids, anti-trust regulation is not strictly judicial either; but it is administered by the government - unlike the Panel, which is self-regulated by the City with a sort of supervisory interest taken by the Bank of England. There are two layers to the anti-trust examination of take-overs, the Office of Fair Trading and the Monopolies and Mergers Commission. They're known as the OFT and the MMC. The OFT is headed by a man called Gordon Borrie, looked upon as rather to the left of centre. The OFT conducts an initial review of all proposed take-overs above a certain size threshold and forms a committee of interested government departments. So, in your case the Department of Trade and Industry and the Department of Health and Social Security would certainly also be involved. On the basis of the review, the Director General of Fair Trading makes a recommendation to the Minister, the Secretary of State for Trade and Industry, that's Lord Young at present, whether or not a full-scale examination by the MMC is desirable. The Minister normally accepts the recommendation and, if a bid is referred, it lapses for the period of the MMC review, which is normally set for around four to six months. When the MMC recommendation is sent to the Minister, he has to accept it if it gives the merger the all-clear but he can overrule an adverse recommendation. If it's an all-clear the original bidder has twenty-one days to resume the process under Panel rules."

"And the reasons for preventing a deal are simply oriented to market share and market power?"

"Well, successive ministers - and Tories in particular - always maintain that that's the case; but the legislation is framed in terms of whether a merger can be expected to operate 'against the public interest'," Peter said, raising a finger on each hand to indicate the quotation signs. "That gives politicians every opportunity to meddle. Often they can't resist the temptation to politick. I'm sure the States is no different in that."

"That's one of the reasons why politicians have no part in our anti-trust regulation."

"Unfortunately that's not the case in the UK; and, to make matters worse, the politicians have two chances for a bite at the cherry - the decision whether or not to refer to the MMC, which is often alone enough to kill a bid, and the decision whether or not to implement the MMC decision. For example Elders, the Australian brewer, tried to take over Allied Lyons back in 1986. There were no conceivable anti-trust implications but the establishment hated the idea of these colonial upstarts getting their hands on one of the commanding heights of UK industry. The Bank of England expressed concern, supposedly because the bid was going to be leveraged, and it was referred to the MMC on so-called public interest grounds. Allied Lyons and Warburgs, who were advising them, had gone into a complete panic, running around like headless chickens, and it's a common view that the reference was really just to give them the breathing space to get a proper defence organised. By the time the MMC had given Elders the all-clear, Allied had swallowed every poison pill it could get its hands on. Elders abandoned the idea and bought Courage from Hanson instead.

"There are two other problems with the process. The MMC reports have, in general, a disturbing tendency to produce politically convenient decisions, even though the members of the MMC are part-time appointees, professionals, businessmen, trade unionists, academics and such-like, and not government officials. For example, a couple of months ago, British Airways got the all-clear from the MMC, on the basis of secret concessions, to strengthen an already dominant position by taking over British Caledonian. I'm instinctively distrustful of that. It looks like championing the flag carrier and to he... blazes with the public," he corrected himself. "Secondly, the OFT officials are all civil servants."

"But that's the great strength of the British system. In the States, every while we have a change of president, the whole administration gets to be thrown out. Your civil service is independent."

Peter was silent for an instant as Hennessy looked at him.

"Isn't it?" Hennessy prodded.

"Well, yes and no, Christopher. Sure that's the theory. I've already confessed to being a bit of a cynic and it's only a personal view; but Thatcher's been in power for nine years now and that's a long enough period to have changed the complexion of senior officials pretty fundamentally. There's not been a lot of promotion for those who sing a different song to that of their political masters. That's one side of it; but the other is that the civil service also has its own self-protective agenda. It likes to ensure that its own role is not diminished. It has always had an instinct to exercise power - and power without responsibility at that. These chaps don't get paid very much. For some, being able to exercise power is reward enough. For others, there's the prospect, if they've been seen to be helpful, of getting themselves a remunerative little number to while away the five years following an early retirement."

"Do they have a lot of latitude to interpret regulations? Surely not."

"Quite a lot. In the case of the Panel, the general view is that the flexibility is helpful. It makes for speedy decisions adapted to particular circumstances, without an unreasonable dependence on precedent. You won't find many people in the City calling for an SEC here. But I'm not so sure in the case of the OFT. When the Guinness bid for Distillers looked like being referred to the MMC on genuine anti-trust grounds - they have an absolute stranglehold on the production of scotch whisky - a grotesque little deal was cobbled together to sell four or five minor brands that were already in headlong decline and the head of the mergers secretariat at the OFT allowed himself to be got out of bed in the middle of the night to approve it."

"We wouldn't allow regulation like that in the States to run our... our...our dog pounds," Christopher sputtered eventually.

"Well, I guess it doesn't really matter anyway," Peter reassured him. "No company in the world has a significant market share in pharmaceuticals and there is no possible combination of Pitcairn and anyone else which could conceivably have anti-trust implications. But I must tell you that Elders said that the only comparable thing to dealing with the Panel was trying to win the Americas Cup - just when you thought you had the winning design, the New York Yacht Club would up and change the rules."

"Okay, okay," Christopher responded, breaking, to Peter's relief, into a brief smile of acknowledgement. "I guess that's enough of that. The next subject is fees," he announced, bringing Peter straight back down to earth. "I want our advisers to be heavily incentivised. Are you in a position to agree a basis with me now?"

"I would have to consult some colleagues before agreeing a final structure," Peter confessed uncomfortably, "but, if you have something in mind, I could take that back to base with a view to finalising it on Monday morning."

"I don't want to be gotten into a negotiation with someone who has no power to negotiate, if you'll pardon my plain-speaking. How are we going to resolve this?"

"Well, I had a discussion with Rod on Monday about a flat fee plus different percentages for different levels of success."

"Yes...yes...yes, I know, he told me."

"Is that what you had in mind?"

"I'm not sure about the flat fee; but, broadly speaking, yes, that would be my objective. Now who can do me a deal on that?"

" No one in Corporate Finance on their own."

"In that case I suggest you arrange for me to meet with Sir James for half an hour on Monday morning and I'll settle it with him. I assume he has the necessary authority," Hennessy concluded with something bordering on contempt.

"Yes, I'll do that and come back to you if there's any problem with his diary," said Peter, glad to be offered a way out.

" OK. That's settled. What else?"

"Did Rod talk to you about our lining up a legal firm to act for Dundas?"

"Yes. This man Lampard. I've checked him out and he seems worth having simply to stop the other side from using him. You can go ahead with that."

"And a new PR firm?"

"Yes, I've checked them out too. You can go ahead with Wordsworth."

"Both of those, of course, are subject to them being willing and able to act; but I'll speak to them both this afternoon and get back to you if there are any problems."

"Anything else?"

"No," said Peter with relief. He never enjoyed these sessions with Hennessy but, with the exception of the 'bible', this one had gone relatively smoothly.

"Okay, I've got one for you. I've been thinking about some new non-executive directors. I met an excellent man at a party some old friends of ours threw Thursday - Christmas Eve; and I've decided to ask him to join the board. Ben Silkin. He's a director of Brocklebank Nobel. Do you know him?"

*****

Don't you think he's a bit old? - Same vintage as Jock Enderby. No harm in some years of experience. He can give us a good five years. Young doers and old brains - that's the sort of shape we like for a board of directors in the States.

Isn't it unreasonable to ask him to take on this role when the company might be about to receive a bid? - Of course I'll tell him that, but he's in the same profession as you, knows lots about take-over bids.

Have you told Lord Enderby? - I think that I'm right to assume that this is a chairman's decision, but I know he will support it.

I'm not sure that he and Ben Silkin are the best of friends (in fact, I know damned well, though I'm not saying it, that Jock refers to him as 'that slimy little shite' and that they hate each other's slowly decomposing guts ever since Ben Silkin got Harold Wilson to block Enderby's appointment as head of the Industrial Reorganisation Corporation in the late sixties). - Like peas in a pod, great combination, no doubt full of excellent advice for us at a moment like this.

*****

By the time they emerged from the study, it was gone one o'clock. Claudia Hennessy was waiting for them in the sitting room. She was dressed in a plain red woollen dress which showed off her slim figure and had matching big black pearls at her neck, her earlobes and her right wrist. The gold Rolex with the absurd circle of diamonds around the face, which Peter remembered from previous meetings, was as usual hanging from her wrist over a bronzed but rather bony hand.

"Hello, Peter," she said, maw-mawing him a kiss on first one cheek and then the other. "I'd just given up on you two and sent for the champagne. Virginia's gone up to fetch Granny."

At that moment the big oak door at the far end of the sitting room opened and a small mobile battalion entered. At its head sat an unbelievably ugly old woman in a chromium-plated wheelchair, a rug of blackwatch tartan across her knees, totally enveloping her legs, if legs she had. Pushing her was a tarty young girl with too much make-up that Peter took to be the teenager with the mop of long black hair who had been sitting in the window when he arrived. Behind them, with the impedimenta, was the maid who had brought Peter his coffee, now wheeling a trolley on which was a large and distinctly over-elaborate Victorian silver champagne bucket, a huge crystal jug of orange juice and six heavy cut-glass champagne flutes.

"Peter, allow me to introduce my mother, Mrs Sabine Zeitlin; and this is our daughter, Virginia. Mummy is deaf and dumb, I'm afraid, but she enjoys company and she loves her champagne. Ginny, you'll do the honours, won't you, dear?"

It had never occurred to Peter that Claudia Hennessy, wife of the mormon midget, was jewish; but the woman in the wheel chair was the image of that old Russian bag who used to run Israel. He extended his hand rather awkwardly and one of the dappled claws that rested in her lap rose to meet it. She was as cold as ice, but a flicker of courtesy, less than a smile, played momentarily across a slightly hairy upper lip as she inclined her head almost imperceptibly to acknowledge him. It was the face of a central european peasant farmer, a barely female Lyndon Johnson without the Texan grin. She had a bonnet of scraggly dark grey hair above a deeply lined brow and wedged between the craggy contours of her jowls was a great tuber of a nose. Her thick black bushy eyebrows surmounted dark experienced tired eyes, sloping down towards the corners, which contrasted strangely with an almost authoritarian mouth.

Peter could not help find himself looking from her to Claudia Hennessy. How could this old crone, utterly devoid of grace and poise, have produced this polished socialite with the complexion and features of ..... Of, course, she's had a nose job! And quite probably a few other nips and tucks beside. The eyes are the same - but not the lids - or the bags. And the ears. She's certainly plucked the eyebrows. And maybe the chin will go that way too. And those bony hands become mottled with years and gnarled with arthritis.

And then there was the daughter, who had parked her grandmother closer to the fire and was now returning to the drinks trolley. Seated at the window reading her magazine, she had seemed like any other teenage girl. Now standing, she was a truly amazing sight. She was no more than seventeen or eighteen and barely over five feet tall; but she had done her best to give herself height with stiletto heels that must have been all of five inches and by piling much of her pitch-black hair on top of her head. She was fortunate to have inherited her father's button rather than a jewish conk and his slight build was probably also responsible for the tiny waist, which she emphasised by a tight broad black leather belt with a large silver heart for a buckle. Her superstructure was breathtakingly out of proportion with every feature of her breasts displayed on the outline of her tight white roll-necked sweater as though sculpted there. Finally she wore a pair of shiny pillarbox red trousers in some sort of stretch material which clung to an extremely pert bum. They were embellished provocatively in the front with a black satin bow at pube level and beneath the bow was a perfectly etched and quite astonishing furrow.

By some ridiculous quirk of fate, her parents had chosen at birth to call this child Virginia. One could imagine the paroxysms of laughter with which each new introduction of this vamp was now greeted. As she busied herself with the bottle, Peter thought, she looked as though, ten years hence, she would be standing on a bar in Bangkok pulling out champagne corks with her fanny.

"I've told cook not to hold up lunch for Oscar, darling. It's just too beastly of him to be late back when he knows we have a guest for lunch. Just half a glass for Granny, Ginny, you know it makes her hiccough. Peter, dear, do you like it straight or buck's fizz? I'm afraid Christopher has all buck and no fizz; but he's rather on his own in this house on that score. I feel that old Dom Pérignon would be spinning in his grave if he caught us adulterating his best with all that citric acid."

Peter felt torn between his client's disapproval of alcohol in general and Claudia's perfectly valid objections to tampering with the ecstacy of the 1976 vintage. He opted for the pure solution but tried to temper his decision with moderation.

"Just a Granny-sized glass for me thank you, Virginia," he said, noting as he did so that the old girls's flute had been conspiratorially topped up to the brim. Unfortunately, on this occasion, Virginia took the instruction at its word.

"Well then," Claudia resumed, "if everyone's ready, can I propose a slightly premature toast to 1988."

They chinked glasses dutifully, Christopher the only one not to have chosen the nectar, and Peter noted with some delight as he bowed towards the old lady in the wheelchair that she had already surreptitiously drained her glass to the level prescribed by her daughter.

"Did you spend Christmas in London, Peter, or were you in the country?" Claudia inquired, as if she only knew people for whom the choice was available.

"Well, actually, I was skiing in Courchevel, but as Christopher's probably told you, we look as though we might have a bit of excitement on the way, so I came back over the week-end."

"Oh, a real white Christmas for you," she beamed, ignoring altogether the disruption to which he had been subjected. "How delightful for you. Of course, we always go to St Moritz, but never until March. I don't think the Carlton would know what to do with us if we arrived at any other time."

"Well, I must admit it's the first time I've skied this early in the season, but we were quite lucky with the snow, certainly compared to everywhere else, and we had a splendid time."

"Then you must have been at the Byblos," she said, naming the most exclusive and expensive hotel in the Trois Vallées. "They say that the lobsters there are as good as at their place in St Tropez."

"Well, I can't vouch for that, Claudia. There were six of us and we had a little chalet with our own girl to do the cooking; so we only ate out one evening while I was there."

"How delightfully homely," she said with what sounded like a tinge of pity. "I believe that sort of holiday is all the rage with you youngsters."

"And what about all of you," Peter turned, trying to involve the rest of the family, "a big family Christmas with crackers and Christmas pud and presents round the tree?"

"Well sort of, Peter, but you know we Americans are more into Thanksgiving. It was really quite quiet here."

"Well, in any event, I thought I detected a rather special Christmas present for your husband sticking out of the garage over there," said Peter, gesturing towards the window.

"No, no, Christopher's had the Jaguar for ages. I'm sure you've seen it before."

"On the contrary, I was thinking of the Bentley."

"Oh, the Bentley's mine, Peter. I ordered it months ago but it's only just arrived. I could have had a Rolls-Royce straight out of the showroom but all my friends say they're just too terribly 'town'. Don't you agree?"

"But the number plate, Christopher Hennessy the Third?"

"Oh, that's just a coincidence, Peter. I'm a CH too, remember. That was the best number that Jack Barclay could get me at short notice. I'll give it to Christopher when they come up with something better. Ginny, I'm sure we can persuade Mr Davenport to have a little more champagne, and I'll have a refill too."

"Very kind, but you must go easy on me. I'm driving."

Virginia did the rounds again with a practiced style. Granny got another whopping glass and Peter, feeling part of this delightful conspiracy himself, endeavoured to distract Christopher and Claudia Hennessy's attention by taking a couple of paces towards the window.

"Did you suffer much damage in the hurricane? It seems to have played havoc with the trees down the road outside."

"We had a few tiles off the roof," said Christopher, "but fortunately we had the constructors here at the time to do a few alterations; so they were able to fix everything up real quick. But, boy oh boy, did the trees come crashing down? It was awesome out there - looked like a battlefield come morning."

"Well at least that lovely oak at the bottom of your drive survived."

"Only after a major dispute with the tree surgeons. They were contending that it was unsafe; but I reckon that a tree that's stood for three centuries and survived a hurricane has hunkered its roots down pretty good."

"I think at this stage we can give up on Oscar," Claudia concluded, draining her glass. "Let's go through to lunch."

The dining room was the far side of the central hall. It was a grand room, beamed and panelled, with another huge inglenook on the wall which presumably shared its flue with the kitchens beyond. The room would comfortably have accommodated a party of sixteen or even twenty but various sections of the dining table had been removed to the corners, leaving a setting for six. Claudia Hennessy sat at the head at the window end of the room with her husband with his back to the fireplace. Peter was placed on Claudia's right with a blank space for the recalcitrant Oscar opposite, on her left. To Christopher's right his mother-in-law was installed in her wheelchair and Virginia sat opposite her, next to Peter. He noticed now that she kept up a rapid and expert exchange with her grandmother in sign language; but also that the old lady's beady brown eyes darted hither and thither as they conversed, as if unsettled by the incomprehensible chatter going on around her. Christopher noticed Peter's insufficiently subtle attention to proceedings.

"My wife's mother has been deaf and dumb for many years," he began to explain. "She was a prisoner of the Gestapo at the end of the war," he added ominously. "Unfortunately neither Claudia nor I have been able to master the sign-language but she and Ginny seem to be able to talk away for hours together. It's quite an expertise. Oscar is as hopeless at it as the rest of us," he added, as Mrs Hennessy tasted and approved what turned out to be a crisp, dry Soave. The multi-faceted Hilda filled the non-Christian glasses, including that of Mrs Zeitlin who, whilst showing no imminent sign of the dreaded hiccoughs, appeared to be working her way towards that condition with a will. Christopher Hennessy stuck religiously to the Perrier.

"Of course, it's a tragedy for us that we can't communicate properly," Hennessy continued, "but God in his goodness has granted her a mind that has remained as sharp as ever. She reads the *Wall Street Journal* and the *Financial Times* from cover to cover and writes out her instructions to her broker every week. She's a marvel really."

Over the avocado with dressed crab - neither the jewish nor half-jewish members of the family appeared to be kosher - Peter politely enquired of Virginia as to her interests. It was only too apparent what one of them was and another popular music; but otherwise she appeared to be almost completely vacant. Peter had just ascertained that she was already seventeen and had only taken her 'O' levels the previous summer at Benenden without conspicuous success. Now she wanted to finish off at a boys' school - more likely finish off a boys' school, Peter conjectured silently - but her parents were understandably showing reluctance. Like putting a piranha in your goldfish bowl, Peter was thinking, when a low-pitched but increasingly loud bubbling of engine noise drifted into the room. It was followed by the unmistakeable crunching of the gravel behind the rhododendrons and a moment later a black-beleathered figure on a huge shiny beast of a Harley-Davidson swept past the window, coming round the driveway as it were the wrong way - or perhaps it was just the left-hand drive American way - and disappeared in the direction of the garages. Two minutes later, now absent helmet and leather jacket but still sporting knee-length boots and brass-studded leather trousers, Oscar, heir to the Hennessys, emerged from the door to the kitchen, his own plate of avocado and crab in one still oily hand and a can of Budweiser in the other.

His mother made only a token protest at his late arrival and none at all at his appearance as he was hastily introduced to Peter and took his seat opposite. He was a truly horrible sight and Peter was glad, by virtue of crab and can, to be spared the obligation of a handshake. He was, Peter supposed, around twenty years old or even a little more, of well above average height - though God alone knew where he got that particular feature in this family - dark and swarthy with almost as much stubble on his chin as on his head. Three quite thick silver rings pierced various parts of his upper left ear and what appeared to be a bent nail was driven through the outer corner of his right eyebrow. His bare arms, below a rather sweaty looking black tee shirt, were heavily tatooed, as were his knuckles, which spelt out on the right hand H-E-L-L and on the left R-A-T-S.

"Oscar's a member of a motor-cycle club," his father said superfluously.

"Pack, Pop, pack," his son corrected; and then to Peter "we call ourselves the Hell Rats."

"Yes, I rather gathered that." Oscar looked a little blank. "From the knuckles," Peter helped him out.

"Yeah, right. We do a burn somewhere most Sunday mornings; but some of us done a few special runs for this week 'cos the roads are so quiet. We did Brighton this morning. Great hill down into up-town," he said without linguistic inhibition, setting to his crab shovel-like with his fork.

As much as anything to distract himself from the apparition opposite, Peter turned the conversation to the subject of the Hennessy's renovations, surmising correctly that beneath every American socialite lay the answer to an interior designer's prayer.

"I must say that this is a wonderful house, Claudia. Did you have to do much before you moved in?"

"Not too much really, Peter. We made a little apartment for Granny and converted the back stairs into a lift for her. And, of course, there weren't enough bathrooms - only four for nine bedrooms."

"By English standards, that's fairly generous."

"Really, Peter, you astonish me. Anyway, we had four more made out of two of the bedrooms and now I think we can just about manage."

The meal proceeded with some wonderful grouse, presented by cook herself, of which Christopher had a conspicuously half portion appropriate to his dimensions. It was accompanied by a glorious burgundy, unfortunately decanted so that Peter could not confirm his suspicions as to its provenance. He dared not ask for fear that Mormon retribution would follow upon such obvious interest in transgression. It was now clear that Hilda too was privy to at least one of the delights of Mrs Zeitlin's declining years, ensuring that the old hag's glass was never less than half full as quickly as the dowager herself was ensuring that it was never more. A stilton of exquisite creaminess and perfect maturity followed and a bowl of fruit before Mrs Hennessy proffered her apologies that they never ate real deserts at lunch-time and suggested an adjournment to the drawing room for coffee. As Virginia backed her grandmother's wheelchair away from the table, a talon emerged from beneath the table and clutched to her lap as she went a good two-thirds of a glass of red wine.

Peter stayed as little longer as he decently could and then made his farewells, bending in front of Mrs Zeitlin's chariot to take her hand and to receive in return a twitch of her left eye which could almost have been mistaken for a wink. He left Claudia, after further ceremonial maw-mawing, in the sitting room with her mother, the children having disappeared. Christopher took him to his car and, as the door to the sitting room closed behind them, a distinct hiccough ricocheted from its interior.

The tall wrought-iron gates were still flung wide when Peter reached the end of the drive. He stopped for a moment before swinging right towards London.

"Jesus H Christ," he said out loud, "what a fucking awful family."

*****

Martin Lampard came round to Gracechurch Street at five o'clock that evening. Peter wanted Timothy Phillips to have the opportunity to meet him although Timothy was complaining that they were never going to get the bibles finished by Friday evening unless the whole team worked on them flat-out.

"Don't worry about that," he said, "I'll be clear of the things I've got to organise by early tomorrow afternoon. You can put me down for some of the cross-checking. This is a man you ought to meet.

Lampard was in one of the smaller conference rooms on the sixth floor. He was standing, wreathed in smoke, at the far end looking out of the window as they entered, a stocky man with black slicked-back hair in a crumpled grey suit. He turned as they entered and Peter made the introductions. A tray of tea had already been delivered and had been placed on a small sideboard behind the door; while Tim poured, the others sat down. As he did so, Martin pulled an enormous white cardboard box of cigarettes from one of the pockets which he always had specially constructed for that purpose inside the lower front of the jackets of his double-breasted suits. It contained fifty or sixty cigarettes, maybe even a hundred, and was of a big square box-like construction which Peter had never seen in anyone else's possession. Martin opened the lid, took out a cigarette and lit it, leaving the box open beside him on the table. Peter hadn't worked with Lampard for a couple of years; but he was nevertheless surprised by his appearance. He wasn't exactly older and he wasn't exactly more wrinkled - though, heaven help us, he was wrinkled enough. But his pallour was, Peter thought for a moment - yes, he was smoked. He was smoked like a sodding kipper.

"You'd better tell me what this is all about," he growled, his voice even deeper and huskier than Peter remembered, like gravel being scraped under a door.

Peter had called him with difficulty from his car on the mobile on his way back from Godalming. The infernal machine had repeatedly lost the connection; but after four or five attempts, he had given Lampard the name of the client, told him that they were expecting an offer, probably hostile, and asked if he could act for Dundas. Martin loved a fight more than anything else in the world and Peter could sense, even down this fuzzy and often incoherent line, that he was hoping against hope that none of his fellow partners was engaged in anything which would give Ashursts a conflict and prevent him from accepting. By the time Peter had reached his office, Martin had been back to his secretary to announce that he would be around within the hour.

Peter took him rapidly through the evidence that had come to light, Martin scribbling the odd note to himself on one of Dundas Brothers' pads and helping himself to one cigarette after another. As Peter finished, he stubbed one out and reached immediately for another.

"We've got two immediate lines of attack," he barked gruffly. "This jobber's trick must be on the fringe of legality, certainly close enough for us to frighten the shit out of Wagstaffs if they got an injunction. Creating a false market. Failure to register a disclosable interest..."

"But," Peter started to interrupt.

"Yes....yes...yes, I know they've got valid defences; but that won't stop them crapping themselves when they find themselves on the end of a writ; and of course Pitcairn's shares will go through the roof once a predator is revealed, making this buying spree of theirs that much more expensive. If nothing else, it ought to slow them down. At present they could be picking up shares faster than a dog breeds fleas. You said you'd put a Section 212 notice on Wagstaffs. When exactly?"

"Monday evening, late. Well after hours."

"Okay and its now Wednesday. I think we ought to start beating them about a bit tomorrow morning. By tomorrow evening they'll have had 72 hours. That ought to be enough for anybody."

"But I thought that all the lawyers took the 'reasonable time' set out in the act to be a week."

"The act says 'such reasonable time as the notice shall require' or some such. We can say that we think 24 hours to be reasonable if we want. It may not be reasonable but it's another way of getting the bastards in front of a judge. Does the notice you sent in give them a week?"

"To be honest I don't know, Martin."

"Who sent it to them?"

"Well, I think it was the company secretary; but it may have been Plummers."

"Sodding pansies! If it specifies a week, get them to bang in another tonight with just 24 hours to reply. And what about Wagstaff's possible clients?"

"Realistically, Martin, it could be anybody. Any one of a dozen companies, most of them overseas."

"There's nothing to stop us banging out 212 notices like fucking grapeshot if that's what takes our fancy," he rasped, sucking a good half inch of cigarette into his lungs in a single inhalation and stubbing out the rest. He reached immediately for another. "If we fire off enough of it, we're bound to hit something."

"Unfortunately," Peter cautioned, "it could be our own foot. We don't yet know for certain that we're a target. There are dangers in raising our profile and putting ourselves into play."

"Well, I'm only here to give you the law. The tactics are down to you," he added in a tone which implied that Peter was also in danger of joining the pansy class.

"There's a meeting here on Monday morning which will be attended by all of the directors. Realistically, Martin, I don't think they'll be bounced into precipitate action until they've been over it all then. But you mentioned a second line of attack?"

"Yes. Wagstaffs are clearly vulnerable to the charge of using insider information. It doesn't matter a toss whether or not it's true."

"The Chairman and I discussed that today. He's keen that we raise the issue with the Panel. I would certainly intend to do so though I have no confidence of success. They were fired by Pitcairn more than six months ago and, on that basis, the overwhelming weight of precedent is on their side.'

"I wouldn't let that deter me," Lampard croaked back. "But I wouldn't confine myself to the Panel. I'd spread the muck around pretty liberally in the press, too. Mud tends to stick and it's something that Wagstaffs like to avoid. They're secretly pretty chuffed at the shit that's being thrown at Caz over the Guinness shindig and more than usually keen to avoid stepping in a turd themselves right now. By the way, who does Pitcairn's PR?"

"As of now, no one. The Chairman fired Charles Barker a few weeks ago; but he's agreed that we should ask Freddie Wordsworth to take it on. I'm seeing him for lunch tomorrow."

"That sounds like the Freddie we know and love," Martin said, drawing proceedings to an end by standing up, popping the huge box of cigarettes back into its marsupial's pouch and dropping a final stub onto the impressive pile that had accumulated in the past half hour.

*****

Freddie's bright-red Roller was already parked, two wheels on the pavement, in that curious little street that leads to the Savoy, the only one in the UK where driving on the right is the norm, as Peter climbed out of his cab. Freddie had not been in his office when Peter had rung the previous afternoon but his secretary had undertaken to track him down and get him to call back.

"Hello, Peter m'boy. Wordsworth here. What are you doing on the bridge when you should be in front of the yuletide fire with that delicious little blonde you brought to our marquee at Henley?"

"Hello, Freddie. Thanks for calling back so quickly. Sadly I've had to leave her skiing in Couchevel. I've got an urgent job and I was hoping that you might be able to help us out. I was calling on behalf of Pitcairn Pharmaceuticals. They need new PR advisers."

"I thought Charles Barker were belayed there," Freddie came back, his knowledge of connections as ever encyclopaedic despite his air of casual tomfoolery.

"They were fired just before Christmas and no one's been appointed in their place. Now we need someone urgently."

"Well, I know we have no other clients in that industry. If you can assure me that there was nothing in the sinking of Barkers that would make us queasy, I'm sure we would like to help out. Can I get someone in the office to call you?"

"The parting with Charles Barker just seems to have involved a clash of personalities. But Freddie, I should have made it clear that we want you heading the account personally."

"Ah, you know how to flatter an old salt, Peter m'boy. I've been intrigued by the way that new American chairman of theirs has been trimming his sails. Plenty of work on board a ship like that for the likes of us. Can it wait till next week? I'm down in the Isle of Wight spending a few days with an old friend."

Peter knew this 'old friend' of Freddie's was the feisty lady who was part of the admin at the Royal Yacht Squadron and who was the 'out of town' half of his curious marital arrangements.

"I'm afraid it's too urgent for that, Freddie. We think that we might be on the receiving end of a bid and it could come as early as Monday. Could I persuade you to come up to London tonight and see me in the morning for a briefing?"

"Don't interefere with an old sailor's nights in a foreign port, Peter m'boy, they are few and far between these days," said the old rogue, aware that Peter knew at least something of his wanderlust. "But if you'll allow me to travel up in the forenoon, I'd be delighted to give you lunch."

"Done," said Peter, much relieved.

"Savoy River Room. One o'clock tomorrow. See you then."

"Thanks, Freddie, you're a star."

Despite the short notice, Freddie was sitting in his habitual table by the window, some hapless Christmas visitors having no doubt been despatched to some less desirable corner of the room. Freddie tottered to his feet as Peter arrived. He had made the point that he considered himself to be on holiday by sporting grey flannels and a blazer, a dark blue shirt and one of his convoy of yacht club ties. He was truly not that short but his immense girth always made him seem so, the width of each trouser leg appearing to be not far short of the length of that part of his legs which was revealed beneath the great skirt of his double-breasted jacket. His beaming face was rotund and, as usual, slightly sweaty, just from the effort of hauling himself to his feet.

"I've asked Bertrand to splice some champagne so that we can toast the new year. I hope you're got going to be like some boring American banker and head back to the office after a glass of Perrier and one tomato stuffed with another. Antonio tells me that the oysters today are the best."

"Well, I really musn't stay too long, Freddie. I've got a team of people working their butts off on this back at the office and they'll all be keen to finish in time to get away to their New Year's Eve parties."

"A light repast m'boy, and I shall then personally take the helm to see you back to your office."

"Yes, I saw that your car was outside. I'm sure they wouldn't let me park my old banger there for a couple of hours."

"Peter, heaven forfend that you should suggest that the staff of the Savoy are the sort of snobs who would be influenced in such decisions by the mere variety of a car. Put it down, if you will, to the cut of my jib, to my innate charm, to my long-standing as a customer of this hostelry, or even to my curious gait..."

"More likely to the tenner you slip the doorman, if you ask me, Freddie," Peter interrupted.

"Oh dear, you bankers can be so mercenary these days. And so perspicacious. Aha, here's the champagne! That's right, Bertrand, the Krug 1982. None of the usual rubbish for my friend Mr Davenport."

They both opted for the oysters, a dozen in Freddie's case and a half-dozen for Peter, to be followed, for the sake of simplicity and speed, by the roast beef from the trolley. Freddie tackled his dozen with relish, his napkin tucked into his shirt collar and spread wide on each side under his armpits. Lemon juice, Tabasco and black pepper were wielded with an efficiency reminiscent of a Toyota production line and a speed to match. Finally, he sat back, a beatific smile on his joyous face and announced to the maître d', who happened at that moment to be passing their table, "Perfect, Antonio, I'll have another dozen."

Peter could not be persuaded to join him and was instead vouchsafed the job of choosing a wine to accompany the beef. He would normally have hated to be put in such a position, which inevitably caused one to vacillate between what one would like to drink and what appeared reasonably priced; but Freddie, about to tackle his second dozen, laid down the fundamental parameters in no uncertain terms.

"Remember m'boy, claret with beef and a fine claret is like a young girl. You must never touch 'em until they're at least sixteen. I don't want to be accused of statutory rape, and by the somelier at the Savoy least of all."

While Freddie squeezed and spiced, peppered and skewered his second dozen, Peter started to explain Pitcairn's predicament. He knew that Freddie was a good listener and would miss nothing despite what appeared to be an all absorbing pre-occupation.

"Okay," he said, as their plates were taken away, "it seems to me, from a PR point of view, that our chairman is our best asset. I can't imagine why he thinks that Charles Barker haven't been doing a good job. He's already been getting good copy. He's tossed the buggers who fucked it up overboard and put the head office crew on half rations. I can't imagine how the institutions who got him appointed could have him keel-hauled now when he's not yet been a year in the job."

Peter was silent.

"Well, isn't that so, m'boy?"

"It's one interpretation, Freddie. I'll give you another version when we've got our beef. This is not something I would like to have overheard. I reckon the staff in here can move markets with the titbits of conversation they pick up."

Antonio himself carved for them from the trolley of ribs - wonderful blood-rare slices of Aberdeen Angus with roasted turnips, crisp brussel sprouts and perfect Yorkshire puddings.

"I don't doubt," Peter began, once they were left alone, "that the general perception of what he's done is favourable, though Charles Eve was frankly a sacrificial lamb and Cyril Greenacre a scapegoat. The fact that the profits have stalled is down to a combination of bad luck with one or two originally promising formulations that failed under clinical trials and under-investment that pre-dates anyone who's been around for the last five years. Kicking most of the head office staff out into suburbia hasn't saved a bean. In fact there'll be big relocation costs to be charged against this year's profits and next year the savings will be substantially absorbed by a combination of the expenses of St James's Square, which costs an arm and a leg, and the Gulfstream which is due for delivery in the spring.

"The man himself has a chronic dose of short-arse syndrome. He is personally, I'm afraid to say, a greedy and self-seeking little bastard; and what makes it worse is that it's dressed up in this sanctimonious aura that you might from a distance take to be christian asceticism. You'll hardly believe your eyes when you see the offices in St James's. The boardroom is like a miniature version of the Hall of Mirrors at Versailles. And his office is like Madame Pompadour's boudoir. No desk. He works from a sofa with a gilt coffee table in front of it. Tapestries and chandeliers and inlaid whatnots everywhere. I hope the other side never get an inkling. Don't ever get the idea of inviting the press round there for a briefing. We'd be toast."

"My dear boy, if it were not for the splendour of this excellent Bordeaux that you have chosen, I might be thinking that you had handed me a poisoned chalice."

*****

"There's no way we're going to get this finished tonight, Peter. Charlotte still has two companies on the A list of potential predators to analyse and none of her output has been checked yet. Rod's just phoned to say that we won't have the updated projections until at least 7.30. We can't run the merger models for any of the possible bidders until we get those and there are twelve separate analyses that we have to input. Each will take at least one man-hour to do and another man-hour to check. And then there's all the photocopying and collating."

It was the sort of lunch from which you returned to the office only as it was beginning to get dark. Already gone half-past three. Tim had asked Maureen to let him know the moment Peter got back. The rosy glow of good food, fine wine and a Montecristo No 2, with which Peter had returned from the Savoy, was rapidly dissolving into a feeling of guilt as he contrasted the pleasure of briefing Freddie with the drudgery of the tasks he had set the team back at the office.

"Okay, Tim. It has to go out tomorrow, even if it's only in the evening, so that they've got time to read it before Monday morning. We can either work as far through the night tonight as is necessary and take the rest of the week-end off, or work until, say, seven-thirty this evening and reconvene tomorrow morning to finish it off. I'll go with the majority decision. Maureen, Tracey and Alison to have an equal say. Agreed?"

Tim nodded gloomily. "I'll go and conduct the ballot," he said rising wearily. "It's really a choice between working with a hangover or working instead of one."

"Maureen," Peter shouted through his open door, "could you find out if Sir James is in this afternoon and if I could have half-an-hour." He pulled a schedule from his pocket on which he had been scribbling in the back of the cab on the way to the Savoy and grabbed a pen to finish it off. At the same time he picked up his phone and dialled his flat. Sophie's flight back from Geneva was due to touch down at one-thirty. She ought to be home around now. The answering machine responded and he left a message for her to call. The week in Courchevel, though it was as long a period as they had managed to spend together, had done nothing to satiate his appetite for her, and he had been missing her horribly. He dreaded the possibility that he might have to cancel their announcement this evening; but she must be getting used to living with a corporate financier by now.

Maureen was standing in front of his desk when he looked up from his papers. "The vote is six-nil in favour of taking the evening off," she announced to Peter's relief. "And Christopher Hennessy is on the phone," she said. "He's on your line."

"Hello...Hello, Christopher...Yes...Thank you for the excellent lunch yesterday...Yes, I've briefed both of them now and they'll be in the City on Monday if anything crops up...Yes...Yes...Of course that's possible.

It'll be a little tight; but we can get it down there on a bike...Sure...
Okay...Bye."

"Christopher Hennessy has used his casting vote. He's accepted
an invitation at short notice to spend tomorrow and Sunday with Tony
O'Reilly at his Irish estate. A plane is picking him up from Biggin Hill
at ten thirty in the morning and he would like his briefing pack there
when he departs."

"Are you going to tell them all or shall I?"

"I'll go round and see them now. Could you please type this up.
Is James Cruso available?"

"He's out until six and he's got to leave by seven-thirty for some
hogmanay bash - London Caledonian Society or some such. His
secretary has already gone home; so we'll have to keep trying his
line."

Peter trailed round to the open-plan area which was occupied by
Tim Phillips and his team. After breaking the news, he settled in
behind a spare desk and began checking through the papers they had
prepared. Tracey and Maureen went backwards and forwards with
revised drafts like automatons. Alison, newly wed to her policeman, was
more or less imprisoned in the photo-copying room. She had just this
week returned from her brief wedding and honeymoon in Bali with her
hair in Bo Derek plaits, a fixed broad grin across her face and, so it was
generally agreed, a distinct bow-leggedness, which was nothing to do
with the constable's bicycle but everything to do with his truncheon.

At six fifteen Sophie rang and Maureen transferred the call from
his office. The flight back had been delayed by an hour and a half but
she was still full of bounce and looking forward to their evening. He
wanted to soften the blow but there was no easy way. Her voice went
flat and she was clearly on the verge of tears. He encouraged her to
join the rest of the gang at Annabel's but felt far from certain that she
would. It was a rotten end to a holiday and a miserable start to the rest
of their lives together; but they were young and in love and by tomorrow
evening the universe would again be at their feet. After all, when exactly
they got engaged was really no big deal.

Rod King's revised forecasts arrived long after eight and at around
nine thirty they sent out for pizzas. The local Pizza Hut, unsurprisingly,
was more incredulous of the order on such an evening than overburdened.

As they all took a short break to eat, Peter realised with irritation that both he and Maureen had forgotten about the brief word he needed with the chairman on the subject of Pitcairn's fee. He would just have to call him at home over the week-end.

A couple of hours later there was still no end in sight to the paperchase but Peter had a brainwave. He popped back to his office for a key and took the lift up to the sixth floor. They always kept a stock of champagne in the fridge in the little kitchen adjacent to the boardroom so that clients could receive the appropriate congratulation on their completed deals; and each corporate finance director had a key. As well as the door that opened directly from the boardroom, there was one from the corridor and Peter would normally have used this for fear of disturbing any other meeting then in progress; but, if he was going to be carrying a tray on the way out, as he intended, it would be easier to have a table on which to rest his burden while he relocked the kitchen door rather than put the tray down on the floor. He propped the double doors to the boardroom open on their catches to make life easier and was surprised to find that the lights still blazed within. He turned right and, unlocking the door of the kitchen, noticed that the door at the far end of the room opening into the chairman's office was wide open. He had the distinct impression that he could hear voices within. It was no effort to cross the room soundlessly on the soft pale-green carpet but the voices still made no sense. He was more or less on the threshold before he realised that he didn't understand a word because they were talking in German. They were making no effort to keep their voices down but one had a distant, almost mechanical timbre to his tone, as if he were talking from under the desk. Perhaps he had his head in the chairman's safe. Peter hesitated now. He felt no inclination to heroism if these were a couple of burglars. The security guards made their rounds throughout the night but there was always at least one spare at the ground floor reception desk. He started to back away. There was a telephone in the kitchen which he could use to summon help.

"OK, Heinrich. Das ist güt. Glückliches Neues Jahr. Wiedersehn."

Silence.

Shit! There aren't two of them. It was some jerk on the squalk-box. The burglar theory disintegrated in favour of one of Juan-Antonio's boys in international for some reason using the chairman's office. Probably talking to a headhunter. Peter decided to put his head round the door. The sight that greeted him made him feel a total prat. Sir James Cruso stood to one side of his desk carefully stuffing the bowl of one of his enormous pipes from the familiar tan leather pouch. He was in full regalia - kilt, sporran, dirk, the lot - and alone. He was a big ruddy man with that sort of pepper and salt grey hair that must have once been red and, in the same variegated hue, those faintly ridiculous nineteenth century tufts of bristles on each cheek that Peter always thought of as 'bugger's grips'.

"Oh, I'm sorry, James. I thought I heard voices in here, and in German."

"You did indeed, Peter. One wee talent I have until now been able to keep hidden from your colleagues," he said, puffing hopefully as he applied a match to his pipe. "I hope you're no gonna rat on me noo."

"I couldn't understand. I was trying to get ten minutes with you earlier on; but your secretary said you were only back briefly, early evening."

"Well, as ye ken see," he puffed again unsuccessfully, tamping down the red-hot embers with a thumb that had apparently been transubstantiated into asbestos at some point in the past, "I was meant to be; but there was someone I needed to talk to and I discovered that he was in flight to Tokyo. He landed there a couple of hours ago but has only just reached his hotel. But, more to the point, what are ye doing here?"

"I've got a team downstairs working away their New Year's Eve. I thought the least I could do was to fetch them some champagne from the kitchen to see in the New Year."

"Good thinking, Peter." His pipe was now successfully under power. "Well," he said, looking at his watch and then sitting down on one of the sofas. "Sit yersel down. Ye've still got twenty minutes. What did ye want to see me about?"

"We're expecting a hostile bid for Pitcairn. Someone's been building up a stake. Christopher Hennessy wants to discuss fees with you on Monday. I wondered if you could find half an hour for him. We have a meeting here starting at ten."

"Let's see," he said, going over to his desk to consult his diary. "I could do 9.15; but I must be away by 9.35 latest. I've got to see some shifty politico at the DTI at ten. Is that okay? But why me? Why can't ye chaps in corporate finance do it?" he said, returning to the sofa.

"He's playing the decision-maker - wants to talk to someone who doesn't have to refer to a committee. I've got a proposal that I've discussed with Cyril and with Bill McAdam; but the schedule's in my office. I'll just go and fetch it."

"No need o' that, I'm sure Peter. The one thing ye chaps can always remember is a fee proposal. What do ye want me to ask for?"

"Pitcairn's current market cap is about £1.8 billion; so the take-out price might be around two point four. We would normally expect ten to twelve million on that if we won and say two-thirds of that if we lost; but Hennessy wants us to be more heavily incentivised. I'm proposing a flat quarter per cent on the final bid value plus a further quarter if they stay independent."

"That's six mill if they get bought for two point four and twelve mill if they get clean away," said the chairman, as ever grasping the numbers instantaneously. "That's not much of a change from the norm; but if I were Hennessy I'd say it was a wee bit rich to pick up your percentage on the whole value and not just the uplift, even if they lose their independence."

"We proposed to do it that way because Hennessy gave me a pretty clear hint that he was opposed to a flat-rate charge in addition to a percentage."

"Sure, I can understand him there; but on your basis, at three bill, which would be a rock-crusher of a bid, you'd only pick up seven and a half. That's not a great reward for the Brothers getting a stonking price for the shareholders. What about collecting one per cent but only on the bit over one point eight if they get taken over and doubling it up if they stay independent? That would make it six or twelve at two point four but twelve or twenty-four on three billion."

"Or only four or eight at two point two."

"If you let them go for two point two, ye'll have more to worry about than the fee, laddie," said Cruso ominously. "Leave it with me," he added in a kindlier tone, "I know what yer after. Now run along and get that champagne. I'll come and have a wee one m'self with yer troops on m'way oot."

Friday, 1 January, 1988

It was gone four in the morning by the time Peter stepped into his apartment. The spot over his desk was not on. Sophie was not yet back. He was glad she had decided to go out with the gang after all - and that they were making a good night of it.

He felt absolutely bushed. Though Timothy and his team were going to be at it for a good while yet, the hard work was finished and he was confident that Hennessy's copy would be ready for the courier by seven. He laid his two briefcases on the desk, switched on the spot for Sophie's benefit, turned out the rest of the lights and headed straight for bed.

He woke with a start just before eleven. He had been thrashing round the bed in who knows what uneasy dream and looked to have been engaged in mortal combat with the duvet. The first drab daylight of 1988 was showing round the heavy curtains.

No Sophie.

He popped his head round the door of the bathroom.

No Sophie.

He walked naked into the sitting room. The spot over the desk was still burning. He switched it off automatically. She must have decided to spend the night with one of their friends. He tried to recall if her mini was in the garage when he got home last night. He thought not; but she wouldn't have taken it out on New Year's Eve in preference for a taxi. She must have driven to the Fordyces or the Mulhollands and left it there ready to drive home this morning. Still, no point ringing around for her. God knows what hour that lot would surface. She'd ring in due course.

He returned to the bedroom for a bathrobe and set off for the far end of the apartment in the direction of a cup of tea. He saw the envelope as soon as he entered the kitchen, propped up against the kettle, his name in her large looping hand, and felt an immediate unease. This wasn't normal. She would usually have left a note on his desk - under the spot. "So and so called from New York and wants you to call back when you get in." "Josh rang to cancel golf tomorrow. Wentworth is closed because of flooding. A lie-in. Yummy!" "My period has started! Phew!"

He tore it open but hardly needed to read beyond the first line. As he looked across the open-plan apartment, he realised that there was nothing of hers to be seen. He slid down onto the polished wooden floor, his back against the oven door, and stared at the single sheet of paper, the tears welling into his already aching eyes.

The phone by the fridge started to ring. He struggled to his feet and leapt at it, clutching the receiver to his ear with frightened, trembling hands.

"Hello," he said feebly, the word barely coming at all, "Sophie?"

"Hello....hello, Peter, is that you? It's Christopher Hennessy. I'm talking to you from the plane."

"Yes, of course, Christopher. Good morning. I trust you've got the papers."

"Yes, indeed. I've just been through them briefly and have been speaking to Ben Silkin. We think there's one thing missing which I'd like you to do some work on before Monday. What poison pills can we swallow? Are there any companies that we could bid for ourselves to make Pitcairn bigger? Or to put a chunk of our shares in some friendly hands? Could we make a bonus issue of loan stock to our shareholders carrying conversion rights? We're not currently exploiting our relative lack of gearing. Could we tie parts of the business up in joint ventures? And anything else you can think of."

"Yes, Christopher, of course; but there are Take-over Code implications." He just prevented himself from using the word 'problems'. "Rule 21," he recalled automatically, "prevents what is called frustrating action without shareholder approval, either during a bid or even when there is reason to believe that an offer is imminent."

"Yes, yes, I know that, Peter; but Ben Silkin says that a clever adviser can always find a way round things like that."

'Fuck Ben Silkin,' thought Peter silently. "Okay, Christopher, we'll do you a paper," he intoned, barely able to disguise the rising crescendo of personal anguish and professional frustration boiling up in his chest as he crushed the phone in one shaking hand and Sophie's pitiless note in the other.

"Good. Anything else?"

"Yes, Christopher. Sir James Cruso will be available at 9.15 on Monday to talk about fees, if you could come in a little bit early. We can then all convene as scheduled at ten o'clock."

"Sure thing, Peter, see you then," he said ringing off.

Peter stared at the now buzzing receiver. He instinctively dialled Sophie's apartment in Chelsea. It rang...and rang...and rang.

"I'm sorry, Peter," he read again, "you haven't got room for a wife. You're already married to the Brothers."

*****

Peter started drinking around noon. He was still unshaven. Sophie had cleared every scrap of her possessions from the apartment. Her wardrobe was empty of everything but the after-redolence of her perfume, which hung in the constrained air, mocking his grief. Her make-up had gone from the shelf in the bathroom, leaving little rings of dust and the odd spillage on the marble surface to remind him of her passage. Her books and her magazines, her CDs and her tapes left vacant hollows in the shelves and cupboards. The photographs of her family, that had stood in silver frames on the big oak beam that separated the dining room from the sitting area, her tennis racket, that always lived in the umbrella stand behind the front door, her spare car keys that hung on a hook in the kitchen; all gone. She had ripped herself out of his life with a violence and rigour that left him feeling that his entrails had been pulled from his guts.

He stood staring at the cold, swirling, dirty river below, a third tumbler of barely diluted scotch in his sweaty and trembling fist. At last he could bear it no longer. He crossed to his desk and rang the Fordyces' number. She was closer to Jenny than most of the rest of their mutual female friends, who were largely just the wives or girl-friends of his mates.

Jenny had been expecting the call but was nevertheless dreading it. She was equally close to them both and had taken an almost proprietorial interest in a match that she prided herself had its origins under her own roof and around her own table. Sophie had been so excited about going to Courchevel that Jenny herself had been speculating hopefully to Josh on the outcome. Indeed only the tie of young children had kept the Fordyces from joining the group.

"I'm *so* sorry, Peter She was very upset too when she called last night; but she seems absolutely to have made up her mind."

"But, if she was so upset, she can't want it to end. I just need to talk to her."

"When we saw her later last night, she wouldn't even hear of talking to you. She said she wanted an absolutely clean break, a new start."

"You mean she came along to Annabel's last night."

"Yes. She didn't arrive until eleven and she wouldn't eat. I think she'd been crying. She looked puffy round the eyes, which is so unlike her, and had more make-up on than usual. Said she'd been moving back into her flat."

"But she's not there, Jenny. I've been trying the number ever since I woke up. Where can I get hold of her?"

"I think it's too late, Peter. Mark Cubit was in Annabel's last night. She left with him. I'm sorry, Peter. I'm so so sorry."

*****

He spent the long New Year week-end in a daze. He didn't leave the apartment and he didn't eat. His bowels voided, as if in terror, the moment he put the phone down on Jenny Fordyce, barely able to reach the security of the loo. The Cubit thing was too much. It was as if she were deliberately trying to revolt him. He was sick a couple of times later, though he retched only fluid. One bottle of Johny Walker was finished ... and then another ... and then another. It didn't help him sleep. He lay in bed from time to time, as if from habit; but, if there were fitful moments of relief from his wakeful nightmare, then they were too troubled to constitute rest and too brief to grant him respite from his wretchedness. He had placed his future life with Sophie in the category of certainties. It had lain there with Mark Twain's death and taxes, with old Cyril Bishop's extraordinary memory and with his own conviction that only his own efforts could make something of the years that separated him from eternity. They had had everything between them. She was beautiful and cultured, well-heeled and, above all, fun. He was successful and well paid and everyone said he was going places. Together there was no end to what they could do. Now he could see nothing worthwhile to lift his life above that of the crude savage that Hobbes had labelled solitary, poor, nasty, brutish and short. He could never love like that again. And, if one could not love like that, was there any point in loving?

He pretended to work on the paper he had promised Hennessy, roping in the long-suffering Tim Phillips by telephone and sending him back to the office to grind out the numbers. Maureen was warned to be in early on Monday to type it up. It was a shoddy piece of crap which even Maureen could see, as she bashed it out, would be unredeemed by more reams of Tim's meticulous schedules.

He had fetched the Saturday *FT* from the local newsagent as usual. He scanned it automatically. Costain had proposed a clever little scheme for sinking an eight-lane motorway under the Thames from Chiswick to Docklands. Peter, more cynical than ever, thought they could go bust waiting for the leaderene's po-faced government to embrace such an imaginative piece of infrastructure spending.

Maxwell had got his way at his New Year's Eve egm, out of sight of the press, which he had excluded. Afterwards he took the trouble to beat his chest a little at the expense of the struggling Murdoch, proclaiming the crash a great opportunity for MMC to acquire assets while the dirty digger remained mired in debt. With a final flourish he had claimed that the Mirror pension funds had moved strongly into cash two weeks before the crash. "The advice originally came from the chairman of the investment committee, and you're looking at him." Peter read the words without taking them in. Not a flicker of a smile passed his ashen contours.

Elsewhere, the pre-Christmas rally, it was noted, had now been completely undone, leaving a trail of abandoned new issues and some infectious-looking underwriting exposures, Bottley included. The Lex column comment caught a note: *"Sentiment, which this year has proved even more capricious than usual, has moved from unbounded optimism to blackest pessimism to a mood of gentle hope, only to take a subtle turn for the worse as the year was all but done."* His own year now appeared to have contained the same swings of emotion but in a savagely altered sequence. He had begun the year as one of the boys, feasting absent-mindedly as and when he pleased on the oriental delicacies of Soo Chan's perfect body, only to be first fascinated, then enchanted and finally besotted by the girl that he had decided was all he ever desired. And he had lost her by taking it for granted that nothing else had to change to accommodate their love. The "blackest pessimism" seemed too trifling a description of the mood that gripped him now.

Monday, 4 January, 1988

"Pitcairn's principal products are forforformulated for the treatment of medical problems associated with what I like to call the fer..four efs - feef...fever, faff...faff...fat," and here George Aladyce paused momentarily, toying with vulgar impropriety as he surveyed his audience around the boardroom table of Dundas Brothers. His mischievously twinkling eyes lit for a moment on Charlotte Mulder as he continued with an innocent smile, "flatulence and fun...fun...fun...fornication." Peter was sure that he heard Rod King, sitting next to Hennessy on the far side of the table, exhale gently with relief.

George Aladyce was looking every bit the mad professor this morning, his wavy mass of snow-white hair billowing hither and thither like the fluffy cumulus clouds of an English summer's afternoon. He was in his early fifties, a big shambolic man in the sort of grey tweedy suit that one could associate with country squires or public school headmasters but hardly with a corporate colossus. His jacket pockets bulged and gaped with their assorted contents and his trousers bagged slackly at shiny knees. His dark blue shirt and even darker blue knitted tie made barely more concession to the City environment in which he now found himself than his habitual brown suedes.

Generally possessed of a voice replete with round and mellow tones, he was totally unfazed by his speech impediment. In fact he rejoiced in it rather like that old Irish cove who was really a lord of something or other and used to appear on long-gone late-night TV chat shows, telling whimsical anecdotes in a stutteringly lilting brogue. He had an occasional problem with almost any consonant but efs were his speciality. 'Pitcairn' itself could on occasions peep-peep-peep for ever before he got it out. Two consonants together seemed to help, unless, of course, they were 'ph'. Thus flatulence and frigging plopped out first time without exception; but 'pharmaceutical' and 'fart' and 'fuck' and 'faeces' could fibrillate furrily fur ever. Indeed every word commencing with an eff and proceeding with a vowel was likely to hang there for such an interval that Peter had a suspicion from time to time that the opportunities for innuendo had become too amusing for George to be interested in any possible successful therapy.

He was standing at the far end of the boardroom where the projection screen had been lowered from its concealed compartment in the ceiling and an oblong panel in the table had opened to reveal a projector with a carousel for 35mm slides. 'The Four Fs' had read the previous slide, now replaced by one which listed the offending conditions. A discerning eye might have detected that this slide did not quite match the layout of the one before. Those around the table more familiar with George's style might then have concluded that the presentation now under way had originally been designed for audiences sufficiently robust to appreciate George's four 'F's in all their original anglo-saxon magnificence.

It was a largish gathering. Christopher Hennessy, who sat opposite Peter, was flanked by Rod King and the empty chair which George Aladyce had occupied until he began his presentation. Hennessy had invited the two non-executives to sit together next to Rodney, so that they would get a better view of the screen; but Lord Enderby had conspicuously avoided the opportunity for proximity to "his old friend" Ben Silkin, and chosen to take up station next to George's now empty chair. Beyond him were Justin Travers-Coe of Gourlay Gilfillan, Pitcairn's brokers, Julian Corrigan from their lawyers, Plummer, Goodspeed and Bleriot, and Freddie Wordsworth. Peter had his whole team with him - Tim Phillips, Oliver Quentin-Archard and Charlotte Mulder, her naturally olive skin deliciously Caribbean-bronzed, Elspeth Watson, dowdy again and with nothing to show for her latest brush with things African but a red-raw and peeling nose, and the ungainly giant, Stuart Robinson, the knot of his tie as usual nearer his breast-bone than his chin. Martin Lampard, a wrinkled old wreck amongst this youthful entourage of advisers, slumped beneath a haze of cigarette smoke opposite Julian Corrigan.

Peter's team had been keeping their heads well down, Maureen having warned them all first thing that her boss was in a foul temper. He looked as though he had the mother and father of all hangovers with great grey-black bags under his bloodshot eyes and a sour ashen complexion. He had held the floor for the first half hour of this meeting but without any of his usual brisk good humour. Rod, like Maureen, unhesitatingly put his condition down to seasonal over-indulgence. Tim, who had first-hand experience of Peter's capacity when he had been a more regular member of the department's bachelor outings, was not so sure. He had never remembered the traditional five or six pints in an east end pub whilst various tarts removed their kit and rubbed baby oil in and bananas up their fannies followed by two or three more and a ring-burner at Khans in Westbourne Grove to have a significant impact next morning on Peter's constitution. Nevertheless, having had first-hand experience of the short end of his director's temper on more than one occasion and well able to judge the mood of the moment, he had not thought it prudent to inquire. Freddie Wordsworth, meeting them at the sixth-floor lift as he arrived, had dared to ask if Peter was feeling well only to be snapped at in no uncertain terms. He put it down to pressure and resolved to keep a low profile until he was called upon to contribute.

They had all had their packs over the week-end and those who had not studied them were not confessing to their indolence with revealing questions. Despite Tim's carefully concealed misgivings, Peter tabled the embarrassingly awful paper on poison pills that the chairman had demanded; but they were rescued from Ben Silkin's eagerness to discuss it straight away by a witheringly alarming warning from Julian Corrigan of the Take-over Panel's determination, post Guinness, not to be bested again. Martin Lampard growled gravelly and pencilled a note of protestation to be passed along to Peter but fortunately held his tongue. Julian's little speech led conveniently into the routine cautions about observing the rules, the importance of secrecy and the restrictions on dealing in the shares and Peter drew the directors' attention to the formal notice in their packs. He went on in the same monotone to warn of the increasing involvement in bids of teams of private investigators only to draw fresh fire, this time from Hennessy himself.

"I am going to take this opportunity to say, Peter, that, whatever the current predisposition of corporations to conduct merger and acquisition activity with the use of underhand and shameful tactics, I will not tolerate such abuses to be undertaken by Pitcairn or, on

Pitcairn's behalf, by any of its advisers. Peter is right to bring to our attention the possibility of such measures being used against us - and we should be on our guard; but we will neither retaliate nor reciprocate."

"Do I make myself clear?" he demanded in response to the ensuing silence, peering leprechaun-like around the assembled advisers over his ridiculous spectacles until he was satisfied that all the heads had nodded enough.

"Seventy per cent of our turd...turd...turnover and over ninety per cent of our operating profits," George continued, "come from three fur...fur...fur...families of products - Toneral for the treatment of hyperperpertension and heartbeat irregularities - that's normally caused by being too faff...faff...fat - Banamet, which is fu...fuf... fundamentally ffffor the treatment of chronic stomach and intestinal disorders - there's your flatulence - and the Myodin range of antibiotics, which are used primarily in the treatment of diseases associated with bacteria - there's your fur...fur...fur...fever - and most specifically gog...gog...gog...gonorrhoea, which, despiepiepiepite all the aspersions cast against the innocent bog seat, is, in my humble medical experience, most commonly acquired as a result of fuff... fuff...fun...fornication."

George at least was enjoying himself, exploiting his fondness for schoolboyish humour of the lavatorial variety. Those who had not previously experienced one of these presentations were certainly already taking notice. But even Rod was held spellbound by the conflict so clearly raging within George's wickedly intelligent brain. Would the temptation to pull the dwarf's tail in front of such an audience finally crack George's far from iron resolve to clean up his public act and lead him into his more normal version of such presentations, effing and blinding and replete with colourful working-class expressions for the parts of the human body?

"I'm only intending to give you the briefest rundown, because frankly this subject's as dry as a ten-day-old ter...ter...turd. For those who like their punishment in bigger dollops, there's a hand-out to foff... foff...follow. I'm going to talk a bit about the industry, a bit about what Peep-peep...Peep-peep the company makes, a bit about what's in our research pie...pie...pipeline and a bit about the competition. You can ask questions if you like as we go along or I'll take them at the end.

"Fur...first, the industry. The world-wide pharmaceutical cay...caper is worth $100 billion and is growing at between fi...fi...five and ten per cent pur...pur...pur a year. We have only about three per cent of the market. Every company has some fo...fo...formulations which are past their best before date, some which are like a bit...bit...bitch on heat and some which are like a pre-pupe...pupe...pubescent schoolboy. You can see on this chart where we stand. In western Europe patents have a life of twenty years; but it can take you ten or twelve years to get your product past the fuff fuff fuff regulators. You've then got only another eight or ten years to milk it for all it's worth. Foff...foff...four years before expiry you have to give the for...for...formulations to any old Tom, Dick or Harry so that he can get ready to knock the stuff...ff...ffing out of your market as soon as your time is up.

"In our case, Banamet reached its patent expiry in October last year and we have no patented product to take its place at the moment. We were pursuing a radically different approach but the particular drug we developed fay...fay...failed in clinical trials too late fo...fo...for us to start again. We're now going to produce an improved version of Banamet - Banamet Plus or some such - but it will be a couple of years before we can get it on the road. Until then we'll have open compepepetition on the original Banamet for...for...formulation with generic copies and, of course, at a much lower price. Toneral, the heart drug, which is what is called a beta blocker, is also old technology. It was selling like hot cakes fife...fife...five years ago but there are better treatments now. Toneral often leads to memory loss, insomnia and therefore, not surprisingly, faff...faff...fat... tiredness.

"Myodin, here, in the middle of this chart, which is Myodil when sold in tablet for...for...form, is currently our best selling product. It's been an absolute winner - a broad-spectrum antibiotic and there's a derivative called Tagadin, which is a specific antibiotic fo...fo...for bacterial infefections of the gut. We make a pip...pip...piss pop...pop...pop...pile of money out of those two.

"Then we've got some new products coming along. All these were only known by code-numbers until a couple of months ago, but we've now chosen the names under which they'll be marketed. I'm pretty pleased with them. There's Impidin and Impidol, new broad-spectrum antibiotics in injectable and tablet foff...foff...form."

Peter was struck by the name, which he hadn't heard before. He knew that George habitually referred to Hennessy behind his back as either the imp or the midget or occasionally even the runt. He glanced over at Rod King and detected the beginnings of a smirk playing on his lips. He returned Peter's quizzical expression with a silent shrug.

"We also think we're quite the beeb...beeb...bees' knees at gonorrhoea - I guess you all know what that is," he added questioningly, in the forlorn hope that someone might give him the chance for a particularly ribald explanation. "New products in this area are important because gonorrhoea has a habit of chewing up new antibiotics and fife...fife... finding them quite palatable in due course. Anyway we've developed Migitin and Migitol, again injectible and tablet, foff...for that little baby."

Rod was now having great difficulty controlling his expression and even Peter, his general depression overwhelming him, could not suppress the briefest of smiles.

"Now, as I say, gonorrhoea's a cun...cun cunning little bleeder," George continued. "It's the commonest infe...fe...fectious disease in the world after influenza and the common cold and, quite apart from having fouf...fouf...found a means of spreading itself around which is feef...feef...fiendishly popular, it only takes a fuff...fuff..few years for it to learn to love whatever it is that quacks throw at it. You might call it the research furf...furf...pharmacist's friend. Syphilis is all very well and good, but there's simply not enough of it about fo...fo...for anyone to make a decent living out of it by compa...pa...parison."

Venereal diseases were George Aladyce's pride and joy and the foundation of his original reputation as a research chemist. He would talk about them happily for hours, particularly since he had come by a chairman whose body language was, as usual, now displaying his intense discomfort with the entire subject.

"Impidin and Migitin will not be going on sale in this country until late 1989 and a year later in the States, which is the most important market - I sometimes wonder if they haven't all got the clap - not you, of course, Chairman - sorry pardon. The Myodin patent expires mid 1988 although Tagadin has another fur...fur...four years until the end of 1991. But we've got a nasty gap between the end of patent protection on Myodin and the fur...fur...first sales of Impidin and Migitin.

"Fur...fur...further out we've got a new heart drug which we think might be a blockbuster. It's what is called an Ace inhibitor which forf...forf...forces the blood vessels to widen imperceptibly and thus causes the blood pressure to reduce. It's a market that's grown from fuff...fuff...fuff sweet fa...fa...fanny adams in 1984 to around £800 million today. It's shared between Squibb with Capoten and Merck with Vasotek; but we think that our product is better than either. We're hopoping to launch that in 1989 too."

"What's that product called?" asked Stuart Robinson, who had been furiously taking notes but now played innocently into George's hands.

"We haven't given it a name yet," Aladyce replied. "On the list here, it's just CF396 but I thought we might call it Runtacene," he added absolutely po-faced. "What would you think of that, Rod?" he enquired, drawing attention to Rod King's spluttering discomfiture.

"After that, we're a bit into the realms of whimsy and at the mercy of clinical trials. We've got some ideas fo...fo...for another new generation of antibiotics for launch in the mid-nineties; and we're working on a drug to counter allergic reactions to anaesthetics - about the same timescale. Quite a lot of peep...peep...people still die on the slab and forforfor a surgeon that can be pretty bloody embarrassing. Fi...fi...finally, rather fur...fur...further off- sex...sex...second half of the nineties, is something else in the fur...fur...fat line which I managed the fur...fur...first research on myself - a treatment to attack the for...for...formation of body fur...fur...fats. That would be something entirely new in the way of a medical breakthrough and potentially hugely profitable, particularly with the entire American race beginning to resemble the arse end of an elephant - begging your per...per...pardon, of course, Christopher," he added tactlessly again.

"There are dozens of other products and derivatives but that's really the core of our business and all I want to say on that subject. Stuart, you'll find some potential fif...fif...figures for sales of the new drugs in the bum...bum...bumf here and I think Rod's given you the past history product by product.

"Now I thought I'd just say a word or two about the competition. I'm going to confifififine myself to UK companies because that's where Peep...Peep...Peter said a bid was most likely to come from; but again there's more infofoformation on our product fif...fif...fit with overseas companies in all this paperwork.

"There are fie...fie...five important UK fur...pharmaceutical companies apapapart from ourselves: Glaxo, Beecham, BMP, ICI and Wellcome. None compeepeepetes with us directly all across the park but most have some competitive drugs. Glaxo is the bear...bear...biggest company and has the most successful drug, Zantac, which is fo...for the treatment of stomach ulcers. Our gut treatment, Banamet, which is for stomach infe...fe...fections, even before the patent expiry, was not directly competitive. Next are their anti-asthma drugs, Ventolin and Volmax, which again are areas we don't cover. Their third big group of drugs, however, is antibiotics - fo...Fortum and fo...fo...Fortaz and Ceftin and Zinnat. We're in direct competition here, though we are currently bigger. Glaxo have a humungus research capapapability and it's rumoured that they're planning to increase it even more. This drug," he said, pointing at the screen, "is to counteract nausea in cancer patients undergoing key...key chemotherapy and will be launched this year. This one's called an agonist and is the fur...fur...first fo...for the treatment of migraine - due out in 1991. This one's an antagonist fo...fo...for the treatment of anxiety. These three are fo...for various infe...fe...fectious diseases, these fo...for bronchial problems and these fo...fo...for ulcers. Any of these could be a potential blockbuster and, in addition, they're believed to be eyeing the market for heart drugs because of the growth rates there. All in all a for...for...formidable cum...cum...company.

"Beecham are rather up the same swanny as us, with a gap between their old range of drugs and their new fo...for...formulations. But of course they've also got a huge business outside prescription medicines in toothpapapaste and Lucozade and Brylcreem and god knows what. In drugs they're currently hugely dependent on antibiotics - Augmentin, Amoxil and Timentin, as you can see here. But they've also got a couple of interesting prospects. Reliflex, here, is an arthritis treatment likely to be launched in 1992; and Eminase here is another heart drug. This is a thrombolytic which is used to dissolve blood clots. Until now Genentech have had this market to themselves with Activase and they've been charging $2,000 per pay..pay...patient. Beecham don't expect US approval until 1990; but a company with Eminase and Runtacene in its portfolio might be sitting in the pow...pow...pound seats, eh Rod?

"Next is BMP. As you know, this is not a pure prescription drugs company either. It's the jack-of-all-trades of the UK industry, which makes its attempts at important research a bit difficult to take seriously. It has an extensive OTC drug portfolio - painkillers, cold remedies, throat lozenges, tinctures, antacids and a shit-load of other bits and bobs. It is also a major producer of generics fo...fo...for which it uses a string of low-cost plants in the fur...fur...Far East. Like us, it is also big in antibiotics - Banzinin is its brand. It's really the only big thing they've invented for themselves; but it's a very successful broad-spectrum antibiotic which was launched three or fo...fo...four years after Myodin and therefore has no immediate problem with patent expie... pie..piry. We don't yet know what plans, if any, they have fo...fo...for its replacement. Or even whether their labs are up to the job.

"They also have a heart drug called Avricor which they are just about to launch. They bought that with Depson Healthcare two years ago. It's what is called a statin which works by reducing the cholesterol level in the blood. It will compee...pete against Mervacor, which Merck launched last year and has been going like shit off a shovel. This is a market which is expected to grow at an annual rate of upwards of seventy per cent fur...fur...for the next fur...fur...few years.

"Fi...fi...fi...finally, there's ICI and Wellcome. FffPharmaceuticals, of course, are only a relatively small part of ICI but they are a significant player in heart drugs. Wellcome traditionally specialises in vaccines, which we don't cover, except to a minor extent. They're currently the subject of huge excitement because of their treatments fo...for herpes and HIV. Zovirax is the herpes drug and Retrovir the HIV treatment. Retrovir has some nasty side effects, such as anaemia, and, although it may retard the onset of Aids a smidgen, I'll bet my balls that it won't cure it; but they're starting to use it together with Zovirax on HIV patients with some early signs of promise. Fo...fo...for good measure they sometimes throw in Pentamidine, which is made by fie...fie... Fisons, and is thought to protect Aids patients against pneumonia, which is actually what often kills them."

"What about Fisons itself, Dr Aladyce?" It was Charlotte Mulder's first contribution. "Are they a potential bidder?"

"I doubt it, my dear," George instinctively replied in the tones he would use towards any young lady, not realising that this dark and deliciously tanned creature did not consider herself anybody's 'dear'. "They're a bit player these days. Intal, their anti-asthma drug, had a good run; but their new one, Tilade, is proving a disappointment. Any other questions?"

"Yes, Dr Aladyce." It was the unctuous Ben Silkin. "Are we doing no research into Aids?" he enquired, with an already proprietorial air.

"A little bit; but viruses are not really our baa...baa...bag."

Ben Silkin looked conspicuously blank.

Rod King had told Peter that George Aladyce had been almost as irritated as Jock Enderby by the way that Hennessy had shoved his new mate down their throats. He now took the opportunity to show up his lack of expertise.

"Would it help if I explained the diff...iff...ifference between a bacterium and a virus?"

"Oh, enormously," exclaimed Silkin.

"Shit and derision," muttered Enderby quite audibly from the far end of the table.

"Pathogens - that is agents that cause disease - are," Aladyce began, with the resigned air of a schoolmaster conducting a first year biology class, "made up of bacteria and viruses. Not all bacteria are harmful; in fur...fur...fact we're all fur...fur...full of them and most are absolutely tickety-bur...bur...boo. But all bacteria are independent organisms - and they're many hundreds of times the size of a virus - so you can grow them in an appropriate medium and, when they are harmful, you can attack them. That's what antibiotics do.

"But viruses are tiny organisms which invade cells and become a part of them. They require the medium of living tissue. So, to attack a virus, you also have to attack the patient. Bacterial diseases are things like wound infe...fe...fections, some sorts of gangrene, tetanus, anthrax, cardiac infe...fections, diseases of the respiratory tract like tuberculosis, scarlet fe...fe...fever, diphtheria, pneumonia, whooping cough, intestinal infe...fe...fections such as tyfoy...foy...phoid and cholera, infe...fections of the urinary tract like our old friend gonorrhoea, general infe...fections like bubonic plague; and there are also bacterial diseases of the central nervous system like septic meningitis. Altogether a pretty gee...gee...genial and treatable bunch.

"Viruses are much sneakier bastards - smallpo...po...pox, chicken pox, herpes, hepatitis, measles, German measles, mumps, poliomyelitis, rabies, yellow fee...fe...fever, lassa fe...fever and influenza and the common cold. Fo...fo...for these diseases the only really efe...fe...fective treatment is vaccination. A number of these bug...bug...buggers have been all but cur...cur...kiboshed now; but it is ballsachingly diff...if...ifficult to make vaccines against some of them. Fo...fo...for example influenza and the common cold. There are many, many varieties of these diseases - what we call antigenic drift - and the vaccine fo...fo...for one variety often will not work against another.

"HIV, the disease which leads to Aids, Mr Silkin," he concluded, with little attempt to disguise the patronising tone, "is a virus."

"Thank you, Dr Aladyce; but it's clearly going to make a lot of money for the company that finds a cure, or even a treatment. You can't deny that it's doing wonders for Wellcome's share price. Can't we have a bit of that action?"

"Chairman," George sighed, "have we got time for a f...f...few minutes on HIV and Aids?"

"Of course, George. I think it would be useful for our advisers, as well as for Mr Silkin - indeed for all of us."

"Very well. To date there have been about 150,000 cases of Aids worldwide and about half of those who have caught it are already dead; the rest will be in the relatively short term. The World Health Organisation is for...for...forecasting that there may be a million cases by 1991. If so, there'll be god knows how many by the end of the century. It appears to have started in central Africa and is spreading there like hot butter. The two things that are certain about the f...fur...future progress of the disease are that the vast majority of those who catch it are going to be very per...per...poor and that any treatment is going to be very expensive. Instinctively I don't like the thought of spending vast amounts of money compee...peeting with the rest of the world in the search for a drug that most patients aren't going to be able to afford; and who are blessed with rulers who are too busy fur...fur...filling up their Swiss bank accounts and buying guns so that they can blow the shit out of their oppo...po...ponents to give a toss about the odd fur... fur...few hundred thousand deaths amongst the general populace. The risk reward ratios are all wrong; and if, against all the odds, we were to succeed, there is then great scope for making oneself unpopular by charging a fur...fur...fancy price fur...for it. It may sound harsh but we're in business to make money - not to make people better. If the two coincide, so be it. If not, too bad. We'll leave it to someone else."

The good Samaritan, Hennessy, nodded his approval to George's charitable interpretation of the company's mission statement.

"In principle HIV is a simple virus and quite difficult to catch," George went on. "You can pipi...pick up some viruses at twenty paces. By comparison the methods by which HIV is most often transmitted - fu...fu...fornication, injection by drug users and buggery - all strike me as pretty invasive procedures. There are, however, three difficulties with HIV. Fur...fur...first, the virus is a poor replicator of itself, so that when it multiplies it tends to produce something that looks slightly diff...if...ifferent every time. That means it can be like lots and lots of versions of the common cold all racing around inside the same body. Second, it is what we call neurotropic - that is it can get into the brain and the central nervous system and go into hiding there fo...fo...for years and years before it decides to become active. Third, the natural human immune response, which it generates like any other virus, is, as far...far...far as we know, never sufficiently powerful to fie...fie...fight it off. Vaccines work by introducing a part of the virus - an antigen - into the body to trick it into producing an immune response - antibodies - so that, when the real McCoy turns up, the body is able to see it off. But, if the human body is incapable of resisting HIV, what the blue blazes is the immune response which the vaccine must be designed to trigger? Nobody's even remotely close to the answer to that one.

"What Wellcome is doing is as different to a cure as shit is from sugar. Retrovir is an anti-viral which attempts to suppress the virus. The sales are tiny so fa...fa...far; but Zovirax, which they use fo...fo...for herpes and shingles, has had some success.

"And, of course, every crank and crook in the business is trying to climb on the bandwagon. There was even some east european ex cycling champion who defe...fe...fected during the Tour de France back in the fi...fi...fifties who was pe...pe...peddling - aha that's good for a cyclist isn't it? - peddling some wonder cure a while back.

"Okay?"

"Not quite," persisted Silkin, to another loud groan from Lord Enderby. "You mentioned that we are doing a little bit of our own research. Why is that if you're so sceptical?"

"It's like this, Mr Silkin: there are vast amounts being spent round the world on Aids and ninety-nine point nine nine nine per cent of it is going to be wasted - pissed against the wall - but one or two pee... pee...people might get lucky eventually. I take the same attitude to it as I take to the fur...fur...football pools - if you don't play, you can't win - but if you wager twenty-five thousand quid every week, you can't win either."

"And what exactly are we doing?"

"Well, we've got a small team in one of our labs doing some research on monkeys."

Peter detected Elspeth stiffening in her chair. Oh, shit, he thought, she's not a fucking anti-vivisectionist as well.

George noticed it too but ploughed on regardless. Not even he regarded Elspeth as forming part of the 'my dear' category.

"They're doing some work on SIV - simian immunodefi.. ficiency virus. HIV stands fo...for human immunodefi...fi... ficiency virus - did I tell you that? The two are very similar but no one knows if they're the same. You wouldn't want to try to catch it from a monkey, would you? By any of the usual methods, eh, Rod?

"Anyway, our people have been trying to develop vaccines to inject into macaque monkeys. The technique is pretty tricky. You have to take the SIV virus and sort of cut away bits of it until you think you have something diffifferent enough not to cause the disease but similar enough to set off the creation of ef...ef...effective antibodies. After vaccinating the monkeys, you expose them to the disease" - a gasp from Elspeth - "to test their resistance. We were getting along quite fay... fay...famously until a month or two back when one of the little buggers who hadn't even been exposed to the disease went down with it. The implication, of course, is that he got it from the vaccine. Back to the drawing board."

"Any other questions for George?" Hennessy enquired.

"Well, just one more," said Silkin. Jock Enderby rose massively to his feet and set off noisily in the direction of the gents. "Are we doing any research into cancer. That would be another winning cure, wouldn't it?"

"Bloody miraculous, Mr Silkin. Quite honestly, whatever they tell you, there is very little known about most types of cancer. Sure, smoking can do your lungs in and salt your stomach; but with most cancers, they don't know what starts it, they don't know what stops it, they don't know why it sometimes goes away on its own and they don't know why some treatments work sometimes. It's probably all down to genes; but I put it in the 'too hard' pi...pi...pile At the moment it's more of a diagnostic and surgical problem. And that's one for the sawbones, not the pharmacists."

"Thank you, George," said Hennessy. "Peter, what else do you want to do this morning?"

"I think we should just have a discussion about the desirability of raising our profile by announcing that we believe that someone may be assembling a stake, or leaking the information, if that looks the better course. That was the final item on the agenda for this morning; so we ought to be able to get away by lunchtime."

Maureen had just bustled her way round the door with a note which she put in front of Peter as Christopher Hennessy continued: "Peter, could you please summarise for us the arguments for and against making this public. Whether we do so formally or informally is a tactical matter on which we should take Mr Wordsworth's advice."

"I think the discussion may be superfluous, Christopher. There's a message from your secretary to say that a director of Grossmanns called Gillian Wilkinson has just been on to her to say that she has Lord Evans of BMP with her and could you ring her back urgently."

"Do you think they're about to announce an offer?"

"I doubt it. A bid would normally come first thing in the morning. I suspect they're going to ask for a meeting. We'd better find out. Elspeth, can you find us a meeting room with a phone with an extension piece? Any of the ones down this side of the corridor would do. Gentlemen, could the rest of you please hang on here a moment. We'll send out for sandwiches if we're going to go on beyond one o'clock."

Elspeth was back in a few seconds with a messenger who led the way for Christopher and Peter down the passage to one of the smaller meeting rooms. It was more modest but tasteful, with two nineteenth century views of Greenwich, one looking down towards the Naval College and the other looking upwards through the Park to the Observatory, a round meeting table and a fine antique sideboard, both in dark mahogany. The telephone stood on a smaller table in the corner and the two men drew up chairs around it. Peter tapped in the number.

"Ms Wilkinson's office," came the reply.

"It's Peter Davenport, Dundas Brothers. Could I speak to her, please?"

"She's in a meeting right now," her secretary replied, as they all did upwards of a dozen times a day. "Could I get her to call you back?"

"I think you'll find that she would like to be interrupted. Please tell her I have Mr Hennessy with me."

"Please hold on."

A moment later Gillian Wilkinson was on the line. The community of corporate advisers in the City was relatively small but Peter had not encountered her before. Her voice was deep - in other circumstances and other moods, he afterwards thought that he might have found it almost sexy - but businesslike. They exchanged a little protocol before agreeing to put their principals on the line simultaneously. Peter and Christopher swapped receiver for earpiece in a ritual that was no doubt being mimicked a few hundred yards away at Grossmann's offices in Gresham Street.

Arthur Evans was jovial, good-humoured, unthreatening but nevertheless determined in a busy sort of way. Peter and his client had agreed to play for time and try to put any meeting off for a day or two if possible, simply so that they might disrupt any predator's plans. Christopher was full of "the need to seize the initiative" - a rather forlorn hope in Peter's view, having had George's confirmation of the continuing gaps in the product pipeline to reinforce Rod's gloomy prognostication on the immediate outlook for profits. In any event it was to no avail. Arthur Evans would not hear of putting off till tomorrow what could be done today and it was no use pretending that the parties were not already encamped less than half a mile apart. It was agreed within minutes that battle would be enjoined, in the most gentlemanly way, on the Brothers' turf, at three o'clock that afternoon. Lord Evans would be accompanied only by his merchant banking advisers. He had no objection to Dr Aladyce and Mr King being present, together with

Dundas Brothers; but he hoped that Christopher would restrict the participants to that extent.

The saving grace of a hastily convened working lunch at 69 Gracechurch Street was that the kitchens up on the seventh floor, whilst for other purposes competent enough to dispense adequate fare, were deemed incapable of producing a few sandwiches at short notice without disrupting their primary duties. Since the sandwiches which they produced officially, at a minimum of forty-eight hours' notice, were a dire reversal of the proper amalgamation of thinly-sliced bread and generous filling, everyone was only too happy to send out to Birley's for the real thing.

Over curried turkey with mango chutney, prawn mayonnaise, avocado and crispy bacon, brie with redcurrant jelly and, for Peter, a single forced half-round of smoked salmon, and with the benefit of near-certainty now over the identity of their would-be bridegroom, they tossed around a few more ideas. The product fit with BMP, even for George, was undeniable, though, as a professional scientist, he thought their research effort to be beneath contempt and their attachment to what he considered quack remedies and old wives' pills and potions bordering on the offensive. Christopher airily embraced this tack with what appeared to be genuine confidence that the "superior quality" of Pitcairn's reputation would see off such an aggressor. Peter could hardly believe that he didn't realise that, at the end of the day, it was only the quality of profits that mattered and that the institutions would sell out any other quality for a sufficient quantity of dough. With Martin Lampard's gruff and belligerent support, Peter was keen to raise the temperature through an immediate cautionary announcement; but Christopher was adamant that the chances of dissuading BMP from unilateral action were good enough for it to be unwise to admit that Pitcairn might be in play.

"But, Christopher, we have to assume that they're sitting on fifteen per cent of your equity already; and, that being so, nothing you can say this afternoon is going to dissuade them," argued Peter.

"If this jobber's trick works as you say it does, Peter, they'll still be able to pull back without risking public exposure when they see how determined we are to resist. Anyway, we can ask them whether they have a commitment, Peter. They could hardly lie to us outright.

And if, as you fear, they are already committed, we can get out an announcement to the Stock Exchange before they're back at their desks. We've got the text all agreed."

Peter knew this was nonsense. The meeting would most likely drag on beyond the close of Stock Exchange business. And, if BMP did not get what they wanted, they might well launch their offer tomorrow morning; but he lacked the will to argue. The week-end's catastrophe had sapped his energy and he was feeling physically unwell.

"More to the point, Peter, you've seen these discussions before. What's their likely approach? What do we need to be prepared for?"

"The normal line follows the rabbit stratagem and I'll be surprised if this is any different."

"The rabbit, Peter?"

"Rationalise, admire, bribe, threaten. Rabbit. I've told you that I don't believe there's a chance that these people will pull back; but, if they stop before they get to the stage of threatening to go over your heads to your shareholders, you'll know that they lack resolve. We'll see."

The meeting broke up shortly after two-thirty, though Jock Enderby had not even stayed for a sandwich. Peter could not help speculating to himself that the old rogue was off to snap up some Pitcairn shares through some anonymous foreign trust. The same thought had in due course probably dawned on Ben Silkin, equally unscrupulous but less quick-witted, who left abruptly with a pile of untouched food on his plate fifteen minutes later. Peter kept Tim Phillips with him but sent the rest of his team back to their desks. He wanted a thorough review of the product and research overlap out of Stuart Robinson as soon as possible and some more detailed analysis of potential BMP offers from Charlotte. Elspeth could help with that if she wasn't still crying over the thought of macaques snatched from their mothers' breasts. Oliver needed to get working with Freddie Wordsworth on refining a specific public response to a hostile BMP offer. The rest of Pitcairn's advisers drifted off, sharing with Peter the certainty that another late night lay ahead.

*****

They arrived on the dot of three. Forewarned by ground-floor reception, he met them at the lift. She was tall for a woman, not far short of his own height despite the flattest of flatties, and absolutely shapeless. Arthur Evans, every bit as foursquare as his photographs, was right behind her, double-breasted jacket flapping unbuttoned and the toes of his polished black shoes pointing cockily outwards. A couple of Grossmann aparatchiks brought up the rear. Peter shook Evans's hand but not the others; then led them down the wide corridor to the board room where they completed the introductions.

"Mr Hennessy, I'm Gillian Wilkinson, Grossmanns." A slightly husky and, Peter could not help thinking, rather inappropriate voice. "May I introduce Lord Evans, the chair of BMP?"

The chair of BMP. The chair of BMP. What, Peter reacted, did this silly bitch think she was saying? Where did a presumably well-educated woman, earning her living in the private sector of a capitalist economy think she was doing when she came out with such pathetic horseshit? A chair, madam, he thought, is something on which to place your scrawny arse, and nothing else.

"Lord Evans," he intervened. "Christopher Hennessy, chairman of Pitcairn," he said, with an emphasis on the gender that was unmistakable. "And this is George Aladyce, chief executive, and Rod King, finance director. And my colleague, Tim Phillips. Please come and sit down. I suggest you take this side of the table."

They settled down opposite each other in a rather lop-sided configuration, Evans occupying the chair facing Hennessy and Gillian Wilkinson across the way from Peter. Her two henchman, pale and both prematurely grey, sat beyond her like ghostly shadows of each other. The three of them looked as though they had just emerged from a dusty and sunless cellar to which they had been confined for months past. By contrast, the ruddy Arthur Evans looked the picture of health. Resolute and statesmanlike but cordial and unpretentious, he began.

"I think that, having asked for this meeting, I should set the ball rolling. First of all, may I thank you for agreeing to see us. We are all very busy people and I therefore want to come straight to the point. We have been doing a great deal of thinking about the structure of our industry in recent months and I should like to take the opportunity, if I may, to share our conclusions with you."

Peter tore a sheet from the notepad in front of him and wrote a small 'R' on the blank piece of paper. He slid it a few inches to his right where Christopher, sitting next to him, alone could read it. He noticed Gillian Wilkinson watching his every movement, like an attentive bird of prey.

"We are, of course," Evans continued, "competitors in some fields - I'm thinking particularly of antibiotics - but in most areas our activities are merely complementary. We've both been taking a keen interest in the increasingly successful new treatments for diseases of the heart, though we're tackling the problem from different directions. We're hugely excited about the prospects for Avricor. We're encountering tremendous interest amongst the medical profession; but we also know from our own market analysis that the Ace inhibitor that you're developing is going to provide some competition to Merck and Squibb that the public health authorities are going to find most welcome. We're also both diversifying our product portfolios away from our traditional strengths into other areas. As I'm sure you know, we're getting some interesting results out of a number of compounds which we've identified for the treatment of infectious diseases; and we're working with confidence on development of a new generation of broad-spectrum antibiotics for the eventual expiry of the Banzinin patents in 1992. We know something of your research programme and it would be our expectation that you too will be able to provide a broader range of products in due course."

There was, Peter detected, just the merest surviving lilt in Evans' speech to betray his boyhood celtic origins. But it might just have been what appeared to be a slightly nasal constriction to his voice, as though he had a cold. Perhaps he was simply carrying around a bit too much weight to breathe as easily as he should. He took another breath through his mouth, as if there were a blockage somewhere behind the bridge of his nose, and continued.

"We all know that our businesses face many challenges. I've been devoting a lot of my time over the past months to an analysis of the long-term trends and the development of an appropriate strategy for BMP. On the one hand, we all know that identifying, synthesising, testing and obtaining approval for new drugs is becoming a very long-drawn-out and costly process. On the other, there is justifiably huge excitement within our industry at the opportunities which our increasing understanding of the gene is throwing up. We face the prospect that, over the course of the next two or three decades, our industry is going to make astonishing progress in pushing back the frontiers of disease, of disability, indeed of the whole ageing process.

"The potential scale of it all is almost alarming and, quite frankly, my initial conclusion was that the resources required by way of capital investment and research were too large for BMP; that we were too small to be a survivor and that it would be best to break the business in two and sell the research-based ethical pharmaceutical business. That's when we started to do some analysis of potential purchasers of that business. The same conclusion kept on recurring. The most obvious partner, the best product fit, the most complementary research programme was Pitcairn's. Only one problem. If my analysis of the industry's potential was correct, you could barely afford to develop your own business, let alone shell out the cash to buy ours. You simply couldn't afford it without a huge rights issue, which would dilute earnings for your own shareholders, or a massive increase in your debts. Either way you'd end up weakened rather than strengthened and unable to exploit fully the potential of the acquisition.

"Then we suddenly saw the answer. Can you imagine what opportunities would lie in prospect in terms of scale and security and financial returns if we were to merge our two businesses. A broadly based ethical pharmaceutical business with strength and depth and breadth of both tried and tested products and new formulations. Behind that a low-cost generics business based out of our Asian factories; so that we could be both the first to replicate our expiring patents and a perpetual thorn in the side of our competitors. And finally a powerhouse for the OTC medicines that stuff the shelves of Boots and Superdrug and will shortly, mark my words, be commanding space in Sainsburys and Tesco and every supermarket in the land as well.

"That, gentlemen, is the vision which I want to propose to you today. I hope that you will find the idea as exciting as we do."

Evans sat back in his chair expansively, throwing his arms wide as if to welcome a response.

"You will have to forgive me Lord Evans," Christopher began in reply. "Naturally, we've been speculating here on the reason that you asked for this meeting; but I have to tell you that any ...rationale," he said, with emphasis on that word, "for a merger of our two businesses is something which has escaped us in our deliberations. Our own analysis of the future prospects for our industry in general, and for Pitcairn in particular, does not suggest that we have any reason to surrender our independence. Perhaps BMP lacks the length and depth of our experience in bringing the fruits of our research to market."

For a fraction of a second, Evans was stung, insulted, by the barb; but he recovered his good-humoured expression instantaneously. Peter had rehearsed the line with Christopher and was watching intently for the response. If not, he would have missed it. He was pleased by the reaction though he did not really know why. He couldn't tell whether Hennessy had seen it. Unfortunately, he had and it made him overconfident.

"We have more than adequate resource to pursue the profitable development of our business and could see some sense in tacking on your ethical pharmaceutical business if you wished to dispose of it."

Oh, shit! You cocky little bastard, thought Peter. That's a sentence that could come back to haunt us.

"The rest of your businesses would be of no interest to us. We are a pure research-based ethical pharmaceutical company and see no advantage in diversification into lower-margin products. That's why a merger makes no sense, as far as we are concerned. In any event, your use of the expression 'merger' implies a combination of the businesses without a premium over the current market price being attributable to our shareholders. We believe that the basis for valuation of a company like Pitcairn, which prospers exclusively as a result of ownership of its own unique technology, should be materially superior to that of BMP, with its lower quality OTC and generics businesses making up a substantial proportion of the group."

"By all means, Christopher. May I call you 'Christopher'?" Evans waxed bonhomously, "and please call me s'Arthur - Arthur," he corrected himself, not entirely used to his ennoblement as yet but adamant for years past that even close colleagues give him the benefit of his knighthood.

"I can't tell you how much regard we have for Pitcairn's research capabilities. Your laboratories are among the finest in the country."

Peter retrieved the slip of paper that lay on the table between his place and Christopher's and added a small 'A' to the single letter that was written there. Ms Wilkinson was transparently beside herself with curiosity, her eyes narrowing in a futile attempt to decipher, upside down, these mysterious hieroglyphics.

"In my own view, pound for pound," Evans continued, "Dr Aladyce here has been running a more productive research operation than even Glaxo. We would not be proposing this merger if that were not so. Indeed, we have the greatest admiration for Pitcairn's business. Your current market capitalisation is a churlish response on the part of the stock market to both your past achievements and your future prospects. It would certainly be our intention to recognise that under-valuation in the terms of the merger between our two companies."

Whilst Arthur Evans larded it on, Peter contemplated his own principal adversary. She was a prototype blue-stocking, ascetic and asexual. Her dark hair, perhaps even a touch ginger, was drawn back from her face so sharply that it looked almost painful and gathered together at the back of her head in an old-fashioned bun enclosed in a net. She looked, Peter thought, nearer forty than thirty and wore not a trace of make-up. Her face was well-shaped and she might even have the benefit of high cheekbones; but the skin was so pale as to appear chalky and he could not really tell. Her eyes, behind slightly tinted round spectacles of what Peter always thought of as the John Lennon variety, were steely grey. After her discomfiture with Peter's note to Christopher, she now sat spectacularly still and owlishly impassive as Evans began his charm offensive. As he did so, his attempt at a beatific smile matched with sweeping gestures was muted by the failure of his adviser to participate in the general good humour. Her gaze seemed destined to turn to stone any unfortunate on whom it alighted. While Evans sprawled in his chair, expansive and sincere, the woman to his right sat upright in hers. Her lips, also uncannily pale, never seemed destined to smile; and Peter was amused to see that the notebook which she held open in front of her in fingers as slender as talons, was covered in a tiny neat script which made it all too apparent that, far from discoursing with good-natured spontaneity, Arthur Evans was following from memory the text agreed in advance with the lady.

"We have no quarrel with what Pitcairn is doing - far from it. We don't want to merge our businesses so that we can change the way you do things. Christopher, we're very impressed by the way you and your new team are tackling the challenges that face you. There's a whole new dynamism and determination about Pitcairn since you took over - a slimmed-down management team, a sensible attack on the cost base, which, I am sure you will admit, your predecessor had allowed to get a little out of hand and, if I may say so, a recognition in Dr Aladyce becoming chief executive that it's research that's got you where you are rather than Charles Eve's fancy footwork on the marketing front. We know that a premium would have to be paid to recognise all that you've done; but we're not afraid of that because we have absolute confidence in the synergies that would result from the merger."

Hennessy fortunately came back with what, though he would not have been able to recognise it, others would have called a straight bat. Despite the invitation to informality, he continued, Peter thought commendably, to address his opposite number with impeccable formality and had now reverted, after his earlier slip, to the previously agreed line.

"Lord Evans, I have to repeat that Pitcairn has no need of a merger to further its long term plans and the business is emphatically not for sale. If you have any proposals which you wish to make, then we will hear them out and I will convene my full board to give them due consideration."

"Come, come, Christopher. There's no call for alarm. We're not here to gobble you up," Evans came back jovially. "We're both professional businessmen. We know the rules. I wouldn't dream of trying to bypass the appropriate procedures; but I wanted to have the opportunity to talk to you face to face so that I could tell you why we think this merger is good for both of us and to explain where I would propose that you and your team would fit in. I'm talking about a genuine merger."

As Evans dropped his voice conspiratorially, Peter retrieved his slip of notepaper and added a small but prophetic 'B' to the two letters already written there.

Evans seemed unnerved for a moment by the procedure, rather like a bridge player trying to interpret an opponent's bidding exchange that he had never encountered before. Were they trying to rattle him? Or was he already rattled? He tried to ignore it and pressed on.

"I like the way you run Pitcairn with a tight-knit group of executive directors. What with all the heads of the business units, a chief executive, operations director and finance director, I'm saddled with six executives on BMP's main board apart from myself. They're frankly not all of them up to snuff. The principal reason that I'm here on my own is so that I can talk freely about the roles that I envisage for all of you without the presence of those who would find their positions shall we say 'threatened' as a result."

The joviality had gone now and he was getting serious. No longer sprawled in his chair, he sat upright with his thick arms and strong, stubby-fingered hands flat on the table either side of his papers. He was short, squat and square; fat certainly, but more barrel-chested than beer-bellied, though, to be honest, he had one of each. His neck, compressed and thick, was almost non-existent so that his head appeared to sit like a gymnasium medicine ball on the broad flat shelf that was his shoulders. He exuded suddenly the reputation that surrounded him, the truculent self-confidence of the playground bully now matured into the genuine commercial article - the fully-fledged corporate thug.

He was almost completely bald save for a dark grey tonsure cut down almost to stubble length. His face was round and ruddy, a slight glistening of sweat on pitted skin, the legacy of juvenile acne. His mouth was wide but thin-lipped so that it formed a straight gash from one side of his face to the other; and when he smiled the gash did not turn up at the corners, but simply became larger and opened a fraction so that he looked rather like a humanoid tortoise.

But it was his eyes that held Peter's attention. The whites were almost non-existent and the pupils so large and brown and dead that one would hardly have disputed, had they not moved as only the eyes of the sighted do, that he was actually blind.

Peter looked at those eyes and that smile and recalled the title to his picture on *The Times'* leading business page on the day of his ennoblement - the Lord of the Rings. Peter thought that what he saw now before him was more like the face of Gollum.

"Mr Hennessy, I want you to be deputy chairman of the new group. I'm intending to retire at the Annual General Meeting in June

1989 when I'll be near as dammit sixty-five. I don't see a successor amongst my people. I'd want Dr Aladyce as head of research, on the main board of course. Jack Beazley won't be around as head of the pharmaceutical division much longer. It looks as though he has leukaemia. And I propose that Mr King should be director of operations with responsibility for administration, personnel and legals as well as finance."

"And what of your existing directors of operations and finance?" It was Rod King's first and only intervention.

"They'll go," replied Evans flatly. "They're both good men; but this is more important than either of them," he added, unaware that he was, by implication, damning Rod King with faint praise.

"I'm afraid your directors' service contracts are also out of line with ours. Given that, and the increased responsibilities which will come with the running of a substantially larger group, you'll all have to accept three-year rolling contracts at around eighty per cent above your current basic salaries. Unfortunately most of that will go to Mr Lawson; but of course you'll each have share options to the maximum permitted under Inland Revenue guidelines. In addition, of course, we provide a pension of two-thirds of final salary to main board directors on retirement, whatever their period of service. I hope you won't object to that," he added, glancing briefly at George and Rod, confident that, whatever Hennessy's own rumoured wealth, he might at least drive a wedge between him and his more modestly placed salaried colleagues.

Whether it was irritation at the accuracy of Peter's prediction or the crudity of Evans ruse, those glances were enough to make Hennessy flip. As far as he was concerned, it was for him to make the decisions and for his colleagues to endorse them. Evans was trying to give these men ideas above their station.

"Perhaps I did not make myself sufficiently clear, Lord Evans," Christopher came back stiffly. Peter could see that he was squaring up now like a little bantam against the prize Christmas turkey opposite, fixing Evans over the top rim of his oversized spectacles and trying to stare him down. "Pitcairn is not for sale and we have no desire to merge with BMP," he spat out pugnaciously.

"But, Mr Hennessy, you haven't even heard our terms."

"Indeed I have not, Lord Evans. All I've heard is a lot of flim-flam. I am not proposing that my non-executive directors, who are also busy men, should be gotten round to pass judgement on such bunkum."

"We are proposing, Mr Hennessy, five of our shares for every eight of yours. That's worth 360p per share for you, an increase of almost 37 per cent over the current market price."

Peter and Christopher had already agreed the response to that one. Anything less than 375p per share, a 43 per cent uplift, which would more or less constitute a knock-out punch, was to get the same undifferentiated derision. For a sighting shot, this was painfully close to that threshold; but Christopher could tell a porky with the best of them.

"Lord Evans, you're not even in the right ball-park. You give me no option. I shall have to speak to my non-executives now; but I can assure you that the response will be negative."

"I should be grateful if you would put it to them nevertheless."

"Very well. I can call a board meeting for Friday this week and let you know the answer next Monday morning."

Arthur Evans was at bottom a crude man; but, over his years in business, he had often heard and grown fond of an expression which appealed to him because, whilst veiled in a cloak of courtesy, it so obviously conveyed the meaning which was its opposite. He had given up on Hennessy and he used it now,

"With respect, Mr Hennessy, I think this matter is more urgent than that. It would be inviting a leak to allow this matter to drag on for another week. Don't you agree, Mr Davenport?" he added, aware that there was another wedge that he might try to drive home.

"I don't see the urgency," Christopher came back before Peter could reply. "You have proposed a merger and we have rejected it," he said, positively inviting the threat which Peter was at that moment initialing on the slip of paper that had passed between them.

"Mr Hennessy, we believe very strongly that a merger is in the best interests of the shareholders of our two companies. We are so firmly of this view and that the institutions would support it that we may feel forced to go over the heads of the Pitcairn board directly to your shareholders."

"That is always your prerogative, though I think you would be ill-advised to take that course," Christopher rejoined spikily, beginning to enjoy himself again.

"My own feeling, Mr Hennessy, is that your institutional shareholders, who have not enjoyed the best of returns in recent years, would find it difficult to understand why you had declined talks with a company that was offering to put you in the forefront of the growing heart drugs market, solve the problem of the forthcoming expiry of your Myodin patents by adding Banzinin to your antibiotic portfolio and give them a more than one-third increase in the value of their holdings. And allow them, through their stake in the enlarged company, to benefit from the improved growth prospects. But so be it," he said, turning to Ms Wilkinson as he pushed back his chair.

"One moment, Lord Evans, if you'll permit me." It was Peter. "Could you please tell us if BMP holds any shares in Pitcairn?"

"What's the relevance of that?" It was Gillian Wilkinson. Again that voice. Husky. Perhaps she smokes twenty a day. If you closed your eyes, you might almost think she was feminine. But he had hit a nerve.

"It might influence our views on whether we ought to put out a cautionary announcement following this conversation."

"Well, I don't see why it should," she snapped back.

"In any event we don't." It was Evans again.

"Are there any commitments to purchase shares?"

"No."

"Any arrangements with holders of shares?"

"Mr Hennessy, would it surprise you if I said that I was beginning to find your adviser's tone offensive?" said Arthur Evans, rising red-faced to his feet.

"Any options to take up shares or orders outstanding for the purchase of shares," Peter continued.

"I think I have answered all the questions on this subject which are appropriate. Good-day, gentlemen. We'll see ourselves out."

"Well, that's seen them off and no mistake," beamed Christopher confidently, when they'd gone. "What do you think, Peter?"

"They'll bid tomorrow morning," he replied flatly, openly endeavouring to prick the bubble of this man's absurd high spirits with his discourtesy. "You'd better tell Enderby and Silkin. I'll talk to Justin, Julian and Freddie."

*****

Hennessy was barely willing to contemplate the seriousness of Pitcairn's position; but Davenport finally persuaded him to put in place some simple contingency arrangements. George would stick to running the company, merely to be consulted as and when necessary. Christopher insisted on taking personal charge of the defence "if that unlikely scenario were to come about". Rod would assist him, which meant that he would do all the work. That suited Peter fine. In the event of a bid, they would meet daily in St James's Square at 8.30am; but, for the moment, Christopher would not vary his schedule. The driver would pick him up next morning as usual at 8.15. He would be in the office around a quarter to ten.

While Hennessy phoned Silkin and Enderby, Peter returned to his office to call the other advisers. His *FT* still lay unopened on his desk and Maureen had put the day's *Evening Standard* on top of it. While he made his calls, he glanced through the papers. The dollar seemed to have been in free fall for weeks but the central banks, sensing the opportunity to spring a bear trap, had used the first day of the new trading year to intervene on a massive scale. Freddie was unimpressed.

"Farting against thunder, m'boy. Mark my words. No more impact than pissing in the Pacific."

"Any whispers on the Street of Shame, Freddie?"

"Well, m'boy, a little bird tells me that Grossmanns have had it suggested to that acerbic little hack, Peter Oborne, at the *Standard*, that there might be some advantage in making an early appearance at his desk tomorrow morning."

"Have you nothing to cheer me up, Freddie?"

"Did you see that the leaderene became the longest serving prime minister this century yesterday?"

"Is that good news, Freddie?"

"It must bring us a bit closer to the end of her reign, old boy. She's only beatification to go for now!"

By the time Peter returned to the board room only Rod was left there. He was on the phone to his secretary.

"What do you think, Rod?" Peter said when he finished.

"It's pretty clever timing from Evans. He's right about the need for consolidation in the industry and he's caught us with our fingers up our bums. We can't produce any real growth until our new drugs come on song. In reality that's two to three years. Next year we'll be lucky to hold profits steady where they are. Is there anything going for us?"

"Well the institutions may still feel obliged to give your diminutive chairman the opportunity to prove himself. After all, they put him there."

"Then we'd better make sure they don't discover the truth. To be fair, though, he seems to have done a pretty good job negotiating your fees."

"Really? I haven't seen my chairman yet."

"There's no flat fee. One-eighth per cent if you lose, which looks a fortune to a farthing odds-on, and three-quarters if you win. Sale to a white knight though only counts a quarter per cent. I wouldn't start spending your bonus just yet. And there's another thing too. Hennessy's joining the board of Dundas as a non-executive. By the way, has anyone told you, you look awful?"

Wednesday, 6 January, 1988

To give him his due, Christopher Hennessy was already in his mock-baroque boardroom with the gilt-framed mirrors and the ridiculous ornate chandeliers poring over that morning's papers with Rod King when Peter arrived at 8.20. The latter had already spent an hour at his desk at 69 Gracechurch Street. It seemed to him that he had still not slept a wink - though, in truth, his relentless tossing and turning must have been interrupted from time to time; but he was bone weary with emotional distress and furry-tongued with the whisky that had failed to provide him with either solace or slumber. His every attempt to contact Sophie had been in vain. Her phone just rang and rang.

Bill McAdam, habitually hyper-active, was in his office when Peter arrived shortly before seven. As ever the master of the succinct phrase, he called to him through his open door as Peter passed.

"What the fook is this fer a fookin press?"

The simplest way to describe Bill McAdam was to say that he was like something you had stepped in, accidentally. Some people said that he was a man you could respect if you could bring yourself to overcome your understandable distaste and get to know him properly. Peter had made what efforts he could; but for many of the directors of Dundas Brothers, predominantly products of the upper or at least professional classes, there were still barriers too high in the Britain of the 1980s for social intercourse with such a creature to be possible. To them he was quite simply a fat, working-class, Geordie slob. To be sure, he was obese and sweaty, foul-mouthed and foul-tempered, scruffy and quite probably dirty. He was very short - less than five feet six - and all of sixteen stone. His greasy-looking greying, unbrushed hair hung curling over his collar and one always had the suspicion that parts of his latest meal lay concealed in his unkempt grey moustache, tinged orange as if with rust. His flushed cheeks were flecked with the broken blood-vessels of the serious consumer and his eyes were bloodshot and bulging. The belt of his trousers strained at the lower reaches of the pot that hung over it and his perpetually wrinkled double-breasted jacket flapped open for the simple reason that it was no longer possible to button it.

He was, as one might have surmised, not a product of the Brothers but had been recruited on an iconoclastic whim by Johnathan Tudor, its chief executive, from Bear Sterns, where he was head of M&A, specifically to take over from Cyril Bishop when he retired. There were other directors of Dundas's corporate finance department, notably Graeme Kent, who had harboured ambitions for the succession; but Peter was too young to be among them and was, in any event, contemptuous of their claims, and particularly those of the cunt Kent, as he was commonly labelled.

Peter had furthermore found himself on one previous occasion on the opposite side of a negotiation with McAdam, then still at Bear Sterns, who was conducting a controlled auction of some UK subsidiaries on behalf of an American client. Though McAdam had been as hard as nails, greedy and abusive, he had proved to be not only a formidably clever negotiator but also scrupulously honest in circumstances in which Peter would have guaranteed his own colleagues to be deceitful to a man. He told the representatives of all the potential buyers that he would shaft them all backwards, front and sideways to get the highest price for his client - and he did exactly that.

Bill had been with Dundas now for just a year, resigning his position at Bear Sterns in unheard of fashion before rather than after the bonus round. He had been thought for some time to be depriving himself of a small fortune in the process but it was discovered, in due course, that he had been more than compensated by a staggering golden hello. He had extraordinary energy for a man who was so clearly digging his own grave with his teeth and was obviously going to run the department in a very different way to Cyril's traditionalist approach; but he made it clear that he considered 1987 to be Cyril's valedictory year and only the future to be his. That future held fears as well as fortune. Peter was sympathetic to Bill's desire to cast aside the parochialism of Dundas's present sphere of operations to go after European and American clients. He had put together an impressive plan for the first phase of that expansion and he had a vision for the subsequent phases which could not fail to enthuse the department behind his leadership. On the other hand, the large increase in personnel that he planned for 1988 and the huge uplift in fee income required to maintain profits in such circumstances was looking badly timed post crash; and the immensely specific targets to which each director was now being subjected were set in terms that made clear that the consequences of falling short were very specific indeed.

There were other jarring notes, not as yet sufficient to cast doubt upon his position, but unnerving nonetheless. First was his management style. As far as hours on the job and energy expended, he was without parallel in leading by example; but the bullying and abuse were already beginning to get to some of the juniors and his reluctance to delegate decisions on anything of importance irritated his fellow directors, used, under Cyril, to the exact opposite. Second was his judgement of people. He had brought in Hank Amadeo, who was as obvious a waste of space as Peter had ever seen, and had bludgeoned through his appointment on grounds of his "wide international experience" against the advice of his colleagues; and he now seemed intent on doubling the number of corporate finance directors by going on a recruitment drive amongst the senior managers of Lazards, Schroders, Rothschilds et al. Sybil Dunwoody had leapt to the task with enthusiasm and was now giving Bill daily briefings on the relative merits of the various targets, as if she knew the first thing about the business. Peter, who had a supernumerary role as co-ordinator of executive recruitment for the department, had tried in vain to persuade Bill that making directors out of people that Dundas's competitors, with first-hand knowledge, did not believe to be ready was no way to achieve excellence; but all that he had done was to cut himself off from the interviewing process altogether as Bill himself subsumed the role.

"What sort of a coont have yer goot andlin yer fookin PR to pick up fookin shite like this?" he spluttered, waving the back page of the *Financial Times* with its all-important Lex column above his head as Peter backtracked into his office.

"Hennessy fired Charles Barker just before Christmas, Bill. I've prevailed upon Freddie Wordsworth to take over at short notice. I grant it's a baptism of fire; but it could have been worse. *The Times* is reasonably kind."

"Fookin nooboody in the City reads the fookin *Times* any mair. Ye'd better get that oold fart to poot some fookin effort into the fookin Sundays. Thoose twats will still print any shite yer give 'em. Well, at least we'll start the year by pickin up a oomoongus fookin fee as yer sooddin client goos doon the swanny."

"I'm afraid not, Bill. It's three-quarter per cent for success but only one-eighth per cent for failure."

"One-eighth per fookin cent! What arsehool agreed to that?"

"It was negotiated directly between Hennessy and Sir James. Hennessy wanted us to be heavily incentivised. We're stuck with it now."

"Well, too fookin right we'll be incentivised. Pitcairn are as good as stooffed before we start. Ye'd better get the fookin white knights ridin oover the hoorizon and sharpish and we'll get our bluddy three-quarter's that way."

"White knights are worth only a quarter, Bill. Success means independence. That's the agreement."

"Jesus fookin wept. What is this fookin half-arsed outfit I've joined?"

Bill, Peter noted for future reference, was not at his most amenable first thing in the morning.

The office car had sped along Victoria Embankment in merciful contrast to the two lanes of traffic on the other side of the dual carriageway splashing their way towards the City through the blustery remnants of yesterday's bitter and torrential rain. The Volvo was held up at the lights just past Middle Temple where cars coming down from the Aldwych or round from the Howard Hotel crossed in front of them. As they waited there, a black cab swung right onto the inside lane of the embankment. A large swarthy man was sitting on the near side of the passenger compartment, his head turned away in conversation with a familiar profile of blonde hair cascading from a dark fur hat onto equally dark and furry shoulders. Peter, sitting on the nearside back seat with his open briefcase beside him, put down *The Daily Telegraph*. The lights changed and Sid, as ever briskly away, rapidly closed on the taxi. Their own lane of traffic was moving the faster and they

Richard Crick

were just coming alongside, Peter staring transfixed at the taxi, when the Mercedes in front of them slowed suddenly, signalling at the last moment to turn right towards the riverside entrance to the Savoy. Sid swore quietly under his breath, pushed his way across into the nearside lane to the blaring protest and customary anglo-saxon salutation of the driver of a Post Office van, and swung back again into the outside lane. The Volvo's bonnet was again level with the taxi's rear end as they passed Cleopatra's Needle, Peter still staring but not yet certain, as Sid slowed to turn right down Northumberland Avenue towards Trafalgar Square. As the taxi slipped onward down the inside lane towards Parliament Square Peter looked down at the newspaper on his knees. His hands were shaking uncontrollably.

"Peter's prepared a routine agenda for these morning meetings, gentlemen," Christopher began, "so we'll run through that before we turn to other matters. I am sure there will be lots of things to discuss today; but I'm intending that in future we'll be able to get away back to our separate desks within half an hour or so. The press is the first item. You'll be leading on that Freddie."

Over the course of the previous frantic day, Mr Wordsworth had become the familiar even of Christopher Hennessy. He had truly been a star to achieve any sort of balance in the press coverage; but it was depressingly clearly first blood to BMP just the same. Evans had telephoned Hennessy's office just before 8.30am. Fortunately his overpaid trophy secretary, who kept barely more punishing hours than Christopher himself, switched her lines through to what George Aladyce called his girl - though she was all of forty-five - when she went home, so that there had been someone there first thing to give Evans the number in Hennessy's car. By the time the two chairman had finished a courteous but frosty exchange, the announcement was already ticking up on the screen. Peter, with Tim at his shoulder, watched it flash up on the monitor beside his desk. As it did so, he read it over to Rod on the other end of the telephone.

The tone was insidiously more in sorrow than in anger, the token attempt to persuade Pitcairn's board to roll over converted overnight into a tragic failure on the their part to share BMP's vision to create a British pharmaceutical powerhouse that, unlike Glaxo under Paul Girolami, would both buy and research its way to market supremacy. The terms, at 3 shares of BMP for every 5 of Pitcairn, were less generous than had been mooted in the privacy of the Dundas Brothers' boardroom, but were nevertheless worth nigh unto a third above Pitcairn's closing price the previous evening. With a pro-forma profit and loss account set out at the back of the press release in notes for City editors showing no reduction in earnings per share for BMP shareholders, before even a penny of savings or synergies, it was clearly a sighting shot. The cash alternative of 327p, provided through Grossmanns underwriting BMP's shares at 545p each had clearly proved a doddle in the sub-underwriting market. The institutions knew that Evans was probably going to have to pay more to secure his prize; but they accepted him as a man who knew value for money and rewarded his inspiration with an unusual rise in the bidder's share price, dragging the value of the bid ominously upwards in its wake. Sure Pitcairn's shares still settled above the value of the offer, the market confident that there was more to come; but the margin was not large, and, in logic, rightly so. The need for a cash alternative had been triggered under the Take-over Code when BMP had also announced that they had acquired that morning 14.9 per cent of Pitcairn's shares at 327p per share. If institutions had been prepared to sell out at least a part of their holdings at such a price, even to get the ball rolling, they must be confident that Evans was not expecting to pay much more for the balance.

An hour after the bid was announced Grossmanns had the brokers' analysts assembled in Goldsmiths' Hall, around the corner from their offices. At 11.00 it was the turn of the financial press. By all accounts, Arthur Evans put up a pair of rollicking performances. Lex in the *Financial Times* compared the new bid with the Hoffmann-La Roche offer for Sterling Drug, announced 24 hours earlier under the title *Drug dealers.*

> *The Hoffmann-La Roche bid for Sterling Drug at $4.2 billion and the BMP bid for Pitcairn Pharmaceuticals at the equivalent of $4 billion are of similar size; but there the similarity ends. Whilst Sterling, like a small part of BMP, is primarily an OTC player, the BMP offer is in reality all about the rationalisation of two big research-*

based pharmaceutical operations. It is difficult to see what benefits a drugs giant like Hoffmann can imagine in taking a shy at the manufacturer of Panadol painkillers, Bayer aspirin and Phillips Milk of Magnesia; but BMP's logic is impeccable. Whilst there are no doubt drug companies on both sides of the Atlantic dusting off their files on Sterling and Pitcairn and there is no shortage of potential counter-bidders for either, BMP has chosen its target with microscopic precision. An under-performer against its sector for five years now and with a potentially damaging gap, which BMP's Banzinin would plug, between the expiry of its Myodin patents and its new generation of antibiotic products, Pitcairn looks hard-pressed to mount a convincing defence. True it has a promising new heart drug for the reduction of blood pressure due on the market next year; but this is just another area where its product range complements that of BMP, which is about to launch a treatment for the reduction of cholesterol. Pitcairn was claiming yesterday that BMP would be seeking to reduce the overall level of research expenditures with a view to maximising profit in the short term; but the more likely outcome is that maintained expenditure will increase the success rate once the two companies' research operations are combined. Certainly the new management of Pitcairn, installed by an institutionally supported coup last spring, has been doing all the right things so far and has earned the right to have its demands for independence given a fair hearing by its shareholders. For that reason alone the present bid is unlikely to succeed, but, given the undoubted synergies involved and the much superior rating of its own shares, BMP can afford to be generous enough to carry the day in the end.

"We can't deny that BMP have got away the first broadside as far as the press is concerned," Freddie began, "but even that Lex piece, though its conclusion is unfavourable, contains the two points we decided to major on in briefing the press yesterday afternoon. First, this is a new management that is turning the business around and selling out now will be making a gift of the benefits of that turnaround to BMP. And second, that BMP has a minuscule record in research with only one significant success - Banzinin. Almost everything else it sells or plans to launch is the fruit of the research of companies it has acquired.

"The Kenneth Fleet article in *The Times* has given our line almost equal coverage to that of BMP. Of course, I have to admit he's a sucker for arguments about maintaining Britain's place in the forefront of technology and inclined from time to time to favour the sort of interventionist strategy which is anathema to the Iron Lady's government.

"Inevitably BMP were in control of events yesterday and were able to take the initiative. We've taken some incoming fire but we haven't been holed below the waterline. I think these arguments we're using can stand some further elaboration, particularly for the week-end papers. Peter, are your people coming up with some chapter and verse on BMP's research record to support us?"

"Chairman, Freddie and I spoke about this last night and I've got Stuart and Elspeth working on it now. We're looking for two things. What products have they bought in rather than developed themselves? And what evidence is there when they have acquired companies in the past that the acquired research facilities have been closed or used to replace their own? The second line's going to be more difficult to support but we'll see what we can do. Justin's people may be able to help us with this; but that's a subject we'll come to later.

"But another thought occurs to me that's wider than the press coverage. If we can genuinely cast doubt on BMP's fitness to run a research activity that will be of national importance, can't we manufacture a case for sending this to the Monopolies Commission on public interest grounds? What do you think, Julian?"

"Well, as you know, that's not my branch of the law but I'll certainly talk to David Stephenson, my trade practices partner, about it. He's going to be primarily responsible for the OFT submissions."

"Okay, gentlemen, enough of that," Hennessy intervened, seeking to bustle the meeting along. "Justin, what's happening in the market?"

"Quite a lot of activity, Chairman, particularly in the June call options, and some in the shares themselves. Anything that comes available is being snapped up. Of course, Wagstaffs aren't doing any buying because the share price is above the value of the cash alternative. They're currently offered at 360p and bid 354p, which is exactly the current value of the share offer, but not in size. It mostly seems to be buying by the arbs; but Morgan Grenfell Securities have been particularly active."

"Do they represent anyone of significance, Peter?" Hennessy asked.

"No one obvious, Chairman, but one never knows which house a US or Continental buyer might use. But it would be very early days for an overseas buyer to be showing interest so soon."

"Well I think that brings us quite naturally to our submission to the Panel that Wagstaffs should be barred from acting as joint brokers to BMP. What news have you got on that Peter?"

"I saw Antony Beevor, the new D-G, late yesterday afternoon. I have to say he was pretty po-faced about our complaint. Said all the precedents were against us after a gap of more than six months. He promised me an answer this morning after he's pulled Wagstaffs in for a grilling; but he made it pretty clear that he'd come down against us unless we could come up with something unusual that they have by way of inside knowledge."

"What sort of justice is that?" Hennessy exploded. "This man Beevor is judge and jury in his own court. We must appeal to the full Panel over the heads of the executive. I've been reading up on the rules."

"Well, they haven't made a ruling yet; but I wouldn't advise an appeal even if it goes against us," Peter ventured. "There's no dispute about the facts. The only grounds for an appeal would be that the executive's judgement was at fault. We'd be casting doubt on their competence. We're going to have lots of occasions to need the Panel's impartiality over the coming weeks. I don't think this is important enough to be worth putting their noses out of joint before we start."

"We'll wait for the judgement. But I haven't finished with this one yet," Christopher rebounded with a note of defiance that Peter prayed was sufficient for him to have established his pugnacity in front of his advisers without in reality taking it any further.

They ploughed on for another hour. Rod King was to take responsibility for briefing the brokers' analysts. The Documents Committee, which would be responsible for drafting circulars to shareholders, would be chaired by Tim Philips, though Rod and Peter would attend when strategic matters were under discussion and Julian Corrigan would take responsibility for the legal appendices - what he referred to as the boilerplate. Rod would also chair the Presentations Committee, which would prepare the various set-piece expositions to be made to institutional shareholders but Christopher, who would make the presentations jointly with Rod, would also attend. Peter was authorised to engage Martin Conradi at Showcase Presentations to advise on the format of the presentations and prepare the material in the most striking format. The OFT committee would be chaired by David Stephenson and would, unusually, also contain George Aladyce in his role as head of research. Otherwise, he was exclusively to mind the shop. Rod would, of course, be responsible for profit forecasts, with the assistance of the auditors. And finally it was reluctantly agreed by Justin that one of his two star pharmaceutical analysts would be dragged over the Chinese Wall to join the defence team and provide expertise on the industry. Thereafter he would be banned from talking to Gourlay Gilfillan's institutional clients for the duration of the bid, an expensive sacrifice of expertise and potential commission income. No doubt Justin would ensure that his firm was richly compensated.

They broke up a bit after ten but Rod motioned to Peter, with Hennessy safely departed, that he would like a separate word. They went upstairs to Rod's embarrassingly opulent office and settled at his over-elaborate inlaid meeting table in the corner.

"Peter, as you suggested, I've had the registrars do some analysis on how Wagstaffs managed to assemble this shareholding - who were the sellers? - what was bought on which days? - who were the selling brokers? - what prices did they pay? And then I've had Justin's people provide figures for the volumes in the market on each day - and the market in the options. The registrars have been through the stock transfer forms as well as the register. A great wodge of paper arrived from them yesterday evening and I put one of the oiks in the accounts department on to trying to make some sense of it. I got him to try to trace in broad terms all purchases and sales of over 20,000 shares - where they came from and where they went. Maybe I set the level too low. Poor sod was up all night," he said, with a twinkle in the eye which denied any hint of sympathy. "By morning his eyes were going round in circles; so I don't know if the little shit's got it right, but I think we've got the pattern.

"They seem to have started buying on Monday, 30th November. That deal for 100,000 the previous Monday," he said, pointing at the schedule set out between them, "was not them - some woman or other. The market took a big dive on the 30th - almost five per cent - but our price only came off from 225p to 220p. The market stayed very fragile all that week and they picked up on average two per cent every day, more the first day, and only moved the price by the end of the week back to 225p. Since then, they've behaved very cautiously. The Footsie has gone from 1583 at the end of that week to 1790 now - that's an increase of 13 per cent - and our price has risen 16 per cent while they've accumulated another four or five per cent. Pretty clever, eh?"

"Wagstaffs were never accused of being fools."

"But there's something a bit curious in the options market. See here. The price in the June futures leapt against the market on that final Friday before they started buying and almost as much in the March expiries. I'm afraid I can't cope with these bloody theoretical option price valuations; but that looks out of kilter with the market to me. During the following days the price settled back to where it was before."

"Are there any other blips like that?"

"Not really. Well, there's one here on Monday this week, the day we met them. But I guess there were getting to be quite a lot of people in the know by that stage."

"Yes, well I wouldn't be surprised if Messrs Enderby and Silkin had something to do with that one."

"Are you serious?"

"Of course. Those chaps are old-fashioned bankers. It was more or less traditional to do a bit of insider dealing in their day. Didn't you see the way they shot out of that meeting like greyhounds out of a trap? That blip at the end of November is probably much the same sort of thing - just the partners of Wagstaffs getting their personal accounts organised ready for the off."

"God, you are a cynical bastard," Rod said with a chuckle.

"Okay, now who's been doing the selling?"

"Well, it's pretty well spread. Mercury, Flemings, Hill Samuel, Schroders, Morgan Grenfell - they've all lightened their holdings - and your people too."

"Basically the active fund managers. The trackers won't have sold, of course, and I doubt if much will have come out of the unit trusts and the life funds. What's that?" Peter said, pointing at the page. "Isn't that that woman again?"

"You're right. That's very strange. I hadn't noticed that. She sold the whole lot on the Friday," Rod hesitated a moment, checking the other papers, "just four days after she bought them and, on the following Monday, the shares found their way to Wagstaffs - there, their first purchase."

He stopped again, going backwards and forwards between the schedules.

"Let's see. She bought 100,000 at 228p on the 23rd and sold them again at 222p on the 27th. She probably didn't even make it on to the register. Let's see," he said, pulling a great sheaf of paper off the floor and onto the table. "Here's the print-out for the end of the final stock exchange account before Christmas." He leafed through it briefly. "No, she's not there. Might have been on the previous one; but I didn't get that one dug out. What do you make of that, Peter?"

"I don't know. It's a curious way to generate a capital gains tax loss of £6,000, plus commissions and stamp duty - about ten thousand quid all told. And a pretty big punt for an individual - best part of a quarter of a million at stake. I wonder if there's anything in it. Mrs Lindsay Cunningham - I wonder who she is."

"Can we find out?"

"Who did she deal through? Was there a broker's name on the transfer form?"

"Sharps. They're regional aren't they?"

"Yes. Birmingham based. The Greasy Chip," Peter mused.

"What are you talking about?"

"Oh, he's just one of their dealers. Les Goodenough. Colourful character."

"Do you know him? Would he tell you?"

"Only by reputation. He's a legend; and I'm absolutely certain he wouldn't."

"How are we going to find out then?"

"We need some private eyes. Are you prepared to defy your chairman?"

"If I can get away with it."

"How about this? I was going to suggest that you ought to get your offices here electronically swept on a weekly basis for the duration of the bid. It's just a precaution against bugs. We do it all the time in Gracechurch Street. I know some people who could do it for you. They're called Harrington Ingram. Quite respectable .... I think. They could also track down Mrs Cunningham. Her address should be on the transfer form. I'll get it off the registrars. You're responsible for clearing all the professional bills. One lady to be traced shouldn't add much to the cost. If I get them to send their invoices to me, I can pass the cost on to you as out-of-pocket expenses."

"Okay. I should be able to clear the anti-eavesdropping stuff with the dwarf. He loves that sort of drama. Make him feel important."

The telephone on Rod's desk began to ring.

"Shit, I told her not to put anyone through."

It kept ringing as his secretary put her head round the door.

"It's for Mr Davenport," she said, "Tim Philips. Yes, Tim, he's still here," she said picking up the instrument and holding it out for Peter as he came over. He pressed the button on the squalk box and put the receiver down.

"Yes, Tim. I'm with Rod. You're on the blower."

"The Panel's turned down our request for Wagstaffs to be declared off-side. No basis for believing they had inside information that was either up-to-date or relevant. And it was not as if they resigned in order to act for BMP. We fired them. Thereafter, within reason, the Panel say they were free agents."

"Very sensible, Tim. That man Beevor could go far. Wykehamist, of course. And New College. Already seems better than that Warburgs wallah Walker-Howarth, of blessed Guinness memory. Thanks."

"Oh, and Peter. Freddie Wordsworth wanted a word."

"Okay, Tim. I'll give him a bell."

Peter dialled Freddie's private line as if Rod's office were his own, but this time kept the receiver in his hand until he could be sure that it was a conversation Freddie wished to share with his client. Having discreetly done so, he again pressed the hands-free button and replaced the receiver.

"Rod, Freddie here. I was just saying to Peter that I was turning this OFT point over in my mind on the way back in the cab and I think we need to open up another front. We can insinuate the idea into the press over the week-end by casting doubt on BMP's credentials as a research outfit - I'm just thinking whether we should try to pull the editor of one of the Sundays over on to our side by promising him exclusivity on a weekly nugget in return - and the legal boys will advise you how to get those arguments over to the officials at the Office of Fair Trading. But, if we're going to get this ship moving, we need the political wind blowing in our sails. Frankly, that's not my bag. Though I've one or two friends amongst them, as a breed, I hate these politicos. They're none of them sailors apart from old Ted Heath, and he's got about as much influence with Thatcher's Government as the shade of Karl Marx."

"We think you're right Freddie," Peter replied, picking up on Rod's nodding agreement. "Do you have anybody in mind?"

"Well, I hate to say it, m'boy, but I suspect that the best man, if I can use that word, for dealing with our slimy legislators is that old queen John Addey. I don't know whether he still makes the claim, but he used to say that he could deliver you a monopolies reference if you asked him nicely."

"Does he still have those curious offices in Wardrobe Chambers, between St Paul's and The College of Arms?"

"I believe so. I always thought it was a wonderfully precious address for him. But please don't ask me to accompany you. It's particularly badly lit at this time of year and I always feel fortunate to get out of there without being sodomised. We don't have much in common, John and I, and I thought I'd never say that I'd like to have him behind me; but, in this case it might just be true."

*****

A gale was blowing up again, the wind and rain swirling off the blackened condemned-looking buildings on either side of the narrow street and making wild cyclonic patterns under the old-fashioned streetlamps as the taxi drew up. An umbrella would have been inside out in a trice. Peter paid off the cabbie through the sliding window between the driver and passenger compartments and made a run for it. He was already dripping when he reached the safety of Addey's hallway. He dabbed at his face with a handkerchief as the secretary took his khaki Burberry trenchcoat.

"Why, Peter, how nice to see you," Addey, holding open the door of his office, exclaimed as if Davenport had made no prior arrangement. "We simply don't see enough of you nowadays, darling. We thought you'd become too grand for us."

Since Margaret Thatcher had resurrected the royal 'we', John had embraced it with a new enthusiasm. He ushered Peter into the room, more salon than office, with deep brocaded sofas in burgundy, piped with gold, a huge Persian carpet in the same hues covering most of the flagstone floor and solid brass table lamps with burgundy shades, also edged in gold. One stood on a small mahogany desk in the corner, which was otherwise entirely clear apart from a telephone. Addey picked it up.

"Boris, Mr Davenport's here if you'd like to join us. And do pick up a bottle of shampoo from the fridge on the way, there's a dear.

"Brilliant boy that; brilliant. You'll love him," John pronounced, replacing the receiver.

Boris appeared a moment later, carrying a silver tray with a bottle of pink Perrier-Jouët and three champagne flutes. Peter never did get his surname. He was not as obviously camp as Addey, soberly dressed in a plain dark-blue double-breasted suit to John's green velvet 'smoking', but boyishly handsome with a thick blond mane, slightly bouffant, possibly tinted, fashionably concealing his ears and resting on his collar.

"Now what can we do for you, Peter," said Addey, settling himself into one of the sofas and waving Peter to the seat opposite as Boris set about the champagne bottle with a little more flamboyance than was strictly necessary. "I presume it's all to do with that big bully Arthur Evans and that nice young American who runs Pitcairn Pharmaceuticals."

"It is indeed, John. I'll come straight to the point. We think there are grounds for asking for this bid to be referred to the Monopolies Commission; but, to get that point across in government circles, we need to strengthen the team with a firm that specialises in parliamentary PR."

"Can't Charles Barker organise that for you, Peter? Cheers, darlings, happy new year," he added, raising his glass. "We'll have to stop saying that soon. I'm sure we're past twelfth night."

"Charles Barker don't act for Pitcairn any longer," said Peter, perversely content that Addey's intelligence was not as omniscient as sometimes it seemed. "Freddie Wordsworth's doing it now."

"Ah, the delightful Freddie has taken over the mantle! What an old trooper he is; but, as you have rightly concluded, not necessarily adaptable enough for all circumstances. Did he recommend us, by the way, or do we have you, my dear Peter, to thank for this assignment?"

"A bit of both, John," Peter maintained without much conviction. "We've both benefited from your particular skills in the past."

"I know. You didn't know where else to turn. We shall take it as a compliment to be thought of as a last resort. But, tell me, Peter, how have the pair of you contrived to make a case for this one to go to the Monopolies Commission? I understand they're still sticking to the Tebbit doctrine - ooh, what an awful man; it makes my flesh creep just to think of him - you remember all that stuff about restriction of competition being the primary criterion for a reference. Well, Peter love, there's just as much competition in pharmaceuticals as there is in flirting; or foreplay come to that. How can we be expected to turn an honest penny if we're only given mission impossible?"

"It's not quite as wild as all that, John. Remember even the Tebbit doctrine had a get-out - 'other than in exceptional circumstances' or some such phrase, that they always said was to protect the national interest but we all knew was in reality to allow them to poke their fingers in whenever they felt like it. Now, whatever problems it has had of late, Pitcairn is generally reckoned to have some of the pharmaceutical industry's leading research laboratories and to have produced more than its fair share of medical breakthroughs. BMP has had one great success - the antibiotic Banzinin. Most of the rest of its pharmaceutical product range consists of drugs it has acquired through a string of takeovers, particularly since Evans became chairman in 1982. There's some evidence - and we're working on putting some flesh on the bones - that part of BMP's acquisition strategy has actually been to increase profits by closing down either part of its own facilities or part or all of those it has acquired. Our contention is that Evans plans to do that again; and that this time he would be destroying a research facility of national importance. That's pretty anti-competitive."

"No competition in the design of the super-suppository, leading to skilled job losses and technological desertification? A monstrosity to stir the souls of madmen as far apart as Heseltine and Wedgie-Benn. A bipartisan cause to unite the Beast of Bolsover and the best of British. Sounds all right if you say it quickly, Peter. But look who we're dealing with here, who we've got to win over. My Lord David Young at the DTI - damned property spiv. Doesn't give a toss for technology unless he can do a deal to privatise it. And his sidekick Kenneth Clarke - a man who thinks that the apex of the cobbler's art is the hush-puppy. Difficult to find what motivates a man who chooses to be shod in brothel creepers, don't you think? As for John Moore at Health and Social Security, do you know what he even looks like? The man's had a quadruple charisma bypass. We're not exactly working with promising material here, Peter. Not like the good old days. At least you knew with Reggie Maudling that you could always pay him off with a choice tip at the right moment. Some of these men haven't got enough character to take a bribe."

"What about Lawson? He could exercise some influence on this if he wanted to. Commanding heights of the economy and all that," Peter suggested in desperation.

"Oh, Peter, I don't doubt he *could*. Any of these men *could*. But Lawson. He likes his food and he loves a good bottle of wine; but, apart from that, he'd be about as incorruptible on something like this as the Mad Monk. Too proud, sod him.

"If they were all a bit closer to getting thrown out by the general populace it would help. They'll all be scrabbling round for their jobs in the City when that time comes. But they've only just got back in. That daft idea for a poll tax will get them in the end; but it's early days yet."

"What about trying to stir up the rank and file of Tory members - a sort of petition to their ministers to stand up for a champion of British technology?" Peter suggested, now scraping the barrel.

"More promising, Peter, but we'd have to, shall we say, *influence* an awful lot of people. Most of those backwoodsmen are pretty well heeled though, of course, if these rumours about Lloyds are well-founded, that will make a dent in a few portfolios. The trouble with dealing with tories en masse is that they're far more prone to zipper trouble than an interest in the petty cash. However, we can't really set a gang of tarts and catamites on them, even if that would be the most effective course. It's the Alan Clark rat-up-a-drainpipe school of politicians rather than the Jim Callaghan how-did-I-come-to-such-a-wealthy-retirement variety.

"What do you think, Boris?"

"We could just rely on the arguments."

"Now there's a radical thought. Don't you think he's brilliant, Peter? Come on, Boris, develop me a theme."

"There's absolutely no anti-monopoly case here. That's a good thing because Maggie can't abide people dressing up self-preservation as an anti-monopoly cause. Here, we're simply saying a reduction in the overall quantum of British pharmaceutical research, which would be implied by a threat to Pitcairn's laboratories, would be against the national interest, the public interest, or whatever you want to call it. That *is* surely an argument we could run with ministers. And it's so unquantifiable, that we wouldn't even try to quantify it. Wouldn't need to. And nor would they. All we'd have to do is generate enough steam to hide the facts."

"Brilliant! You see, Peter, I told you he was brilliant. We'll do it."

"There's just one problem," Boris cautioned, "Arthur Evans."

"Arthur Evans? Arthur Evans? Why should he be a problem? He's just an ex-nationalised industry boss getting his snout in the trough like all the rest of them. The likes of you and I, Boris dear, are not going to be outsmarted in the corridors of Whitehall by that Welsh wanker."

"That Welsh wanker, John, is one of Maggie's closest industrial confidantes and it was she who put him on the Court of the Bank of

England. BMP have given the Tory party £100,000 a year for the last three or four years. He's closer to her heartstrings than her Marks & Sparks 36B cup brassiere."

Tuesday, 19 January, 1988

Although Peter's distaste for politicians knew few bounds, his most withering contempt was reserved for civil servants. The group into whose shabby conference room George Aladyce, Rod King, David Stephenson and Peter were now directed encapsulated the causes of his disgust. They collectively oozed bureaucratic self-importance, power without responsibility, threadbare academia and the working-class politics of well-educated envy. The senior of the five - four men and a woman - was a sallow grey-suited man with a nondescript tie that had seen better days, twisted to reveal the label, *Cecil Gee*, and brown, rubber-soled lace-ups. He shook hands clammily with each of his visitors in turn and motioned them to the four chairs ranged opposite his team at a cheap, metal-framed table covered in what had once been white formica.

"My name is Christopher Snaithe. I am the senior case officer for this proposed merger", he began in a tone rather over-precise and strangely high-pitched. The word "senior" was emphasised by a wrinkling of his nose, a mannerism which could only lead one to conclude that no junior case officer existed.

"On my immediate left", he went on, "is Dr Martin Ryan, our economic adviser, and on his left Simon Masters, the secretary on this case. On my immediate right is Daphne Phelps, who is our healthcare industry specialist and on her right Geoffrey Peabody, who is one of our consumer affairs advisers.

"I will begin by explaining the overall procedure which we will be following with a view to advising the director general on his recommendation to the Minister; and then I will go on to explain the particular purpose of this initial meeting."

While Snaithe droned squeakily through his ritual introduction, his nose wrinkling occasionally as he felt that he had turned a particularly neat phrase, Peter gave free rein to his prejudices as he summed up the OFT team. The economist, Dr Ryan, he had come across before. He was a beetle-browed man of Scottish extraction, short and significantly overweight with thick curly ginger hair and a red beard too scraggy to conceal a flabby neck. He was dressed in a cheap grey tweed jacket, a blue nylon shirt with grey knitted tie and, so Peter observed under the table, dark brown trousers. His eyes were deep and heavily lidded, his nose broad and his cranium, even beneath the mop of marmalade hair, forebodingly large. Peter remembered him from an attempt, unsuccessful, two years before to persuade the OFT, on behalf of one of the national brewers, that his client should be permitted to do a grubby little deal with the Wapston family whereby his client would buy and then close the Wapston brewery, thereafter supplying the Wapston chain of pubs from their own super-brewery in Burton-on-Trent. Dr Ryan had put Peter's client through a well-deserved but withering hour of cross-examination during which he had clearly demonstrated that it was an excellent transaction for all parties other than the beer drinkers of North-West Shropshire. Dr Ryan was a clever man and one of strong convictions; but none of them were remotely capitalist.

Daphne Phelps was a typical Whitehall spinster, tall, plain and pallid. Her lank straight hair was of shortish length, raggedly cut and unmistakably greasy. Her pale green woollen dress, shapelessly calf-length, screamed 'Oxfam Shop'. She was one of those unkempt women who could be anything between 26 and 45. Her nose was thin, straight and pointed and her pale brown, loveless eyes, which seemed unnaturally close together, gave her the air of a bedraggled weasel emerging from a muddy ditch. No make-up; no jewellery; just a cheap gent's watch on her right wrist on a strap of brown imitation leather. She sat tall with her head back and her thin lips curled slightly downwards at the corners so that she appeared to be sniffing wildly through large unsightly nostrils at the noxious fat cats ranged before her.

Geoffrey Peabody, beside her, was a washed-out old has-been in his late fifties, shuffling unnoticed towards an index-linked civil service pension. His face was ruddy, as if he'd been out too long in a bracing wind, his eyes blue but watery and a whispy grey fluff was all that he had left for hair. For all that he must have witnessed these farces on countless previous occasions, he nevertheless bore a slightly startled expression almost as if, rabbit like, he expected the carnivore at his elbow to turn its attention upon him as a potential meal.

Snaithe himself was still holding forth self importantly, as much for the sake of demonstrating his superiority over his minions as for the benefit to his visitors in having the ritual of merger references and clearances explained. He was an almost painfully thin man in his mid forties, inexplicably, at that age, apparently still rather inexpert with a razor. His sideburns were ragged and uneven; he appeared to have taken a nick out of his neck so that dried blood flecked the collar of his almost white shirt; and beneath his left ear was a small clump of grey bristles which he appeared to have completely overlooked for a week or more. His hair, which was straight and fair but now going grey and thin, was combed in no particular direction. It looked as though it had been styled, as indeed it had, in a suburban kitchen by a dutiful but sadly unskilful wife. His face was intelligent and inquiring; but the affectation which he used in addressing his listeners of furrowing his brow and wrinkling his nose, which he thought to be friendly and reassuring, Peter found at best mannered and at worst condescending. This was a man who relished his ability to require the rich, the powerful and the famous to come before him as supplicants, for whom the process of bureaucracy was more important than its outcome and for whom the exercise of power was a religion. Peter detested him instantaneously.

At the far end of the table, the secretary to the working party was an earnest young man with a round, almost cherubic face, wide eyes and fair hair cut in a perfect pudding basin. Though Snaithe was still engaged on his introduction, he was already scribbling notes frantically. Peter was gratified to see from the breast pocket of his pale blue suit that he was admirably prepared with a row of fresh ballpoints in a variety of colours.

Snaithe was beginning to wind up his introduction when the door opened and a grimy metal trolley preceded into the room a short and enormously fat black female, who waddled in on an old pair of carpet slippers for all the world like the caricature Alabama maid from the early Tom & Jerry cartoons. She proceeded, without enquiry, to fill nine cups from her urn with pre-mixed milky tea and banged a cup and saucer in front of each participant. Few saucers on arrival were less well-filled than the cups. With a final flourish, she threw a handful of wrapped sugar-lumps and another of plastic teaspoons into the centre of the table and shuffled out without a word. Snaithe's flow was never interrupted.

As meetings go, it was an unmitigated disaster. David Stephenson had insisted that it was essential to go into the meeting with a number of different grounds on which a case for referral could be founded; this although he himself admitted that the national interest in preserving the UK's overall level of pharmaceutical research was the only one of any conceivable merit. The result was rather like the defence of a petty burglar pleading his innocence on the grounds that he was in bed at the time with a lady whose name he couldn't remember, or alternatively that he had been seen in the area but it wasn't him what did it, or alternatively that they were his fingerprints on the window catches but that was only because he had an identical twin who was a window cleaner, or alternatively that, although the silver candlesticks were under his bed, it was only because the police had put them there.

A ludicrous argument that doctors prescribed either Myodin or Banzinin in the treatment of over 35% of UK cases of whooping cough in 1986 was daft enough, given the ineffectiveness of antibiotics as a cure and the rarity of the disease now that most kids were vaccinated against it; but it was the contention that over 85% of cases of Glaswegian gonorrhoea were treated with one or other antibiotic that attracted Ms Phelps's most withering contempt.

"Would I be correct, Mr Stephenson, in conjecturing that the equivalent figure for Myodin alone would be in excess of 80% and would you - or perhaps Dr Aladyce would be better placed to do this for me - please explain, if you can, what characteristics Banzinin has which are not possessed by either Fortum or Augmentin and which make the common ownership of it and Myodin a uniquely powerful monopoly?"

By the time the Pitcairn team got to the only argument of any importance, they were trailing forty-love. What might otherwise have been the reasonably impressive statistics that Stuart Robinson had put together to show that BMP's overall research expenditure had grown at the slowest pace of all the major UK players and had shrunk dramatically in recent years as a proportion of sales were, as a result, shrugged off as of little interest. It became rapidly apparent that the BMP team had been here before and, alerted by the intensity of Freddie's press campaign and warnings from their political friends of Addey's machinations, they had sought to destroy this dangerous fox cub in its earth long before it was old enough to get amongst the chickens. Evans and his senior executives had pounced on a number of the statistics which Dundas Brothers had put out on behalf of Pitcairn, complaining to the Take-over Panel that they could not be substantiated and forcing Davenport to retract them. At the same time, they had prepared and placed before the OFT an intensely detailed plan for their future expenditures in this area which made Pitcairn's independent efforts appear paltry by comparison.

The bureaucrats in all probability believed neither party; but didn't really care either way. Even the intensely socialistic Dr Ryan opined facetiously that, if BMP found that a particular level of research expenditure was compatible with the maximisation of the value of their business, they were simply responding to an immutable law of economics and good luck to them.

By the time they left, it was coming down in buckets again. A pall of failure stunted conversation in the entrance hall as the Pitcairn team buttoned their raincoats and pulled up their collars at the soaking prospect of a futile search for taxis around the corner in Chancery Lane, followed by a resigned and humiliating dash for the tube.

*****

It was almost a fortnight now since BMP had announced their bid - a period for Peter of unrelieved professional buggeration and personal calamity. His appetite was quashed by alcohol and insomnia ground him down. Josh and Jenny Fordyce had invited him round to lunch on Sunday. As she opened the door, her shock at his appearance was all too clear.

"Well, you did say very casual, Jenny," he said looking down at his jeans and trainers.

"Yes, yes, of course, Peter," she said, pecking him briefly on the cheek. "Come on in, quick. God, it's cold out there. You should be wearing a coat in this weather."

"Jenny, I've only walked from the car across the road there."

"Well, you don't look at all well. I hope you've been looking after yourself. It doesn't look like it. You're looking far too thin."

"I've lost a bit of weight since Christmas, Jen; but that's probably no bad thing. And I've just come from the gym. I feel absolutely knackered.

In reality, he was more than bushed. It was his first time at Cannons since ..... well, since the new year and he felt weak as a kitten. He had never been a hunk but it was as if all his muscles had disintegrated, leaving him like a consumptive child. There had been hardly anyone there except for two gigantic blacks in the free weights area, who seemed engaged in a private competition to raise larger and larger lumps of metal above their heads on bars that sagged at either end under the load; and a delicious far eastern lady that Peter had spotted there before Christmas was there too. Whilst he had withered in the interim so that he found it necessary to pull tight the lace within the waistband of his shorts, she had apparently used the intervening month to grow the one part of her anatomy which had failed to her satisfaction to respond to gymnastic exercise. Her physician had not stinted on the silicone and, as she repeatedly hammered the chest press together between her elbows, her chin all but disappeared behind the twin eruptions of her new-found volcanoes.

Peter finished with the bicycle, puffing and feeling thoroughly out of shape, and followed her to the chest press. The weight was barely more than half his usual but he left the toggle where it was, gripped the two handles and pressed his elbows together in front of him. After four repetitions the sweat was pouring from his brow and the muscles in his arms were twittering with pain. It was the same with half a dozen more machines and worse still when he lay on his back to exercise his abdominals. In desperation he turned to the treadmill - after all anybody could run - and found after barely a mile that now he couldn't do that either.

"I'm afraid you're in for a pretty boring lunch. Josh had to fly off to Los Angeles this morning at short notice and the kids are round at their friends the Pattens for the day. Anyway I didn't cancel because I thought you might be just as lonely as me. Come on down to the kitchen and you can have a drink while I cook."

He followed her down the stairs to the lower ground floor. It was a sunny day, though cold, but as always the lights were on down here.

"There's a bottle of white open in the fridge and the glasses are over there in the cupboard above that fruit bowl."

"Do you mind if I have a scotch instead?" he asked.

"Not at all, Peter. There's a bottle of Bell's in here or I can get you something better from upstairs."

"No, no. Cooking scotch is fine."

He poured her a glass of wine and put a more than generous measure of scotch in a tumbler for himself, filling the balance of the glass with no more than a splash of sparkling water from a bottle he found in the fridge.

"Cheers," he said

"Cheers, " she replied, taking a sip. "A bit early for the hard stuff, isn't it? Is it awful inside that silly head of yours?"

"It's not too good. I'm having a terrible time at the office - defending a bid for Pitcairn - you probably haven't seen it - it's fairly stressful - but it will all be over by Easter."

"You know that's not what I meant," she said gently. "And I have seen it. Just because I'm a housewife and Josh is in television doesn't mean we don't follow the markets. I saw your name in the business section of *The Times* last week," she scolded.

She was a slight, pretty girl with straight black hair which hung to just above her shoulders. Her waist was tiny and she bemoaned playfully the fact that everything else was too. In the case of her hips, this had led to both her children being born by caesarean section and, in the case of her breasts, to two brief periods around their birth when she rejoiced all too briefly in a cleavage before resorting to her traditional shape, which she described as concave. She had been married to Josh for eleven years now but it had been seven before the first of their children arrived. The strains had begun to tell and Peter and she had been slipping down that slope towards a consolatory affair with the inevitability of doom when he returned from a month-long job in New York to find her pregnant. He was glad now that they had never crossed the line. It was an acknowledged but unspoken secret between them that had left her closer to him than any woman save Sophie had ever been. He couldn't think of many decent things he'd done in his life; but not shagging her those few years ago when he'd had the opportunity now seemed like one of them. It was probably just a matter of chance.

"I can't say that I'm the happiest bunny right now, Jen. I still don't understand what's happened. I can't turn my love on and off like that; and I wouldn't have thought that she could either."

"I don't think she can, Peter; but she made a conscious decision that it wasn't going to work. She's seen all our friends having affairs," Jenny said, looking at him knowingly. "She didn't want the temptation put in her way of having a part-time husband."

"Then why didn't she tell me? We could have worked something out. I don't have a contract that says I have to work all hours."

"You don't need one, Peter. It's in your genes. You could have promised her any number of things; but you know that being home for dinner is the one promise that you'd never have kept. She's decided to fall out of love with you and hurt you now rather than hurt you down the line. She's in much the same state as you right now - except that she's getting fat. Cubit doesn't care. He thinks it puts off rivals. You'll both heal in due course. Come and sit down. I'm going to make you eat, even if I have to put you in a high chair."

*****

Hennessy had proved almost as difficult as Gillian Wilkinson over the course of the last fortnight. In the end he had reluctantly acquiesced to the Panel's decision to allow Wagstaffs to continue as joint brokers to BMP; but Rod and Peter had agreed that the subject of sweeping the offices for listening devices should not be raised until that trauma was safely negotiated. As a result, Peter could not see Harrington Ingram until the Tuesday. He went round to their offices in Eastcheap mid morning and wearily climbed the narrow staircase to their unprepossessing suite of rooms.

Peter Harrington was around sixty, big, shambling and pasty. Like all these people, he was rather coy about his background either on genuine grounds of previous undertakings to confidentiality or, more probably, because a certain amount of mystery might tend to elevate rather than debase his assumed prior standing. There were mumblings of 'special forces' and 'security services' and 'overseas embassies' and such like; but, in any event, former spy or not, in Peter's experience, he got the job done. The electronics side safely put to bed, they turned to the subject of Mrs Cunningham.

"We don't have the first idea who she is and it may all be entirely innocent. But, just in case it isn't, we don't want her alerted to the fact that we're on to her. We just basically want to know who she is and what she does at this stage. Then we can decide later if we need to go any further."

"Pictures?" Harrington asked.

"What for?"

"If she is up to something and we need to pursue it further it's useful to be able to show the boys who have to follow her what she looks like. I'd recommend it. It's not going to add much to the cost now; but it will if we have to go back and do it separately later."

"Okay, Peter, but discreetly."

"With these modern telephotos you can count the whiskers on a gooseberry at a hundred paces. Don't worry, she won't know a thing about it."

*****

The 15th had been a particularly bruising day. All the business pages that morning had carried a summary of Pitcairn's press announcement, released the previous evening after the Stock Exchange had closed. In reality, under Freddie's supervision, the reporter covering the deal for each of the broadsheets had been separately briefed, on a non-attributable basis, by Stuart Robinson during the afternoon. It was difficult to know what they might have made of him, a combination of the premature eccentricity of the true genius and a body that seemed to have carried on growing, like a tryffid, long after it had reached the normal limits of homo sapiens. Stuart Robinson was the sort of man who was so tall that he would instinctively have ducked to pass under Admiralty Arch. A fraction under seven feet, his muscular control seemed somehow inadequate to the extraordinary length of his limbs so that he gangled along all arms and legs. His head, already balding, was massive and his long, almost ostrich-like neck contained a prominent and intensely over-active adam's apple which battled constantly for supremacy with the knot of his tie. The adam's apple was invariably victorious. His suits, of course, ought to have been bespoke but were in reality obtained on the cheap from his local branch of *High & Mighty*. As a result, he managed, through his general dishevelment, to avoid any pretension to appearing tailored. He bought extra-long shirts but, presumably because his neck size, minus the adam's apple, did not match his body, never long enough. As a result, he always seemed to work the tail free so that it flapped behind him.

The gist of what the gentlemen of the press had heard from him was an attack on BMP's research record and an assertion that each of the four significant pharmaceutical business acquisitions made by BMP over the previous five years had been used as an opportunity to reduce research costs. The figures in the press announcement to support the principal contentions were relatively sketchy; but it could be proved that, as a proportion of BMP's sales, research expenditures had declined over those years from around 4% to a little under 3%. Pitcairn's current equivalent was 5% and had risen over that period from 4.4%. Such figures were deeply flawed and blatantly misleading; but it didn't matter. They were true as far as they went. The figures in Stuart's briefing went far further into the flights of theoretical fancy. The reporters, baffled by Stuart's esoteric formulae and his incomprehensible talk of exponential smoothing, resigned themselves predictably to a form of regurgitation which betrayed a common source.

The Panel, no doubt gouged into action by Ms Wilkinson, were on the phone before ten o'clock summoning Peter to their offices in the Stock Exchange tower. The mild and avuncular Peter Fraser, from the Panel's permanent staff, was presiding. Grossmanns had pointed out, as Peter knew they would, that calculating BMP's research costs as a proportion of total group sales, which included hundreds of millions of pounds of products which required minimal research support, was deliberately specious. As a proportion of pure pharmaceutical sales, BMP could claim that they were spending more than Pitcairn rather than less. Grossmanns, it turned out, were encamped in another of the Panel's conference rooms and an argument raged back and forth between them all morning about what exactly was included in the term 'research and development'. It was all too easy to inflate the numbers by the inclusion of the expenditure, including capital investment, required to gear a new product up into full-scale production. Peter should know because he had conspired with Rod King to do just that with Pitcairn's figures.

"We're very concerned about the figures that you published yesterday. We believe that they are highly misleading and we are minded to require you to make a formal retraction," Fraser intoned in Panel-speak as the toings and froings reached their crescendo.

"But surely, if BMP are unhappy with what we've said they're at perfect liberty to put out their own statement to refute it," Davenport protested, knowing that a retraction was going to look much worse for his client than an exchange of rival claims between the two protagonists.

"We've two objections to dealing with the matter in the way you suggest. First, we deplore public exchanges of rival claims which cannot be objectively supported. If we leave this to Grossmanns to refute, you'll only try to pick some holes in their figures and set off into another round of claims and counter-claims. Second, we believe that it should have been obvious to you that your original statement was so highly subjective as to be on the verge of being wantonly deceptive. This is what we're asking you to put out today," Fraser concluded, passing over the draft of an announcement. "We'll leave you for a few minutes to study it. You can talk to your client over the phone there - it's nine for an outside line - and you can get me back on extension 4908. We'll accommodate reasonable changes to the text; but not such as to alter the meaning."

Peter and Tim Philips spent the next twenty minutes on the telephone to Rod King. It took half that to persuade him that they were not going to get away with their preferred option of an endless confused and confusing exchange of barbs with Grossmanns and the other half to frame an alternative strategy. It was mid-afternoon before Fraser and Davenport wearily settled upon a form of words which both could reluctantly tolerate. The words "likely to be misleading" had been softened to "might have been open to misinterpretation" and "unreservedly retract" had given way to "withdraw". It had fortunately ended up as a dull little six-liner which it was going to take more than Ms Wilkinson's flair to convert into anything that the average financial hack was going to do more than mention in passing, particularly for a Saturday column.

*****

By the time Peter got back to his office, Maureen was waiting with a message that Harrington was ready to call. He got him round straight away.

"Well, the first thing is that she works for Pitcairn. You've spent a grand getting me to send a man up to Leicestershire to find out what's on your client's own damn personnel records."

"Are you sure, Peter?"

"Of course, I'm sure. Do you want chapter and verse? My man's been extremely diligent. Mrs, or I should rather say Dr Lindsay Cunningham, is employed as a research chemist at Pitcairn Pharmaceuticals' Peterborough laboratories. She drives a black Nissan Patrol - ugly great thing, don't see many of those except with the genuinely horsey brigade, company car, I shouldn't wonder - registration D439 BFS. Here she is," he said, passing over a small sheaf of slightly grainy photographs of a rather prim and not unattractive brunette, wrapped up in what looked like a camel overcoat. In some she was perched behind the wheel of her 4x4; in others walking from or to it, briefcase in hand.

"She was widowed last October from one Gerald Cunningham. Shooting accident, by all accounts. He'd bought a share in a pheasant shoot with a few of his muckers earlier in the year and that's where he died. I know these things are likely to arouse a suspicion of suicide; but he was by all accounts as happy as a pig in shit and the police say there was absolutely no reason to suspect foul play. It was one of his own guns and he just seems to have set it off whilst he was putting down the one he'd fired and picking up the other. My man went round to the offices of the local rag to rifle through their back copies for the report of the inquest. Misadventure. We'll get hold of a copy of the coroner's report in due course; but I'm sure it wont tell us anything. After all, he certainly had no reason to top himself. He had a local estate agency business which he'd sold out to the Prudential about a year before.

Rumoured to have collected about a million pounds from that. And they seem to have been doing very nicely thankyou even before that from the looks of their pad. Damn great farmhouse sort of thing just outside Melton Mowbray with three or four horses in the stables and sodding great paddocks. She goes out hunting with the local pack according to the neighbours. Here are some pictures of the house. Looks like the sort of person who might be able to invest a quarter of a million at a pop. Anyway, just to be sure, we've been down to the records office to have a look at her husband's will. Basically he left about one and a half million, including the house. There was probably some life assurance too and that would normally fall outside the estate. It all went to her - so no inheritance tax; and they were childless; so he left her pretty comfortable."

"Still, a bit odd to buy a big chunk of shares in the company you work for. A lot of eggs in one basket. And then, more to the point, why did she sell them? Anyway, I guess we don't need you for that now. We can get Pitcairn's personnel department to ask her."

*****

They had gone straight to the OFT's offices from their regular morning meeting that Tuesday. It was interesting only for Rod's report of an interview that Pitcairn's head of personnel had held with Dr Cunningham the previous afternoon in Peterborough. Interesting but of no use. As a research chemist, she had no inside knowledge of Pitcairn's financial position, of course, but with her husband's death an avalanche of cash had fallen in her lap and she had wondered what to do with it. It was her husband who had always looked after the family finances. Some years before, he had organised for her to become an underwriting member of Lloyds. It had always been a profitable and tax-efficient way for the rich to invest and, although she would have an unlimited liability for any losses she incurred, that remote possibility could only make her bankrupt and could not put the estate agency, the principal source of their income, at risk. She herself had taken no active interest in any of these things and she was perplexed, now that she found herself a widow, to know what to do with the money she had been left. A friend had suggested that the sharp fall in the markets since the October crash was a good buying opportunity and that she could do worse than invest in the shares of her employer. Her bank manager had not discouraged her and she went ahead. It was a disaster. Within a couple of days she had a letter from her underwriting agency to warn of serious losses on her Lloyds account as a result of asbestosis claims, which the members would have to make good. The stock market was continuing fragile; but her Pitcairn shares had not fallen too badly. She decided to cut her losses.

Peter and Rod shared a cab on the way to the OFT. With the connivance of George Aladyce, who of course knew her well and could claim that her name had been mentioned to him by Rod on the offchance, they had managed to disguise from Hennessy the fact that Mrs Cunningham had been unearthed by an outside agency. But they both felt a little chastened that their foray into a little skulduggery had ended so tamely.

"I suppose it has to be possible that BMP are fighting this clean," Peter mused out loud. "Are we just getting paranoid because they pulled this share purchasing trick on us?"

"I thought you were saying the other day that nothing in the City was clean these days. Look at all these articles in the papers. There was another one this morning on Guinness saying that there was evidence that they got their mates to purchase ten million shares in Distillers at way above their bid price. And wasn't there something about Burtons in the FT last week?"

"Yes, the DTI has launched a slightly unusual sort of inquiry into Burton's past dealings. You remember they bid for Debenhams. It was a hell of a scrap but, at the end of the day they won because Philip Harris and Gerald Ronson - two of the usual players - delivered up seven or eight per cent of the target at the last moment."

"And the DTI investigation is to find out if there was a *quid pro quo* ?"

"That's the implication. But it isn't a DTI investigation. It's a DTI inquiry."

"What the hell's the difference?"

"Quite interesting really - for the connoisseurs of these things A DTI investigation is one of those grand affairs normally presided over by an old legal buzzard and an accountant to look into one of these big *cause celèbres* , like the takeover of Harrods by that crooked Gyppo slimeball. And I'd be pretty certain that Guinness is heading that way too as soon as these court cases are out of the way. But a DTI inquiry is an altogether more Kafkaesque affair. It's conducted by an officer of the DTI and it can demand to see whatever it likes and can require explanations from whoever it likes. I think it can even charge them with a criminal offence if they fail to answer a question but can also use anything they say as evidence against them. They're pretty horrible but not all that rare; and they've been cropping up more and more often recently and making people in the City a bit nervous."

"The usual suspects?"

"Oh, certainly an element of that, Rod. One inquiry is into Next's takeover of Grattan. That was an agreed deal. The only reason that the DTI are poking their nose in seems to be that Roger Seelig was advising Next and my Lord Patrick Spens was looking after Grattan. There's a witch-hunt on and, given the role of those two in Guinness, Thatcher wants to see them burnt at the stake."

"Quite literally no smoke without fire, then?"

"Possibly, Rod; but there are grey areas and the pressure has been on merchant bankers in recent years to win at all costs. They've taken to pushing back the boundaries. It's been a bit of a lottery as to whether the authorities cry foul or not."

"For instance?"

"Do you remember Woolworths being bid for by Dixons a couple of years ago? Woolworths' advisers bought one point four million of their own client's shares during the defence to keep them out of Dixons' hands. They sold them a month or two after the bid, taking a gigantic loss in the process - anything up to twenty million. But they denied that Woolworths itself had indemnified them, which would have been illegal, and no one has openly alleged otherwise. On the other hand, something similar happened last year when AE were defending themselves against Turner & Newall. This time Hill Samuel, who were advising AE, but not AE itself, indemnified the people who did the buying. Again not illegal; and I think they would have got away with it altogether if Hill Samuel hadn't panicked and dumped the shares clumsily into the market as soon as the bid was over. The Panel blew the whistle and let Turner & Newall have another go."

"It sounds as though it rather serves them right. I seem to remember that the righteous were all on Turner & Newall's side."

"Yes; but they didn't have to rely on righteousness alone. It was said that Ivan Boesky and some of his mates were busy buying AE shares at above the bid price and selling them on to Turner & Newall at a loss. Now why would they have done that?"

"So where does that put us, Peter? BMP have seized the initiative by the short and curlies with this share-buying spree. You're so sceptical of the OFT even before we get there that you're trying to get some pooftah to seduce a few back-benchers; and we've just drawn a blank with Mrs Cunningham, who we'd persuaded ourselves had the whiff of scandal about her and turns out to be a sweet-smelling widow with more money than sense."

"My sleuth wants us to let him tail Evans. Says he doesn't know anyone who hasn't got something to hide."

"Now that, as you know, is strictly against the poison dwarf's instructions."

"I know, Rod, but Hamilton had quite a cunning ploy to bring him round. He suggested slipping a tramp fifty quid to get himself found going rather noisily through the Hennessys' manorial dustbins. It would be assumed that BMP were behind it, whatever their denials, and our little chairman would unleash our own hellhounds by way of retaliation. What do you think?"

"First, there's a danger that he'll just demand we turn the other cheek. I can never tell when he's going to be sanctimonious and when he's going to be spiteful..."

"Sort of new testament samaritan versus old testament God of wrath?" interrupted Peter with a chuckle.

"I suppose so, if you want to be so damned intellectual about it. But second, it'll be impossible to work that scam without publicity. That in itself would put Evans on his guard against retaliation and make him ultra careful. If he's got anything to hide, he'll be alert to making it more difficult for us to find it. Let's wait and see how Christopher's meeting with Young goes on Thursday before we decide. I don't have much hope for it, particularly after that restatement of government competition policy last week. Maybe, if Young sends our little man away with a flea in his ear, he'll begin to realise that we need to get serious."

Friday, 22 January 1988

"Freddie, notwithstanding that bollocking from the Panel, we've simply got to find a way of hammering away at this research expenditure point. The difficulty is that we can pull out a whole lot of statistics that imply that Evans has cut back; but BMP simply don't publish enough information for me to be able to prove it."

"Ivan's keeping a berth for us on Sunday, Peter m'boy, but I've got to have some rations to throw him. You'd be forgiven for thinking otherwise but these journalists haven't actually got the imagination to make it up themselves. I need some fresh bait."

"We can't risk being quoted, Freddie. The Panel is pretty pissed-off with us already. Alexander has already rung my chairman to tell him that I need to be put on a tighter leash. We can't even risk being implied to be the source. Stuart's done an enormous amount of work but the results are all too circumstantial."

"How does he write?"

"Stuart?"

"Yes, Stuart."

"What do you mean, how does he write? Like a crab on anabolic steroids, Freddie. You've seen him. His limbs are in all the wrong places to be able to guide a pen properly."

"I'm not talking about his best joined-up writing, Peter. I'm talking about his style."

"Freddie, he's a bleeding biologist, fresh out of a university lab. He writes as though he's trying to find the literary substitute for Mogadon. They all do."

"I thought it was probably like that. Still, let's give it a try. Get him to put together the article that you would like a competent investigative reporter to have written and get it over to me. No more than 500 words. We'll translate into Ivanspeak and present it to our friend with a promise of the rarest scoop to come since Jeffrey Archer bought off that whore a year or so back - and hope for the best."

*****

"I'm calling you from the car, Peter. I've just come from seeing David Young at the House of Lords. It really was a very good meeting. I'm very encouraged by what he had to say. The Prime Minister's apparently taking a keen interest too. I hadn't realised she'd majored in chemistry.

"He'd obviously been very well briefed. Your man Addey had done a first rate job. Lord Young was right on top of all the issues and very sympathetic to the line we've been taking. I thought his interest in the whole subject of research verged on obsessionality. He assured me that they wont be rushed into this by BMP and that they've gotten every intention of taking a long and careful look at it. He more or less assured me it would go to the Monopolies Commission if there was a shadow of a doubt about it - and he said that he started from a position of extreme scepticism.

"You've gotten this white paper, or whatever it is you call that thing they put out last week, all wrong. He said that their *primary* concern is any diminution in competition, because that's normally all that's involved; but that they can't afford to be non-interventional when national interest is involved.

"He said he'd also spoken to Moore, who is responsible for public health. Says they've all gotten very concerned at the unabated rise in the cost of drugs and the drain on the treasury which this causes the hospital service. He said that they were far from accepting that there was no substantive anti-trust case to answer, particularly in the supply of antibiotics.

"I've come away feeling very confident that the government are on our side.

"Could you just give me John Addey's number? I want to call and thank him for all his help. See you in the morning."

*****

"Have you seen the screen, Peter?" It was Tim Phillips on the line. "They've posted the offer document. Our copies haven't arrived yet but Grossmanns have promised they're on their way."

"Shit. I hadn't seen it," said Peter, immediately scanning back over the recent announcements on the stock exchange screen. Tim, that's timed at 12.50. It's as near as dammit 1.30 now. Where the fuck is this messenger? I think you'd better get George to send one of his men round there straight away. If they're all out - and they usually are when you need them - get one of your troops over there. Don't leave it to a secretary. They might have to be a bit forceful to get Grossmann's front desk to disgorge."

"Will do."

"Have you called the company?"

"Not yet."

"OK, I'll do that. You get the documents." "Maureen! Get me Christopher Hennessy or, failing him, Rod King prontissimo, will you."

A marginally pained acknowledgement reverberated back from the exterior of Davenport's glass box.

"And then get me a print-out of the BMP stock exchange announcement - it's timed at 12.50. And fax a copy over to Pitcairn."

While he waited for the connection, Peter scanned the press announcement that had accompanied the release of the offer document. Maureen, despairing of his refusal for weeks past to go up to the directors' mess for lunch, had brought him a sandwich, an apple and a coke. He had torn the tab off the can and taken a couple of sips and a couple of bites from the apple. The sandwich looked destined to curl up and face jettison, as had most of the others since she had tried to impose this regime.

The press announcement was pretty standard stuff - with one exception. 'In discussions between the two chairman in advance of the offer' - a nice little phrase that perhaps implied more than one meeting and certainly more mutual acknowledgement that there had ever been a basis for agreement than was actually the case - 'Mr Hennessy indicated that there was sense in putting together the two ethical pharmaceutical businesses, provided that Pitcairn's management supervised the process' - nothing the institutions hated more than a management that put its own interests ahead of the shareholders. "Nice one, you spindly bitch," he said out loud with genuine venom as Maureen appeared round the door, checked at the insult, and gathered her arms somewhat haughtily across her considerable chest.

"Not you Maureen", Peter protested, bemused that she could have taken such a description to be her own. "Gillian Wilkinson unfortunately appears to have got the measure of the poison dwarf."

"Mr Hennessy," she intoned formally, as if not entirely convinced, "is playing squash at the RAC and not expected back until 2.45. Rod King is on a conference call but will ring back when he's finished. And Mr Word..."

As if on queue, Peter's telephone began to ring. It was Tim.

"Oliver's just called on a mobile from Grossmann's reception. They say the bulk print hasn't arrived yet and the BMP team say there aren't any spare copies. We'll have to wait for the messenger. They say he was told to come straight here after the stock exchange and the panel. It's obviously a put-up job. In reality he was probably told to go and sit in a pub for an hour or two. But what can Oliver do?"

"Okay, leave it to me, Tim. Tell Oliver to hold on there. I'll call the awful Ms Wilkinson."

"Gillian Wilkinson," she answered immediately. Again that extraordinary voice. It was as if the sultry tones of an Eartha Kitt had been wrapped up in the unappealing angular body of a Virginia Woolf.

"Gillian, it's getting on for an hour and a half since you released the offer document and we haven't had our copies yet."

"Well I wouldn't worry, Peter" - a little emphasis on the Christian name - "I'm sure they'll be with you in a moment," she came back with no attempt to hide the patronising tone.

"Your messenger seems to have gone astray; but I've got one of my team downstairs in your reception. I'd be grateful if you'd let him have half a dozen copies right away."

"I'd love to help you, Peter, but there's nothing I can do. Your copies are with the messenger. I'm sure he won't be long. All the copies we have here at the moment are already allocated. I'm expecting a few hundred from the bulk print later in the afternoon. Get your secretary to call around five to see if they're here."

Patronised and then provoked.

"Gillian, I'm sure you know the requirements," he said, reaching for his copy of the Take-over Code and flicking through to the relevant page. Rule 19.7 - 'Copies of all documents and announcements bearing on an offer etc, etc.... must at the time of release be lodged with the Panel and the advisers to all other parties to'...."

"...the offer. Outside normal business hours, such advisers must be told of the release without delay, if necessary by telephone," she intoned.

It wasn't quite word perfect but damned close. She wasn't reading it. Christ almighty, the fucking harridan knows the whole sodding book by heart.

"I'm aware of the rules, Peter. I've told you, your copies are on their way by messenger."

"But the delivery arrangements you have made have not met the Take-over Code requirements. There is a remedy sitting in your ground-floor reception area and I'm asking you to use it."

"Well your remedy will just have to sit there. Your copies are with the messenger."

"Gillian, I hope you're not going to force me to make a complaint to the Panel - and to the press."

"You must do what you think is in your client's best interests, Peter. Good-bye."

*****

"Mr Wordsworth is in the boardroom. He called saying he wanted to see you urgently. He's been there for about twenty minutes. I thought you'd have been off the phone earlier."

"Sorry, Maureen. I'll go straight up."

There was no sign of Freddie when Peter opened the door to the boardroom. He assumed the old boy must have gone for a pee.

Peter walked slowly round the table to the huge plate-glass window. He felt tired and physically shattered. He'd been unable to absorb the thrill of the chairman's almost ecstatic report at the meeting this morning of his interview with Lord Young the previous evening. And now this petty squabble with that bitch round at Grossmanns. It was bucketing down again; but this time there was clear evidence of sleet in the icy splashes that battered against the glass before slithering downwards one after another. He could well believe the reports that this was going to be the wettest January since the war. He stared outwards at the Barclays headquarters opposite on the corner of Lombard Street, every light there blazing too against the prematurely darkening day. The room behind him was reflected in the glass.

Something moved. He spun around startled.

Freddie Wordsworth, fast asleep in the chairman's high-backed chair, stirred slightly and settled again into a rhythmic pattern of contented and almost soundless slumber, like a round fat dormouse.

"Freddie.....Freddie," he called quietly.

"Hm.....what?.....what? Good gracious, m'boy, I must have drifted off. Serves you right for keeping a chap waiting after a good luncheon in the wardroom."

Freddie had called from The Army and Navy Club in Piccadilly around two o'clock, following an early lunch, and had spoken to Maureen. She'd had a long and innocently flirtatious relationship with Freddie over the years; but it had almost all been conducted over the phone and she found it even now difficult to disentangle the occasions when he was well-fed but serious from those when he was simply well-fed. On this occasion he left her in no doubt that he wanted to see Peter urgently. She had checked Peter's diary and had arranged with Freddie that he should come straight round.

"Now where was I, m'boy? Couldn't whistle up the galley for a pot of tea, could you?"

Peter walked over to the door to the little kitchen. As he popped his head round the door he almost collided with the messenger bearing the customary silver tray.

"There you are Freddie. Your wish is my command."

The messenger set down the tray and departed. Peter poured. Freddie stretched.

"I've just been having lunch at the In and Out with my minister friend, Alan. It's convenient for his rooms in the Albany. He'd come straight from a cabinet committee this morning. They were all there. As you know, he can't stand most of his colleagues - quite fancies the leaderene herself - probably finds power sexy - but thinks her new men are parvenu philistines and the old party faithful like oyster eyes are thick aristos who should be confined to their farms. Still he can be very amusing. Of course, he's wildly indiscreet but he's normally reliable. He knew of my dealings with Pitcairn - but that didn't stop him. Has the independence of thought of the truly well-heeled.

"Anyway, his interpretation of the government's attitude to a potential combination of BMP and Pitcairn was rather at odds with that report we had this morning from our diminutive helmsman. There's not a prayer of a referral, Peter. Maggie wouldn't hear of an obstacle being put in the way of Arthur Evans. Quite apart from the bullion BMP ships round to Tory Central Office every year, Arthur is described as 'one of us'. 'We're not letting that stunted American runt stand in the way of Arthur building a British drugs colossus' was apparently the way that it was put. All that reassuring guff from the DTI was just hot air."

"Shit. I suppose we should have suspected that the little man might have been legged over by Young. These Americans are always suckers for anyone with a title, even when the ermine's been draped round the shoulders of a creep like that."

"Well, you warned me not to have great expectations of Mr Hennessy. I suppose one has to be pretty gullible to swallow all those Mormon fantasies. Pretty sound views on the place of women; but you should never put your faith in a man who wont take his grog. I'm sorry, Peter, that looks like it."

"What about Addey? He's been claiming oodles of potential support on the backbenches."

"The whips have told the backwoodsmen in no uncertain terms to forget it. Addey is yesterday's queen and not tomorrow's was the way that Alan put it. Maggie has more subtle ways of rewarding the faithful than were fashionable in Addey's day. These chaps have been a long time in office now - too long separated from gainful employment not to have perfected other ways of looking after themselves. The patronage system is a wonderful honeycomb and at the centre sits the queen bee herself."

"Have you told Hennessy?"

"No. To be honest I thought he'd swallowed Young's bait so gleefully that he'd never believe me now if I told him there was a barb in it. Do you want to tell him?"

"Not much. I think I'll talk to Rod instead. We're running out of options," he sighed wearily.

"You're not taking this too seriously are you, Peter? You've not been looking yourself these past few weeks."

"Sorry, Freddie, one or two things on my mind."

"You've got woman trouble, haven't you?"

"You could put it that way."

"I knew it. You're wasting away. It's always the blondes that are the most dangerous. You may not believe it; but I suffered at the hands of the odd lady in my day too. It wont come as much consolation to you now; but I found the solution in numbers. It's an invention of modern naval engineering, m'boy. Its called the twin screw and I heartily recommend it."

Wednesday, 27 January, 1988

"That coont Sellar has asked fer a time when yer and I can goo and see 'im. De yer know what the fook this is aboot?"

The morning meeting of corporate finance directors - often called prayers, though you would have been hard pressed to imagine a less theological, moral or devotional occasion - had just broken up on the previous Tuesday. Bill McAdam had spent much of it berating his colleagues for what he considered piss-poor marketing efforts. He had rounded on one director after another, demanding their whereabouts the previous evening. Peter, finalising the result of the Bottley rights issue till gone seven and thereafter in a meeting to consider the latest draft of the Pitcairn defence document until half past eleven, had got off relatively lightly.

"Doon't yer have a friggin manager on the joob to do that shite?" Bill had snapped.

"Tim Philips normally chairs those sessions but the finance director and I were there last night to review the whole shape of the document."

"Ok," McAdam came back grudgingly. "What aboot yer, Seymour? I cooldna raise anyone at yer oom last night; yer'll ave bin oot wi a client, I would ope?"

Peter could see Farquharson weighing up whether to risk a porky before he lamely settled for "I had to take my wife down to Charterhouse to see a possible new housemaster for my son this September."

"Yer noot paid to squire yer wife roond Surrey lookin for a coomfy boolt-hoole for wee Johnny. That's the poorpus o' wives, ye know. It's jest another wasted bluddy marketin opportunity. Ther've been far too fookin many roond this room this mornin. There's a soddin jungle oot there and I expect to see yer all doin a damnsight more 'untin than is evident today.

209

"OK, that's enough for this mornin. Peter, I still need a word wi' yer."

"I assume it's about the Bottley rights issue, Bill. Sellar was pretty miffed that we stuffed him with ten per cent of the sub-underwriting. It's all part of an agreement with DAM that's been in place for yonks."

"What fookin agreement? I've niver oerd o' it."

"It's one of those typical pacts between sworn enemies. DAM interpret it as a right to a ten per cent share of any of our underwritings. We interpret it as their obligation to take a ten per cent share. Actually it's both. Of course, on the vast majority of occasions, it's a comfortable way for the Brothers to keep a chunk of the sub-underwriting commission in house. But Sellar was very aggrieved at having to take ten per cent of the Bottley rights and, with all bar a smidgen left with the underwriters, he's no doubt spitting tin-tacks this morning."

The Bottley issue had closed the previous afternoon. The share price had been as sick as a parrot from the moment the rescue had been mounted back before Christmas and during the last two weeks it had sagged to 95p, a level which deprived investors, other than those accustomed to signing anything which fell on their doormats, of any incentive to subscribe for new shares at a pound a throw. The whole thing had been left to the institutions. Bottley and Dundas had both been on the receiving end of further maulings in the financial press that morning, as the dismal outcome was reported.

Just like Corporate Finance, Dundas Asset Management was located in separate and secure offices, this time on the third floor of the building, to which executives of other parts of the organisation did not have access. McAdam and Davenport were collected at DAM's reception desk by Sellar's rather sniffy secretary and escorted to his office, which lay in a row of three, the other two occupied by lesser-brained members of the Dundas clan. Dundas Brothers' chief executive, Johnathan Tudor, about whose attendance they had not been warned, was already there, his tall but conspicuously lived-in frame draped into a comfortable armchair to one side of Sellar's desk. He was pulling on his customary Marlborough. Sellar himself, behind his desk in a wing-backed leather chair that rotated and tipped and swivelled and levitated, was on the phone. As he finished the call, he waved Bill and Peter to a couple of hard-backed chairs that had been drawn up opposite. It was the arrangement for a court martial; at the very least for an interview of the visitors by those already there.

"I asked Johnathan here to join us because I wanted to discuss something which is conceivably of interest to the group as a whole - certainly of separate and perhaps conflicting interest, what? - to corporate finance and asset management."

Sellar's diffidence in dealing with his colleagues was emphasised by an ability to speak without effectively opening his mouth, as if conversation with lesser mortals could not justify the effort required. In full flow, the sentences which he felt to be particularly conclusive were rounded off with an imperious "what", like an eighteenth century monarch, and usually also a self-satisfied smile, amounting to no more than a straightening of his firmly closed lips. The "what" was certainly not interrogatory; more a confirmation that what he had just uttered could not be seriously doubted. Peter had never heard him laugh, even at his own quips, which were always sealed with a particularly confident "what" and a more than usually seraphic grin.

He had begun confidently this morning, not merely as he always did from atop his lofty pedestal of wealth and breeding, but also as if he had separate reason to expect that he would win whatever exchange was to come. Peter had the uncomfortable presentiment that Tudor was already squared. The old underwriting agreement was on its way out. Peter couldn't get excited about that. It had been a matter of convenience; but it was looking a touch archaic now. If the government's privatisation programme got going in a big way, these funny old arrangements were going to be swamped by competitive underwriting tenders and god knows what other new techniques. An in-house deal with only one of around twenty important UK asset management groups was going to be impossible in any issue that was of international interest.

"We've decided that we want to take advantage of the interest in Pitcairn - by selling our shares in the market, what?"

Sellar dropped his news deliciously and pitilessly, like a live lobster into a boiling cauldron. The outline of his mouth straightened, on the verge of a smile, as he relished the impact of his words.

"The logic of the decision is impeccable. At over four per cent, it's one of our largest holdings and worth a short hundred mill. It's one of the few holdings we have where selling would have a measurable overall effect on our cash liquidity - and that's something I've been looking for as we dive further into this bear market, what? Added to that, the shares have underperformed their sector for five straight years, they're now sitting at a premium to a bid which doesn't look as though it's going to need improvement to carry the day and, for reasons which I don't understand, there's some good demand out there from the arbs. It's too good a opportunity to miss, what?

"Of course, I appreciate that it will excite some comment short-term for Dundas Asset Management" - Sellar never used the abbreviation DAM universal both within Dundas Brothers and in the City at large - "to be selling shares in a company advised by our own CFD colleagues; but that will be a passing cloud. It'll blow over quickly enough; but not without just enough comment to demonstrate the independence of our separate decision-making processes, what? It may have come as a slight shock to you," he observed, relishing the horrified expressions opposite, but I'm sure you'll agree at the end of the day that it's the right thing for us to do, what? Anyway, I wanted to let you know - as a matter of courtesy, what?"

"It's absolootely out o' the fookin question!" roared McAdam, spitting instantaneously with rage. "I've niver oerd anythin soo godamned ootrageously fookin stoopid in my whoole soddin life. Dundas CFD are defendin Pitcairn against an unwelcome bid. We have a fee o' the best part o' 20 million poond ridin on the ootcome - that's more than twice the fookin profit that DAM makes in an entire fookin year - and yer, as the biggest sharehoolder bar Mercury, propoose to pooll the fookin roog from oonder us."

"To be fair, Bill," said Tudor, endeavouring to cool things a little, "your most likely fee on this transaction is closer to £3 million..."

"Too bluddy right it is, if we canna even rely on our oon sooddin colleagues fer suppoort."

"Now be reasonable, Bill, we're just being neutral," Sellar resumed, unruffled by McAdam's outburst and, Peter suspected, positively relishing the working-class reaction he had provoked. "Back last spring we agreed, at Peter's request, not to support the institutional coup which led to the previous chairman's removal. Peter felt it would be prejudicial to his neutrality as adviser for it to be suggested that Dundas itself was siding with one party rather than another; and we were happy to go along with that. Isn't that so, Peter?"

"Yes, David, but...."

"Hang on a moment, Peter, let me make my point. You can't ask us to be neutral at one point, when that's what suits your book, and then uncritical supporters at another when something different tickles your fancy."

"David, I hardly think these two occasions to be comparable. Our stance last spring was entirely for appearance's sake. We already knew that Jock Enderby had enough support for his palace revolution without your adding your weight to it. Here you're talking about taking action which threatens to present over four per cent of the shares to the other side."

"No, no, no, Peter. It's again just a matter of appearances. Selling into the market is entirely neutral on our part."

"Peter, it's not as if David's proposing to accept BMP's offer," Tudor suggested, still languidly draped across his chair. "I can see that it would be embarrassing for the Brothers as a whole if our investment management division were responsible for delivering the deciding votes - as it were the *coup de grâce* - in favour of BMP. As chief executive, I would have to take a view about that; but here we're just talking about selling into the market, and definitely not selling to BMP because they can't buy. The market price is standing above their bid. There's always a danger if David sold later on that he would be passing the shares direct to BMP. In that sense, there's much to be said for him getting out now."

"With respect, Johnathan, I hardly think that makes a difference. BMP can't buy them now; that's true. But David will simply be putting the shares in the hands of someone who'll be looking to sell them on at a higher price if BMP are forced to up their offer to win. And, by the way, someone who may have to cut his losses and sell to BMP anyway if that's his only way out."

"Well, Peter, if you don't want them to go into the hands of the arbs, it's always open to you to find some other buyers. We won't be unreasonable," Sellar crowed, meaning the exact opposite and now really beginning to enjoy himself. "We'd be prepared to give you a week to come up with a friendly buyer at the market price."

"You know that's not possible, David. The only potential buyers apart from arbs are other potential bidders. We'd be taking a decision that Pitcairn was going to lose its independence one way or another before BMP have even posted their offer document."

"Now look," said Tudor, straightening himself in his chair, as if he had suddenly realised that he was going to have to take the decision himself. "I think that CFD must accept that David's first obligation is to his clients, the holders of the funds which he manages."

"Well, moost o' those are just the fookin footsoldiers who've bought his friggin unit troosts or are waitin fer their sooddin pensions," said McAdam. "They're ardly goonna coome oowlin for David's balls just because e hasna soold oot woon capitalist arsehoole to anoother."

"Actually, it's divided about half and half between the unit trusts and various pension funds - and there's also a little bit in private clients. It's all very well for Bill here to say that we're under no pressure from the unit trust holders; but Johnathan you know how sensitive our sales are to our standing in the unit trust performance tables, what? And, as for the pension funds, every quarterly meeting with trustees now is turning into a battle to defend your performance against whichever manager is currently leading the charge. Bill, you can't say we're too far removed from those to whom we're responsible not to feel the heat. In your game ultimately you're responsible to your client's shareholders; but it's the directors and not the shareholders who pass your fees. With us it's the trustees."

"But, David, this is surely marginal," pleaded Peter. "You have so little to lose by holding on to see the outcome. If, at the end of the day, BMP win, then you can accept."

"I don't like that route, Peter, for a number of reasons. First, I can get out - in cash - now - and above the bid price. The bid's currently worth 354p and the cash alternative only 327p; but I might get 360p in the market for such a big parcel. Second, BMP might cut off the cash alternative when they win, which would leave me with BMP shares. I don't even think Pitcairn makes a very good acquisition for BMP; so I wouldn't want them. Third, if the market shares my view, BMP shares will fall if they do get control of Pitcairn. Then I'll be selling into a falling market. Now I can sell into one that's rising. It might look marginal to you; but the difference between the top of the performance table and the bottom is a whole series of marginal decisions. Still, if you think it's marginal, why don't you give me an indemnity, what?"

"Joohnathan." It was McAdam, now leaning forward in his chair, his face flushed and sweaty, damp rings at the armpits of his shirt. At this angle his eyes were level with Tudor's and he held him in his direct piggy gaze. "I willna toolerate DAM sellin these shares," he said slowly and deliberately. "If yer conclude that they can sell, yer do so wi'oot me. Do I make mysel entirely clear?"

Less than a month into his new role as head of CFD, for which Tudor himself had recruited him, McAdam was shrewd enough to know the power that he could wield through a threat of resignation. Tudor had gone out on a limb to take on a man so out of step with the Brothers' traditional gentility. For the moment at least, he was forced to act as the new man's sponsor in the inevitable internal rivalries. But Sellar was also a difficult man to deal with. He had shamelessly used the advent of ever more solid Chinese walls between the bank's various operations to secure himself independence of action and had fostered the personal loyalty of his managers by the creation of a separate DAM culture. Investment management was an increasingly important area of the business with enormous growth potential. If Sellar walked out on him, he was likely to play the pied piper with a stream of his subordinates and perhaps ultimately clients too. He was wealthy enough to do so at any time without suffering a pang of hardship; but he was fortunately also sufficiently greedy for Tudor to have held him so far in harness with the aid of ever juicier carrots dangled before his haughty muzzle.

On this occasion too, Tudor suspected Sellar's motives. The discussion that they had had the previous evening had begun with Sellar's complaint about the Bottley underwriting and only subsequently moved to the subject of the Pitcairn shares. Tudor had a more than shrewd misgiving that, on this occasion, revenge lay at the heart of Sellar's motivation for what he was proposing. It was the selling of the shares - the disruption of CFD's plans for Pitcairn's defence - that in all probability featured higher in his objectives than the protection of his clients' assets.

"I think we must find a way around this problem," he said at last. "How much money are we talking about?"

Peter pulled an HP-80 from his pocket. He pressed a few keys.

"The difference between 360 and 327p on 27.4 million shares. That's nine million pounds near enough."

"How do you feel about indemnifying David to the tune of nine million pounds, Bill?" asked Tudor.

"Sood off, Joohnathan."

"Bill, you've got to find me a solution."

*****

"Peter, yer've gootta find me a fookin solootion, mun. It's noo use coomin ter me whingeing aboot oow the Coode doesna allow undisclosed indemnity arrangements. Everyboody's been ferretin their way roond that shite fer years."

"Bill, you know the rules have been tightened up. Everything's disclosable now - indemnities, options, arrangements, agreements, inducements - for all practical purposes, nods and winks. Anything that would encourage someone to deal or dissuade them from dealing."

"What doos Lampard say? If anywoon knoows a sooddin trick, it'll be that fookin roogue."

"Nothing he'd ever put in writing. The Code's completely all-embracing as regards these arrangements; but, even so, it carries a specific warning to consult the Panel on anything that's borderline. They're quite simply trying to stamp it out."

"Of course they're tryin to fookin stamp it oot," he roared That's not the bluddy point, Peter. We're gooin to fookin do it. Now, how do we fookin do it soo we doon't get caught?"

"OK; we set it up as a bet. That's not a securities transaction at all. Bets don't come under the financial services regulations and they don't fall under the Code. At least they're never mentioned, even if they might be caught by the sweep-all clauses. But to make it even more remote, Johnathan's private office enters into a series of bets with CFD and a series of bets with DAM on the share price of Pitcairn 24 hours after the bid closes. Nothing direct between the two of us. Each bid is in relation to a specific share price and the overall effect is that DAM wins if the share price falls below 360p and CFD wins if the price is higher."

"Fookin marvellous, Peter! As far as it goos. But CFD are fookin stuck with payin Sellar 9 million poond out o' a fee that could be as loow as three."

"It's even worse than that, Bill. If we lose the bet, the money goes substantially to David's clients. It's not an internal transfer. The Brothers in general and CFD in particular would be down £6 million. Johnathan's not going to stand for that."

"And what's yer answer, Peter?"

"We've got to get a stay of execution, Bill - at least until we can see if there's a possibility of flushing out a higher offer. We need Johnathan to insist that DAM holds the shares for the time being. In return, we could just about afford to give Sellar a 10p per share indemnity in the short term."

"And the loong term?"

"My feeling is that this stunt of Sellar's is principally to get his own back over Bottley - but, if there's one thing that's likely to motivate him more than revenge, then it's greed. If we can provide him with some potential upside from holding onto the shares, then he might be prepared to risk some downside. At the moment he's right. Pitcairn looks dead in the water. A referral to the MMC would be marvellous but I'm sure we're not going to get it. But if we can put up a strong enough fight for it to be clear that BMP will have to raise its offer, or that there might be another bidder, he would see the possibility of the price going higher. Then we might be able to do a deal with him that gave him half the upside if we took half the downside."

"I don't see how a soodin monoopolies reference would help wi' that. If Pitcairn get clean awa, the shares'll go into a fookin' noose-dive."

"But we'll get a fee of 18 million quid, Bill."

"T'woold break my fookin' eart to give that bastard the alf of it; but laeve it wi me. Mr. Tudor an' me need to ave a few choice fookin' words."

*****

"We're sure he's up to something, Peter" said Peter Harrington. "But we're damned if we can work out what it is."

"What do you mean?"

"Well, as you know, he lives in Northamptonshire - quite the country squire. That's where he went on Friday evening when we started tailing him. He didn't budge from the house - or at least the grounds - all week-end, though his wife went into the village on her bicycle to do some shopping. A van turned up from Burrups - they're one of the City printers aren't they? - I thought so - that was Saturday mid-morning. Then there was another courier on a motorbike - just any old outfit that one, so we couldn't tell who sent it - on Sunday around lunch-time. He set off back for London, driving himself, around 7.30 and checked in to the Grosvenor House - that seems to be where he normally stays - around ten.

"He was all over the place on Monday - at Grossmanns first thing - his driver turned up to collect his car from the Grosvenor House car park and take him there. Then he went back to his office in Hammersmith. He was back in the West End for lunch at the Carlton Club - we think with Kenneth Clarke - he's the minister for industry under Lord Young, isn't he? - then back to Hammersmith. He had a meeting back in the City at Wagstaffs around six in the evening and then went off to dinner at the Savoy with his finance director and Piers Pottinger from Lowe Bell, their public relations people. Then back to Grosvenor House. The driver left the car there and made his own way home. I guess that's slightly unusual; but he seems to drive himself backwards and forwards to Hammersmith morning and evening.

"Of course, we don't know what his normal pattern is - and, even if he has a normal pattern, it's probably disrupted at the moment - but Tuesday was much the same, except that he was at Hammersmith first thing, spent the middle part of the day in the City visiting institutions with people from Wagstaffs and....."

"Which institutions?" enquired Timothy Phillips.

"Let me see - Philips & Drew and Commercial Union in the morning, then they went back to lunch at Wagstaffs - may have been joined by someone else there - then the Prudential."

"Okay, go on," said Peter.

"From the Prudential he went straight back to Hammersmith where he stayed until about 7.30. Then we come to the unusual bit. He left, driving himself, and turned west down the M4 to a little village near Sonning where he booked into a country house hotel - on his own - and spent the night before driving back to Hammersmith this morning."

"Perhaps he fancied a change of scenery."

"And a change of name?"

"What?"

"He didn't book in as Lord Evans or Arthur Evans or Sir Arthur Evans."

"How do you know?"

"Seamus O'Shea - he's my man - he'd be here now if he wasn't continuing to follow our little bird around - rang the hotel and asked for him. He thought he might get lucky and have a young lady answer the phone in his room. But they'd never even heard of him. Curious that, isn't it?"

"And did Mr O'Shea see him leave in the morning?"

"He did. Mr O'Shea has the unusual trait of requiring no sleep to speak of. Useful quality in his profession, don't you think?"

"And was Evans alone?"

"Yes."

"And did any ladies leave on their own in the morning?"

"Not a single one. He waited till the car park cleared instead of following Evans back to London."

"Perhaps he meets a man. I guess that might be even better from our point of view."

"To find that he was a bum bandit," said Timothy, "would give a whole new meaning to that title, the Lord of the Rings. Don't you think?"

Friday, 29 January, 1988

It is not thought to be the natural inclination of any animal to wallow in its own excrement. A dog can readily be trained to shit anywhere that someone else intends to walk; a rabbit will spread its pellets around - but not in its own burrow; a cat will take readily to its own litter, or someone else's garden. True, the elephant, the horse, the deer and the cow will crap on the move; but at least, in so doing, they generally leave most of what they have done behind them. What they splash down their hind legs appears to be due to a design fault rather than their own inclinations.

For these reasons, amongst others, Peter found himself at a loss to understand the state of the interior of the average family car. His brother's was a classic. Sure, Charlie and his wife had two small children who had perfected the art of synchronised travel sickness and who could therefore divert the attention of their parents to the problems of the one performing on the grass verge while the other was simultaneously spraying the interior. This, and Charlie's wife's insistence, on animal rights grounds, on the sort of cloth upholstery which made every manifestation permanent, at least in olfactory terms, always gave the interior of their Espace a certain piquancy. But the general mayhem within their car was, in other respects, typical. Newspapers, cassette tapes, cassette boxes - always separate - tissues - new and used - empties of every sort - but usually not quite and still dribbling - bananas that had seen better days, broken toys, plastic carrier bags - invariably from Tesco - half tubes of polo mints, leaves, conkers - in season and out - odd shoes - never pairs - and half-spineless umbrellas.

Peter was not generally an admirer of other people's driving; but it was detritus that was the principal reason for his aversion to anything but his own car, a chauffeured limousine or a London cab licensed by the Hackney Carriage Office.

His experience on the afternoon of 28th January had confirmed his worst expectations. Seamus O'Shea picked him up from the office around 5.30 in his Y registered Escort. It had a scrofulous, lived-in interior with the sediment of years stuffed into every nook and cranny. The front passenger seat was obviously used as a combination of desk and dining table. O'Shea cleared it by the simple expedient of tossing the debris across the rear seat; but, if Peter was to become a sleuth, this at least he could ascertain. Seamus O'Shea lived off a curious diet of boiled sweets, McDonald's fries and unfiltered cigarettes, all washed down with some liquid which lurked, as yet unidentified, in a thermos flask jammed between the two front seats in such a way as to maximise its obstruction to the operation of the handbrake.

They drove in near silence, interspersed by a terse interrogation consisting of single sentences separated by long periods of quiet concentration.

"Wull he be knowin yer?"

"Who?"

Silence.

"This Evans mun. Wull he be recognisin yer?"

"Face to face, I would think so; though we've only met once."

Silence.

"Recent?"

"What?"

"When yer met 'im?"

"Yes, just three weeks ago."

Silence.

It was starting to drizzle.

"A cowt?"

If that was what he was asking, it was not apparent, to Peter at least, why this particular piece of motorised surveillance should need one.

"A hat?"

Peter had got into the car with nothing but a copy of the afternoon edition of the *Evening Standard*. It was obvious, he would have thought, even to a sleuth.

"Hm."

221

Silence.

It was as well, Davenport concluded early on, that Seamus O'Shea was close to monosyllabic because he was one of those drivers with the irritating habit of turning his face full towards you when he spoke. He did it with such assurance and such absolute disregard for the traffic around him that the consequences of travelling with him as a rear-seat passenger were too frightening to contemplate. He was a swarthy little man of indeterminate age with dark heavily-lidded eyes and a humourless expression of utter dedication to his unusual metier.

They drove west across the City and joined the Embankment by Blackfriars Bridge, followed it along the north bank of the river and then turned right to cross the south-east corner of Trafalgar Square and went on up via The Mall, Constitution Hill, Belgrave Square, Pont Street and Beauchamp Place onto the Cromwell Road.

"Anytin to eat?" O'Shea enquired, turning once again to face him.

Did this mean 'Have you got anything to eat with you?', the answer to which was as obvious as that to the previous questions, or 'Have you had anything to eat?' This seemed to Peter the more logical, notwithstanding his experience of Mr O'Shea to date.

"I had a bit of lunch. I'm not hungry," he replied.

"Will you no be by mornin?"

Silence.

"Drink?" This one was more perplexing, but Peter decided on an all-purpose response.

"No," he said.

Silence.

O'Shea turned right into Warwick Road and pulled over into the Shell station, where he parked some way from the pumps. He scorned the handbrake, ramming the gear lever into reverse. He got out, opened the boot and rummaged around in there for a while, appearing at last with a grey trenchcoat that had seen better days and a brown flat cap.

"Put tese on," he said, before disappearing into into the forecourt shop. He returned a couple of minutes later with a handful of plastic-wrapped sandwiches, a dozen or more tubes of boiled sweets and two packs of Senior Service, all of which he dumped onto the back seat amongst the existing rubbish.

"Bovril."

"Sorry?"

"De yer drink Bovril?"

Ah, the contents of the mystery flask.

"No, not really," replied Peter, almost gagging at the thought.

"Coke, Doiet Coke, Fanta, Pepsi, Doiet Pepsi, Seven-up, apple joos, orange joos, tropical fruit joos, Ribena or water, sparklin or still?"

"I'd be very happy with sparkling water."

O'Shea returned to the shop with a shrug of disdain at Peter's unprofessional lack of preparation and a parting "You'll be needin to put dat cowt and hat on."

Peter got out and did as he was told. O'Shea returned with a large bottle of Perrier which he chucked onto the back seat with almost contemptuous resignation. He drove up past Olympia and turned right into Blythe Road. BMP's head office had been built on part of the site of the old Lyons complex. Behind the anonymous concrete and glass block O'Shea turned round and pulled up adjacent to the ramp leading down to the basement car park. It was a little after six.

From where they sat, they could see a policeman working his beat down the Hammersmith Road. He glanced towards where they were parked, stopped and headed towards them. O'Shea had parked on a yellow line. No parking permitted until 6.30. Shit, thought Peter, he's going to move us on. O'Shea ran down his window as the policeman approached and proffered his pack of cigarettes.

"We're tinkin of tombin a lift," he said inexplicably - and incomprehensibly as well as far as Davenport was concerned.

"He's still in there," the policeman replied, pulling from the cigarette pack a neatly rolled blue note. He turned and walked off back to the Hammersmith Road to resume his beat, unfurling the note, examining it as if he expected a forgery as he went and finally stuffing it into his back pocket.

They sat in silence. It was too dark to read the paper and O'Shea would not let Peter put the light on. O'Shea, who apparently prided himself on never smoking whilst he was driving, lit up. Each cigarette was followed by a boiled sweet and each boiled sweet by another cigarette, as though he had found some magic prophylactic against lung cancer. The windscreen fogged up at regular intervals. O'Shea responded by turning over the engine and directing blasts of hot air mostly into their faces. Peter was beginning to feel both kippered and broiled. Shortly before seven, it started to rain more heavily, so that O'Shea had to operate the wipers every couple of minutes for them to see even the forty odd yards to the ramp.

Every vehicle emerging was a new source of expectation to O'Shea and fifty or more consecutive disappointments did not appear to blunt his appetite for the next. By now Peter was positively racked by ennui. He asked if he might turn on the radio for the seven o'clock news summary. O'Shea consented but it was evident that he was bemused that the excitement of the current mission was not enough. The Birmingham Six had been sent back to prison with a flea in their ears by the Lord Chief Justice. Peter just managed to suppress a 'bloody Irish'; but the report excited no reaction from O'Shea in any event. Klaus Fuchs, the atom bomb spy, had died in East Germany. Britain's balance of trade in 1987 was the worst for 13 years. And Lester Piggott's much-betrayed wife had been granted her own training licence by the Jockey Club.

"Now what was the porpus of sendin im to jail?" said O'Shea. "Only ever interested in savin money and makin the weight for his next roid. Prison most be te perfect place to do boat."

The end of the news was followed by ten minutes of the Archers. That was too much for Peter, who switched off.

Shortly before 7.30 O'Shea withdrew from his lips the only cigarette that had not been burnt down to a half-inch stub, dropped it out of the quarter-light onto the little pile that had been accumulating in the road, popped another boiled sweet into his mouth and started the engine. A moment later, his curious premonition fulfilled, Arthur Evans' dark-coloured Daimler emerged at the top of the ramp, his lordship himself at the wheel, turned right across the road in front and, on reaching the Hammersmith Road, turned right again heading west.

"He'll not be goin back to te Grosvenor tonoit ten," said O'Shea as he moved off in pursuit. They followed him around the Hammersmith one-way system onto the A4 heading west. It had stopped raining but the traffic was congested as a result of roadworks in the near-side lane. Evans had pushed his way into the outside lane, as had O'Shea, but the Daimler was some six or seven cars ahead. Inevitably the lights changed at the Hogarth roundabout with Evans through and themselves stranded with two cars still ahead of them.

"Shit," said Peter.

O'Shea seemed blithely unconcerned as the Daimler disappeared behind a line of traffic joining the road from Chiswick and Turnham Green.

Ten minutes later, they came off the overhead section of the M4 and the motorway widened to three lanes.

"Right," said Peter, "we might have a chance to catch up with him now."

There was no perceptible change of pace on the part of O'Shea.

"Aren't you going after him?"

"Look, sor," said O'Shea, turning again to face him, the 'sor' being delivered much as a drill sergeant at Sandhurst might have addressed an officer cadet, contemptuous but correct, "tere are a good sixty or seventy cars in te outside lane between him and os right now, tey are all movin at exactly seventy-tree moiles an hour, tose in the middle lane are moving at around sixty-eight and te inside lane not much slower, te road is wet and slippery, dat Daimler has a V12 engine of foive point tree-five litres against moi 1400, and ABS, te Thames Valley police are te greatest nabbers of speedin cars dis soid of Singapore, oi've got te Lord knows how many points on moi licence, moi loif insurance is not paid up, oi'm colour-bloind and moi noit vision is medically defective."

Peter was not sure whether he was more stunned by the reprimand or by O'Shea's sudden discovery of sentence construction. Above all he was terrified by the experience of travelling at over seventy miles an hour down a rainswept motorway under the charge of a man who had not once glanced at the road throughout the last half minute. He concluded that imitation of his companion's code of silence was the best response and perhaps the only route to survival.

"Anyway, oi'll be reckonin te bastard's going to te same place as before," said O'Shea, "and, if oi'm wrong, tere's a homin devoice which oi taped to te insoid of his rear bumper," he added, leaning across Davenport to open the glove compartment, again sublimely indifferent to the need to watch the road. He broke into an unexpected grin. "Witin a ten-moile radius, tat little box wit de flashing red loit can guide us roit up his jacksy if we need it."

They drove on past Heathrow and the M25 interchange and on to junction ten where they switched onto the A329(M) in the direction of Reading. Peter was increasingly uneasy at the prospect of setting off down another stretch of motorway supposedly in pursuit of a car they had not seen for upwards of half an hour; but O'Shea leant over in front of him for a terrifying ten seconds of blind driving as they swept round the interchange to check the blinking red light in the glove compartment and came away utterly unfazed. Peter had instinctively leant the other way to seize the wheel as O'Shea dived to his left and had to disentangle himself with an embarrassed apology as O'Shea returned to an upright position. When Peter looked down again from the road, the little red light was still keeping up an irritatingly persistent and monotonous flickering, almost like a defective neon bulb that never quite goes off before it comes back on again.

"It'll be tellin us we're about to lose him if de gaps get to more dan about a second. Wit it flashin loik tat, we must be witin a matter of a few hondred yards," O'Shea observed confidently.

They went on to the end of the short stretch of motorway and turned right at the roundabout heading back east on the A4. Shortly afterwards O'Shea took a left down a narrow road heavily overarched with dripping trees and a few moments later they were into the genteel old village of Sonning with its mixture of black and white half-timbered cottages and mature redbrick houses. O'Shea turned left again and followed the narrow winding streets down to the river. They crossed the old single-lane stone bridge across the Thames, passed the old water mill on the left and went over the second more substantial bridge. Immediately afterwards, O'Shea pulled off the road on the left opposite a smartly-painted white building a hundred years or so old with two steep-tiled roofs and tile-hung gables. From the wall above the entrance a black inn-sign with a brass french horn hung from an elaborate twirled iron-wrought frame. A rough gravel car park large enough for fifty odd vehicles occupied that side of the road opposite the hotel. The little red eye in the glove compartment was continuously lit now. Inky puddles of rainwater shimmered in the headlights between the twenty or so cars already parked there. Among them, Peter quickly identified the dark Daimler Double-Six. The internal light came on as they watched and Evans was visible within, holding the phone to his round pugnacious face. O'Shea switched off his headlights but left the engine running. A couple of minutes later, the light inside the Daimler was extinguished momentarily and then came on again as the door was opened. Evans climbed out, briefcase in hand, went to the boot, from which he extracted a small soft overnight bag, locked up and set off across the road to the front door of the hotel with that rolling open-toed cocky swagger that Peter remembered from the meeting at 69 Gracechurch Street. Evans safely out of the way, O'Shea rearranged their parking position so that, sideways on to the rows of cars, they could more or less see them all but also had a clear view over to the entrance of the hotel on the far side of the narrow lane.

Over the course of the next hour and a half there was an incessant coming and a lesser going of cars as people arrived in ones and twos, threes and fours for the night, for dinner or a drink. Their transport was mostly what one would expect of the up and coming representatives of a well-to-do enclave of the semi-rural south-east - Mercedes and BMWs, the odd sports car, lots of four wheel drives and Volvo estates, an old Aston Martin DB5 and an even older Jensen Interceptor. You didn't see many of those any more. O'Shea noted each arrival in a notebook, ruled with columns for time of arrival, type of car and colour, registration number, a brief description of the occupants, and time of departure. From time to time it was pretty frantic as two or three cars arrived more or less simultaneously. Peter, at first almost excited by the novelty, called out descriptions as O'Shea wrote in the semi darkness of the car's interior. God knows, he thought, how the man had managed to do this on his own; but gradually it became clear that O'Shea, whatever the disordered nature of the interior of his car, was immensely methodical in other respects and, despite his previous claim to defective eyesight, observant to a quite remarkable degree. A Granada came in on one side of the car park and, a moment later another 3-series BMW and a Jaguar XJS, which parked close together on the far side.

"Four people in the Granada, two men and two women, four more in the BMW, also two of each, and two in the XJS, also one of each, girl in a fur coat with trousers," Peter called out.

O'Shea scribbled without apparently looking up as they disappeared into the French Horn.

"No," he said, "ta girl was in te back of te Jag when tey came past, two men in te front. Passenger soid had a limp. Only tree in de BMW, two of dem women, one wid glasses drivin."

"Are you sure?" said Peter.

"Will yer be tellin me what te women in te Granada were wearin?"

"Well, I think one was .... no, I can't remember."

"One, te tall one wid de dark hair, had an overcoat, possibly camel-hair. Te shorter, te blonde, was wearing a dark raincoat. And te men?"

"Both in suits I think."

"Wrong again. Te chap who was droivin, wit de moustache, was wearin a blazer. T'other you couldn't tell. He was wearin a mac but he had suede shoes."

"Okay, you win," Peter conceded. "I'll stick to banking."

They paid special attention to women on their own and those with overnight bags. There weren't very many of either. They thought a dressy dark-haired girl in a trouser suit and heels of a height which made her progress through the gravel rather comical to be promising material and, later on, a rather too well-rounded lady wearing a headscarf and a dark duffle-coat, who turned up in a white Range Rover.

"Could be interesting," said O'Shea. She was ear last time."

Those who were obviously checking in for the night mostly looked like businessmen. There was a quite elderly couple, she driving, him with a stick, in a Vauxhall with an Avis tag still hanging from the rear-view mirror, who hurried across the road in one of the frequent showers and sent one of the staff from the hotel back for their two substantial bags. The man who had emerged from the Jensen, in another downpour, was sensibly got up in an Australian drizabone and a bush hat, his eccentric equipage completed by the old-fashioned gladstone bag that he carried.

"Anoter of tare regulars," O'Shea observed.

Otherwise, there was an overweight bearded individual in a Volvo estate which later observation confirmed to be loaded with boxes of glassware, a metallic silver XJ6, driven by a man in a sheepskin coat who, Peter thought, looked like a bookmaker, another Granada containing two men who looked like a more conventional variety of accountants, a little chap in a big merc, who looked like a jockey - another regular by all accounts - and a Citroën 2cv driven by a young girl in jeans, a light-coloured polo-necked sweater and a baseball cap, who heaved a rucksack off the back seat and looked totally out of place as a potential guest of this establishment.

"Won't some of these people be staff?" Peter enquired, realising he was complicating matters but trying to show some initiative.

"Ah, terl be tat, but most of tem park round de back of de hotel, which is where tat gate over dere leads," he said pointing a little way further down the road, "particularly tose of tem tat live in; but oi tink oi've got all teir nombers from moi previous visits. By and large tey've got cars like tis rater tan tat monster tat your friend droives. We'll check tem out layter."

By nine o'clock, there was relatively little movement and the rain had stopped again, at least for the time being. O'Shea set off round the car park to pick up the registration numbers that they had between them missed and to undertake a quick survey of those parked round the back. He had explained that access to the police computer that could match the owners was simple enough if you knew the right people and were known for your unfailing generosity. When he returned, Peter, who was bursting for a leak, was allowed out, rather in the manner of a bladder-full dog, he thought, but ostensibly also for a discreet exploration of the hotel grounds. As he got out, O'Shea leaned across to the back seat and retrieved a small pair of binoculars.

"Will yer be seein if yer can spot anyting in te doining room," he said. "Te windows overlook te gardens leadin down to te river. But don't get yerself spotted."

Peter crossed the road near the bridge and slipped into the hotel's grounds, keeping close to the sweep of the water's edge. The river was, Peter guessed, abnormally swollen because the bank had disappeared and the water was lapping up onto the lawn. The ground was soft, horribly muddy in places, and the grass long and rain-soaked. Within ten paces he could feel the moisture entering his inadequate city shoes and soaking into his socks and the bottoms of his trousers. Fortunately, however, there were plenty of mature shrubs dotted around the lawn and he was able to make his way unobtrusively around the bend of the river to where a large willow, slightly bent towards the water, trailed its bare curtain of branches into the swirling water. It was as good a place for a pee as any.

That function performed, Peter turned his attention to the dining room which lay behind a grand semi-circular bay window looking over the lawn towards the river. It started to rain again, quite hard, but he found a reasonable vantage point behind the trunk of the willow, from which almost the whole interior was visible. The tree, though bare, provided a token of shelter. He scanned the scene through the binoculars. It was more or less full. He took his time trying to match the faces one by one to their previous observations. He could pick out the elderly couple who had arrived in the hire car sitting at a small table near the window; and the six people who had between them arrived in the XJS and the BMW turned out to be a single party, all quite young, which now occupied a large round table in the centre of the restaurant. The two he had labelled accountants were there and had been joined by another man, perhaps the man with the Jensen; and the bearded glassware salesman was also identifiable, on his own. Of Evans there was no sign. Perhaps he was at one of the tables over on the right which were obscured from this position. Peter picked through each group carefully. He was looking particularly for the brassy brunette in the trouser suit and the chubby lady who had arrived in the Range Rover. The brunette was definitely not visible. Of the other one he couldn't be sure. There were several ladies there who would not have missed a kilo or twain and the one he was trying to spot had been wearing a headscarf which had hidden her features too thoroughly for his inexpert eye. The 'bookie' was with a lady that could have been her. Perhaps O'Shea could do better. After twenty minutes or so Peter gave up, slipped the binoculars back into his pocket, turned up the collar of O'Shea's old mac and set off back across the grass as inconspicuously as possible. Halfway across, he stole a glance over his shoulder towards the corner of the restaurant that had been hidden from behind the willow. There were two or three tables there but Peter felt unable on the open ground to risk stopping and getting out the binoculars for a proper look. He returned to the car, sopping wet from the soles of his feet almost to his knees.

"Will yer be tellin me, Columbo, how did yer do?" asked O'Shea more than a mite facetiously, half-eaten sandwich in one hand and an evil-smelling plastic mug of Bovril in the other, as Peter closed the door.

"Well I couldn't see Evans, nor either of our prime suspects - at least not positively. The lady in the Range Rover maybe. But I couldn't get a squizz at the tables on the far side of the restaurant - at least not through the glasses. There are some people there, but it's difficult to find somewhere to stand to get a good look without being ridiculously exposed. How about you?"

"Oh, we've been havin no problems here; te bourgeoisie continue to come and go but tere's been a terrible lack of single women. Neiter of te ladies you've picked upon has left yet and none of tose we'd identified as overnoighters. And no more have arrived. So what are we left wit? Tose two birds from de MGB GT over tere and de Range Rover over here or te youngster in te little French car tat looks loik a tomato box on wheels. Not much of a bag, Mr Davenport, but it may be enough."

He turned on the wipers and cleared the windscreen.

"Oi'll be tinkin it's easin off a bit." He flicked his cigarette out through the quarter-light. "Oi'm goin to take a drink at te bar and see if oi can take a peep into te restaurant as well. Meanwhile could yer try and keep tis notebook up to date?" he asked without much confidence. "Help yerself to a sandwich. Oi won't be long."

They were starting to leave by now. Within fifteen minutes, O'Shea's meticulous notes were in a state of utter and humiliating disarray. The final straw came when the party of six with the BMW and the XJS emerged, one couple got into the XJS and two men into the BMW. The two remaining women walked straight over to the chubby lady's white Range Rover, which she had apparently left unlocked, and drove off in it furiously, spraying gravel as they turned too sharply into the lane and roared off away from the bridge.

Peter was still sitting there, totally perplexed, when O'Shea came trotting back across the road as the heavens opened again. O'Shea flicked despairingly through the notebook while Peter recounted, by way of excuse, the tale of the Range Rover, convinced he had been the witness of a blatant case of theft.

"Well, tere you are, sor" - that condescending formality again - "shows you can't take anytin at face value. Tat old biddy wit de Range Rover was sittin in a corner of a little room at te back of te bar wit tat chap who arroived in te BMW 6-series - te very tall man wit te sloit stoop - I could tell it was her because tat headscarf of hers was on te table. About twenty odd minutes ago, a girl in her early twenties pops her head round te corner, walks up to te old dear, takes te keys right off te table and walks out again."

"What, and she didn't even notice she was being robbed?"

"Oh yes, she noticed. You see te girl said 'Tanks, mommy. We'll see you later', said O'Shea, grinning broadly.

"Okay, okay, okay; well that's the end of that one," said Peter, trying to disguise his irritation at O'Shea's little joke. "Anything else going on in there?"

"Not much. Te bar and more particularly a luvvly open fire is bein monopoloised by te gin and tonic brigade. Tey're all millin around tat Parkinson man, who's letting dem all boy him drinks and bask in the sun shoinin out of his arsehole. It's one of his acts. He was in here doing it last week too. "

"Parkinson?"

"Yes, you know tat chap on the telly who makes a profession of bein a Yorkshireman. Tat one who got so angry when tat chap's stuffed ostrich attacked him. He's a place round here somewhere. Bray I shouldn't wonder - the purgatory of te nouveau riche."

"Any sign of Evans?"

"Not a whisper."

"Not in the dining room?"

"Not when oi took a look - tough one of tose tables you couldn't see - and a small one at tat - was just bein cleared; so oi might have missed him."

"And the trouser suit and stilettos?"

"Anutter Parkinson groupie. Sorry."

"The girl with the Deux-Chevaux?"

"No sign of her. A bit on te young side, I'd have taught, but perhaps tat's te way he loikes tem."

*****

It was one of the most excruciating nights of Peter's life. O'Shea seemed to be able to take a never-ending series of cat-naps but to wake instantaneously at any movement. It was clearly a trait in which he had perfect confidence.

"Wull yer go ahead now and get some sleep," he said, pouring more Bovril and lighting another cigarette. "I'll wake you if tere's anyting interesting," he urged, as the last car which they had not identified as belonging to overnight residents or live-in staff set off unsteadily into the gloom.

He was not to know that Peter was having trouble sleeping in his own bed these days, let alone on a Ford Escort's cramped and poorly upholstered front seat with, as he soon discovered, a broken reclining mechanism. It was increasingly cold, particularly where his feet had still not dried out, as well as uncomfortable, pitilessly monotonous and miserably unproductive. Peter was almost inclined to call it off but dared not mention any such qualms. O'Shea, he had come to realise, was the sort of man who saw every task through to the bitter end not just with the fortitude of a man on the end of a life sentence but with a sort of absurd enthusiasm to emerge having ticked off every box.

It was too early in the year for there to be anything like a dawn; but as the first lights came on in the hotel around six in the morning O'Shea was already squirreling through his notes, mug of Bovril in hand, the first cigarette of the new day attached to his lower lip, anticipating the action to come. The 'Aussie' in the Jensen had, O'Shea said, left very early during what was apparently a brief moment of sleep for Peter. And the jockey.

"Off to te da harses at Lambourn," said O'Shea confidently.

Otherwise Evans himself was the first away, between seven and seven-fifteen, a powerful, confident man setting out on the new day with purpose and assurance. They let him go. Perhaps a taxi would turn up for someone else in due course. Over the next hour and a half, all the rest trickled out, save the elderly couple in the Avis car whose bags preceded them just before ten. Only the Deux-Chevaux remained.

"Well, Mr Davenport sor, it looks loik te girl or notin," said O'Shea, fishing out the bulkiest of mobile phones from somewhere under the dashboard and mechanically pressing the digits for a well-used number.

"Hello, George. It's Seamus. Compliments of te mornin. How're yer doin? I hope te vouchers for Majorca have arrived. Tey have. Oh, good. I'm so glad. Yer and te missus'll love it. Great to get away from England tis toim of year. Yes. Well, of course, ye're right, George. Yes, actually tere is. HGK 829Y. Citroën 2cv. Cream and maroon - half and half. No, not left and right. Top and bottom. Yes, I'll hang on." He waited silently for no more than half a minute. "Yes, yes, yes. Okay, I might have known it. No, no problems. Tanks, George. Enjoy te holiday. Bye."

He pressed the 'end' button on the phone and put it back under the dashboard.

"Sorry, Mr Davenport, your juvenile temptress lives over te shop. She's te daughter of te manager. Wasn't around last week."

*****

Peter's phone rang. It was Maureen.

"Lady Henderson-Ball on the line for you."

"What on earth can she want? Okay, put her through....Hello."

"'ello, luv, it's Rita 'enderson-Ball."

"Hello, Rita, how are you?"

"Oh I'm fine, luv. Look, I know you and Timofy 'ave been 'avin' a bit of a spat over this and that; but I'm sure it's nuffin' reely. I agree with you that it's 'igh time the old geezer eased off a bit. All be forgotten by summer. I've always enjoyed 'avin' you up 'ere; and that Sophie's got real spunk...."

"Yes, well, actually that's...."

"Anyways, look, luv, that's not why I called you. I was just flickin' through the business pages in my *Daily Mail* this mornin' - you know I like to check up on my investments," she said giggling, trying on an accent she would have called 'oity-toity, "and I saw that you're 'avin' a right set-to with that Welsh git, Arfur Evans. Timofy and 'e sees eachuvver sometimes but I 'ate 'im meself. Fat bastard comes over all posh wiv me like as if 'e comes from a better class o' gutter than wot I do. I don't know if it could be any 'elp to you but his sekertry used to be one o' my girls. Sally Rogers she's called. Name quite suits 'er reely, when you fink about it. Anyways she always was a sorta top sekertry

234

but she liked it so much that she used to sorta moonlight for me. Quite a looker. Tall girl wiv lots o' blonde 'air. Sorta beehive it used to be in them days. Gents used to say she could suck a golf ball down a garden 'ose, if you get my meanin'. Any 'elp to you, luv?"

"Well it could be, Rita. It's very kind of you to call."

"Oh, fink nuffin' of it, Peter luv. Now when are you and that Sophie goin' to get 'itched? Don't you dare go leavin' me off the guest list just 'cos you and Timofy are not on speaks."

"Well, actually, Rita, I'm afraid that's all off," he said quietly. "She moved out around new year."

"Oh dear, luv, you sound all sad. What got into 'er, silly girl?"

"Oh I guess she got fed up with me spending nights with people like your husband rather than her. She's gone back to an old flame."

"And what about you, luv? I 'ope you're not wankin' yourself to sleep. A man needs a bit of noofy to come 'ome to."

"Nothing on the horizon at the moment, Rita. I'm not getting much time for such things."

"Rubbish, Peter, dear. You can always find time for a fuck. Tell you what, luv, I'll give you the name o' a friend o' mine in Bayswater. She'll sort you out wiv somefing to tide you over."

*****

"Peter Davenport."

"Hello, Peter Davenport. Robert Maxwell here."

It can't be, thought Peter. Authentic-sounding deep voice, full of rounded confidence; but it can't be. He'd get a secretary to make his calls. It's some prankster pulling my wire.

"Ye..es," he answered cautiously.

"Mr Davenport, I've been taking an interest in your defence of Pitcairn Pharmaceuticals and I shall be making an announcement on the subject on Monday morning. I'd like to discuss the situation with you before I do so. I wonder if I could ask you to come round and see me - ninth floor, Mirror Building, on Holborn Circus."

"Whe..en?" Peter mumbled hesitantly, still trying to decipher which of his friends was lurking behind this facade.

"Let's see; seven-thirtyish now. Could you be round here by eight?"

"Could you give me a clue as to what you want to talk about?" asked Peter, envisaging even now the embarrassment of being turned away by some minion at the *Mirror* who'd never heard of him and returning to the office to the guffaws of his colleagues or a crowing fax from someone to whom he'd done something similar at some time or another.

"I told you - Pitcairn Pharmaceuticals - I don't think the details are something we should discuss over the telephone, Peter," the still perfect imitation intoned, slipping lightly into the familiar.

"I'm sorry, Mr Maxwell; but I don't really know that it's you, do I?"

"Well you will when you get here, Peter. I wouldn't advise you to miss what I've got to say; but you'll have to please yourself. If you're coming, you'll find a separate lift on the left-hand side of the lobby that's labelled 'Publisher's Office'. The security man will alert my girl to meet you from the lift."

"I'll be with you as soon as I can get a cab," Peter heard himself say, falling limply into the trap.

There was a smartly dressed homely looking woman standing in the hallway as the lift opened onto the ninth floor of the Mirror Building. She was about the same age as Peter, perhaps a little younger, her medium-length hair, the blonde side of mousey, casually parted in the middle. Not heavily made-up, she wore a generously-cut beige tweed suit, the skirt to mid calf. She was not pretty but not plain, with the sort of soft undefined features that might betray a girl who'd put on some weight in later years.

"Hello, Mr Davenport. I'm Andrea Martin, Mr Maxwell's personal assistant," she said, extending her right hand and smiling broadly. She led the way into a well-organised office where she apparently presided over three other ladies who were all still busy over their word processors, notwithstanding the hour.

"Let me put your coat in the cupboard here. And could you just let me have your business card. Then I'll take you straight in to Mr Maxwell. He's got Peter Jay with him but he's expecting you and told me to interrupt."

She led the way down the hallway to the next door on the left. Opposite was a little glass box of an office not unlike his own rabbit-hutch back at 69 Gracechurch Street. The door was ajar and the lights still burned, but it was empty. Its size was an immediate contrast to the huge office into which Peter was now led. It was oddly out of keeping with what Peter had seen of the rest of the building, a modernised square sixties block of aluminium windows and coloured facades. Inside it was all dark mahogany furniture and plain dark wood-panelled walls, expensive but unimaginative - the comfy bolt-hole of an east european refugee rather than the opulent showpiece of a media tycoon, the best he could imagine rather than the best that he could afford. Opposite the door, under a heavily curtained window, was a large meeting table with upwards of a dozen chairs. Away to the left were two enormous sofas facing each other across a gigantic coffee table. And over in the far corner beneath another curtained window, the ponderous but familiar bushy-browed bulk of the Captain himself, his slicked hair jet black, unnaturally black, like his brows, in immaculate white shirtsleeves, a scarlet bow-tie at his well fed throat, loomed over a massive desk, covered in screens and telephones and papers, and the figure of another man facing him, not obviously young but with brown tousled hair, his back turned to Peter, who was awkwardly, almost timidly, writing notes on a pad balanced on his knee.

"Mr Davenport! How good of you to spare me your precious time," he bellowed, rising with surprising agility and coming forward, right arm outstretched. He shook Peter's hand warmly, cupping it over with his left hand and enveloping his visitor with a welcome which perfectly combined professional respect and fraternal familiarity. He held Peter's eyes in a warm, almost parental, embrace for what seemed like half a minute before gesturing him to the comfort of one of the long, deep sofas and, turning over his left shoulder toward the man with the note-pad, airily dismissed him with an "Okay, Peter, that's all for now. Get on with that document straight away. I'll want it first thing in the morning."

Her Britannic Majesty's former ambassador to the government of the United States of America in Washington, and now, with Maxwell's unerring eye for a lickspittle, the Captain's chief of staff, obediently hurried out without a word.

The door had barely closed when another over in the wall behind the meeting table, which Peter had barely noticed, swung open and a frock-coated waiter appeared bearing a huge silver tray by handles on either side on which were plates of thick open smoked salmon sandwiches, blinis with sour cream and caviar and an ice-bucket from which emerged the unmistakable transparent yellow neck of a bottle of Louis Roederer Cristal.

By the time the butler had uncorked and poured the champagne, Maxwell had already consumed a smoked salmon sandwich and a couple of blinis. As the man disappeared in the direction of what was apparently the kitchen, Maxwell raised his glass.

"To Pitcairn!" he beamed with a knowing twinkle.

Peter raised his own glass without a word and sipped cautiously. It was delicious but he could feel the need to have all his wits about him. He registered the Captain's avuncular gaze, notwithstanding the deep brown St Bernard eyes, as the hypnotic leer of an all too poisonous serpent.

"I'll be announcing on Monday morning that we control 5.6% of Pitcairn. You'll have seen that there's been some action in the market over the last few days; and now you know the reason."

"Are you still buying?"

"Oh, as and when. As and when," Maxwell replied, relishing the mystery. He took another sandwich, wolfing it in a single mouthful.

"And your intentions?"

"The game of life, Peter, the game of life," he said still chewing. "A man has to have a bit of fun. Didn't you see JAK's cartoon in the *Standard* earlier this week. They even think I'm going to be a white knight for Britoil. Here, there's a copy of it here," he said, rifling through a pile of newspapers at the far end of the table between them and turning up Tuesday's cartoon of a mediaeval castle flying the Britoil flag. As a knight on horseback approached, the lookout shouted to an old defender up on the battlements 'The good news is a white knight approaches. The bad news is it's Robert Maxwell!'.

"Not bad, eh? You see, sometimes we play the tables in Monte Carlo, sometimes the markets in London. Some days we play at the Alhambra, some days it's the Palladium. But we always play to win."

"And what exactly is the game on this occasion, Mr Maxwell? Or, is it not a game but a show?"

"Now don't get smart with me young man. I'm not in the best of humour after the fuck-up that those farts at the Football League have made over my investments in their silly little sport. At the moment you and I are on the same side. Every share that I buy in Pitcairn is one that Arthur Evans can't have."

"Unless you sell them to him."

"I don't think Arthur Evans and I see eye to eye on the price; but I haven't asked him yet. Do you think I should? I hate dealing with that woman from Grossmanns who's advising him. Never trust a woman who wears skirts down to her ankles. Always have awful legs."

"You'll have to do what you think is best," Peter parroted from another conversation, cursing himself for his stupidity as he did so. He wasn't going to penetrate this man's motives with antagonism. "We'd agree with you that what he's offering at the moment isn't very attractive."

"Exactly, Peter. And I'm going to see to it that he has to pay up or see somebody else walk off with the prize." He raised his glass and drained it in a single gulp.

"You don't envisage an independent Pitcairn at the end of the day then?"

"All things are possible, Peter. I want you to look upon me as an ally. A more than interested bystander in your struggle for Pitcairn's future - whatever that may be. Perhaps you will find a wealthier mate than Arthur Evans. Perhaps you will confound those who write you off as an ugly duckling and emerge as a gracious and profitable swan. Either way I can help you. But you would be ill-advised, Mr Davenport," he added, reverting ominously to Peter's surname, "not to confide in me sufficient of your plans to keep me on your side. Now drink up and have some of this excellent Beluga. My friend Mikhail Gorbachov sends it over for me personally."

*****

"Well that's Maxwell for you, Rod. But now that I've thoroughly fucked up your evening, there's something else that I need to tell you. I've decided to call the dogs off Evans and switch them onto his secretary."

"What on earth for?"

"Rod, I spent the whole of last night sitting in a Ford Escort with a mad Irish private detective in the car park to a hotel where Evans was supposedly engaged in an adulterous tryst. I estimate that during the night I passively consumed at least sixty cigarettes. My eyes are still burning and my throat is raw. And the evidence we unearthed was precisely nil. We checked everybody who came for dinner in and out, we checked everyone who went there for a drink and we checked the contents of every car out of the car park this morning and there wasn't an unattached woman amongst them. It may be that Evans likes little boys, though I can't say that there's any evidence of that either, unless he goes for jockeys. But I have found out that his secretary used to be a call-girl."

"You cannot be serious!" Rod protested, in imitation of John McEnroe.

"I have it on the authority of the woman who used to be her madam."

"You know, Peter, I've never taken you for the sort who goes to prostitutes. What's the fascination? I know that some people get a thrill out of paying for their rumpy-pumpy. Or is it just a banker's jealousy of the only profession that's older than your own?" he teased, chuckling down the telephone.

"Never mind how I found out. You wouldn't believe me anyway. I don't know whether we'll unearth anything at the end of the day; but I have a feeling that there's something about BMP that smells. I just wanted to let you know that I'm investing some more of Pitcairn's money with Mr Harrington."

"Peter, you're beginning to rack up some serious expenditure for an exercise which the midget has specifically forbidden. Are you sure this private detective nonsense isn't generating a momentum all of its own?"

"What else do you suggest, Rod? We've only spent about twenty-five thou so far. Another week won't take it much above forty..."

"A touch pricey for an electronic sweep of half a dozen offices and a boardroom, don't you think."

"I know, I know, Rod; but between us we'll hide it somewhere. KPMG are going to charge you a multiple of that to review those profit forecast figures you sent round this morning and frankly, from the cursory glance I've had at them, they're not going to go very far towards getting you off Arthur Evans' hook. They're barely above last year's numbers and you'd have taken a pasting for those if you hadn't had the previous chairman to blame."

"I know, Peter, but we've still got the possibility of the Monopolies Commission. The share price is still way above the offer. And you've said yourself that the institutions ought not to tip out Tom Thumb until he's had a chance to prove himself."

"Be realistic, Rod. You know that Freddie's version of the government's attitude to this bid has more of the ring of truth to it than the dwarf's. We now know who's been propping up the share price. If the Captain's still standing in the market when we announce that profits are running flat, that price could come off quickly enough for him to get killed in the rush. The likes of the Prudential and Mercury are full of support for management when it suits their book; but a year ago we were in a bull market and now we're in a bear. Cash shouts a lot louder than loyalty in markets like these," he added, ruefully recording the appalling deal he and Bill McAdam had made to keep David Sellar from dumping his Pitcairn shares.

"Peter, we're not even posting the first defence document until next Friday and you talk as if we're already running out of options. You're the fucking adviser. What do we do?"

"If the OFT decision goes against us, we've got to be ready to go looking for a white knight. The one thing that will keep Maxwell on our side, still rolling the dice, is the prospect of an auction."

"That's not the sort of talk that will go down well with our little chairman, Peter. I have to warn you, my friend, that he's been talking about bringing Goldman Sachs onto the team. Thornton's been all over him like a rash - he's here every other evening with a huge team. Loads of ideas and some of them pretty daft to my mind, but always backed up by reams of analysis. You know these yanks are suckers for paperwork, even when it's churned out at the press of a tit. Sometimes Hennessy looks at these Ivy League jerks as though he's witnessing the second coming."

"And you, Rod? Do you think Goldmans have anything to add?"

"It doesn't matter what I think, Peter. You know their line. You must have heard it so often you could do it for them. The US angle. The predominance of US companies in the pharmaceutical industry. The weight of American institutional investment. The more sophisticated valuation techniques of the New York market. The leading international specialists in take-over defence. I may think it's so much horseshit; but that won't count for anything if Hennessy concludes that he wants to hire them. I'm sorry, Peter, but I'm not putting my head on the block for you on that one."

Friday, 5 to Wednesday, 10 February, 1988

"O'Shea used something he called the flower gambit to identify her. He sent a big bunch of flowers to her at the office and then waited until she came out carrying them. Worked a charm apparently. It was such a colossal bouquet that she had to take a cab home; and he followed her. She's certainly up to something, Rod, though I'm not sure it's necessarily of any relevance to us. Most likely just continuing to work evenings as a call girl. She's no chicken but quite a looker from the photographs. Like one of those Roger Vadim creations gone a bit blowsy. She seems to base herself on the Bonnington Hotel in Bloomsbury. She was there for a couple of hours last night between six and eight - basically just dropped these flowers at her flat in Bryanston Square and went straight there. Of course, what we need is a list of her customers but that's quite a big hotel and it's difficult to separate her punters from the regular guests."

"For heaven's sake, Peter, we're fighting a bid; not investigating the London call-girl market. Hennessy will have our guts if he finds out we're spending money on this - and I'm not altogether sure I'd blame him. I really can't support you on this one any longer. So Evans has a secretary who's a harlot in her spare time. There's nothing illegal in that. It might be interesting if you could show that Evans gets his leg over in between dictation; but unless this O'Shag or whatever he's called is going to disguise himself as the office cleaner and find us a used french letter in the chairman's waste-paper basket, you'll never prove it. I'm damned certain he's no idea what this Sally Rogers does in her spare time - and, if he does, he's just being broad-minded. Lord and Lady Evans look to me like a devoted couple. He seems to live like a monk during the week and the biggest thrill his wife gets when he's away is from the saddle of her bicycle. For fuck's sake, let's give it a rest and concentrate on the defence. This document we're sending out to shareholders today needs some decent follow up. When are we going to get some reaction from the institutions?"

"Okay, Rod," Peter replied with resignation, "I'll talk to Harrington." He knew that Rod King was basically right. Reality told him that he had just been pursuing all these fruitless leads out of a sense of frustration. At the same time there was a little voice in his sleepless nights that told him that all was not as it appeared. Dr Cunningham's curious share dealing. Evans going incognito. His apparent unwillingness to spend two nights running in the same bed. His secretary's disreputable past, perhaps even present. There just had to be something behind it all. Or at least something behind one bit of it. But the painful truth that kept coming back to him was that he was simply looking for an escape from the professional humiliation of Pitcairn going down, on his advice, with barely a murmured protest.

"As regards the institutions, Justin and his people are going to have a good ring-around on Monday and give us a full report at our meeting first thing Tuesday morning. Then we'll start lining up the individual presentations. What about this invitation to lunch with Maxwell? Is Christopher prepared to give it a go?"

"The answer is no, Peter. He says that it's bound to leak out and will look like weakness on his part. I think he's right. He shouldn't be seen to entertain negotiations with that fat gangster."

"But, Rod, he's a six per cent shareholder, the largest we've got apart from BMP. We can't ignore him just because he's a lying crook. The poison dwarf can't confine his dealings to those as saintly as himself. He's going to have to get his hands dirty at some stage."

"Well, fortunately he's got an answer to that one, Peter. He's said that I can go. He doesn't mind me getting my hands in up to the elbows in the brown and smelly stuff provided he retains the scent of violets. He can deny that I have authority to do anything other than listen and report. Tuesday is the suggestion, isn't it?"

"Yes, one o'clock at his offices. I'll come and pick you up at 12.30. I don't think either of us should risk being alone with him. I'm bringing Tim along too."

*****

"All shareholders with over 0.1 per cent are listed down the left-hand column of this schedule. A lot of these are nominees; so, to the extent that we know their real identity, that's listed down the next column. It's a bit complicated because some of the big fund managers have investments which they hold for various different groups and some can be managed on a discretionary basis, where effectively the fund manager takes all the decisions, and some may be non-discretionary. For example, if you look at Barclays, they've got a total of 3.2 per cent. We've divided that up because about 1.3 per cent is in Barclays Unicorn, the unit trust management arm, where the managers will have discretion, and a further 0.15 per cent in private client funds. Some of these clients will have given Barclays discretion and others not. The balance of the holding is in pension funds that they manage and a large part of that is invested in tracking funds, which aim to mimic the performance of the index. The tracker funds merely follow the market. They never lead it; so they never accept a take-over bid until enough of the rest of the shareholders have accepted to make the offer's success certain.

"The next column shows whether or not the fund is subject to tax on any gains - that may make a difference as to whether or not they would sell and whether they would take cash or insist on deferring their tax liability by rolling the shares over into another investment. The next column shows their holdings in BMP - again that may influence whether or not they are prepared to accept an offer. Some people may think that Pitcairn is under-valued by the current offer but are nevertheless ready to accept it because they will get the benefit in the increase in the value of their BMP holding.

"The final three columns are the critical ones. They show our current assessment of those likely to accept BMP's offer, those unlikely to accept and what we might call the dont-knows, the undecided."

"And your conclusion, Justin, if I read this right," said Hennessy, "is that BMP can only currently count on around 20 per cent, we can rely firmly on around 35 per cent and the rest is all to play for. Am I right, Justin?"

"Absolutely, Chairman. Of course, we'll have to keep updating this schedule as we go along and fund managers firm up their views. Naturally, some people will never tell us what they're going to do; but we'd expect to whittle down the undecided figure as we go along and be reasonably confident of who's going to support us before we reach the closing date."

Shit and derision, thought Peter, why on earth am I saddled with this deadbeat upper-class twit whilst BMP have Wagstaffs to rely on? Evans will be looking at a schedule from Carradine with a totally different complexion to this simpleton's heap of crap.

"Well, that looks like a pretty fine start to me. I think we can build on that. Wouldn't you agree, Peter?"

"I have one or two prob.... refinements that I think we might ask Justin's team to make to this schedule for our next meeting, Christopher."

"Okay, Peter," Hennessy came back, catching the choked-off criticism in Davenport's reply. "I think this is a very fine piece of analysis; but if you've got a positive contribution to its improvement, let's hear it."

"Well, Christopher, I think we might have a more realistic measure of the task that faces us if we divided the likely attitude of the shareholders into rather more categories. For example, I would have a category for weak holders of our stock and I would take Maxwell and all the holdings that have gone into the hands of arbitrageurs over the course of the last few weeks out of the dont-knows and put them there. If you were to add that category to BMP's firm supporters, you'd have something pretty close to equality in the support for us and them."

"Oh, surely that's too negative, Peter. We mustn't assume that everyone who's not declared that they are with us is against us."

"No," said Peter hesitantly, desperately searching for something to redress the balance. He could all too easily lose this man's confidence and find himself saddled with Goldman Sachs as joint advisers. It came to him.

"Equally, we should determine what proportion of our shares are held by people who never respond to anything. They range from people who never even bank their dividend cheques - because they're dead or gone away - to those who simply never send in proxies for annual general meetings. We can certainly count on the missing as our supporters - because Evans needs 50.1 per cent of everybody - and probably a good proportion of the rest of the lethargic."

"Well that sounds fair enough. Go on."

"I'd use six categories to analyse shareholder support where Justin currently has three. At one extreme certain backing for BMP - basically the shares they've bought - then likely BMP supporters - I'd include Grossmann's managed funds in that, for example; then weak holders - Maxwell and the arbitrageurs; then dont-knows; then likely Pitcairn supporters - for example the Prudential and Britannic, who support management as a matter of principle; and finally certain Pitcairn support - the dead and missing and the index-trackers. I fear you'll find that the last two are materially less than 35 per cent."

"That sounds reasonable to me, Justin," Hennessy responded. to Peter's relief. "Don't you agree?"

"Well, it's a bit precise for this stage in the game; but we can give it a go."

"Good. As you say, it may be a little pre-mature; but why don't we just run through the big names on this list and see where we'd put them on Peter's basis?"

"Well, as Peter says, our likely backers must include all those who traditionally support management - that would be the Prudential, Britannic, Norwich Union, M & G, Mercury, Scottish Amicable...."

"Not Mercury, Justin!" Peter interrupted. "I know that's their mantra; but you know as well as I do that Carol Galley woman has a record of selling out to the highest bidder in the end."

"I agree they have done that from time to time; but they were part of the group which supported the appointment of the new chairman."

"Perhaps I'm being too cynical", Peter conceded, "but I think they take these decisions one at a time. At best we should put them with the dont-knows. That's the group we're going to have to concentrate on persuading to stay with us; and Mercury will need all the attention we can give them."

"Fair enough, Peter. Now other likely supporters. The Pearl are normally reliable and I presume we can put DAM in that category too."

There was just the hint of a question in Travers-Coe's voice and Peter remembered that he was an old Etonian mucker of David Sellar. Had they talked, he wondered? Justin was watching him closely. He had clearly been peeved at Davenport's criticism of his analysis and Peter was increasingly certain that he was looking for revenge.

"Well, we maintain strict Chinese walls," he intoned, not quite promptly enough, "so I haven't spoken to them; but David Sellar is normally pretty sensible. Have you talked to him, Justin?"

"I was naturally looking to you to deliver DAM," Travers-Coe replied, avoiding the question and continuing to fix him in his sights.

"I don't think my understanding of Chinese walls should prevent you talking to your investment management colleagues, Peter, provided you don't disclose any confidential information," Hennessy chimed in unhelpfully.

"Well, we'll need to decide exactly how they should be approached," Peter came back, trying to close down the subject.

Travers-Coe would not let him wriggle away. Either he knew the truth from Sellar or he had detected Davenport's discomfiture.

"I hope you're not suggesting that we need to put them amongst the dont-knows."

"Oh, I'm sure not," Peter came back immediately, having decided to brazen it out.

"Good. Well then, we'll leave that one to Peter, Chairman," Justin concluded, satisfied that Davenport was now firmly nailed to the wall.

They ran through the rest of the list without major disagreement and totted up the sums. Pitcairn's likely supporters now totalled only 31 per cent and 4.15 per cent of that was made up of the DAM holding. The agreement that Bill McAdam and Peter had cobbled together with Sellar would hold those shares at bay on a temporary basis but, at the end of the day they would need to be categorised with Maxwell and the arbs. Peter did a swift piece of mental arithmetic to put together the total for BMP, the Grossmann funds, the Wagstaff private clients, the arbs, including Maxwell, and DAM. It came to not far short of 40 per cent. He kept it to himself.

*****

"Can we talk in the car?" he whispered conspiratorially to Peter, his eyes motioning towards the driver on the pavement, as he climbed in.

"Sure, no problem on that score."

"You having trouble with DAM?" Rod enquired before Sid had even got the door closed.

"What makes you say that?" Peter defended automatically, realising immediately how pathetic it sounded.

"Come off it, Peter. We're in this together. I may be new to this game but I can detect a frisson in the air."

"Did Hennessy detect it too, may I ask?"

"I don't believe he did. For all his Christian principles, the little bugger can lie his socks off with the best of them; but he tends to believe what other people tell him. Strange that, isn't it?"

"David Sellar has told us he wants to take advantage of the offer to sell out for cash in the market. We've done a ...... we've persuaded him to hold off for a while."

"But he's a weak holder is what you mean."

"Does a bear shit in the woods? Is the pope catholic? Are the Kennedys gun-shy? Does Muhammed Ali still do the shuffle? Take your pick, Rod. He wants out."

"I've only had four pension fund meetings with that man since I took over. What a shit. I know you're all toffs but he's not like you. He's not my type of toff. I'm not sure what the difference is."

Tim in the front seat let out a spontaneous peal of laughter. Peter cuffed him over the back of the head with his newspaper..

"I'm a toff by education. He's a toff by breeding. He's a moneyed toff. Tim and I are just salary slaves disguised as toffs."

"Well, what if I tell him that, when this is all over, it'll give me the greatest pleasure to tear up his management contract for our pension fund and stuff it up his well-bred backside. There's the thick end of half a billion quid in there."

"It won't do any good, Rod. We're talking power, not size. He's decided you're carrion. A maggot doesn't feel threatened by the elephant it's eating."

"And Harrington? Have you stood him down?"

"Sort of."

"What exactly does that mean, Peter?"

"He's bringing me round some photographs later. See if I can identify anyone. That's the end of it. Promise."

"Okay, let's concentrate on Maxwell. He's a bigger shareholder than Sellar now. What's the line?"

"I'm convinced he's just here for the arbitrage. He'll want to sell to a higher bidder and it won't matter a fuck to him whether that's Evans or someone else. I don't think he'll have invited us because he wants our company. He wants to know if an auction is going to develop. It's in our interest not to deny that possibility; but we must be very careful what we say. I don't want to see a headline tomorrow saying 'Pitcairn in talks with other bidders'. We've had enough statements forced out of us by the Panel already. That's why there's strength in numbers. I've been kicking myself for seeing him alone last week, wondering what words he might have put into my mouth. And remember, we may well be taped."

Sid came off Fleet Street along Fetter Lane and pulled up before the corner with Holborn.

"I'll be here again from 2 o'clock," he said. "There's no parking here; but if I get moved on, I'll go round and round the block."

It was raining again and blowing up stormy as they bolted across the wet and windswept pavement for the unlikely and unprepossessing sanctuary of the Mirror Building. There was a man outside protesting about something or other. He had pulled an olive-green souwester down over his ears and his placard seemed about to take flight.

Andrea Martin, again with the heavy gold rings at her ears which had been her only adornment when Peter had first met her, relieved Rod and Tim of their business cards to add to her collection and led them along the corridor past the grand door on the left and Peter Jay's pathetic goldfish-bowl on the right. A little further on, she opened a door on the left and ushered them into a rather modest windowless dining room. A slight but wiry young man with a narrow, almost gaunt, face, heavy squarish tortoise-shell-framed spectacles and dark, curly hair stepped forward to meet them. He wore an inconspicuous grey suit, a pale blue shirt and a narrow featureless burgundy tie.

"Hello, I'm Kevin Maxwell," he said. "My father will be with us in a moment. Can I fix you some drinks?"

Rod and Tim stuck to tomato juice spiced with Worcestershire sauce and Peter settled for a Perrier. The increasing quantities of scotch which he seemed to be consuming every evening had not dulled his appetite for another; but this was not the moment. Kevin stuck to small talk. He was as blatantly uninterested in each successive subject as were his guests. The minutes ticked by. Tim and Rod had a refill; Kevin likewise.

"I do apologise. My father was on a trans-atlantic call. I'm sure he'll be with us shortly," Kevin was saying as the door swung wide to frame the Captain's bulk. He was wearing a blue worsted suit, not quite as dark as City manners would have dictated, his habitual white shirt and a blue silk tie with a loud red zig-zag running down it, like a bloody lightning strike. He looked even larger with his jacket on than Peter recalled from their earlier meeting. He went straight to Rod King and smothered him in that two-handed handshake.

"I'm so glad to meet you, Mr King." That gruff voice, that same perfect English, almost too perfect given his east European origins. "Forgive me for keeping you waiting. I've come straight from a meeting with Brenda Dean. Easier on the eye than your average trade unionist - but just as garrulous," he added, smiling broadly at his little joke.

Kevin looked sheepish as his father turned to Peter.

"My dear Peter. How very excellent to see you again." For a moment Davenport thought he was going to kiss him as he took him by both shoulders; but it was only a prelude to an even more fulsome hand-wringing. Tim Philips got barely a nod.

"I think we should sit straight down since I've kept you waiting so long. Mr King come and sit here on my right; Peter here with Kevin there, and ... you there, next to Mr King."

Maxwell took up station at the head of the table and pressed at a button concealed beneath it to summon the food. The first course arrived almost instantaneously, scallops with a mild and creamy curry sauce. It was accompanied by a Gewürztraminer too rich for Peter's taste.

"So, how are you getting on in your efforts to get away from the iron grip of the Lord of the Rings, Mr King?" Maxwell began, diving into his food the moment the waiter had departed. No talking in front of the servants. Not an environment in which Sid's brand of confidentiality could be guaranteed, thought Peter, making a half-hearted effort at chewing on a scallop. And not very kosher either.

251

"Oh it's early days yet Mr Maxwell," Rod replied. "We only put our first defence document out last Friday and it'll no doubt be a while yet before the OFT decides whether the bid should go to the Monopolies Commission."

"There's no chance of that, mark my words. You're going to have to look elsewhere for your saviour on this occasion. I don't doubt that what you say about Arthur Evans' attitude to research expenditure and what he's done with every other BMP acquisition has the ring of truth," he added, displaying a knowledge of the detail of the defence that Peter found surprising, "but, talking as an ex Member of Parliament, I can tell you that's not a kite that's going to fly with this government."

"We'll have to wait and see on that one; but, even if you're right, there are plenty of other lines we can pursue."

"Ah, alternative merger partners. I thought as much." Maxwell had already cleared his plate. He quaffed vigorously at his wine.

"No, no no," Peter jumped in too nervously. "Of course, there's always the possibility that we will receive other approaches; but I'm sure Rod was merely talking about other defence arguments. The current bid seriously undervalues the potential profits from Pitcairn's research pipeline over the next few years."

"Oh I don't doubt that Arthur Evans' balls can be put through the wringer; but in my view you'll need someone to turn the handle. He'll fall more deeply in love with the girl when he sees someone else canoodling up to her. And in my view there should be wealthier and more attractive suitors for....."

Over on a little table against the wall to Peter's right and Maxwell's left, a telephone began to ring. It was tiresomely shrill. Maxwell stretched over to it.

"Yes, Andrea, yes. Put him on. Hello. Hello."

Maxwell dropped unhesitatingly into a language of which Peter caught not a word. He was pretty certain it was east European, slavonic perhaps, maybe Russian. There were intermittent silences during which Maxwell did most of the listening, nodding and interrupting occasionally, apparently for clarification. The exchange was finally terminated.

"I do apologise, gentlemen. I had to take it. It was Lech Walesa. Such a brave man - I think he'll be president of the Poles one day. He needs me to speak to François Mitterrand for him rather urgently - and confidentially. Unfortunately gentlemen, whilst I am certain that your English public schools will not have provided you with Polish, I am not so confident of the inadequacies of your French. I will have to talk to Monsieur Le Président from my office. I won't be long. Continue with your lunch. Kevin, please take care of our guests." And with that, he rose and departed as the waiter reappeared.

The main course was pheasant. There was another rich sauce redolent of port and redcurrants and a heavy Bulgarian cabernet fit to make your eyelids droop. The visitors were all commendably abstemious as they reverted to the younger Maxwell's small talk. His father rejoined them, just as they were finishing. As the door closed behind him, the figure of Ian Maxwell, his other son within the business, could be seen scurrying away down the corridor.

"Sorry about that," the great man apologised again without feeling, as if such affairs of state were routine.

He waved away the efforts of the waiter to ply him with the pheasant, contradicting the evidence of his capacity for indulgence displayed around his waistline, but eagerly alighted on the cheeses that followed as soon as Rod had done with them and took himself a generous tranche each of the Stilton and Camembert before passing the platter on to Peter.

"Gentlemen," he said between mouthfuls, "I have a proposition."

He waved to the waiter to pour him a glass of the red and waited again for him to retire before continuing.

"I agree with you that Arthur Evans would be a dire custodian of your business. He's a boor," he said, stuffing a three-inch stick of celery generously mounted with stilton into his mouth.

"A nationalised industry man, an organiser of generally inefficient and largely unskilled labour on a massive scale. He had some success because he knows how to wield an axe and he's not squeamish at the sight of blood."

He quaffed vigorously and reached for the bottle.

"The PM likes her men like that. But Evans knows nothing of real science. I publish more pure research through Pergamon Press every month than he would tolerate in a lifetime running Pitcairn. He has no vision of the future as we do here. His background is in trying to make the best of Britain's crumbling engineering base. Well, I've tried that with Hollis too. And with that bid for AE. Thank the Lord it didn't succeed. The future's with science, technology, electronics, medicine. Your sort of business, Mr King," he added, masticating vigorously.

"If you'll support me, if you'll give me the necessary information to let me do it, I'll put together a bid to blow the gonads off Arthur Evans and I'll make Pitcairn the core of a giant European medical business to give the Americans a real run for their money. What do you say to that, Mr King?"

Peter jumped in rudely before Rod had a chance to recover from his astonishment.

"As you know, Mr Maxwell, we're only here to listen and report back. It would be going outside our mandate from the Pitcairn board to give you a reaction. But, if you wish to put forward specific proposals, we'll ensure that they're given the appropriate consideration."

"Now fuck you, Mr Davenport," Maxwell came back angrily. "We don't need your mealy-mouthed formulae. We need some passion. And, if we're going to have some passion, you'll need to get your knickers off. I'll put together a bid. Don't doubt that I've got the capacity. But Michael Richardson and Goldman Sachs...."

Goldman Sachs! A conflict for Goldmans, thought Peter with as much elation as he had experienced this year. What a Godsend! He glanced at Rod who caught his brief moment of absurd triumph.

"....... will need to have the projections to support the financing. Mr King, I hope your position is not as narrow as Mr Davenport portrays it"

"Then I'm sorry to disappoint you," Peter heard with relief. "I go along with everything he says."

"Well, I'm sure that's a very loyal stance towards your advisers; but I warn you, you can't find a way out of the predicament you're in by sitting on your bums. We work together on this, or we go our separate ways and you take the consequences. You can get back to me on it. But now, gentlemen, you'll have to excuse me, I've got work to do. Kevin will give you some coffee and see you out."

And with that he rose impatiently from his chair, offered a perfunctory handshake to each of his guests in turn and made an unsmiling and ungracious exit.

Ten minutes later, as they departed, they had to stand back at the lift to let out two strikingly pretty far-eastern girls, probably Thai thought Peter. They were a little too sharply dressed for the normal visitors to the publisher's offices and each wore a pair of improbably high heels.

"And what do you think those two hoo...." Tim began, until quickly silenced by Peter placing a finger to his lips, as the lift doors came together.

Sid's Volvo was outside, sandwiched between two other chauffeur-driven cars, a Rolls-Royce in a curious shade of greyish pink with the number plate 'MCC 1' and a dark green Jaguar, its chauffeur dozing happily with the peak of his cap pulled down over his eyes..

"Well, what did you think of all that Mitterrand and Walesa guff, Peter?" Rod asked, as they climbed quickly into the back out of the rain; "true or false?"

"Well there is some evidence that he knows a whole lot of these east Europeans. Remember, he's one himself - the bouncing Czech, as *Private Eye* calls him - but this time I've got a hunch. Sid, could you please just go up Holborn a little way, do a uey and pull in over there, where we can see the entrance over on this side."

Sid did as instructed. Two minutes later he had parked the Volvo on the north side of Holborn, a couple of hundred yards east of the redbrick gothic mass of the Prudential building. It was not a parking zone; but the road was wide enough here and there was little danger of being moved on. He left the engine running to operate the heating and, more particularly the windscreen wipers. They sat there for ten or twelve minutes, Peter's eyes glued to the *Mirror* entrance forty or fifty yards away across the street. There was the occasional anxious moment as the bulk of a slow-moving double decker wholly obscured their view. The protester in the souwester was still at it, though he had abandoned attempts to keep his placard aloft in the high wind and had left it against the wall behind him. He was handing damp copies of a flysheet to all those emerging from the building who would accept one. Since most had more preoccupations with their attempts to prevent their umbrellas being blown inside out, his success rate was low. Tim, however, had been sufficiently curious to accept one.

"He's objecting to the *Mirror* carrying cigarette advertising. Apparently he's been at it for months. I should think, standing on that corner, he's absorbing more carbon monoxide in 24 hours than the average cigarette smoker inhales in years," Tim was saying, as again there was a movement behind the man and he turned to press his flysheet on the two figures emerging from the revolving doors. They turned towards the green Jaguar, heads down against the weather, but the lady in the voluminous brown raincoat, testily waving the protester away, was unmistakably none other than Gillian Wilkinson and the belligerent open-toed swagger of the bulky bruiser at her side belonged to none other than Arthur Evans.

*****

Tim Phillips bounded up the steep staircase to Peter Harrington's offices two at a time with Davenport trudging steadily in his wake. The weeks of amnesia, of fretting over Sophie, of finding every mouthful of food a chore, of drinking too much Scotch too late into the night, of fighting, it seemed, a wearisome battle whose only possible outcomes would all amount to professional failure, weighed on him like a decade of drudgery. Right now it seemed the final straw to have discovered that he was being two-timed by such an unlikely tart as Robert Maxwell. But at least it had dished Goldman Sachs.

Harrington's ridiculously enthusiastic assistant, Nicolla Duckworth, had pinned the dozens of enlarged photographs round the walls of the drab conference room. In the top left hand corner of each was yesterday's date, 8 February, and the time in hours, minutes and seconds. They were arranged in meticulous order, four high, at more or less eye level, starting around half past four in the afternoon to the left hand side of the door and snaking all the way round the windowless room until they stopped just short of the door again at eight thirty-five that evening.

"She got to the Bonnington just before six. That photo with the blue dot there is the picture of her arriving; and she left at eight seventeen - the red dot over there. Our van was parked about twenty yards down the road from the entrance so that the photographer could take pictures through the one-way glass in the back door. They're not all the same quality and sometimes one person is a bit obscured by another; then there are side views and some just backs; but he assures us that he got a picture of everyone who went in and everyone who left from three o'clock until nine. If there's no one you recognise in this lot, we can try the other films - but we haven't had them enlarged yet. Thought we ought to concentrate on the time she was there and the immediate period around that. We've..."

"Won't he have missed people when he needed to change the film?" Tim enquired, dubious of any claim for one hundred per cent infallibility.

"No. He had three cameras and an assistant reloading as he went along; and, because he was basically taking every picture at the same distance, he didn't have to waste time on refocussing. Of course, it was dark by the time she arrived; but the entrance is pretty well lit and he was using a very fast film - 1000 ASA. In general we're pretty pleased with the quality. I think we were right to opt for black and white. I suggest you just begin at the beginning and go on round. You need to start there and go down each column of four pictures and then up to the start of the next column. There are a couple of magnifying glasses there, if you need them. Meanwhile can I get you something to drink?"

"Thanks, scotch and soda," said Peter automatically.

"Coke, thanks," added Tim.

It was a god-awful thankless chore. Tim at least started with enthusiasm and was down the first wall in no more than twenty minutes, by which time Peter had covered barely half that distance. The drab grey photographs of drab grey people wrapped up against the cold of an early February evening in their drab grey clothes were almost hypnotically soporific. The airless room was over-heated. A second scotch had arrived unbidden but unrejected. Peter began to doubt if he was taking anything in. His own brother might have passed him by unrecognised amongst this black and white mob. He rubbed his eyes and sat down for a minute before wearily hauling himself to his feet to resume the search.

"That's Julian, isn't it?" Tim announced a few minutes later, well down the second wall. Peter hurried over. Sure enough, Julian Corrigan, one hand deep in his overcoat pocket, was paying off a cab with the other and a moment later, in the next photograph, disappearing into the hotel.

"What the fuck is he doing there? If that bastard is running with the hares and hunting with the hounds I'll have him eat his own sodding giblets on toast. What's the time on that? 19.36."

257

Diverted, they pursued the following photographs frenetically.

"Isn't that Robert Sutton from Macfarlanes?" asked Tim after a few moments.

"Yes, and that's Byam-Cook from Bird & Bird. And that's Robert Lane from McKennas. It's a fucking Law Society dinner. Shit, shit and more shit!"

It took Peter all of ten minutes to find out where he'd got to after they resumed. If anything, blundering into the familiar faces that spattered the images from around seven-thirty to eight, presumably the time for the dinner, made things even more confusing. Even Tim was slowing down.

Around nine-thirty, Peter finally turned onto the final wall. Tim had finished and was starting again.

"8-2-88 20:06:18," Peter intoned, as he started on the fresh column. "Now who's this shifty bloke?"

To be honest, the man wasn't the least bit shifty - just another nondescript character emerging from the Bonnington's revolving doors. With one hand he was tugging up the scarf at the throat of his overcoat against the cold blast of the evening air. In the other he carried a simple briefcase. Actually he was looking quite jaunty, pleased with himself, improbably puffed up - like a man who's just had a particularly wonderful and gloriously satisfying.....

"Well, I'll be buggered! I know you, don't I? Tim, come and have a look at this. I am going to castrate, hang, draw, quarter and fucking crucify this cunt."

Peter unpinned the photograph.

"Come on, we need to find out when he arrived."

It took them all of three-quarters of an hour going backwards and forwards over the earlier shots. The first time through they missed it altogether. Then Peter worked backwards from the gap that had now appeared in the grey montage and Tim forward from the start. They repeatedly snatched the original photograph from one another as they tried to match a figure partially obscured; but eventually Tim found it. A back view only. The time in the top left hand corner read 8-2-88 18:22:53.

*****

"Can't you just burst in on them and snap the traditional picture of the bastard hammering away at her with his bare bum in the breeze? Isn't that the original purpose of private detectives?"

It was gone eleven and Peter Harrington was far from pleased at being dragged back to his office from his home in Islington. Eventually Davenport had seized the telephone from Nicolla.

"Peter I want you here and I want you here this fucking minute. Now do I make myself one hundred per cent crystal fucking clear," he bellowed, as the colour rose to Nicolla Duckworth's cheeks. "We've got to nail this cunt and I've no idea whether we've got twenty-four hours to do it, or forty-eight, or none at all."

"Peter, what you've got here is the most circumstantial of circumstantial evidence. Four photographs - two of her and two of him. Not together. You may be right to add two and two and make $64,000 - but you've got to give us time to substantiate it and to get you proof."

"I haven't got time, Peter. I need action and I need action right away. If this happens again tomorrow night, I want that bastard in flagrante delicto."

"Be realistic, Peter. This isn't the wild west. Hotel bedrooms have locks. And it's not Chicago. We can't batter down the door. It's not James Bond either. We can't set up a video camera to do a *From Russia with Love* on them."

"Can't you follow her to her room and get a man to hang around in the corridor waiting to see who joins her? Grab a shot of him with a concealed camera. Dress someone up as a chambermaid, for god's sake!"

Nicolla had been doing her best to quieten the rising crescendo of Davenport's frustration; but plying him with scotch, she had now realised, had badly backfired.

"Peter, be realistic," Harrington said again. "I don't run to ersatz chambermaids; and you can't hang around in a hotel corridor looking innocent. It's not a sodding airport lounge. We'll do what we can. I'll put separate tails on them twenty-four hours a day. It'll mean a sharp rise in costs. We'll need a team of at least four for each of them to maintain round the clock coverage."

"How much?"

"Seven or eight thou per day. Is that okay?"

"Sure," said Peter.

Friday, 12 February, 1988

"Rod, I've been spending some more of your money."

"Christ Almighty, Peter, what now? I hope it's not more of this private detective shit."

"No, it's lawyers this time."

"I'd have thought we'd got enough of those bastards too. Between you and the poison dwarf, this is beginning to look like a City benefit match."

"What the hell has he done now?"

"Nothing yet; but since we put Goldmans off side, he's been going on about those two chaps who've just walked out on First Boston. You know the ones I mean; they sound like a Costa Brava menu - Paella and Holstein or some such."

"Wasserstein and Perella?"

"Yes, that's the pair. Do you know them?"

"Well, I've met them both. To be honest I was interviewed by them a while back when First Boston were looking for someone to set up a corporate finance department for them in London."

"And?"

"We didn't get anywhere. Our discussions sort of fizzled out. I wasn't sad. It would have involved reporting to a namesake of Hennessy's who's one of the investment banking world's classic bastards."

"Not and that, you berk; and what are they like."

"Oh, sorry, yes; well, very clever, very influential, very well-connected, ruthless like you wouldn't believe."

"What, worse than the dwarf?"

"Different. I always think he's ruthless for the sake of ruthlessness. Like he's trying to prove himself all the time. Comes from his size, I suppose. These chaps don't have anything to prove. They're the biggest of the big swinging dicks already. When they're ruthless, they're ruthless for a purpose. And the purpose is usually money. Someone else's money that they have in mind to make their own. They've been making a fortune for First Boston and it's not surprising when you think that every big deal employs them just to make sure they're on the inside pissing out and not the outside pissing in. Bruce Wasserstein's sort of shambolic and dog-eared but horribly clever - not really presentable. Joe Perella is tall and intense - sort of like a conquistador. They're quite a team."

"You sound enthusiastic. You fancy sharing your fees?"

"Rod, those two don't share with anyone. They're extra."

"Would they be useful?"

"Well, I suppose if I say 'no', you'll say I'm just talking my own book. But, truly, I think we're better off having them out there looking for counter bidders. Sure that suits the Brothers too. If you ask him, that won't be Wasserstein's view, of course, because everyone likes working for the chap who's on the receiving end. In any bid, there's only one big fee that's certain - and that's from the victim. If the defence succeeds, the adviser gets the gold medal. If it fails, he still walks off with the silver or at worst the bronze. But there could be a dozen potential bidders and, at most, only one of the advisers will strike gold. The rest are all last. You may not like it, but from the point of view of Red Riding Hood's shareholders, the more wolves there are out there the better."

"You're talking like someone who's given up the prospect of Pitcairn being independent at the end of the day. Have you forgotten you only win gold if we show everyone a clean pair of heels? Otherwise it's dross. That argues for having the fastest adviser - even if he's got four heads and eight legs."

"The fastest adviser never has four heads and eight legs, Rod. Haven't you ever heard the one about the camel - the horse that was designed by a committee? But I assure you I'm still after gold," said Peter, sounding to Rod at last a little more perky than the hang-dog defeatist of recent weeks. "That's why I've told Justin to hire the best trade practices QC and get him briefed to argue our case with the Monopolies Commission - if we get there, of course."

"Peter, you're going soft in the head. Maggie Thatcher will be caught in bed with Ken Livingstone before this'll go to the MMC. At the very least, you're premature and, at the worst, you're pissing away our shareholders' money."

"Well, you never know," said Peter, blithely ignoring the reprimand. "It's best to be prepared; and we don't want BMP snaffling all the best brains. I doubt if they've retained anyone - too bloody confident - so I thought we should grab the pick of the bunch."

"And what would all that cost?"

"Well, of course, it won't just be the QC. He'll need a junior. None of these chaps will go for a pee without someone to hold it for them. Justin reckons it'll be about £25,000 to get him briefed and then about £2,000 a day...."

"Shit, you can get a barrel full of accountants for that."

"Sure, Rod, I know; I know. Then there'll be 50 per cent on top of that for his junior."

"Who will no doubt do all the fucking work."

"'Twas ever thus, Rod. Thank God. It might be the turn of thee and I in due course."

"I forbid it, Peter. Do you hear me? I forbid it."

"Too late, Rod, I've done it," Peter blundered on. "But actually, that wasn't why I called. I've got something else I want to go over with you. Can I come round later? - say about eight-thirty nineish? Will you still be there?"

"Reckon so, but I warn you I'm bloody irritated with what you've just said. Meanwhile I'm trying to find a few more million to add to this sodding profit forecast. I could go on all night with that."

"Okay, I've got to go out to see someone right now. I'll call round when I get back."

"Maureen," he called as he replaced the receiver. A moment later she popped her head round the door.

"Could you nip round to Thomas Cook in Cheapside some time tomorrow and see if you can find me somewhere to go for a fortnight or so, starting at the end of next week."

"You thinking of resigning, Peter?" she said in jest, only immediately afterwards realising that it could just be true and feeling suddenly guilty. "I can't say you look as though you're enjoying it much these days," she said, trying to take it back.

"I just need a rest."

"And who's going to look after Pitcairn, may I ask?" she added.

"I don't think they're going to need me much for a couple of months."

"I didn't think you were going to throw in the towel so easily," she said, with a hint of rebuke, now realising that her previously guilty feelings were misplaced. "Anyway," she said, in a tone that seemed to abandon all hope for him, "what sort of thing? They say the snow's much better now."

Remembered joys tugged at his guts.

"No. No more snow, Maureen. Somewhere hot. Caribbean, Pacific, something like that."

*****

Peter was not a fan of the tube. He never used it to travel to or from work. It was occasionally convenient to get from one side of the West End to the other; but he couldn't have recalled a journey of more than six stops since he had ceased to be an articled accountancy clerk with a flat in Highgate back in the mid seventies. This was forever. And rush hour. The train rattled along noisily on its decades of underinvestment, squealing at the fiscal incompetence of Wilson and Heath and Callaghan as it crossed the junctions, filthy from Thatcher's love affair with her people, the car-owning middle classes, stopping and starting with incompetent management, and throwing its contents this way and that as some 'memberrr' of that big Glaswegian oaf's union confirmed his surly indifference to anyone's 'interrrests' but his own.

"I've never seen so much sodding humanity jammed up one another's armpits. Everyone covered in layers of winter clothes, everyone sopping wet, the heating going like we're on our way to Hades. It was like the drying room in a rugby club. That awful smell of wet wool wrapped round sweaty flesh. Half of them seemed to have colds and none of them handkerchiefs. All that sniffling and sneezing. It's no wonder you bastards make so much money stuffing your pills and potions down their throats. And the garlic. Do these people cook in it or use it for bath salts? Between a Paki on one side and what looked like a Greek on the other, I thought I was going to up-chuck."

Peter stood to one side of the double doors so that, at each station he could observe whether his quarry, in the next carriage, was alighting. He had an immediate anxious moment at Holborn as the platform appeared on the left-hand side of the train instead of the right where he had got on and he was forced to fight his way through to the doors on the other side to check on the passengers who were getting off. How could that happen? The Central Line was just one line west to east with a couple of branches off at either end. Harrington had told him that the man could be expected to go right through to the end of the line at West Ruislip; but he was taking no chances. He got back onto the train as the doors closed and, to the undisguised hostility of his fellow standing passengers, clawed his way back through the crowd again at Tottenham Court Road as the platform once again appeared on the right-hand side. There were huge comings and goings at Oxford Circus and, if his quarry had slipped in amongst the crowd on the platform, it was doubtful if Peter would have spotted him - except perhaps too late as the train got underway again. But luck was with him. A motley collection was disgorged at Lancaster Gate and again at Queensway in the Arab quarter. Most of what was left of the smarter set departed at Notting Hill and Holland Park; but it was still standing room only at Shepherd's Bush. Shortly before White City, the train suddenly emerged from its subterranean passage into the dark and dreary winter night. At White City itself the platform switched back to the left again but he was by now one of the few standing passengers and was able to move from side to side without a problem. As they pulled out of the station, he was able to find a perch on one of those little shelf-like ledges at the rear of the carriage. The grimly-lit facade of Wormwood Scrubs prison emerged on the right and at East Acton, the next stop, a sprinkling of Japanese departed into suburbia. The stops were becoming more widely spaced as the West Indian and Pakistani communities became the majority of the passengers and everyone found a seat.

At North Acton Peter, abandoned his carriage, walked a few paces down the platform, and slipped inside the rear door of the next. It was only half full by now and no one was standing. He was able to park himself in the seat closest to the door. From there he had a clear view diagonally along the length of the carriage to where the man was sitting, almost as far away from him as it was possible to get. He had one of the broadsheets carefully folded in his lap and a ball-point in his hand, apparently absorbed in the crossword. Peter opened his *Evening Standard* and arranged himself behind it in what would have been obvious to any interested observer was an absurd attempt at concealment. At each station, as the train slowed down, he took a squint over the paper to make sure that the other man wasn't about to get out. The entire carriage took not a blind bit of notice.

The two seats next to the man, away from where Peter sat, were occupied by a large West Indian lady and, between her and the man, her son of perhaps six or seven. Beyond her, an unfolded baby buggy effectively blocked off access to the door at the far end of the carriage. For her part, she cradled in her lap an infant a year or so old that she was trying to feed with a bottle. The head of the baby lay towards the young child, who was kneeling on his own seat, peering over it, giggling at his sibling and playing with its waving hands, thereby distracting it from the task his mother had in hand and at the same time wiping the soles of his trainers against the raincoat of the man next to him. From time to time this man glanced at him with irritation but fortunately he made no attempt to relocate. Not politically appropriate to flee from colour, thought Peter; but, if the child had been white, he wouldn't have hesitated. In desperation, the mother eventually rummaged inside the plastic bag at her feet and brought out a can of some fizzy drink. For a moment the child settled back in his seat with the can apparently glued to his lips but by Hanger Lane he was fidgeting again, back on his knees with his nose pressed against the window, peering into the gloom outside as the art-deco rear of the old Hoover factory on the A40 swished by on the left.

At Perivale there was a further significant exodus, and another at Greenford, which included the West Indian lady staggering under packages and children and their paraphernalia. There were now only half a dozen people left in the carriage and the man at the far end was sitting in total isolation. As the doors closed Peter folded his newspaper, got up, picked his way down the carriage and settled quietly into the seat beside him. The man next to him was naturally a bit surprised that someone should come and sit right next to him in an almost empty carriage. He turned and glanced at the new arrival.

"Hello, Mr Snaithe," Peter said. "I don't know if you remember me. I'm Peter Davenport from Dundas Brothers. I'm advising Pitcairn Pharmaceuticals."

"Oh yes, Mr Davenport, of course. Well, what a coincidence," he added in that sort of prissy high-pitched precise voice that Peter now remembered. He had found it bloody irritating when he had first heard it and this time it only served to heighten his contempt.

"Do you live out this way?" he added.

"No, and it's not a coincidence, Mr Snaithe," Peter said. "I've followed you from your office because I wanted to talk to you."

"Well, that's very irregular, Mr Davenport. You know we've had answers to all the questions we've put to Pitcairn through their lawyers and matters will now take their course. I hope you appreciate that I can't elaborate on any of our other enquiries. You'll be familiar with the standard procedures that we use; but I can assure you that everything will be done to expedite the announcement of the minister's decision in due course. I hope you won't press me further."

He was still taking it at face value, more irritated than nervous. Peter noticed again his inadequacies with a razor. There were a few stray bristles under his left nostril.

"Well, in that case I'm going to disappoint you Mr Snaithe," Peter said, "because I'm going to ask you to ensure that the BMP bid for Pitcairn Pharmaceuticals is referred to the Monopolies Commission."

He preened himself like the petty functionary he was and came back with a "Mr Davenport, you know that's not something that's within my power. These matters are decided by a committee formed for each particular transaction. It makes a recommendation to the Director General, who in turn makes a recommendation to the minister. I'm a very small cog in that wheel."

"Oh, surely not, Mr Snaithe," Peter said, patronising, "but, in any event, I'm asking you this entirely for you're own sake, you understand," he added with a deliberate touch of menace.

"You're not threatening me, are you Mr Davenport," he came back. There was a touch of nervousness now but only as if he thought Peter might be about to hit him. There was even now no indication that he realised what was coming.

"I'm not threatening you, Mr Snaithe," Peter said. "I'm simply telling you that, if this bid is not referred, I'm going to tell the press that you've been shagging Lord Evans' secretary."

For a moment, there was absolute silence.

"Well, that's utterly preposterous. Where could you have got such a ridiculous idea?"

"Now which papers do you think I should use?" Peter mused. "I see you're a *Guardian* man yourself," he said, with a wave of his hand to the little pile of newspapers in Snaithe's lap. "I think I'd have guessed that; but, what about your wife. Perhaps the *Mail* appeals more to her. Perhaps we'll cover them both."

In twenty-one years of marriage it was Snaithe's first experience of adultery. Lacking the recklessness of the habitual philanderer, he thought he had been desperately careful. Perhaps this man was just playing a hunch; but the reality must be that he had no proof. It was just a question of bluffing it out. "I don't know what you're talking about, Mr Davenport, but it seems to me you're playing a very dangerous game."

That too high pitch again; but he was steadying himself, not yet defeated.

"As you know, Mr Snaithe," Peter said, sure of his facts and beginning to enjoy the game, "it's the truth. That hotel was not as secure a venue for your trysts as you might have imagined."

"What hotel?" He went even higher pitched. And he was getting angry by now. And thoroughly frightened.

"The Bonnington, Mr Snaithe, you know, the Bonnington in Southampton Row."

He tried another tack. "Even if it were true, it would be an entirely private matter. You have no right to peer into an individual's private life."

"Oh, but I disagree with you," Peter said. "I think it's a matter of great public interest that you're getting a leg over Sally Rogers."

"Whatever there may be between Miss Rogers and myself is entirely private. It has absolutely no bearing on the Office of Fair Trading or your client's affairs; and you have no right to treat it as such."

Peter wasn't entirely sure that he didn't believe him. Perhaps Evans had just gone too far in stitching up every angle. He already had the government in his pocket and this was an unnecessary embellishment. Meanwhile, he reckoned, this pathetic little runt thought it all a coincidence and that he had finally found true love. It was the moment for the *coup de grâce* . He didn't hesitate.

"Mr Snaithe, I had a man standing at Miss Rogers' elbow last night when she settled the bill for your room. Did you know that she used her company credit card? BMP have been picking up the tab for your little affair. Now that's what I call public interest."

Snaithe gasped in genuine surprise; but by now he realised he was hopelessly nailed.

"It can't be true," he pleaded. He was ashen now, trembling, desperately calculating to see if there was a way out, scurrying this way and that searching for a release from the trap.

"It's out of my hands," he wailed. "It's a political decision at the end of the day."

"Oh, Mr Snaithe, Peter assured him condescendingly, "I think you underestimate the power of the civil service to get its way. I'm sure the minister wouldn't wish to overrule his advisers on such a trivial matter. I've every faith in you."

"But I'm only one voice amongst many. There are a number of departments represented. There's no guarantee that whatever opinion I express will carry the day."

"Oh, I realise that," Peter said, "and, if it were down to logic I'd have to agree with you; but there's one way you can get them to support you."

"What's that?" he asked pathetically, looking into Davenport's eyes and practically begging for salvation.

"You'll have to go to Gordon Borrie and tell him the truth," said Peter pitilessly.

"And what did he say to that?"

"He didn't say a thing, Rod. His face sort of contorted and there was suddenly this awful smell. I swear to God he actually shat himself. Saints alive, it was a wonderful sensation. I haven't felt like that since I broke the Teddy Hall stand-off half's leg in the Cuppers final. They said you could hear the crack 300 yards away."

"Christ Almighty, Peter. Did you play wing forward?"

"Sure."

"I thought so. All the worst shits were wing forwards."

"That's a bit much, Rod. Where did you play?"

"Wing forward," he admitted, smiling. "But I hope you haven't gone too far."

"How? He deserves everything he's got."

"But what happens if he goes and does something daft? Suppose he's suicidal?"

"No chance of that, Rod. I'll wager he's not the sort of fanatic who's got the courage for that. But he's intelligent enough to work out that those bastards will protect him. Not necessarily Borrie. He's got a pretty straight reputation for a socialist; but the rest of them will insist on it. I'd stake my life on it. You seldom see a minister resign to take responsibility for a cock-up these days; but you never, ever, ever see a civil servant take the rap. Can you imagine the sheer fucking conceit of a bunch of clerks to call their trade union the First Division Association? Who do they think they are, Paul fucking Gascoigne? They'll pension him off quietly or move him somewhere out of harm's way three months down the road. But when he thinks it through he'll realise that he won't go down for this. Sending it to the MMC will be a small price to pay for hushing it up. No skin off anyone's nose but Arthur's. And, if he complains to his friends at Tory Central Office, it will no doubt be pointed out to him that he brought it on himself by sending his glamour-puss out to catch that worthless ferret. So be it. Evans will just have to bide his time until the MMC gives him the all-clear, which I'm sure it will. But at least it'll give us four or five months to produce a proper defence - or at least for you to fiddle the figures."

"I guess you're right, Peter. Well, what a turn-up. And to think I'd given up on Harrington and his crew."

"Yes. I wasn't going to mention that."

"Like hell you weren't, you bastard," Rod exclaimed, breaking into a broad smile. "I think I owe you one. Thank God you're on our side. You're the dirtiest fighter I've ever seen. Let's go and have a drink."

"Now remember, Rod, not a word of this to anyone. John Addey will take the credit and send you a bill for a couple of hundred thou; and the dwarf will think it was all down to him and his influence with his mucker, Lord Young; but we say nothing ... not to anyone ... not now ... not later ... not ever."

269

"Okay, Peter. Don't worry. It's what I think we're now obliged to call a lady of Afro-Caribbean origin."

"What are you talking about, Rod?"

"Very satisfying from time to time," he smirked ... "but not something you talk about."

Thursday, 18 to Saturday, 27 February, 1988

At Flight Departures in Terminal 3 there was a huge queue for the security check, shuffling slowly forward with barely-suppressed ill temper. Only three out of the five x-ray machines were in use and BAA were playing their usual profitable game of providing the minimum level of manpower necessary to avoid a riot. The milling crowd in front of him as he emerged from an even more than normally surly inspection of his boarding card was surging this way and that as his fellow travellers sought the most advantageous of the three lines of passengers snaking towards the x-ray machines and metal detectors and their bored and indifferent operators. Away up in the front of the middle of the three queues a girl in more or less skin-tight jeans and a pale blue sweater with cascading blonde hair and a familiar curvaceous figure had popped her hand luggage on to the conveyor and was waiting while the man in front of her emptied his pockets onto a plastic tray. As he stepped through the metal detector, collected his things and moved away, the face of the man operating it flashed a spontaneous and without doubt reciprocated smile at the blonde girl coming through behind him. Peter felt his heart quicken. He was absolutely sure it was her. The resolve with which he had set off from the office earlier that evening to forget what had passed and start his life afresh seemed to fall from his weary shoulders and settle dismally around his ankles like a whore's faded skirt.

It was another fifteen minutes before he reached the far side of passport control. He looked around the lounge frantically and did a quick tour of duty-free, WH Smith and the café before concluding reluctantly that she was nowhere to be seen and heading dispirited for the Qantas executive lounge. As the door swung open, he saw her immediately. She was standing at the bar, mixing herself a bloody mary. As she turned towards him, heading back to her seat, she looked him full in the face and flashed the automatic, beaming smile that had so enlivened the man at the security check-in. She was all of fifty years old. Peter smiled sheepishly back. He was shaking uncontrollably but surprised to find himself relieved.

Three-quarter's of an hour later, and with two large whiskies and soda in the executive lounge already under his belt and a third on its way, he was settled in a window seat in the business class cabin of the Qantas 747. He congratulated himself on the decision to upgrade from economy, the only time he had ever done so at his own expense. There was no one beside him and he was able to spread himself out. He had brought with him a fat briefcase full of unread or only partially scanned newspapers and business magazines, the latest thick wodge from Freddie's press-cutting service with reactions to the surprise decision on Tuesday to refer the BMP bid for Pitcairn to the MMC, a raft of Dundas Brothers' internal memos, a pile of reports on his various clients from brokers' analysts, and the glossy annual accounts of various less than glossy companies. There should be enough in that lot to occupy his mind until the flight touched down in Sydney at dawn on Saturday morning; but, just in case, there was also a copy of Tom Wolfe's first novel *The Bonfire of the Vanities* , just released to rave reviews and instantly *de rigueur* amongst actual or aspirant masters of the universe.

Peter started with this week's *Economist* that had just arrived before he left the office. He felt sure there would be a comment on the Pitcairn referral but it would not be on the Wordsworth Wallis press cutting service until tomorrow when he would be far away. He scanned the contents page quickly and turned up the appropriate section. Under a heading *'What competition policy?'* he read:-

> *Once again this week doubts have been raised over the consistency of the British government's policy towards referrals of proposed mergers to the Monopolies and Mergers Commission.*
>
> *Since early last month, Pitcairn Pharmaceuticals, a UK drugs business specialising in antibiotics, has been the subject of an unwelcome take-over approach by BMP, a*

larger and more diversified UK rival. Pitcairn bombarded members of parliament and the press with the argument that a combination of its own highly regarded research effort with that of BMP - a more brazen upstart that has expanded its pharmaceutical product list largely through acquisition - would be likely to diminish the sum of British drugs research to the detriment of the national interest. The possibility that this argument might fall on receptive ears at the Department of Trade and Industry (DTI) seemed much diminished following last month's white paper which, whilst recognising that the procedures for scrutinising competition issues needed to be streamlined, reasserted the doctrine that the restriction of competition should be the primary criterion for the referral to the commission of a proposed merger. True, the DTI reserved to itself, as usual, an escape clause in the form of the words "with rare exceptions"; but it was claimed that this might be necessary from time to protect "the public interest". Few experts had hitherto thought that the public interest included the amounts which individual firms might choose to spend on research and development.

The government's decision on this occasion looks at best inconsistent and at worst downright capricious. It does little to dispel the suspicion that expediency plays too large a part in these deliberations; though quite what the expediency was on this occasion is hard to guess.

Quite so. You tell 'em, he chuckled to himself, as the hostess, a well-built dark girl in her twenties with an unfortunate greenish complexion, perplexed at his reaction, apparently to her attentions, set down his scotch and soda. He put *The Economist* down, saving its convenient size for reading matter over dinner, and pulled the pile of broadsheets from his bag. He confined himself largely to the business pages; but he couldn't help reading the piece in *The Times* on how the media had turned the absurdly gauche myopic figure of Eddie 'the Eagle' Edwards into the cult ski-jumper of the Calgary Olympics; and how the Tories on Haringey Council had exposed what the awful Gillian Wilkinson would have called the chairperson of the Tottenham Labour party, a champion of gay and lesbian rights, as the former Magnificent Mandy, a voluptuous 20 stone 62 inch topless kissogram girl. *The Sun* not being included in his habitual reading matter, he was spared the inevitable archive photograph.

No investment banker can experience a greater sensation of joy than that at the public humiliation of a competitor; and a classic toffee-nosed example appeared to have been unfolding over the past few days as the Blue Circle cement company, advised by Lord John Verulam at Barings, sought to turn itself into a conglomerate with a bitterly contested bid for Birmid Qualcast, which made lawnmowers and heating systems. Last week, Cazenove, part of the Birmid defence team, had started buying up Birmid shares that had already been assented to Blue Circle, at above the offer price to boot, and promptly withdrawing their acceptance. Notwithstanding their efforts, the bid had closed on Saturday with Blue Circle claiming victory by the narrowest of 50.01% margins and Barings had promptly placed quarter-page ads in the financial press crowing that the whole thing had been 'FINELY JUDGED.....FINELY EXECUTED'. Now it had turned out that Hoare Govett, Blue Circle's broker, had miscounted and the bid had in reality been lost. To add insult to injury, BZW had dithered over whether to accept, finally told the Blue Circle chairman that they were going to give him their 1.5% and then not done so. Barings, Hoare Govett and BZW all covered in shit by a single well-aimed turd.

Peter turned back to the beginning of *The Economist* as the cabin crew started to busy themselves with the food trolleys. *'Advantage, Bush'* read the cover headline alongside a photograph of the US vice-president, proclaiming his success in the early primaries. More to the point in the way of personal interest, was an article headed *'Lawson's lazy budget'* which basically claimed that the chancellor could afford to sweep away all the higher rates of income tax, remove the ceiling on employees' national insurance contributions to give a combined top rate of 34%, tax investment income at the same rate, and sit down feeling that he had done a more than prudent job. Fat chance of generosity like that, thought Peter, though it was looking increasingly likely that this was at last going to be a budget that would see him a little better off.

Dinner came and went. He picked at it, but with some determination; and drank a good few glasses of wine, an up-front oaked-up chardonnay from the Barossa Valley and a Coonawarra cabernet sauvignon with a mouth-filling explosion of blackcurrants and summer fruits and the silky depth of a draught Guinness. With a final glass and already feeling drowsy, he slipped down a couple of Temazepam, which he kept in his overnight flight kit and had entirely overlooked throughout the last weeks' crazy insomniac nights. He had barely reclined his seat when he was instantly asleep.

He slept all the way to Singapore and woke as they descended with a mouth like a calcified kettle. On the second leg, he tackled the rest of his reading, set about dinner with something approaching gusto, and repeated the successful cocktail of the night before in a quantum undiminished. Barring a day's growth of stubble, that he removed at Sydney Airport, and a severe dose of dehydration, which he attacked with about half a gallon of orange juice in the coffee shop of the departure lounge, he felt the best he had all year as he boarded the plane for Cairns with Tom Wolfe under his arm.

*****

From Cairns, it was only an hour or so by helicopter out to Turtle Island, a long thin sand-fringed ribbon of palms and lush green vegetation astride the Great Barrier Reef. Peter shared the helicopter with a middle-aged German couple, he teutonically spare and spectacled, she just as trim but also blonde and bejewelled, and an American husband and wife with an unlikely age gap of thirty or so years between his surgically improved septuagenarian features and her over-indulged midriff and broadening buttocks. One of the men reeked of Aramis. Peter sat up alongside the pilot and it wasn't him, a long laconic Aussie

275

in khaki shorts and bush boots, who might once have found his chosen profession exciting but had clearly long ago come to the dire realisation that he was no more than an airborne bus driver. For those in the back, conversation was more or less impossible above the clatter of the rotors; for Peter, equipped, like the pilot, with earphones, the impediment was not physical, but just as discouraging.

Around one o'clock it became apparent to Peter that the expanding speck on the hazy blue horizon to which they were heading was indeed their destination and a moment later this was confirmed by a crackled conversation between the pilot and someone on the ground. In a single touristic gesture the pilot took them right down the western side of the island and banked sharply round the southern point on which the resort was perched before heading back north. He followed the line of a dirt track, dust swirling behind a vehicle heading the same way, to where the scrub had been cleared for a rough landing ground about the size of a football pitch. As the whirling blades slowed to a drooping halt and the dust subsided, a small white Toyota minibus drew up alongside.

They were taken straight down to lunch, a buffet of all manner of shellfish, cold meats, salads and exotic fruits set out under an awning beside the pool, while the man in immaculate white shorts, shirt and long socks who had met them from the helicopter busied himself with their bags. There were only about a dozen tables, all of oiled reddish teak, with blue-cushioned arm chairs to match, and no more than half were still occupied. Peter sat alone and a little self consciously over to one side, feeling uncomfortable in the long trousers and long-sleeved shirt which he had now occupied for a day and half and which seemed to him absurdly out of place in this palm-fringed sub-tropical oasis.

"Mr Davenport?" enquired a voice at his elbow.

"Yes."

"I'm John Soldatis, the manager. Welcome to Turtle Island," he said, shaking Peter's hand. "We've put your bags in cottage sixteen - it's the last one you come to on that side, right on the beach," he indicated, gesturing to the eastern side of the island. "It's no more than a couple of hundred yards and I think it's got the best of our views - not that any of them are less than spectacular. There are no keys here, no formalities and no extras. Help yourself to whatever you like and, if there's anything you can't find, just let us know. It's all pretty simple. As you can see, the pool's here, beaches either side; there's a little harbour with our boats round the corner. There's always someone there to sort out fishing rods, water skis, scuba equipment etcetera. We just like to know where you're heading. The tennis courts are just beyond the harbour. We have a little tournament once a week if you're interested - that's Wednesday afternoons. The dining room is up there but guests normally take breakfast and lunch out here. The bar and indoor lounge and the library are round that side, towards the tennis courts. There's normally someone there too; but just help yourself if there isn't. You can find all our wines there too. They're in temperature-controlled cabinets; so just take whatever you want in to lunch or dinner and one of the staff will open it for you. There's a little map in here of where to find everything," he said, handing Peter a little pack in a soft green leather folder, "and all the information we could think of. Is there anything you particularly wanted?"

"I don't think so, thank you. I'm just here to relax. Are you full?"

"More or less for the fortnight you're here; but we only take a maximum of 40 guests. You won't find much here to disturb you if you want to take it easy."

"How big is the island?"

"It's only four and a half miles from end to end. You can walk the beach the whole way round in about three, maybe four hours. The hotel only occupies the southern extremity."

*****

The cottage was magnificent, a sort of two-storied thatched rondavel set into the slope leading down to the beach. The entrance on the top side led straight in to a sitting room with a dark polished wooden floor which occupied the whole of that level. There was no ceiling beneath the wigwam of beams that supported the thatch and, on the sea-facing side, there was a great sweep of unpainted wooden sliding windows which looked out over a small veranda to the white sand, the azure sea and the reef itself. There were two deep sofas covered in a thick red and gold striped brocade and heavy solid wooden tables with bowls of fresh fruit and sprays of blood-red bougainvillaea. To one side, behind the doors of a long wooden sideboard were three cabinets, one with glasses, cups and saucers, and a variety of teas and coffees, nuts and nibbles, another with bottles of wines and spirits and a third containing a substantial refrigerator crammed with champagne, white wines, beer, mineral water, mixers and juices. On the other side, a matching but smaller cabinet opened to reveal, on the right, a TV and video machine and, on the left, a CD and cassette player. It was a room of warmth and tropical island simplicity but also one which contained a more than lavish share of modern comforts. Peter was beginning to see how the $350 a day that had made him wince when Maureen had presented him with the cheque to sign could evaporate so easily.

A little staircase over to the right of the sitting room gave access to the bedroom below from which sliding full-length glass-panelled wooden doors gave directly onto the deserted beach of pure white sand. The big double bed was another solid affair with a wooden headboard padded to match the bedspread. Beyond the bedroom was a beautifully equipped marble bathroom with shelves of fluffy white towels, toiletries of every description and sun-tan creams of every factor.

Peter unpacked quickly, showered, changed into shorts, polo shirt and deck shoes and set off to explore.

A gravel path led from his cottage past seven well-separated similar structures facing out towards the Pacific. A matching path led away from the hotel itself up the western side of the promontory with another eight cottages in much the same style but apparently somewhat larger. Two ladies appeared from the second as Peter walked up the path. They were strikingly similar in the face but one perhaps in her forties and the other not yet out of her teens. The younger was peachy blonde, slim and leggy, her mother slightly gingerish, perhaps from a bottle, still good-looking but less firm fleshed, the cut of her swimsuit identical to her daughter's but too high in the thigh for her years. She gave Peter the sort of swift but intense examination reserved for new arrivals and Peter nodded a mumbled "Hi" in return as they passed.

Between the two paths which led to the guest cottages, where the low central ridge of the island began was the start of the road leading out to the helicopter pad and, almost completely concealed behind the waving palms on either side of that track the low wooden buildings that were apparently occupied by the resort staff.

The main building of the hotel, beyond a sweep of gravel where the two paths and the roadway met, was no more than another larger rondavel on a single level with a floor consisting of slabs of steely-grey slate. Its centre, which was inaccessible to guests, was presumably occupied by the kitchens and other domestic offices. On the side facing north towards the cottages was an informal reception area, to the left lay the dining room and to the right a large lounge with a bar at one end and a wall of books, magazines and videos at the other. Between the two were groups of low tables, sofas and chairs in the same solid wooden and well upholstered style as Peter's own cottage. Thick woollen rugs covered in tribal designs were scattered everywhere. All around the circumference of the structure was a low wall into which were set the solid wooden uprights which supported the huge thatched roof which overhung the wall by two or three yards all around, providing shade and presumably, in some circumstances, also shelter. Thick canvas sheets which could be let down and fastened to eyelets set into the wall in the event of inclement weather were rolled up and concealed under the roof so that, as was now the case, the entire building lay open-sided to the views all around. Outside, down a few steps, was a broad terrace that ran in a semi-circle round that half of the building that faced east It was here that they had set out the buffet earlier and where now one or two groups were sitting, under broad sunshades, playing bridge or backgammon.

Below this terrace, to the left, down a few more steps, but a little way above the beach was a lovely pool, its sides and bottom also slate-grey, full to the brim so that, at the far extreme, its inky black waters seemed to cascade over the edge into the blue blue ocean beyond. A dozen or more loungers, upholstered like the chairs on the terrace, in a blue canvas, piped with white, were arranged around it and there were more, down a few wooden steps, on the beach itself. There were only eight or ten people around the pool - two rather paunchy men with bushy moustaches and pale skin, now rather reddened, who were propped up on their loungers under a large umbrella, reading books and a quite elderly Japanese with a girl who was young enough to be his daughter had she not been a filipina who clearly occupied a different status. Under another sun shade, an ancient couple were asleep on their backs, she with a sun-hat over her face, the man snoring far from gently; and, out in the full sun and lying face down, their swimsuits rolled down below their waists to show their evenly-tanned backs, were the mother and daughter that Peter had encountered earlier.

He climbed back up onto the terrace and walked on round. The bar was here, one side, with a row of stools, facing outwards towards the terrace above the pool and the other, on the interior, with more stools, occupying this end of the lounge. There were more steps down from here to a little jetty on one side of which, moored stems towards the quay, were four identical speedboats of about twelve or fourteen feet, each with a fat outboard motor now folded forward out of the water. On the other side of the jetty and moored alongside it, fore and aft, was a more substantial boat, perhaps forty or fifty feet in length with a high superstructure and what appeared to be the wherewithal for some serious fishing. A dark-skinned man, perhaps aboriginal or mauri, was washing it down with a yellow hose which coiled back to a tap in the wall below the terrace. A pair of doors in this wall were opened wide and within was a well-ordered store of scuba suits and air tanks, flippers and snorkels, masks and skis.

"Are you wanting a boat, sir?" called the dark-skinned boatman.

"No, not right now. I've only arrived today and I'm just exploring," Peter replied, "but I'll maybe take you up on that in a couple of days."

"Any time, sir."

Beyond the boats, the coastline curved around towards the north and headed off towards the cottages on this side, the first one of which Peter could just make out amongst the trees. Between here and there, however, were two brick red hard tennis courts, side by side, with a pole for the floodlights at each corner of the enclosure. They were unoccupied save for a Hennessy-sized Japanese with a jet-black wig who was mechanically practising his backhand against a grass-green cannon which was firing identical balls at him one after another at twenty second intervals.

Peter walked round the courts and found a path down onto the beach on the western side of the island. The odd palm projected outwards over the water at a crazy angle, dividing the white coral sands into individual beaches, as the coastline stretched away into the distance, more or less straight. Peter took off his shoes and paddled along the shore line. The water running over the hot sand was warm but a little further out where it lapped his knees one could tell that it would still be cool enough to be refreshing. He walked on past the final cottage for a few hundred yards along the beach. It was utterly deserted.

*****

Around seven he took another shower, put on a pair of khaki slacks and a pale blue cotton short-sleeved shirt and headed for the bar. The broad-bottomed American who had shared his helicopter was already there. She was perched on a stool, legs crossed, with one long heel resting on the tubular steel of the stool's support. Even sitting, one could see that the satiny black catsuit into which she had been, for all practical purposes, decanted was showing obvious signs of strain at bust and belly and bottom. As yet minus sugar daddy, she was whiling away the time until his arrival with a dry martini. From her flushed and excited exchanges with the barman, Peter could guess that it was not her first.

The barman himself was clearly more interested in his two other customers, the blonde mother and daughter, also perched on bar stools but neither overlapping the circular upholstered seats in the same way as their competitor for this man's attention. They were both dressed in white trousers, the girl in a white T-shirt on which was Ken Done's colourful but ubiquitous interpretation of the Sydney skyline, opera house, bridge and all in bold simple lines of red and blue, yellow and green, her mother in a pink shirt unbuttoned at the throat rather more than one might have expected.

"What can I get you, sir?" Peter was asked as he arrived.

"The champagne's awfully good," said mummy, in an accent which Peter found hard to place - English certainly, but in some way artificial - but familiar too.

"Well, that sounds like a very good idea. Thanks. By the way, I'm Peter Davenport," he said, extending a hand.

"Hi. I'm Jacqueline Fortescue," she said, taking it, "and this is my daughter, Jade."

"Delighted to meet you," said Peter, reaching across to take the daughter's hand. It was cooler and smaller, less sinewy than her mother's, almost vulnerable. He held it a little longer than was necessary. She really was very lovely.

"And I'm Susan Bradley," said a loud American voice to Peter's shoulder.

It was like a reprimand from a lady slighted. He turned swiftly round, embarrassed, and extended his hand again.

"Peter Davenport. We shared a helicopter."

"Sure did, honey. How're you doin'?"

"Fine, thanks. What have you done with your husband?" he added, trying to fend her off. She was a bit too gushing for his taste.

"Milton. Why he's gone off to bed complainin' o' jet lag. I guess that's what you gotta expect when you go marryin' an older man. Just remember that, Jade honey."

Oh, shit, she's looking for a dinner companion, thought Peter. The consternation obviously registered on his face. He took a sip of his champagne. Jacqueline Fortescue jumped in, apparently to rescue him.

"You've just arrived, haven't you Peter? We saw you this afternoon. I think we must be neighbours."

"Yes to the first and no to the second; actually I'm in one of the cottages on the other side. I was just having a snoop around, getting my bearings."

"Are you here on your own then?"

"Yes."

"Well, would you believe that, Jade? We were beginning to think that single men were banned here - apart from those who are together, if you know what I mean. It's not been much fun for Jade."

"Oh, mummy, that's not true. I've had a super time," Jade rejoined. Same accent - Sloane - of course! Same as her mother. Same as Sophie. Same as Sophie's mother. All the bloody same.

"We're doing a trip around the world before Jade goes up to Oxford."

"Mummy, it's just secretarial college. You make it sound like the university."

"So important for a girl to see the world when she's young, don't you think?" her mother went on, making the best of the destruction of her little pretence. "Before she settles down. Dan, what about some more champagne?" she said, turning to the barman.

"And another martini, Dan. Then Peter and I are going to go in to dinner, aren't we, honey?"

What could he say?

"Well, why don't we all have dinner together?" he spluttered quickly, hoping at least that the lovely Jade would be there to brighten the scenery.

"I'm sorry, Peter, we've promised to have dinner with the Radziwills. They've invited us to stay with them in Gstaad this summer. Eleanor is such a sweetie. Jade, there's Igor now. Darling, he's terribly short-sighted. Do go and tell him we're here. I think they'll want to sit down in some of the comfortable chairs. Please excuse us, Peter. Perhaps tomorrow night. Do enjoy your dinner. Susan."

It wasn't "Do enjoy your dinner, Susan," Peter thought. It was "We want to get away. Do enjoy your dinner, (Peter). Goodbye, Susan." Subtle difference that. Not that it did him any good. He turned to find Susan Bradley smiling and flushed. She was swaying a little on her stool.

"And then there were two," she said triumphantly.

He drained his glass and Dan, returning from attending to the Radziwills at the far end of the lounge, poured him a refill. Susan Bradley pushed her glass forward clumsily across the bar for another. She was smashed and there was a danger she was going to topple over. He couldn't face the scene.

"Why don't we go and sit in some comfortable chairs too?" Peter suggested with resignation. "I'll bring the drinks."

"Shure, hun," she slurred, climbing unsteadily from the stool and swaying a little as she headed for the nearest arm-chair.

Dan gave Peter a knowing wink as he poured yet another martini from the shaker and added a fat green olive. He thought of making a run for it, condemned himself for cowardice, and picked up the two glasses. He walked over to the chairs she had chosen and set them down noiselessly on the table between them. She was fast asleep. He waited a few minutes to be sure, sipping his champagne, and a few minutes more while he selected two half-bottles of wine from the cabinets beside the bar. The manager was on duty in the foyer. Peter explained. It appeared that she was not the first of his ladies that had needed to be put to bed.

*****

Peter could not have said that he had ever enjoyed dining alone; but he considered this occasion a pleasure. He selected a table in the far interior which had a good view of the entire room and settled comfortably into the chair which afforded him the finest view of proceedings. Most people were dining in couples, the Fortescues and Radziwills being one of only two exceptions. They were away to Peter's right at a table at the edge of the room under the eaves. Igor Radziwill, it turned out, was the afternoon's ancient snorer by the pool and Eleanor, his wife, though probably not a great deal younger, had the taut slightly startled look - like clingfilm - of one who'd been washed and ironed a good few times.

The Japanese were also a foursome, though Peter doubted that they were two couples. The little man with the wig, still more obvious now, who had been practising his tennis, had also got a young filipina to play with off court. It was a variation, Peter thought, of the traditional Japanese golfer's holiday. They left home with their clubs and flew to Manila, dropped them off in left luggage at the airport, selected a tart downtown and off they went. Coming back, they returned her to her master, paid him the balance due, collected their clubs and flew home to the little wife. She knew what her husband had been doing, and he knew she knew. It was the custom - like going to a karaoke bar with your mates on Friday evening and then to the turkish baths in Kawasaki for a body massage.

The food got off to a wonderful start - half a dozen Moreton Bay bugs, like little fat langoustines, grilled over charcoal and served with mayonnaise, and a rack of Australian lamb with a rosemary and garlic crust that was so tender that you could have cut it with a feather.

The Japanese, who had clearly dined as close to their usual early evening hour as Turtle Island's kitchens would permit, and who no doubt also had other pursuits in mind for the remainder of the evening, were the first to leave, soon after Peter had arrived. The four tiny figures were dwarfed as they departed by the arrival of three more girls, two white and a black in a spectacular flowing tribal gown of blue and green. They were big, all of them, tall and broad as they sallied down the length of the dining room and settled at a table under the eaves, the black girl in the middle, her back to the interior of the room and the white girls, one mousey and the other dark, on either side. They were loud and boisterous, perhaps a little drunk. Snatches of their conversation drifted unintelligibly right across the room between their peals of laughter. He strained to see if he could catch the words but it was hopeless.

He nibbled at some cheese; and then an exotic little fruit salad of fresh pineapple, mango and strawberries doused in lime juice and curaçao; and felt suddenly and wonderfully tired.

*****

Sunday dawned fresh and bright. He woke early and flung open the doors onto the beach, hesitated on the threshold for a moment as he contemplated the temptation of a swift naked sprint across the sand before middle-class decorum got the better of him and he returned for a pair of trunks. The sea was flat and crystalline and the temperature was perfect. Shoals of tiny fish in brilliant blues and yellows played in the shallows and brushed the hairs on his legs as he waded out from the gently shelving beach. A few hundred yards out, less than half a mile, one could see the water lapping and occasionally crashing over the reef itself but here, inside was a vast and relatively shallow pool of perfect tranquillity. He struck out with a purposeful crawl but after no more than a couple of minutes dropped into a lazy breast-stroke and thence onto his back, breathing heavily and flapping his arms and legs feebly for locomotion. He waded back to the shore feeling absurdly weak and started to plan his regime.

After a breakfast of fresh papaya with lime juice, eggs benedict and coffee, he repaired to the tennis courts. On one a couple in their twenties were just packing up. He was dressed in a pair of black shorts and an orange singlet which laid bare a hugely muscled pair of broad shoulders and bulging biceps; but the overall impression was horribly spoilt by a black baseball cap, worn back to front, and a protruding lower lip, which, like its upper companion, was plastered with some sort of protective cream in a bilious shade of lilac. Together these embellishments gave him a countenance of neanderthal stupidity. She, a coarse-looking tart, overdeveloped front and rear, was wearing a pair of skin-tight white hotpants, a matching top, like a sports bra, and a bright red eye shade from which cascaded a mass of raven black hair. Peter wished them good morning as they passed and received the inevitable g'dyes in return. He chose the court which the diminutive Japanese he had seen the previous afternoon was using, switched the cannon from the single mode in which it had been left so that now it would oscillate at random from side to side and set to work. The sun was not yet high but it was absurdly hard going and he was reduced to a panting and sweaty shambles long before the machine had exhausted its stock of ammunition. He sat on the bench to one side and consumed the better part of a litre of water, reloaded the hopper and did it all again. By the time he finished a half hour later, his legs were aching and the muscles along the top of his right arm were tight and tender. He was fit only for the pool and his book.

He had planned to jog around the island on the beach after lunch but it was already apparent that his ambitions overreached his capabilities by a comfortable margin. It was getting pretty hot and, after a couple or four beers and a light lunch, feeling decidedly mellow, he dozed for a while beside the pool. When he came to, the German couple were also there, he processing up and down the pool purposefully Prussian, she half propped up on a lounger, topless, small but remarkably firm, slowly turning the pages of *Der Spiegel* and occasionally stopping to read an article. She looked damned good. Another sensation swept over his body to add to the stiffness of his bones and the increasing lethargy of his relaxation. It was time to move; but for the first day at least a walk was going to be enough.

It was still only just after two o'clock when he set off up the beach on the Pacific side. He had observed during his swim that morning that the palms appeared to come right down to the sea a little further along the beach, obscuring all but the first 400 or 500 yards or so of the shoreline; but, if the manager was correct, it should be possible to walk right around the island. Sure enough, as he approached the trees, he could see that there was a well-worn path between them and, as he emerged again, that there was another stretch of open sand, like a private beach, deeply fringed with tropical foliage, which ended with a rocky outcrop a further 300 yards away. There he could see three girls he took to be the rather brash party that he had seen at dinner the previous evening. They were emerging from the sea carrying snorkels and flippers. They had found, he thought, a perfect spot. They could not be quite the brats he had taken them for if they forswore the pool for a haven such as this. He walked slowly along the foreshore towards them, his deck shoes in his hand, paddling in the water lapping up onto the soft, white sand.

By the time he had reached them, two had resumed their sunbathing on the beach. The other, the black girl, was sitting some way off on the rocks, cross-legged on one of the hotel's blue beach towels, applying crimson varnish to her nails. She was very dark - Africa black in the flamboyant way which only francophone Africa seems to stamp upon its women. Her long hair was a mass of small plaits pulled back from her face and fed through a thick gold ring on the top of her head. Another heavy gold band adorned her right wrist, an expensive gold watch her left. Her face was smooth and elegant, a small tribal scar, no more than a nick, high on each cheek and her thick lips moist with fresh lipstick She was big boned though truthfully not fat; but her bare breasts were more than large and each ended in a huge wrinkled jet-black nipple. She wore, beside her jewellery, only a tanga which was composed of diagonal stripes of the brightest red, gold and green. A bow of identical colours held the mass of her hair in place.

The girl closest to him as he strolled along the sand was lying on her belly but from her broad, round and scantily-clad bottom, it was obvious that she was not just big. Lying face-down and with her head turned away from him, there was no reason to think that she was aware of his approach; but she seemed to smell his advance and turned over and sat up as he approached as if alerted by sheer testosterone. Her hair, not quite blonde, was tousled over her shoulders, her face round except for the slightly squarish jaw of so many Australian women, but quite pretty in a podgy sort of way and her bare breasts less droopy than one would have expected for their spectacular mass, the pink nipples the size of small saucers. She exuded a musk of sensuality that caught Peter's slightly tipsy mood.

287

Her friend was as dark as she was fair, olive-skinned, brown-eyed and brown-nippled, less pretty but even more earthily sexual, as if the advancing years that weighed down her huge breasts left too little of her man-eating days ahead of her.

"Hi, we haven't seen you before," said the mousey one, her accent the brashest that Sydney could muster.

"Oh, but I saw you at dinner last night," Peter contradicted.

"Well, you must have been hiding. We were propping up the bar till late."

"Mummy makes me go to bed early," Peter replied.

"Naughty mama," said her friend, who was clearly not Australian, but as yet Peter could not place the accent, "I would also if you were mine."

Spanish? French? Italian? Greek? Peter remained unsure. The complexion could certainly be Mediterranean.

"And what brings you here?" It was mousey again.

"Oh, just a holiday. I come from London. It's pretty horrible there this time of year."

"No, not here, here," she said, spreading her arms wide suddenly so that her naked breasts wobbled like blancmange, "here, here," she went on, pointing at the sand with both hands. "Most of the people here don't stray more than 50 yards from the pool - or the bar - the wrinklies even less."

"I was just trying to see if I could walk round the island."

"In this heat, you must be mad. Anyway, you can't run off like that. We haven't seen a man all week and we're leaving this evening. It'll be cooler to walk in an hour or two. Sit yourself down. Catch a few rays. Have a swim. There are towels and snorkels and things over there. Help yourself."

"I'm not much of a sun-bather. I burn too easily."

"No sweat, sport. We got all the sun-tan lotions. We're trying to use up Albertine's share before we go, isn't that right princess?" she called laughing to the black girl, listening but not participating, still a little way off on the rock, now intent upon her toenails. She smiled back, flashing a mouthful of purest porcelain. She was really very striking.

Female company was pretty appealing right now - even these three. They weren't much to look at, and one of them was black, not one of Peter's specialities; but they seemed quite fun and Peter was easily diverted.

The two white girls, it transpired, worked for the Cameroon Embassy in Canberra and had been nominated to take Albertine, who really was a princess, off for a week's holiday while her father, Chief Alphonse of Bandiagara, was doing his rounds of the Government. Donna, the more forceful one with the digger accent, was pure-bred Australian but had done well at French in school and spent a couple of summers in Nice, working in various hotels and restaurants and generally having a good time; Brigitte, whose father had been out in Australia for ever, with Michelin, was genuinely French. The language appeared to be the only qualification for the Cameroon Embassy. Neither looked destined to be a diplomat.

The princess, now satisfied with her nails, spread her towel on the rocks and lay full-length, her eyes closed. African gymnastics, Peter thought. He chatted to the other two for a while, principally the recipient of their gossip about their fellow guests. Most of this was speculative. They seemed to think that Igor Radziwill's nephew was married to the sister of Jackie Onassis and they had decided for some reason or other that the two queers with the bushy moustaches were a pair of Catholic priests from Baltimore. Brigitte claimed that she had actually seen them doing 'eet' on the beach one night after dinner, though mercifully she did not describe exactly what 'eet' involved. They couldn't make out Mrs Fortescue and daughter at all. That Peter, as a newcomer, already knew their names gave him, he thought, a certain cachet in their eyes.

"She never seems to let the poor girl out of her sight. We tried to be friendly when we arrived - suggested we take a boat out together - but we got fair squashed by the mother. Bit too much of a stuck-up pair o' pommies for the likes of us. That's probably why she's only prepared to speak to a posh bastard like you," she added.

Only in the case of the Japanese had their speculations been put on firmer ground and this as a result of cornering their young companions in the ladies loo. They were indeed, as Peter had suspected, working girls but from Jakarta rather than Manila. They had apparently had a pretty easy time. The old boy was a big noise in Mitsubishi, but that was the only thing that was big about him, and the little one with the wig was a member of parliament who came if you tickled his feet.

It was hot and Peter was beginning to feel the sun on his bare shoulders. He crossed his arms and put a hand on each.

"I'm going to burn if I'm not careful. Where's that suntan cream?"

"C'est içi," said Brigitte instinctively, throwing him the bottle.

He started to unscrew it and then stopped.

"Actually, I think I'll just have a swim first. Can I borrow some flippers? Who's got the biggest feet?"

"No doubt 'bout that, sport. Albertine's your girl. Those black ones over there. She's sorta colour-co-ordinated," said Donna, throwing back her head and laughing at her joke so that her breasts heaved up and down uncontrollably.

The flippers made a lot of difference. He must remember, he thought, to pick up a pair from the store ready for his early morning swim. He adjusted the snorkel and swam out a little way using only his legs, peering through the mask clear to the bottom below him; but this morning's teeming schools had disappeared. Something to do with the sun maybe. He returned to the beach disappointed, hoping desperately that what he had witnessed before breakfast was a daily occurrence rather than an aberration unlikely to be seen again. He towelled himself down in a perfunctory sort of way, applied cream to his shoulders, torso and legs and sat on a towel next to the two girls. They had turned on their tummies and were silent. He picked up a copy of *Paris Match* that Brigitte had been reading and alternately flicked through it idly and gazed lazily at the captivating reef. They were right. It was still too hot to walk and sitting here still you could feel yourself roasting. After ten minutes or so, he turned on his tummy, then remembered the suntan cream, shook some into his hand and started trying to apply it awkwardly to his back.

"Don't worry. I 'elp you," said Brigitte suddenly awake and seizing the bottle.

He gave in and settled on his tummy, his head to one side. She took an inordinate time about it, applying the lotion little by little to his shoulders, neck and arms and massaging it into his skin. He couldn't say it didn't feel good; but the pleasure was manifestly not all his. After a few minutes he felt another pair of hands join hers, starting round his ankles, and turned his head the other way to find Donna kneeling there, her enormous rump towards him. The material of her bikini bottom, scanty enough in any event, had ridden up the cleft between her buttocks and a clump of brown pubic hair had emerged on each side at her crotch. It ought not to have been but it was strangely provocative and he felt reassured that he was lying on the evidence of his interest. After a few minutes more, they let him be, though not before Donna had applied cream all the way up the backs of his legs and attempted to protect parts of the inside of his thighs that the sun could not possibly penetrate.

He must have dozed off a little after that because the next thing he knew was a slap on his bottom and Donna saying "I reckon it's time we turned this barbie over."

He struggled sleepily over onto his back only to discover that they were ready for him once again, Brigitte's pendulous brown-tipped breasts swaying before his eyes as she started on his chest and Donna already attacking his feet, insteps and ankles.

"Come off it, Donna. I'm not the little nip. That tickles. I can't stand people touching my feet."

"Okay, sport," she giggled, moving up his shins. Soon she was above his knees and he could feel the uncontrollable hardening of his loins that was the inevitable result of four female hands working on his body. Donna was still concentrating on his legs, now paying particular attention to the higher portion of the inside of his thighs. Brigitte meanwhile knelt above his head She was so close that he could smell her as she leaned over his head to rub cream into his torso and stomach, contriving to allow her pendulous breasts to fall towards his face. The teats seemed excitedly erect. He licked at one. It tasted salty from her swim. "Ooh, méchant," she said. "Donna, regarde ce que ce type fait à moi."

"Yeah, an' I reckon he's got a hard on," said Donna, putting a podgy hand on the rising bulge in his trunks.

"Ooh, let's see eet," said Brigitte, suddenly holding Peter down by the shoulders while Donna, needing little encouragement, tugged at his waistband until his cock, released from the confines of his shorts, sprang out to stand pointing skywards like a steel flagpole.

"Oh la la la la, celui-là me parait délicieux," said Brigitte, "Albertine," she called, "princesse, je pense que nous devions trouver une place pour jouer avec ce que nous avons içi."

To be fair, he didn't need a lot of encouragement. He was feeling as horny as all hell and these girls seemed to make up for what they lacked in looks in sensual enthusiasm and an obvious sense of fun. They were all sharing one of the larger two-bedroomed cottages on the far side of the island; so it was natural enough that they ended up in his, just a few hundred yards down the beach. Donna on his one side and Brigitte on the other, their beach bags slung over their opposite shoulders, made a play of frogmarching him down the beach and Albertine brought up the rear with a slow and regal stride. Sliding open the double doors directly off the beach into the bedroom he stood aside for them to go in. He didn't know exactly what was coming next but he thought it was going to be fun. Suddenly, Brigitte seized one of his arms and Donna the other and pulled him back onto the bed. Albertine sprang at him like a tigress, knocking the wind out of him and pinioning him between her knees. He wasn't altogether sure that this was quite what he had in mind and started to fight to get free, yanking first on one arm and then on the other and trying to buck the girl from his midriff; but these three were carrying the better part of 500 pounds between them, and it was hopeless. Within no more than a couple of minutes he found himself like a naked starfish, his left and right arms tied to the bedposts with Donna's and Brigitte's bikini tops, his shorts pulled off and his feet tied with towels to the legs of the bed. In fairness the bonds were not tight but they were nevertheless effective. He could move his arms a bit, also his legs, but there was no way that he could break free.

Having got him thus secured, they all stood up, the two white girls, unfit and overweight, breathing heavily, Albertine, for all her size, showing little sign of the exertion other than a gentle rise and fall of her ample bosom. The sexuality of the struggle, the flesh on flesh writhing and the sheer animal lust of the girls had left Peter feeling shamelessly horny. Arms spreadeagled by his lightly tethered wrists, his head propped upon the pillows at the head of the bed, he looked down over his chest and stomach to his cock, bolt upright, beyond. Albertine stood at the end of the bed, her full red lips wet and shiny. She ensured that she had his full attention, turned around, bent over and peeled the bottom half of her bikini down her long and muscular legs and off. Remaining bent over away from him, she parted her legs and slid her hands slowly over her bottom to open the black lips of her vagina with her long crimson-tipped fingers, displaying the wet pinkness within. Between her legs and her huge swinging breasts, she observed with satisfaction the impact which her display was having upon him. Evidently satisfied, she turned, knelt on the bed between his splayed legs and bent to take the top half of his penis into her mouth, holding him firmly with her lips whilst her tongue played ecstatically around his glans. After no more than a minute, by which time he felt his member throbbing with anticipation, she suddenly withdrew, leaving a perfect ring of lipstick around the centre point of his shaft as clear and distinct as the red sash across the label of a bottle of Mumm champagne.

'Okay, babes," she said, "accordez cet instrument. Je vais avoir sa langue." And, with that, she clambered over him to take up position, kneeling still, her fanny a half-inch from his mouth. She smelt of musk and sex, sweat and pussy as his tongue snaked out to taste her. She teased herself and him for a while, holding her slit just beyond or barely within reach of his darting tongue; but as she began to thrill to the feel of his occasional successful foray, she shuffled herself closer and gave her clitoris to the fullest enjoyment of his attentions.

Nothing in the room was visible to him other than Albertine's thick mound of curly black pubic hair, but he could feel her friends also settling themselves on the bed and it was soon apparent to Peter that they were in turn licking up and down the length of his shaft like two kids sharing a lollipop. The sensations were mesmeric, the taste of minge above him, the two hands, which didn't somehow feel like a pair, grasping the base of his cock, the distinct separable sensation of two tongues measuring its length. From time to time Albertine shouted regal instructions over her left shoulder.

"Keep him going." "Don't make him come." "You'll get your turn." "Donna, take your bottoms off." "Okay, I'm getting close. Climb on him. Back to back with me."

He felt Donna's hand clasp his cock, shoving it unceremoniously up into her cavernous hole as her huge buttocks settled on his stomach.

More instructions from the princess.

"Brigitte, can you get at his balls?" "Okay, tu peut les lecher." A second later he felt her hot tongue snaking over his scrotum. He plunged his tongue deeper into the wet slit above him. thrust his hips against Donna who was now writhing in his lap, all the while a wet half-tickling, half-massaging sensation at his testicles. The explosion could only be moments away. Suddenly, Albertine's movements changed, pushing her mound forward to him and back; forward again and back; and then, as she came forward again, she threw back her head and bellowed in orgasm as Donna, triggered by his own massive ejaculation, gasped in ecstasy and sat on him so firmly that he was almost winded again.

The room fell silent save for the panting of three sweaty and exhausted bodies. Donna wriggled down to enjoy the last dregs of her orgasm. Albertine, utterly in bliss, climbed over his torso to bring her face next to his so that she could explore with her own the tongue that had just given her so much pleasure. She was soon, however, aware that Brigitte had been missing out.

"Hop off, Donna," she ordered. "Climb on his face, Brigitte, il a une langue comme un serpent."

Peter's tongue, in fact, felt far from snake-like. In reality, he already thought that his exploration of Albertine's pussy had strained the roots by which it was attached to the back of his mouth.; but that, it was soon made clear, was not going to spare him further duty.

Albertine climbed off the bed to fetch her cigarettes and Donna pulled herself off him and joined her on the settee, leaving Brigitte in sole charge. His dick hung limp and slimy as she turned towards it, planting her bum in his face and offering him her slit. God, this is like a wine-tasting, thought Peter, clarets against burgundies. In fact it was very similar. Sure, when you had two back to back like this, and he never had before, they had a strong generic likeness. They were two wines though from different regions or perhaps from different grapes. In this case, certainly more than two of the same wines from different vintages. Was that because Albertine was black and this girl white? Perhaps. They always said that a black girl smelt different from a white and the princess had been noticeably more musky and stronger flavoured than this one. Quite the connoisseur, thought Peter, his satiated condition allowing him the luxury of a little analysis. This one was more tangy, the sort of thing a wine bore might have called lemony, zestful, but not as deep and complex as the African cultivar. He labelled her a riesling against Albertine's cabernet/merlot blend, a young Alsatian against the Pauillac princess.

"I don't think he's concentrating properly," complained Brigitte and Peter had to agree that he was tasting rather than quaffing at this stage.

"Je pense il est seulement paresseux," said Albertine. "Tu dois donner sa bitte un peu de la pipe."

Peter felt the big girl move above him, the angle at which she presented her fanny to him changing as he felt her grip his knob. A moment later she had him in her mouth. She was not as subtle as Albertine, slobbering greedily rather than probing and playful; but he had been too long without female company for there to be any semblance of resistance to such stimulation. He felt himself harden within seconds and, as his own pleasure mounted, so did his attention to the clitoris above him. They were shortly both down to the short-strokes and the frenzied workings of her tongue as she reached her climax sucked a second orgasm out of him.

"Okay," said Albertine, "I think we should give him a little rest while we decide what to do with him next. I want that cock good and hard for what I have in mind."

"Do I get any say in this?" asked Peter.

"Pas grande chose, cheri," replied Albertine. "Pour moi c'est presque la premier fois comme ça - surtout avec un blanc - et c'est magnifique, n'est-ce pas?"

"Well, what about a beer. Quite apart from anything else, I've got an assortment of pussy hairs stuck between my teeth and, since I can't use a toothpick, I could do with a mouthwash."

Donna fetched drinks from the fridge upstairs, peeled the tab off a can of Carlsberg for him and knelt across his torso, tipping the beer gently between his lips. His own and her juices trickled from her stickily into the hairs on his chest.

"Don't you think it's time to untie me?" he suggested, between sips. "I'm awfully good with my hands."

"Hear that, princess? Pommy bastard says he's awfully good with his hands," she mocked, imitating his clipped English accent, then giggled and leaned forward to smother him between her tits, as if to confirm it was all in jest.

"Bien sur, mais je pense qu'il est mieux comme il reste maintenant. C'est tellement rare n'est-ce pas? Extra sexy."

"There, you heard it, sport. Princess likes you the way you are. Now, how's that dong of yours," she added, turning herself sideways and seizing his flabby dick with her podgy right hand. "Now don't you think you can go off to sleep, cobber," she addressed it firmly, "reckon you've still lots of work to do before we fly away."

For the next hour and a half, they were all over him, breasts and buttocks, tongues and teats, mouths and muffs, perspiration and pussy, sex and sweat, nipples and navels. It was a battle of diminishing returns in one sense, as each successive erection took more effort to effect than the last; but also a war of attrition that took every advantage of the longer and longer gaps between his orgasms. Eventually each of them mounted him in turn, plunging up and down on him as they sought their own climax while, for his part, the thought increasingly uppermost in his mind was what was increasingly tender and ultimately downright sore. Albertine finished him off, gripping his member with astonishing resolution as she slowly and deliberately slid him up and down inside her, assiduously bringing them both to a final denouement as painful, in his case, as it was pleasurable.

A huge and exquisite ivory smile lit up her face as she slipped herself off him, quickly untying the brightly-coloured silk scarf that held up her hair. Leaning forward, she bent over him and carefully tied it in a perfect bow around his member.

"Et n'inquiete pas," she said, "pas de SIDA. Je te promis. Nous étions tous examinées avant de partir de Canberra."

AIDS. Christ, he hadn't even thought about it. The Africans were meant to be bloody-well riddled with it, according to George Aladyce. What a let-off.

It was around six-thirty when the maid who came in to turn down the bed found him there. His shoulders, spread crucified for the past four hours, were aching viciously for release and his mouth was unbearably dry.

"Could you untie me, please?" he croaked, as she stood at the bottom of the stairs, transfixed in wide-eyed astonishment. She blushed scarlet and hesitated for a moment before stepping gingerly forward to untie the princess's silken bow.

*****

Every muscle in his arms, shoulders, back and thighs howled in protest as he hauled himself off the bed next morning. He felt as if he'd gone twelve rounds with the incredible hulk - and then stuck his cock in a bee-hive.

The evening had been predictably embarrassing but, after an endless shower, an even longer soak in the jacuzzi and a couple of beers upstairs, he had steeled himself to face the dining room. The girl at reception had just finished checking in some new arrivals, who had no doubt come in on the helicopter by which his amorous assailants had made their escape. She flashed him a smile that was more like a snigger. As he crossed the lobby towards the dining room, the manager emerged.

"Well, hello, Mr Davenport," he exclaimed as he passed by. "Good to see you up and about."

The maître d' was also in on the secret.

"Hello, Mr Davenport. Are you tied up for this evening or are you dining alone?" How long had he been rehearsing that one? The chef was also in on the act. Unbidden, Peter's dinner was completed with a little plate, which had notably not been offered elsewhere, which his waiter announced grinning from ear to ear as three gobbets of sorbet - blonde (lemon), brunette (mango) and black (chocolate). They were presented together with a banana around which the kitchens had cunningly created a bow of fresh mint and added a dollop of fresh cream.

Notwithstanding his protesting body, he repeated his regime of the previous day - a swim first thing, a healthy breakfast and a punishing bludgeoning at the barrel of the tennis automaton. He ached everywhere but was surprised to find that he was already sharper, the machine's hopper actually exhausted before he felt compelled to take a rest. His muscles didn't like it but he reloaded twice more and batted them all back, albeit with diminishing effect, before the lure of the pool and an ice-cold beer overcame him. It was slightly overcast, less warm than the previous day, as if bidding him not to weaken; and he decided to take up the challenge. He took a small salad for lunch, forswore the third beer in favour of sparkling water, and, deciding against his previous day's direction of travel, was setting off boldly up the western beach with only another bottle of water for company before most of the guests had got their hands round their knives and forks.

What with the odd fallen palm, some rocky coral-encrusted outcrops that made him wish he had worn his trainers, and his general feeling of decrepitude, it was more a stiff walk than a jog; but John Soldatis proved as good as his instructions and around four o'clock, having been heading back south for a good while now, he felt that he was approaching familiar territory. Sure enough, as he scrambled up to the top of another sharp-stoned little rock, he saw the familiar beach set out before him. He paused briefly, searching for any trace of what had transpired, as if he suddenly felt now that it might have been nothing more than an erotic dream. One of Turtle Island's endless army of invisible hands had gathered up all the snorkels and masks and flippers that the previous afternoon's revellers had left there. Not a footprint remained. At that moment the soft sand shifted momentarily under a gust of ocean breeze, and he looked back to see his own tracks now barely visible. He was proceeding gingerly down Albertine's rock, opining to himself racially that she must have the hardened soles of generations of Africans notwithstanding her aristocratic title, when something caught his eye. It was wedged in a tiny cleft, scarcely visible unless one were on top of it - a small bottle of crimson nail varnish. As he picked it up, the top, which was still unscrewed, tumbled off and he clumsily trickled a thin vein of the contents down his khaki shorts.

He ran into the ocean, peeling them off and scrubbing irritably at the stain which spread effortlessly under his ministrations from a red line no longer or fatter than a baby's finger into a man-sized hand-sized maddeningly pinkish splodge. The mark of Albertine would confine those shorts to the bottom of his drawer for ever.

A couple of hours later, rested, showered and changed for the evening, Peter left his cottage and set off in the direction of the Fortescues'. Passing that morning on his way out and their way in to breakfast, Jacqueline, the mother, had chided him gently for his failure to appear in the bar the previous evening, where she said they had planned to inveigle him into joining them for dinner. She insisted that they make it tonight and suggested he come over to their cottage for drinks first - to avoid Mrs Bradley's intoxicated attentions. She had apparently made quite a spectacle of herself again. At least his fellow guests, as far as he could so far tell, did not appear to have been appraised of the spectacle that had been made of him.

Jacqueline herself opened the door. She was dressed in an absolutely plain white cotton shift, ending well above the knee - barely more than a shirt. The suntan she had put on over the last couple of days suited her and she was looking good for her age, Peter thought. It was not surprising that Jade was such a stunner.

The cottage was quite a bit bigger than Peter's - presumably with two bedrooms on the lower level - but essentially of the same design. More deep comfy armchairs, larger sofas, one almost as deep as a bed. Jacqueline Fortescue settled herself onto it, tucking her long bronzed legs half under her, out to one side, and motioning Peter to the chair opposite. Her dress unbuttoned down the front. It was open to a level where a bra, had there been one, ought surely to have made itself known. Dusk had descended swiftly and the rich warm woods and soft fabrics appeared to absorb the suffused light of the three of four table lamps around the room; but not a hint of underwear appeared visible from where Peter was sitting.

"I think that daughter of mine is still in the shower; but let me fix you a drink, Peter. What's it to be?"

"Does your bar run to campari and soda? I asked them specially to put some in mine."

"Well, let's see," she said, now on her feet, opening the door of the cabinet. "Yup, your request was superfluous. It's clearly standard issue. Would you like that in a tall glass," she said over her shoulder.

"Excellent. Do you want some help?"

"No you just sit there and relax."

The glasses were in another cabinet, above the drinks, and she was standing on tiptoe now to reach into it. The hem of her dress, which Peter had already found startlingly short, rode upwards as she stretched to reveal ...... nothing. The slightly less than perfectly rounded cheeks of her bum - more pear than apple - were absolutely naked.

Now going braless is one thing, thought Peter, but you don't just forget to put your knickers on, do you? I suppose she could be wearing one of those string things - but no, she bloody well isn't, he gasped, he felt as if it were aloud, as she bent to the lowest shelf of the refrigerator and a fringe of pubic hair was etched between her legs against its interior light.

She might have noticed the expression on his face as she turned with their drinks - a gin and tonic for herself - but, if so, she gave no hint of it. Was it all deliberately staged? She handed him his campari and resumed her position on the sofa opposite. Now, of course, he was mesmerised by the shadowy point at which the hem of her white shirt met the tanned thighs beneath. Was that her pussy? Or just a trick of light and shade? He had to take his eyes off it. He hauled them deliberately to her face. She beamed at him contentedly, lifting her glass to him.

"Cheers," he said.

"Bottoms up", she replied, her smile even broader now and her eyes twinkling. "Peter, I've got a confession to make. I particularly asked you to come round because I want to enlist your support. In the short time since you arrived, you've already got yourself quite a reputation and I'm sure you're the man I'm looking for."

He felt his face redden with embarrassment. It was ridiculous for a man of his age, he thought, but he could not suppress it. Was he being teased? Seduced like an older woman's teenage toy boy? Was it just another stage in the conspiratorial piss-taking in which half the staff of the establishment had spent the day participating?

"You see, Peter, I've got a very specific need for a young man's help." Her fingers were at the buttons of her shirt. "Not too young a man, of course." She was definitely not wearing a bra. "I need a man of some expertise but not so experienced as to be intimidating." She slipped her left hand inside her shirt and caressed her right breast. He had felt this morning that his dong was going to need at least a month's convalescence; but now she was making him feel unbelievably horny. Amazing how the more you get, the more you want. Suddenly she rose. Her dress was unbuttoned to the waist now. "I'll show you," she said, holding out both hands to him and pulling him to his feet. She stood before him, his hands still in hers, and pushed them inside her shirt onto her naked breasts. The nipples were desperately erect, pointed, although

300

the breasts to which they were attached were far from firm. Her mouth came up to his, open, wet, urgent, and she pressed her belly against the now solid bulge in his thin cotton chinos.

"Jade needs our help," she whispered, as their lips parted. "I promised her she'd know everything she needed to face the world at the end of this holiday. But we haven't found anyone suitable until you. We leave the day after tomorrow and then it's just India and home. And we can't do it with a coolie, of course. Please help us. You're ideal," she gasped as she fastened herself again to his tongue and clawed at his bottom with nymphomaniac hands.

"But where does Jade come in to this?" he spluttered. "You're not expecting me to do it in front of her, surely?"

"Of course not, silly. We're all going to do it together. We'll show her how it's done and then she can try it with you for herself. She's just waiting downstairs for me to tell her that you've agreed. Please say you will," she said, rubbing one hand between his legs.

It was all downhill from there. Jade appeared in answer to her mother's call wearing, briefly, nothing but a towel and a gorgeous, eager smile. They would start, her mother explained, as if to justify the educational angle, with a couple of Latin words.

Two hours later, all slightly flushed, they were very much the final guests to take their seats in the dining room. In one corner Susan Bradley was in the midst of a loud-mouthed row with Milton. They'd got to the stage of peddling mutual abuse.

"You're pathetic," she slurred. "You shell out all that alimony to marry me and then you can't even get it up any more."

For himself, Peter felt happily weary, still a bit sticky despite a quick visit to Jacqueline's shower, where she had attempted unsuccessfully to get a final and exclusive shout out of one flagging and tender party. The pair of them had been astonishing; the mother, in Peter's albeit medically untrained view, technically addicted, the daughter, whatever her lack of experience, apparently without scruple or embarrassment in this department - rather like those stories of the Polynesian island girls first encountered by eighteenth century sailors whose willingness to do it for a couple of nails started to cause whole ships to fall apart. Their bodies, once Peter's initial lust had been satisfied, were a fascinating comparative study. They were as alike as a mother and daughter could be; but nevertheless always different. Jacqueline's skin was healthy and youthful with barely a wrinkle beside the light crow's feet that her tan laid bare, the lines that appeared around her mouth as she gasped or groaned or gobbled and the slight sagging of parts which should have been more tense. But Jade's flesh had an astonishing combination of yielding softness and firm invisible muscle that would have made even Soo Chan jealous. As they climbed enthusiastically all over him, Jacqueline's breasts swayed and danced, but Jade's just bucked and bounced. Peter closed his eyes and felt the flesh all over him, a buttock here in each hand, both marvels of carnal temptation; but it was impossible to mistake their separate owners. But it was more subtle than that even. These two tongues that licked alternately at his vitals, the one hot and greedy, the other somehow a cooler, gentler caress. The two pubic mounds pressed towards his face, the one a fraction less blondish, a fraction more coarse, a fraction more frequently and more rigorously trimmed. Those nipples competing for his mouth, identical in complexion, but the one ever so slightly distended by attention, the other as perfect as a Botticelli. And inside them too, how could it be? A whirlpool of desire in the one pulling him towards the abyss; a long gentle slide into a delectable ecstasy with the other. It was hard to believe this was her first time. A girl like that could cause a lot of grief.

*****

Next day, for the first time in an age, Peter slept almost till noon. His brightly coloured playful little fishes had gone from the shallows as he wandered out for his now habitual swim. He could feel the tenderness in his trunks but somehow he was also beginning to feel restored. He snorkelled around for half an hour, albeit with flippers, without a sensation of strain or breathlessness. Commenting later to himself that he had shat and shaved, shampooed and showered, he now set off on the short walk to his lunch feeling genuinely hungry.

He had heard the helicopter clattering in again as he emerged from the shower and, sure enough, there was a couple, their backs towards him, busy with the receptionist as he passed, heading towards the bar.

The man, who was apparently trying to cough out a tickle in his throat, was really tall, perhaps as much as six foot seven or eight, blond and wirily thin, the girl very shapely in the bum in a tight pair of jeans with long auburn hair tied in a pony tail.

"Could you just send off a couple of faxes for me", she was saying to the receptionist as Peter passed.

He didn't turn. He didn't need to. It was a voice he was sure he recognised, hard though it was to associate it with the body in the tight-arsed jeans.

*****

There was a bigger, though not much bigger, turnout for the tennis competition than Peter had expected. Beside the little Japanese and the Australian with the muscles, they were joined by the bespectacled German, who turned out incontrovertibly to be the source of the haze of Aramis, and the wiry giant, a Scandinavian by the name of Lars. John Soldatis, who was there to supervise the draw, announced at the start that, with five participants, the competition would take the form of each man playing two sets against each of the other four, two points for a win, one point for a draw; in the event of two being equal at the end, they would play the best of three sets against each other. A couple of minutes later, emerging from a huddle with Lars, he declared that it was too hot for the possibility that anyone might have to play eleven sets and that the format would be changed. The draw would be Helmut against Junichi, the winner to play Peter for a place in the final, and Lars to play Ross, the neanderthal, for the other place, each match the best of three sets. Peter was not about to complain. Avoiding the ape-man in the first round looked like a distinct advantage; and whichever representative of the former Axis powers emerged victorious from that contest would be conceding him the better part of a couple of decades.

Those accorded a bye to the second round settled themselves in the shade to observe the battle of the wrinklies. The Jap, true to his race, had been practising the wrong aspect of his game. He turned out to have a magnificent double-handed backhand and a precise though hardly penetrating service; but his forehand, which he also hit with both hands was woefully wayward. Helmut by contrast had a bit, though not much, of everything. His advantage was that he never hit anything out and that he used his eyes. He served first and lost the game to love as Junichi sidled deliberately onto his backhand for every shot, driving the ball precisely into first one corner and then the other. The Jap won his service too but that was the end of it. Helmut had got his measure and never put another ball anywhere near his backhand, emerging 6-2, 6-0 in not much more than half an hour. He looked no more stressed than when he emerged from pounding up and down the pool for half an hour and was ready to get back on the nearside court with Peter before Lars and Ross had even finished knocking up on the far court.

The twenty-odd years separating them did not turn out to be much to Peter's advantage. The German, he soon concluded, was chronically fit, he himself merely a little less of a wreck than he had been a week before. Furthermore, far too much of his recovering strength had been spent on or rather in the female form. The sun was at its height and he felt himself sweaty and lethargic by comparison to his sprightly opponent who moved about the court with the utmost economy of effort, hoisting lob after lob into the broiling sun or worse still over his head into the back of the court. At least there was a lot of effort being expended on the other court. Peter had no time to observe more than the odd rally as he and Helmut were changing ends; but the neanderthal, who was now being watched in rapt admiration by what turned out to be his new bride, was a grunter not merely on his serve but on each and every shot. By contrast to the relatively gentle stroke and counter stroke that he and Helmut were engaged in, the other game consisted of a ceaseless cannonade of roars and grunts and whipcracked bullets of gut on rubber. The ape-man was apparently pummelling his opponent to death against the back netting. It was no surprise that they were finished well before Peter and Helmut embarked upon their third and deciding set. Peter had won the first solely by virtue of his serve and lost the second as he turned for the umpteenth time to scrabble hopelessly in his backhand corner for yet another exquisite lob. And then it all fell into place. He got in a good number of aces to relieve the pressure on his own service game and he stopped advancing to the net so that he couldn't be lobbed. The German was still not hitting anything out but his middle-aged muscles and slender frame were no match in a baseline duel against an opponent so much younger. Peter found his serve relatively easy to break when he stopped trying to be subtle and ran out 6-1 in the final set, feeling almost restored.

The rest of the participants, except Ross, who was nowhere to be seen, were sitting in the shade with Soldatis as he and Helmut came over.

"Fine match. Congratulations to both," said Soldatis. "Lars has kindly suggested that you shouldn't start the final until six. The heat will have gone out of the sun by then and you can take a dip in the interim, if you like."

"Oh, but I thought," Peter started. "Great idea. I could do with cooling off."

"At six o'clock I see you then," Lars intoned in that melodious Scandinavian rise and fall; but he was wheezing a bit, thought Peter, as he set off for the pool.

*****

Lars Stenhammar was, Peter discovered, before they had even finished knocking up, no ordinary tennis player. He barely moved about the court and he appeared to expend no effort on the shot; but he used his immense reach to the full and he flicked the ball backhand or fore, at knee level, at shoulder height, above his head or off his toes, with exquisite timing. He could impart backspin so heavy that the ball seemed to stop like a fallen brick or roll a topspin half-volley so that it sped away as if suddenly turbo-charged. He swerved his services massively to left or right at will and got them to kick up or dive under Peter's racket without warning. It was not yet twenty to seven when Peter found himself serving to save the match.

He got an ace in straight away but the next three, which he thought were just as good, came back like arrows, one at his feet and one each down the line left and right. 15-40. Peter's first serve was again good, wide into Lars' back-hand court; but the return came back hard and deep down the line and Peter was only just able to reach it with a forehand flick to offer up a feeble lob which hung in the air as Lars advanced at walking pace towards the net, invited to smash it into Peter's unguarded backhand court. Peter scrambled to recover his ground towards the centre of the court behind the baseline only to observe the awful inevitability with which Lars changed tack and stroked the ball past his wrong-footed opponent into the forehand court which he had just vacated.

Peter ran to the net to shake his hand. "Congratulations," he panted, "I'm afraid you found that all too easy."

"Not at all," replied Lars, not a bead of perspiration on him but catching his breath with a noticeably harsher wheeze.

"You make me run around like crazy. Come and have a drink, and let me Samantha introduce to you."

"Samantha? Oh, I thought you were with someone I'd met before. She must be her double."

She met them at the top of the steps leading from the courts up to the veranda bar. She stood on tiptoe to kiss Lars, he in turn arching down and holding her by the shoulders at barely chest height. "Well done, big boy", she said. "Are you alright?" The husky voice sounded full of a concern that Peter would never have expected from that particular shrew.

"Yes, sure," he said breathlessly but he didn't sound it. "Peter, I'd like you to meet with Samantha Wilkinson. Samantha, this is Peter Davenport. He's met your double."

"Remarkable coincidence that. She's called Gillian Wilkinson. You must be identical twins," he said, holding out his hand to shake hers.

She extended her hand coldly. "Not exactly. There's only one of me. My first name is Gillian and that's how I'm known at work."

He quickly took her in. It was the same girl alright, but what an extraordinary change in appearance. She looked a good ten years younger than he recalled. Gone, of course, were the small round unflattering spectacles and the hair scraped back into a bun; but she also seemed altogether less pale and drawn as though a single day in the sun had somehow opened her like a sudden rainstorm can reawaken dormant desert flowers. Her face was certainly quite broad, as he remembered it, but was now framed by a mane of thick golden-brown hair. The fringe at her forehead stopped above well defined, almost bushy eyebrows of the same reddish hue. Matching collar and cuffs, he said to himself. The eyes, set with a slightly slavonic upturn emphasised by high cheekbones, were translucent green. The nose was straight but no button. Her nostrils seemed to flare slightly and her full lips formed a wide and sensuous mouth. Altogether she had an animal beauty like an untamed and potentially dangerous exotic jungle cat.

She was wearing a pair of smartly cut dark blue shorts and a sort of sleeveless white singlet with a few buttons at the collar, all undone. Her sunglasses, slung in the gap, pressed the material against her chest. She clearly wore no bra and the gaping armholes of her shirt gave tantalising glimpses of naked breasts whenever she moved her arms.

"I see you had the same idea for a holiday after our little fracas," he said, "but I seem to have stolen a march on you. I've already been here four or five days."

"I had to get the barristers briefed for the MMC. You probably left that to your minions," she said, implying that he had been neglecting his duty.

"On the contrary, I did all that some time ago. I knew we were going to get a reference."

She did not rise to the bait but Lars, who knew at once that they must have been on opposite sides of the Pitcairn bid, swiftly moved to defuse this resumption of hostilities.

"Well, I suggest that for the next couple of weeks you put aside your little ding-dong" - this said again with that particular Scandinavian vocal rise and fall. "Now, come and drink a potion of peace," he said quickly.

It struck Peter that Samantha, Gillian, whatever, took Lars by the hand and led him to the bar almost as if he were an invalid. She settled him on a stool and waved the barman over.

"A bacardi and coke in a long glass, Dan," she said, "and I'll have a XXXX. What about you, Peter?"

"I'd rather have a beer," he responded belligerently, "they've got Carlsberg here."

"Now, as a Dane, that I like," said Lars with what started as a laugh but rapidly deteriorated into a wheezing, spluttering cough. At length he got it under control. Ms Wilkinson was looking genuinely anxious.

"You know you shouldn't have played, big boy. I hope you're going to take it easy tomorrow."

"I'm fine, just fine. No worry. I have tonight a nice long sleep and tomorrow Jonah takes me after the marlin."

"Lars, that's really not wise. You know what the doctor said."

"How I live my life the doctor cannot decide for me. Jonah and I will leave at dawn. We'll be back by mid afternoon - unless we are lucky in big way. Peter will look after you, won't you Peter?"

*****

Around eleven o'clock she appeared at the top of the stone path leading down to the pool. She was wearing a brightly-patterned parea, predominantly red and green, which was tied in a knot above her breasts. A large off-white canvas bag was slung over her shoulder and on her head was a broad-brimmed straw hat around which was tied a silk scarf in brightest emerald. Her long red hair fell in coppery waves to a point halfway down her back. The large Yves St Laurent sunglasses covered much of her face.

He stood to greet her.

"Good morning. With all these Germans around, I've kept a spot for you."

"My word", she said - that wonderful, slow, gravelly, voice -, "you're taking this chaperoning very seriously."

Having thus belittled him, she put her bag down beside the sun-lounger, adjusted it so that it was almost flat and laid one of the hotel's aquamarine beach towels along its length, placing the other as a pillow. Then she untied the knot that held her parea, folded it carefully and put it in the bag. She was standing with her back to him now as she reached casually behind her back, unclipped the top half of her bikini and dropped it too into the bag. 'Christ, do women know how sexy that movement is?' Peter thought. 'No, of course they don't. Even when they're not misbehaving , they take their bras off at least once a day and they do it as casually as a man takes off his tie. But, for the effect it has, they might as well be reaching down to unzip one's fly - and that's before she turns around.' He tried desperately to keep his eyes, at least substantially, on his book as she sat down, delved in the bag for a bottle of suntan lotion and proceeded to apply it from neck to foot. Finally she lay down on her back, took off her sunglasses and placed the wide-brimmed straw hat over her face.

It gave Peter the opportunity to examine her unabashed. It was scarcely credible that this was the anaemic, pinch-faced, blue-stocking that had accompanied Frank Evans to the meeting in the Dundas boardroom. She was magnificent. Her feet were graceful, the toenails painted in the brightest crimson, as were her fingernails. Her legs were long - not too thin - shapely, almost athletic. The bottom half of her bikini, emerald green like the silk scarf around her hat, was cut in two deep vees, back and front, revealing sensuous upper thighs, an expanse of flat belly and an area of groin that must have been perilously close to the display of pubic hair, however trimmed. But it was her breasts which were perfection. For Peter, a tit man through and through, they were sensational - as large as a good figure would have allowed and, even now, with her lying almost horizontal, far from unobtrusive. When she stood, he had seen, they hung and parted slightly from their own weight, promising to be wonderfully fleshy to the touch. The nipples were large, surprisingly dark for a girl with a fair complexion and, when she stood, gazed at you, slightly upturned, from a point a little over halfway down the orb of her breasts. As she lay there now, they were still mindful of the attention she had liberally afforded them with a cupped handful of suntan lotion and were standing slightly proud. Around the teats the large aureola were speckled with a dozen or more tiny bumps, a feature of womankind which Peter had always thought both fascinating and sexy. She had an inclination to produce the palest of freckles as she tanned and there was a wonderful plunge of this darker skin starting at her neck and covering the area which had been exposed by years of open shirts, low necklines and bathing costumes. She was positively edible.

After a half hour or so on her back, during which Peter found he had made precious little further progress with *The Bonfire of the Vanities*, she stood and proceeded to anoint her back as best she could. The legs and shoulders were easy but not, of course the centre of her back. He was not surprised to receive no request for assistance - but felt deprived nevertheless. The memory of where the last such exercise had led produced a further reactionary hardening in his groin. Finally she lay down again, this time on her stomach, her hat laid to one side and her face away from him. He was grateful. It gave him the opportunity to neglect Tom Wolfe in favour of a critical perusal of the other side of this goddess. It was no less pleasing. The legs stretched upwards faultlessly to the bright green vee of the scrap of material that covered most of the crack of her well-rounded buttocks. Many would have said that her bottom could have been smaller, or flatter, but the roundness appeared to invite a man with a firm grip to grasp her to his loins by these delightful handles. From above the crack of her bum, the top inch of which was revealed by her bikini, her perfect straight spine curved upwards through the small of her back. The expanse of it, all the way to her lightly freckled shoulders, glistened with what could have been beads of perspiration or possibly residues of suntan lotion. It was ravishingly inviting. To keep cool - it was now climbing steadily into the eighties, she had swept her auburn mane to one side to reveal a long and slender neck, the back of which was covered with the finest down. Her dark reddish hair fell in thick waves and shone like burnished copper in the bright sunlight.

The girl's sense of discipline extended to her sunbathing. Half an hour and no more than two or three pages of his novel after she had turned over, she rose, stretched like a cat, turned, walked the half dozen paces to the edge of the pool, and dived in. She swam effortlessly, but with purpose too - five lengths of breaststroke, followed by five lengths of crawl, five of backstroke, five more of breaststroke and finally five more of crawl. Finishing at the far end from where Peter sat, she paused hardly a second before grasping the edge of the pool and hauling herself easily out. This exit gave him the added pleasure, surreptitiously pretending all the while to be deep in his book, to watch the grace with which she walked half-naked the length of the pool. Every male eye around the pool, even those which had not been observing her aquatic progress, followed her. She was not like Albertine, who walked with her head still as if she had a gourd of water balanced upon it; but she had the gazelle style of the girls on the catwalk he had once been dragged off to see with Soo Chan. Up at the bar, Dan's eyes and (had it been possible to see) his gonads too followed every inch of her progress. When she reached her chair, she attended first to her hair, wrapping a towel expertly around her head in an elaborate turban and, in so doing, pulling her breasts up magnificently.

To the cognoscenti amongst the boys from soixante-neuf, there were five levels of attainment amongst topless sunbathers. The debutantes were those who would lie on their tummies and unfasten their bra straps but who would quickly refasten them before turning sunny-side-up. They were of a species called totti modesta. The next level would turn over on their backs but retain an entirely prone position - totti supina. The third group were prepared to sit up, adopting a posture which in all too many cases brought about an unfortunate collision between what was pendulous from above with what was over-inflated around the middle - totti tumula. The more confident group were those who, like the first of the hominids, went upon their hind legs - totti erecta. But the summit of achievement belonged to those who played volleyball. They were called totti tempestua and Samantha was, he decided, one of them.

"What about a drink after all that exercise?" he asked.

He had barely moved to raise his hand when Dan leapt from behind the bar and bounded in their direction. He arrived in time to be disappointed as Samantha took her other towel, wrapped it round herself and tucked in the top corner above her left breast. Nevertheless, Peter detected a noticeable bulge in his crisp white shorts.

"What would you like, Samantha?"

"Oh, I don't know - it's so hot. What's really refreshing?'

"I recommend a long campari and orange juice; that's what I'm having."

"Sounds okay. Make that two" she said with what Peter was astounded to behold was truly a softening. Not a smile. Certainly not a beam. But distinctly a 'let's be civil' sort of acknowledgement.

She adjusted the lounger to give herself a sitting position and sat down, her long legs out in front of her. Peter thought he could risk a conversation.

"I hope you don't mind me asking about the Great Dane, but has he been ill?"

"The Great Dane. Not exactly original but he'll like it. I must tell him. No, Lars has not been ill. Well, not really. He's going to be. He's got HIV. He had to have his appendix out a couple of years ago and they gave him a contaminated transfusion. He used to smoke like a chimney and now he seems to have got emphysema or tuberculosis, or maybe both. It's always terminal, of course, but no one knows how long. In his case it seems to be galloping. He might have five years. It might just be five months. He tries to carry on as if it nothing had happened; to imagine it isn't there; but you can see for yourself that it is."

"Oh, I'm so sorry," he said automatically. "Aren't you worried about....?" he tailed off embarrassed.

"Oh, it's not like that, whatever the appearances." She laughed, a little contemptuously. "All the cottages down that side," she said, with a wave of her hand, "have got two bedrooms. And not as good a view as on your side either, by all accounts. We're just great buddies. We used to go skiing together. And play golf too. He was a fantastic athlete. Danish junior tennis champion. You did well to get a few points off him. Not that, of course, you would have done, when he could still run around."

He noted the put-down.

"And what does he do now?"

"He's senior foreign exchange dealer at Den Copenhagen Bank. I don't have City friends but he's the exception. It's complicated enough having all your telephone calls recorded without finding that the compliance departments of two separate banks have you on tape and are comparing notes."

"So Grossmanns really are the control freaks everyone says they are."

"Perhaps. Let's just put it this way. I have my work and I have my life. I can happily keep them apart."

Dan brought the drinks and set them down on the table between their loungers.

"Thanks, Dan," Peter said, and then , turning back to her, "And what made you decide on Turtle Island for a holiday? You must admit it's a bit of a coincidence."

"Lars and I were just looking for something that would suit us both. There's the big fish for him - that's still just about allowed - and the scuba-diving for me. He used to love that too; but of course that's out of the question now. What about you?"

"Well, I'm hoping to do some diving too. I've just been getting myself in better trim over the last few days. I don't find being torn between Arthur Evans and Christopher Hennessy very conducive to maintaining a general level of fitness."

"Funny little chap, that Hennessy. I expected rather more after all that Harvard Business School and KKR stuff. Is that really all there is to him?"

Peter was tempted to be indiscreet but settled on something more likely to be advantageous but sufficiently close to the truth to be plausible.

"Well, what you see is what you get. He's got a classic dose of small man syndrome, which makes him aggressive enough to bite anyone's bum, particularly when someone like Arthur Evans tries to sit on him. What about your man? The ideal client? I suspect not."

"Evans. He's a copper-bottomed, silver-plated, gilt-edged shit - but everyone knows that. A ruthless pig without an atom of genuine charm - and proud of it - so I'm giving nothing away there."

"So how do you come by the short straw of looking after him?"

"Oh, you know how it works. I used to be the manager on the account and when I became a director, I just sort of carried on with it. And I must say it's fun. No one minds a client whose always dishing it out so long as most of it is in the direction of the opposition."

"How long ago was that - that you became a director?" He knew it must be pretty recent and saw no harm in ramming it down her throat that he was a more experienced hand.

"Nearly a year ago. Mid '87."

"Got used to supping with the devil yet?"

"Don't worry, I know how to use a long spoon. And you."

"You'd better know that I'll sit on his lap and share his spoon if that's how I get to win," he said ominously.

A silence descended between them. He was pleased with it, let it linger, but broke it eventually.

"And how did you come into this business?"

"Oh, you know, the usual thing - law at Cambridge and then Linklaters."

"I was at the other place and then accountancy."

"I know. I've seen your file. Winchester, New College of course - no problem getting in there as a Wykehamist - an undistinguished second in PPE and a half-blue at something or other athletic you can undoubtedly no longer do, and Price Waterhouse. If you remember, you applied for a job with Grossmanns in 1978. Failed the graphology test, I seem to remember. I won't tell you why."

"Well, that's a bit sneaky on the part of your personnel department," he said, considerably more piqued than he cared to let on. "Is there anything you people don't have tabs on?"

"Well, I wouldn't mind knowing why your lot appointed Bill McAdam head of corporate finance. Bear Sterns were desperately keen to get rid of him and no one else would touch him. He asked us to take him, of course, but one doesn't need a handwriting analysis to see that there's plenty wrong with him. Is he as awful as everyone says?"

"How can I put it? He's more or less like your description of Arthur Evans - but without the veneer of culture."

She laughed at that. She genuinely laughed, rocking forward and banging her fists on her knees. "Oh, I do like that," she said at last. "I might be tempted to use that one."

"Privileged information. Non-attributable."

"Okay, okay; but we don't know everything about you. For instance, I take it that there is no Mrs Davenport."

"No, well you're really to blame for that. My intended was not best pleased with the time I devoted to you over the Christmas holidays."

"What do you mean? We didn't approach you until 2nd January."

"I got wind that you were on your way on Boxing Day and cut short my skiing holiday. We were due to announce our engagement at a party on New Year's Eve back in London. I got stuck in the office and never made it. When I finally got home, I found that she had walked out."

"I'm sorry." She sounded no more genuine than he had over Lars.

"Oh, there's no need to be really. It was quite a shock at the time. I guess I took it for granted that she knew what was involved in being tied up with a merchant banker. It was probably better that it happened before we got married rather than after." That sounded alright, he thought to himself. I really am getting over it.

"Had you been together long?"

"Not really, about as long as you've been a corporate finance director."

Now it was her turn to note the put-down. She tried to smooth it over.

"Were you very upset?" She was a good actress, sounding positively human though it was hard to believe, given his past experience of her.

Just trying to gauge his degree of vulnerability. He searched for a plausible line.

"Yes, I suppose I was at first; but life goes on. This bid has made me too busy to fret", he said untruthfully. Then more light-heartedly, he decided on a bit of flirting, "just as well she didn't know I was seeing Grossmanns' most attractive corporate finance director."

"I'm not sure that's a compliment", she grinned automatically. "I'm the only female corporate finance director of Grossmanns and I suspect that 'attractive' is not the word you would apply to the males."

"Too right. Not the ones that I know anyway."

"How did you find out that the bid was on its way? We were more careful in our preparations for that bid than any other we have ever done. I even told BMP's board at the start of December that it was going to be nasty and that they should watch out for private investigators."

"Sorry, that's a trade secret but it's nice to know you're not omnipotent."

"I think that's enough of business," she said suddenly, as if any more was going to get her irritated and she didn't want to be. "Another drink, or shall we go and have some lunch?"

"Lunch, I think."

"Okay, just give me a couple of minutes to tidy myself up."

She re-emerged from the ladies' room under the bar a few minutes later as she had first appeared that morning with the big straw hat, dark glasses and flowing parea, but, Peter thought he detected, without the bikini top beneath. They chose a table up on the terrace under a broad umbrella, which decided her to remove her hat. She put it on top of the big canvas bag beside her. Peter was pleased. Her hair was simply the most wonderful colour. Too bad the dark glasses stayed in place. There was something about green eyes.

"Are you happy for me to go and choose some wine?" he said.

"Provided it's white and will go with a dozen oysters and a lobster salad."

"Hm, you bet. You can order that for me too."

Peter reappeared five minutes later with two ice buckets. In one was a bottle of Veuve Cliquot and the other a fine Australian chardonnay. A waiter hurried over to open them. He poured them each a glass of champagne.

"What are we celebrating?" she asked coolly.

"The cessation of hostilities?" he enquired in return.

"The temporary cessation of hostilities," she conceded, raising her glass. "Mmm, that's good. Right, we've done with business. What else can we find to fight about?" she suggested, smiling now.

"Let's start with politics and then go on to religion," he quipped.

"Okay," she responded to his surprise, "when it comes to politics, I hate them all. I'll bet you're a conservative."

"Well, I'd have to confess that I have voted for them...."

"There you are, I knew it," she jumped in. "Gotcha!"

"But that doesn't make me an adherent. I'm not a party member or anything like that. It's just self interest. They're likely to steal less from me than the other lot, that's all."

The waiter set down a large earthenware platter piled with oysters and poured more champagne. They each started on the ritual of selection and preparation with similar enthusiasm.

"Anyway," he added, "I'll bet you've voted for the Iron Lady too."

"Certainly not. Wouldn't vote for any of them. The whole system stinks. British politics is riddled with corruption - probably no more than the French or Italian - but that's no excuse."

"Well sure there's a lot of you scratch my back and I'll scratch yours but not many fingers in the till," he said, spearing another oyster.

"Back-scratching, old boy network, jobs for the boys - it's all the same. Stealing a job is no different to stealing money. And the civil service is just as bad. Worse. Look at all these ex-permanent secretaries with their cushy little numbers. Not to mention that MMC reference of yours. I don't know how you did it but I'll wager somebody pulled a fast one."

He let the specifics pass.

"Look, I've no more time for civil servants than you have - ghastly little creeps in my experience - but what's your alternative? You don't want to kick them all out every time there's a change of government - like the Americans - do you? By God, these oysters are good."

"Fantastic. Sure I would. Fixed terms for governments and turn over all senior civil service posts at the same time. And preferably at much less than four or five year intervals. Politicians and civil servants are like nappies. They need changing frequently - and for much the same reason."

"But it's hardly practical, is it? You'd get no continuity."

"Too right you wouldn't and there's another excellent thing. Government would either oscillate from one party to the other so that they never got time to do anything before they were thrown out again; or there'd be endless coalitions where nobody could ever agree to do anything. It's no coincidence that Europe has done so much better than the UK since the War. Despite having nominally socialist governments most of the time. Stalemate. Perfect. And these oysters, too."

"You're teasing me because you think I'm a tory drone. I don't believe you haven't got a sneaking admiration for what Thatcher's done. She must appeal to the women's lib in you if nothing else."

"Women's lib! Don't give me that horseshit, Peter. The one thing I do admire about that awful woman is that she doesn't stand for women's lib. She doesn't go in for all this whinging about glass ceilings and sexual discrimination. She just gets on with it and, if that requires a bit of female guile, so be it."

The eyes of Caligula and the lips of Marilyn Monroe, thought Peter. Was it François Mitterand who said that of her? You might apply it equally to Samantha Wilkinson. He poured her another glass of champagne and they each selected a few more oysters. He was beginning to have a sneaking admiration for this girl.

"And what about all that 'let me introduce you to Lord Evans, the *chair* of BMP'. Isn't that the language of the sisterhood?"

"One's got to keep up appearances, Peter," she said, wiping her chin with her napkin and, Peter thought, smirking at him from behind it.

"And that's another thing. You weren't exactly dressed to kill for that meeting either. What's the game?"

"In a predominantly man's world we girls have enough advantages over you guys without needing to rub it in. Grossmanns is first and foremost a meritocracy, but it's also a pretty masculine environment. There are lots of things a girl can get by wearing a short skirt; but promotion at Grossmanns isn't one of them."

He laughed. The waiter cleared the platter of oyster shells and poured the last of the champagne.

"And those horrible little spectacles," Peter added. "Not exactly your Yves St Laurent, are they?"

"I like them; and I can't wear my lenses twenty-four hours a day. Anyway spectacles are for looking through, not for looking chic."

The YSL sunglasses betrayed the lie, but Peter said nothing. The waiter returned with the lobsters on huge elliptical plates which they nevertheless comfortably overlapped. He poured the chardonnay for Peter to taste. It was big and alcoholic. Peter nodded his approval.

"You see," she said, as the waiter parted once again, "he pours you the wine to taste. I might be a master of wine. I'm Jancis Robinson for all he knows, but you're the man. I can live with that. It's not important for me and it makes you chaps feel macho. I choose the ground where I want to fight. My God, these lobsters look good. What's that?" she said, sniffing at a little jug the waiter had left. "Mm, garlic butter. Wow."

They each anointed the lobster tails and tasted the dense white meat.

"Fantastic," he concluded.

"Wonderful."

"So you're an anarchic, meritocratic, man-hater and, don't tell me, you're a zen-Buddhist to boot."

"I'm not a man-hater," she protested, "I just think there's no point in making out that men and women are the same - or that they're equal. You're more equal than me at some things. I could never run a four-minute mile - or whatever it was you almost used to do. But I'm more equal than you at others. Probably more in the latter category, admittedly," she said, touching his arm to emphasise the tease. And I'm not a zen-buddhist. I'm a lapsed catholic."

"Almost as complicated," he said, cracking a claw and drawing out the perfect pink interior. "Don't tell me you're a convent girl. They're always the rebels."

She laughed. A hoarse, smoker's laugh, though he'd not seen her with a cigarette. A little garlic butter ran down her chin. She wiped it away with her napkin. "You're beginning to get quite prescient, Mr Davenport. The Sisters of Our Lady, the Virgin in Limerick."

"Irish? I might have known it from your hair - and the green eyes." The wine was getting him relaxed. "What's happened to the brogue?"

"The same as has happened to your Cornish, Peter." She pronounced it authentically 'cairnish' with the accent on the first syllable. "Eroded by the imperceptible advance of Oxbridge elocution."

"And why lapsed?"

"Teenage hesitations turned to the adult scepticism of disappointment and finally full-blown disbelief by the crimes of the cardinals."

"What do you mean?"

"I was a real believer." She said it with such conviction that he could imagine her misty-eyed behind the sunglasses. The wine was getting to her too. "I can remember now - August, 1978 - how excited I was when John Paul was elected. It seemed like a new beginning. A genuine people's priest - not one of these awful greedy academic princes of the church. I was nineteen, going on twenty, just starting my final year at Cambridge."

He did some mental arithmetic. Went up aged just seventeen. Not normal, a bright lady. But how could anyone get excited about that horrible reactionary Pole who goes round kissing airport tarmac like some people go sniffing glue. What was the one before him? Did he have the same name? Peter seemed to remember he'd barely got that bee-hive thing onto his head before he keeled over.

"I'd had my doubts," she went on, "but suddenly they were all blown away. He'd been a wonderful Archbishop of Venice and now he was going to come and take Rome back to what real people needed from the church. The smiling pope."

She grinned, Peter thought almost tearfully, as if in imitation of her recollections of him.

"You could see he was the sort of chap who thought all that crap about contraception was the mumbo-jumbo of monks to whom it was of no interest other than as a tool to impose their will. This damned Polish bigot is just obsessed with it. So he keeps his flock in perpetual over-populated poverty. He's no better than Stalin or Mao-tse Tung. Hitler, Stalin, Mao and the Church - the four mass killers of the twentieth century. At least the Church might have been spared entry to that roll-call by Albino Luciani."

She stopped. Her husky voice caught with passion and suppressed emotion. "And, as suddenly as he came, he was gone. It didn't seem fair. Righteous. It just wasn't the sort of thing that his and my God would have allowed to happen. And then, there were questions. Why no autopsy? Why all the contradictory press releases from the Vatican? Why all the lies? And then, after a few months, the rumours began; and finally David Yallop published that book in 1984 and it all became clear. They killed him. The cardinals bloody-well killed him."

"I never knew anything about all this," he said with truthful ignorance and more than a little scepticism. "If that's so, how did they keep it quiet?"

"They just ignored it all. Those bastards share a lot with the mafia. The vow of silence above all. It wasn't in the interests of anyone with power to pursue it. He was the pope of the people, not the politicians or the priests. They only elected him because they thought they could manipulate him, that he was so humble that he wouldn't rock the boat."

"But why did they kill him?"

"Because he was about to rock the boat big time. He was about to change the absurd doctrines that they'd been ramming down the people's throats for decades, kick out a corrupt little French bastard called Villot, who was head of the Vatican admin, and he'd found out how they'd been stealing the church's wealth to play politics and feather their nests."

"Banco Ambrosiano, Roberto Calvi, God's banker, Blackfriars Bridge and all that."

"Yes that was part of it. There was worse. A lot of it was run by a Chicago thug called Marcinkus, who was head of the Vatican Bank, and an archbishop, would you believe. He was in up to his neck with Calvi and above him Michele Sindona and above him Licio Gelli." She was silent for a moment.

They were all names he vaguely recalled. Not Marcinkus; but he felt sure the rest had all been tied up with that P2 Freemasons ring that used, for all practical purposes, to run Italy.

"For me it was the final straw," she said at last. "If these cardinals thought they could kill the pope without needing to fear eternal damnation, it was no use Father Malloney telling me I risked fire and brimstone if I missed confession. I never went again. Gradually it dawned on me that the whole thing was obviously one big fib to allow these bloody priests to ride on the backs of the faithful and part them from their money. And then I realised that all the other religions are garbage too." She smiled again and started back on her lobster. "That's how I lapsed."

He poured her some more wine and they fell to with concentration. It got a bit like that scene from *Tom Jones* with much cracking and slurping. He wished he could see her eyes.

He finished at last and sat back, wiping his chin with an already saturated napkin. The waiter was there in an instant with a dish containing two ice-cold wet face towels.

"Okay, so you're an anarchic, meritocratic Irish atheist and I'll accept that you're not a man-hater if you say so but all your hate figures seem to be men."

"I'm beginning to see why I've had so much trouble with you over the last couple of months, Peter," she protested, her face alight with fun. "You enjoy twisting the truth." She seized a wet towel and dabbed at her wide sensuous mouth.

"And I thought you were the one causing the trouble. Now what are you going to do all summer whilst the MMC is deciding whether we resume hostilities? Where shall I be seeing you? Wimbledon?"

"Of course. Lars gets special tickets, so I can avoid the awful Grossmann's marquee with its watered-down Pimms and cucumber sandwiches with Flora margarine."

"Is it true? Are they really that mean?"

"Every bit, believe me. The old man himself goes through every director's expenses."

"On that basis Covent Garden and Glyndebourne must be out."

"No, not for the most rewarding clients; but I don't care. I hate it. A bastard art form. The eighteenth and nineteenth century equivalent of The Sound of Music - but with even worse actors and a more pretentious audience. Only the ballet is more dreadful - all those squeaking floorboards."

"The Lords' test?"

"What, with the MCC not admitting female members. Even I've got to draw the line somewhere, Peter."

"Ascot?"

"I love it - it's the Irish in me," she laughed again, husky, provocative.

"Silverstone. The Grand Prix?"

"I'd rather watch paint dry."

"A girl of black and white views, would you say?" he said, teasing. "I admit it's better on television, waiting to see when Murray Walker trips over himself. And what about Henley? A chance to watch the boys with the muscles?"

"Awful! Like a cocktail party by the river in fancy dress. My worst. I prefer the sea to rivers. I don't like fancy dress. And I hate cocktail parties."

Peter declined to comment on the disguise she had worn at their first encounter. "Do you know that one about cocktail parties? It was a character in one of Lawrence Durrell's novels - one of the Alexandria quartet, I think..."

"I know what you're going to say," she jumped in, "they were, as the name implies, invented by dogs. They're simply bottom-sniffings elevated to the level of social occasions.....or some such."

"That's the one." They beamed at each other, shaking helplessly with tipsy laughter. "A desert, some fruit, coffee?" he asked as they regained control.

"I'll share a mango with you. Have you tasted them? They're orgasmic."

Peter called the waiter over and ordered. He poured the last of the chardonnay.

She was right. The mangoes were divine - practically without any of the fibres that normally attach to the stone, firm yet sufficiently juicy to require resort to another pair of ice-cold facecloths. They raised their glasses with the last of the wine and clinked them together conspiratorially as the waiter set down their double espressos. Peter delved into his bag for his cigar case and took out a slim six inch Montecristo Especial.

"Ooh, can I have one of those?" cried Samantha.

"Of course," he said, pulling the leather top from the case of four tubes and offering it to her.

"Yummy. I daren't smoke in front of Lars anymore and these are my favourites. I'm sorry, I don't have my cutter with me; could you do it for me?"

He cut the cigars and lit them and they sat there wreathed in grey-blue smoke and exchanged contented smiles.

*****

He opened the door of his cabin and stood aside for her to go in. The north-west facing room no longer caught the direct sun, which made the aspect beyond the sliding doors leading out onto the terrace seem all the brighter. She walked straight over to the windows, drawn by the spectacular view - the white sand of the beach beyond the palms, the still pale blue waters within the reef and then the waves of the dark blue Pacific crashing onto the reef some six hundred metres beyond.

He came up behind her, gently placing his hands on her lightly freckled shoulders.

"There, I told you. It's wonderful, isn't it?"

It was a gesture he might just get away with if she wasn't thinking what he was. As if for answer to his secret thoughts, she turned, untied the knot that held the parea above her breasts and let it fall to the floor. Her arms came around his neck and his about her waist and they kissed; gently at first, exploring the taste and texture of each other's lips, mouths and tongues; then gradually more probing, eventually more urgent, ultimately more ravenous. He ran his hands over her waist to the round cheeks of her bottom, bare on either side of the briefly-cut bikini. He felt the fleshy softness of her large breasts pressed against his chest and she the gathering hardness inside his trunks pressing against her mound.

At last they separated and he stood to admire her. The softness of the flesh on her firm breasts had been everything he imagined, the teats now standing erect in their large aureolas.

"Siesta time", he said. She nodded.

He led her down to the bedroom. She sat on the edge of the king-sized bed and he bent to kiss her. But she pulled him, standing towards her, and pulled down his trunks releasing his engorged penis which stood to face her as she took him into her mouth. He allowed the wonderful sensations of her tongue and lips to play over him for a while and then withdrew, gently pushed her lengthways across the bed, and slid her bikini bottom down over her long thighs and off. Her pubic hair, reddish brown, was carefully trimmed for her bikini but luxuriant. He parted her legs and buried his face in her, separating the lips and probing the pink, wet slit with his tongue.

He felt her tingle with excitement as his tongue first touched her clitoris and heard the long sighs as he licked up and down the length of her slit, stopping at the top of the stroke to pay particular teasing attention to her button. Soon her hips began to respond. She opened her legs wider still, pressing her clitoris towards him, wanting his tongue to be constantly upon it. He responded by sucking at it and probing it feverishly with his tongue. She arched her back, her head shaking from side to side. She began as a low murmur but was soon crying out "I'm coming, I'm coming, oh Peter, I'm coming" and then, at the moment the first climax exploded in her groin, she pressed her thighs hard together, locking his head between them. As she relaxed, he began again, licking and probing, sucking and gentling. Moaning, she came twice more, her thighs trembling, her head thrown back as she pushed her clitoris into his mouth and her whole body shuddered with the thrill.

At last she calmed, taking his head between her hands and pulling gently to indicate that she wanted his mouth on hers. He obediently moved up her body, kissing her mound, her flat belly, the wonderful breasts with the large brown nipples and her neck, until, as his mouth reached hers, his manhood, unaided, slipped into her wet and parted vagina. He lay still on top of her for a moment and was glad to see his smile returned. It wasn't too urgent to be fun but his own climax would not wait much longer. They kissed; a long, wet, probing exploration of each other's mouths. Then he moved his mouth to her ear and began to nibble gently at the lobe. As he began to move, slowly at first upon her, her long legs entwined around his back and she responded. He kissed her again, gently brushing her lips with his. Their hips moved as one, he keeping his loins locked close to hers to minimise the friction and hold back his ejaculation, until he could feel her arousal growing as her movements urged him to pump faster.

"Harder, Peter, harder, please harder", she whimpered between his kisses until half crying, half screaming, half sighing, her climax was detonated as he exploded within her.

They lay panting and satiated, he still inside her, kissing at her green eyes and lightly freckled nose until, light-headed with wine and sex, they drifted briefly into sleep.

He came round, a warm, wet and sensuous feeling in his loins, and looked down to find that his groin had apparently grown a carpet of thick red hair. Her face was pressed between his hips, her long coppery hair obscuring the attention which she was giving his rapidly recovering member. She had its base firmly gripped in her right hand, ever so gently toying with his balls with the other. All the while she was drawing a good proportion of his length in and out of her mouth, pausing every few strokes to tease the throbbing glans at the tip with her tongue. He reached down to touch her hair and to caress the back of her neck and she took this as a sign of encouragement to activity, alternately drawing him deep into her mouth and using her tongue with exquisite effectiveness. It was only minutes since his previous orgasm and this enabled him to prolong the pleasure of her ministrations; but eventually there was no holding back and, as she drew him again into her, the throbbing sensations became uncontrollable, he arched upwards and climaxed over her warm tongue. She held him for some time in her mouth, greedily drawing all the fluid from him. At last, she looked up at him enquiringly.

"No wonder Lars felt that you needed a chaperone", he said, pulling her upwards to him, cupping a hand under her left breast and hugging her lovely body to him, kissing her all over her face and fondling her nipple between his thumb and forefinger. She had satiated him for the moment but her own sexuality was now in the ascendant, heightened by the last ten minutes she had spent teasing his cock between her lips and tongue. He could detect her need and shifted his hand from her breast, replacing it with his lips and nibbling gently at the teat. His hand slid over her pert buttocks as the sexual trigger mechanism of her nipple parted her legs and brought his hand to the inside of her thigh, close to but not at the point she most desired it. The flesh of the inside of her thigh was silky smooth as he ran his fingers up through the curly hair beside her labia. He ran his fingers through the soft down of her mound and traced his finger around and around the outer lips of her vagina. She pressed herself urgently towards his hand but he kept her on tenterhooks for what seemed to her an age. Eventually, able to stand it no longer, she took her hand from where she cradled his head against her breast and grasped the hand that was probing the inside of her thigh. With a determination that brooked no further delay, she clamped his hand onto her sodden and hungry slit. He slid his fingers into her. She was wetter than any woman he had ever known, wonderfully soft and wet here, hard and wet there where the clitoris stood erect like a pearl soaked in oyster flesh. He teased it between his thumb and forefinger and she pressed herself against him, moving her hips back and forth, slowly at first but soon with increasing urgency. Soon she was moving with such power that he found it impossible to keep a grip on the slippery button and simply planted his middle and forefinger in the slit while she pounded away against his hand.

"I'm coming, Peter", she moaned breathlessly at last, "I'm coming, I'm coming, I'm coming" and then as she let out a shriek of pleasure, her whole body shook with the orgasm and she clamped her thighs together around his hand like a nutcracker, shaking and trembling with orgasmic aftershocks.

The sexuality of the girl was breathtaking and the interlude had allowed Peter's previously comatose penis to start again to take some interest in the situation. For her part, she was instantly ready for more. Peter rolled onto his back and pulled her on top of him. She kissed him hungrily and then, placing her knees either side of his hips, rubbed her pussy gently against the tip of his again stiffening cock. As she did so, her large breasts dangled from her chest so that he was able to take first one and then the other nipple into his mouth, kissing, sucking, nibbling and chewing on them in a way which seemed to drive her wild. She reached between her legs, grabbed his cock and rubbed the swollen head up and down the length of her slit. When at last he came up for air, she sat back onto his lap, her vagina by now so sodden and distended that, despite his more than adequate size, it was pulled into the gaping crevice as if by suction. She began to ride him like a rocking horse, slowly at first. The wet softness in which his cock was buried, the fluid flowing from her that soaked his own pubes and the exquisite squelching sound were erotic beyond belief. He had the wonderful sensation of being milked as she rose and fell, her knees clamped to his hips; but, as she sensed that she was bringing him close to climax, she began to buck more violently, her breasts, now beaded with sweat, bouncing up and down and slapping against her body as she strained for the sensation of simultaneous orgasm. He pressed himself towards her, trying to pump in time with her increasingly furious movements but she was now unpredictable, bouncing and writhing almost hysterically. At the moment that he thought that her frenzy was in danger of doing his dearest limb permanent damage, he felt her beginning to spasm. Seizing a round buttock in each hand, he pulled her to him, thrusting his throbbing cock as deep into her as he could and bringing her and himself to a tumultuous sexual convulsion.

She drew herself off him and collapsed at his side, the pair of them now soaked in sweat, her head on his left shoulder, her left leg flung across his thighs.

"The handwriting queen was right", she said, "you're dangerously over-sexed!'

"And what about you, may I enquire?"

"It must be the impact you have on me. I passed the test, if you remember - though, to be honest, I got a friend who I thought more Grossmann's type of girl to write out my CV for me."

The whole idea of the Machiavellian house of Grossmann being duped so splendidly reduced him to gales of laughter in which she joined spontaneously.

*****

They spent the next couple of days intermittently like a curious *ménage à trois*, though, as if by an unspoken understanding between Peter and Samantha, it was always Lars who appeared to be her partner and Peter merely a newly-acquired friend. He never knew if Samantha told him the truth. Lars, returning early evening, found them at the bar overlooking the pool, sipping, to his great amusement, Carlsberg.

"Samantha, I see he has you now converted. This is a glorious day for Denmark."

He was looking terribly tired and clearly finding it difficult to catch his breath, but also wildly exhilirated. Immediately, he triumphantly led them back down to the quay where he was ceremoniously photographed alongside the huge marlin he had caught, almost two feet taller than himself as it hung by a sling round its grand fan-shaped tail.

They dined together that evening, late, after Samantha had more or less ordered Lars to take a couple of hours' rest. It was a warm evening without a breath of wind and they sat outside under the sort of intensely dark sky that you can only get hundreds of miles from the nearest city's polluting sources of night-time light. From one horizon to the other countless billions of stars danced and shimmered in the southern hemisphere sky. Beyond the beach, the faint crashing of the waves on the reef drifted to them on the clear, still air. Samantha and Lars sat side by side on one side of the table, Peter alone on the other, the toes of Samantha's right foot, invisible under the floor-length table-cloth, buried gropingly in his crotch. He was beginning to think she was the most remarkable girl he had ever encountered.

Next day, with a non-alcoholic picnic box already on board, Jonah loaded up a boat with scuba gear for them and pointed them in the direction of the two best coral outcrops on the outer side of the reef. There was only one good channel out of the lagoon up towards the northern point of the island but it was helpfully marked with buoys, as was a point some way to one side of the undersea cliff which, Jonah had assured them, was the site of the most vibrantly coloured coral on this part of the reef.

The water was too warm to need wetsuits but, safely secured to the buoy, Samantha and Peter donned the rest of their kit and carefully checked each other's equipment before sitting on the port side of the speedboat, one at a time, and summersaulting backwards into the water. They hung on to the side of the boat and checked their watches with Lars for a final time before their steady side-by-side descent to the bottom some thirty metres below where the buoy was anchored to a big rough cube of concrete. It was flat and sandy here, the odd brightly coloured starfish and green-brown sea cucumber scattered about but few fish of any great interest. Above them they could see the hull of the speedboat against the lighter background of the sky above, Lars' head peering over the side at them, but no sign of the reef. Peter checked his compass and pointed in the direction it should be. He set his wrist at right angles across the heading so that he could see it as he swam and they set off side by side, Samantha's copper tresses streaming out behind her like a mermaid of yore.

The coral cliff rose almost sheer from the sandy bottom no more than a hundred metres distant, a dazzling hanging rock garden of flower coral, pinks and blues, yellows and reds, whites and greens, here the lightest filligree patterns, like saffroned broccoli, through which tiny brightly coloured fish darted hither and thither, there spiky leaves waving in the currents like undersea palms, here again the big knobbly staghorn corals in reddish brown which were the habitat of another vivid species, striped tigerish in orange and blue, that glided in and out of the antlers. Above a shoal of something larger, silver with black streaks along their sides, raced past overhead. They set off to their right for a while, maintaining their depth, checked their tanks and their watches, rose slowly to a depth of twenty metres and swam back along the wall to their left, stopping to point out to each other everything that caught their eye. By the time they reached the point which they estimated to be above where they had begun, they had been down just over fifteen minutes. Their maximum dive time at this depth was twenty minutes. Peter pointed outwards from the reef in the direction of the boat and Samantha signalled back her agreement. Again using the compass, they set off in the direction they had come. They didn't turn out to be too far out though they had missed the concrete block to which the buoy was anchored away over to their right before they looked up and saw the hull of the speedboat on the surface. They swam across to the cable, checked the state of their tanks and began the slow ascent. Lars had spread a towel on the flat area at the prow of the boat and was lying there on his back, fast asleep.

They dissuaded him with difficulty from helping them out of the water, Peter, instead unclipping his buoyancy control device and leaving it with Samantha while he clambered over the side after his flippers. He hauled it on board and then took hers, before she, considerably more graceful, came over the side as easily as she had emerged from the pool. They stowed the equipment and dried themselves off while Lars busied himself with the picnic box. For all its simplicity, it was another triumph of Turtle Island cuisine, sandwiches of crab and prawn dressed with baby lettuce and home-made mayonnaise, the tastiest sausages Peter had ever tasted with a dip of honey and mustard, succulent pink loin chops of lamb, trimmed of fat and presented with the freshest of mint sauces, miniature tarts filled with a mixture of strawberries, raspberries and red and blackcurrants, all washed down with flasks of iced fresh orange and grapefruit juice and Perrier.

After lunch, they started up the huge outboard, cast off from the buoy and headed back south down the outer side of the reef. After about a quarter of an hour they found what they were looking for - a little bare white sandy atoll poking out of the surrounding ocean like a friar's tonsure. It was, so Jonah had told them, simply the tip of an undersea mountain - more a hill really - rising from the sea bed some seventy feet below. While Lars began a slow revolution of the island to find the mooring buoy, Peter busied himself with the tables to calculate when they could safely go down again and how long they could spend at that depth. If they started kitting up in in the next few minutes, they would have left a full hour and a half since they had surfaced before they went down again. Their residual nitrogen would by then have reduced sufficiently to do a second dive to a depth of twenty-two metres, which was what they needed, for up to 28 minutes. According to the tables, waiting another forty minutes before they went back down would only yield them an extra four minutes on the bottom.

Twenty minutes later they were back on the bottom with fresh bottles of oxygen. The coral was less spectacular here but the sea was teeming with fish. A few small sharks cruised about overhead and a stingray shuffled off ahead of them like a ghostly magic carpet. Everywhere there were schoals of fish, some, like the barracuda, grim and purposeful as they headed off heaven knows where, others skittish and undecided darting off at once in this direction only a moment later to turn, as if as one, and set off somewhere else. A huge mottled potato cod all of five feet long came to have a look at them before turning to resume his patrol. They swam off together after it as it traced the side of the hill, For such a large, fat and cumbersome beast, it moved with surprising speed and had soon disappeared beyond their view. They stopped together and looked upwards. The hull of the speedboat at the surface had now disappeared beyond the far side of the atoll. They checked their watches and the state of their tanks. As he looked into her mask, the green eyes sparkled back at him and he wanted her like crazy. A moment later, their masks in their left hands and their mouthpieces in their right, their lips were pressed together. A gush of bubbles raced towards the surface as, between gulps of air, she pulled off one of her flippers so that she could get free of the bottom of her bikini and he clumsily pushed his own trunks down around his knees. She came to him, weightless in the water, her long legs spread to entwine around him, his hands cradling her buttocks and as two gigantic turtles flapped by close above their heads, they floated backwards and forwards to a slow and breathless climax.

*****

For Saturday Lars had pre-arranged a small private helicopter to take Samantha and himself further up the reef with the hope of spotting some whales. They could put down at Lizard Island to refuel and have some lunch there before returning late afternoon. By now Peter could hardly bear to be away from her; but he was feeling the strain of acting the platonic part he had assumed and could see the sense, for the sake of Lars if not himself, in going his own way for some portion of what remained of his time on the island, provided they would as usual dine together. He was already thinking of their life back in London too, when such pretences could be put behind him. For the moment, he decided to revert to his earlier regime for the morning but, Helmut having by now departed, reluctantly arranged to have a game with Ross, the young Australian honeymooner, in the afternoon. It turned out to be much as he had feared, a service of extraordinary pace and aggression and everything that he returned, wherever it was, leapt upon regardless and lashed back at him with a grunt or a roar. It was even more one-sided than his match against Lars and made it extraordinary that this brute had been seen off by the Dane with such apparent case. To make matters worse, Mrs Neanderthal who, Peter had thought, had simply hauled herself up the ladder into the umpire's chair for fun, insisted on intoning the miserable score with more than a hint of smug gratification, as if she were a Roman emperor counting off christians against lions. At 6-0, 5-0, they were changing ends for what was undoubtedly the last time when Tina, the girl at reception, came down to tell Peter that he was required urgently on the telephone.

"Hello, Peter Davenport speaking," he said breathlessy on reaching the little cubicle.

"Weor the fook are ye, Peter? It's bin like callin fookin Timbuctoo to get hold o' ye."

"I'm in Australia, Bill, on the Great Barrier Reef."

"What the hell are ye doin there? Actually I don't give a toss weor yer are or what yer doin; get yer arse over here and pronto."

"I can't make it before Monday midday, Bill, at the earliest," he said, calculating the connections quickly, "probably Tuesday now."

"Now look. There's a meeting o corporate finance directors in my office at seven o'clock sharp on Moonday moornin and it's a three-line fookin whip. You just better be there."

"What's the problem, Bill?"

"There's nae fookin problem, Peter. We're just bein taken oover, that's all."

Peter leaned round the door of the kiosk. He had been sweating profusely and it was like an oven in there. It was pouring off him now.

"Tina, when's the next helicopter going out to the mainland?"

"There's one just about to leave. The next one will be tomorrow afternoon."

"Can I get on the one going now?"

"Not really. He's got to leave by 4.45, fifteen minutes at most. There's a thunderstorm drifting down the coast and he needs to be in Cairns before it arrives."

"I'll be ready for the minibus in ten minutes," he said over his shoulder, bolting for the door.

It was only when they were already airborne, still in his tennis kit and sitting in a pool of perspiration, that he realised he'd left the ape-man waiting to finish him off. And he didn't even know where Samantha lived.

Monday, 29 February, 1988

They were all there, crammed into Bill's glass-walled office, only slightly larger than Peter's own. Peter still thought of it as Cyril's although Bill had already left his slovenly pawprints all over it. One of the chairs having collapsed and now lying in bits by his filing cabinet, and another being piled high with papers, Blackstone and Amadeo were standing for lack of seats. Farquharson, in shirt sleeves, was sitting on the floor in one corner like a naughty schoolboy, McAdam himself, tieless, with an electric razor in one hand, was behind his desk and Kent in the only other chair opposite. Apart from Bill, who was buzzing up and down his stubble, his shirt open at the neck to reveal a grey mat of chest hair, each had a press release in his hand. Bill interrupted their reading impatiently as Peter dropped his bags outside and squeezed round the door, self-consciously unkempt, dirty except for a new pair of jeans he had bought at Sydney airport. Bill did not even acknowledge his arrival as Peter took a press release off the pile on his desk.

"Will, mun, wi canna sit aroond all day readin this shite. The meat o' it is that RheinHeim Bank is makin an agreed oooffer for Doondas at 640p per share in cash, a tootal of a bit oover 400 million poond, thirty-five per cent oop on Friday's cloose, which was a good bit oop on the day."

"But well below last year's high," Seymour pointed out sulkily.

McAdam ignored his intervention. "There'll be a loon stook alternative. So yer can all avoid tax on yer share oooptions," he added with a scowl, knowing that they were all aware that he, who had only been with the Brothers five minutes, had more than the rest of them put together and that his latest dollop had come at the post-crash price at which the senior directors had topped up.

"It'll be annooned at eight-thirty when the market oopens. It's fookin marvellous. We're gooin to be the first prooperly capitalised European crooss-border merchant bank and we pick oop RheinHeim's brookin and market-makin operations into the bargain to becoom a fool service investment bank. It fills in joost the gaps wiv been wooried aboot."

"Will Dantzics become a subsidiary of Dundas, then?" asked Graeme Kent.

"Noobody's yet decided the stoocture and quite how much we'll be integrated. But they've noo big hitters at Dantzics so we're sure to coom oot on top. And we'll have access to unlimited fookin deutschmarks which will enable us to blow thoose bastards at Warburgs and Morgan Grenfell and Groossmanns and Schrooders clean out the bluddy warter and go ead to ead with BZW and County. In a coupla years time, we'll be able to snap up Morgan Stanley or Goooldman Sachs like a bluddy appetiser."

"Any conditions, Bill?" It was Kent again.

"All the usual crap. The oonly extra ones are some regulatory approovals in Germany and six weeks' due diligence, startin today."

"Really," said William Blackstone. "And what exactly would be the nature and scope of that due diligence?"

"Search me. The usual. Two doozen articled clerks, still wet behind the ears, to tick the books, I guess." Peter thought he was being shifty.

"But it's not at all usual, is it Bill," he ventured. "Not for a public company, and a bank at that, to be crawled all over by another before it decides whether or not to make an offer."

"Ah, yer back from the beach, I see." Peter could tell that McAdam was annoyed. Since that fracas with Sellar, McAdam had treated him as something of a protegé, a co-conspirator. He was not meant to voice public doubts about the party line. "But yer've left yer brains doon under. Every ooffer's got coonditions, mun. Yer know fookin well that noo one has to go through wi an ooffer if it doesna suit them. Material adverse change. Ninety per cent acceptance. There's always a way oot if you want it."

It wasn't entirely true but Peter thought it best to let it ride.

"What's this about Tudor - bottom of page five?" Hank Amadeo broke in. Not understanding a word of the discussion about regulatory approvals and conditions, he had ploughed on through the press announcement. "Heinrich Röhrer, chairman of RheinHeim, will become deputy chairman of Dundas," he read, "and Sir James Cruso, chairman of Dundas, who is fluent in German, will become a director of RheinHeim and join its executive committee. Johnathan Tudor, currently chief executive of Dundas, has offered his resignation and will be leaving the group with immediate effect. Pending appointment of a permanent replacement in consultation with RheinhHeim, the duties of chief executive will be undertaken by Jeremy Stone, who will remain head of commercial lending."

"That's reet. Johnathan didn't want to goo along wi' a looss of independence. Too bad but soo be it. Now get on the foon to your clients. The line is this is grate for Doondas and grate for them."

They started to shuffle out, Peter, closest to the door, in the lead.

"A wee word, Peter," McAdam called after him. "Cloose the fookin door," he said, as the last of them left. Peter felt a bollocking coming on.

"This is noo time to coom oot wi yer fookin doots, Peter Davenport. We're stook wi this deal and wi'd betta make it wurrk. I noo it's not of our makin, but it's as good as it fookin gets."

"How did it happen?"

"All very sooden but the fact is wi've bin stitched oop by Crooso. He's doon it imself. Wid ya believe it, this kraut, Röhrer, was one of 'is fookin guards at Coolditz."

"Did you know about it, Bill?"

"Not a fookin thing till Friday evening. Crooso says Röhrer called im outa the blue last Tuesday."

"I don't believe it," said Davenport automatically.

"And why noot?"

"Oh, things just don't happen like that - out of the blue," he replied, matter of fact, now keeping his recollections of New Year's Eve to himself. "But what about advice? It's required by the Code, even for investment banks."

"Corporate Finance was noot consoolted. They went to fookin Schrooders for advice."

"But this due diligence thing's absurd."

"Of course it's fookin absurd," McAdam bellowed. "It's the moost stoopid fookin piece of negootiation I've ever fookin urd of. I've fookin alf a mind ta think that fookin Schrooders did it on poorpuss. If it goos through, we get swallowed by German bureaucrats, who'll stifle every initiative we ever ave. And, if they pull oot, all our clients will boolt fer the door woondering what it was that they didn't like the smell of."

"Shit. And what about Tudor?"

"Stoopid bastard. He spook oot against it. In particoolar this fookin due diligence noonsense. Your friend ennessy asked for his alternative plan and he didna ave woon. At which point Gallaher, that ong Kong prooperty tycoon Tudor was at school with, who he poot on the board last year, says, in that case you'd better goo. Nice sorta friend to ave, eh, mun? And ennessy and Gallaher boondled him oot. He was fookin fired, Peter."

"What about the rest of the departmental heads? Were any of them asked for an opinion in advance?"

"Not as far as I noo. Except Stoon, of course. And you couldna expect him to say noo. The rest of us were called in on Friday evening. That coont Sellar" - they might just as well by now be hyphenated, thought Peter - "was o'er the fookin moon. He's goot bookets o' Doondas shares. As has Maguire - he's bin well oover thirty years' ere. The ooptions are coomin out of is fookin arse. And Villareal's father-in-law is Baron von soomethin or other, who toorns out to be on the RheinHeim soopervisory board."

"And what about a permanent replacement for Tudor? Are we going to get a kraut?"

"Noo, I doon't think soo. Crooso's too prood fer that. Stoon's well placed if e doosna fook it oop but ees a bit cloose to retirement. Sellar'll fancy his chances and soo will Morrissey."

"And you, Bill?"

"It's not croosed me mind, Peter."

"And where does all this leave us, Bill?"

"In soomeone else's shite. I dinna like wallowin in me oon but at least it smells familiar. Dantzics have their oon corporate finance people and they'll want to come oot on top. They ave the advantage of already being part of RheinHeim and of bein so fookin rich after RheinHeim bought them oot that they can afford to be stooborn. They'll be pressing for the top joobs. We'll ave a fight on er ands. Meanwhile I've a meeting with their ead of corporate finance this afternoon. Robin Pentland. Do yer noo im?"

"Only the name."

"We're to discreetly explore pootential conflicts of interest with a view to woon or other party steppin back," he intoned his instructions in as conventional a dialect as he could manage but with a split infinitive that could not possibly have been in Cruso's original. "When you've spooken to yer clients, I want yer to do me a list. Things we're workin on that are pooblic and separately things that are not yet pooblic."

"OK, Bill."

"And Peter, ear to the groond. I want to noo what's gooin oon; so you and I can keep controol."

Peter retired to his own office and shut the door. He didn't trust Bill out of his sight - all this stuff about you and I - but there could be some advantages in at least appearing to share confidences. If sharing wasn't all one-sided. And dangers too. With Tudor gone, Bill had lost his sponsor. He had a powerful enemy in Sellar and no very obvious friends either at group board level, or amongst his fellow departmental heads. All that about not having his own shy at the CEO's job was so much guff. Bill would have to go for it. If Sellar got it, he'd be finished. And Peter too in all likelihood. In Sellar's eyes he was in all probability an appendage of that fat slob. How had he got himself in this position? Peter hated office politics and didn't think himself very good at it. He felt fatigued, unkempt, disoriented, unprepared for the sudden change from advising companies in such circumstances to finding himself, albeit without influence, on the receiving end. He thought about his mortgage. Would the bonuses still be paid? They weren't due until the salary payment at the end of next month. They'll probably be put on hold - if only to stop people leaving. And he thought about Samantha. What the hell was he going to do about her?

It would be a while yet before Maureen was in; or any of his clients at their desks for that matter. Except perhaps Rod King. Presumably Hennessy knew enough about the niceties of his separate roles not to have told him.

"What are you doing back, Peter? I wasn't expecting to hear from you for another week......Oh, you needn't have called about that. Christopher told us all on Friday."

"What do you mean, told us all?"

"We had a board meeting Friday afternoon. He told us then."

"Were the non-execs there by any chance? Silkin and Enderby."

"Sure, of course, why do you ask?"

"What time did you finish?"

"Oh, let me see, not much before six. We were taking them through the MMC procedures. Plummers were there - Julian Corrigan and David Stephenson. Shit, did they make a meal of it."

"Did you break at all?"

"No. I remember that distinctly because I was bursting for a pee by the end of it. But what are you getting at, Peter?"

"Did anybody leave at any stage?"

"Well, let me see. Oh yes, I'm sure Enderby went out at some stage - but you know what his bladder's like."

"Was that before or after Hennessy told you about the Dundas deal?"

"Ah, I see what you're getting at. He told us right at the start. He was very excited. I think he'd been at your shop in the morning - so it was immediately afterwards. Did the share price move?"

"True to form. I don't suppose your telephones are recorded are they."

"I should bloody-well think not."

"Well, a lot are you know, particularly in the City. Not this one, as it happens, but our dealers are. Anyway it's a pity. It would have been good if we'd put in a system for you along with those sweeps for bugs. I wouldn't mind having something on that old bugger. He might need watching when BMP come back. Arthur Evans might think he could strike a deal with Jock to split the board."

"Well, thank you for that vote of confidence in our MMC submission, Peter. Why didn't you stay on holiday?"

"Rod, I may be a cynical bastard but it's done you well so far. Don't let yourself be spooked by those lawyers into thinking this MMC fandango is anything more than a farce. Next time round, this bid's going to be for real and Grossmanns are going to roll out the really heavy artillery."

"I thought we all agreed that blue-stocking was as awful as you could get."

"I've a feeling they'll be putting someone more experienced on it when the time comes. So long. I'll catch up with you later in the week."

"What are you doing here?" It was Maureen.

"No time for explanations. Get me this lot on the phone - one after another," he said, handing her a list, "and read this while I'm talking to them, if you want to know why" he added giving her a copy of the press release. "Oh, and get me copies of the *FT, Times* and *Telegraph* for the days I've been away, and the Sundays, and when we're done with the calls, get me a cab home. I stink."

*****

It was a horrible icy winter's day. Hail blew against the windows and bounced on the little balcony outside. He had unwisely turned the heating down before he left and it was taking an age to warm through the old brickwork and fill the huge space left by the vaulted ceilings to anything like a comfortable level. At least the water was instantly hot. Shaved and showered, he sat on the sofa with thick socks, corduroys, a polo neck and a heavy sweater, ploughing through the week's events. There was a record current account deficit, as usual. Wales had beaten Scotland and France Ireland the previous week-end. There was a pompous *FT* review of *The Last Emperor* by Nigel Andrews full of precious criticism of Bertolucci's communism but rather lacking in the appreciation that everyone else seemed to have found for the film itself. That perennial collector of golden handshakes, Michael Julien, had done it again, leaving Guinness for what sounded like no job at all - chairman designate of Storehouse - three and a half years hence. That silly bid by Barker & Dobson for Dee had failed but Marks & Spencer had been inveigled into paying a daft price for Brooks Brothers. George Magan had done a Wasserstein Perella, setting up a boutique with Rupert and James Hambro and Alton Irby. I suppose they'll try to muscle in on Pitcairn now, thought Peter.

He made a couple of phone calls and popped down to the local corner shop for a few supplies, picking up a copy of the *Evening Standard* in the process. The prospects of tax cuts in the budget were thought to have taken a pounding from the record £905 million January trade gap; but there was a very amusing photograph of the Duchess of Pork, attending some do in Los Angeles, got up like a prize poodle in a dress

339

like a pair of silk curtains, more of the royal mammaries on view than was elegant or becoming.

Around five, half an hour late, Peter opened his door to a man in a dark blue overcoat with an old-fashioned astrakhan collar which had seen better days and a paisley scarf in blue and gold. Peter took his coat and showed him in. Like his overcoat, he was dapper but faded, a little grey pencil moustache and small pale brown observant eyes that might once have been twinkly but now seemed just tired and disappointed. His grey three-piece suit was shiny at the elbows and knees and the uppers of his black lace-up shoes, though highly polished, were cracked with age. Peter guessed he was the wrong side of sixty. He had found him in the yellow pages under 'private investigators', a modest box ad - Tobias Hastings, Hastings Associates, private investigation, personal service, surveillance, matrimonial, missing persons traced. Peter already supposed the Associates to be amongst the missing persons.

"I want you to find a home address and telephone number for me."

"Well that's entirely in my line, Mr Davenport. Do you have the name of the person concerned?" He took a cheap notebook from his imitation leather briefcase, rather like a shorthand pad.

"Yes, she's a Miss Wilkinson and her first names are Samantha Gillian, I think in that order. To be honest, I can't remember. Maybe the other way round. Anyway, she's a director of Grossmanns, the City merchant bank."

"That doesn't sound a very tall order, Mr Davenport. Perhaps I ought to tell you I have a minimum fee of £500," he said, ceasing his note-taking and looking up. "Have you tried the telephone directory?"

"She's not listed."

"And British Telelecom inquiries? I find the telephone directory not often up-to-date."

"Ex-directory."

"And have you tried Grossmanns?"

"No, you're not to do that. There's to be no recorded evidence of any enquiry."

"Recorded, Mr Davenport? I'm only talking about ringing up their personnel department."

"All their telephone calls are recorded."

"Are you sure, Mr Davenport? That's very unusual."

"I'm quite sure."

"Do you have a photograph?"

"No."

"A previous address? The names of any acquaintances? Family? Schools? Universities? They usually keep tabs on the whereabouts of their old pupils."

"She was at Cambridge - I don't know which college - and before that a convent in Limerick - I think it was The Sisters of Our Lady the Virgin - but I'm sure they won't have her present whereabouts. After Cambridge she was at the solicitors Linklaters & Paines but I doubt if they'd have her address or that they'd tell you, if they had. Anyway, I'd rather you didn't make any enquiries which risked them calling her."

"And she's with Grossmanns in London? What's that, Gresham Street, isn't it?"

"Yes, quite right. But she's not there now. Not right now that is. She's on holiday - on Turtle Island - on the Great Barrier Reef - off Australia. I guess due back next week-end."

"Mr Davenport, you seem to know a great deal about this lady without knowing where she lives. Are you sure you really need me?"

"I do know a lot about her, Mr Hastings. But not the one thing I want. Her home address and telephone number."

"But you don't seem to want me to use any of the information you have to find her. What are you proposing I should do?"

"I thought you might use the flower gambit?"

"The flower gambit, Mr Davenport? You've lost me."

"Oh, I thought it must be a general trick of the trade. You get Interflora to deliver her some flowers at work. Anonymously. Then, when she emerges with them on her way home, you follow her."

"Suppose she leaves them at work - in a jar on her desk. Brighten up her office."

"Grossmanns' offices aren't like that."

"Or just puts them in the bin. An anonymous gift. She might take offence."

"I don't think women are like that, Mr Hastings. Do you?"

"Well, perhaps you're right, Mr Davenport. But suppose she drives to work. You say she's a director. If she comes out of some undergound parking garage with the flowers in the boot - or on the back seat even - I'd never spot them would I?"

"Mr Hastings, I don't think you know Grossmanns. This is one of their newest directors and, I'll wager, the only woman in that position. She's no more likely in my view to have been allocated an office parking space by that mob than a private helicopter."

Tuesday, 15 March, 1988

It was a bloody wonderful day. The rain was coming down in grand thick gobbets and he'd tried in vain for a cab before pulling up the collar of his Burberry, hoisting his umbrella, and splashing off across Gracechurch Street, the wet tarmac shiny black under the street lights, in the direction of Bank tube station. It was like a day of national celebration, as though we'd just won the war or at least the World Cup. Every oncoming face seemed to wear a smile, a nod of greeting towards each passing stranger, a glow of bonhomie.

The real news had come too late in the speech for the *Evening Standard* but that didn't stop everyone from buying one and the vendor at the bottom of the steps was dishing them out two-handed to the crowds hurrying past towards the ticket barriers. 'Lawson's treble...' read the headline over a rather tame summary of expected Budget giveaways. But they hadn't got the tenth of it. The top rate was down from 60 per cent to 40 per cent. It was worth £14,000 odd on his salary alone and another £20,000 on his bonus. The clamour at Dundas to get them paid forthwith rather than wait for the RheinHeim bid to be finalised had turned instantly to a universal hope and expectation that they would be delayed until after the new tax year began on 6th April.

The Uxbridge Arms was heaving with celebration by the time he got there, the vast majority of customers now in the happy position of earning enough for a treble in the time it had previously taken them to trouser enough for a double. As he turned from the bar with his own large scotch and soda, he was fortunate to find a seat in the corner by the window in the process of being vacated. From there he could see the few steps up to the front door of No 12 a little way down the street at which he had rung to no avail a few minutes earlier. He settled himself

343

down with his paper. It was as miserably thin as ever. There was a big article on the front page covering the coroner's report on the previous week's royal avalanche headed 'HUGE BLOCK OF ICE KILLED CHARLES' PAL'. There was a report on page two on the funeral of the IRA terrorists shot dead by the SAS in Gibraltar, which the police had quite cleverly turned into a damp squib by separating the cortege from its 3,000 or so supporters and sending it off down the motorway without them. The US had executed a couple of its longer serving but nonetheless deserving murderers in the electric chair. Curious device that, thought Peter, and very American. Savage but scientific. A sort of twentieth century version of burning at the stake. And Richard Ingram, former editor of *Private Eye* , had presided over what was called the inaugural Robert Maxwell Lookalike Contest at the Garrick but which was in reality a celebration party for Tom Bower's book *Maxwell: the Outsider*, which the great man himself had tried unsuccessfully to throttle in the Courts.

The Cheltenham Festival was in full swing again - Champion Hurdle Day. His memories tracked back a year and, notwithstanding his purpose in being in Notting Hill that evening, the black dog leapt at his throat with a familiar spring. He was not going to fall like that again. Softly, softly with this one, Peter, he said to himself. But at least she knows the pressures. Almost nine o'clock and not yet home. He struggled through a barely diminished crowd to buy himself another, now uncertain if the wait to get served had perversely coincided exactly with the moment of her return. I'll give it another fifteen minutes and then go and check, he thought.

He'd exhausted anything of interest in the *Standard* and was staring, almost absent-mindedly out of the window. Dundas was a pit of swirling intrigue. As far as corporate finance was concerned, Bill was playing his own game and a dangerous one at that. He was attending what were supposedly regular exchanges of information with Robin Pentland at Dantzics' offices in Finsbury Circus but Peter doubted if either party was dealing a straight hand. As he had suspected would be the case, Bill told him nothing of substance of these meetings. They were discussing a number of different options for the future structure of the enlarged department. They were comparing remuneration packages. They were thinking about how they should tackle the European markets in due course, and the States. They were tossing about ideas for how they might strengthen the department. Who they might try to take from other banks. Which specialisations they should try to embrace. Where they could take advantage of Dantzics' research expertise - in oils and minerals, investment trusts and retailing - a long way from Peter's motley collection of clients in engineering, property, housebuilding and pharmaceuticals. Which headhunters they should use. More ominously, where they could make savings. Nothing to be rushed, of course.

It just wasn't Bill's style, careful planning. Not in detail anyway. He was into the broad sweep. The big picture. The instant decision. He'd be going along with it, of course; but something else had been absorbing his time. He was closeted frequently with Sybil Dunwoody and he'd missed morning prayers for meetings 'on the continent' - everyone assumed Frankfurt - three or four times since the RheinHeim bid was announced. The truth, which he had called in the directors to announce only yesterday, was much more dangerous, both to the department's immediate profitability and to the chances of a smooth integration with Dantzics and RheinHeim.

"I wanted ta bring ya oop ta deat wi whear our plans are headin poost the merger. Dantzics have noo European ambitions soo I've decided we shood press ahead as befoor. We'll be oopenin corporate finance oofices in Paris, Frankfoort and Milan on foorst April. Hendrik Cornelius and Philippe de Montfort, who are booth coorrently directors of Mooorgan Stanley will be joining oos to roon Frankfoort and Paris respectively and Solo Quattrone froom Banca Commerciale will roon Milan."

"Solo what?" muttered Seymour, who was sitting next to Peter, under his breath. "What the hell is he - a man or a pizza?"

"They'll booth be at prayers oon Friday and the annooncement will goo oot same day," Bill went on, fixing Farquharson with a glare of contempt. "They'll each be recrootin a team of five oor six to start with and are all expected to be proofitable in 1989."

Other than Seymour's whispered quip, a stunned silence had greeted the news. Peter had hung about afterwards on some pretext or other. He'd didn't expect that a private rather than public airing of his doubts would spare him a foul-mouthed tirade but he thought he might get closer to the truth of what was going on.

"Bill, I know this was all in the original departmental plan; but is it wise to be carrying on regardless?"

"Doon't coom yer fookin wisdom wi me, Peter. Oor instrooctions were to carry oon as befoor save oonly to avoid findin Dantzics and oorselves on the ooposite sides of a bid."

"But Frankfurt, Bill. It's in RheinHeim's back yard."

"Soo?"

"Well shouldn't they at least be told in advance?"

"Why, mun? They're not a bluddy merchant bank. They're the fookin Midland Bank of the Ruhr, or soom sooch. We're gooin ta be their investment bank. We canna start oof by askin them when and wheor and whether we can goo an ave a pee."

"But does Sir James know - and Jeremy now as well?"

"Of coorse they bluddy knoo. It's in the plan, mun."

"But the timing, Bill. Do they know it's happening now?"

"Whayay, mun. It's in the bluddy plan for the second quarter. What's foorst April if it's noot the fookin second quarter?"

April Fool's Day, thought Peter but he uttered not a peep. He'd had another call from a headhunter that afternoon - Korn Ferry this time - 'we're looking for an experienced corporate finance director to play a leading role in an expanding team for a US investment bank in London. We wondered if you might have any ideas for us.'

He was so lost in his thoughts that he hardly noticed her. She was at the door of No 12 now, obliquely lit by one of the street lamps. She wore a long raincoat, almost to her ankles, with a hood that was pulled up against the continuing downpour. A fat briefcase. It must be her, he thought, though it was impossible to tell. He gave her five minutes, downed his scotch, pulled on his coat and fumbled under the table for his still sopping umbrella.

"Oh, it's you," she said, putting a hand to her face, almost as if to shield it, and at the same time removing her glasses. That voice again, inimitably husky, uniquely feminine. "Come in," she added, almost standing behind the door in the narrow hall to let him pass. "Go in there, on the right. Fix yourself a drink. I'll be right down."

She turned her back, dropped the glasses onto the little table in the hall and bounded away up the stairs two at a time, leaving Peter, still dripping, staring after her, the bluestocking in flight. He took off his coat and hung it up with an assortment of others, some more feminine than the rest, on a row of hooks he found a little way down the hall. His umbrella dribbled relentlessly onto the carpet until he found a big copper pot behind the coats which was apparently used for this purpose. There was a bag of golf clubs there too. He came back down the hall towards the front of the house and turned into the doorway to which he had been directed, absent-mindedly picking up her spectacles as he went. He looked at them before setting them down on the mantelpiece. They were quite peculiarly unattractive things, wiry, cheap-looking, shapeless with a sort of smokey glass that was really too grey and flat to call tinted. He tried them to see how short-sighted she was.

The room, which had clearly originally been two, ran all the way from the front to the back of the house. It was all white, walls, ceiling, woodwork with a pale cream carpet and beige sofas and chairs which matched the full-length curtains at either end. The back half was a study and the front a sitting room. The desk was a modern slab of what looked like teak and there were matching bookshelves and cupboards in the same simple but expensive-looking design. The only significant colour in the room was provided by half a dozen bold and striking abstracts, two or three apparently by the same artist who had applied the thick oils with a distinctive knife-stroke. There was almost nothing personal save a vase of flame-red tulips on the mantelpiece, the battered black briefcase that she had set down beside the desk and a framed photograph on one of the bookshelves, a big rough-looking man standing behind a five-bar gate, a girl of no more than four or five, red-headed, perched on his shoulders and his left arm around a sturdy, handsome young woman clutching an armful of daffodils.

The entire room was teutonically tidy as if it had just been spring-cleaned, or even redecorated. There was not a shred of paper on the desk, not a magazine or a book on the teak coffee table in front of the fireplace, not a butt in an ashtray despite, Peter thought, that slight aroma that only a cigar can leave. Peter found the drinks cupboard and poured himself a whisky and soda.

"Can I fix you a drink?" he called up the stairs to no reply. He thought he could hear the sounds of showering.

It was a full twenty minutes before she reappeared, her hair brushed and coppery but still slightly damp. She wore jeans and a fluffy grey sweater with a floppy collar and the tan, which he was sure he hadn't noticed when she opened the door to him, seemed to make her glow with health. He stared at her wordlessly. She smelt of something exotic and looked fantastic.

"I owe you an apology - an explanation," he said. "Just leaving like that."

"Oh, I thought it was odd at the time; but I used to get a daily fax from the office with the news and suchlike - and eventually it became pretty clear what had happened."

"But not, I guess leaving without a note?"

"Is there any other way to leave. I told you I'm used to living in a man's world. When you leave, you leave."

"But it wasn't like that, Sam. I had a call from your friend McAdam telling me to get back immediately and there happened to be a helicopter waiting to take off for Cairns. I had ten minutes flat to pack."

She looked unconvinced.

"And what brings you here?"

"I wanted to see you."

Her expression was unchanged, sceptical, hardened. But why had she bolted upstairs to get out of that dreadful disguise she wears, he thought, if she just wanted to be done with him.

"I was desperate to see you, Sam. I've never met a woman like you. I didn't know how to find you. Not how to find Samantha rather than Ms Wilkinson. I wanted to see you without trespassing on your Grossmanns territory, on your professional life. I am afraid I was responsible for the tulips."

"Ah, so that funny little man on the tube with the fur-collared overcoat was following me. I've heard of that trick before." She smiled, just briefly, still guarded.

"I'd have given you a call here but he couldn't get British Telecom to divulge your number. He tried everything. Long-lost uncle. Solicitor calling about major inheritance. Police trying to trace owner of stolen goods. Did they ask you if you'd accept a call?"

"Never."

"Oh well, I'm not surprised. I don't think he's a very convincing detective. I got him out of yellow pages."

"Oh my God, Peter Davenport," she said, bursting out laughing, "and to think I told the board of BMP that you were likely to set the best that Kroll could muster to follow their every move. And now I find that all you could come up with was a little man who looks like Monsieur Poirot playing Monsieur Poirot."

"Okay, Sam, guilty as charged," he said, raising his hands in surrender. "Now let me take you out to dinner. Didn't I pass an Indian on the corner down there behind the Coronet Cinema?"

"The Malabar. It's wonderful. My favourite. And you'd love the proprietress - very dishy Indian lady. But I'm not going out with you, Peter. Back here we're at war, remember?"

"But Sam, we were at war in Australia too. This shindig's not going on for ever." Christ, he thought, it's over before it's begun. What is it with this hard-arsed bitch?

"No public appearances till then, Peter, and certainly not round here. Half the City lives within a few hundred yards of here. Help yourself to another drink while I go round the corner for a pizza. What do you like, Reine, Neptune, Sicilian - that's the hot one with pepperoni, Quattro Staggione?"

Peter erupted with laughter. It was mostly relief.

"What's so funny?" she said.

"I'm sorry. It just reminded me. Bill McAdam told us yesterday he was recruiting some Italian. One of my colleagues thought he had a name like a pizza."

"I know - we've got lots of them - like all those daft snippets in IFR about the movers and shakers in the eurobond markets. They've always got names like GianLuca Belmondo and Joachim Saxe-Coburg and they're described as veterans of Credit Suisse First Boston when they've just been there two years."

"That's it. Apparently there's a chap at BZW called Roberto Magnifico, would you believe? We've got a German and a frog coming as well. I can't remember the names but they sounded just like that. I'll go and get the pizzas. I've been sitting in the pub opposite waiting for you to get home. I'm a couple of drinks ahead of you."

Downstairs was a kitchen cum dining room, also starkly modern in teak and glass and stainless steel. They sat at the table by the flame from a fat white candle. She had conjured up a green salad by the time he returned and a thick tannic Barolo to accompany the meal. Afterwards she made coffee and fetched her humidor, choosing a Davidoff Château Lafite for each of them and cutting a neat wedge-shaped incision in his cigar before she handed it to him to light.

"Who's that in the photograph upstairs?"

"It's me - and my parents - in Ireland," she ended as if on a down note.

"Are they still there?"

"My dad was killed the week after that photo was taken. His tractor turned over on him."

"I'm sorry. Do you remember him?"

"Of course. He was my hero. They say it used to happen to farmers all the time before they had proper cabs."

"And your mother?"

"He was her hero too. She couldn't live without him. She drank herself to death before I was eight. Then I was brought up by my grandparents. They're both dead now too. But I don't miss them."

"Not a happy childhood?"

"No worse than many others."

"One to make one tough."

"Tough enough."

There was a long silence. She was tough enough; but he saw her eyes were moist. They pulled on their cigars.

"You don't wear contact lenses, do you?" he ventured at last.

"No."

"And those glasses of yours are fake, aren't they?"

"Yes, just tinted glass," she admitted flatly.

"Why do you wear them?"

"It's an image. A bit theatrical, I confess, but I've always liked dressing up."

"Or dressing down in your case. You practically told me the frumpy clothes were deliberate. The whole thing's deliberate isn't it - the clothes, the glasses, the deathly complexion. How do you do that?"

"It's just pale make-up."

"Why?"

"When I was coming down from Cambridge I got turned down for articles by Coward Chance, Slaughter & May, Ashursts and Clifford Turner. All the partners who did the interviews were men and you could see they all thought I was just an Irish bimbo. There was an awful bald charmer from Slaughters who tried to get into my knickers and the senior partner of Ashursts propositioned me in so many words. He was horrible."

"Martin Lampard."

"You know him."

"A bit."

"My last interview in the milk-round was with Linklaters. I decided to try a different tack. I changed my name and bought a long skirt and the mask and it worked. There never seemed any point in changing - particularly not once I moved to Grossmanns. Captains of industry don't take advice from redheads with freckles."

"So that's how Samantha became Gillian. But Wilkinson's not very Irish anyway, is it?"

"I wasn't Wilkinson at Cambridge. I was O'Flaherty."

*****

He woke disoriented and turned over. There was an indentation in the pillow. It smelt of sex and what he now knew to be Opium; but he was alone. He flicked on the light and took in his surroundings. Just after seven. His clothes were all neatly folded on a chair in the corner, not flung about as had been the reality of their undressing. His shoes were beneath the chair. He padded into the bathroom for a wee. It was unlit. He called down the stairs to her. There was no reply. He tucked a towel round his waist and went down the two flights of stairs to the basement. Still dark. The table had been cleared and he found last night's dishes and glasses in the dishwasher. He returned to the ground floor and looked into the sitting room. The heavy briefcase that had been by the desk at the far end had gone. He looked around for a note. Nothing. She'd got her own back.

Sunday, 17 April, 1988

The traditional first act of a new medieval monarch, and particularly one of a new dynasty, would be to remove the heads of those who might conceivably harbour claims to his newly assumed throne. Though no student of history, the lesson was not lost on Stephen Gallaher.

In a piece headed "Dirty Deeds at Dundas", John Jay's column in the *Sunday Telegraph* commented:

> *There were three internal candidates at Dundas Brothers for the position of chief executive vacated when Johnathan Tudor decided to resign rather than go along with the sale to RheinHeim Bank - Jeremy Stone the head of Commercial Banking and acting chief executive during the interregnum, David Sellar, the well-connected head of Dundas Asset Management, and Bill McAdam, the chief of Corporate Finance. None of them got it; but all three were subjected in one way or another to the immediate vengeance of Stephen Gallaher, for having dared to covet the prize, when he emerged as the new CEO following RheinHeim's abrupt withdrawal from the deal last week.*

> *David Sellar, an old Etonian whose father was also a director of Dundas before the War, is widely credited with making DAM one of the leading active fund managers in the City and in successfully increasing its market share*

against the apparently irresistible tide of index-linked fund management, led by Donald Brydon at BZW. Although in his mid-fifties and, as a result of long family association with Dundas, the occupant of an office in DAM's "Millionaires' Row", he clearly had another executive role left in him. By all accounts one of the best managers within Dundas, he was a front runner for the succession because he appears to possess a sure-footed understanding of the dynamics of market risk and an ice-cool skill in handling the billions that DAM has at risk in the markets every day. Gallaher has immediately added to his duties and threatened his enduring reputation by parachuting him in as chairman of Dundas Life, whose investment portfolio, particularly in secondary US properties, is widely rumoured to be the motivation for RheinHeim's disillusionment.

Bill McAdam is the intensely ambitious but earthy ex-chief of M&A at Bear Sterns who was recruited only last year by Dundas to take over as head of corporate finance on the retirement of Cyril Bishop, a much-respected City figure. He is said to have immense strategic vision but is difficult with both clients and staff and is so hyper-active that his waking hours are filled with a frenzy of successive meetings and telephone conferences. Both detail and courtesy, it is said, are frequently overlooked. Stephen Gallaher had a special form of humiliation in store for him when he instructed McAdam to send out a note to his entire staff cancelling a project for the establishment of offices in Paris, Milan and, improbably in view of the then proposed deal with RheinHeim, Frankfurt, which he had launched with a great internal fanfare only a fortnight before.

As for Jeremy Stone, the cerebral lending banker who had steered Dundas clear of the rocks of property speculators, loans backed by non-income-producing assets and underperforming manufacturers, on which the reputations of many of the City's banks have foundered in the 1980s, he was the man to whom Sir James Cruso turned to steady the ship in readiness for the RheinHeim merger. As Stephen Gallaher called the loyal servant Stone in to his office last week to administer his summary dismissal, Cruso, it seems, simply looked the other way.

Morality is not a concept much admired in today's City but the callousness of this act will not be lost on the staff of Dundas Brothers as it tries to recover its feet after the RheinHeim debacle. Perhaps it will not be lost on its clientele either.

Peter flung the paper to one side and heaved himself to his feet from the settee in which he had been sprawled. He switched off the lights; but it was too dark and he put them back on again. He wandered heavily to the window. Yesterday's torrential rain had been superseded by a light grey drizzle descending intermittently from a flat grey sky. It was alright for the London Marathon but for little else. It had been a perfectly dreadful week on every level.

The economic news was universally gloomy. Despite intervention by the Bank of England and a reduction in the base lending rate, the pound was rising inexorably towards 3.15 Deutschemarks. The trade deficit was assuming alarming proportions, growth was sputtering to a halt and inflation on a clearly upward trend. House prices were, as tradition required, already out of control. Lawson was caught between raising interest rates to choke off the threat to price stability and lowering them to calm the exchange rate. He and the Lady were clearly not seeing eye to eye. The US deficit was looking even worse and had pulled the Dow and the dollar sharply lower. No end to the bear market was likely in these circumstances.

The politics were even worse with the government apparently intent on squandering its majority on the ludicrous poll tax proposals and that dog-eared, fag-ashed shit, Nicholas Ridley, was now trying to buy off the rebels in his own camp with a string of concessions which only went to prove how absurd the whole idea was in the first place. Lawson's tax reductions were going to be short-lived if the Tories managed to hand the whole thing over to that imbecilic windbag, Kinnock.

Closer to home most of the merchant banks, save the dreaded Schroders, which looked most like Dundas and would therefore tend to show the Brothers up, were having a tough time. Kleinworts had announced sharply lower profits but the game was potentially being raised by Barclays, and its BZW subsidiary, with a vast rights issue which the Lex column described as "breathtaking both in its size and arrogance".

The background news for Pitcairn was not good either. Peter's hopes that, despite his scepticism, the MMC might buy the research argument had been raised by a House of Lords Select Committee report that more government money should be made available to modernise medical research laboratories; but their lordships' stupidity was exposed within twenty-four hours by Glaxo announcing that it alone was going to spend over £1 billion on research and production facilities over the next decade and increase its UK R & D staff to 3,500. It was clear that the cash mountain that Girolami had accumulated was going to go into filling up his Aladdin's cave of new products and not into a counterbid for Pitcairn. Peter was going to have to look to white knights with lesser resources. Maybe Beecham. Their shares had been rising on favourable reports on the new Eminase heart drug.

Peter had also been on the end of a bruising couple of marketing failures to which Bill had not taken kindly. Although, thank God, not amongst his personal targets for the year, Kleinwort Benson had landed the job of advising the Government on the sale of the electricity industry the previous month. Now the ex- Cazenoves super-smoothie Michael J de Rougemont Richardson of Rothschilds had got another pay-off for all his sucking up to Thatcher by securing, as expected, the job of advising all the individual electricity boards as a job lot, thus depriving their competitors of a dozen significant separate roles. Seymour Farquharson had taken the brunt of that one but there was enough collateral damage to catch a few of the other directors on the ricochet.

The particular projectile that had collided with Peter took the form of McAdam sending him off to the States at the end of March to persuade General Cinema that they should be having a go at Rowntree, which they could afford, rather than Cadbury Schweppes, which they clearly could not. There was an elaborate plan for cashing in the holding they had built up in Cadburys by way of contriving an auction between Nestlé and Unilever against the cost of a dawn raid on Rowntree. Bill had almost gone into orbit when Suchard had popped up on Wednesday with Warburg in tow and snaffled enough Rowntree shares to take them up to 14.9%. Of all the activities in corporate finance, the ambulance chasing of other people's deals was the one that Peter found the most depressing. Bill, on the other hand, was the sort of deal junkie to whom the next fix was worth any amount of hare-brained schemes, humiliating telephone calls, sheets of computer print-out and wasted all-night preparations, particularly when it was the brains, the humiliations the computations and the wasted midnight hours of his minions that were at stake. The discovery that Nestlé had already engaged Peter St George of County NatWest with regard to Rowntree and had no need of the Brothers simply set off a round of fruitless pursuits of Mars and Hershey and heaven knows who.

And then there was the cauldron that was 69 Gracechurch Street. RheinHeim's withdrawal had whipped the bank's entire strategy from under it. The majority of the directors had always been uncomfortable about the decision to sit out Big Bang without acquiring a securities trading capability. Those of their competitors, notably Schroders and Rothschilds, who embraced that line always looked to be doing so for the simple reason that they didn't have the wherewithal to do otherwise. And Rothschilds at least had a substantial stake in Smith New Court. Being taken over by the krauts in order to get one's hands on Dantzics wasn't everyone's idea of heaven; but most found it more comfortable to believe that the flock of City sheep were right rather than the lone goat.

To be told now that they had to go back to their clients and say that it didn't matter a toss after all whether you were a full-service investment bank or not was too risible to warrant consideration. Bill, who had been instructed to tell them what they were to say at the same time that he was told to cancel his continental foray, went through the motions in a torrent of barely contained apoplectic rage. William Blackstone, who found it more difficult to dissemble than was natural in his profession, was unwise enough to seek further guidance.

"Bill, we must have more cogent arguments than the abrupt tergiversation of the RheinHeim management to persuade our clientele that our antecedent strategy was superior to that from which we have been mercifully vouchsafed. Otherwise they'll simply micturate all over us."

"William, mun, I doon't understan a fookin weird of what yer fookin sayin and I doon't gi a fook what ye tell yer fookin clients. Jus goo an fookin tell them."

At least things were going reasonably well with Sam. She thought that creeping out and leaving him to wake up alone in her house that first night in Notting Hill was a huge joke.

"But you were sleeping like a baby, Peter, and I had a full briefcase of papers that I'd been intending to read before I was hijacked by you and your libido."

But this hole in the corner existence on which she insisted was a pain. A month now and they had not been out once together. Not out, that is, rather than in. He longed to resume the life of a normal couple, to meet her friends, to show her off to his. It was made worse because Jenny Fordyce and Julia Archer were in the midst of an obliviously good-natured but intensive campaign to introduce him to every remotely eligible girl within their acquaintance.

"This is like having an affair with a married woman," he had complained to Sam that Friday evening, "while at the same time being paraded around like a prize bull. I'm beginning to know what Prince Charles must have felt like when they made him marry that Spencer girl to smarten up the gene pool while all he really wanted was that soldier's wife."

357

"What do you know about having affairs with married women, Peter Davenport? And anyway, it's you that keeps saying this Pitcairn thing's not going on for ever. Have a bit of patience. I'm going to finish you off pretty quickly when the MMC gives the all clear."

"That's fighting talk," he cried, pulling up his guard as if to box her ears but rushing in to take her in his arms. "Sam," he said, pulling back and looking her full in the face, "you know you're going to have to hand this over to someone else. Why don't you do it now? It'll get terribly messy if you leave it till later on."

She pulled herself free and stood to face him, her legs apart, planted foursquare, and her hands on her hips.

"Why don't you withdraw if you think it's such a good idea. Give it to that cunt Kent, as you call him, if you can't see it through. I'm not going to withdraw - and that's final."

He was surprised by her strength of feeling - and the anger - but in no mood for an argument. What could you expect from a redhead. That's why he was falling in love.

"I'm sorry, Sam. I've had a dreadful couple of days. Let's have a drink and forget about it. I could use one straight into the vein."

*****

They'd parted around 4am during Saturday night - as late as he dared leave it if he were to get home before the roads were closed - and he'd driven back to his flat in Wapping. They'd agreed to devote Sunday to their week-end reading. But he'd got up very late and had hardly worked. All the business pages were full of speculation about Dundas. The shares had fallen like a stone after Friday's announcement but had closed off the bottom, just below 400p. 'Even a dead cat bounces' some wags had observed. There were profiles of Stephen Gallaher, chronicling his rise to fame and modest fortune in the property sector, first as finance director of London Estates and then as chief executive of Central and Kowloon Developments, the property arm of one of the great Hong Kong houses. There was also some gossip, with barely disguised suggestions that he was a serial gold-digger who had sniffed around Christina Onassis - *Private Eye's* 'thunderthighs' - until she had seen him off. He had ended up with the brassy heiress to an Italian engineering group and a large estate in Ireland, no doubt with favourable implications to his tax status. All in all, he didn't sound a very nice man and he wasn't. But they didn't mention that he had a dose of halitosis that could have felled a tree.

There was also lots about Dundas Life and most of it sounded horribly true. The Germans were not as clumsy with their PR as they were often thought, and on this occasion had organised the Friday night drop to perfection. The problems in US real estate, as everyone knew, were most desperately manifested in Texas, round Houston and Dallas, and there were lists of office buildings and shopping centres, every one of them practically unlet, in which Dundas Life was apparently heavily invested. The clear implication was that the Brothers were going to have to dig deep into their coffers to make good the life company's solvency ratios. Until now it had been widely assumed that Dundas Life was in the share price for nothing, a steadily encrusting jewel that would be spun off in due course to the Pru or the Pearl for fabulous riches. The implication now was that it was a bottomless pit.

There was also speculation about other possible bidders. *The Sunday Times* commented that the board of Dundas, having unwisely recommended such a hugely conditional offer, would now be hard pressed to turn down a half-way decent bid from another quarter. And a halfway decent bid, unless the bogey of the rumoured problems in Dundas Life could be convincingly laid to rest, which seemed unlikely, could fall a good way short of RheinHeim's 640p. Peter could only take comfort from the knowledge that Jock Enderby had in all probability filled his boots at around 500p - serve him right.

Peter gave up pretending that he was going to work and mixed himself a bloody mary. It seemed the right sort of thing for a time of day which might have looked suspiciously inappropriate for the consumption of alcohol. He cleared up the mess of the Sunday papers spewed about the floor and decided to fix himself an early supper and get an early night. Though he had been in bed for some part of the previous night, Samantha had made it clear that she had no intention of letting him sleep and, what with the shenanigans of the last few days, he realised that he was dog-tired.

He had poured himself another and was assembling the ingredients for an omelette and salad when the phone went.

"Peter, I need a weird."

"Okay, Bill, go ahead. I'm not in the middle of anything important."

"Not over the phone, mun, heear."

"Can't it wait till morning, Bill. I'll be in first thing and I haven't got any meetings after prayers until lunch-time."

"I need ya fuckin heear, mun."

"Okay, Bill," he said with resignation. "I'll be with you in twenty minutes."

"De yer know weear I am?"

"Yes, Bill, Islington. Remember, we all came to dinner with you in November."

"No, mun. Nancy and I have split. I'm in Holland Park - 2 Holland Park Mews. De yer know it? You go doon the Bayswater Rood through Notting Hill Geat..."

"Yes, yes, yes, I know, Bill. All my rich friends live in Holland Park."

*****

It was a good deal smaller than the large Georgian terraced house to which Peter and Sophie had been invited with all the rest of the corporate finance directors and their wives the previous autumn. It had been by way of a welcome to Hank Amadeo combined with an advance farewell to Cyril Bishop. The younger element of the directors at least, Peter himself, William Blackstone and Seymour the Serpent, had been agog to get their first view of Mrs Amadeo."

The 'famous international beauty', in terms of entertainment value at least, had not been disappointing. Mrs Amadeo was a big girl, towering over her husband in her perilous stilettos, and showing an alarming amount of leg. In certain areas, notwithstanding the bounty with which God had endowed her, she had seen fit to enhance his gifts with silicone and collagen. She would have done better to arrange a transplant of cellulite from her bottom, which was almost of hottentot proportions. The whole thing was encased in a shocking pink satin suit which had been made for someone three inches shorter, a good twenty pounds lighter and at least ten years younger. What the jacket was unable to accommodate sat naked but uplifted upon the open lapels, putting colossal strain on the top button and jiggling at the slightest provocation. Cyril, seated next to her at dinner, was clearly at a loss to know where to look. The rest of the men were transfixed by the spectacle. There was enough mascara on her eyelashes to do a decent job on a giraffe and enough paint on every visible surface to do the entire cast of an average pantomime, dame included. It was difficult to say if she had ever been a beauty but it was quite certain that she had thought herself so, and, seated in front of her mirror, probably still did. A case of beauty in the eye of the beholder.

There had been fourteen of them in all. Even so the dining room, an extraordinary combination of House & Garden and northern counties' nouveau riche, presumably assembled by the erstwhile Nancy, could have comfortably held a few more.

Fourteen people in No 2 Holland Park Mews would have occupied every corner, upstairs and down. The sitting room cum study was up a few stairs. It was all burgundy velvet and gold brocade with elaborately mounted prints of nineteenth century botanical drawings on the walls in too pretty frames and dark claustrophobic paintwork in a variety of colours. Bill had clearly bought it off the shelf fully furnished and interior designed. It wasn't Bill at all but he was at least doing his level best to turn it into a designer pig sty.

"Beam me up, Scotty!" demanded his tee-shirt in bold crimson script on what had once been a white background, stretched across his fulsome gut.

He swept a pile of old newspapers off one of the velvet armchairs.

"Sit doon, mun. Drink?"

He disappeared down the stairs towards the kitchen without waiting for a reply.

"there's no intelligent life down here!" his back complained above the builder's bum. He returned a minute later with two cans of Newcastle Brown Ale - no glasses - and handed one to Peter. He put it unopened among the detritus on the table beside his chair.

"I've jest had a call frem Michael Milken at Drexel Boornham." He pulled the ring on his can and froth exploded from the aperture, foaming over the top, running down the sides and dripping onto the carpet. He took a slurp and wiped his moustache with the back of his hand, at the same time rubbing the still bubbling damp patch into the dark blue carpet with his trainers. "They're interested in buying oos."

"What? Buying Dundas Brothers?"

"No, mun, course not. Corporate Finance, mun."

"Are you sure? What for?"

"They're tryin to build oop a London corporate finance presence. They've doon everything there is to do in America. Remember they took on Swete and Roshier, those two chaps Hill Samuel fired last year."

"But, Bill, Drexels are under investigation by the SEC. For months Milken has been expected to be under arrest any day. He was in over his head with Boesky. And Boesky has been shopping everyone. It was the deal that he did. Drexels are history."

"They're fookin not, mun. The emphasis has changed since the crash - more conventional corporate finance and less joonk bond trading. Boot the joonk bond market hasn't collapsed like all the noo-alls said it wood; and they're still doin deals. And financin them. And all this stoof about Milken - I doon't believe it. It's twelve moonths since Boesky was sent doon. If they canna pin anythin on Milken in twelve moonths, they canna pin anythin on 'im at all."

"I'm more in the no smoke without fire camp, Bill. There's an evil smell about it all."

"Milken assoored me personally, there's not a shred o trooth in the accoosations. He's absolootly clean and they're ready to start buildin oop their business again. He thinks we're perfect for them."

"What the hell do they want with a UK business, Bill. It doesn't make sense."

"It doos make sense, mun. They're ready to goo after UK clients with the oofer to foond their taykoover bids through the joonk bond market. Don't you see, mun, it's a fantastic opportunitee. Noobody else ken tooch them at this game. And after the UK, it's Europe."

"What do they want?"

"They want the hool of oos, loock, stoock and barrel. The hool department. What dya think, mun?"

"Difficult for the Brothers to agree to that."

"Sod the fookin Broothers, Peter. Doondas in corporate finance is dead, mun. We've admitted the need for a fookin securities business and then failed to fookin get it. We've joost becoom a booteek, mun, and a booteek attached to a fookin black hool at that."

"So what's the deal?"

"The deal is he wants to buy oos."

"So why doesn't Milken ask Cruso if he'll sell?"

"Doon't be fookin stupid, Peter. He canna do that until he noos that we'll all agree to join im. There's nothing to the department sept oos, mun. If we all walked oot, he'd have paid for noot."

"And what's the deal for us?"

"Salaries for the hool department oop twenty per cent. Directors to get a hoondred and fifty thoosand a year, what Milken calls a living wage, and a guaranteed million a year boonus for three years, loower guaranteed boonuses for managers and executives."

"Dollars or pounds?"

"Dollars or poonds. I doon't noo, mun. I didn't ask im. Boot there's no deal oonless I and at least foor other directors agree to join them and twenty executives."

Peter wasn't inclined to venture an opinion. The money was heaven-sent but the whole idea of junk bonds still stuck in his toffish craw. Not the currency of gentlemen. And Drexels stank.

"You'd better get the directors together and ask them," he said.

"Will you support me, mun?"

"If it's a good deal. You'll need to put some flesh on those bones. The difference between dollars and pounds matters to me, even if it doesn't to you. And I'd want to know a lot more about where things stand between the SEC and Drexels."

"Ken I trust them, Peter?"

"Drexels? Of course not. I'd want everything in writing."

"Not Drexels, mun. The directors?"

"To do what?"

"Keep it quiet until wear readie?"

"Most of them, probably. Blackstone will give his word and that'll be that. Seymour is greedy and will want to swim in the bigger pool. Hank'll love it - being able to act as go-between - explaining American ways to the Brits and vice versa. And that leaves Kent. Remember he normally acts as corporate finance adviser to Dundas itself. He's often the first to know if anything's going on. Or always was in the past with Tudor. Who knows with Gallaher?"

"Wid better coont him oot."

"Not wise, Bill. He's got some major clients. Better to tell everyone, get their reaction, get their authority to go back to Milken for a detailed proposal. Get them all to commit together in each other's presence to take it to the next stage. That way they're all equally tarred. Then play for time with Milken. Offer to meet in a month or so. And if Cruso or Gallaher tackle you on it in the interim, you'll more or less know that it was Graeme who spilt the beans."

"But it's more oorgent than that, mun."

"Why?"

"Because weear stoofed. We canna win new business. We canna recruit. Ye noo as well as me, we're all sittin aroond with oor fingers oop oor arses, woondering what to do next. We're a wasting fookin asset, mun. We cood waste a fookin way in anoother moonth."

"There's something in that. What do you want to do, Bill?"

"I want you to get oover to New York and talk to Milken. Bring oos back a propoosal. You can be there an back in a day on Concoord. Noobody'll noo you're gone."

Except you, thought Davenport, and, if it all gets nasty with Cruso, you can say it was my initiative. Not bloody likely.

"Milken doesn't work from New York, Bill. His office is on the West Coast - Beverley Hills."

"Well, I'm sure he'll meet you half way."

"I understand he doesn't leave his office for anyone. Bill, you go if you want; but I think we should proceed more slowly."

Saturday, 7 May, 1988

He was over the moon. His little man under the arches of London Bridge station had serviced the Morgan and returned it to the office car park yesterday afternoon. When he got down there to pick it up after dinner, he was delighted to see that he'd given it a clean too. When he'd got it out of the garage this morning into the bright early sunlight, he realised that it had been given a polish to boot. Now, tearing down the A30, hood down, the Rover V8 engine bubbling like a hookah and the canary yellow paintwork glistening in a perfect spring morning, he was singing at the top of his voice to the infrequent passing traffic like Placido Domingo himself.

It was the first time she had agreed to meet him outside her house or his flat and he had no intention of deviating one iota from the strict conditions she had laid down. We tee off at 7.30. I'll drive myself down. I'll meet you on the first tee ready to go. I'm not going into the club house, before or after. I know the whole place is full of nips and nouveau riche estate agents just sold out to a building society, but I'm not taking the risk of bumping into some smart alec broker with you in tow. And we leave separately to return to London. I'll get something in for lunch. And we play the West course.

"I'll need a handicap certificate to sign you in. They're very picky."

She delved in her handbag and produced a dog-eared sheet of paper, folded repeatedly. He unfolded it, glanced at it without comment, refolded it and put it in his pocket. She was a six at Bally-something or other in Ireland that he'd never heard of, four shots below him. He was fucking impressed but buggered if he was going to let on.

The directors of corporate finance met for dinner in one of the seventh floor dining rooms at 69 Gracechurch Street. It seemed an

365

unlikely too-close-to-home venue for a group of conspirators. Bill, in setting it up, had, at Peter's suggestion, just labelled it a post-RheinHeim review of divisional strategy, which, in a sense it was. Bill had wanted to come straight out with the Drexel approach and seek the backing of his colleagues to open negotiations. Peter had, with some difficulty, persuaded him that that was too unsubtle; that they first needed to secure a general recognition that the status quo was what William Blackstone would have called unconscionable, that action was required, and that they, the directors, had a right for their own part and an obligation in respect of their subordinates to attempt to shape the solution. The solution, Peter wanted to emphasise, with more than one eye on Graeme Kent, had to be acceptable to the Brothers as well as to Corporate Finance. Today that had become even more the case.

Bill had been more than a little irritated that Peter flatly refused to put together a position paper to commence proceedings. He had no desire for the pride of authorship of this particular gunpowder plot; but he agreed to make an opening statement of the dilemma that faced them. Even so, to Bill's rising impatience, he had declined to do so until the waiters had withdrawn at the end of dinner leaving the small party wreathed in brandy and cigars, a pot of tea untouched on the sideboard, save by William Blackstone, who still considered it a point of honour.

"Bill has asked me to summarise where we stand in the hope that we can have an agreed starting point for our discussion this evening," he began. "It's three weeks now since RheinHeim withdrew its offer. We haven't, for certain, lost any clients during that period but I doubt if I'm alone in saying that client response to our re-proclaimed go-it-alone strategy has been muted, to say the least, perhaps even bemused would be more accurate. And we certainly haven't won any new business. On the personnel side, we know that Fred Jarvis and Henry Fitzmaurice have both had offers. The fact that they've told us, rather than simply resign is a fair indication that they might be prepared to stay if they could blackmail us into an improved package or promotion; but, though they're both promising managers, the general opinion at their latest reviews was they were at least a year away from being directors, in Henry's case probably more. Bill tells me that an assistant director at Lazards that he was trying to recruit has decided against and none of Messrs Cornelius, de Montfort and Quattrone are prepared to

My Word Is My Bonus

hold further discussions about opening new European offices for the foreseeable future. In terms of revenues, we're well behind budget; though, it's fair to say, that we already had some catching up to do before RheinHeim came along. And there's a reasonable amount of work in the pipeline for later in the year - if we don't lose it and if the markets get no worse. Bill is confident we'll land some work from Richard Branson for a major expansion of Virgin despite all the rumours that he's going to take it back private. But, unless Pitcairn produces a bonanza fee, which, as I've told you many times, is less than even money, we're not going to hit target. And that will mean another year of downward pressure on the bonus pool."

There was a general mutter of agreement round the table. Whatever their experience of Bill's hitherto constant and soaring optimism, this greedy bunch could be relied upon to have more concern for their back pockets than anything else. It had always been the same with Peter but he was feeling separate from them now, uncomfortable in their presence. He wasn't sure he was enjoying this job any more. He hadn't really finished his little speech. For the sake of what he had agreed with Bill, he was thinking that he was going to have to come to an unfavourable, some would say disloyal or even treasonous, conclusion; but he was spared it by William.

"It would appear to me that the continued independence of Dundas Brothers," - Blackstone was too precise ever to use the shorthand version 'the Brothers' - "is open to dialectic discursion but, one way or the other, it is surely ineluctable that the Corporate Finance Division's status as one of the pre-eminent City houses is already terminated unless there is intervention by another vendee of RheinHeim's particular character and ambition."

"That, I would agree, is a widely held view, William, both within the bank and outside," Peter concurred, hoping that would wind up his contribution.

"In my view, we should be looking to put together a management buyout," Farquharson chimed in. "In terms of assets, the division has nothing and valuation parameters would point to a low take-out price at the moment. At the same time, from the point of view of ourselves as buyers, our reputation and our client list are both currently intact. It could be a steal."

"It would be equally logical," Kent opined ominously, with the slightly supercilious confidence of the insider, "for the Brothers to look to replicate the advantages of RheinHeim as a parent company, with another substantial banking group, international or otherwise."

"Like who?" enquired Amadeo, dubiously.

"There are any number, Hank. Credit Suisse First Boston lack a UK presence, UBS have only Philips & Drew and Citibank have only Scrimgeours. Deutsche Bank, Commerzbank and Dresdner too all have a need to get into mainstream UK investment banking, even Paribas. And that's before you even look at the predominantly domestic players. Lloyds have got to decide whether they're going to let this market pass them by and Barclays have got to do something with all that rights issue money. The Brothers would tack onto BZW pretty neatly and give their investment management business some active skills to add to the position they've got in trackers."

It was lost on none of them, save perhaps Amadeo, that this was a list that Kent had been compiling for his client, Stephen Gallaher.

"Oh, yes, I suppose so," said Hank sheepishly.

Peter, mindful of what had occurred that afternoon, was intent on dropping a coded message of loyalty, lest his opening remarks could have been misinterpreted.

"Graeme, if that were a process that Sir James and Stephen decided upon, what do you, as the group's adviser, think would be the appropriate level of involvement of corporate finance? Should we be seeking to promote particular solutions for the group, or for corporate finance separately, or should we be simply reactive?"

The sly Kent could detect a manoeuvre and he side-stepped it neatly.

"Oh, I think personally it would be appropriate to do all of those things, Peter. Don't you, Bill?" he added.

But Bill, Peter had seen from the corner of his eye, was becoming increasingly impatient, fed up with this pussy-footing around the issue.

"I've had an approoch froom Michael Milken of Drexel Boornham. They want to buy the entire division," he said straight out, elaborating immediately on the financial packages supposedly proposed. The numbers had all become pounds, though Peter had no idea whether that had been officially confirmed by Milken. On balance he thought it more likely a McAdam embellishment. But they were all sitting up, even Kent, Peter thought. It was expensive keeping up with the social ambitions of a wife like his.

"Drexel's are not exactly the gold standard, are they Bill," William Blackstone said as he finished. "A little too proximate to Boesky's besmirched escutcheon, some would opine. You may have observed on today's tapes that Meshulam Riklis..."

"Isn't he married to Pia Zadora? You know, the actress." Hank Amadeo chipped in, ever abreast of the social whirl.

"Indeed so, though the designation actress might be stretching a point; but more relevant to our deliberations is that Riklis is another running-dog of Boesky and Milken. He illegally concealed a large holding that Rapid-American built up in Guinness, then his Schenley subsidiary mysteriously acquired the US distribution rights and then Guinness had to buy Schenley to extricate themselves. Now he's sold his Guinness stake. Do we really want to be associated with people like that?"

"I'm absolootly assoored by Milken that there's noothing in any of that or the oother roomors that are bein poot aboot. Weell, what d'yoo al say? Doo I goo ahead and talk to them soom moor?"

Peter was frightened he would turn to him first, seeking out a presumed loyal co-conspirator to start the ball rolling. He gazed intently at his cigar, pretending he was having some problem with it, trying to avoid McAdam's eye. He needed have no fear. Bill knew who to nail first.

"Graeme, mun, what dya think?"

"I think it's worth exploring, Bill."

"Seymour?"

"Certainly."

"William?"

"Affirmative, but with reservations, Bill."

"Hank?"

"Sure thing."

"Peter?"

But Peter was already far away. Well, not so far in reality, merely one floor below where they now sat and a mere six hours ago.

369

"Ah, Peter, come and sit down, laddie."

Cruso was in his shirt sleeves - cream silk - monogrammed JC at the breast. Jesus Christ the juniors called him behind his back but to his face everyone who was vouchsafed direct dealings with him called him James. There was no less respect for all that. He'd done them all proud. They were where they were in corporate finance basically because of him, the clients he had won and the swashbuckling triumphs he had inflicted upon their opponents. Now he took one of his precious pipes with a huge polished golden walnut bowl from the rack on the window ledge behind his desk and came over to join Peter on the facing sofa, already engaged in the elaborate ritual of transferring half a handful of tobacco from the leather pouch.

"And how are things in corporate finance, Peter?"

Maybe it was just a ruse to get Peter to talk for a couple of minutes while he got stoked up; but Peter couldn't resist voicing his concerns about morale. He was confident he could talk more or less openly. Cyril Bishop had been a protégé of James Cruso and Peter had been a known protégé of Cyril. There was an assumed chain of loyalty under fire.

"We're all a bit bewildered to be honest, James. We'd all gone overboard on RheinHeim and then they sailed off without us. I guess now we've seen the promised land, we don't like where we are any longer. It may not be logical - after all it's where we were before all this happened - but it's a fact."

Cruso was entirely hidden for a moment behind a huge cloud of aromatic grey-blue smoke. As he emerged, Peter realised how tired he looked, almost deflated from his normal robust stature. Less colour in his cheeks, though they were still adorned with those absurd tufts.

"There's a good deal of concern, James, that Dundas Life is going to drag us down - or at least put a brake on our progress for a good long while."

"Aye, I ken understand that laddie; but ye must gi me time to get it sorted. It's true those buggers down in Croydon have put us in a pickle; but it's nothing that time won't solve. The whole of Texas has just stopped building; finito; but it hasna stopped growing. All that crap our chaps have invested in will get absorbed within a few years. Meanwhile, if the policy holders don't have enough funds to carry the cost, we'll have to carry it from the group. But we'll get it back outa their with-profits policies eventually. That's the beauty of owning a life company. The policy holders are always going to be the winners or losers eventually. We're just going to be winners or big winners. There's nothing in there to stop us pursuing the future of the investment bank, whether that's in securities trading or internationalisation or both. I really didna expect the laddies in corporate finance to swallow all that tosh about going back to square one. That was for the rest of the group. Ye'all know tae much for that. But it's time we need noo, laddie - and results."

He sat back and took a couple of vigorous puffs at his pipe. It responded with a hot glow and more billowing smoke. Peter didn't get the impression that he was required to speak.

"I had a wee chat with Christopher Hennessy this morning," Cruso said eventually. "About Pitcairn. He's very happy with the team and the advice ye've bin giving him. He's confirmed there'll be noo change of advisers when it comes oot of the MMC."

Christ, thought Peter, maybe it's meant to be flattering; but it sounds to me as though Sir James Cruso is reduced to begging one of his own non-executive directors to keep his business with the Brothers while he tries to sort the firm out. He thought he'd try to probe the deal with Hennessy a bit deeper.

"Does that mean no additions to the advisory team either? There've been a lot of rumours about his relationship with Goldmans. And Hambro Magan might try to muscle in too. I believe George has done one or two things for Jock Enderby in the past."

"Noo additions at the expense of our fee arrangements. Is that good enough for ye, laddie? I canna ban him from taking on the world if that's his inclination."

"No, of course not, James, but you know how awful these joint advisory roles are. It's portrayed as an extra pair of hands; but it always turns out that you have to use one of your own to fend off the knives from those who are supposedly on your own side."

"I'm confident that ye ken handle that, laddie." He paused. "But Stephen and I are noo so confident that we ken keep the headhunters away from ye." He paused again, quizzically. Now Peter had no doubt he was expected to reply. But before he could do so, Cruso leaned forward and held his eye.

"Doon't start lying to me noo, Peter."

Peter hesitated. Had he been intending to lie? He wasn't sure.

"There've been some approaches," he said at last, "but nothing I've followed up."

"Yet."

"Yes. Yet."

"We need to win this Pitcairn thing, Peter, and be seen to win. Not just for the fee, though I'd grant ye that that'ud be welcome. But most of all we need to win it for us. We need to be winners. We need to be seen to be winners. D'ye get my meaning, laddie?"

Peter nodded.

"I'm going to offer ye a deal, Peter. Ye'll get 20% of the Brothers' gross fee for defending Pitcairn if ye stay and see it through. Do I need to remind you how much that is?"

He didn't but he did.

"That's £570,000 where we stand now and £3.75 million if you see off a bid of two and a half billion. I'll get Miss Dunwoody to put it in writing."

He was taken aback by the sheer scale of it; but still fast enough in his wits to spot a danger.

"Couldn't you... couldn't you just get Hildegaard to drop me a note?"

"Aha, so ye don't trust the den o' dykes to keep a secret either," the old boy said with a chuckle.

Peter was unaware that corporate finance's nickname for the personnel department had reached so high.

"Let's just say that I'd rather not put temptation in her way."

"Okay," said Cruso, grinning mischievously. "But one other thing, Peter. Ye must keep yer team together - anyone that Christopher thinks is important - and ye ken offer them part of yer pot to do so. Just let me know if you do."

He stopped and tamped down his pipe with the brown asbestos thumb.

"But I'd like to think yer'll keep it all for yersel, laddie."

*****

The course was a picture in the early morning sun. As he drove into the estate, the solid banks of wild purple rhododendrons were in flower on both sides, broken only by the secluded driveways of the seriously rich. He slowed down for the sleeping policemen, here and there glimpsing a mansion through high closed iron gates. The trees were in that first flush where their new leaves seem light and green enough to eat; and the fairways, after all that rain, looked lush and thick and freshly mown.

She was standing on the men's first tee, above the road leading up to the club house, waiting for him at 7.25 when he emerged from the members' changing room, a tartan skirt (O'Flaherty presumably, if there was such a thing) two inches above the knee, her bare athletic legs still apparently bronzed, a loose long-sleeved polo shirt in emerald green and a sun visor to match against her flowing auburn pony tail. She looked edible but, he feared, not necessarily easily digestible.

"What are we playing for?" she enquired.

"Am I getting strokes?"

"You're ten on the board inside."

"I thought you weren't going into the clubhouse."

"Do you expect me to have a pee behind a bush in some plutocrat's back garden? I'm not going in there with you. Anyway that's three-quarters of four - three strokes. Or I'll play you level off the back tees. Please yourself."

He thought for a moment. A woman off six was never off the fairway and would have a short game to die for; but she'd have been lower still if she could get the distances. And coming back up the Burmah Road for the final holes he would have the advantage of being able to reach the greens. No woman could do that off the championship tees.

"Let's play level," he said, "and the game?"

"Loser to withdraw from advising either BMP or Pitcairn," she said immediately.

He felt his knees buckle.

"Well, I'm not sure you quite realise..... not sure that's quite.....quite what I had in mind."

"Why not? You've said often enough that you wanted to sort this out. Here's your chance. Once and for all."

"But.....but....."

'I'm not sure you've got the same to lose as me,' is what he wanted to say but didn't dare. It came out as "But.....but.....is that handicap of yours genuine?"

"It's two years old but I haven't played a dozen times since - and not since October last year. And I've never played here. Do you think you've got enough of an advantage, now, or do you want to back out - play for a ball on each nine and one on the match?" she added contemptuously.

"We'll stick to your original suggestion," he said, terrified, knowing he'd been goaded into it unnecessarily but at the same time knowing no way out. And then, just as he was thinking how he'd explain to her afterwards, if he had to, that Cruso's offer must supersede everything.

"Okay, you're on, Mr Davenport," she snapped back, "but no reneging if you don't like the result."

"Your honour," he said, stepping back to offer her the tee.

She took just a couple of practice swings, huge arcs of the club that had her entire torso, stretched wonderfully against her shirt, facing the hole at the finish. Save for the unbridled movement of her breasts, it wasn't like a woman's swing at all. None of the deliberate concentration, none of the emphasis on timing rather than power, technique instead of testosterone. Then she stepped up to the ball and, with no further preliminaries, smacked it off the tee. To be honest, it wasn't a great drive. It didn't get up enough into the air and it started drawing long before they lost sight of it over the ridge. She'd be lucky if it wasn't in the long stuff on the left - but the one thing it wasn't was short.

Peter took his time, trying to get control of his knees. Getting one up going into the second was just the sort of start he needed, particularly if that was just a rusty shot on her part. This was the fucking Grand Slam - the Open, the Masters, the US Open and the PGA all rolled into one. He was out of his sodding mind. He was little better than a bloody week-end hacker and he was playing for a minimum of five hundred thou, perhaps as much as four million fucking pounds. Or, he thought suddenly, the end of their relationship. He already knew her well enough to have no doubt whatever that reneging would cost him that.

He stood over the ball for an age. Watch the grip. Check the stance. Bend the knees. Slowly back. Head down. Rotate the hips through the swing. He repeated the mantra over and over again. And then he hit it. There was a dull clunk and it took off like a quail and sailed over the ridge down the centre of the fairway. He gazed after it, already exhausted. The awful realisation dawned that he was going to have to hit another fifty odd shots like that - and putt like God himself.

Sure enough she was behind a bush on the left over near the first tee of the East course. An awful lie, deep in the long grass, wet with the overnight dew. She did well to hack it out more or less level with his drive in the middle of the fairway. There was still 230-odd yards to go across the dip and up again to the green. To his surprise, she went for it with a fairway wood. She wasn't far short either; but that draw was obviously a feature of her game and she ended up in the deep bunker on the left below the front of the green. He played the percentage game with a three iron down the centre and a wedge into the green. Not close to the flag but a certain par five. She was in the bunker for three and he was already counting himself one up. But she fluffed it out with a great golden spray of sand to within six feet and dropped the putt; and they went to the short second across the gully all square.

He judged she had a seven or eight iron in her hand but she gave it no air, drilling it low at the green as if she'd topped it. But she found some backspin from somewhere and it stopped two feet from the flag, over on the right above the bunker, as if it had fallen in a fresh cow pat. He hit the green too; but he was short of the flag on the left hand side and never looked like making the twenty foot putt. She made her birdie. One up.

They were both in greenside bunkers for two on the next, she inevitably to the left, he to the right. The three-tier green sloped sharply down towards her but she thumped it out again onto the top level where the flag was placed. He, playing across the upper slope, left himself with a horrible curly one of ten feet and missed it. She made no mistake. Two up.

He got one back at the fourth, the long left-handed dog-leg downhill, when she was again too far left with her drive, leaving no direct route to the flag. With her bum in a holly bush and forced to play out wide, she scuffed it into the ditch over by the furthest to the right of the three bridges and had to take a drop. She played a majestic approach from

160 yards to finish within four feet; but he made a safe par to her bogey. Back to one down.

They halved the next three. An undistinguished pair of fours at the short fifth. Two more bogeys at the sixth as he sliced his drive into the bunker on the right but she obliged with a quick hook into the bunker on the left. Two more bogey fives at the seventh, downhill and then up, where they both had hanging lies in the short rough and failed to take enough club to get up the final hill. She was looking less assured now, he told himself; and she wasn't used to all these trees. Bally-whatever-it-was was clearly a links. Trees couldn't grow and low-handicap golfers learned to survive by keeping their ball below the incessant winds blowing in off the Atlantic. The odd hook didn't matter if you only ended up in slow-growing seaside grass beside unwatered fairways. This was different. This was the Augusta of England and her concentration and silence revealed that it was not to her liking. On the other hand, he felt that he was starting to hit the ball more solidly now and his confidence was growing.

The eighth at Wentworth is that slight dog-leg to the left with water in front of the green to left and right. They both hit fair drives to the left centre of the fairway, leaving themselves about 180 yards to go. To his surprise, playing first, she layed up short of the water, giving him an ideal opportunity to haul one back and go all square. He took out a four iron - there was no point in being short - and promptly lifted his head, spraying it into the right-hand pond. To her credit, though her gamesmanship had done it, she didn't say a word. They were both playing in near, almost self-conscious, silence. But she pitched her approach right into the centre of the green and picked up a five to his six. Back to two up.

They halved the next five, the long par four ninth with bogeys, the short tenth with pars, and the shortish but uphill par four eleventh. At the long twelfth, she was perilously close to the ditch on the left with her second but somehow scrambled it through the gap between two silver birches onto the green from a unspeakable lie to match his par. At 440 yards uphill, the par four thirteenth was too long even for her but, though he trickled his up the final slope onto the fringe of the green, she put her wedge from 45 yards dead and took one putt to his two. Still two down and running out of holes.

The fourteenth is that difficult par three up the hill. From the tee, you can only see the top of the flag, which is usually on the upper level of the two-tier green. He hit a humdinger of a four iron and got up there to find it six feet from the hole. He took his time about it and managed to get control of his knees sufficiently to roll it in for a birdie. Back to one down.

At 460-odd yards, neither of them could get to the fifteenth in two. Their drives were level with the bunker on the left and that fancy mansion behind the trees on the right with the faintly Palladian columns. He hit the better second but was still well short and they settled for a half with solid bogeys. The sixteenth, much shorter and less hazardous, they halved with fours.

They both comfortably cleared the road with their drives at the seventeenth but she was too far left again, under the oak trees. With her draw she had a chance of pulling it round the corner but, though she appeared to strike the shot quite perfectly, it caught an overhanging branch. The ball ricocheted right onto the fairway but stopped dead. She had all of 300 yards to go and still no view even of that weird house that looks like an ocean liner above the left hand side of the sunken green. She took two more to get on while he played his irons steadily up the middle. For once, playing from the rough on the right, she didn't get her approach shot close and they walked down off the seventeenth green all square. It was all on the last.

The eighteenth is a much shorter par five and the back tee was closed for some reseeding, bringing it down to around 480 yards. He took an age over his drive but successfully got it down the left-hand side of the fairway, level with the back of the furthest bunker and perhaps just long enough to get the green. She hit hers left again too but it ran off the fairway and just trickled into the back of the first bunker, leaving her with no room to get any sort of long iron behind the ball. She did well to blast it out but she was still 40 yards short of the ditch, on the downslope, and with all of 200 yards to go. He had a three wood in his hand but he put it back in his bag and took an iron for safety instead. He hit it well, short of the green but only by twenty or thirty yards. She went for it with a fairway wood and hit a beauty; but for once the draw deserted her. It finished up just on the green but it was way back on the right, all of sixty feet from the flag, which was tucked in behind the bunker front left. She'd do well to get it down for two more from there. He hit his wedge to seven feet, giving himself an excellent chance of a four. She had none at all.

For once she got down to have a look at the line. Peter had been back right on this green so often that he knew it well from there. It wasn't easy - a long one, slightly downhill turning from left to right and gaining pace in the final few yards. And then she walked up to it and hit it. It was a good line but it was struck far too hard, swooping across the green towards the flag like a freshly-fucked ferret. The moment she struck it, he knew it was going to go a good ten or twelve feet past. He pulled out the flag as it approached to watch it sail right off the green; but it hit the back of the hole, jumped a couple of inches into the air and fell back into the cup with a clunk that did his mind. He'd been looking at a certain win and now he needed this for a half. He was instantly liquidised. Almost actually shitting himself. It was only seven feet but it might just as well have been seventy. There was no way he was going to get it in. He prowled around looking at it from every angle but in reality just trying to get a grip of himself. He knew it was straight; it was just a matter of hitting it straight. But with his hands and knees shaking the way they were, he wouldn't have been confident of getting it in from seven inches. Finally he knew he was going to have to hit it. He'd decided it wasn't going to get any better and was just settling over the ball when she walked over and picked it up.

"You can have that," she said. "I can't stand watching a grown man going through all that for such a piddly little putt," she added, breaking into a broad grin and wrapping her arms around him, the flagpole still in her hand.

*****

They raced each other back to London, shamelessly carving up other motorists pottering about between their garden centres and their hypermarkets. She drove a Golf GTI and she drove it like one possessed. He hauled her back on the straight bits as the Morgan's three and half litres came on song; but on the bends and the roundabouts she was all brake lights and burning rubber. When they got to the motorway, he was confident of showing her the way home; but there were only the briefest opportunities to wind it up down the outside lane and they were insufficient to counteract her ploy of overtaking slower traffic to right or left at will. As they got towards town she brazenly jumped a red light at the Hogarth roundabout and he lost her completely. In many ways he was glad. His nerves had suffered enough damage that morning without a white-knuckle chase down the Cromwell Road, diving in and out of the traffic from one lane to another. He relaxed and pottered along to Kensington High Street and up through Campden Hill Road. By the time he reached Uxbridge Street and had found himself somewhere to park, she had unloaded her clubs, poured the beers and was starting to put together one of her exquisite warm goat's cheese salads. Overcome with relief at his escape, affection for a creature who had brought so much excitement to his life and the sheer animal beauty of her, he put lunch on hold and took her straight to bed.

They parted in the afternoon to 'do' their briefcases before getting together again at his place for dinner. The weather promised to be warm enough for them to sit out on his little balcony and he promised her a fillet steak with a sauce of crushed green pepper, cognac and cream and a strawberry soufflé that would blow her mind.

She arrived a little before eight with her little overnight bag. He'd in reality not brought home that much reading and had used a good bit of the afternoon to prepare something really spectacular. He'd popped into the fine wine section at the back of Oddbins in Notting Hill after he left her and bought a bottle of 1982 Dom Perignon Rosé, a 1970 Pétrus - carefully remembering Freddie's admonitions on the subject of the statutory rape of young clarets - and a half bottle of 1976 Château d'Yquem. The knowledgeable young man who had helped him find what he was looking for was pretty impressed and, for two and a half bottles, the bill was pretty impressive too. Then he popped along the road to Chalmers & Gray, the fishmongers, and bought two dozen fines claires. Seven days into May, they were not really kosher; but he thought it worth stretching a point for such an obvious aphrodisiac. Now they were freshly shucked and sitting in the fridge on his largest dish. The sauce for the steaks was made and needed only to be reheated and the mixture of fresh strawberries, strawberry juice, caster sugar,

Cointreau and beaten egg yolks was ready in one dish with the whites of the eggs ready for beating in another.

She was wearing a pair of tight white jeans that hugged her perfect bottom and, wisely distrusting the temperature of an early May evening, a fluffy grey rollneck sweater flecked with gold. He took her in his arms. As usual she smelt divine, as though she had just stepped from a bath of Opium. Her breasts pressed against him.

"Sam, I've been meaning to ask you. Do you own a bra? I thought at least you might wear one for golf."

"What for? I reckon if I get them behind the ball, it gives me an extra twenty yards. You can't get that without bounce," she giggled huskily, shaking her breasts from side to side against him.

He brought the champagne and they sat out on the balcony where he'd already laid the table.

"Wow," she said when she saw the bottle, "what are we celebrating?"

"I'll tell you in a minute."

They raised their glasses and sipped. It was yeasty and delicious.

"But I need to have a serious chat with you first." He'd intended to leave it until after dinner; but it was pressing on him, nagging. He was wondering whether he wanted out of the City. In due course he might now have the dough for it. She thought he looked fretful and decided to make a joke of it.

"What's wrong? Do you think I should become a golf pro? Join the ladies' circuit? Or do you think I lack the killer instinct?"

"That would make me pretty happy."

"What?"

"You becoming a golf pro. You've got the talent if you practised."

"Don't be ridiculous, Peter. I'm a merchant banker."

"Sam, you must ask Grossmanns to take you off the BMP account. There's still a couple of months before a decision is due from the Monopolies Commission; so somebody else will have plenty of time to play themselves in."

"No, I've told you, Peter, it's out of the question."

"Why?"

"We don't know that the MMC will clear it," she protested, knowing that this was irrelevant to his argument.

He responded nevertheless. "Of course it will be cleared. For one reason or another, they felt that they had to send it there," he said, brushing over his own rather unconventional role in securing the reference, "but Thatcher's not going to let the MMC stand in the way of her favourite industrialist. If necessary, it will be fixed for him. Better to tell Grossmanns now. Nobody will be pleased to have this sprung on them when the clearance has been announced."

"How many times do I have to tell you, Peter, it's out of the question." She said it firmly but without rancour, suppressing her rising anger. "If you're so worried about it, why don't you ask to be relieved of Pitcairn?"

"I can't."

"You bloody nearly were this morning."

"Things have changed. It's no longer possible for me to back out."

She began to boil over with his presumption that his was the only solution. "Why not? Why should you bastards always assume that a woman counts less, that her career is unimportant? And what's changed since this morning?"

"Nothing's changed since this morning, Sam. I can't bear to think what would have happened if you'd let me take that putt and I'd missed it. I should never have let you inveigle me into that bet."

"There you go again, you bloody male chauvinist. I had exactly the same thing on the line as you. More. This is my biggest deal ever. You've been at this lark for yonks."

"I can't back out, Sam. After that RheinHeim fiasco, the Brothers are desperate to win this one. You know about fuck-you money? A pot that's big enough for you to tell the world to go fuck itself - for ever. Well, this is my fuck-you money. Cruso's promised me 20% of the gross fee, that's a bonus of around £4 million if I pull this one off. One way or another, there's going to be a change of ownership at Dundas. So it's not going to be these particular Germans; but there'll be others - Germans or Swiss or Dutch or French - maybe another British house. Worse still some Americans with their own ideas of how things are done and a corps of corporate financiers ready to show us how. I could be out of work by the end of the year. I've taken on a mountain of debt to buy this apartment. Interest rates are on the rise and the job market is not easy. I need that bonus."

"Then you'll have to fight me for it," she snapped immediately. She had been momentarily dumbstruck by the number, but, as always with her, it was the principle that mattered. She had no such expectations from Grossmanns. Indeed the old man himself had called her in last week, she thought at Evans' suggestion, and asked her if she wanted a second, more senior, director to handle the bid jointly with her. Julius Grossmann, to his credit, had allowed her to win the argument but he had left her in no doubt that, particularly since it was at her insistence, if she did not pull off the required victory, she would go the way of others who had failed him.

"Look, Peter, I'm the only female director in Grossmanns corporate finance and I'm the newest. This is my first big job in charge and I've got to win it. I think I love you but I'm not sure yet. What I do know is that I'm never going to be dependent on a man the way my mother was. I have my own career and I'm going to keep it that way. If you make me choose between you and that shit Evans, I'm going to choose Evans. It will hurt; but that's the way it is. And I'd rather make that choice right now while I don't know if I love you than wait until it's too late to be anything else but heartbroken."

"Sam, be practical," he pleaded, taking her hand in his. "How can we fight a take-over battle day after day for the best part of three months, scratching and clawing at each other for 18 hours a day and then fall into bed with each other every night?"

"If you don't want to end this now, we'll have to." She pulled her hand away and sprang to her feet, feeling the need to be firm but secretly doubting her resolve, deciding that she must get this settled quickly before she weakened.

"It can't work, Sam. We can't keep it hidden for that long anyway. Either your sleuths or ours will be onto it and the shit will hit the fan in a big way."

She knew the impracticality of what she was suggesting. But though she felt the tears welling up behind her strong exterior, she pounded on. "I'm going home. Think about it. If you feel it can't be done, so be it. You'll never see me again out of a business suit." She turned on her heels, swept up the overnight bag she had dropped on a chair by the door and ran from the apartment, slamming the door. By the time she reached her car, she was sobbing uncontrollably.

Thursday, 16 June, 1988

Davenport had caught Hennessy eyeing Charlotte Mulder from time to time in meetings with what he took to be more than just concern for her eternal soul - or whatever Mormons have. To be sure, she was a delicious creature and looking her very best today in a slinky sheath of turquoise and pink silk, one of a collection with which she had appeared after a holiday in Thailand the previous year. She had the Siamese figure for it, petite but pert, and the dress slit to well above the knee revealed a shapely leg. The matching wide-brimmed shiny straw hat, pulled down low to shield her dark, dark eyes, gave her a coquettish, Lolita-style charm. Mindful of Cruso's instruction that Hennessy wanted the Pitcairn team kept together and certain that Charlotte was one of his favourites, she had seemed an inspired choice as Peter's companion for the box at Ascot on Ladies' Day. A good bit cheaper than cutting her in on his deal too. Sid had brought them down in the Volvo early, picking Charlotte up from her Chelsea flat en route, so that they could be in situ before their guests began to arrive.

Freddie was the first there, partly perhaps with a view to getting in a few sharpeners as soon as the noon gun was fired, but more particularly, Peter thought, to avoid any subsequent embarrassment by explaining to him, on one side, exactly which of his wives was his companion that day. Actually it was the real one - the town mouse rather than the country mouse - possessed, appropriately for the wife of a submariner, of a torpedo-shaped pair of breasts and, on this occasion at least, a conning tower of a hat in steely naval grey.

"Any gossip from your ministerial friend about the MMC, Freddie?" Peter enquired, whilst he had him alone out on the balcony, Charlotte meanwhile attending to Jemima Wordsworth inside the box.

"You'd hardly believe it, m'boy, but Alan says there's a view that some of them are actually going to swallow this bilge about competition in research." And then, as a cheque for four million-odd quid swam before Peter's eyes, he added: "But Central Office have told Evans in no uncertain terms to run up a better line of signals. Of course, I haven't told Hennessy any of that and, if you're agreed, I'm not going to."

"I think you're right, Freddie. I don't want the Pitcairn people easing off, thinking they're winning."

At that moment Sir Timothy and Rita Henderson-Ball arrived. Peter had suffered grave doubts about the combination of personalities that he was proposing to entertain; but Rita had more or less invited herself - they had been his guests for Ladies' Day two years running - and, given her unknowing contribution to Pitcairn's MMC reference, he had felt it churlish to ignore the hint. In any event, Sir James had put on a typically bravura performance at Bottley's recent Annual General Meeting, praising the outgoing chairman to the ionosphere, and, what with one thing and another, the ice was slowly beginning to thaw as regards Peter's relationship with the old boy. Rita, barely wearing a little pale-blue chiffon number, backless to the waist and gaping perilously at the front as her unfettered and startlingly tanned bosom tussled with the inadequate material, came bounding out onto the balcony where Peter and Freddie were still conspiring and planted a huge candy-floss coloured kiss directly on Peter's lips. Rita was not into maw-mawing. Freddie could hardly contain himself as he waited for Peter to make the introductions and was clearly more than contented to be left alone with such a floozy while Peter went to make continued peace overtures to her husband.

Stephen and Fay Harcourt and George and Felicity Aladyce arrived more or less simultaneously. Fay was a pure and simple English rose and Felicity as perfect a middle-aged townie brunette as her husband was a bucolic shambles. No doubt what had been no more than a couple of hours previously an immaculately pressed and laundered Moss Bros grey morning suit, supplied on hire to his exact dimensions, was now bulging at the pockets and sagging over his gut like his habitual tweedy suits. His topper, which had somehow been supplied in unmatching black, might or might not have been the correct size for his head but had taken no account of his generous head of snowy curls and was perched atop them like a circus clown's bonnet. It was also apparent that no end of searching of his wardrobe had revealed a pair of black shoes to replace his usual brown suedes. Sir Timothy, whose own suiting had required a certain amount of rebuilding over the years to accommodate his expanding girth but who nevertheless maintained the gentry's obsession with appearances, was transfixed by the spectacle.

"Aladyce. Aladyce. Don't I know that name from somewhere?"

"Dr Aladyce is chief executive of Pitcairn, Sir Timothy," Peter assisted.

"Pharmaceutical suppliers to the fer...fer...fer...fucking world, Sir Timothy," George added for good measure.

"Well, yes, jolly good show, I'm sure," Henderson-Ball came back, apparently far from convinced.

It was another splendid summer's day, as it had been all week, and they all drifted out onto the balcony with their champagne. In the box immediately to their left, towards the winning post, were Sir Ernest and Lady Harrison and their guests. Ernie, as usual, was looking exceptionally dapper in the palest and sharpest of grey morning suits. Peter recognised John Coates, the Racal finance director, Bob Clark of Hill Samuel, now absorbed by TSB, and John Thornton of Goldman Sachs. There were also a couple of rather military-looking men, presumably procurement chiefs from the Ministry of Defence or retired brass-hats cashing in as consultants to sell Racal's array of communications equipment. It was already a gathering of raucous good humour and Ernie, the ultimate East End boy made good, was leading the party.

On their other side, towards the straight start, things were more muted but no less well-heeled. Sir Owen Green, chairman of BTR, was the host and, among his guests, the avuncular Anthony Forbes, joint senior partner of Cazenoves, his ex-colleague Michael Richardson, now deputy chairman of Rothschilds, and George Magan, long BTR's favoured adviser while at Morgan Grenfell and now independently established outside the house that Guinness had humbled.

Her box was beyond Sir Owen's. Peter could make out Lars Stenhammar standing alone at the balcony rail, as if gripping it for support with two long, bony-fingered hands. He had become cadaverously thin, his sunken cheeks so pale that his grey stubble was his only colouring and there was a yawning gap between the collar of his white shirt and his emaciated neck. Five months, Peter thought, looked like the sum of it.

She had her back towards Peter. He could recognise now the range of her disguises. They were extraordinarily clever. Without her turning, he could see that this one was of a plain woman doing her bit to look her best. She was wearing a straight navy blue dress, or perhaps skirt, which came to mid calf, and a jacket in the same colour, cut deliberately wide and square at the shoulders to disguise her curves and long enough to conceal her bottom. She had also gone in for a wide-brimmed straw, this time in black with a sky blue ribbon, tied in a bow at the side. He would wager she was wearing a high necked blouse in a matching shade of blue. He couldn't see her shoes but she was looking her full height, hiding for a while all but the shiny black top hat of the man to whom she was talking. Then she turned to her right to offer her glass to the waitress for a refill to reveal the unmistakable bolt-upright figure of David Carradine, his strong Roman nose and broad smile as usual quartering his noble face. As inconspicuously as possible, Peter climbed the two steps back up towards the box so that he could get a view over the heads of the BTR party. Sure enough there was the stocky figure of Arthur Evans discussing his race card with an attractive young lady less than half his age. Charlotte sidled up to him.

"You see who's in the next but one box?" she enquired. Perhaps he hadn't been as obvious as he thought.

"Yes, but who's the girl talking to Evans?"

"I don't know but I'm sure I've seen her picture," she said, and then, as her husband joined her at Evans' side, "of course, Pandora Maxwell, Kevin's wife."

Christopher and Claudia Hennessy arrived just before one, he looking like a child dressed up for a wedding, she just a little bit OTT with very high heels and a bright red pillar-box hat that made her a good foot and a half taller than her husband. Peter led them out onto the balcony and made the introductions. The BTR party had gone inside for lunch and Peter was keen to get his mob seated too. There was not much point in wasting time while Christopher had an orange juice. He began to shepherd them up the steps to the box, Rita bringing up the rear.

"See your friend Arthur Evans is over there," he whispered, as he guided her by her naked back.

"Yeeuk - he gives me the heebie-jeebies. Haven't seen 'im since last October - worst week-end of my bleedin life."

"Why?"

"Sorry, Peter, I don't want to talk about it. Ever."

He took the head of the table with Claudia Hennessy on his right and Fay Harcourt on his left and put Sir Timothy in charge at the other end between Jemima Wordsworth and Charlotte Mulder. This had a number of advantages. It made old Henderson-Ball feel important but kept him too far away from Peter for direct conversation to be possible. He didn't yet feel that relations were sufficiently restored to survive extended exchanges. Then, he was able to put Christopher next to Charlotte, where he was sure he wanted to be, with Rita in the middle of the table to liven things up, and George between Rita and Claudia. Freddie he put between Fay Harcourt and Felicity Aladyce, where he thought he could come to no harm, and Stephen on Felicity's right.

"Stephen's the expert at your end of the table, Sir Timothy," Peter called out, as they started on their asparagus, "so I think you should get him to mark your cards."

"Not really fair, Peter," Stephen protested, "you know I'm a jumps man myself."

"Must be much 'fe same - a leg at each corner," said Rita, a little tipsy. "Freddie, what d'ya fink?"

"I'm afraid I just go by the names; but my *Times* this morning was recommending Handsome Sailor for the first and, for an old sea dog like me, that's irresistible."

"What about you, Claudia?" Peter enquired. Have you got a system?"

"Oh, I think one must be loyal to one's friends. Dear Robert Sangster has a couple of runners and that darling Sir Philip Oppenheimer has one. And then the Queen has a couple too. She's invited us to her garden party on the sixth of next month, you know."

"Ere, Freddie, fere's a Sovereign Fleet in 'fe second and a Sailor's Mate in 'fe fourf. That gives ye a bleedin treble," said Rita, waving her race card. "Timofy," she demanded, her voice rising above the babble of conversation at his end of the table, "whatya gonna do in 'fe first, luv?"

"Dowsing. I'm sticking with all the ones owned by the bloody arabs, my dear. I figure they've had enough off us this past year to owe us one."

The asparagus was followed by fresh salmon with new potatoes and salad and they finished off with summer pudding and clotted cream. By the time the cheese board went around, most of the men were off to the Tote windows to place their bets for the first whilst the ladies were gathering on the balcony to watch the royal procession.

Peter popped out with only three or four minutes to go before the off. As he hurried down the passage towards the Tote, he found Samantha coming towards him. He had been right about the sky-blue blouse but she had added a feature that would never have occurred to him but which explained her height - a pair of those awful ankle-high lace-up boots, perversely popular amongst the young adherents of fashion, that make a woman look like something between a witch and a crow. They passed with just a nodded acknowledgement.

He put a tenner each way on Posada for no very good reason other than that he had won last time out and was getting 21 pounds from the favourite, Freddie's Handsome Sailor, which seemed an awful lot extra to carry, even over only six furlongs. They were already running when he got back to the box and by the time he'd checked the colours, Posada was home and dry by a good three lengths. Jemima had backed it too but everyone else was down the pan.

"Charlotte tells me that's Kevin Maxwell over there with Lord Evans in the Grossmanns' box," said a voice at his waist. "What do you think he's up to?" Peter manoeuvred as discreetly as he could to arrange little Hennessy one step above him on the balcony terracing rather than one below.

"Difficult to say; but it's safe to assume that his father's not given up on interfering in Pitcairn's affairs. He was making a great hoo-ha last month about changing the Hollis operation from an engineering group into a service provider for the health industry. It could all just be part of the smokescreen. I still think he's unlikely to put in a bid himself; but it will not have been lost on Evans that it would be a nuisance if he did.

Grossmanns obviously think it's worth cultivating him. Somehow or another, they need to pick up his stake without paying over the top."

"Has Freddie got any information on the MMC?"

"Nothing I'm sure that he hasn't already told you."

"Any further thoughts on the Nestlé clearance?"

Both Nestlé and Suchard had been given clearance to proceed with bids for Rowntree without reference to the MMC.

"Well, I never thought, within the Tebbit doctrine, that there could be any case for referring either of them - although that hack Anthony Hilton in *The Standard* was still claiming up to the last that Young would do it for the sake of expediency. But perhaps I'm not the one to judge. After all, I didn't see the case for referring us. Though I thought we put it very elegantly," he added, securing a little smile from Christopher which was close to the sum total of his sense of humour.

Peter took Fay Harcourt and Felicity Aladyce down to the paddock to have a look at the runners for the Norfolk Stakes. Superpower, with five wins out of his last five outings, didn't look like one to bet against; but they all did, nevertheless, stopping at the bookies' stands on the way back to the Grandstand. Superpower was being offered at evens. Fay and Felicity both opted for an each way bet on Time To Go Home, which had won five times out of the last six, but in indifferent company. They both got four to one; but Peter, seeking richer pickings, got 25/1 about Desert Dawn, which was a nice-looking two-year-old and would produce good money, even for a place. They watched the race from the rails, Superpower predictably leading them home, but Desert Dawn following on with Time To Go Home third. The ladies got their money back and Peter trousered sixty odd quid to go with the hundred he had picked up on the first. The sensible thing was to sit out the rest of the afternoon; but he knew he wouldn't.

Back on the balcony of the box, Sir Timothy and Freddie had been left consoling each other on the combined nautical and arabian failures of the first two races whilst the bulk of the rest of the party, sounder of limb, had headed for the paddock to see the Gold Cup field. It was a foolish choice. It would be a hell of a scrum by now. George Aladyce had opted out too and Peter took advantage of the opportunity to get him on his own.

"What did you think of the Beecham results, George," he asked, sitting down beside him.

"The fur...fur...figures were not that special when you think how much interest they've saved by selling some of that consumer product crap. But their antibiotics are still going well, which makes sense. Ours are ter...ter...too. All the excitement is in selling Eminase in the States through Upjohn. Interesting to see how much more they're spending on research. Up another thirteen pur...per cent."

"And Glaxo?" Peter enquired, still his other major hopeful as a counter-bidder.

"I cunt...cunt...can't understand it. It's by fafafar the best cum...cum...company in the business and it has the weakest share price. Of course that nu...nu...nutter Girolami never seems to give a toss if pee...pee...people don't want to buy his shares, but I see he's apoy...poy...pointed some City gent as finance director; so, maybe he's trying to do something about it. What's his name? Something like Hinge and Bracket?"

"John Hignett."

"What's his gay...gay...game?"

"He was head of corporate finance at Lazards. Did a spell a few years back as director-general of the Take-Over Panel."

"Is that a sign that je...je...Geronimo is about to break the habit of a lie...lie...lifetime and start bibibidding for things? Like pee...pee...Pitcairn?"

"Would he make an acceptable white knight, George?"

George looked around carefully. Having confirmed that his chairman was nowhere to be seen, he leaned over towards Peter, his voice barely above a whisper.

"The mi...mi...midget, of course, won't hear such tor...tor...talk. But, I'm a mere boff...boff...boffin, pee...pee...Peter, and their research is the best. I know you think we've been over-eck...eck...egging this research poy...poy...point; but Evans would be the fur...fur...fucking pits. We owe it to our pee...pee...people to key...key...kick that bastard in the ner...ner...nuts."

Peter was reflective for a while. Then he changed the subject.

"Talking about your people, George, that doctor in your research labs who bought all those shares. The widow. I don't know why but she still bothers me. I've listened to the story and it's logical enough. I've heard of other people being warned that their Lloyds' syndicates are in the shit. But it still seems strange to buy all those shares in one company, and your own employer at that, only to panic and sell them a week later. I keep asking myself what's her real problem?"

"Aids."

"She's got Aids?" Suddenly it seemed to be getting everywhere.

"N...n...no, pee...pee...Peter. She's in charge of Aids research. Lie... lie...like I said awhile back, it's only a small team, fur...fur...fiddling around with some mun...mun...monkeys. Same as everyone else. They've got n...nowhere. Bur...bur...but if it poo...poo...puts your mind at rest, I'll tay...tay...take a closer look at what she's been up to. There's not much else we can do while we're waiting for the sodding MMC."

"Thanks, George. You're right. It would set my mind at rest."

The Gold Cup was a shambles. El Conquistador, who had led the field, hit the rails and came down on the final bend as the favourite, Sadeem, and then Royal Gait between them came up to pass him. Royal Gait ran away to win by five lengths and was then disqualified for causing the fall, with Sheikh Mohammed's Sadeem being declared the winner and the third and fourth horses moved up to second and third. Peter, looking for something to beat the favourite at good odds, had invested fifty quid of his winnings on Royal Gait at 9-1. At least Sir Timothy had a winner, though at 7-2, his winnings would barely cover his stakes on Daarkom and Shimshek, which had both come in down the field.

The Ribblesdale Stakes and the Chesham Stakes took back most of what was left of Peter's winnings but, though the final race, the King George V Handicap, looked like a lottery, he couldn't resist joining Henderson-Ball in a flutter on the two Al Maktoum horses. Sir Timothy, sticking to his guns, invested in the three Sheikh Mohammed horses as well. He must have lost a pot, Peter was thinking, as he handed the Tote another forty quid. He turned to go to find she was at the next window.

"Supping with the little devil again, I see," he said.

"You're just jealous he's not in your box," she replied waspishly, as she swept up a fistful of twenty pound notes that the girl had given her and turned on her heel.

Charlotte organised a fiver a head sweepstake for the final race with the ladies pulling the names of two horses each out of Peter's topper and the men one. Sir Timothy picked up what he called another bloody a-rab.

"A message from the office," Charlotte whispered to Peter as he pulled out Ile de Chypre, the second favourite.

"It'll have to wait till afterwards," he replied testily. It couldn't be that important.

Ile de Chypre was leading by a mile as they came round the final bend, which was just as well as his bets were nowhere. He was just calculating that the pot would put him back safely above square when the damned animal suddenly took a stride to the left, leaving Greville Starkey going straight on, pitched unceremoniously onto the grass. There was a communal gasp from the crowd and Thethingaboutitis, which bloody Christopher had drawn, came galloping home by two and a half lengths. The little bugger accepted the congratulations of all concerned as though he'd actually chosen it.

They all had a few more glasses of champagne, except Hennessy, of course, who celebrated his triumph with a glass of Perrier, and drifted out onto the passageway to listen to the band down below and watch that old biddy with the huge hindquarters who conducts the singing of old music hall favourites.

It was nigh unto seven by the time they'd got rid of everybody, tipped the waitresses, and found Sid double parked in the road outside.

"Morrissey's resigned," Charlotte repeated. "I popped out to call my secretary and she said it had just been announced."

"Why would he do that? It doesn't make sense. He's got a pisspot full of options and it's a pound to a penny that someone else is going to bid for us."

He called up Bill from the phone in the car and got his secretary.

"Bill's on the other line. I'll just read you the announcement and, if he's finished by then, I'll put you through.

'*Stephen Gallaher, the chief executive of Dundas Brothers, has concluded that there is unnecessary duplication between the roles of chief executive and group finance director. It has accordingly been agreed with Henry Morrissey that the latter should resign with immediate effect. Terrence Chung, presently finance director of Central and Kowloon Developments,*

will be joining Dundas Brothers next month as director of group finance.'
That's it."

Peter laughed out loud.

"Well, that's bloody hilarious," he said.

"Wait a minute, Peter. Bill's off the phone now. I'll put you through.

"Whayay, mun, soo the news has penetrated darkest Ascoot, has it?"

"What the hell's going on, Bill?"

"Yer can see what's gooin on, mun. Gallaher's surroondin imself with his fookin croonies."

"But why that extraordinary announcement? What the hell's the difference between a group finance director and a director of group finance?"

"Compensation, mun."

"What do you mean, compensation?"

"Soomtimes, Peter, I think you're bluddy thick. If he'd joost fired Morrissey, Henry woodveadim for wroogful dismissal. Gallaher coodna claim he coodna do the job, mun. He's bin finance director for years. Three years' salary, pension rights, benefits in kind, unexpired ooptions, pain and sooferin. Soo ees aboolished the position of groop finance director and joost made im redoondant. Statutory redoondancy pay and a flea in his fookin ear. It's a Sybil Dunwoody special, mun."

"Bill, I've never had any time for Morrissey; but that's a bit rough."

"Ay, mun, it's a roogh oold woorld."

*****

There were no messages. He switched off the answering machine, picked up his mobile and pressed a single digit.

"How did you get on?" she asked without waiting for his voice.

"I made 160 quid on the first two races and then blew it all on the rest. How about you? You were picking up a fat wad when I last saw you."

"I ended up £690." They taught them to be exact at Grossmanns.

"How on earth did you do that?"

"I did £50 each way with the Tote on all the Eddery rides - both of them. I had two seconds and four thirds. We Irish know what we're doing when it comes to the nags. Not bad, eh?"

Their reconciliation had been untidy and filled Peter with foreboding; but at least it had been swift. They had each spent the Sunday after their row in a turmoil. When he got home from work on Monday, late, there was a message on his answering machine. He had left a string of messages on hers too. He drove straight over to Notting Hill.

"If you really thought I should give up Pitcairn instead of you giving up BMP, why did you concede that putt?"

"Don't exaggerate, Peter. That putt was only for a half. I've never suggested you should give up Pitcairn."

"But you have."

"I haven't. I simply said that I wasn't going to give up BMP. It's never bothered me if we both carry on advising Evans and Hennessy through to the end. It was always you who said it was impossible."

"Well, it is, more or less."

"I don't claim it will be easy. But, if we can survive that, we can surely survive most things. And, if we can't, then it's probably better not to go on trying. Do you want to try?"

"Of course I do, Sam. But the money."

"Don't be so bloody mercenary, Peter. One or other of us, or both, are going to make a pot of money in the next ten years. Does it matter if it's not this year?"

"I think it does to me. I'm not enjoying it any more."

"An unwise confession. You won't find me easing up just because your heart's not in it."

"Okay. Rules of engagement?" he conceded.

"Pitcairn and BMP are banned subjects. No, all business would be safer."

"Agreed."

"No meetings in public places."

"Okay."

"And no visits to each other's places without prior arrangement. I don't want you popping round to find I'm working on the next offer document with papers strewn all over the floor."

"You don't strike me as a mucky worker. No calls at the office, of course."

"I don't want any calls here either."

"Why not?"

"Grossmanns normally pay my home telephone bill. I didn't put it in last quarter because of you. They require an analysis. It will be thought suspicious if I stop claiming altogether. Anyway, I don't want you checking up on my movements."

"And you've already told me I can't call you on your mobile for the same reason. How are we going to communicate, Sam? Pigeons?"

"There's always the post."

"Be sensible, Sam. Even next day delivery is a joke nowadays."

"Well, what do you suggest?"

"I don't know," he said wearily. "Yes, I do. We'll buy two more mobiles. Just for us. No answering service. We just leave them switched off when we can't take a call."

Thursday, 28 July, 1988

8.25am. The whole team was in his cramped little office, crowded round the monitor waiting for the stock exchange announcement to flash up. Tim, enthusiastic even when hungover, as he clearly was today, had been so insistent on it that Peter had reluctantly taken them through the motions of a review meeting of where they stood ready for a resumption of hostilities. Charlotte was a little full of herself, having spent the previous day, at Hennessy's invitation, in the Pitcairn box at Glorious Goodwood. He wondered whether the sanctimonious little runt was really trying to lay her. Stuart Robinson, his shirt-tail still flying around outside the arse end of his trousers, had reams of fresh analysis, his latest theory being that the US drug company Smithkline Beckman should be the preferred white knight. The company had issued a profit warning in June as sales of its top drug, Tagamet, had been overtaken by Glaxo's Zantac - which was much the same in terms of efficacy but only required two shots a day to Tagamet's four - and yesterday James Cavanaugh, the head of its US drugs business, had been shown the door. Nevertheless Smithkline had some interesting new products, notably the Dyazide diuretic for high blood pressure and treatments for asthma and hypertension. Stuart's thesis, which was not daft, was that the product range would be complemented by Pitcain's, that Smithkline needed an acquisition to strengthen its position in Europe and that now it needed some new blood as well. What it did not of course need was a new chairman and Peter couldn't quite see even the mighty midget coming out on top of the urbane and distinguished Henry Wendt.

It had not been all that unusual for Freddie to call him at home last Sunday. He often did if there was something in the financial pages that he wanted to discuss; but, going through them all scattered about

Samantha's bed that morning, reeking of fresh sexual activity, over a decadent and late breakfast, more a brunch really, Peter had seen nothing. Nevertheless there had been a message on his answering machine when he got home early that afternoon.

"Alan invited us to dinner last night at his castle in Kent. These vegetarians are very odd coves at the best of times but he's about the oddest. He eats game you know, but that's fuck all use at this time of year. If I'd remembered I'd have asked him to fit us in a fortnight later. But he splices a damned good bottle of claret, just the same.

"Anyway, that's by the by. It was a pretty big gathering, a third politicos, a third academe, a third general ne'er-do-wells like yours truly, but they all got well rat-arsed, including our host and his interminably suffering wife. I reckon he'd probably bedded a good half the ladies at dinner, Jemima no doubt included. Anyway Jane, lovely girl. I was going to say I can't understand why she hasn't left him - but I suppose it's pretty obvious. He makes me look like a pauper. And he's a damned witty rogue for all that his prick usually has the upper hand. Anyway, he came out to our car with us when we left. Just as well, I don't think I could've found it on my own. To be honest I was in no state to navigate, let alone steer a steady course, but Jemima, God bless her, was even worse. Alan and I exchanged a bit of gossip and by the time I slid in behind the helm she was asleep.

"The upshot is that the MMC have sent their report in to the DTI and, would you believe it, they've come out against it. Turned it down on grounds of diminution of competition in pharmaceutical research."

"That's bloody incredible, Freddie. Fantastic news."

Freddie could not have known how fantastic. Four million fucking quid. Now all he had to do was find a way to pick it up in such a way that Nigel Lawson couldn't get his podgy mitts on forty per cent of it. Never mind that it would have been sixty per cent a few weeks ago. He was sure there was some wheeze about going abroad for a full tax year. He thought he could bear to sit it out in the Turks and Caicos Islands if Sam would come with him. To think he had nearly lost her; and all for nothing.

"Have you told the dwarf, Freddie?"

"No. I thought you and I might keep it to ourselves for a few days. It's sure to be announced within the next week or so. There's apparently a cabinet reshuffle in the offing which might hold it up for a couple of days. You know these buggers can't even put in an hour or two in the office while there's greasy-pole-climbing going on. But it won't do him any harm not to know until then and there's always the danger he might blurt it out to someone. This is one particular source I don't wish to risk compromising."

"I might just tell Rod King. He can keep a secret."

Rod was out playing football in the garden with his kids. His wife called him to the phone. Peter could hear the kids' shrill protests in the background, deprived of their goalie.

"Mum's the word as regards shortie, Rod, but Freddie's had word that the MMC have come out in your favour."

"Well, Mr Smart Alec, didn't I tell you we put in a damned strong case. I think it's my turn for a toldya so."

"You go right ahead," said Peter laughing, "but need I remind you that you wouldn't have got in front of the MMC at all if I hadn't nailed that shit Snaithe."

"Okay, okay. Of course, John Addey would dispute that - and I've got his bill to prove it - but we'll call it deuce. But what now? Can anything go wrong from here?"

"Well it could in theory but it's bloody unlikely. In a few days' time we'll get a call from some twerpish functionary to say that his lordship, the Secretary of State, will be graciously pleased to make an announcement at 8.30 the following morning and would we please ensure that we are hanging over the screens for that event respectfully tugging our forelocks. And then it'll all be over and I shall be pleased to send you my fee note."

The cabinet reshuffle had come on Tuesday. It had some relevance to their case and might explain a few days' delay. Kenneth Clarke was moving out of the DTI, where he had been number two - what he liked to call 'Lord Young's representative on earth' - to take over the Department of Health, also relevant. Tony Newton was taking over at the DTI.

"Here it comes," shrilled Elspeth excitedly as it came up on the screen.

'Secretary of State gives clearance for BMP to bid for Pitcairn.'

Peter stared at the monitor. He felt immediately sick, disoriented, barely able to read the text as it flashed up. The kids were all excited, exultant actually, wanting all along to fight a proper fight, right through to the sixtieth day, not content with a mere technical knockout. They were loving it. He couldn't bear it. Testily he sent them back to their desks with an "Okay, you've got plenty of work to do now" before settling down to read the text.

Freddie had been right. The MMC had recommended against, albeit only by a majority, with two dissenting voices, and the politicians had overruled them. The Secretary of State was entitled to do so; though it was rare. Taking orders from on high? One way or another, Arthur Evans and Tory Central Office had got their way.

Hennessy was apparently still doing the English season with another day at Goodwood, this time for his legal friends. During Peter's fourth or fifth telephone conversation of the day with Rod King, George Aladyce had come on the blower to say that the two of them would like a private chat round at their offices that afternoon. Tim, listening in on the earpiece, had been disappointed but nevertheless Peter left him behind.

They sat in George's absurdly opulent gilded office, a ridiculous contrast with its scruffy, rather bohemian, down-at-heel proprietor.

"Pee...pee...Peter, this is an off-the-record did...discussion" George began, after his secretary, having left them tea, departed. "Rod will be mum...mum...mother. Sir...sir...sir...so what happens next?"

"Well, in simple terms, BMP have got twenty-one days to announce a new offer; and then we start all over again with them having up to twenty-eight days from that announcement to post the formal offer document and up to sixty days from posting to secure a majority of the shares for that offer, or a higher one. You can't put out any new information after day 39 and they must have put their final offer on the table by day 46 - all that of course provided no other company intervenes. If they do, all the competing offers have to adhere to the timetable of the last one out of the traps."

"All that, Pee...Peter, even I know. What I me...me...mean is what are wee...wee...we going to do?"

"By way of defence?"

"Egg...egg...egg...exactly."

"Well, the strategies would include putting forward a profit forecast which would show the offer price to be mean, perhaps an increase in the dividend, some fuller particulars of what's in the research pipeline to allow analysts to justify a higher rate of growth in future profits than is currently assumed, perhaps some measures to cut costs, gear up, return some cash to shareholders, increase market penetration, attack new overseas markets. Then there's the opportunity for knocking copy against BMP, seeking to depress their share price and thus lower the value of their offer. Cast doubts on the benefits of integration. We've got the support of at least two members of the MMC - and the scientists at that. Convince the institutions that there's nothing to be gained, perhaps something to be lost, by having shares in one enlarged company rather than two. And you'll have the opportunity to visit all the major institutional shareholders, put your points face to face, answer any questions they have, demonstrate that you know what you're about."

Rod had poured the tea and handed it round. George sat po-faced.

"And," he said at last.

"And what?"

"Wee...wee...will that work?"

"A realistic opinion, Peter," Rod added. "No bullshit."

"It might."

"No fer...fer...fucking bullshit, Peter," George repeated, his voice now raised.

Peter felt sick again. He'd been going through all this over and over again in his head all day.

"No," he said at last, "to be honest, I think not."

"That's what we think too," Rod said.

"And." It was George again.

"And then we'll have to decide whether to press the white knight button. See if we can get a better offer from somewhere else."

"Not quite that simple, is it pee...pee...Peter? It takes two to tat...tat... tango, doesn't it? We won't get another come...company to make an offer just because we'd like them to. If we could get him to come...come...come just like that, we'd all be round pulling Geronimo's wire right now, wouldn't we?"

"True, but companies often take a different view about making an offer if they know they're welcome."

"But there's not much worse for egg on chairman's face than making a recommended offer as a white knight only to find that the shareholders opt for the bugger who's opposed. Isn't that so, my friend?"

400

"Well, of course you're right, Rod; but one would hope that one could tell a preferred suitor things that would remove some of the uncertainties of the bidding process. Not in so many words. That's not allowed of course. You're supposed to give everyone the same information. But there are ways and means. The three year forecast accidentally left open on the table when you go to take a leak. That sort of thing. Justify the white knight tossing the highest price into the ring. Let him think he's doing the right thing by paying up."

"Pee...Peter, I've been in this mim...mim...malarkey thirty odd years now. I reckon I know jew...jew...just about everyone there is to know in the industry - certainly on the research side. Would it surprise you to know that in the ses...ses...seven odd months since Evans bid for us, non...non...not one pup...pup...pup...person has cast a fer...fer...fly over me about beeb...beeb...being a white knight? Not a fer...fer...fucking one?"

"Perhaps they've gone to the chairman."

"Peter, we're off-the-record remember." It was Rod. "Don't be a fucking prat. Who'd go near that runt when they'd been in every brothel from Bangkok to Bogota with George?"

"Strictly for research purp...purp...purposes, you understand."

"Okay. So you've also concluded that a white knight's going to be hard to find. Are you saying you want to roll over? Sue for peace? Get the best terms possible? A few seats on the board? Three year rolling contracts? I might warn you that Arthur might not be feeling so generous now you've given him the run around all these months."

"I hope you haven't gone soft on us, Peter. It's not too late to find another adviser, you know."

"I'm all for fighting, Rod. There's never been a bid I want to win as much as this one. But you asked me what are the chances and I've told you."

"You've given us the cun...cun...conventional defence and we agree it whoa...whoa...won't work. Now fififind us something that fer...fer...fucking will."

"George and I are going to fight this, Peter. And we're not fighting with one arm tied behind our back by that pious pint-sized bigot that we happen to have for a chairman. We'll use all the usual means; but we're not going to stop if we have to fight dirty. I told George that I thought that was your speciality. I hope you're not going to disappoint me. Now are you with us or not?"

What had he got to lose. One way or another, he was increasingly feeling that this was his last year in the City. It certainly would be if Pitcairn won.

"Sure. Let's go for it," he said.

"Right. War...war...what do we do?"

"George, it's not that simple. Well, in essence it is. We have to stop BMP acquiring our shares. A large number of shareholders will accept the offer and a large number will not. It's what happens at the margin that counts. How many shares they can buy in the market. To stop that our share price has to be above what they're allowed to pay in the market - the value of their cash offer - and they'll be trying to find ways to get round that one if need be. As I've said, depressing the price of their shares would help because it reduces the value of a share exchange offer or the price at which they can underwrite their shares to provide a cash alternative. But fundamentally, when you've exhausted the conventional means of attack and defence, it's the operations in the market that are critical. And for that you need huge amounts of firepower, either to buy shares at prices above what they're worth or to sell them at prices below what they're worth.

"The Guinness pranksters were doing both. They had people buying Guinness shares to keep the value of the offer above where it would otherwise have been and they had others buying Distillers shares at above the value of the offer and then taking a loss by selling them to Guinness at the offer price. For us it would in principle have to be the other way round - selling BMP shares short to depress them, buying Pitcairn shares to keep them high. But the amounts involved can be huge. And without certainty of result. For all I know the other side in Guinness were at it too. Who knows?. And now it's all been exposed, it's also damned difficult. The same names used to appear over and over again - the usual suspects. Ronson cropped up in Guinness but he was also a buyer of Debenhams shares to accept the Burton offer. Sir Ralph Harris was with him on that one. People have alleged that Halpern, the five-times-a-night knight of Burton, might have needed to return a favour. Then there are all the Americans - Boesky, Milken, Lindner, Riklis, Saul Steinberg, Tisch, Perelman, Icahn - plenty of others wanting to make a fast buck too. And now of course they look at everything that Roger Seelig or Patrick Spens was ever involved in. There's a good deal of tittle tattle that it was only the scale of the Guinness exercise that made it different to standard underhand practice."

"Sir...sir...so what are you going to do for us?"

"Right now, I don't know, George. We've got to find something different or somebody different. These chaps are all running scared. Sure they might be able to steer some deal through a Liechtenstein anstalt or a Caymans trust; but what for? These men are all billionaires. Why risk five years in a dungeon to make another ten million dollars out of you? The important thing, from my point of view, is to know where I can find receptive ears. Your chairman sometimes makes me feel like a leper."

They were all silent for a while, hopelessly racking their brains for something new.

"Have you done anything more about the lady with the monkeys, George?" Peter said at last.

"Not yet. She's away on a cun...cun...conference the week after next with most of her teat...teat...team. I thought that might be the opportunity to have a sneak around at my leisure. But I wouldn't hold out any hope. She's an impe...pe...peccable record of research."

"Maxwell?" It was Rod.

"Now you really are digging deep. He's got the money. He wants to play. He's got a Liechtenstein anstalt where he can hide his dealings, he doesn't give a monkey's nuts for the rules; but is his a bed you want to share?"

"Isisis there all that much did...did...difference between his and our...our...Arthur's?"

Monday, 15 August, 1988

She announced the new offer at 8.30 after a mercifully unsuccessful effort to persuade the institutions to sell her some more of their shares. Not that the offer wasn't serious enough. She'd really got the gloves off now. When BMP's previous offer of three of their shares for every five Pitcairn had been sent to the MMC it was worth about 350p per Pitcairn share. During the months of inactivity since, the market as a whole had gone nowhere and Pitcairn had drifted off to 328p. The announcement that BMP were cleared to bid again had shot them up to a shade over 380p but ominously BMP shares had risen too, albeit not as sharply, so that they now stood at 605p bid and 615p offered. The new offer was two BMP shares for every 3 Pitcairn and was worth almost 407p per share. And she'd got David Carradine round at Wagstaffs to organise an underwriting to provide a full cash alternative of 385p per share. Next day, Lex, under a heading *'Pitcairn under pressure'* was as usual on the button.

> *Having cleared the MMC hurdle, albeit with the aid of political sleight of hand, BMP's new offer for Pitcairn, though rejected as adamantly as its earlier approach, is clearly more than the sighting shot with which Lord Evans launched his campaign to create a British pharmaceutical powerhouse back in January. That said, the unwillingness of any institutions yesterday to sell out to the higher offer indicates unanimity that BMP has another shot in its locker. Shareholders will want to see if the new management's*

defence includes a forecast of the long-awaited improvement in Pitcairn's performance. Even if it does not, it will not have been lost on analysts that, at the present level, BMP needs less than £20 million of annual pre-tax savings on combined turnover of £4.4 billion to avoid dilution in earnings per share. That hardly looks a tall order for a man with Lord Evans' track record and accounts for the continued strength of BMP shares. Meanwhile the arbs were out in force again yesterday, driving Pitcairn's shares at one stage above 420p. It also looks safe to assume that Robert Maxwell's idiosyncratic intervention in this affair is not yet at an end.

They had been on permanent alert ever since BMP had been given the go-ahead and the defence committee was in session, as was now the case every weekday morning, round at 5 St James's Square when Oliver Quentin-Archard phoned through the news that it had gone up on the screen. They had the usual riposte, already on the stocks - wholly inadequate and conceptually flawed - out within the hour. Christopher Hennessy, marching up and down Pitcairn's absurd Versailles board room like a strutting little Napoleon, clearly thought that he had everything under control.

Justin Travers-Coe, on the phone to his dealing room at ten minute intervals throughout the meeting, was coming back with news which increasingly indicated other forces at work. Morgan Grenfell Securities had been active in the market even before the announcement - no doubt alerted by Wagstaffs' efforts to prise shares loose of institutional holders - and were undoubtedly adding to the Captain's holdings.

"How much do they think Maxwell's picked up this morning?" Peter asked.

"Well, they think Morgan Grenfell could have got as much as 25 million shares - that's getting on for four per cent. If it's all for Maxwell, he could be getting close to ten per cent by now. But it seems to me unlikely that it is him. He's just bid the best part of $2.5 billion for

Macmillan and, according to the *FT* this morning, he's sitting on his yacht in Corsica. He flew a whole bunch of journalists out there yesterday for a briefing."

"What's your analysis of what he's up to, Peter?" It was Rod.

"I don't think we can take it for granted that it isn't him. That same article said that the Lady Ghislane is bristling with communications equipment and satellite links. I don't think he lets go of a single lever of power wherever he is. And I think he's mad enough to think he can do any number of things at once. And his advisers - Goldmans and the rest," Peter could not resist the barb," are greedy enough to give him every encouragement. As regards Pitcairn, he's so mercurial that I don't think that you can assume that he's made up his own mind what he wants to do yet. He's quite capable of thinking this idea of forming his own pharmaceutical grouping is feasible; but, at the same time, he'll reckon he's got little to lose by putting himself in a position to be the power broker if that comes to naught. He's got to be taken seriously. If it is him, he's spending big money - getting on for £100 million this morning to add to the £130 million odd he spent back in January/February - but he's also sitting on a fat profit on what he bought back then."

"Up to £30 million by my reckoning," said Tim Phillips, after a few seconds on his Hewlett-Packard. He was wearing a black tie in mourning for the death of Enzo Ferrari over the week-end and was obviously not at his sharpest.

"Only at the current market price," Charlotte Mulder corrected him. "If he picked up his original holding at an average of 350p and today's at 420p, he'd only be showing about £10 million profit if he had to accept BMP's cash alternative. That would barely cover his dealing and financing costs."

"Sure, he's a gambler," Peter came back, a little irritated by her intervention. He didn't want anyone there, and particularly Hennessy, who now seemed to hang on her every word, underestimating what danger Maxwell presented. "He's gambling that, at worst, he can force BMP higher. Or someone else. That hardly seems unreasonable. If BMP are having trouble finding shares to take themselves above thirty per cent on the forty-sixth day, a holding of around ten per cent would have critical importance."

"Remind us of the significance of that," asked Hennessy, for a moment pausing in his perambulation of the room. The little runt, Peter concluded, had not been studying his Take-over Code as diligently as he claimed. Perhaps his prick was getting in the way.

"The forty-sixth day is the last on which an offer can be revised, Christopher," Peter obliged, deliberately addressing his reply to the chairman personally, notwithstanding his inference that there was a general need for enlightenment. "An offer made by someone who already holds over thirty per cent of the shares has to have a less stringent acceptance condition, and no others - basically they can't back out simply because more than fifty per cent but less than ninety per cent of shareholders have accepted the offer. So they could end up with awkward continuing minority shareholders who prevented them from integrating the two businesses. At the same time, because you can't revise your offer after Day 46, it follows that you can't increase a holding of less than thirty per cent to one of more than thirty per cent after that day. You're effectively prevented from buying control in the market."

"Quite so. Quite so," Hennessy quickly asserted. "It's important that everyone on this committee is aware of that. And with BMP already holding 14.9%, buying a Maxwell stake of around ten per cent would get them most of the way there."

"Precisely," Peter confirmed, confident that the implications of this little exchange had not been lost on the professionals round the table.

"But we don't even reach Day 0 until they post the offer document, do we?" speculated Hennessy, compounding his already apparent lack of technical competence.

"Indeed."

"Peter, what's your view of when they're likely to post now?" It was Freddie. "It has some relevance as to how we try to get the Press facing fore and aft."

"Well, I can't think they'll want to hold it back very long. The underwriting costs will be ticking now and you only get twenty-eight days for your original outlay. After that it's a further quarter per cent for every seven days. That's over £6 million by my reckoning. I think BMP will want it out as soon as possible.

"The other consideration, though, is how the sixtieth day would fall. In my view, Grossmanns will want that ideally to be a Sunday and for that, they need to post on a Wednesday. It seems pretty unlikely that they'll be able to get it out within forty-eight hours from now; so I suppose I'd go for Wednesday week."

"But they didn't post on a Wednesday last time round, Peter." The chairman's memory was not, after all, to be underestimated. "And you at least would have said, I seem to recall, that they should have had no reason to expect a reference to the MMC." So he had taken Peter's not so gentle belittling on board.

"You're right, Christopher, and frankly I don't understand why they didn't. It's not universal practice; but there are a number of advantages to ending on a Sunday, particularly if the outcome is likely to be close. First, it means that every acceptance coming in by post has to be there by Friday, or Saturday at a pinch, and that gives extra time for checking - even more important with a big share register like yours. No bidder wants to fail simply because his registrars haven't had time to do all their sums; but some have. Even more critical, if the count on Friday shows the bidder one or two pips short, he's still got time to contact institutional shareholders who haven't accepted - and they'll have all the home numbers of the relevant managers - to try to effect some last minute changes of mind. Maybe they were more complacent first time round; but I don't reckon they will be now."

To be honest, he had expected some intuitive help from his contacts with Samantha; but she was being staggeringly enigmatic. She maintained effective radio silence for days at a time - her mobile switched off - so that he was on tenterhooks waiting for some development that never came. Then she would come on the line, as she had done on Sunday, offering to be round at his apartment by bed-time. They had set off for their separate offices on Monday morning, after another wonderful night, as if it were any other day, and an hour and a half later she had the offer on the screen. While he had been hoping merely to be provided with some clues, she was positively using these mobiles as another tool in their professional conflict; and, as in most things, Peter was finding, she was a damned sight better at it than him.

As he had suspected all along would be the case, he was finding the strain of it all horrid. She seemed, perhaps much as he had been six or seven years before, to be enjoying every minute of it and the fact that she was doing battle with him apparently just added to the piquancy of the experience, every experience - the bid, their relationship, their feverish and frantic couplings. Together, he was constantly biting his tongue to avoid forbidden territory; she was apparently oblivious, gabbling on huskily about anything and everything, what films she'd seen, what galleries she'd visited, what books she'd read. How did she find the time? He was almost resentful that she could have a life apart from him, and be able to enjoy it. He just wanted to be with her.

But she'd had a low point too. On 3rd July she'd been at Wimbledon with Lars for the men's final between Becker and Edberg. It had started four and a half hours late and had to be stopped after only five games as the rain resumed in torrents. By the time she got Lars back to his flat in Knightsbridge, he was shivering uncontrollably and she sent for his doctor. They whisked him straight into hospital but he went into a coma that night. On 21st July, a foul damp month in which it rained almost every day and which eventually turned out to be the wettest for two generations, he finally succumbed. She allowed herself barely a week of sadness, like some throwback to her renounced catholicism, before BMP's clearance to bid again suddenly lifted her spirits and away she went again.

But, whether or not it was the association of rain and death or the sun-drenched memories of Turtle Island, she kept on saying how they should plan a winter holiday together in the sun. She never said "when this is all over" - she never made a reference even as oblique as that to their present predicament - but that was the implication. And it gave Peter an idea. But it was a dangerous one which would require him to share a confidence.

Rod motioned to Peter as the meeting broke up. Once certain that Hennessy had disappeared into his office and having sent Tim and Charlotte back to base, Peter took the lift to Rod's suite up on the third floor. The secretary showed Peter straight into Rod's office. George was already there. He hadn't been at the defence committee. His primary job was nominally to mind the shop; but Rod had been busily briefing him.

"Tit...tit...time to contact mum...mum...Maxwell, do you think, pee...pee...Peter?"

"Personally I think not. I agree that there's a risk that he just sells out to BMP but I think it would be a betrayal of his Jewish roots.

Did you see that article about him in the Observer column last week? Apparently he was on Israeli television dishing out some shit that his role in life was to help mankind. How, if he was a woman, he'd be constantly pregnant because he can't say no. And how he'd been offered a peerage but had turned it down. He's a born spinner of yarns, a born gambler and a born trader. And I can't see him selling out to Evans until he's asked us whether we've got a better offer. And there's no reason for a white knight - whatever your scepticism, George - to do other than take a general interest until he's at least seen what BMP are likely to have to pay in order to win."

"Anyway, Peter, that's by the bye. I was just talking to George about him because that's what cropped up today. We really wanted to bring you up to speed on Dr Cunningham."

"It's basically no die...die...dice. Not that she'd told us the truth, or not all of it. She may or may not be about to lose a pipipipile at Lloyds. I've no way of knowing. It seems to me just as likely that she thought of having a pup...pup...punt to restore her fof...fo...fortune as that she sold our shares because she thought she'd lost one. But she certainly had some reason to buy pip...pip...pip...pip...Pitcairn shares last November. She thought she had an HIV vaccine or at least one that worked for the simian equivalent of HIV, SIV. You remem...mem...member I said that her team were trying to develop vaccines that they then gave to macaque monkeys and then expo...po...po...posed them to SIV by injecting it into their bloodstream. And then the whole experiment went down the pap...pap...pan when one subject that had been given the vaccine but not exposed went down with it. Implicay...cation - vaccine caused infef...fef...fection. Well it di...di...did but it di...di...didn't."

"You've lost me, George."

"A mum...mum...monkey did go down with SIV but it was in a third group which was not given the vaccine but which was exposed to SIV. The object was to be able to compare the results of treating with the vaccine and not treating with the vaccine in subjects similarly exposed. With a view to seeing if the vaccine delayed the onset of SIV even if it did non...non...not give permanent protection. Somehow or another there was a co...co...cock-up. These subjects are all given code numbers - they're electronically tat...tat...tagged with a chip just under the skin - and, as fer...fer...far as I can see, two digits in the code were transposed by some lab assistant feef...feef...feeding the results into the computer. As a result this subject was originally assumed to be in the group vaccinated and not exposed and not in the group vaccinated and exposed or, as was the truth, in that not vaccinated but exposed. She fur...fur...found the error herself at the end of November and seems to have got very excited - her notes indicate that she thought it was a real breakthrough. But a week later another subject in the vaccinated but not exposed group was confur...firmed to have gone down with SIV and the whole experiment fer...fer...fucking fer...fer...fell apart."

"Bugger. I was convinced there was something about that woman that was going to be useful. Certainly more useful than a bit of insider trading gone belly up. I'd even asked Peter Harrington to send me round his file on the woman, just to see if anything would ring a bell. I'll give him a call and tell him to forget it."

"Any brainwaves yet?" Rod enquired.

"Just a thought about profit forecasts. I know you don't think what you can put forward for the year to March '89 is terribly exciting - and, from what I've seen so far, I agree. What about trying to do a detailed forecast for the year to March 1990? It would be virtually unprecedented to go that far into the future and we might have to put the auditors over a barrel to get them to put their stamp on it - but I guess there's a price for everything. We could even make a virtue of a flattish current year by pushing some of this year's profit into the following year, making it look as if things were really about to take off then."

*****

There was another meeting of the Brothers' corporate finance directors that evening. Things had got no better. Branson had indeed decided to take Virgin back private and Dundas would have no role in it. Bill had also made a big push to get appointed to advise the water authorities in the forthcoming privatisation; but it had been announced at the beginning of August that it had gone to Rothschilds. Bill was incandescent and had set Seymour the Serpent off on another wild goose chase to find an alternative bidder for RHM, which was being pounced upon by the Australian company, Goodman Fielder, already holding thirty per cent.

Three months had now elapsed since the Drexel approach. In the interim Graeme Kent, Bill had observed to Peter, had been "oop and doon to Stephen Gallaher's oofice moor ooften than a whoor's drooers". But there was no reason to believe that Gallaher had been alerted to Bill's discussions with Milken, which continued, albeit at the glacial pace on which the directors had insisted. This evening Bill was intent on bringing things to a head.

"We've bin fooking aboot with Milken for three moonths now. Absolootly noothing has coom of all this crap aboot the SEC bringing charges and I think it's time we got oon with it. Oor business is wastin away and we're recrootin noo one. We've goot a proopoosal from Drexel ninety per cent complete and I think Peter shood goo oover to Los Angeles at the end of next week - the bank hooliday weekend when noo one will miss him - and fill in the gaps. Then we take it to Crusoo and get the hell oot of this sinkin ship."

"I'm sorry, Bill," Peter jumped in frantically. "I can't get away while this Pitcairn thing's in progress. Hennessy would go apeshit if I even suggested it."

"Well who shood goo, then?"

"I think you should, Bill." It was Graeme Kent. Was it genuine or was this his push for power? He'd apparently played it clever so far in keeping it from Gallaher. He more than anyone would know if there was a future for an independent Dundas Brothers. It seemed unlikely. Cruso had more or less told Davenport as much. He only needed time. But Kent would know if there were other potential partners in succession to RheinHeim and whether CFD would have a future with them. If there were, he now had the opportunity to get McAdam hoist, as the leader of this bid for independence, and then present himself as the loyal alternative.

Bill was shrewd enough to see all that and cunning enough not to be caught.

"Ookay, Graeme mun. You coom with me."

There was a chorus of agreement from the rest of the directors, who had been tensely waiting to be fingered. This was brilliant. The two men in the department they all most feared forced to present a united front, unable to pitch separately for their support. But Peter Davenport breathed a sigh of relief for a different reason.

*****

Wordsworth Wallis occupied a little Georgian property to the north of Fleet Street, conveniently placed for El Vino's, one of Freddie's many favourite watering holes. Peter had been to the offices for lunch a few times, to their pre-Christmas cocktail party (though he had missed last year's courtesy of Bottley) and to the odd press conference in the basement suite. But he had never before been in the inner sanctum of Freddie's office. On this occasion, however, he was a supplicant.

To be exact, it wasn't Freddie's office but the partners' office with one simply enormous antique mahogany desk at which they sat face to face, all of ten feet apart. Wallis, mercifully, was absent. He took his holidays in August, or had since Freddie's sailing days were over and he no longer attended Cowes week. Freddie went to Cowes for other purposes these days and with greater frequency.

It was basically the drawing room of a Georgian townhouse, simple but elegant with three tall sash windows overlooking the little courtyard outside. One of those tasty peaches and cream Sloane Square girls with which all PR offices seem to be replete brought them tea. They sat in a couple of deep soporific armchairs in one corner of the room in front of one of two exquisite fireplaces with carved wooden surrounds. Peter had the feeling that afternoon naps were frequently taken there.

"Well, Peter, to what does our humble wardroom owe this unusual and mysterious visit?" Peter had called Freddie from the taxi on his way back to Gracechurch Street from St James's Square that morning. He had refused to tell Freddie's secretary what it was all about and then, to Freddie's surprise, after she put him through, Freddie himself.

Peter was fighting embarrassment.

"Freddie, I need to confide in you and to ask you a great favour."

"My dear boy. What has got into you? Have you got some gal in the family way and are looking for the name of a friendly gynaecologist? Have you fallen victim to John Addey's charms and think you've got Aids? No surely not. Have you got a dose of the clap? I would have thought George Aladyce was the best chap to turn to for that. Don't tell me you've been rodgering Claudia Hennessy and our minuscule client has caught you in flagrante. Or he's been rodgering that comely assistant of yours. Now that, I shouldn't wonder, is more likely from the way I've seen him looking at her. I can't think of much else, on a personal level, where an old fart like me would have any experience with which to help you. And I thought you'd been looking so much better recently. You were a real wash-out back at the start of the year, when this storm first blew up."

"It's really much more embarrassing than any of those, Freddie."

Friday, 26 to Monday, 29 August,1988

The flight down to Nice Côte d'Azur was as chock-a-block as you would expect for the Friday afternoon preceding a bank holiday weekend. Peter found himself wedged between a French boy of around ten or twelve, apparently unaccompanied, and a slightly familiar looking woman in her late thirties, rather smartly dressed in a beige cotton suit with a Hermès scarf at her throat. Carol Galley, he asked himself. He couldn't be sure. Her fame as Mercury Asset Management's star fund manager and the fear generated by the ruthlessness of her decisions on successive take-over bids meant that he'd seen her photograph in the papers often enough; but he'd never had any direct dealings with her. Just the same, it was enough of a suspicion to keep him from his plan to have a flick through Peter Harrington's file on Mrs/Dr Cunningham. His call to tell Harrington Ingram to forget it had crossed with the messenger. Now that he had it, he had thought he might as well give it a flick through. He abandoned himself to *The Economist* instead.

The Goodman bid for RHM had been referred to the Monopolies Commission by Lord Young the week before. To Peter's surprise, *The Economist* had let the opportunity for a sardonic comment on government inconsistency go by and had merely reported the facts. 'The DTI,' it said, 'is worried by the amount of debt the Antipodean buccaneer wants to take on board.' Officially there were said to be 'possible effects on competition, especially in the market for bread, arising out of the financing of the proposed acquisition'. Bread for heaven's sake. Young was a 'let them eat cake' sort of man. It was palpably as daft a decision as Pitcairn had looked at the time and, after a huge hoo-ha by MPs, it had been clearly made on political grounds. Peter wondered if John Addey had again been involved.

415

The miserable sandwich and dishwater tea were as bad as only British Airways can manage, worthy aerial successors to British Rail in the paean of rotten British catering to captives. The French boy waved them contemptuously away, asked for a Perrier, and delved into the haversack at his feet to produce a baguette all of a foot and half long, a Swiss army knife and a large bar of dark chocolate. He carefully slit one side of the baguette from end to end, broke the chocolate into squares and distributed them evenly throughout the long thick envelope of bread. Satisfied at last with his creation, he settled down to his croc monsieur au chocolat with considerably more relish than Peter could summon for what had been set before him on a flimsy plastic tray.

The driver who deposited him on the quayside in Monte Carlo harbour an hour and a bit after landing was every bit as avaricious as the reputation of the Nice taxi mafia required, parting Peter from the equivalent of not far short of a hundred pounds and vocally unimpressed with his modest tip. Wandering Cloud, Freddie's sixty-five foot motor cruiser, was moored stern to the quay and at the top of the passarelle, on the open canopied aft deck, stood the unmistakable and, as usual, spectacularly attired figure of Madame Maxine Dubarry, Freddie's boating factotum. Peter had met her a couple of years back when he and his girlfriend of the time, and a couple of other guests, had enjoyed a week of Freddie's hospitality aboard. Freddie had been accompanied by his Royal Yacht Squadron 'wife' and between them they had put Peter through a sufficiently intensive course of seamanship and navigation as to give Freddie confidence that his pride and joy would be safe with Peter, under Mme Dubarry's guidance.

Maxine Dubarry, who was all of fifty-five and well-rounded, dressed to around half her age. Her honey blonde hair was in a permanent chignon, worn a little loose, perhaps to match her inclinations. She was a balloon-breasted female with a penchant for items of underwear inadequately engineered for the structural stresses and load-bearing requirements to which they were subjected. Today she was wearing a baggy pair of thin white cotton trousers, lacy at the ankles, and a matching blouse, lacy at the wrists and the deep décolletage. Little of what was beneath this costume was left to the imagination. There was a lot of gold jewellery at her throat and wrist and an elaborate belt of interlinked gold coins. Her shoes, barely more than slippers really, were also in gold and emblazoned with the interlocking G's of Gucci. She greeted Peter as a favourite aunt would a favourite nephew, clutching him to her bronzed bosom and planting a kiss on each cheek.

Peter and Sam were to be installed in the owner's suite for'ard of the saloon and below the flybridge. It boasted a big double bed, roomy teak wardrobes and dressing tables, solid brass fittings and a substantial marble bathroom, in which Mme Dubarry had laid out piles of fresh white fluffy towels. Below the comfortable saloon with its dining table at one end and seating area and chart table at the other, Peter recalled, there were two delightful guest suites, as well as a powerful pair of Caterpillar marine diesels. Aft of the saloon and below the rear deck lay Mme Dubarry's domain and the galley. Freddie had commissioned the boat from a Scandinavian yard seven or eight years before when he decided, after a particularly hairy Fastnet, that his sailing days were at an end. Save for the nuclear power plant which would have been his preferred means of propulsion, it had been built entirely to his demanding specifications, immaculate joinery, pleasing proportions, hedonistic comforts and utter seaworthiness.

"Quand est-ce que la mademoiselle arrive, Pierre?" She insisted on using the French version of his christian name and, although her English was, though heavily accented, more or less perfect, she liked to tease her guests by forcing them to make the effort.

"Une heure, j'espère, peut-être deux. Son vol était vers une heure et demi après le mien."

"Bon, et nous partirons toute suite quand elle arrive. I ave already refuelled and checked zee engines ready for start-up," she said, taking no chances with his comprehension when it came to the technicalities.

Peter quickly unpacked his soft bag, slipped into a pair of shorts, a polo shirt and deck shoes and arrived back on deck just as Sam's taxi drew up, a good while before he had expected. He raced down the passarelle, kissed her fondly, and grabbed her bags from the boot.

"Cinquante-cinq francs," said the driver.

"Etes-vous sûr?" Peter asked, surprised. "I don't understand this, Sam, my taxi was almost 900 francs."

"You didn't come all the way from Nice by taxi, did you, silly? I got the helicopter from the airport. Really, Peter, I can't see the point

417

in the Brothers wanting to make you so damned rich when you've got so little style," she teased.

Peter introduced her to Mme Dubarry. Her French, it was immediately apparent, was infinitely superior to his own, which got her off to a very good start, and her husky tones were ideally suited to the language. But he could see that Mme Dubarry was dubious as to the comeliness of Peter's choice, this straight-laced looking woman in the shapeless grey suit with unattractive spectacles and her hair in a dowdy bun. He sent her down to change whilst he went up onto the bridge to start up the engines. They were planning to slip out of Monaco and head round west to Cap Ferrat where they could anchor for the night in the sheltered waters off the eastern side of the promontory.

It was a perfect Mediterranean summer's day, still the hot side of warm in the late afternoon, with only the lightest of breezes. Behind the harbour, the extraordinary high rise enclave of Monaco, shimmered in an arc of pastel shades, the odd rococo villa, the pink toy-town palace of the Grimaldis, the grand Victorian casino, standing out as exceptions to the universality of the towering apartment blocks perched on the steep-sloping hillsides.

Under Mme Dubarry's watchful and still-bemused gaze, Peter stowed the passarelle, dropped the mooring chain for'ard and watched it sink, slipped the stern moorings and raced back up to the flybridge to ease the boat forward from her berth. Once safely clear of the boats to left and right, he slipped the port engine into reverse and the starboard into forward and, spinning the wheel anti-clockwise, brought her round before engaging forward for both engines and heading slowly out towards the harbour entrance. He heard an audible gasp from Mme Dubarry somewhere astern and suddenly Samantha was at his side, clad only in her emerald bikini bottom, dark glasses and her huge straw hat. She slipped an arm round his waist as he stood at the helm.

"Happy now?" she asked.

"Ecstatic."

Now they were heading slowly down the line of the huge sleek boats of the mega-rich moored, one after another, sterns on to the southern leg of the harbour wall, the bow of the largest of them all, the Saudi royal family's Abdul Aziz, jutting out a couple of hundred yards ahead of them immediately to this side of the harbour entrance.

"Peter Davenport," an announcement suddenly boomed out away above them to their right, impossibly loud, even the electronically-distorted voice grotesquely familiar, "what the fuck do you think you're doing here at a time like this when you should be behind your goddamned desk?"

As one, their faces turned, stunned, to the source of the voice and there, ahead and to starboard, was the massive, graceful all-white form of the former Khashoggi yacht, with her classic elegant superstructure, two satellite pods to port and starboard at the highest point of the stern superstructure. One chain stretched out taut from the gaping black anchor port at her bow, the other still belayed in its housing. The name Lady Ghislaine was picked out in bold golden capitals along the level of the second deck amidships, behind the bridge. And there, on the top-most level of the forward superstructure stood the Captain himself in a huge baggy pair of scarlet swimming trunks and a black New York Yankees baseball cap, a powered megaphone in his right hand, a pair of binoculars in his left, and his round fat white belly trembling uncontrollably with laughter.

"Shit. What if he recognises you too?"

"Peter, you are wonderful. Do you think I dress like this when I go to see him?" she exclaimed, turning towards Maxwell and waving to him with both arms for all she was worth, her naked breasts jiggling at him provocatively.

The Captain blew her a kiss in return as they disappeared from his sight beneath his bow. Peter didn't look back; but she was still in fits of laughter as, a couple of minutes later, they rounded the harbour wall and set out into a mill-pond Mediterranean.

It took them only fifteen minutes at a steady twenty knots to reach Cap Ferrat. Peter headed for the Anse de la Scalletta and edged Wandering Cloud in slowly to a position a couple of hundred yards off the shore. He turned her into the light south-easterly breeze, from which they were largely sheltered by the Pointe St Hospice, checked the depth, multiplied by four, and dropped anchor into the sandy bottom on eight fathoms of chain. He put both engines into reverse and very gently pulled back to ensure the anchor was embedded; then cut the engines.

There were grand villas, secluded in lush gardens, that climbed the rocky cape but no one else was anchored out here. In the sheltered waters, the big boat's rise and fall was barely perceptible.

"I want a swim," she announced.

Armed with the snorkels and flippers that Mme Dubarry had found for them in a big fibreglass box on the aft deck, they slipped off the bathing platform at the stern and splashed out towards the shore. There were masses of fish, shoals of tiny little silver things that swam in clouds, simultaneously changing direction as if somehow orchestrated, different species of dorade, some grey, some pink, some of a bluish tinge with a heavy yellow brow like a fishy early hominid. The water temperature was perfect, cool enough to be refreshing, warm enough to feel no chill even as they emerged after an hour or so of paddling about. There was a fresh water shower on the bathing platform and Mme Dubarry was ready with more piles of fresh towels, these dark blue, as they climbed the few steps up onto the aft deck.

"Est-ce que vous voulez dîner dehors?" she enquired, and then added, having made up their minds for them, "je crois c'est plus romantique. Vous devez vous habiller pour ça. Il ne fait pas froid but de temps en temps, il devient un peu frais le soir."

He put on a pair of navy slacks and a short-sleeved pale blue cotton shirt, she a long white dress, buttoned all the way down the front and provocatively transparent. By the time they re-emerged on the aft deck, the dining table to one side had been laid, apparently for a feast, and on the other side, where there was an upholstered u-shaped sitting area, a bottle of champagne was sitting in a bucket of ice on the low table with a couple of flutes to hand. Peter was just setting about opening it when Mme Dubarry, now in her apron, emerged from the galley. She would have none of it.

"C'est mon plaisir de vous servir cet week-end. C'est pour vous, Pierre, seulement d'être le capitaine. C'est pour mademoiselle de faire ce qu'elle veut, mais, si non, absolument rien."

Sam protested in her fluent husky French that she couldn't leave everything to madame; but for once it didn't look as though she was going to get her way. It was as much as she could do, and a triumph at that, to have Mme Dubarry share a glass with them; but she only wetted her lips before scurrying away to her galley.

They sat and sipped champagne as the sun went down and a pale dusky pink moon rose on the southern horizon, travelling west as it mounted the sky and brightening first to creamy yellow and finally, long after they sat down, to burnished silver.

Just as they were starting to feel peckish, Mme Dubarry emerged to light the wicks in the glass lamps and to summon them to the table. Dinner was a marvel. First there were bright orange courgette flowers stuffed with foie gras and wild mushrooms, a sauce of morilles fit to take your breath away. Then a whole sea bass each, the local loup de mer, with a sauce of melted butter, lemon and fenouil and fat crisp sautéd potatoes. To drink there was iced San Pellegrino for their thirst and for their palates, a wonderful crisp but fruity white Château de Bellet, from the extraordinary chalky vineyards high above Nice. Then there was a plate of local cheeses, exclusively goat and ewe, chèvre and brebis, with hunks of brownish baguette, baked *à l'ancienne* from unrefined flour. And finally, with a glass of muscat, Beaumes de Venise, an exquisite tarte Tatin, not made with those awful floury golden delicious that the French normally favour, but with beautiful crisp granny smiths.

Then there was coffee and calvados and Montecristos and suddenly Mme Dubarry was gone, leaving them to the glittering moonlight, the warm night air, the lights twinkling in the mansions of St Jean Cap Ferrat, the steady, pulsing sweep of the lighthouse on the point, the low far-away buzz of Beaulieu-sur-mer and the sea lapping gently on the hull.

He took her down to their cabin and undid every button, peeling off her panties and stripping her naked. A tear rolled down her cheek.

"You wouldn't believe it, Peter. I've got the curse. It started on the plane. You could set GMT by me normally; but now I'm five days early. I'm sorry," she said, burying her head on his shoulder.

*****

They hadn't pulled the curtains to and he woke early as a shaft of sunlight, streaming from the east through one of the portholes, touched his eyelids. She was still fast asleep, her head framed by the great coppery shield of her tresses. He got up quietly, arranged the curtains as

421

noiselessly as possible, slipped on some trunks and a shirt, and grabbed a handful of small change.

He climbed the few steps up onto the fly bridge and took the cover off the tender, which was stowed on the canopy above the aft deck, and released the fastenings that held it in place. There was a little crane which was used to launch it over the side. He had just worked out how the controls functioned and raised the tender a few inches out of its chocks when Mme Dubarry appeared at the top of the steps from the quarterdeck. She was in pink today - all in pink - shocking pink - tee-shirt and shorts - both far too tight - nipples joyously erect - with more gold bangles, different from the day before.

"Bonjour, Pierre. Est-ce que vous avez bien dormi? Qu'est-ce que vous voulez faire?" she enquired, apparently not at all convinced that he knew what he was doing.

"J'ai pensé que c'est l'heure pour la boulangerie. Je vais aller chercher les croissants."

"Pierre," she said sternly, "je vous ai dit que c'est à moi de faire les choses comme ça. Il y a deux boulangeries, un à St Jean et l'autre à Beaulieu; et une autre au Port des Fourmis, mais c'est terrible. Vous ne savez pas qui est la meilleure."

He looked sheepish.

"Est-ce qu'il n'y a pas possible de me dire?"

"Non," she said with finality, and then softening, "peut-être, mais j'ai beaucoup des autres choses de faire pour mes courses. Si vous voulez, vous pouvez aller vite chez le boulanger et on peut arrêter à Antibes plus tard pour aller au marché là."

"Oui, bon idée," he agreed.

She supervised him as he lowered the tender over the side and gave him strict instructions as to where he was to go and what he was to buy. A couple of minutes later, he was scudding over a flat-calm sea in the direction of Beaulieu, a frothy bow-wave spreading out in his wake.

By the time he returned Sam was already having a swim. She waved for him to join her over towards the shore. When Peter had handed his packages to Mme Dubarry and she had carefully checked and approved the contents, he stripped off his shirt and jumped over the side. Sitting behind the wheel of the tender in the full sun it had already been getting warm enough to perspire and the cool of the water was a sensational tonic. He swam over to Sam. They kissed, long and lingeringly before swimming back out to the boat.

Mme Dubarry had been right about the boulangerie. The croissants were incredible, clearly made with nothing but butter so that they left your fingers decadent with grease. They ate them with honey direct from the comb and washed them down with freshly squeezed orange juice and big cups of dark aromatic coffee.

The capitainerie at Port Vauban-Antibes at first replied over the radio that there were no berths available at Antibes, even for an hour or so; but Maxine Dubarry was having none of that and was evidently sufficiently influential to insist on tying up to the Quai d'Honneur whilst she did her shopping. She was very dubious about allowing Peter and Sam to accompany her. Freddie had apparently laid on pretty thickly the importance of them not being spotted in public together and Madame had embraced the conspiracy as only the French can embrace such things. One could have suspected that national honour depended on her preserving their secret whilst under her care. And Pierre, to her intense chagrin, had already been exposed by that vulgar man in Monaco harbour. Ultimately, however, even she had to accept that Sam this morning was not readily identifiable as the lady who had arrived in Monte Carlo the previous afternoon. On the strict conditions that she would wear her sunglasses and straw hat, she was eventually allowed ashore.

They followed the narrow road through the arch into the old town and walked up the hill to the big covered market, Maxine Dubarry striding purposefully ahead with a huge shopping basket over her arm. She seemed to know every stallholder in the place. Kisses were exchanged with the man with the immaculate pyramids of shiny black aubergines and perfect onions, fat courgettes and tiny shallots. But you didn't buy your tomatoes there. Oh, no. There was a gnarled old lady further down who had tomatoes on the vine but her lettuces weren't as good as the old boy opposite with the pipe and the rusty moustache. Then there was the man with the hams and salamis, who was also on kissing terms. He sold the best parmesan, brought over the border from Italy; but he didn't have the choicest chèvre. That was the old girl up at the end, now confined to a chair whilst her daughter busied herself with the customers. Then there was a young man from Corsica whom she addressed in a dialect so strange as to be incomprehensible, even to Sam, but he had something special in the way of a rosé and Pierre was deputed to carry a little box with half a dozen bottles of which one was an extra virgin olive oil, green as grass. There was a dour middle-aged couple half way up on the right hand side with tapenades and terrines and pâtés de campagne and cooked meats that looked like ambrosia; and they even smiled briefly for madame as they took her money. And the fishmonger who, quite apart from his loups and his dorades and his monkfish and skate, had live crabs, sporting a thick green rubber band about each claw lest they should get ideas about a final nip before their boiling adieu, and prawns and langoustines and lobsters and scallops and bigorneaux and oursins and all manner of strange and twisted shellfish that neither of them could identify.

Finally Madame was satisfied that she had adequate supplies to last the twenty-five odd miles that separated them from St Tropez where further emergencies could be addressed if necessary. They set off back down the hill to the harbour, Peter with the rosé under his arm, Maxine Dubarry reluctantly sharing the weight of her pannier of purchases with Samantha. The handsome young man from the capitainerie on the quay at Port Vauban was the final man ashore to get the kiss on both cheeks treatment and less than a half hour later they were pottering into the broad square bay of the Anse de l'Argent Faux at the southern end of Cap d'Antibes where Peter dropped anchor in around ten metres of water under the rocky cliffs on the north-east shore.

The rosé was chilling in an ice bucket when they came back from snorkelling around the rocks. It was delicious, like a wine of Provence crossed with a chianti, light but peppery and alcoholic. And to accompany it was a plate of crevettes with garlic mayonnaise, jambon with fresh figs and a selection of tapenades and terrines worthy of the wonderful fresh bread with which they ate it.

After a serious and sexually enervated siesta, they emerged again to a knowing regard from Madame Dubarry, who had apparently been lying out on the foredeck above their cabin nominally at least to renew the bronzage of her embonpoint. She was in no particular hurry to put them away, displaying herself somewhat coquettishly to Peter when he asked her for her view on where they should spend the night. St Tropez was the decision but they would anchor off rather than join the scrum in the harbour. She insisted that they be within a quick sprint in the tender of an appropriate source of croissants in the morning; but Madame was also convinced that every other boat berthed there would contain someone intent on discovering her charges' secret and Peter was prepared to humour her. He loved St Tropez as much as anyone without the trippers but it would be seething this week-end and, she was right, an unwholesome proportion of them would be les anglais. The Anse de Canebiers was the spot they selected, about a mile to the south-west of the harbour entrance where they could drop anchor up against the eastern shore and protect their dinner and their subsequent slumbers from any south-easterly swell.

For the moment, however, it was still a flat calm and Peter and Sam took the tender out for an hour or so after they got there to do a little water-skiing. They were both about the same standard but there was no doubt who drew more of the admiring glances from the passing boats. There was always something spectacularly vibrant about a topless girl on a water-ski, like a topless girl on a windsurfer, somehow separated by miles from her modesty; and no one could look more vibrant than this tanned redhead with the long athletic legs, spraying great arcs of water to one side and then the other as she turned this way and that, her coppery hair streaming out behind her.

At least they were getting some exercise between madame's attempts to fatten them up. That night it was an incredible foie gras followed by an astonishing bouillabaisse, which she had prepared from the morning's purchases in Antibes. First there was the thick orange fish soup poured over croutons spread with crushed garlic, rouille and grated parmesan; then the fish which had previously been cooked in it, chunks of red and white fleshy meat, fat langoustine tails and big lobster claws. Then more cheeses, this time a selection of bleux; and finally fresh raspberries and tiny wild strawberries. There was more champagne with the foie and chablis with the fish and a thick red local bandol with the cheese. Heaven could not be far away above the stars twinkling in the sky.

Sam insisted that it was her turn to do the croissant run in the morning. She was gone a while and he was sitting on the aft deck, increasingly anxious, until the tender reappeared around the point. He went down to the bathing platform to meet her.

"What kept you?" he asked.

"Can I have permission to break one of the rules?" she asked in return, stepping out of the tender grinning from ear to ear, as he tied the painter to a cleat.

"Which one?"

"Not talking about you know what - it's so funny," she exclaimed, giggling helplessly.

"Okay," he said, intrigued, already sharing her infectious laughter, though he knew not why. "Go ahead."

"There was a message on my answering machine. 'This is Robert Maxwell'," she imitated, with devastating accuracy, "'that prat Davenport is away for the weekend on a boat in the Med bonking a tart with big tits. If you want to talk about buying my stake in Pitcairn, my dear, now's your chance!'"

They fell into each other's arms, helpless with laughter.

"Can you imagine? There was a man waiting for the phone box and he didn't know what to make of it. I was standing there with the phone in my hand and I almost pissed myself."

Gradually they got control of themselves and Peter stepped back.

"Did he name you a price?" he asked.

"Shit, you're impossible, Peter Davenport," she said, planting both hands on his chest and pushing hard so that he toppled backwards off the bathing platform into the water.

*****

Madame dispatched the crabs later that morning. They had been marching around her refrigerator, she complained, keeping her awake; and she served them for lunch, exquisitely dressed, as they lay at anchor in the Calanque de Maubois. They were on their leisurely way back towards Monaco now. It was another beautiful anchorage with a little beach at its head, 800 metres to the north of Pointe de Cap Roux under the towering bare peaks of the Massif de l'Estérel, pink washed in the afternoon sun.

Another tempestuous siesta, another of madame's understanding looks of sexual complicity, another swim and they weighed anchor yet again. This time Peter set course almost due east, out beyond the Iles de Lérins, with their dense week-end coterie of boats anchored in the narrows between Saint Marguerite and Saint Honorat. When they were far enough out to clear Cap d'Antibes, he turned north-north-east and set course for Villefranche. They had neither of them been able to get late afternoon flights back to London on the Monday and would have to return Wandering Cloud to her berth in Monte Carlo next morning. But tonight they would be at anchor again and madame had commended Peter's choice of the Anse de l'Espalmador on the eastern side of the Rade de Villefranche, sheltered to the south-east again by the bulk of Cap Ferrat.

As if she had to date barely been trying, Maxine Dubarry was clearly intent tonight on something special for their final evening. Sam, though strictly prohibited from doing anything much to help, was normally welcome to join her for a girly gossip in the galley; but not so tonight. The whole thing was under wraps. A cork was pulled from something which she had decided needed a good two hours to breath and they heard the quick staccato chopping of the serious cook as they went forward to their cabin to get out of their wet costumes. An ambrosial smell of fresh herbs and serious baking wafted into the saloon as they went back up on deck to find vintage Krug awaiting them there in the ice bucket. They sat and sipped it in contented silence, his arm around her, her head upon his shoulder. She smelt fantastic. She felt divine. The whole thing was fucking absurd. The day after tomorrow they would be having to pretend again that they hated each other's guts and she, who had laughed with him and loved with him for the last two days without ceasing, would be doing everything in her considerable power to rob him of four million quid.

He was startled out of his nightmare by the shimmering appearance of Maxine Dubarry in her slinkiest number yet, an ankle length backless gold sheath, which hugged every extraordinary curve of her body. She carried a dish piled with scallops which gave off a wonderfully subtle aroma of fresh cumin, ginger and cream. She set it down, summoned them to the table with a theatrical flourish and filled their glasses with more champagne.

The long-pulled cork turned out to have belonged to a 1970 Haut-Brion. Freddie had apparently pronounced this the only way he could get through what he had bought of this particular vintage. He thought

427

he would be long dead before it reached a state of maturity where you could pull the cork and drink it straight away. To accompany it was fillet of beef. It had been peppered and then heavily but briefly charred on the outside, barely cooked within and it was incredible, served with a ratatouille of vegetables that was pure essence of Provence.

There were more wonderful cheeses to follow with the balance of the red wine and finally an astonishingly delicate millefeuille of oranges and lemons, apples and pears, which melted in the mouth.

And afterwards they went up onto the flybridge with their coffee and their calvados and a shared Montecristo and sat on the big comfy bench there watching the stars, his right hand cupped inside her shirt over her firm cool breast. And they pretended it would never end.

Wednesday, 7 September 1988

The defence committee was in session for much longer than usual that morning. She'd got the offer document containing BMP's new offer out on 17th August, a week before Peter had forecast; but timed, as he had suspected, so that the final closing date - the 60th day - would fall on a Sunday. It was now the first closing date - Day 21 - and, though it was inevitable that the offer would simply be extended because there was no possibility of them gaining sufficient acceptances to declare victory today, it looked like a suitable time for a review of progress.

They were all there, even, unusually, George Aladyce. The pretence had apparently been at least partially abandoned that the subject of white knights was taboo. Furthermore, there were developments at Beecham that needed to be aired. John Robb, managing director since Kenneth Keith's boardroom coup in November 1985, had 'resigned' last Friday. Bob Bauman, formerly of Textron, who had been installed as chairman almost exactly two years before, had clearly kicked him out. George had been using his extensive contacts within the industry to find out what had really happened.

"Berb...berb...Bauman has been getting a grip on the reins of power, Christopher, making sure all the chiefs owe their pop...pop...positions to him," he said, addressing the chairman directly with a knowing smile. "The heads of pharmaceuticals, coc...coc...cosmetics and coc... consumer products had all been made to report to him direct, leaving John with bub...bub...bugger all to do. It was baub...baub...bound to lead to a bust-up at some stage. But I think something else is going on too. They've announced that the consumer products division is going to be turned upside down. I think they're getting ready to do something big in pharmaceuticals and it may be us. Whatever it is, it has to be berb...berb...Bauman's plan and not Robb's."

"Should I put in a call to Mr Bauman, Peter?" Christopher asked.

It was the question, and in its most direct form, that Peter had been dreading since the subject of Beecham had been raised that morning. He still didn't have a clear idea whether it was a line of defence that Hennessy could tolerate and, if so, who was his favoured partner. He knew that George would choose Glaxo, and probably Rod too. Would Hennessy prefer to deal with a fellow-American? Or would he consider the cerebral Girolami more his intellectual equivalent. In normal circumstances, Peter would have had more opportunity to search out the answer that the client wanted to hear; but until now, with the chairman at least, the subject of white knights had been off-limits. And he was still convinced that Geronimo was determined to go it alone.

"Could we just first ask George for his thoughts on developments at Glaxo, Christopher," he stalled. "Their results for the year to end June are due the week after next."

"Sure thing," Hennessy came back. "George?"

"I dodo...don't expect their results to be spectacular; but they'll be adequate - certainly by coc...coc...comparison with ours. And that's after spending well over £200 million this past year on research and planning to take that to £450 million by 1993. The research pipe...pipe... pipeline is fur...fur...formidable. The migraine treatment is on track and the product for counteracting nausea associated with chemotherapy for cancer patients. Then there's Fluticasone for inflammation, Sufotodine for ulcers, Interleukin-2 for cancer and Salmetorol for asthma all due within the next few years; and they're followed by a whole string of bib...bib...bits and bob...bob...bobs for schizophrenia and depression and blood pressure and thrombosis and intestinal did...did...disorders that are only known by code numbers at this stage."

"Does that mean they're more to your liking, George?" Peter asked, knowing the answer but wanting Hennessy's own chief executive tied to the white knight rack before he had to commit himself. In terms of his bonus, a white knight was worth double where he stood at present and was as good as he was going to get. A million quid, less 40% tax, wasn't exactly fuck-you money; but it was better than a poke in the eye with a sharp stick.

"I dodo...don't look upon them as an option, pee...pee...Peter," Aladyce neatly side-stepped. "Girolami won't allow any discussion of acquisitions. I have that on goog...goog...good authority, at board level."

"So, Peter?" Hennessy wasn't letting go.

"It would undoubtedly be helpful to know what Beecham are up to," Peter ventured, trying to feel his way carefully through this minefield, "though I have a feeling that too much might be read by them into a chairman to chairman contact - and, of course, by others if it leaked or was leaked out deliberately. It might be better for George to give the head of their pharmaceutical division a call - I'm sure you know each other well," he said, turning towards Aladyce, who had to confirm his suspicion with a nod, "just to ask what's going on. If they have any designs on Pitcairn, one might expect to get a hint."

"I'd go along with that," said Hennessy, maybe appreciative of Davenport's dexterity, maybe simply happy to be able personally to avoid the role of mendicant.

Next they turned to a review of the press. It was running neck and neck at the moment. Few thought that BMP were going to get away without a further increase in their offer but few doubted that they were going to succeed in the end. Freddie had managed to get one or two flattering profiles of Christopher Hennessy into the papers without having to give the journalists concerned access to the Palace of Versailles or allowing them to discover the presence of the absurd Gulfstream. Rod had told Peter that it spent most of its time on the tarmac in the section for private jets at Heathrow, eating its head off in airport charges, but that it was being borrowed most weekends by Stephen Gallaher to fly back and forth to his estate in Ireland. Fortunately it was the silly season for news, and the reptiles were even more than usually prepared, without checking, to be fed with articles for simple regurgitation.

But Freddie, Peter thought, did not seem at his most chipper. He looked tired and peaky, a bit flushed, slightly sweaty. Maybe it was just that it was damned hot today, the sun already high in a cloudless sky, though the air conditioning was humming away quietly beneath some mock Louis XVI decorated panelling in the Pitcairn board room. He'd apparently been at his very best only last Friday when Peter had taken him out to lunch, partly to thank him for the fantastic hospitality that he had arranged for his tryst with Samantha, and partly to celebrate the return to a month with an 'r' in it with a mountain of oysters at

Bibendum, Terence Conran's rather classy restaurant in the old Michelin building at the top of Sloane Avenue.

Freddie had been embarrassingly well briefed by Mme Dubarry, who had not only regaled him with the strange behaviour of the man on *The Lady Ghislane* as they left the harbour at Monte-Carlo, but had also reported the incidence of blood-spattered towels soaking in the bath every morning.

"I gather you spent most of the week-end playing red indians. These ladies never seem to be able to keep these things quite as ship-shape as they should, despite the intervention of modern medical science. Perhaps we should ask George Aladyce to find a solution. Still, I gather you did your bit. You wouldn't think a bank like Grossmanns would employ such a noisy girl. Apparently hollers like a bosun's mate."

"Enough, Freddie," Peter reprimanded him gently. He was a very good friend, though more than twenty-five years his senior; but he could be a bit of a schoolboy. "What do you think of this Chablis?" he asked, trying to change the subject.

"Excellent. Now what I really don't understand is that everyone says this Wilkinson woman's a blue-stocking's blue-stocking, a dreadful harridan. I know that beauty's in the eye of the beholder and all that stuff; but I distinctly remember you once told me yourself that she was well to the ugly side of plain. Now Mme Dubarry tells me she's an absolute stunner."

"She is, Freddie. I told you she wears this disguise. She does it for effect. I can't wait to introduce you."

"Nor yours truly, m'boy. Nor yours truly."

The next item on the defence committee agenda was the profit forecast. Rod had recast it yet again, this time larding the year to March, 1989 with provisions for this and that, disguised as genuine costs, only to discover, as if miraculously, dramatic improvements in margins for the following year. The result was a current year forecast, at £228 million, only six per cent up on the previous year; but a following year, at £294 million, 29% up on that. The auditors, however, simple as they were, had scented a plot and were still playing hard to get.

"I'm not bloody surprised," Martin Lampard had told Peter when he discovered the plan, "and Dundas should be bloody careful too. You'll have to sign off that profit forecast as well as the auditors. If your client gets off the hook, the chances are that no one will ever know any better. But, if BMP win, and let's face it, no one would give you even money right now, I'd advise Arthur Evans to sue the balls off the pair of you when the truth comes out."

Peter wasn't sure that he cared. Either way, he didn't intend to be around when that particular chicken might come home to roost.

"Can you talk to the auditors for us, Peter?" Hennessy inquired. "I'd do it myself, of course, but I fear that anything I say might be misinterpreted as a threat to their retaining the account. As a chartered accountant, I'm sure you're best placed to explain to them that what Rod is proposing is entirely reasonable. And, of course, you'll be taking responsibility for the assumptions behind the profit forecast, won't you? It's only the math that flows from that which is down to them. I'm confident you'll carry them with you."

Next it was a review of the share register, under Justin Travers-Coe's direction. It was another area of potential embarrassment for Peter with DAM's four per cent plus holding assuming ever greater marginal importance as the total stakes of BMP, Maxwell, the supposedly independent Grossmann and Wagstaff funds and known arbitrageurs came to account for a larger and larger proportion of the shareholders' list. Peter already made that figure over 37%. Add in DAM and you were well north of 40%.

The schedule that Justin distributed, like all its predecessors save the first to which Peter had so objected, now analysed the shareholders into six categories - BMP known support, BMP likely support, weak holders, don't knows, likely Pitcairn support and certain Pitcairn support. Many of the original list had gone, bought out by Maxwell's raids or simply sold into the market so that they had disappeared into the hands of various speculative funds. Even some of what might have been regarded as institutions who normally supported incumbent management, had lightened their weightings. Ominously Grossmanns' funds, treated as independent behind their Chinese walls for the purposes of the Take-Over Code, had edged up theirs over the intervening months.

The deal that McAdam and Davenport had done with Sellar to hold back from selling had so far put the thick end of £20 million on the value of DAM's holding at the market price. There was no sign of gratitude on Sellar's part - just a growing haste to lock in his profit. He was constantly ringing Peter to ask if he had found a friendly buyer, reminding him that the indemnity agreement had now expired and that he was increasingly inclined to consider himself a free agent. He wasn't exactly that. Stephen Gallaher's desire to put all his senior executives in their place had led him to agree to Bill's demand that Sellar give 48 hours notice of an intention to sell, and get Gallaher's approval. There was no great sacrifice in that for Sellar, who was in the camp of those who believed that BMP could be induced to pay a bit more, and that, at the end of the day, Gallaher, shrewd enough to know that Pitcairn was going to lose anyway, would welcome the opportunity to irritate McAdam a bit more.

Justin continued to give Peter the impression that he was aware of his discomfiture. Reviews of the shareholders' list never passed over the DAM holding, its loyalty assumed.

"I take it DAM are still on side, Peter," he said on this occasion.

Rod fixed Peter with a knowing stare as Davenport replied.

"That's my understanding from my side of the Chinese wall; but, as I've said before, you must treat them like any other institution. They'll expect to receive a presentation from management like anyone else. I wouldn't expect them to take kindly to you dealing through me."

He knew that in reality these efforts to distance himself from the inevitable were in vain, tossed on the wind to deaf or defiant ears, as the case might be. There was going to be one humungus shit of a row at the end of the day.

*****

The corporate finance directors got together again that evening, officially at 7.00 pm, though Bill didn't turn up until about 7.20 and Amadeo was still on a call to the States that had been going on forever. Bill had angrily called his secretary to get him off the line and send him up; but to no avail. He had eventually started without him, distributing the terms of Drexel's offer. Peter didn't like it at all. The money was good. Seymour was positively drooling. And Kent, who had managed to get out of any personal involvement in the negotiations, Peter thought, by feigning a bout of food-poisoning and who could normally be relied upon to find something objectionable in anybody else's deal, appeared to be warming. Peter just took that as a sign that nothing much else that he was working on with Gallaher was making much progress. Blackstone, never the most imaginative of men, seemed increasingly willing to accept the inevitable.

"Had I been told when I embraced this profession that it would one day revolve around high-yield bonds" - junk was too short a word for William and the concept too imprecise - "I believe that I might have remained an auditor; but perforce one must transmogrify oneself with anno domini."

What bothered Peter was that it all seemed so unprofessional. It wasn't exactly set out on the back of an envelope; but it wasn't exactly a draft contract either. True, the numbers had all become pounds sterling; but there wasn't a shred of Drexel's headed notepaper in sight. He didn't doubt that Bill had seen the junk-bond impresario himself and that Milken and his colleagues had talked of a deal; but he didn't entirely feel that Drexels, who had invented the highly-confident letter in the days before they had the resources to give a firm guarantee, were necessarily wholly committed. And what the Brothers were going to get out of parting with their corporate finance department was not entirely clear either - 'an appropriate sum' was all that Peter could find in the papers. Dundas certainly looked doomed long-term; but, even so, he didn't doubt Cruso's ability to negotiate. Or even to walk away if he didn't get what he wanted. And even with the worst outcome for Pitcairn, Peter personally was going to have a damned good year. He didn't feel inclined to give that up for less than a copper-bottomed contract.

Bill, however, was in a hurry.

"I want yer unanimoos agreement to take this to Crooso. Seymour?"

"Yes, Bill."

"Graeme?"

"Yes."

"William?"

"Affirmative."

"Peter?"

He didn't want to go along with this. At least not now. Even losing Pitcairn, he now stood to gain a £600,000 bonus. Drexel's first year bonus of a million pounds didn't look quite sufficiently certain for the odds to be good enough to ditch that. His Pitcairn bonus, and then Drexel. That would be another thing. He hesitated, wondering how he was going to put it, and at that moment the door opened and Hank Amadeo hurried in. He was flustered, slightly wild-eyed.

"Bill, I got something here you need to know. The SEC have charged Drexels and Milken with insider trading. It's coming over on the tapes just now."

"One cannot claim to have been entirely deprived of divinations of that possibility."

"William, mun, will yer shut the fook up."

*****

They talked on for an hour or so, throwing around other possibilities. Seymour thought UBS were disillusioned with the drones at Philips & Drew and would welcome some merchant banking backbone. Hank was carrying a torch for Citigroup, god knows why. They were clearly already suffering with their purchase of Scrimgeour Vickers, which had, in desperation for more business, begun a competitive narrowing of market-maker spreads only a fortnight before. William knew someone at Lloyds, for whatever that was worth. Kent wasn't participating, Peter suspected, because he already knew the attitude of every party that Gallaher had approached. And Peter, despite Bill's bullying, had had enough of this farce for the moment. He didn't like any of the names being bandied about because he didn't like the City any more. Bill's standby was BZW. They'd tried to pick up Hill Samuel's corporate finance department a year before only to find the whole shebang go to TSB of all people. A dozen of the Hill Samuel men had gone over the wall; but Richard Heley, BZW's head of corporate finance, was still hungry for more.

Bill had more or less forced them into allowing him to return Heley's call when the phone on the little table in the corner of the conference room rang. William, who was nearest to it, could reach it, leaning back in his chair.

"Blackstone. Yes, Maureen. Yes. I see. Yes. Yes. I'll tell him."

He put the phone down and turned to Peter.

"I believe Freddie Wordsworth's working with you on the Pitcairn defence. Maureen says he's just suffered what she should have called a myo-cardiac infarction."

"What the fook's that?" said Bill.

"It's a heart attack, Bill," said Peter, hurrying out.

*****

They'd taken Freddie to St Barts on the edge of Smithfield Market. Peter drove straight round there, parking in the circus of West Smithfield close to The Bishop's Finger. He hung around the hospital for hours, pressurising alternately hassled young house doctors and mature stony staff nurses. None of them would allow him anywhere near Freddie, who was in intensive care. Around 1.00 am, as the throughflow in casualty began to abate, he managed to get a bit of attention. Freddie had suffered a big one. For the moment he was holding his own, though unconscious; but the prospects for any sort of recovery were not good.

"Your friend is significantly overweight," said the young intern, stating the more than obvious in a tone of some reproachfulness. "A heart can only stand so many years of that. There's no possibility of you seeing him before noon tomorrow, if he survives till then. You can give us a call after that to see how he's doing. His wife is with him now."

Which one, Peter thought, but he kept it to himself. He walked slowly back to his car, parked below Weddel House, the old headquarters of Union International, the Vestey empire. He'd worked on the audit there from time to time back in his years as an articled clerk. It was a monstrously inefficient, old fashioned, almost Dickensian establishment and in those days hordes of articled clerks were thrown at the job of ticking away at the mounds of handwritten ledgers. At lunchtime, outside on the pavement in summer, they would spend unconscionable hours downing pints of real ale at what was always known as The Episcopal Digit. No one missed you if you took the odd day or two off and the fee was so large that you could safely fill your time sheet with 'Union' when you were doing nothing in particular. It was what was known as a 'dustbin' job.

The articled clerks had one particular trick that they used to play to while away the time. There was a public telephone box over on the other side of the circus outside the hospital and they used to ring the number from time to time and watch what happened from their office opposite. It was never long before some passer-by, hearing the persistent ringing, would stop and pick up the phone.

"Look, I'm terribly sorry," one of them would say, "but I'm a surgeon and I'm operating in a theatre on the third floor of the hospital here, just a few yards down the road from where you are now. I put my scalpel on the window sill for a moment and it's dropped onto the pavement outside. I wonder if you could just go and pick it up for me and bring it up here.

"Well, I would send a nurse but we're terribly short staffed. One's trying to keep this chap anaesthetised and the other's got a finger on his aorta. If she lets go he'll bleed to death.

"No, I can't come down myself. I've got his left lung in one hand and the phone in the other.

"You can't see me waving to you. Well, I can see you. You're wearing a dark raincoat and a trilby. It's dropped down just by that blue Ford Cortina with the crumpled front nearside wing."

On a good day they could have upwards of a dozen people crawling around in the gutter, peering under cars and searching the pavement on their hands and knees, inch by inch.

Peter smiled. Old Freddie would have loved the story. He hoped he would still have time to tell him.

Wednesday, 28 September 1988

They called off the plan to publish a profit forecast and let Day 39, the last on which Pitcairn was allowed to publish new information in their defence, pass with a lot of bombast but not much substance. Actually, since Day 39 was a Sunday, 25th September, they sent out the circular overnight Friday/Saturday, thus giving themselves the opportunity to put the week-end *Financial Times* and the Sundays in the picture but depriving BMP of the chance to have their response included. There was a ritual howl of protest to the Panel by Grossmanns, claiming that the *FT* journalist had clearly seen a copy of the circular, as indeed he had, whilst the rule required the Panel and the bidder to get it first. Peter brazened it out, claiming that the *FT* had been briefed but no more, confident that the journalist concerned would protect his sources. In Freddie's absence, the redoubtable Wallis had stepped into the breach.

They made the best of a bad job without the profit forecast, publishing detailed projections of sales and margins for individual new products coming on stream over the course of the next couple of years but declining to add up the figures. For good measure, they proposed dividend increases of twenty per cent for each of the current year and the year following. It was sailing as close to the wind as they dare. The stockbrokers' analysts had enough information to put together their own sums, many with some off-the record assistance from the gangling Stuart Robinson. Overall the desired impression of management's confidence in rapid growth two years out was got across without resort to a formal forecast; and Pitcairn were able to put the blame on the narrowness of the Panel rules as the cause, however far that was from the unvarnished truth. The Panel were very unhappy about it all and kept on mumbling about retractions; but they couldn't find what exactly Pitcairn was meant to retract.

In truth, there had been more fighting within the defence team than between the supposed protagonists. Peter had tried very hard to do a two-year profit forecast. He considered it no skin off his nose if the whole damned thing was a lie. But the audit partner was absolutely adamant.

"You wouldn't even get a third tier accounting firm to go along with what you're suggesting, let alone one of the Big Five, like ourselves," he had said.

The truth gradually dawned on Peter. BMP, as they grew, had surprisingly retained the services of a little-known firm of accountants. The chances were that Arthur Evans found them more compliant with the deviations from standard accounting practice with which he massaged his results from time to time. But BMP were seeking to become substantially bigger and the enlarged audit was clearly going to be beyond the resources of their incumbent auditors. Who more appropriate to turn to as joint, or perhaps even sole auditors, than those who had been responsible for Pitcairn's audit - provided, of course, that they had done nothing to make themselves unpopular with BMP. Peter couldn't be certain; but he had a more than shrewd suspicion, so hard was this normally unassuming little man digging in his toes, that Arthur Evans had already dangled that particular carrot before him.

And then there was Martin Lampard. He hadn't actually said he would resign as Peter's lawyer; but he had said that failure to heed his advice would make his position "fucking untenable".

"I don't mind you twisting the Panel's tail till the bloody thing comes off in your fucking hand," he had said, drawing deeply on yet another fag, "but this is a matter of tort - and that's my bailiwick. This forecast is a lie and you know it. If Evans sues you over it, there's a good chance he'll blow such a fucking hole in your professional indemnity insurance that you'll all be able to disappear into it up to your sodding armpits."

BMP didn't wait for Day 46 to put out their final offer, but had banged it out today, Day 42 and set the closing date as 12th October, Day 56. It was a rock-crusher - 3 of their shares for every 4 Pitcairn - worth over 461p per share, more than 13% higher than the previous offer and more than a third higher than where they'd started back in January. Even so, as the Press were eagerly urged to note, Evans had to wring less than £50 million a year in savings out of the combined operations to reap an immediate improvement in BMP's earnings per share. A head office here, a research laboratory there, combining the international sales force, firing the Pitcairn board; that sort of number was child's play. And on the back of it, David Carradine had done his bit again, underwriting the whole thing at an even finer discount, to produce a cash alternative of 440p per share, over 14% higher than the previous 385p.

It had been good enough for the Captain who had sold them 64.68 million shares for cash. He had other things on his mind. All that crap about a new pharmaceutical grouping had gone down the pan as he went head to head with KKR for control of the Macmillan publishing group in the States. Yesterday evening he had slammed in an offer of $89 per share in cash - over $2.5 billion in total. Credit Lyonnais and Samuel Montagu were finding most of the money; but the $420 million odd that he had got for selling out Pitcairn would go a long way towards providing Maxwell's own contribution.

It had also been good enough for most of the arbs. BMP had picked up another 40.59 million shares in the market and could now claim a total of almost 31%. There was now no practical obstacle to them buying their way through to control. To aid them in this enterprise, Sellar had called Peter as soon as he saw the new offer, and presumably Gallaher too, to say DAM wanted out.

The defence committee that morning had been a long drawn out but scarcely productive affair. The list of institutions still holding out - the Pearl and the Pru, Scottish Amicable, Britannic, Norwich Union, M&G, General Accident, Commercial Union, Scottish Widows, Standard Life and Barclays Unicorn also contained the funds managed by Mercury, Schroder and Flemings, mercenaries to a man, or woman in the case of Mercury. In total about half appeared in the 'undecided' column on Justin's schedule; and the others in those inclined to support management. But DAM were still shown erroneously over in the Pitcairn camp. Peter did his own separate sums. 30.9% BMP, plus Grossmanns and Wagstaff, 37.25%, plus DAM, 41.4%, plus acceptances already received and not yet withdrawn, 44.65%, plus Mercury, 48.9%.

For once it was Hennessy who called him aside after the meeting and took him into his office.

"You've gotten it into your head that we're going to lose, haven't you, Peter," he said, almost before they were both seated. Hennessy was perched in one corner of his Marie Antoinette sofa, Peter in a straight-backed but ridiculously gilded armchair.

"Oh, I think it's too early to be as gloomy as that, Christopher. There's still two weeks to go and the institutions don't make up their minds until the last minute. In our final push, we've got to persuade them to stay with us."

"And what line of argument have we gotten that we haven't already used?"

"Nothing exactly new, Christopher; but it's only now we've seen their final offer. Seen how much they have to cut costs to justify the price. £48 million pounds a year is half our current annual research bill. It enables us to show that our argument was right all along. Evans is going to decimate the research spend. That's no good for the future of the enlarged company."

"You see, Peter, even you reckon there's going to be an enlarged company."

"I didn't mean that, Christopher. That was just a slip of the tongue. I just meant that, if BMP were successful with the offer, institutions would have to doubt whether growth could be sustained."

"Sure, and if they don't think so, they can take the cash."

"It's not quite as simple as that. Many would have to pay capital gains tax."

"But many would not. The retirement plans - whatever you call them - the pension funds, for example."

"Individual shareholders would all find themselves paying tax."

"They don't call the shots here, do they, Peter? We're talking institutions."

Peter didn't reply. Hennessy got up and walked to the window. He looked out on the sun-drenched leafy square for a while; then suddenly turned around. He dropped his chin to look over his glasses at Peter. They lost their grip on the end of his nose and bounced onto his chest on the end of their string,

"Peter, Justin told me about Dundas Asset Management some weeks ago." He didn't use the abbreviated form either. It was too close to a profanity. "I've had it confirmed by Stephen Gallaher."

"Oh," said Peter.

"It makes Pitcairn's position much more serious, doesn't it?"

"Yes."

"4.15% less in our support and 4.15% more in theirs is a swing of 8.3% in their direction, isn't it?"

"Yes."

"Enough to take them to what by your reckoning?"

"44.65%."

"Mine too."

"I don't think it was smart of you not to tell me."

"No," Peter confirmed."

"Then why didn't you?"

"I was still hoping to find a way to persuade them not to sell."

"And how did you think not telling me would help?"

"I don't know."

"But you haven't found a way?"

"Not yet."

"We're running out of time, Peter. I think you and I should have been working more closely together."

In many ways Peter would have preferred the blazing row he was expecting. He couldn't work out whether Hennessy was putting on a display of christian forgiveness or cold indignation. He put his glasses back on the end of his nose for no particular purpose; for he surveyed Peter again over the top rim.

"Stephen also told me about your bonus."

"Oh."

Shit, he's going to get me fired from the job, thought Peter. I'm not even going to pick up third prize. Shit, shit, oh fucking shit.

"I didn't begrudge it you when I heard about it. I wanted Dundas incentivised and that meant you more than anyone. What are we up to now as regards your share? Three-quarters of a million if we lose, one and a half for a white knight, four and a half for success?"

"About that, a little more," Peter confirmed. He knew the sums by heart. Hennessy was looking out of the window again, his back to Peter. He turned abruptly again. Peter braced himself for the worst.

"Good; then I guess you still have a will to win."

Peter felt weak in the gut.

"Take me through the implications of BMP bringing out their final bid four days early."

Peter tried to gather himself together.

"Well, it's enabled them to set the next closing date four days early too. You remember I told you way back that I thought they would launch the initial bid on a Wednesday so that the 60th day would be a Sunday - and that's what they did. A Sunday closing makes the final count more relaxed, because, for all practical purposes, everything is received by close of business on the Friday. And, in addition, if you still find yourself a couple of pips short, you have the opportunity to bribe or bully one or two of the institutions into accepting over the week-end."

"You're not seriously suggesting they would bribe a fund manager into accepting?"

"I know it's not your style, Christopher," he replied, almost choking on his insincerity, "but this is the real world. It wouldn't be the first time.

"But setting their next closing date on Day 56 is another twist. I think the reasoning goes like this; day 56 is so close to Day 60 that they could well get the vast majority of likely acceptances in by then - perhaps, if they were going well, enough to declare victory. But, if they were close to victory at that stage but still short, they would know exactly what they had to make up. Normally, with a bid that closes on Day 60, all that is guesswork on the part of the brokers; informed guesswork through talking to individual fund managers, but always with an element of uncertainty.

"Now, suppose BMP had a total of 48% on Day 56; they could extend for a further four days and know that they needed to secure just another two per cent during those four days to win. They could get that in a number of ways: they might persuade two per cent more of the shareholders to accept; if the market price of your shares was below 440p, the level at which they're allowed to buy, they might find shareholders willing to sell another two per cent to them; or, if the price were too high for them to be allowed to buy, they might persuade someone friendly to buy at above 440p and take a loss by accepting."

"Why would anyone want to do that?"

Peter looked at him quizzically. It was a look that said 'work it out for yourself'. Hennessy worked it out for himself.

"Because they were bribed into it?"

"Perhaps," said Peter, pleased at having trapped him into an unchristian conclusion, "though I could put an entirely innocent spin on it if I had to."

"How?"

"Imagine I'm an institution. I have a small shareholding in Pitcairn but I've been a long-term follower of Arthur Evans and I have a bigger holding in BMP. Arthur tells me that securing Pitcairn would be very good for BMP and my shares in it; but, even though I've accepted the offer in respect of my small shareholding in Pitcairn, he needs just another two per cent. How would I feel, he says, about going into the market and buying two per cent at 441p, 442p - whatever it takes - and accepting BMP's offer for them, maybe even selling them to BMP for 440p? Take a small loss on two per cent against the big profit I've already made on my Pitcairn shares and the major benefits still to come from a BMP victory. There's no difference between the outcome based on slipping me a brown envelope stuffed with fivers and the one based on how I've succumbed to logical argument."

"But what would the Panel have to say about that?"

"The Panel has waved that argument through on countless occasions. It stinks but the Panel has a selective sense of smell."

"I see," he said. He paced the room for a while in silence. At last he returned to his sofa.

"Right, now tell me about this Minorco bid for Consolidated Goldfields last week," he said. "What's all this about insider dealing?"

"Well, as you know, Minorco, which is based in Luxembourg, is the offshore vehicle for the Oppenheimer family, which controls a huge proportion of the private sector in South Africa through Anglo-American and de Beers, the diamond operation. They've always wanted to get their hands on Consgold, initially for Gold Fields of South Africa - the Oppenheimers have never been able to abide competition in anything. But now apparently they want Consgold for its overseas interests. They say they'll put those into Minorco and sell the South African business. They've had several goes at Consgold before and picked up 25% in a dawn raid several years ago. All told they have around 29% now. The insider dealing row has erupted because there's been some quite extraordinary activity in the options market for Consgold shares in recent weeks."

"That's what I thought. And wasn't there something similar in our shares at the back end of November last year, before BMP made their approach?"

"Yes, though you remember Wagstaffs accumulated all their stake in the shares themselves. There isn't normally enough volume in the options market to mount a raid that way. In the case of Consgold, only about three per cent of the company's shares, and that's exceptionally high, are now accounted for by call options - that's options to buy shares..."

"Yes, I know, I know. Go on."

"Even that level of activity has driven the price of options to about twice what they ought theoretically to be in relation to the underlying shares. So there's clearly been something going on. There's speculation that either some people with inside knowledge have been jumping in for a private punt or, more seriously, some part of the Oppenheimer empire has been secretly accumulating shares that way."

"Has the buying been coming from Luxembourg then?"

"No. Switzerland. Swiss Bank Corporation through their Savory Milln operation here."

"Was that the same with the options on our shares?"

"Some of them. Quite a large proportion were bought by one of the Swiss private banks. I forget which one now. It was tiny by comparison with the activity in Pitcairn shares all told, something like five or six thousand contracts, each for a thousand shares, less than one per cent of the total outstanding capital."

"Well, if it wasn't BMP, who do you think it was?"

"It's impossible to say, Christopher. Rod and I did some work on it; but we never got to the bottom of it. And when BMP popped up with 14.9%, frankly it looked like a side-show. Of course, I would have said it was too much activity to be entirely innocent - like in the case of Consgold - but by the time a bid like that is launched, there are likely to be a few dozens of people who know what's going on and it's easy for one or two of them to get tempted."

"Although the option market is so small that a relatively small amount of buying of options will drive the price sharply higher, and betray what's going on?"

"Well it betrays that something's going on but not who's responsible. Anyone doing something like that is likely to hide his tracks pretty carefully. The Stock Exchange's record of getting those responsible into court is pathetic."

"And if one wanted to drive a price lower?" Hennessy asked.

"You could sell in the options market."

"And, in the same way, presumably a relatively small amount of selling would send prices lower?"

"Yes."

"And eventually."

"Well, if it's persistent enough, it will tend to spill over into the shares themselves and drive them higher or lower."

"So one could push BMP shares lower or Pitcairn higher without necessarily selling or buying the shares themselves and with much more modest capital commitment."

"That's certainly the theory, but I'm not sure that it would apply to Pitcairn shares right now. If you're going to buy an option to purchase shares, someone who already owns them has got to sell you that option. BMP's buying has already taken a large chunk of shares out of the market. I suppose if you pay someone a big enough premium for an option to make it worth his while holding onto the shares for future delivery should the option be exercised, then, within reason, the market will provide the shares you want. But it's an unusual situation. I'm no expert but I would have thought that normally the options market would dry up. That wouldn't be the case with BMP shares of course. Driving their share price down would reduce the value of their offer. But only the share exchange offer; their cash offer is underwritten firm. To keep our share price out of their reach, we really need a physical buyer of our shares, not a punter on the fringe."

"Okay, I think that's what I thought. How long have we got with Dundas Asset Management?"

"I probably can't hold them off for more than a day or two now that the final offer is out, maybe more if I could hold out the prospect of something a little better from another quarter. But now that most of the arbs have thrown in the towel and there are no other buyers around other than BMP, you would expect our share price to drift back towards the value of the cash alternative. And BMP, of course, will then snap up anything they can."

"Tell them that."

"Who?"

"Dundas Asset Management."

"Tell them what?"

"To expect something a little bit better."

"Is that realistic?"

"I don't care if it's realistic or not, Peter; I want the breathing space. Tell them any flim-flam you like, but buy us a bit of time. Now tell me, what would happen if we were to announce a research breakthrough."

"What, now?"

"Yes, now."

"In what?"

"I don't care. Cancer. Prevention of heart disease. Parkinson's. Alzheimer's. It doesn't matter."

"Well, strictly speaking it's not allowed."

"What's not allowed?"

"The offeree announcing new information relevant to the defence after Day 39."

"Who says?"

"It's Rule 31 of the Code."

"What sort of tin-pot dictators do these people think they are? Is the advance of medical science automatically suspended by the magic of their Day 39?"

"Well I see your point but we'd have to expect a row. I don't think it's ever been tested in this form before. We could certainly argue that something that genuinely emerged after Day 39 and had material relevance to the value of Pitcairn had to be disclosed or shareholders would be prejudiced. But you can see the scope for argument can't you? Did it genuinely come to light after Day 39? Is it material? Would shareholders be prejudiced? Is it just a defence tactic? It might all back-fire terribly if the press and the market concluded that converting the research into a product was too far distant to be of great value. There would be sure to be a lot of scepticism. And then there's what concessions BMP might demand in return? I could see the Panel ruling that Day 60 should be extended - and Day 46 too - so that they could put in a new offer and give shareholders a fortnight to accept it." He was lost in thought for a moment. Riches again floated before his eyes. "Is it true, Christopher," he said eventually. "Is there something new?"

"I haven't decided yet. I want you to meet me at seven tomorrow morning at the private aircraft terminal at Heathrow. Do you know where that is?"

"On the south side, east of terminal four."

"Sure thing."

"May I ask where we're going?"

"We're going to Paris. We're going to see Monsieur Guillaume de Fontaubert, the Président of Générale des Chimiques."

"But they've said publicly that they're not interested. They said it again last week."

"We'll see."

Saturday, 1 October 1988

Freddie was hanging on in there despite everything he had done to abuse his body over a sustained period of decades. It had been a full week after his heart attack before they let anyone but family see him and Peter had been shocked by his appearance. Quite apart from the fact that he was wired up as though he were about to be blasted off into space, he looked horribly drained. It would take more than a week on a drip-feed to make Freddie's round and ruddy cheeks go sallow, but the mere absence of colour seemed to diminish his natural corpulence. He was propped up on a mound of pillows in an extraordinarily gaudy silk nightshirt, broadly striped in gold and black, which at least retained for him a certain amount of panache; but his speech had not returned beyond an incoherent mumble and his wise old eyes had lost their twinkle. They opened wider as Peter sat down by his bed; but that was as far as signs of recognition went. Davenport wasn't good with sickness. He didn't like hospitals and he never knew what to say. The art of the one-way conversation was beyond his limited sense of care for his fellow men. He decided to summarise for Freddie what had happened over the past week; but there was no indication that Freddie had heard him, let alone comprehended. In any event, after only a few minutes one of those thick-set domineering nurses with which every hospital appears to be equipped came in and hustled him away.

A week later, there was no perceptible improvement that Peter could detect though he found a doctor who pronounced that they were satisfied that Freddie's condition had stabilised. From here on, he declared, they could expect some improvement.

Peter popped in again on the Tuesday evening but found him asleep. The following weekend was much better. The eerie sepulchral light in which his room had previously been shrouded had been exchanged

450

for too-bright hospital-issue neon; but there were flowers everywhere to lessen the harshness of the bare surroundings A lot of the medical paraphernalia had been removed but there was still a machine in the corner, its monitor blipping iridescent green in time to Freddie's heart and a plastic bag of some or other clear liquid dripping into a tube inserted into his left forearm. A huge bowl of sweet peas on his bedside table clashed catastrophically with a new Freddie confection in the form of a nightgown of bilious imperial purple. He smiled as Peter entered the room and held out his right hand to him. His speech was slurred but it was returning, little by little, and there was every sign of comprehension. Peter told him about the extraordinary trip to Paris on Thursday.

"I hadn't expected him but George Aladyce was there too. What a bloody plane, Freddie. Business tool, my arse. There must be configurations for a Gulfstream that would seat a dozen or so executives in comfort. But Pitcairn's isn't one of them. It's pure self indulgence. Full-time stewardess on the payroll as well as the pilots. It's even got a sodding bedroom; but even so it would only take six if two spent the whole damned flight in bed."

"Avarishious little bigot," opined Freddie, to Peter's heartfelt joy. "It'sh alwaysh the shupposhed shaints who've got both trottersh in the trough."

It would be hard to imagine anyone who'd put more trotters in the trough than Freddie; but that was different. It was his own money. Or at worst his great great grandfather's. And he'd never pretended to be remotely saintly.

"You just wait, Freddie. When it comes to the seven deadly sins, our diminutive client has a pretty full house.

"We put down at Le Bourget. Fontaubert had sent his car to meet us. Not a little Citroen either or a Renault 5. Top of the range Merc. Guillaume de Fontaubert is French when it suits him and European when it doesn't. And boy is he patrician? Perfect, slightly old-fashioned formal English. Like you'd imagine Churchill talking to the king. He makes Giscard d'Estaing look like an upstart. God knows what he made of George in his brothel-creepers. Of course he's filthy rich as well as diplomatically polished. His family still more or less controls Générale des Chimiques. The headquarters are a stunning block of blackened glass and stainless steel just off the périphérique and his office makes even Christopher's look cramped. It's modern of course and so quiet it must be quadruple glazed; but there are wonderful modern tapestries and sculptures everywhere in marble and bronze. I'm sure one of them was a Rodin. And then he's got acres of black marble flooring - well, I suppose it's granite really - and when his secretary comes in - one of those willowy Parisiennes with five inch heels, legs up to her armpits and seams in her stockings - she clickety-clacks about fifty yards from the door to his desk. Very sexy. And she knew it."

"Of coursh, m'boy, in my day a pair of legsh with sheamsh in their shockingsh were guaranteed never to be parted - practically welded together. Now, ash I undershtand it, they're the onesh you can rely on never to closhe. Funny that, ishn't it?" he added with a chuckle.

"Well that's natural selection for you, Freddie," Peter said, joining in the schoolboy humour. "But I tell you she could waggle her arse as she walked like it was two little boys fighting in a sack."

"Down boy. Behave yourshelf or I'll tell Shamantha."

"Not allowed, Freddie. No disclosure of what I do in the cause of Pitcairn; even if it's only lust. Actually it was hardly all I did do. We asked Fontaubert if he would reconsider making an agreed offer and he said no - in the most charming way possible of course - and then Hennessy sent me out. Said he and George needed a word with Fontaubert in private.

"So I sat in his waiting room for a couple of hours in a rather uncomfortable but terribly fashionable-looking leather chair reading the paper and drinking espresso."

"And ogling hish shecretary?" Freddie enquired with another rumble of mirth.

"When the opportunity presented. She was in and out of Fontaubert's office a dozen times or more, wiggling her tail, fetching bits of paper and typing them up. And then Christopher and George came out all smiles. There was a bit of exchange of smalltalk. The old boy apologised for keeping me hanging about; more than Christopher did, of course. Then he showed us to the car and we went back to the plane and flew home. And on the way back Christopher dropped me in it from 25,000 feet."

"Whatsha mean, Peter?"

"You won't believe what he'd done, Freddie. First of all he says 'Peter, you were not entirely honest with me over the subject of Dundas Asset Management and now I must confess that we - that is George - has not been entirely honest with you.

'You will recall Dr Cunningham, the lady who's been leading our research into a vaccine for Aids. I believe George told you that her experiment had failed and that was probably why she sold those shares she had bought the week before, when she thought it was going so well. Well, George has gotten into some rather unusual things about her research. George, why don't you tell him?'

'You purp...purp...probably recall that she first thought the whole thing had fafe...fafe...failed when one of her monkeys was mis-identified. She had originally thought it to be in the group that was vaccinated but not then exposed to SIV - so that the vaccine itself was thought to be at forf...forf...fault. Subsequently she ferf...found that the little bleeder was in the group that was not vaccinated but exposed. That seems to have been her buying signal. Then, a week later, another was identified with SIV and he was in the vaccinated but not exposed group. Selling signal.

'Well I think there was a lot more to it than that. He wasn't in that group at all.'

'What on earth do you mean, George?'

'I think she gog...gog...got the idea from that original transposed code number that she could use mis-identification as a means to keep the results to herself. All she had to do was make sure that she alone knew their true identities.'

"'I thought that was impossible,' I said, 'you told me they they were identified with electronic chips implanted under the skin.'"

"'They are' he says, ' but our little lady started moom...moving the chips about. I had a good look at the two subjects which were identified as having contracted SIV. I noticed something unusual about the second one and I started having a shoofty at some of the others. I'm quite certain that some of the tags had been interfief...fief...fered with. There was too much scar tissue around the tag foff...foff...for a single insertion. They'd been moved around. But the upshot was, when you'd got everyone properly identified, that to date none of her SIV-vaccinated subjects, even those subsequently directly exposed, had contracted SIV.

By being the only one who knew which individuals had the right tags, she alone was able to monitor the true results. We don't know whether HIV will behave in the same way; but, if it genuinely is the case that the disease jumped the species barrier, it should. And, of course, there are some side effects we have to clear up still. All that could still take several years. It's not a blockbub...bub...buster yet; but our competitors would give their baub...baub...balls to have got this far.'"

"'How long have you known all this, George,' I asked. 'We only spoke about what you'd discovered amongst her papers a couple of weeks ago.'"

"'Well, to be honest, Peep...peep...peep...Peter, I've known this since that weekend I dididid her lab over. I just thought that Christopher mime...mime...might be able to maim...maim...make better use of it than you. Sorry.'"

"'Why should she be behaving so secretively?' I asked. 'It must be impossible for a research chemist to appropriate a bit of work like that to herself.'"

"'Who knows her mome...mome...motives,' said George. 'Maybe she thought there was more glory in it if she could keek...keek...keep it under her hat until she was fur...fur...further advanced.'"

"'Have you told her that you've rumbled her?' I asked. I was getting pretty baffled by now as to what the pair of them were up to."

"'No,' says George, 'she's doing very well on her own and now I know where she keeps the real inforff...forff...formation, I can pop into her lab occasionally when she's not looking and check up what's really going on. Of course I'm not happy that she's being devious towards us as her employer, but I think we've got this tite...tite...tiger very fur... fur...firmly by the tate...tate...tail.'"

"You mean Pitcairn'sh hit the shodding jackpot."

"Well, it's not quite that simple, Freddie. There's a very long way to go between where they are now and getting out an effective vaccine for HIV. At the very least years to get approval; and that's only once they've got the product perfected. What they've got now seems to have some unfortunate side-effects. Apparently the vaccinated group shows increased susceptibility to other viral infections and George says that he doesn't begin to understand why; but it's certainly the most significant advance in Aids research to date."

"It'sh brilliant. The sharesh'll go up like a fucking dishtresh flare when you announsh it, m'boy."

"We're not going to announce it, Freddie. It's too late. He's sold it."

"Shold it? What do you mean, shold it?"

"Christopher's sold the research to Guillaume de Fontaubert. That's what he and George were doing while I was watching that tart's arse going in and out of his office."

"Why the hell did he do that?"

"I think it was the result of a conversation I had with him last week. He was asking what I would expect to happen if they announced a research breakthrough at this stage. I didn't really understand the reasons for his questions; but I told him there was the problem with the Code - announcing fresh information after the 39th day; but that could possibly be overcome if BMP were allowed an equivalent extension to the final day. But I also said there was a danger that an announcement at this late stage would be treated with some cynicism. He'd obviously been turning it all over in his mind. To be honest, I got the impression when he talked to me about it originally that he might be thinking of inventing some research story; not that he really had something."

"Sho whatsh he done?"

"He's sold her research to Fontaubert for a pound."

"For what?"

"For a pound. And not to Générale des Chimiques either, mind you; to Guillaume de Fontaubert personally. In return Fontaubert has granted Pitcairn an option to buy it back for £50 million, provided there is no change in control of Pitcairn within a year. Then he's separately undertaken to get his family's Liechtenstein trusts to spend up to £250 million buying Pitcairn shares, if necessary above the offer price. Starting yesterday. If BMP wins the bid, Fontaubert will walk off with the Aids research and sell it to Générale des Chimiques, more than protecting himself from any small loss on the Pitcairn shares he purchases and boosting the value of his own stake in the company. If Pitcairn successfully fights off BMP, it would exercise the buy back option. That would give Fontaubert a personal profit of £49,999,999 and the subsequent announcement of an Aids breakthrough would probably send Pitcairn's share price higher still, giving him a further profit; or at least prevent it falling when the bid lapses. Our Christopher's given Fontaubert a no lose deal and, as for Pitcairn, he's used the Aids research to take shares off the market that might otherwise have fallen into BMP's hands. You could argue quite strongly that all that's a more effective defence against BMP than making an announcement of a research breakthrough."

"Clever little shod."

"All that toing and froing and arse wiggling was Hennessy drafting contracts - he's a lawyer remember - but he needed George there to give him technical back up on the medical side. Fontaubert may be the biggest smoothie since Casanova; but his father prepared him thoroughly for the succession. He's got doctorates in chemistry and biology. Apparently he really put George through the wringer."

"I don't know the Code like you, Peter; but I can't believe all thatsh kosher, ish it?"

"Of course it's not fucking kosher, Freddie," said Peter, raising his voice. Then he remembered the rather unfriendly nurse lurking down the ward and reverted to a conspiratorial whisper.

"There are at least two violations of the Code. You're not allowed to dispose of material assets during a bid without shareholder consent - Rule 21 - and you're not allowed to enter into agreements for the purchase of shares without disclosing the purchases, the prices paid, who has made them and for what inducement - Rule 8 - with which I assure you Hennessy and Fontaubert have no intention of complying."

"Sho?"

"So I told them. And do you know what Hennessy said? He said 'I thought that was probably the case; so I thought I ought to spare you the embarrassment of consulting you in advance. Frankly I long ago came to the conclusion that we were spared the need to act exactly by the book when Evans started the whole thing off with that trick to buy up 15% of our shares last December.'"

"But if BMP win," I said, "and Evans finds you've sold this research gem, he'll go ape... beserk."

"'So he'll go beserk,' said Hennessy. 'It's only the Code. It's not law. This is a legally enforceable contract. And he's no reason to think Pitcairn has this gem, as you call it; so he has no cause in law for complaint.'"

"'But what about announcing the share purchases?' I said. 'That's not just Code requirements. Holdings over five per cent must be disclosed under the Companies Act. And the Code is more restrictive. During an offer period transactions by holders of over one per cent have to be announced.'

"'Oh, Guillaume won't have any problems with that,' he said. 'He'll set up a dozen different trusts and spread the shares around.'

"'He could still get required to disclose his identity.'

"'How? You're being very negative, you know, Peter,' he says.

"'Section 214. A holder of ten per cent or more of your shares - ie BMP - can requisition you to send out a 212 notice; and you have to make public disclosure of the information you receive in reply.'

"'So? The names of a few anonymous trusts.'

"'Operating from the same Liechtenstein address?'

"'Perhaps, though I expect Guillaume and his advisers are a little cleverer than that. But, even so, what can Lord Evans do? I've looked at the Companies Act, Peter. If Guillaume's family trusts choose not to disclose their identity, Section 216 would enable Pitcairn to apply to the courts for the rights of those shareholders to be suspended; but we would have no obligation to disenfranchise them. BMP can requisition us to send out 212 notices until - I believe the English expression is - they're blue in the face; but they can't requisition us to deprive shareholders of their rights.'

"'Then there's section 151 of the Comanies Act', I said, '- financial assistance by a company for the purchase of its own shares. Pitcairn's giving away a research gem as a means of inducing someone to buy its shares. That must be pretty close to financial assistance, by any definition. That's a criminal offence.'"

"'I wondered when you'd get to that,' says Hennessy, 'but I don't think you're right. Fontaubert's under no obligation to buy the shares. He just told me he would. And, as for transferring Pitcairn's research to his care, I've made it clear in the contract that our motivation is purely humanitarian. We have no confidence that Evans, given his research record, would invest what's necessary to take Dr Cunningham's discoveries forward. We're really just protecting mankind from his boorishness. In the circumstances, I don't think you could make that charge stick.'"

"'Maybe you're right, Christopher,' I said foolishly.

"'I know I'm right, Peter,' he snapped back, like he does.

"'But that won't stop the Panel putting me under intense pressure to find out what's going on.'

"'But you don't know, Peter, do you? Any more than I do.' Then he put those enormous glasses on the end of his nose. You know the way he does. And he looked over the top of them at me and he said: 'I feel sure I'm right that you don't know anything about these trusts. That's the beauty of our interests coinciding so exactly, isn't it Peter? I'm sure you understand my meaning. Your interests. My interests. Guillaume's interests.' Of course he knows I'm over a barrel too with this bonus arrangement with the Brothers. 'If we see off BMP, no one will ever know about today's discussions. Rod will have to find somewhere in the accounts to put £50 million of costs; but I don't doubt he can do that. And, in the unlikely event that we fail, BMP will have secured Pitcairn at the price it proposed. So how could it claim to have been disadvantaged.' You've got to hand it to him, haven't you Freddie. He'd thought it through."

"Sho that was Thursday. What happened yeshterday?'

"The little bastard had me line up DAM for first thing in the morning. The shares were standing in the market at 442p offered and 440p bid - Wagstaffs for BMP, of course. They were still picking up the odd bit here and there when someone dropped their price to the level of the cash alternative, but nothing significant. Then DAM offered their shares - all 27 million odd of them - at 441p and Pinsent Securities popped up and bought the bloody lot. Well the market had a fucking cadenza. Immediately concluded there was a white knight about and the shares shot up to 460p. They closed at 455 bid, 460 offered but there was no more volume at all.'

"Brilliant. We're going to fucking win. Absholutely fucking brilliant."

Freddie was genuinely animated. He looked so much better. His old joviality returning. But he caught the sceptical look in Peter's eye that he'd been doing his best to suppress..

"Well, ishn't it?"

"Yes, Freddie it is. But, at the same time, it does expose the limitations of this ploy. Fontaubert spent £120 million yesterday. That's bloody near half our firepower to take out someone whose loyalty to the Brothers should alone have kept on side. Practically everyone in the defence team, bar that shit Travers-Coe who's known about this problem all along, would have assumed that to be so - and no doubt the opposition too. I know we've gained some ground; but everyone else, including Fontaubert himself, would have assumed it was ground we already held. That I find frankly depressing."

A quiet descended between them. Peter was sorry to have turned the conversation negative. Freddie had only just now been bubbling with some of his old spirit. He was just wondering how to revive a more optimistic tone, when the sounds of a commotion further down the ward drifted in through the half-open door. There were raised voices - female - one the brusque nurse, Peter thought, the other, was it possible? A moment later, the door to Freddie's room was opened wide and Samantha strode in, undisguised, sister snapping angrily at her heels.

"You can't go in there," she was still saying. "It's strictly one visitor at a time in this ward. I shall have no alternative but to call security to have you ejected."

But Freddie, though he had never met her, had heard enough about her from Maxine Dubarry to know exactly the identity of this tall redhead in the tight white jeans.

"Shamantha, my dear!" he exclaimed. "How wonderful of you to come and shee me."

"Mr Wordsworth, this is not permitted," the nurse continued to fuss.

"Oh do be quiet, shishter, there'sh a good girl. I won't tell a shoul."

"This is all highly irregular, Mr Wordsworth. Rules are rules", she muttered, retreating in sullen defeat.

But Samantha, never for a moment doubting her victory, was already leaning over Freddie to kiss him on both cheeks, as her opponent scuttled away.

"I've brought you a little something to speed your recovery," she said, delving into her bag and producing five half bottles of old claret, one of each of the first growths. Now just make sure you don't share these with anyone. Not best accompanied with hospital food; but I reckon even mince tastes pretty good with Margaux. I'll pop them in the cupboard here out of sight," she added in a husky, conspiratorial whisper. "They just need to lie there for twenty-four hours to settle. And I've brought a corkscrew too, in case they don't run to one of those in here."

She came over to hug Peter briefly and then returned to sit on Freddie's bed. He loved it. He was in his element, beaming joyfully as they chattered together. She had no inhibitions about hospitals and no reticence with this old boy that she had only just met. His boat had been the essence of him and she felt she already knew him well. Freddie, originally intensely suspicious when Peter had confessed his new love but attracted to the female of the species even more than he was to food and drink, found her everything he had been told to expect. Her eyes sparkled, her wide, sensuous mouth was parted constantly in laughter to reveal her even white teeth. They joked and tittle-tattled, touching each other constantly with affection.

Peter sat and watched them as they giggled and flirted, as she told him about Maxwell, demonstrating how she had waved to him, wiggling her breasts from side to side under her thin jersey to Freddie's gleaming delight. Peter felt utterly without jealousy and utterly superfluous.

She stayed for no more than twenty minutes but by the time she left Freddie was in love. More than that, he had a joy in his face that made Peter know that his old friend was going to pull through.

Peter had walked the length of the darkened ward with a fresh spring in his step and was waiting on the big brightly-lit empty landing for a lift. There was a bank of six of them; but they were those huge things into which you could wheel a bed and every one that stopped was occupied by some poor sod on the way to or from the operating theatres or casualty down below.

"Mr Davenport. Mr Davenport." It was the sister, still obviously smarting from her put-down. "Could you come back a moment. Mr Wordsworth says he has something terribly important to say to you. He was absolutely insistent."

Peter hurried back after the nurse. He was filled with anxiety. Even more so when he saw Freddie. His eyes were closed and he was breathing heavily. Sweat stood out on his pale forehead and trickled greasily into his thin hair. His nightshirt was stained dark with perspiration at the neck. His insistence over the nurse had clearly been dearly bought. Peter took his hand. The eyes opened wearily.

"Sho why did she shell the sharesh?" he said at last.

"Who? What shares, Freddie?"

"Dr Cunningham, shilly boy, Dr Cunningham," he whispered and was instantly, snoringly, asleep.

Saturday, 8 October 1988

Peter woke alone in his apartment. He felt wretched. His mouth was furry and alcoholic and his head throbbed. His guts were queasy and his thirst prodigious. There was no disguising it. This was a hangover. He hauled himself out of bed and padded naked towards the kitchen in search of a cup of coffee and an aspirin. On the low table in front of the sofa an empty bottle of Laphroaig and a tumbler watched him guiltily as he passed. He stopped and picked up the tumbler, taking it with him.

He found a packet of Codis in the top drawer in the kitchen and put a couple of tablets in his mouth as he automatically filled the tumbler with water from the tap. He nearly gagged at the smell of whiskey as he put the glass to his lips and again as the pills, too large to be easily swallowed in one, began to crumble, bitter and chalky in his mouth. He quickly took another gulp and turned to the coffee machine.

While it was brewing, he pulled on a pair of jeans and a tee-shirt and slipped painfully out for an *FT*. At the little newsagent round the corner, they had all gone. He looked at his watch. It was almost noon. Eight bells, he thought wretchedly. He settled for a *Times*..

Back in his flat, he nursed a black coffee and turned the pages of the newspaper. By virtue of a government minister's presence to deliver the eulogy, Freddie's funeral yesterday had made the back page. He felt only sadness again now; but it had, in truth, been a spectacular occasion. Three women in the front pew contesting widowhood as Maxine Dubarry out-flounced both Jemima and the lady from Cowes with an astonishingly short skirt and a breathtaking décolletage in black satin. Four or five hundred people packed tight under the ornate domed ceiling of St Mary-at-Hill, a clutch of admirals and retired sea-dogs, bedecked with scrambled egg, hunched submariners from the other ranks with rows of medals and handkerchiefs to their eyes, the editors of every leading national newspaper, the Governor himself, industrialists, stockbrokers, bankers, the maître d' from the Savoy, Marmaduke Hussey, the Chairman of the BBC, Samantha, a few yards away from him, in public still beyond his care, her eyes red-rimmed behind those awful specs, Wallis with the nubile staff from their little Georgian office off Fleet Street, even his competitors, Tim Bell, John Addey, Piers Pottinger, Roddy Dewe - all bidden by his last will and testament to turn up in their glad rags to say adieu and to adjourn thereafter down the hill to Watermen's Hall for a gargantuan piss-up, substantially at the expense of the chancellor of the exchequer's bill for inheritance tax.

He had been Freddie's last visitor. Wallis had called him at home early last Sunday morning to say that he had suffered another massive heart attack during the night and had died without regaining consciousness. Peter was racked with guilt and helpless with rage. Had it been the excitement of the visit that had done it? His report on the developments to the Pitcairn saga that had unfolded in Paris? Meeting Samantha for the first time? Their giggling flirtatious exchanges as she sat on his bed, holding his hand? Or his struggle with that bossy nurse to have her fetch him back? Which of them had killed him? It was too awful to be numbered amongst the suspected, even in his own conscience; worse still to think it might have been her. Better to blame the nurse. I'll bet she pinched that claret, too. Poor Freddie.

"Why did she shell the sharesh?" He could hear him now through the nausea and his pulsing head. "Shilly boy, why did she shell the sharesh?"

Why did she sell the fucking shares? If George was right, she sold them just at the moment when she knew she was onto a winner. She should have been adding to her holding; not getting rid of it.

He'd spent that Sunday in a ferment of frustration and guilt. He couldn't find the Harrington Ingram file on Dr Cunningham anywhere. Strictly speaking it was forbidden, but he'd gone over to Notting Hill to deliver the sad news in person. With less than a fortnight to go, they were keeping their distance more than usual. Their phones were constantly ringing, the bid pervading every hour of day and night, and there was scarcely any difference between the home and office environment. She was desperately upset and he had stayed there the rest of the morning, trying to comfort her but only upsetting himself more as he thrashed around in his recriminations. At last he could stand the waiting no more. He felt sure it was in his office and headed there on his way back to Wapping. As usual it was far from well ordered and he turned it upside down without success. There was no reason for anyone else to have it. It must be in one of his briefcases back at home. By now he was utterly convinced that there was a clue in that file somewhere. At least there weren't so many places to look back at the apartment; but he turned out three briefcases without success and then his desk, drawer by drawer.

Around four o'clock he had phoned Maureen. It rang and rang. She had no answering machine. He called her at ten minute intervals for a couple of hours without success and then tried Peter Harrington at his home number. There was a message on his machine but no clue as to his whereabouts either.

He spent the rest of that afternoon at his desk, *The Sunday Times* spread in front of him, alternately dialing Maureen and Harrington without success. There were two articles on the bid, the first accompanied by one of those huge photographs that sunday business sections use to disguise their vacuity with filler. This, clearly a library job, showed Arthur Evans on horseback in hunting pink, sporting a slightly self-conscious version of that unsmiling smile. The caption read: *'Speculation continues as to the reason for BMP setting the closing date for its bid for Pitcairn as Wednesday, 12th October and not Sunday, 16th October, the 60th day of its offer. Sources close to the company say that Evans, a spirited huntsman (pictured above with the Quorn), is confident of success and keen to avoid losing another Saturday of the early season to this long-drawn-out battle which started way back in January .'*

The second, a mere paragraph within John Jay's column but written, one would assume, with a rather later deadline, referred to the mystery buyer who had entered the market for Pitcairn shares on Friday and asked whether a last minute white knight was about to appear. *'All will be revealed by an announcement to the Stock Exchange tomorrow'* it concluded.

Evening came and there had still been no reply from either Maureen or Harrington. Peter put down the telephone for the umpteenth time only to have it ring back at him immediately.

"Who the fook ha yer bin oon the foon to all fookin afternoon?" said Bill, without waiting for him to speak. "Weel, niver mind, I've got yer noo. Listen, can yer get roond here?'

"Oh, not again, Bill," Peter had said; but he had been bullied into it just the same.

Bill's squat in Holland Park had become significantly more lived in over the intervening months. The sitting room had become an extension of both the kitchen and the bedroom, an assortment of plates and glasses, those disgusting little polystyrene cartons in which McDonalds peddle their ersatz beefburgers and thin square cardboard boxes from PizzaExpress fighting for space on every available surface with odd socks and dirty shirts. Scotch, however, had replaced Newcastle Brown Ale as the booze on offer; but there was no ice and no soda. First of the day. I must be feeling better, thought Peter.

"Hev yer foond a replacement foor that Woordswoorth mun to do yer PR?" he opened sympathetically and then, without waiting for a reply: "Anyway that's not what I wanted to talk to yer aboot. Look, Gallaher called in all the heads of department this moorning. He wooz sittin there wi that coont Kent at his fookin elbow an he says there's bin an approoch from Fidelity Bank for Doondas."

"Ah, I might have known it. Lord Enderby."

"What the fook's Enderby got to do wi it, mun?"

"Jock Enderby joined Fidelity as a non-executive director when they converted from a building society. Supposed to give them credibility, a bit of gravitas. But I suspect he's been nursing a loss on some Dundas shares he bought a while back and this way he gets out from under scot free. He probably put them up to it."

"Well I doon't care who the fook poot them oop to it. They're still a fookin buildin society as far as I'm consoorned and I'm not fookin workin for them. They woodn't knoo a coorporate finance department froom a girls' school."

"Is an announcement imminent, Bill?"

"They're aiming at stitchin it all oop by next week-end ready to annoonce it on the Moonday, what's that," he speculated, picking up that Sunday's *Telegraph* , which was lying in its disparate parts in crumpled heaps on the floor, and looking at the date, "the tenth. I've toold Tom Camoys and Richard Heley roond at BZW they'd better get their bluddy skates on if they want to do a deal."

"But Fidelity won't want corporate finance, will they, Bill? It's not part of their business. They'd just put us up for sale."

"Aye, mun, and we'd goo to the highest fookin bidder. Well that's not my idea of lookin after yer oon fookin destiny. We all agreed," he exaggerated slightly, "that BZW wood be ower preference and that's wear wear gooin to goo. I wanted to tell you becoos I might need yer help with negootiations later in the week."

*****

Maureen had been late in the next day. She's been staying with her sister in Norwich for the week-end and got the train back to London that morning.

"Oh I sent that back to Harrington Ingram weeks ago," she said in all innocence as he tackled her in a mounting rage when she appeared a little after ten. "You'd put it in your out-tray and I assumed that's what you wanted me to do with it."

"Well, get it back. I need it and I need it right now. I've been hunting for it all sodding week-end."

"Okay," she said, refusing with some justification to accept the blame, and turned on her heel. Tim Phillips passed her on his way in.

"Why's Maureen got her nose in the air and her nipples to attention?" he asked. "Sad about Freddie."

"Yes."

"Heard anything about the identity of our mystery white knight?"

"Not a thing."

"Oh well, I guess there'll have to be an announcement this morning. I've scheduled a meeting for the whole team here in your office for twelve o'clock."

"Eight bells."

"What's that?"

"Twelve o'clock. Eight bells on the forenoon watch."

"Yes. Sure," he agreed, somewhat bemused. "There'll have to be an announcement by then and we'll need to think through our response.

I've told Rod to stand by for a meeting of the full defence committee early afternoon at St James's Square."

"Ok. Maureen!" he shouted through the open door, "what news on that file?"

She appeared a few seconds later, unhurried. "Nicolla Duckworth says they've sent it back to archives. Thought it wasn't needed any more. She's sending for it straight away but it won't be back before this afternoon."

"Saints pre-fucking-serve us," he bellowed in frustration. "OK, Maureen, quick as possible."

11.55. They were all gathered in his office, staring at the screen, the girls twittering with excitement, the boys trying to adopt the nonchalance of experience. No announcement yet. There wasn't going to be one; but he couldn't tell them. He didn't know anything about it, did he?

He got the first of many summonses to the Panel that week within a couple of hours. It started relatively low key; just Peter Lee and some seconded lawyer for the Panel, Peter and Tim for Dundas.

"You'll know why we've asked you to come and see us," Peter Lee began.

Davenport said nothing.

Lee looked at him quizzically. He still said nothing.

"There was a buyer in size of Pitcairn shares in the market on Friday. It was estimated that around five per cent of the company changed hands and first thing this morning Dundas Asset Management confirmed a sale of around 27.4 million shares - that's about 4.15%."

Davenport still felt no need to proffer a contribution.

"There's been no announcement by the purchaser this morning, as required by Rule 8.3."

Peter remained silent.

"Do you know why?"

"No."

"Do you know the identity of the purchaser?"

"No."

"Have you any suspicions as to the identity of the purchaser?"

"No."

"Have you or your client had any discussions with a party which might be the buyer."

"Not as far as I know."

"What do you mean 'not as far as you know'." There was a slightly more hostile air now.

"As far as Dundas Brothers is concerned, 'no'; as far as Pitcairn is concerned, not that I am aware."

"Have you asked the question?"

"We are in constant touch with regard to all matters concerning the defence."

"But have you asked the specific question? Do they know who it is?"

"They tell me that they do not."

"Mr Davenport, have you got your client under control?"

"They have been made aware of all their obligations under the Code, if that's what you mean."

"The purchases were conducted through Pinsent Securities."

Davenport reverted to silence in the absence of a direct question.

"Have you spoken to Pinsent Securities?"

"No."

"We have. They tell us that they purchased shares for a correspondent bank in Liechtenstein on behalf of a number of clients; but that they have no reason to believe that any one has acquired a holding of one per cent or more. Does that seem likely to you?"

"If that's what Pinsent Securities say, I'm sure they're right."

"But does it seem likely, Mr Davenport?"

"It's not for me to speculate; but, as I say, if Pinsents say that's the case, I'd take their word for it."

"*Prima facie* I would say that there's evidence of a concert party. Wouldn't you?"

"Oh, I think I would leave it to the Panel to be the judge of that," he proffered condescendingly.

"Have you or your client or your client's lawyers served a section 212 notice on Pinsent Securities?"

"No."

"Why not, may I ask?"

"We don't see any reason to."

"If, you'll forgive me, that's a rather unusual attitude to take in the course of defending a bid. Could you please explain your reasoning?"

"I think we have to assume that somebody buying Pitcairn shares in size right at this moment is doing so out of motives other than pure investment. It could be that it's someone who wants BMP's bid to succeed or it could be someone who wants it to fail. If these shares had been purchased next week, I'd have wagered a pound to a penny that BMP had put someone up to buying Pitcairn shares above the offer price on their behalf."

"You know very well that's not permitted in terms of....." Lee started to protest, but Peter cut him off.

"Yes, quite so, quite so; but you and I both know that there are ways of doing this that the Panel has found perfectly acceptable in the past. Now, in this case, with over a week to go before the closing, and BMP unable to tell their friends how much they need to win, we think that Pinsents' clients are on balance more likely to be opposed to BMP's take-over offer for Pitcairn than in favour."

"Yes. So? Go on."

"So if, within the law - and the Take-Over Code," he added portentiously, "they decide that they do not wish to make themselves known, we see no reason to frustrate their wishes."

"I assume that you are aware, Mr Davenport, that BMP, as a ten per cent plus shareholder in Pitcairn, can require you in terms of the Companies Acts to issue a section 212 notice."

"Of course."

"Very well, then I guess we must advise Grossmanns that that's what they should do."

"If you'll forgive me, Peter, I don't think it's beholden on the Panel to advise one or other of the parties to a take-over as to what tactics they should adopt."

"Quite so. Quite so. But you'll be aware that that's obviously what they'll do next."

"As for my part," Peter concluded with wholly unnecessary sarcasm, "I shall be awaiting their next move with baited breath."

*****

The Harrington Ingram file on Dr Cunningham was sitting on his desk by the time he got back to the office.

"Tim, ring Rod and tell him to expect a section 214 requisition from BMP in relation to those dealings."

"What do you want them to do about it?"

"Well, they must comply with the law, of course," Peter said, closing the door of his office and shutting off the world. He opened it again a moment later.

"But call Martin Lampard. Ask him how long he thinks they can delay between receiving the requisition and sending out the notices. And ring Rod and tell him the answer. That poofter Corrigan will want to send them out before he's even been asked."

"But, Peter, what's the point in delaying?"

"What's the point in not? It'll irritate those bastards round at Grossmanns, if nothing else."

He closed the door again.

The file bore the unmistakable marks of Seamus O'Shea. On the front cover was the ring left by a mug - Peter could almost smell the Bovril - and down the spine inside there were fine powdery traces of cigarette ash. And then there were sheaves of meticulous notes, all in that tiny neat script that he remembered from that awful night in the car park of The French Horn. The file was divided into sections. First there was the subject herself - name, age occupation, a cv, photographs. A lot of the information must have been supplied via Rod or George by Pitcairn's personnel department. It went right down to her annual appraisal, the various projects she had worked on, her promotions, ultimately to team leader, her salary history, tax code, bank account number, holiday records, a photocopy of her medical history from the company doctor. She was on the pill. Just renewed her prescription. Shit, this is really not on, he thought.

Next there was a section on whereabouts - a map showing the location of her house, the route she habitually took to the Peterborough laboratories, the location of her own office and labs within the complex. There was a map of Melton Mowbray and environs which noted where she shopped, where she got her newspapers, where she had her hair done, where she filled up with petrol and god knows what else. There were pictures of her house from every angle, a painstaking pen and ink map of the grounds, showing the location of the paddocks and the stables and the various outhouses. There were notes on where she played tennis, who helped her look after the horses, when they exercised them, who did the gardening and maintenance of the property, where they lived, even what they were paid.

There were detailed notes on the two days of surveillance that Seamus had carried out - the thirteenth and most of the fourteenth of January, by which time who she was had become obvious - with her every movement minutely recorded.

Then there was a section on the share dealings that had first brought her to their attention with photocopies of all the relevant information that the registrars had supplied to Rod.

Finally came a section on her late husband. It was not as detailed on him as the earlier section on her; but it had his birth and death and marriage certificates, a summary of his education and subsequent career, a brief history of the firm he had established and a summary of the terms on which he had sold out, a copy of his will. But then there was a big chunk of material about his untimely death, police reports, the inquest. A lot of this was contained in newspaper clippings, mostly from the *Melton Times* , the local rag for which it had been the biggest story that week. LOCAL PERSONALITY KILLED IN SHOOTING PARTY TRAGEDY read the headline. The following week's edition had carried coverage of the funeral, including a photograph of the hearse leaving the house, the grieving widow, supported by her elder brother, and various mourners arriving at St Mary's Church. Peter's eye was drawn to the familiar bearing of a smartly-dressed woman in one of the photographs. She was only a figure in the background, the image was grainy and she was wearing a hat but.... He was almost sure. Maureen kept a little magnifying glass in the top drawer of her desk. She'd gone home now - last in, first out today - and her desk was locked. He rummaged around in the plastic whatnot on her desk with the paperclips and the Post-its, erasers and elastic bands. Then he tried the earthenware jar with its assortment of pencils, felt-tips and ballpoints. Sure enough, there was a spare key in the bottom. Back in his office, he switched on his anglepoise and hunched over the photograph. Under the magnifying glass, it began to dissolve unhelpfully into dots of printer's ink, but he was nevertheless sure that he was right. It was Rita Henderson-Ball. No sign of the old boy; but that slightly too brazen look was unmistakable. Now what on earth was she doing there?

He had sat and thought about it for a good long while before he had delved into his book for the Henderson-Ball's home number. It was going to sound like a pretty odd inquiry; but what else could he do? It was the only lead he'd found.

The telephone at Marsham Hall rang and rang. He knew there was always someone there; so he let it ring. Eventually what he supposed was a housekeeper picked it up.

"Marsham 'all," she said with more stiffness than was appropriate to her bucolic tones.

"Hello, my name's Davenport. Could I please speak to Lady Henderson-Ball."

"She's not 'ere."

"When are you expecting her back?"

"Who are you," she enquired curtly, with typical Yorkshire grace.

"Peter Davenport. I have business dealings with Sir Timothy."

"'e's not 'ere neither. I'll give you t'phone number of Bottley Engineerin. You can ask 'em there."

"No, actually, it's Lady Henderson-Ball I need to speak to. I do advise Bottley Engineering; but I need to speak to Lady Henderson-Ball on a personal matter."

"Well, I don't know 'bout tha'. They're neither of 'em 'ere. They're on 'oliday. Won't be back 'til Sa'urday."

"Can I contact them wherever they are? Do you have a telephone number?"

"I don 'ave no number. They're on one of 'em safaris, see. Ain't no telephones where they be."

"Whereabouts are they?"

"Africa somewhere," she said helpfully, narrowing his field of enquiry somewhat.

"Do you know where in Africa?"

"No."

"Would Sir Timothy's office know?"

"I don't think so. She organised it all, see. Sort of surprise for 'is birthday. Some swamp or other, I think she said. Didn't sound much of an 'oliday to me."

"Okavango Swamps?"

"Ar, I think that's right, whatever you said 'swamps'."

Shit, he thought, there really won't be any telephones there.

"When are they due back?"

"Sa'urday."

"Do you know when on Saturday. It's very important."

"'Ang on a minute." He heard her open a door and shout out:

"'Ere, Jim. when you gotta go down London to fetch 'im and 'er? Yeah, I know it's Sa'urday. Chap 'ere wants to know when on Sa'urday."

He could hear a door bang and her come shuffling back.

"Early. Jim's got to be at 'eathrow at eight in t'morning. Should be 'ome some time in t'arternoon."

"Okay. Thankyou. You've been very helpful."

"Shit, shit, shit and a thousand times shit," he said out loud as he put down the phone and slammed the file shut.

*****

He'd been summoned to the Panel twice more on Tuesday and twice again on Wednesday. No more significant numbers of shares changed hands on the Monday as the market awaited the emergence of the expected white knight; but as the afternoon had worn on without news, the price of Pitcairn shares began to drift back. Next morning a few institutions started to offer parcels of their holdings, tentatively probing for the mystery buyer. Pinsents were there for everything at 441p.

"Mr Davenport, could you tell me if your client has received a requisition in terms of section 214 of the Companies Act.?"

"They have received something which purports to be a section 214 requisition."

"What do you mean, 'purports to be'?" asked Peter Lee from across the table in one of the Panel's meeting rooms.

"Well, we're consulting our lawyers as to whether it's a valid notice."

"How can there be any doubt about it?"

"Oh, I don't know, I'm not a lawyer. But I think you'll agree that it's fair that they should opine."

"Very well, and how long will that take?'

"Oh, I don't know. Not long, I shouldn't think."

"Okay, I want you to call me as soon as you have that opinion. But not later than three o'clock."

Peter never called back. He was in front of the Panel again at four-thirty. The temperature had been raised. Antony Beevor, the director-general, tall, spare, dark, distinguished, had now taken charge, Peter Lee at one elbow and Lee's sidekick at the other.

"Mr Davenport. have your lawyers confirmed that the requisition received by your client under section 214 of the Companies Act is valid?"

"Up to a point, Antony."

They'd both been at the same school, and the same college at Oxford, but Beevor was ten years his senior; so their paths had never crossed at either. Nevertheless, it felt a bit silly to address a fellow corporate financier by his surname, just because he was the latest to be fingered for the job of director-general.

"What do you mean 'up to a point'?" Beevor came back, not very friendly.

"They've confirmed that it's in a format that's valid. We're just checking with the registrars now that the requisitioner is on the company's register and has the required proportion of the company's share capital for the requisition to be effective."

"But that should just take a phone call. And it could have been done simultaneously with the lawyers checking the format."

"Maybe it could have been; but it wasn't. And, in the circumstances, we do feel that it's necessary to have the registrars' confirmation in writing."

"How long will that take?"

"Oh, I don't know. Not long, I shouldn't think."

"Mr Davenport, you should put yourselves in a position to act on that requisition today."

Peter noted that he was not considered to be on christian name terms. He adopted silence mode again.

"I don't want to get the impression that you or your client are dragging your feet."

"Oh, I certainly hope not, Antony."

"Why are we dragging our feet?" Tim asked as they took the lift back down to the ground floor of the Stock Exchange tower.

"I don't know, Tim, it seems like about the only initiative we can take at the moment."

Martin Lampard had advised that they could safely spin out the sending out of the section 212 notices until the Wednesday morning without fear of the other side applying to the court for an injunction. Peter gained a certain wry satisfaction from the fact that this advice was coming from Ashursts, where the director-general himself had learnt his law. Nevertheless he was back in front of him early that afternoon. There had still been no announcement to indicate the identity of the mystery buyer; but the British Rail Pension Fund, who had held over three per cent, and Schroders nearly one and a half per cent, had both issued releases to the effect that they had reduced their holdings. And then the floodgates had begun to open. By lunchtime on Wednesday, Gourlay Gilfillan were estimating that almost £230 million, 7.9% of Pitcairn's shares, had been acquired through Pinsent Securities since the buying spree had started on the previous Friday.

With access to the computers of the Stock Exchange's Surveillance Department, Antony Beevor's figures were more precise.

"Mr Davenport, 52,164,000 shares in your client have now been purchased through Pinsent Securities since last Friday. They inform us that, in addition to a number of Liechtenstein trusts, they have also been buying for investors in the Netherlands Antilles, the Bahamas and the British Virgin Islands. Is it still your contention that you and your client are unaware of the identity or identities of the purchasers?"

"That is correct."

"And what measures have you now taken to ascertain their identities?"

"Those that we are required to take by law."

"To be exact."

"We have put section 212 notices on Pinsents in response to the requisition from BMP and have received a list of names and addresses from Pinsents. We are currently preparing section 212 notices to send to those addresses."

"How long will that take?"

"Oh, I don't know. Not long, I shouldn't think."

"Mr Davenport, I want you back here at six o'clock to confirm that those notices have been despatched."

"Very well."

That afternoon there had been a new development. Institutions, and some large private investors too, had continued to unload Pitcairn shares in the market in dribs and drabs and Pinsent Securities had continued to mop them up at 441p until just before four o'clock when they suddenly stopped. Justin Travers-Coe or one of his colleagues had been on the phone to Peter at regular intervals all day. Now he rang to say that Warburg Securities had offered a parcel of 100,000 shares at 441p, for whom they didn't know, and found no takers. They had dropped the price to 440p and Wagstaffs had snapped them up.

Shit, Peter thought to himself, Fontaubert has blown the whole 250 million - and still they're coming. It's a free-for-all for BMP.

He was fifteen minutes late for his appointment with the Panel, by design.

"So?" Beevor began. Distinctly hostile.

"So," Peter replied. All innocence.

"Have you sent out all those section 212 notices?"

"Yes."

"Very good. I want to see copies."

"Can we send them round in the morning?"

"Yes, but I want them here first thing. Nine o'clock at the latest. I've noticed you're not the best of timekeepers, Mr Davenport."

The two of them couldn't keep the mischievous grins off their faces as they walked back through Royal Exchange Buildings and St Michael's Alley into Lombard Street and back to 69 Gracechurch Street. Tim didn't understand exactly why Peter was being so difficult with the Panel; but he was enjoying it nonetheless.

"Better reckon to be back there by 9.30 tomorrow morning," said Tim.

"Maybe 9.15 if they're on their toes," Peter replied.

It was in fact nearer ten o'clock Thursday morning by the time they got there. Nothing seemed more important to the Panel these days than their internal meeting first thing every morning.

"We've received the copies of your section 212 notices but we appear to be missing the cover sheets. We'd like those as well."

"What cover sheets?"

"For the faxes. You did send them by fax?"

"No. We didn't have any fax numbers. We popped them in the post."

"You did what? To the Bahamas? To the Netherlands Antilles? To the Virgin Islands? It's now the sixth. The next closing date is the twelfth. This bid will potentially be over before you get any replies."

"Quite possibly. We're just complying with the law."

"I don't think that's good enough, Mr Davenport. I want to adjourn this meeting for a few minutes while I consult with my colleagues. Please stay here."

He returned ten minutes later with reinforcements. There were now five of them versus Peter and Tim. Beevor did the talking.

"The Panel Executive is not prepared to allow this bid to run its course without Pitcairn making every possible effort to identify all its shareholders within the time available. We will therefore be instructing Pinsent Securities to obtain fax numbers for all these purchasers and will be supplying them to you this afternoon. You are to make arrangements for fresh section 212 notices to be despatched immediately. I want those out today. And you are to require replies to be faxed back to you within twenty-four hours. The time difference is very inconvenient. Unfortunately, with the best will in the world - and that is a commodity which I am increasingly inclined to believe is lacking on your part - I don't think you'll have all replies by close of business tomorrow. But I want you here at ten o'clock on Monday morning with a schedule of the responses and photocopies of each of the replies."

*****

He consulted his watch for the umpteenth time. One thirty. At least the coffee was beginning to make him feel better. He tried Marsham Hall. They were not back yet. Jim had rung from the Rolls at Heathrow to say that the flight from Johannesburg was expected to be almost an hour late. He turned the pages of *The Times* with mounting nervous tension. He was beginning to place absurd reliance on Rita providing him with a clue to the answer to Freddie's question.

They were having to reprint the autobiography of that polecat Norman Tebbit in order to delete an alleged libel against Cecil Parkinson's former mistress. It was too much to hope that the cost would be taken off his royalties. RTZ had sold a great chunk of shares in Lasmo and there was speculation that they were clearing the decks ready to be a white knight for Consgold. On the sports pages were the results of the second round of the Suntory World Matchplay at Wentworth. Woosnam, Faldo, Lyle and Ballesteros were through, though Seve had been four down at one stage, in the car park adjacent to the sixteenth again in the second round, and never in the lead until he won at the thirty-seventh. Thank God Samantha hadn't suggested back in May that they go on to sudden death.

And then there was an article on the great October storm last year in which winds in Sussex had reached 98 knots, thirty people had been killed, fifteen million trees lost and one in six houses substantially damaged.

"Oh, ullo, luv. You're lucky to get us. We're just back from 'oliday. 'Ang on a minute; I'll jest get Timofy."

"No, Rita, actually it's you I want to talk to."

"What, you still lookin for a bit o' 'elp to find yerself some nookie, Peter? I don't fink you're tryin 'ard enough. I fought myself that girl you were wiv at Ascot looked more likely to find 'erself got up by the funny little American than you, luv."

"No, I've sorted that one out thanks, Rita. Well, not her, you understand. She just works for me. I'm not quite sure how to put this, Rita, but I've been trying to find out something about a man called Gerald Cunningham and I saw a picture of you in a newspaper attending his funeral."

"Peter, I told you at Ascot it's not somefing I ever want to talk abart."

"No you didn't, Rita; that was Arthur Evans."

"Same fing. He was there too."

"What, at the funeral?"

"No, luv. Well, he was there...but.." She was quiet for an age. He was just thinking they'd been cut off when she added "when 'e was killed."

"Arthur Evans was there?"

"Yes, luv. Lord fuckin Arfur Evans," she shouted, almost hysterical.

"Rita, I'm sorry. This is obviously painful; but I've got to know what happened. You can't conceive of how important this is."

He heard her draw a deep breath.

"Okay, luv, I can't imagine why you want to know but I trust you; so 'ere it is. I told you that Timofy and Arfur Evans went shootin togevver sometimes. Well, not togevver really. They jest sometimes find themselves on the same shoot. Gerald Cunningham was one of Timofy's muckers. I liked 'im. He was nice. She's a bit o' a cold fish - pretty but cold; but 'e was great fun. They used to come up here for the cricket sometimes. You might have even met them. Anyway, that week-end 'e an 'is wife invited us to stay. And unfortunately Arfur Evans an his fat-arsed wife as well. Timofy and Arfur and Gerald an the rest of his mates wot owned the shoot would go off for the day after the pheasants an Lindsay, that's 'is wife, would take the wives to Bram... Borough... Bligh, somefing House, some stately 'ome or uvver, back near the A1."

"Burghley House."

"Yes, that's right. Anyway then we'd all 'ave supper at their place. Only when we got back, the police were waitin an they said that Gerald had been shot. That he was dead." He could hear her catch her breath, trying not to sob. "Peter, it was awful."

"What had happened?"

"There were eight of 'em. Of course they draws for pegs and on this drive Timofy was right out on the left on the uvver side of a high stone wall which surrounded some woodland wiv Gerald the uvver side of the wall just where the trees finned out, and then Arfur Evans. The beaters drove the birds up frough the woods and they fired away. Timofy was a bit surprised because lots seemed to be going clear over where Gerald was and 'e was normally a bloody good shot. An when they'd finished the drive, Timofy goes back to the gate to get back into the wood an the uvver side of the wall he finds Gerald wiv half his 'ead blown away an 'is two guns lying by his side. Well 'e shouts for everyone to come an of course Arfur's just next peg along but e'd seen nuffing neiver. Seems it just went off in his 'and. The police came along and they took statements from everybody; but it was obviously just an accident. It was awful. We was staying in 'er 'ouse. Timofy and Arfur's cloves was covered in 'is blood from where they'd picked 'im up. I know she's a doctor and, like I said, she's a bit cold; so she wasn't hysterical or nuffing. But we couldn't just get up and leave her alone in that great big place. And there was Arfur Evans lording it about an organising everybody. An fussing over Lindsay like she was 'is to look after. Arranging fings. It gave me the creeps the way he sort of took charge, knew what to do an all."

"You mean like he was expecting it?"

"Yes....no....well... What on earf are you saying, Peter?"

*****

He called Rod as soon as he put the phone down. Rod drove straight up to London and met him at his flat.

"You chaps do alright for yourselves, don't you," he said, surveying the apartment.

"Just no kids to sop up the salary, Rod," he explained. "Drink?"

They sat down with a couple of beers and Peter explained what had happened.

"You've been reading too many thrillers, Peter," Rod said as he finished. "You're not putting two and two together and getting four; you're putting fuck all together with sweet fanny adams and thinking you've hit the bloody jackpot."

"Now come on, Rod, that is just not true. Sure I can't find an explanation to fit all that we've got; but there are some pretty odd facts. Take them in chronological order. This is incontestable. The husband of one of your research chemists is killed in the presence of the chairman of one of your major competitors. That research chemist is in the process of making a major advance against the most frightening of modern epidemics. She deliberately conceals what she has discovered. She makes a significant investment in your shares and then sells them again at the very moment she should have been buying some more. Your major competitor launches a bid for you. Its chairman, to say the least, behaves oddly. He sends his secretary to seduce a senior official of the Office of Fair Trading. He himself spends a couple of nights a week in one or more hotels under an assumed name."

"I'm not quite sure what you're suggesting he should be accused of, Peter - apart from murder that is; but I'll give you the defence case just the same. The inquest reached a verdict of misadventure - Gerald Cunningham was killed by accident with his own shotgun - and no one for a moment has contested that verdict. Dr Cunningham is a greedy bitch who thought she could make a buck by punting our shares. She got a simple dose of cold feet. She knew her research would have to come out eventually. She tried to delay the date - she's still trying - to put as much distance as possible between her silly attempt at insider dealing and the moment all is revealed; and she'll be able to say of the delay at that stage that she just wanted to be certain before claiming a breakthrough that would attract so much attention. Evans is a control freak who thought he'd take the risk out of the OFT deliberations by buttoning up the official responsible. And he likes to escape the pressure a couple of times a week by retiring from the limelight."

"Come off it, Rod. We don't live in a world of such innocence."

"Alright, give me an alternative scenario."

"Lindsay Cunningham is Arthur Evans' mistress. The French Horn at Sonning is their love nest. Maybe there are others. They plotted her husband's murder together. When Evans gets the opportunity and nobody else can see, he walks over to Gerald, picks up his spare gun and blows his head off. BMP's interest in Pitcairn may not have been her idea; but, whether or not it was her who suggested that BMP bid, keeping the results of her Aids research quiet would have been a huge bonus to a successful bidder. As you say, she's a greedy bitch and can't resist a punt. Why she sold I don't know. I can't work that out."

"Peter, you haven't got a shred of evidence for any of this. The police investigated his death. They look at fingerprints on triggers, ballistics or whatever they call it, trajectories of the buckshot and so on - and wouldn't a murderer be covered in blood too?"

"He was. Rita said as much."

"But no more so than Sir Timothy. And if Henderson-Ball was first to the body, what would Arthur Evans be doing turning up all covered in blood?"

"Maybe Timothy never noticed. He doesn't notice much these days. And within a couple of minutes, they were as messy as each other. Perhaps Evans would have accepted that he had to be first on

481

the scene if he had been badly spattered; but I guess the blood would fly away from the man who pulled the trigger rather than towards him. Wouldn't it? So he wasn't too bloody, which was a bonus. He could leave Henderson-Ball to discover the body."

"And the fingerprints."

"I don't know, Rod; perhaps they didn't take any. Or Evans could have pulled on a pair of gloves. Anyway I don't suppose Inspector Plod looks too hard when he finds out that the chaps each side of the deceased are City bigwigs and knights of the shires."

"Trajectory of the shot?"

"He could have shot him from in front, like it would have been if Cunningham had been picking up the gun and it had gone off. And it's odd that both guns were lying by his side too. If you were using two guns and didn't have a loader, you'd expect him to lean the one he wasn't using against a tree, or the wall; not just drop one on the ground and pick up the other. But that's just how it would be if the murderer picked up his spare gun and dropped it when he'd killed him."

"Perhaps a lot of birds came over all at once; got him flustered. He didn't have time to prop up the one he'd just fired."

"Then it would be empty."

"Perhaps not both barrels. Maybe that's what he forgot; that there was still one up the spout."

"You must admit it's possible he was murdered."

"What's the motive?"

"Her."

"And what about fat-arse, Lady Evans? Or are you suggesting she's next for the chop? Perhaps we should get her put under police protection," Rod added with a grin.

"What about what Rita said about Arthur being all over Lindsay Cunningham."

"I don't remember what you said she said being quite like that; but what about your night in the car park at the French Horn? Was she there? What does she drive? A Nissan Patrol, wasn't it? Any sign of one of those?"

"No, everything but. But maybe she hired a car," Peter blurted out as an explanation occurred to him.

"So every time she fancies a fuck, she hires a different car. Just in case Sherlock Davenport's hiding behind a tree sucking on his meerschaum. Come off it, Peter. You accounted for everyone in that car park. Evans wasn't with anyone. He drove up in his Daimler. On your theory shouldn't he have gone off to Hertz to get himself a Fiesta? And since, according to you, they got rid of her husband a year ago, why doesn't he just go up to her place in Melton Mowbray when he fancies a knobbing. It's not that long a drive when your dander's up."

"Perhaps he's taking no chances about being followed. Even fat-arse may have her suspicions."

"Peter, I know you've got the best of intentions; but I think we ought to be concentrating on the shareholders. Old Fontaubert may have shot his bolt; but at least he's taken out the weakest eight or nine per cent of the shareholders, including that bastard Sellar. We've still got a chance if we can hold the rest of them steady.'

"Rod, I know it's just circumstantial evidence; but I'm certain there's more to Dr Cunningham than meets the eye."

"You've not been listening to what I've been saying, Peter? It's not circumstantial evidence you've got. It's not any fucking evidence at all."

Sunday, 9 October 1988

It seemed he hardly slept a wink, churning it over again and again in his mind. There was no point lying in bed although the dark clouds swirling over the Thames which greeted him as he parted the curtains promised an awful day. He slipped out quickly for the papers and bought all the broadsheets. They would contain their final verdicts on Pitcairn's chances of survival. They all had theories about the mystery buyer; but, having noted that the buying had dried up and that BMP had resumed market purchases, most were dismissive of a last minute intervention by a new bidder. The absence of an announcement that a single purchaser had picked up most of the stock that had changed hands led *The Sunday Times* to conclude that a coterie of European and US fund managers had decided that victory for BMP was going to be a bonanza for the company and they had decided to climb aboard through the medium of Pitcairn shares. They would all accept the offer and BMP would walk it. The last thing Pitcairn needed now, Peter thought, was a BMP bandwagon, however misplaced the reasoning that generated it.

The Sunday Telegraph was equally depressing from a different direction. It declared authoritatively that there had been a leak of talks with a white knight and that the spivs had piled in; but that the talks had now collapsed and that they would be forced to accept the BMP offer in order to cut their losses. It urged shareholders who wanted cash to sell in the market to BMP for immediate settlement rather than wait three weeks while acceptances were processed.

It was Faldo versus Lyle for the World Matchplay. They'll need their waterproofs, Peter thought, as a vicious gust of wind swept a cloudburst of rain against the windows of the apartment.

By eight o'clock he was threading his way up through Islington and Canonbury onto the A1. It was coming down in buckets by now, exposing the inadequacies of design in the Morgan's soft-top. A particularly irritating drip was falling on his right trouserleg, making it look as though he'd pissed himself. But it could have been worse. On anything but a Sunday, the road would have been infested with heavy trucks hurling fountains of dirty spray rearward. Today there was hardly anything. At the roundabout just before Stamford he passed the signs for Burghley House and shortly after came the A606 that ran by the north shore of Rutland Water, normally a forest of sails but devoid today of weekend boating, towards Melton Mowbray.

As he came over the pretty railway bridge, the town was dominated by the church on the hill to the left of the road. From the *Melton Times* clippings with its photograph of the massive-towered stone church, he knew this to be to be St Mary's. This was where Gerald's funeral had taken place although he had apparently been buried in the churchyard of the village where they lived. He pulled over for a moment to consult O'Shea's map, then followed the signs for the A607 towards Leicester. He slowed down as the sign announcing the village of Kirby Bellars came up after less than five miles and peered through the torrential rain down the incline towards the open countryside on the right where he expected to see The Priory. It was unmistakable; a substantial two-storey stone house, perhaps 300 years old, with the windows of the upper level set into five identical gables in a steep-sloping slate roof. It lay two or three hundred yards from the road at the end of a sweeping gravel drive, the land between the road and the house and again over to the left devoted to a series of paddocks, the furthest one set with a number of painted wooden jumps. There were no animals to be seen, save a lone donkey which sheltered under an enormous horse chestnut, its leaves now starting to yellow autumnally, half way down the drive.

Peter turned into the entrance and stopped. There were stone pillars either side with black ironwork lamps on top and black iron posts with matching lamps at intervals the length of the drive. The paddocks to left and right were fenced off with iron railings. He took a deep breath, rehearsed his story and let out the clutch. The wet gravel crunched beneath the tyres.

Peter couldn't see how deep the house went but it was wide. In the centre was a great stone archway in which were set double oaken doors, studded with iron. It seemed absurdly large for a couple, let alone a woman on her own. And rather forbidding under the continuing downpour.

The door had one of those bell-pulls beside it. He could hear the bell clanging loudly inside and shortly thereafter a woman's light footsteps approaching over a flagstone floor. She opened the right hand of the double doors and regarded him, a questionmark in her eyes. He was glad he had dressed respectably - blazer and flannels, shirt and tie - though she was in jodhpurs and riding boots. She was an unusually tall but pretty woman with a startling resemblance to the wife of that crook, Jeffrey Archer. Her complexion was perfect; her face framed by her dark hair, conservatively styled. Her figure was good; but athletic rather than curvaceous. You could imagine a judge describing her too as fragrant as he directed his jury to acquit her. You could hardly conceive of her as a conspirator to murder and Peter had second thoughts. Butter wouldn't melt in her mouth.

"Dr Cunningham?" he enquired.

She nodded very briefly but did not actually acknowledge it.

"Hello, I'm sorry to appear unannounced like this; but I need to talk to you urgently."

She stood her ground, still quizzical, though there was little shelter where Peter stood from the pouring rain."

"My name's Peter Davenport. I work for Dundas Brothers and I'm advising your employers, Pitcairn Pharmaceuticals, on the bid by BMP."

"Yes." She still gave no ground, though something registered. But it was only for an instant, no more than a widening of the eyes. She inclined her head slightly to one side and the questionmark repeated itself.

"I need to ask you some questions," he said, producing his business card, trying to improve his *bona fides*. "Would you mind if I come in?"

She stood aside. Progress. Then shut the door behind him. It was a large hallway, stone-flagged, as betrayed by her footsteps, with a substantial staircase ahead, also in stone, that turned left and left again as it rose to the next floor. She led the way beneath it to the back of the house into an enormous kitchen. It had been expensively done out in Smallbone country style, a vast jet-black Aga, rust-coloured granite worktops, cupboards in dark natural wood, burnished copper pans hanging from the beams, original flagstones, polished and indented by the feet of ages. She sat on one of the upright wooden chairs to one side of a big, rough oak table and motioned him to the seat opposite. She wasn't hostile; but she wasn't friendly. Almost resigned. Peter recalled Rita's words. A cold fish.

"Dr Cunningham," he began. He had decided to stick to the 'doctor'; he thought it put more emphasis on her status as an employee, questioned her right to go dabbling in the shares of her employer. "You will know that Pitcairn Pharmaceuticals is currently the subject of a take-over offer by BMP."

Again she nodded briefly, almost imperceptibly. She was neither gentle nor severe; just calm, detached, almost serene. It was her eyes. They were dark and very beautiful. Not twinkling. More smiling. Smiling with intelligent comprehension. Peter recalled Evans' eyes from that meeting at number 69. Dark too. Dark as death.

"I lead the team at Dundas Brothers, the merchant bank that is providing advice to the board of directors of Pitcairn. The directors, advised by us, are of the view that it is not in shareholders' best interests to accept BMP's offer. Nevertheless, we recognise that the outcome is likely to be close and, as you might imagine in those circumstances, we're trying to contact as many as possible of those who own Pitcairn shares with a view to persuading them not to accept the offer."

"But there must be a mistake, Mr ..." She hesitated for a moment as she looked down at his card in front of her on the table, though she didn't look like one to forget a name so quickly. "Mr Davenport," she went on, "I don't own any shares in Pitcairn."

"Oh. But I'm sure you bought some back in November last year - actually quite a large holding for a private individual."

She was still impassive. For a fleeting moment he had the impression that she was thinking of denying it all. But there were calculations going on behind that bland exterior. Perhaps she thought of putting it down to an error on the part of her broker, then remembered the enquiry earlier in the year from the head of personnel. If she was lying, she was clever enough to remember the lie that she had previously touted.

"Yes, I did buy some shares shortly after my husband passed away. He died very suddenly, about a year ago - in a shooting accident. I really didn't know what to do with all the money that came from his life policies; but I sold the shares again very soon - for personal reasons."

The whole thing was intended to shut him up, appeal to his courtesy, keep him from deliberately touching a tender spot. She didn't know that, at the best of times, Davenport wouldn't have cared; though he knew the formulae for appearing solicitous.

"I'm sorry. But could I be rude enough to ask you what sort of reasons made you sell so quickly?"

She hesitated again. She could have chosen the moment to turn aggressive, to tell him to mind his own business, but she remained imperturbable.

"Actually I was warned that I might be facing some rather severe losses at Lloyds. It was something that Gerald - that's my deceased husband - had organised for me. He thought it would give me some income of my own; but it all appears to have gone wrong. Anyway I was told that I ought to remain - I think the word is liquid, isn't it?"

"Quite so. So you sold the shares?"

"Yes, almost as soon as I'd bought them."

"And you don't have any other interests in Pitcairn shares?"

"No. None whatever."

"Then, I'm afraid this has all been a mistake. I'm sorry for disturbing you," he said, starting to push back his chair. He stopped.

"Oh, one other thing, Dr Cunningham. Do you know Arthur Evans?"

"Why, yes, of course. Gerald and he used to go shooting together sometimes and I see him from time to time at the hunt. We both go out with the Quorn. It's the local pack."

Peter remembered idly watching a television documentary about the famous hunt some years back. It had a reputation for many things, including men of large appetites. A phrase from the programme came back to him. *'The air over Melton Mowbray heaves with the sighs of adulterers.'* Odd that she didn't refer to the fact that Evans was present at her husband's death, Peter thought. He stood up. He was contemplating a flyer but the phrasing took some working out. It had to be susceptible to protestations of innocence on his part; but its insinuation had to be unmistakable.

"I don't suppose Lord Evans told you that BMP was about to bid for Pitcairn?"

"Certainly not." As a response, it was a little more enlivened.

"Oh, I just thought he might have done. As a result of your relationship, you know."

She took it as she was intended. She coloured and the serenity flew from her face.

"Mr Davenport, are you suggesting something improper?"

"No of course not," he blustered, certain that he'd hit a nerve although he had no proof. In for a penny, in for a pound, he thought. "But you might have told him you were secretly on your way to discovering an Aids vaccine. That would be quite something for BMP to find hidden in Pitcairn's laboratories when they'd got control."

"Don't be so absurd, Mr Davenport. You may know something about companies and take-over bids; but you clearly know very little about pharmaceutical research. I think you'd better leave now. Your tone is starting to become quite offensive."

"I wonder what the press might make of it," he mused out loud, walking away from her across the hallway towards the front door.

"I wouldn't risk it Mr Davenport and you can expect to hear from my solicitors in the morning to that effect."

She stood in the open front doorway and watched him as he crossed the driveway to his car. It was coming down in buckets again and he was thoroughly soaked for his attempted display of nonchalance. He climbed into the Morgan and turned it round. As he set off up the drive, he looked over at her, still framed in the stone doorway. He expected a look of undisguised malevolence but she was perfectly composed again behind those beautiful dark, gentle eyes. If he for one moment had thought he had any evidence, they seemed at once to dismiss it.

Emerging from the drive, Peter turned right and drove slowly on up the hill. At the top was a sign indicating the centre of the village down a road to the right. He followed it for a few hundred yards past prosperous-looking houses of various eras as it descended into the vale. At the bottom a bridge crossed what he took to be the railway line again and the road continued on for two or three hundred yards before it disappeared into a farm track. At that point and to the right stood a pretty old church with a little square tower in creamy stone. It was tiny by comparison to St Mary's in Melton Mowbray and one could see how it had not been adequate to accommodate the funeral of a significant local businessman. From the number of cars outside, there must have been a service in progress and Peter had to turn and park the car some way back towards the railway bridge. He got out, hoisting a large golf umbrella as he did so and walked back down the road. There was a little iron gate, set below an arch of ironwork and surmounted by a lamp of yellow glass. A handwritten notice, encased in clear plastic against the weather, and headed 'St Peter's Church' announced harvest festival for 9th October - today.

The gravestones set amongst the wet grass on this side of the church were all old and grey. Peter walked down the pathway past the vestibule. The weedy singing of an English congregation, barely audible above the organ, drifted from the closed door. Not a very spirited thanksgiving for harvest home, Peter thought. He followed the path round to the back of the church and emerged the far side where there was a clear view over the sodden countryside. Newer departures were laid out in a couple of neat rows, chronologically. There were only two since him. Gerald Matthew Cunningham - Born 13th August, 1939 - Died 10th October, 1987. That was all. Plain black marble - like Fontaubert's floor - with gold lettering. No 'Loving husband of Lindsay'; no 'Tragically taken before his time'; not even a 'Rest in Peace'. A year ago tomorrow.

The rain was easing off though it looked as though it was going to start again soon, more darkness over to the west. He returned to the Morgan, drove back up to the main road and turned back towards Melton Mowbray to pass her house for the final time. He drove slowly. She appeared to have taken advantage of the brief respite in the weather to get out and exercise one of the horses, though, in waterproof cape and hat, he couldn't have been sure that it was her on the big grey tracing the perimeter of the furthest paddock.

On a whim he turned down a single track road to the right, opposite The Priory's driveway and found an open gateway where he could pull off into a field. It was foolhardy. The ground was sodden and muddy.

He'd be lucky to find enough grip to get the car out again. He pulled on his anorak but left the garish umbrella behind as he set out on foot.

Back on the road, he turned right. Sure enough, he thought he had seen a secondary entrance to the property. It was in reality a farm track with a cattle grid on one side and a little pedestrian gate to one side. It appeared to run around to the back of the house, where there were presumably the stables. There were hedgerows on both sides but he felt nevertheless absurdly conspicuous. What on earth did he think he was doing? She appeared to be alone on the property; but it would only take a dog to alert her that he was snooping about.

He emerged cautiously from the far end of the lane. There were half a dozen loose-boxes on the side of a cobbled yard facing the house, but not all were apparently occupied. One door was completely open, presumably the grey's, and the top halves of two others, from which the inquisitive heads of a bay and a chestnut, ears erect, observed him suspiciously, but mercifully in silence. There was also a tack room, its door too wide open. On the far side of the yard a five bar gate gave access to the paddock beyond and a stone archway, at right-angles to it, apparently led through to the gravel driveway in front of the house. Between the gate and the loose-boxes was a long low barn of ancient provenance. At one end were stacks of hay and some sacks, presumably of feed; in the middle a two-horse trailer, a small tractor and a gang-mower; on the right were two wide double doors, later additions. One stood slightly ajar.

Peter crossed the yard. He was feeling desperately furtive and his heart was pounding. There was no reason to be here. It was just looking for trouble. As he reached the double doorway, he heard the bolt on the five-bar gate being drawn back, followed by the squeal of the hinges; and, just as he ducked inside what turned out to be a garage, a horse crossing the cobbles. He hardly dared breathe. Hopefully she'd saddle up another one and take it out, but he could see through the slightly open door that it had stopped spitting and was beginning to rain in earnest again. Within moments it was coming down as hard as ever. He tried to get a glimpse of her but could find no crack in the planking of the doors. There was a slight gap where the door was hinged but his field of view was very limited. She crossed it once or twice on foot but he could not figure out what she was doing. Unlikely that she'd be going out again in this. She seemed to be an age. Presumably she's got to unsaddle it. Rub it down? Get it some feed? And the others? There was much toing and froing and banging of doors but he still couldn't make out what she was about.

He started for the first time to explore his surroundings. The conversion of this end of the barn into a garage was relatively recent, he guessed. There was a concrete floor and the doors were obviously new. But the uprights which supported the roof were original. They divided the space naturally into bays for three cars. Her Nissan Patrol was over there at the far end, a gap to this side of it, and immediately behind him an old Jensen Interceptor. His heart turned somersaults as he tried to picture her on the grey. The broad-brimmed hat, the oilskin cape. That 'Australian' at the French Horn. Circumstantial evidence at last; but he wanted more. He was just going down on his knees to check the registration number when he heard her coming towards him. He froze onto his belly and then, as he heard her actually at the door, tried to slide noiselessly feet first under the car. She slammed the door shut and he was plunged into total darkness. As he lay there he heard the key turn in the lock and bolts at the tops and bottoms of the doors slam into their slots.

"I wriggled out from under the car. I tell you I was crapping myself. The tiniest chink of light came from under the double doors but there were no windows and I could make out nothing more than shadows in the darkness. I went back down on my hands and knees in front of the Jensen, trying to feel the contours of the letters on the registration plate. It ought to have been one of those old-fashioned types with raised letters and numerals; but it wasn't and I couldn't make out a bloody thing. I thought that perhaps I could put the sidelights on; that would probably give me enough visibility; but then I was worried that they might be seen from outside. Probably not if it was just the sidelights. I decided that I'd have to risk it. But, so what; now I was bloody-well imprisoned.

"Anyway, first things first. I'd get the number. Well, you wouldn't fucking believe it. The car was locked; driver and passenger doors. Well, perhaps I could get enough light from the Nissan, though I'd have to use the headlights on that if it was going to get diffused to the other end of the garage. No chance. Also locked. All the doors. All sodding five of them.

"So what am I going to do? I could stay there all afternoon and all bloody night. In the morning she'd come and open up to go to work. I could possibly hide under the Jensen while she got the Nissan out. But, so what, then she'd lock me up again. I could, of course, pop up bold as brass as she opened the doors in the morning. 'Hello, surprise, surprise, it's me again!' I didn't think so. Perhaps I could find a way to break out of there. I crawled all round the walls, looking for something loose that I could prise open. Fat chance; that barn was built like fucking Fort Knox."

"So, how did you get out and why are you calling me at six in the bloody morning."

"Don't start whingeing to me, Rod. At least you've had a night in bed tucked up next to your warm little wife. I've been lying awake on cold sodding concrete waiting for the firing squad at dawn. And she was up at dawn, if not before. Apparently she likes to ride before she leaves for work. Actually it was all in O'Shea's report but I'd forgotten that. Explains what she was doing leaving Evans' hotel so early in the morning too. Anyway she opened the garage door and drove the Nissan out round to the front of the house. I was under the Jensen. I just slid out and bolted for it across the yard before she came back again."

"And did you get the registration number?"

"I did. LRP 416K."

"And is that the one?"

"I don't know yet. I need to speak to Harrington. Get him to look it up. But let's assume that it is. It must be. Would you accept that as evidence now, your honour?"

"Yes. Still circumstantial; but strongly circumstantial."

"Sho why did she shell the sharesh?"

"You alright, Peter?"

"Yes. Sure. Just rather tired."

"Let's be logical about this. The motive for buying can only have been greed." Rod was concentrating now. Previously, he had been so dismissive of Peter's theory that he really hadn't been prepared to give it a second thought. "So maybe she told him she'd bought some shares. He said it was a damned silly idea for her to appear on the register. We'd be crawling all over it when we realised what was happening. But Wagstaffs hadn't started buying yet; so she should get off the register again before they began and maybe we'd never notice she'd been there."

"Is that all? Throw up the chance to make a hundred k just like that."

"Possibly not. You remember that activity in the options market in our shares. That was about the same time. I'll have to check the dates. Perhaps he told her there was a better way. More profitable too. Lower outlay for more shares. Remember she has no financial background."

"And more anonymous too. Weren't those orders generated in Switzerland?"

"I think so. I'll have to check. Look, I'm going straight into the office. I'll call you in an hour - no more than an hour and a half. Where will you be?"

"I've got to go home, Rod. I'm covered in mud from head to foot. I'd parked my car in a field; and what with all the rain, I couldn't get it out. I had to pile half my clothes under the rear wheels to stop them spinning. And I'm due in front of the Panel again at ten o'clock."

"Okay. I'll talk to Justin. See if we can get more of a handle on that options dealing. You check the registration number with Harrington and we'll talk again when you're done with the Panel. See where we go from there. If your evidence still stacks up."

"It will, Rod. I'm convinced of it."

Monday, 10 October 1988

"What do you mean 'there have been no replies'?"

"What I am saying, Mr Beevor, is that there have been no replies to our latest section 212 notices. Not a single one."

"Well, that's a clear breach of the law."

"You're the lawyer; but I've been advised that it's not quite as open and shut as that. It's all a question of what's a reasonable time. We put in twenty-four hours - like you told us to - but it might be said that that's too demanding."

"It's perfectly normal nowadays. And we're running out of time. I think you'd better make immediate application to the court under section 216 to have the shares disenfranchised so that they can't affect the outcome of the offer."

"No."

"What do you mean 'no'?"

"What I mean is that we are not going to make such an application. We have no obligation to do so in law and we have no such obligation in terms of the Code. We are simply not going to do it."

"But BMP can instruct you to do it."

"I think not. If they so wish, they can requisition an extraordinary general meeting of Pitcairn and propose a resolution which, if passed - and that is far from certain - would instruct the directors to make an application to the court."

"But that would take weeks."

"That's the law, so I'm told."

"But there is clear circumstantial evidence of a concert party. That most certainly is a matter for the Panel."

"What evidence?"

"I would have thought that was obvious."

495

"I don't think it's circumstantial evidence that you've got. I don't think it's any evidence at all."

"Mr Davenport, the Panel executive will not let this matter rest. You may expect to hear from us again."

*****

When he got back to the office, there was a message to call Justin Travers-Coe urgently.

"Bad news, I'm afraid, Peter. That lady dog from Grossmanns has been going round some of the institutions with David Carradine recruiting fund managers to buy Pitcairn shares above the offer price and sell to BMP for cash at 440p. She's close enough to know exactly what she needs and it's a small enough figure to know she can find the shares in the market."

"Do you know who she's got signed up?"

"Well, nobody is signed up yet. It's conditional of course. She has to guarantee them that the bid will succeed. So she won't press the button until the total of what she's got to date and what these people are prepared to do equals 50.1%. And, in addition, she's got to find them sellers of enough shares to square the circle. But we know she's been to Schroders and Flemings and they've agreed to play the game."

"What about Mercury?"

"She's been to them too; but no dice."

"Well, thank God for that. I'd given up on that four and a quarter per cent. So the calculating Carol Galley's got a human side after all."

"No, Peter, you were right first time. She went round to see Hennessy first thing this morning to tell him to his face that they'd decided to accept. That they are going to accept is what's tipped the balance for Grossmanns. Apparently Galley said magnanimously that she wouldn't do anything else to help the bid succeed; but she didn't really need to. I reckon they've now got 48.75% in the bag or promised. They only need another eight million odd shares or so to be home and dry. They're probably just waiting for Mercury's acceptance to arrive. I'm afraid it's all over, Peter."

"Have you told the chairman?"

"No. I thought you'd prefer it if I left that to you."

"Thanks, Justin," he said, hanging up. Toffee-nosed bastard.

He called him back immediately.

"Justin, did Rod ring you this morning to ask you to check the timing of all that activity in the options market back at the end of November last year?"

"Yes, something to do with that research scientist who bought and then sold a parcel of shares. To be honest, I didn't really understand what he was going on about. I thought she was history."

"And?"

"And what?"

"When were all those options purchased?"

"Oh, I see what you mean. Yes it was apparently the same day that she sold; but I can't for the life of me see what Rod's getting steamed up about. If you ask me, he'd be better dusting off his service contract and checking that his expense claims are in order," he concluded with a stifled Etonian guffaw.

Peter looked up to see Bill McAdam coming through the door into his office. He was sweaty and disheveled, dark patches at the armpits of an unironed blue shirt, a button burst to reveal an unappetising portion of white, hairy belly. He shut the door behind him.

"Whayaye, mun. It's doon and doosted," he said, rubbing his podgy-fingered hands together and sprawling all over the chair in front of Peter's desk. "BZW hev agreed it all. I'm jest gooin to goo an tell Gallaher that wear oon our way. Terms are as we discoosed."

"What's the state of play with Fidelity, Bill?"

There had been a hitch at the end of the previous week and they'd missed the targeted announcement that morning. Just as well for Bill, who had needed the week-end for BZW to get the deal past the crusty old farts on the Barclays board. Gallaher and Fidelity had been beavering away all week-end too.

"Kent says it's back oon track. Annooncing Wednesday moorning. It's poorfect timing. Simooltaneoos, like. Coorporate finance to BZW -- the rest doon the swanny to Fidelity. De yer want to coom oop and see Gallaher wi me?"

497

"Love to, Bill, but I'm up to my ears in Pitcairn right now. I'm due at St James's Square five minutes ago."

*****

"Hello, hello, is that 0483 495367?" Peter couldn't make out the female voice on the other end of the line. It wasn't the snooty Claudia trying to do her English counties accent; and it had a twang that didn't fit with Hermione or Hilda or whatever the housekeeper was called.

"Sure is."

"Oh, it's Peter Davenport here. Is Mr Hennessy there please?"

"Oh hi, Mr Davenport. It's Virginia. Remember we met once a while back. You came to lunch."

"Yes, yes, of course. Is your father there?"

"Yes, I think he's out in the garden somewhere. I guess he'll want to take your call in his study. Can you hold on a minute?"

"Yes, of course."

The minute became three or four; but eventually there was a pronounced click and Hennessy came on the line.

Peter had spent all afternoon round at St James's Square with Rod and George Aladyce.

"It all fuff...fuff...fucking fuff...fuff...fits together circumstantially, pee...pee...Peter; but fuff...fuff...for example, there's no evidence that he's actually fuff...fuff...fucking her, is there?"

"Why's this little widow on the pill then, George?"

"Well, as a matter of fuff...fact, pee...pee...Peter, there are medical cun...cun...conditions for which general practitioners prescribe the pip... pip...pill which are nothing to do with fun...fun...fornication. But anyway, there's none...none...nothing against a girl taking precautions in cake...cake...case she gets lucky."

"What? With her husband barely cold? This isn't a matter of luck, George. Arthur Evans actually murdered for this bit of pussy."

"Look, even I'm not sure about that, Peter," Rod broke in. "You could never make that stick. I'm still bothered by the fact that she didn't have him cremated. You'd think that they'd have wanted to destroy every bit of evidence they could."

"Well, I dododo...don't gogogo...go along with that Rod. You could exhume the purp...purp...poor bub...bub...bugger every which way up you lie...lie...like; but you'd still discover his head half blown off with his own shotgun."

"What about fat-arse?" It was Rod again.

"Well, I don't suppose they're planning to do her in as well, Rod. That's a bit too obvious. It's the divorce courts and a generous pay-off for her, I should imagine. She'll probably be delighted to see the back of him."

"Difficult to see what this little doctor sees in him, if she's as tasty as you say, Peter."

"It's power, isn't it, Rod. The seductive influence of power. Practically every despot in history was a leg-over legend - except for Hitler that is - and he only had one ball by all accounts. And the money too."

"She hardly needs that after what she's inherited, Peter. She's got plenty already."

"The greedy can always find room for a bit more. And she's not got it on this scale, Rod. If the two of them were behind the purchase of all those option contracts by Oberoi et Cie on 27th November, right now they're sitting on a gain of ten or twelve million quid. The great thing about buying the options instead of the shares is that they've got a hell of a lot more bangs for their bucks. Even if it's only a business arrangement between Evans and her and she contributed just her quarter million, she's made the best part of three million quid. And they'll neither of them be telling the tax man about it either. You don't necessarily have to believe that her husband was murdered or even that she and Evans are having it off. There is undoubtedly contact between them - O'Shea has confirmed that the Jensen at Sonning was definitely hers - and she has certainly been playing jiggery-pokery with her research results."

"Well, it's all very interesting, Peter; but you can't prove it can you," Hennessy said, as Peter finished his rather more muted version of the report. "What do you think we should do next? I guess you should go round to the Panel and lay it all on the table."

"That won't work, Christopher. As you rightly say, there's no evidence that can't be countered with a simple denial from Evans - or from Dr Cunningham come to that. Added to that, frankly I've blown away all possibility of the Panel executive leaning in our favour with all the delaying tactics I've adopted over the activities of our friend in Paris. The Panel would sit tight on anything like this right now. They'd hate the thought of admitting that it even might be true. I could see them not even bothering to ask Evans just to keep it off the record and protect their own backs if it subsequently came to light. Better to dismiss all we say as malicious tittle-tattle and let the bid run its course. Difficult to argue with that judgment from their point of view. The last thing they want on their hands is another Guinness."

"But we can't just let Evans get away with this. He's suborned one of our research staff at the very least and in all probability used the bidding process for his personal gain. We've got to nail this guy once and for all."

You never knew with Hennessy, Peter thought, whether he was going to be the Old Testament God of wrath or the New Testament God of forgiveness. At least he seemed to have fire and brimstone in his belly this evening. And he was not short of an appeal to a bit of covetousness either, as he added: "I thought you at least Peter had reason to fight this to the very end."

"Oh indeed I have, Christopher, and I'm certainly not proposing that we give up now."

"What are you proposing then?"

"Christopher, in my view what we have here is a very powerful loaded cannon; but we only have one cannon ball. If we fire it in the wrong direction, it will explode harmlessly and the opportunity will be gone forever. I think we have three potential targets. The first is the Panel. I'm against firing it at them for the reasons I've explained. I suspect they would just absorb the blow and do nothing about it; but even if they were to call on Evans to answer the charge, I'm sure he'd follow up his denial with an application to the courts for an injunction to smother anything we might want to say. And I think he'd succeed.

"The second possibility is for us to go to the courts ourselves. I don't think that would work either. I don't think the judge would be prepared to listen to us if we didn't have legally acceptable levels of proof and hadn't exhausted the conventional route for complaint - the take-over code - first."

"And you've already dismissed that."

"Quite so; and again we would be giving Evans the opportunity to use the law to silence us."

"So which target are you proposing for this salvo?"

"The press."

"Now come on, Peter, I'm a lawyer and I know something about your libel laws over here. They're a whole lot tougher than ours. No Brit newspaper would dare publish stuff like this without third-party corroboration."

"I can imagine circumstances in which they would."

"Go on."

"They'd publish it if it came directly from you. I propose you call a press conference tomorrow and present the evidence - all circumstantial I know. But we believe we know what it points to; so why shouldn't the press?"

"You want me to get up in public and accuse Lord Evans of murder?"

"Well not necessarily that. Gerald Cunningham's death could just be presented as a background fact. Let the press draw its own conclusions. But the rest of it, yes."

"Peter, you can't expect me to get up in public and come out with all this. Don't you see? Evans will deny it all. You've got no more than a few unrelated items of circumstantial evidence. The press will be too scared to swallow what you've got, even if they wanted to; and I shall be a laughing stock."

Yes, Peter could see. Hennessy could play the eye for an eye or the arm for an arm; but, only inches north of a dwarf, he couldn't stand the prospect of being laughed at.

He replaced the receiver.

"Oh, Freddie," he said out loud, "this is when I needed you."

Tuesday, 11 October 1988

'*NatWest and Midland set stage for battle in credit card market*' read the *Financial Times* headline; but that wasn't the article that Peter was reading, hunched over his desk, palms spread either side of the newspaper, still standing in his Burberry, his briefcase dropped on the chair. The bottom half of the page was devoted to an article headed in only slightly smaller type than the main headline '*Dundas dismisses corporate finance chief for planning defection*'. The article below read:-

> *Dundas Brothers, the City merchant banking group, yesterday dismissed the head of its corporate finance department for holding what it called "unauthorised discussions" about the possible transfer of his department to another company.*

> *Mr Stephen Gallaher, Dundas Brothers' chief executive, said his conduct was "reprehensible" and "totally inconsistent with his responsibility as a director". The executive concerned, Mr William McAdam, declined to comment publicly last night.*

> *One of the groups Mr McAdam is believed to have been negotiating with is Barclays de Zoete Wedd, the relatively newly formed investment banking arm of Barclays Bank, which recruited around a dozen senior*

502

members of Hill Samuel's corporate finance department in similar circumstances a little over a year ago. BZW's corporate finance department is headed by Mr Richard Heley, a former director of Hill Samuel.

Mr Heley confirmed last night that BZW was interested in acquiring Dundas Brothers' corporate finance staff and business. But he said BZW had indicated its interest formally to the Dundas Brothers group, and he denied there was a connection with these talks and yesterday's dismissal.

Other groups might have included US investment banks keen to establish themselves more strongly in the City.

The dismissal comes less than 6 months after merger talks between Dundas Brothers and RheinHeim Bank of Germany collapsed unexpectedly, leaving a questionmark over Dundas Brothers' future. There was considerable speculation that the group would subsequently suffer defections.

According to sources in Dundas Brothers, the corporate finance department was disappointed by the failure of the merger talks, which it hoped would raise the group into the big international league.

After the collapse, Mr McAdam contacted a number of banking groups to negotiate a move which would have included a large number of his colleagues. Dundas Brothers' corporate finance department has 65 people and 6 directors and claims to have one of the most active client lists in the City.

BZW was likely to be interested because of the limited success of the group's previous raid on Hill Samuel and its continuing keenness to build up its corporate finance business which is new and relatively small. However, news of the negotiations got back to Dundas Brothers' headquarters at the end of last week, and Mr McAdam was called to account.

Although there have been several mass defections from City institutions before and after Big Bang, Dundas Brothers took the view that Mr McAdam was acting beyond his powers in negotiating the transfer of a major proportion of the group's business and its staff without the board's knowledge. Mr McAdam is believed to have argued that he was acting in the best interests of his department.

There was a reference at the end of the article to a comment in the Lex column. Peter turned to the back page. *'Walking the plank at Dundas'* read the Lex headline above three balanced paragraphs.

The latest upheaval at Dundas Brothers looks like being a test case for the ethics of the new City. In planning the secession of an entire corporate finance department, the sacked executive was doing nothing new in principle, though there is a touch of novelty about the scale. Analytical and other teams have been marketing themselves collectively for years, and though Dundas argues that the executive concerned was in breach of his fiduciary duty as a director, there is doubtless precedent for that as well.

The ethics of the case are complicated by the fact that Mr McAdam took the initiative in disclosing the outlines of the deal to his employers, whose agreement as principals was taken to be necessary. But Dundas Brothers' response, though unusually vehement in City terms, is hardly surprising in a wider context. One pictures the reaction of an ICI board, say, on being told by a divisional head that he had been privately negotiating its sale to a BASF or a Dupont.

In acting as it did, Dundas Brothers may well have frustrated the deal with the mystery buyer, at least in its planned form. But either way, the damage seems done. The whole debacle sheds an unwelcome light on the state of morale after the collapse of the RheinHeim talks, and any executive who felt ready to join the original defection will scarcely feel more settled now. The 20p fall in the share price yesterday to 475p looks like balanced recognition of the increased certainty of a bid, and the reduced value to a bidder.

Peter took off his raincoat and threw it onto its customary spot on top of the filing cabinet. He hung his jacket over the back of the chair and walked across to Bill's office. It was a glass box like his own, just a little bigger. Peter tried the door. It was locked. He peered inside. It looked as though a small army of spring-cleaners had attacked it overnight. Gone were the usual higgledy-piggledy messes of papers and documents, plastic cups, battered briefcases, cardboard boxes, the odd bit of clothing, never too clean, the cluttered shelf of tombstones, miniaturised advertisements set in blocks of perspex to celebrate bygone deals, the ballpoints and broad red felt-tip marker pens with which Bill had rubbished everything put before him; and in their place, nothing. A clear desk, empty chairs, the glass-fronted bookcase, the two filing cabinets, the credenza with its grey keyboard and blank monitor screen. There was no more of Bill in there than a couple of dark stains on the pale blue carpet tiles.

Over the course of the next hour, the department drifted onto the floor in dribs and drabs. The executives scurried hither and thither like ants, forming tight little groups one moment, then breaking and reforming somewhere else. The directors were no better, though Kent was nowhere to be seen.

Though he had intended to send Tim Phillips in his place, Davenport, for lack of anything else to do, went off to St James's Square for the defence committee. When he got back shortly before ten, Sybil Dunwoody, the personnel director, was waiting for him by his desk. Not a message; the dyke herself. Stephen Gallaher wanted to see him.

Sybil Dunwoody was a dumpy lady with short grey hair, slightly bulging eyes and a thick scarlet slash of heavily painted lips. She had a huge wardrobe, but unfortunately one entirely of her own devising. Whilst she had mastered the mechanics of sewing cloth together, she was sadly devoid of the shape which would make her an agreeable mannequin or the style to disguise it. Her reaction to these deficiencies was to use only two patterns, one for a suit and the other for a dress. The dress was basically shaped like a sack and the suit like two sacks, one above the other. Neither had a waist; but, then nor did she. She apparently found a squarish shape to the shoulders easiest to cut and, as a result, her torso always reminded Peter of one of those Soviet generals lined up to take the salute at the May Day parade atop the Lenin Mausoleum. Some variation might be found in the length of her skirts but her feet were frankly the best part of her legs and it was downhill all the way up after that. Any disclosure of ankle, calf, knee or, heaven forfend, thigh was destined to be acutely undesirable. Today she was wearing another suit, nondescript in a muddy brown with its jacket apparently modeled on the back of a substantial armchair.

Gallaher's office, what had previously been Johnathan Tudor's, was adjacent to Cruso's with a shared office for their two secretaries between them. His own secretary was not at her desk but Hildegaard von Schulzendorff, the grävin herself, was sitting imperiously behind her word processor daring it to defy her will. She gave Peter a knowing look, almost a wink, as Sybil opened the door of Gallaher's office without knocking and ushered Peter in. It was a little smaller than Cruso's office and of a very different style with four soft modern-looking armchairs in grey leather to one side and a desk of smokey glass supported by tubes of stainless steel to the other. The windows which filled one side of the room were permanently shaded by an expensive-looking venetian blind in a light veneer which matched the window sill and there was one of the bank's collection of three Hockneys on each of the walls.

Gallaher was in shirt-sleeves, a pale blue silk shirt and darker knitted silk tie, which set off his late-summer but more or less permanent tan and his longish, silver-streaked grey hair. He motioned Davenport amiably towards one of the armchairs. Dunwoody wedged herself uninvited into one of the others, a square brown peg in a square grey hole.

"Peter, I think I should start by telling you that I know you were aware of the negotiations that McAdam was conducting behind our backs with a view to robbing Dundas Brothers of the value of its corporate finance department."

Though it hadn't really got him anywhere, Peter decided to adopt the same approach with Gallaher as he had been using on the Panel. He said nothing. Sybil Dunwoody's presence said enough. Gallaher wasn't going to let him get away with it.

"You were aware, Peter, weren't you?"

"I wouldn't describe what Bill was doing in the terms that you've used; but yes, I was aware that there were some discussions."

"Well, be that as it may, I've decided that, having made an example of McAdam, I'm going to leave it at that. There's not going to be a witch-hunt. The rest of you are safe."

Gallaher looked at him quizzically. He leaned forward in his chair towards Peter, giving him the benefit of a whiff of his appalling breath.

Peter got the impression he was meant to say 'thankyou'. He wasn't going to. He knew full well that Gallaher realised that, if he fired all the accessories to Bill's supposed crime, he could end up destroying whatever was left of the value of corporate finance.

"You are also aware that we are close to agreeing a deal for Fidelity Bank to acquire Dundas Brothers?"

"Yes."

"There are still a number of matters outstanding which I am hoping to resolve at a meeting with Fidelity this afternoon so that we can make an announcement tomorrow morning. One of those matters is the future of corporate finance. Frankly it's not part of Fidelity's business and I doubt if they will want to make it so. They want the Brothers for the commercial loan book - they've got practically nothing outside mortgage lending; also the international business, the treasury activities, and above all asset management. So we're thinking, with Fidelity's agreement, of selling corporate finance to BZW. What do you think of that?"

"It seems sensible," Peter confirmed, steering clear of the hypocrisy of it all.

"BZW did not consider McAdam's continuing presence in the department to be essential to a deal; and they agreed that I had no alternative but to fire him."

Again he looked at Peter as if seeking a response. Peter decided against. He had noticed out of the corner of his eye that Sybil Dunwoody was taking notes and had decided to redouble his wariness. Even with Pitcairn going down the pan he stood to pick up a bonus of over three-quarters of million quid from the fee and he wasn't going to put that at risk by giving this bastard an excuse for his summary dismissal. He'd in all probability still be entitled to what Cruso had promised him; but he didn't fancy trying to find a solicitor who would take on the Brothers on his behalf.

"BZW would, however, require the rest of the directors of corporate finance to be locked in and they have specified you in particular, Peter."

Again the interrogatory. What was he meant to say? 'Oh, Stephen, I do feel flattered.' Forget it. He wanted out more than ever with or without enough money to tell the world to fuck off.

"They want you to sign up for three years at 50% above your current salary with a guaranteed bonus equal to five years' salary at the end of that period."

Peter maintained his silence.

"Well?"

"Well what?"

"Will you sign up on that basis? I'm calling all the corporate finance directors together at eight o'clock this evening to sign their commitments. There'll be lesser deals for the rest of the executives to follow. But I want to know now that you're going to agree to yours, if that's what BZW require."

"I'll think about it, Stephen."

"Thinking about it is not good enough, Peter."

He had started off amiably enough by what Peter knew of his standards but was showing a flash of frustrated anger now. You could see him thinking who does this sullen little shit think he is that he can hold us all to ransom.

"For heaven's sake, Peter, it's only a few weeks since McAdam went to BZW begging them to make you all offers so that you could walk out on the Brothers en masse."

"That's not the way I understand it, Stephen."

"Well, that's what I'm telling you happened."

"That's not what Bill told me."

"Peter, it's a fact. I've spoken to BZW."

Peter was getting fed up with this. He felt tired and angry enough himself. The whole Pitcairn thing was collapsing round his ears while he spent the time he should have been devoting to finding some way to screw Arthur Evans fencing with this scheming shit. Gallaher was expecting an answer again.

"Are you calling me a liar, Peter Davenport?" he said eventually, again bringing his disgusting breath obnoxiously close.

"Stephen, Bill McAdam may not be your idea of a best buddy; but he's too damned simple to lie to his colleagues. If you're asking me to call Bill McAdam a liar, you can forget it."

*****

Maureen was waiting with a message from Beevor to call him urgently. Peter summoned Tim Phillips to listen in on the extension piece and then called the direct line.

"Mr Davenport, I told you yesterday that the Panel is very unhappy about the non-disclosure of the purchaser or purchasers of Pitcairn's shares and in particular your refusal on behalf of your client to seek to have those shares disenfranchised. I also warned you that we did not intend to let the matter rest. The Panel executive believes that there is *prima facie* evidence of a concert party and I am now going to inform you of what action we intend to take to deal with this situation.

"If we are correct in suspecting the existence of a concert party, it could have the intention of supporting BMP or Pitcairn or conceivably a third party. We wish to be even-handed with regard to any one of those possibilities. We have therefore decided that, for the purposes of the final count of acceptances on the sixtieth day, all those shares acquired by unidentified purchasers through Pinsent Securities will be excluded from the total of Pitcairn shares outstanding. The result is that 56,690,000 of Pitcairn's shares will be deemed not to exist and a simple majority of the remaining shares will be deemed sufficient for BMP to declare their offer unconditional at that time. In the event that any or all of the ultimate beneficial owners of those shares make themselves known before 1.00 pm on the sixtieth day, they will be automatically restored to the total of Pitcairn's outstanding shares. We shall, of course, though wish to examine the nature of the disclosure to ensure that there has been compliance with the Code and reserve to ourselves all rights to take further action in the event that we are not so satisfied.

"Do you understand exactly what I am saying?"

Peter raised his eyebrows towards Tim, who had been taking notes even more frantically than Sybil Dunwoody fifteen minutes before. Tim nodded.

"Exactly," Peter replied.

"This is an unprecedented situation," Antony Beevor went on, "and the Panel executive has felt it necessary to take unprecedented action. For this reason we believe that you may wish to appeal the decision of the executive to a hearing of the full Panel and, in the circumstances, we would have no objection to your so doing. It is also possible, of course, that BMP may wish to appeal the decision and we are extending that option to them also. Do you have any questions?"

Peter looked up again at Tim Phillips. Tim raised a finger. Before he could speak, Beevor added: "Of course, none of this affects any ability of BMP to declare their offer unconditional in advance of the sixtieth day - for example at the next closing date, tomorrow afternoon, using the full total of Pitcairn shares outstanding as the denominator."

Tim Phillips nodded.

"That's what I wanted to ask," he whispered.

"No questions," Peter replied, replacing the receiver.

"Shit. That's a death sentence, Peter. He knows we'll have to appeal it. By my reckoning that means they only have to get 45.7% to win. That's so unfair. With Mercury's acceptance promised they must be home and dry already."

"Not until Sunday, Tim. Let's concentrate on tomorrow's closing date first."

"Sure; but we must put the appeal in motion too."

"On what grounds?"

"I'd have thought that was obvious, Peter. How can we be held responsible for these purchasers when we don't know who the hell they are?"

Peter said nothing.

"We don't know who they are, do we Peter?"

"Of course not, Tim," Peter replied.

*****

Graeme Kent's office was next door to Peter's. Just before twelve-thirty, he put his head round Peter's door.

"Peter, I've just got to pop out to the dentist. I've got a terrible toothache. I'm due at a meeting with Gallaher at Fidelity at two-thirty. Cindy's already at lunch. Could you tell her I should be back well before then. In the meantime, if Stephen needs anything, it's all on my desk."

Peter didn't need a second invitation. Kent was fastidiously organised. The latest drafts of the agreements with Fidelity and BZW were in a neat stack on the left-hand side of his desk, leaving the fresh blotter clear. On top of the pile was a draft press announcement on Fidelity's paper, extensively annotated in red with suggested amendments in Kent's stylishly italic script and a handwritten list of points outstanding in the same hand, divided between 'BZW' and 'Fidelity'.

The BZW list was headed with

1) Will PD sign up?
2) If he won't ? acceptable if they get all the others.
3) Terms for managers.
4) Terms for executives

Under items *3* and *4*, there were some proposed salary hikes and, in the case of the managers, guaranteed bonus provisions for the first year, 1989. Peter thought they looked generous enough. The final points were

5) Client confidentiality
6) Ownership of records
7) Responsibility for pre-deal actions
8) Client fees

Peter flicked through the pile to the proposed BZW agreement and looked up the particular clauses. They seemed to have been pretty sensibly dealt with on the whole, though there were a few suggested elaborations and amendments. The corporate finance department was to take with it all its records relating to current clients but leave the rest behind under the control of the Compliance Department, who would be responsible for preserving ongoing confidentiality. Any clients wishing to terminate their relationship with the corporate finance department as a result of the change of ownership would obviously be free to do so, as they always were at any time, and Dundas was to bear responsibility for any claims from this or past actions. No problems there. It was simply recognising the *de facto* situation. There was just a hand-written note *'inform professional indemnity insurers of continuing liability tail'*. Finally there was a provision for BZW to pay Dundas, one month after completion, in addition to the agreed price of the acquisition, a sum equal to any success fee in respect of the offer by BMP for Pitcairn, less twenty per cent, which was to be disbursed by BZW in accordance with the terms of a side letter. Peter hunted for a draft without success. Well at least that cunt Kent hadn't been given access to that. Not that it was all that exciting any more. Peter turned to the Fidelity list.

It was dominated by

1) *Compensation terms for non-exec directors*
2) *Compensation terms for JC*
3) *Compensation terms for SG*
4) *Confirmation of Divisional Heads in place*
5) *Roll-over of directors contracts*
6) *New share options for directors*
7)*Pension provisions for directors taking early retirement*

Nice to know that shareholders' interests featured so highly in the final deliberations, thought Peter, straightening the pile and heading quietly back to his office.

*****

If not at eight itself, all the corporate finance directors, save Kent, were gathered in the Dundas Brothers boardroom by shortly thereafter. There was another terrible gale blowing up outside. Seymour Farquharson, who had somehow managed to adapt his stock exchange monitor so that it could pick up television for the cricket, said that the BBC had interrupted broadcasts to warn of possible structural damage overnight.

"I hear the sound of one Mr Michael Fish shutting stable doors after bolting quadrupeds," opined William Blackstone. "If, following his meteorological miscomputations last October, we are to be subjected to the admonitions of Cassandra every time the wind blows, we shall be confined supine to our beds for eternity."

The rattling bursts of rain against the west-facing windows and the dense darkness of the night skies only served to cast a further pall over proceedings. There were none of the joys of a new beginning in the faces of those milling about forlornly in the huge room. Not even the promise of lucre to come seemed to diminish the sense that they were presiding over a sad passing like the heirs at an old and much loved patriarch's deathbed. Even the magisterial Gordon Dundas and the dashing Sir Alastair seemed to gaze out of their portraits with sadness at the passing of their progeny, rebuking those who were about to sign it into history for a mess of pottage.

The time passed. Someone sent in a drinks trolley a little before nine but there were still no contracts to peruse, let alone to sign. Graeme Kent joined them about twenty minutes later.

"Not much longer, he said. A few further discussions to which I am not privy."

He carried a fat folder under his arm in a sickly shade of pale green but he kept it there as he headed for the drinks trolley and poured himself a pretty stiff gin and tonic. Peter sidled up to him.

"Any problems, Graeme?" he enquired quietly.

"None as regards Fidelity."

"BZW then? Am I still required to sign up?" He still wanted out; but he had been toying with the idea of just going along with it all for the sake of his colleagues and then seeking to bail out later when it was a *fait accompli* .

"Oh we've discovered they don't really give a tinker's shit about you, old boy," said Kent. "You could sign up if you want to or go to hell if you don't," he added, taking a large snort of his gin and then beaming malevolently at Peter. "They'd be quite happy with anything they could get."

Peter decided to ignore the calculated insult. It was what endeared Graeme to his colleagues.

"Well, what the hell's the problem then?"

"We don't like the terms of the indemnity arrangements."

"Why not? They look innocent enough to me."

"How the fuck do you know?"

"Oh, come on Graeme, you couldn't have given me a more obvious hint to go and take a look at the drafts."

"You little shit."

"Well that's as may be; but what's the problem?"

"We're not prepared to take responsibility for the actions of corporate finance under our past stewardship once it's under new ownership."

"Why on earth not? The Brothers take responsibility for that now. That's why we carry professional indemnity insurance. It's a non point."

"Those were not my instructions, Peter. The deal with BZW is off. But, don't worry, Fidelity are going to take the bloody lot. We're all going to work for a fucking building society. Stephen's just going to come in and tell us all about it once he's finished sorting out how many millions he's going to get out of it all."

Wednesday, 12 October 1988

The defence committee met as usual in the gilded boardroom of 5 St James's Square but at seven-thirty, an hour earlier than usual. Unable to find anything more expensive or quintessentially English, Hennessy had taken a suite at the Connaught for the night; Rod and George had booked into the Cavendish in Duke Street, two minutes' walk around the corner from the office. It was just as well. The BBC's meteorological predictions had been more or less correct this time around and the road network in general and British Rail in particular were in chaos.

As the months had ticked by, the composition of these morning meetings had changed from day to day like the ebb and flow of a tide. At moments of tension, all the big wave-makers were there. On other occasions Tim Phillips had had to deputise for Davenport and the same was true of the other professionals. Often there was no more than a single representative of the brokers, the lawyers, public relations, Dundas, the company. But they were all here today, partners and their deputies, double banked in places round the long table, Christopher as ever at his place in the middle, perched discreetly on a little gold velvet cushion, that he claimed was for his back, Rod to one side and George the other. All except poor Freddie. It was like a great graduation party without the heady sense of achievement, a wake without the gaiety of good times remembered.

Rod looked tired; as tired as Peter felt. The news from the Panel the previous day had blown away the last shreds of hope to which they had all been clinging. Rod felt it more personally than the rest of them. The professionals would all move on to the next deal. You couldn't be in this game without taking your share of the knocks. The poison dwarf would bugger off back to Boston and pick up another cushy number from the husband of one of his wife's socialite friends. George Aladyce, for all his eccentricities, had a first class reputation as a research scientist and Roche or Pfizer or umpteen American companies would be falling over themselves to snap him up. The chances were that even Arthur Evans would try to keep him on board. After all he hadn't been involved in the day-to-day minutiae of the defence and the gratuitous insults and hints of misconduct, sexual and professional, which would have reached Evans via their separate contacts with the press could predominantly be traced to Rod.

Of late these meetings had barely occupied more than a half to three-quarters of an hour. Not that they achieved less for all that; but background could always be taken for granted so that only what was genuinely new needed to be addressed and familiarity with the subject made for rapid exchange and quick decisions. Hennessy had not exactly been responsible but he loved it nevertheless, priding himself on the economy of saving fifteen minutes from a gaggle of advisers each chalking up several hundred pounds an hour. Sure he hated to lose; but Peter felt it was the loss of the power to preside that was going to hurt him almost as much as the loss of face.

But today it was going to be different. From the start it was obvious that everybody wanted their say, their last fifteen minutes in this bit of limelight at least. Peter was called upon to report the Panel's decision and its implications though everyone present had already had a note on the subject. There was then a debate on whether, or more particularly when, they should appeal. Rod and George, Peter thought to their credit, said not a word but Hennessy denounced the Panel's interference as a monstrous conspiracy against fair-play in general and his personal probity in particular. It was only with the utmost difficulty that Peter, while agreeing that it was utterly unreasonable to assume that the chairman knew something which he clearly did not, persuaded Hennessy that, since it could not affect the outcome for today's closing, tomorrow was the day they should appeal. Even Peter was getting fed up with lying. Christopher, it appeared, was just getting into his stride.

Then Justin Travers-Coe went through the shareholders' list yet again; but this time not with just the updates. The whole catastrophe from Abtrust Nominees to Zurich Insurance. It got no less depressing for being more detailed. It was clearly going to be a very close call this afternoon. By Sunday, with or without the Panel, and with Schroders and Flemings waiting to dive into the market the moment they were given the off, Sam was going to walk it. He hadn't seen her for a week; not even spoken. He found himself hoping she'd finish him off today. He didn't want to wait until Sunday to start his life again.

He was pulled from his reverie by Hennessy demanding another attack on the Panel, this time for permitting the Schroder/Fleming tactic which Justin had just explained was in the offing. That it had all been done before and that the procedures and requirements had been agreed with the Panel cut no ice with Christopher. He wanted the whole thing gone over again. The lawyers were close to despair.

Then there was the day's review of the newspapers, Wallis painfully aware of how inadequately he filled Freddie's place in either their respect or, in the case of Peter at least, their affections. Then they went through draft press announcements with Pitcairn's proposed reactions to the results of this afternoon's counts. Predictably Hennessy had ordered the suppression of the only draft that counted, acknowledging defeat.

It was near ten o'clock by the time they split up, after being called to an embarrassing minute of communal silent prayer by the chairman. It was his only acknowledgment that today was going to be it. On his way out Peter popped upstairs to Rod's office to collect a banker's draft in favour of Dundas Brothers for £4,376,109.30, including VAT. That at least was not going to be left for a subsequent argument with Evans. As he emerged from Rod's office, he almost collided with a sheepish gaggle of Travers-Coe, Corrigan, Wallis et al, a collection of pin-striped buskers, all cap in hand. Back downstairs, he bumped into Christopher, squash racket in one hand and kitbag in the other, on his way to the RAC. As Peter hoisted his umbrella against the continuing downpour and set off in the hopeless search for a cab, the chauffeur held open the door of the Jag as Hennessy set off for the 300 yard drive to his game.

*****

Peter sat in his office alone. There was nothing to do but wait. The announcement of Fidelity Bank's agreed offer for Dundas had apparently gone up on the stock exchange screen first thing, as planned. The market had given it a resounding raspberry, knocking eight per cent off Fidelity Bank's shares on the turn. Who cared? For the purposes of Peter's modest tally of options, and because of Stephen Gallaher's rather more substantial pile, it was an all cash deal. There wasn't a bank analyst worth his salt who didn't know that Fidelity's management was going to be hopelessly out of its depth next time a recession started to expose the weaknesses in the Brothers' loan book; and there were already dark mutterings again about the black hole that was Dundas Life. For good measure, Gallaher had persuaded these imbeciles to pay a price even higher than that at which RheinHeim had taken fright.

Davenport took out a pad and started drawing up a personal balance sheet. The apartment, the Pitcairn bonus, cashing in his options; it came well into seven figures. Then he knocked off the mortgage and 40 per cent tax on the bonus and his fuck-you money crumbled to dust before his eyes. Oh well, he'd just have to stick with it. He and Sam would have a damned good income between them. They could sell her house and maybe buy something quite substantial in the country for weekends.

His phone broke the spell.

"Some girl for you," Maureen said helpfully, "sounds foreign, and in a state. Shall I put her through?"

What did she expect him to say? 'No, tell her to fuck off.'

"Okay, Maureen, go ahead," he said.

"You're through," he heard her say.

"Peter Davenport."

"Mr Davenport, it's Virginia....Virginia Hennessy. I'm so glad I've found you. I've been trying to get daddy but he's gone off to play squash or something. Mom went up to London with him yesterday afternoon and I can't get her at the hotel either. And something terribly important's happened and something awful too. I don't know what to do. Please, please help me."

She was like the child she really was, almost hysterical, the way only an American girl can be when things get out of hand.

"Why don't you start at the beginning, Virginia. I've got all day."

"But you haven't. I know. I know. You've only got till three o'clock. You see, I stayed on the line when I put you through to daddy on Monday evening. I was listening in all the time. And I thought it was all so unfair. And then you'd done all that work to find out about that horrible man Evans. And then daddy wouldn't help you because he's just too proud. So I signed it all over with granny and she made me send some faxes and during the night a whole lot of faxes came back. And I'd missed them because I got up late. And I don't understand it, but granny says one of them's terribly important and that you've got to have it right away."

"Okay, Virginia, I'll just give you the fax number and you can send it through to me."

"But I can't. Don't you see? That big tree by the front gate came down in the storm last night and it's fucked all our phone lines. I'm calling you from a call box up in the village. Oh, how I hate this country. Why doesn't anything work?" she bawled.

"Have you got the fax with you?"

"Yes."

"Could you read it to me?"

"Well sort of. There are two pages and the first page is in French and I'm not very good at that; but it says something like 'cheer Sabine, jesper cur curliew key est cur too ass besoyne, bizooks, Rudolf'. Does that make any sense to you, Mr Davenport?"

"Not a lot to be honest, Virginia. Who's Rudolf?'"

"Granny says he was a little boy she hid during the war when the Germans killed his parents. She said he was something called a grand laygoom in Switzerland now."

"What about the second page, Virginia?"

"Well that's a lot easier cos it's in English; but I still don't understand it."

"Just read what it says slowly, Virginia."

She did as she was told.

"Granny was right, Virginia. That is very important indeed," he said when she finished. "Now, how are you going to get it to me?" he mused. "I could send a courier; but he wouldn't have time to get down to you and back. I know. What about that big brother of yours?"

"What, Oscar? Oh, he stays in bed till lunchtime when mom's not here."

"Well, you run back to the house, Virginia, get the lazy little sod out of his nest, stick him on that chromium steed of his and tell him to ride like hell and get that fax to me by two o'clock latest or he'll have more than the wrath of his mom to worry about."

"But he can't, Mr Davenport, don't you see?"

"Why not?"

"I told you that tree's come down right across our gateway. We'll never get his Harley over that. It weighs a ton."

"Shit."

"Wait. I've got an idea. He's got a scrambling bike too. We could probably lift that over the tree between us."

"Good girl. Now, will he be able to find my office?"

"Dundas Brothers. Sure. He knows all the banks. Daddy made him do a summer job as a courier in the City. He loved it."

Davenport put down the phone and looked up. Sybil Dunwoody was standing in front of his desk, foursquare, today in a purple sack made of something shiny that most certainly contained no natural fibre. She turned and shut the door, then sat down facing him.

"You're going to be fired," she said without preliminaries.

"Oh," he said, "any reason in particular?"

"You called Stephen Gallaher a liar."

"I did no such thing," Peter protested. "But I do remember refusing to call Bill McAdam a liar," he added, "if that's any help."

"You called Stephen Gallaher a liar. I was taking notes at the time and I wrote it all down immediately afterwards. In the circumstances there will be no notice period and you will not be entitled to any compensation. Your Dundas options will lapse in accordance with the provisions for dismissal following gross misconduct. I shall escort you off the premises forthwith. You will leave everything but your raincoat. Anything personal will be sent on to you shortly."

"Sybil, do you think I was born yesterday? I knew what you were up to when I saw you scribbling away there. I made my own note immediately afterwards too. It's your word against mine; and, as it happens, I sure know which one of those I'd believe. And I've consulted a lawyer. Are you and Stephen aware of what will happen when I make a claim for wrongful dismissal?"

Of course he'd done no such thing. He knew he ought to have done. He knew it at the time. He knew it even more when Gallaher eventually appeared in the board room last night, as cocky as a bantam, to tell them he'd cut a deal with Fidelity to include corporate finance in its purchase of the Brothers. It was the way he addressed Peter as though he were the only one present, outlining how Fidelity were going to improve their packages to keep them on board, how those who stayed would get the same from Fidelity as they would have got from BZW, how taking out their options would be organised to avoid them having to pay tax. It just had to be that Gallaher had something special in mind for him by way of revenge.

But the bluff was enough for the moment to pull simple Sybil up in her tracks.

"If you insist, I'll put what you say to Stephen, but I don't expect there to be a change in his position. You're not to leave your desk. I'll get back to you immediately, within the hour."

"You do that, Sybil. Now cut along then, there's a good girl. I've got work to do."

He picked up the phone, without waiting for her to leave and dialed Grossmanns.

"Gillian Wilkinson, please," he said, as the Grossmanns switchboard answered, as always, on the very first ring.

*****

Peter, waiting in reception on the ground floor of Dundas Brothers, heard him long before he saw him. First there was this horrible high-pitched whine, like a rusty chain-saw gone berserk, down by the approach road from London Bridge. And then there were the sirens. A moment later Oscar Hennessy appeared, performing a two hundred yard wheelie up the length of Gracechurch Street. He dived across in front of the oncoming traffic, causing a minor shunt as four cars, a taxi and a red double-decker bus, moving off from the traffic lights, banged into each other nose to tail, and screeched to a halt in front of Dundas Brothers, a grin on his face as wide as the prairie. His bike looked as though it had just crossed a ploughed field. With a flourish, he unzipped his leather top and handed the fax to Peter as three squad cars, sirens howling and blue lights flashing surrounded him, entirely blocking the junction of Gracechurch Street and Fenchurch Street. A moment later another appeared at the top of Lombard Street and gridlock was complete as Oscar was pinned against the wall of Dundas Brothers, his legs spread as rough metropolitan hands explored his person.

Peter, concerned less the law should turn its clumsy attentions to the recipient of this clearly illicit package, set off at a run down Fenchurch Street, then dived left up Lime Street into Leadenhall Market, turned left again at Bull's Head Passage, and emerged back on Gracechurch Street. He slowed to a brisk walk, hoisted his umbrella and pulled it well down to hide his face, just in case, then crossed the road and set off down Cornhill in the direction of Bank en route for Gresham Street.

*****

They kept him waiting. For a while he was beginning to worry that she was actually going to keep him waiting past three o'clock and announce that BMP had won despite what he'd told her over the phone. Tim had put his head round the door half an hour before he left to say that Justin had called to say Wagstaffs were in the market at 445p, presumably on behalf of her Schroders and Flemings co-conspirators. She had obviously decided that the time was right to close the net.

It was a nice little room; good view of the Guildhall if the weather had been kinder; a decent antique mahogany table - George III he guessed - and a sideboard of about the same period, perhaps a little later. It didn't quite fit with Grossmanns' reputation for austerity. Nice chairs too and some framed eighteenth century cartoons that were all rather rude about foreigners. I don't suppose they use this room for eurobond signings, he thought to himself.

Just as he was beginning to get quite anxious, the door opened and a short, burly messenger appeared, pin-stripe trousers and black jacket, cauliflower ears. Tight-head prop, Peter thought.

"Ms Wilkinson and Lord Evans will see you now, sir. We need to go down one floor. This is the chairman's dining room. Stairs all right for you, sir?"

"Of course."

He led the way down the passage, down a flight of stairs, along another, knocked at a set of double doors and entered without waiting for a reply. It was the Grossmanns boardroom, almost as gigantic as that back at number 69, but rather more utilitarian. Save for one end, which had been cleared, the table was covered in papers. It was the war room of a hostile bid in its final days. Lord Evans was sitting on the far side of the table in his shirt sleeves, bullet-headed, she at its head, hair pulled painfully back from her pale, pale face and those ridiculous grey-tinted glasses, devoid of magnification.

She rose as Peter entered and extended her hand. He wanted to hold it for ever but shook it briefly and turned towards Evans. He remained rooted to his chair, barely acknowledging Davenport's presence. Peter could see clear through the disguise now that he was used to it; but it was, every time he saw it, unnerving nonetheless, as if it were her but really it wasn't. Jekyll and Hyde. She waved him to the chair opposite Evans.

"Now what's all this nonsense?" he opened gruffly. "I shall be damned annoyed if you're just wasting my time. I've had quite enough trouble with you already, Mr Davenport. In my view the way this defence has been conducted has been an absolute disgrace."

Peter said not a word. By way of reply he merely opened his briefcase and took out a sheet of paper which he put on the table. He turned it around to face Evans and pushed it across the table to him.

"What the hell's this?"

"Insider dealing, Lord Evans, and, as you know, it's a criminal offence which carries a prison sentence. What we have here is an order dated 27th November, 1987 to Oberoi et Cie in Geneva to buy 5000 contracts to purchase options in the shares of Pitcairn Pharmaceuticals against monies held in your numbered account. You'll note that it bears your signature, Lord Evans - the one we've been seeing so much of on all these offer documents recently."

"It's a bloody fabrication. I tell you, Gillian, there're no depths to which this defence won't sink. We've seen all too much evidence of that in recent months."

Samantha Wilkinson reached over for the paper to take a look. Evans rudely snatched it away.

"Well, here's what I think of your little forgery, Mr Davenport," he said, taking up the sheet and suddenly tearing it across and across and across again half a dozen times before finally flinging the pieces in the air so that they drifted down around him and onto the table like a ticker-tape parade. "I'm not getting set up by another of your attempts to blacken my reputation. Well now you've got no evidence anyway; so you can get back up on your hind legs and fuck off out of here."

"I thought you might do that," Peter said, "so I took the precaution of popping into a shop on the way over here and doing a few photocopies. That was one of them," he said, gesturing at the little fragments of paper all around them. "Not that shiny paper you get with faxes, you see." Shit, he was enjoying this so much that he was in danger of almost mocking Evans' Welsh accent. He must watch it. "Would you like another?"

He opened his briefcase again, this time on his knee, wary of the possibility of a full frontal assault on its contents, took out two more sheets and handed one to each of them.

Samantha read it through carefully.

"Can you assure me that this is a forgery, Lord Evans?" They were the first words she'd spoken and, bar their brief telephone exchange earlier in the day, the first he'd heard from her in ten days. That wonderful, deep, bewitching, husky voice that betrayed, if only you had eyes to see, what sort of a woman this really was.

"Of course it's a fucking forgery, Gillian. These people will stop at absolutely nothing. I've a good mind to go to the Governor about them. And don't you think I wouldn't, young man," he added, leaning across the table to shake a stubby finger threateningly in Peter's face. "I'm on the Court of the Bank of England and I can get Sir Robin Leigh-Pemberton on the phone just like that," he said, snapping his fingers. "You're going to find yourself driven right out of the City if you're not careful."

"It is not a forgery," Peter said quietly. "I can assure you of that, Ms Wilkinson."

"Of course it's a fucking forgery," bellowed Evans. "Everybody knows the Swiss have bank secrecy laws tighter than a cat's arsehole. The proof of it is that this man just wouldn't dare to use this shit. Or he wouldn't be round here now, trying to blackmail us with it."

"Oh, we'll use it alright, Lord Evans. I'm really just being kind to you. I'm giving you a choice. You can let your bid lapse this afternoon or I'll take this to the *Financial Times* right after this meeting. Your choice."

"They'd never dare publish crap like this. Their lawyers wouldn't let them. They'd know they were exposing themselves to the libel claim of the century."

"They would if they had an indemnity against the costs of any action against them."

"And who the hell of any value would give them that. They're not going to take it from a whipper-snapper like you. Of that I can assure you."

Davenport took a deep breath.

"Dundas Brothers," he said. "I have my bank's authority to offer the *Financial Times* an unlimited indemnity."

Epilogue

Leaving Grossmanns, Peter went straight round the corner to the City police station in Wood Street.

"I think you've got a young man called Oscar Hennessy here. How much do you want for him?" he asked, slapping his cheque book on the counter.

The spotty young policewoman opened a huge ledger and ran her finger down the page. Nails bitten down savagely. She found the entry she was looking for and turned over her shoulder to an older officer seated at a desk at the back of the office.

"Sarge, how much do we want for that young tearaway with the motorbike? He's not due in front of the magistrate until tomorrow morning."

The sergeant ambled arthritically over to the counter. He put on his spectacles and examined the ledger.

"Speeding, dangerous driving, driving while uninsured, in possession of an unlicensed vehicle. Let's say a hundred and fifty quid for the fine, sir, and a couple of hundred for the Police Benevolent Association."

Peter opened his chequebook and began writing a 'P'.

"Better just make out the one cheque to cash, sir. We'll sort out where it all has to go. More convenient that way."

Peter crossed out the 'P', initialed it and started again. The sergeant turned to a young policeman typing out a report in the far corner, painfully one-fingered.

"Constable, fetch that American oick with the nail through his eyebrow out of the cells; and tell him to get his filthy fucking bike out of my yard."

*****

527

He picked Sam up from her place in a taxi. She was looking absolutely stunning. She put her lips to his gently, preserving her lipstick. She smelt wonderful.

"You didn't have that indemnity for the FT, did you?" she said as soon as she was seated beside him.

"Of course not, but I knew he wouldn't take the risk, even if you would. Right now, Sam, I don't even know if I'm still on the Brothers' payroll. I've had a bit of a run-in with Gallaher over the last couple of days. My only concern was that you might still go ahead and declare it unconditional and then throw that bastard to the wolves afterwards."

"I wanted to. Old man Grossmann wouldn't let me. Unfortunately we had no arrangement for a success fee. Old Julius would have happily shopped him if there'd been a couple of million riding on it. He has a very precise view of the value of loyalty and it doesn't amount to much. But I made him give me fifteen per cent of our fee for compromising my professional reputation."

"What, including the underwriting?"

"All three underwritings and a flat fee of five million. We made over £36 million gross all told."

"Shit, that's £5.4 million for you. That's more than I got."

"I should bloody well think so. That's how I calculated what I wanted. After all, for all practical purposes I won. I had to intercept MAM's acceptance. It's still in the drawer of my desk."

"If old man Julius is so mean, why did he give you all that money?"

"He didn't exactly. He charged it up to Evans. Told him he would have to pay it personally, or else."

"What's the Panel saying?"

"They've gone incandescent; lighting up the night sky. Apparently no one's ever lapsed an offer with four days to go and 47.9% already under their belt."

"So what did you tell them?"

"I said it was all your fault."

"What?"

"Well more or less. Too much uncertainty over these unknown shareholders. We might never have been able to mop up the minorities and get 100 per cent control."

"Oh, I always assumed those chaps were allies of yours, friends of BMP."

"Like hell you did."

*****

They had a big round table in the centre of Bibendum. There was a magnum of champagne, of course, and a disgracefully large bowl of Beluga caviar, glistening translucently grey, in the centre of the table with plates of blinis and sour cream and lemons and chopped hard-boiled egg, the whites and yolks separated. Beside each of their plates was a polished golden spoon with a long, long elaborately carved ebony-black handle.

"What's with these crazy long spoons, man?" asked Oscar.

"My guess is that they're a warning," Sam replied.

"A warning? What of, man?"

"That tonight you're supping with the devil incarnate."

Virginia looked askance at her brother, newly released from the police cells, and dismissed the idea. He was too lazy to be the devil. She looked at Peter and then at Sam, and then from one to the other.

"Which one of you's the devil then?" she asked.

"Him," she said. "Her," he said. Together.

Printed in the United Kingdom
by Lightning Source UK Ltd.
110603UKS00001B/174